An Uncommon Courtship

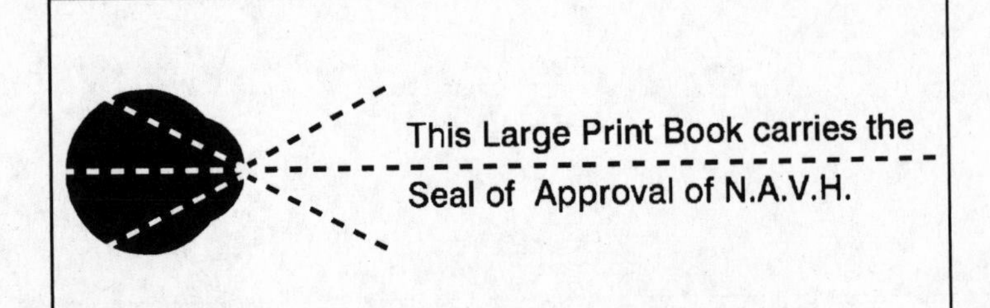
This Large Print Book carries the
Seal of Approval of N.A.V.H.

HAWTHORNE HOUSE

AN UNCOMMON COURTSHIP

KRISTI ANN HUNTER

THORNDIKE PRESS
A part of Gale, Cengage Learning

GALE
CENGAGE Learning

Farmington Hills, Mich • San Francisco • New York • Waterville, Maine
Meriden, Conn • Mason, Ohio • Chicago

Scripture quotations are from the King James Version of the Bible.
Thorndike Press, a part of Gale, Cengage Learning.

Thorndike Press® Large Print Christian Historical Fiction.
The text of this Large Print edition is unabridged.
Other aspects of the book may vary from the original edition.
Set in 16 pt. Plantin.

LIBRARY OF CONGRESS CATALOGING-IN-PUBLICATION DATA

Names: Hunter, Kristi Ann, author.
Title: An uncommon courtship / by Kristi Ann Hunter.
Description: Large print edition. | Waterville, Maine : Thorndike Press, a part of Gale, Cengage Learning, 2017. | Series: Hawthorne House | Series: Thorndike Press large print Christian historical fiction
Identifiers: LCCN 2016051757| ISBN 9781410497154 (hardcover) | ISBN 1410497151 (hardcover)
Subjects: | GSAFD: Regency fiction | Love stories.
Classification: LCC PS3608.U5935 U53 2017b | DDC 813/.6—dc23
LC record available at https://lccn.loc.gov/2016051757

Published in 2017 by arrangement with Bethany House Publishers, a division of Baker Publishing Group

Printed in Mexico
1 2 3 4 5 6 7 21 20 19 18 17

To the Creator and Giver
of Perfect Love.

1 John 4:16

And to Jacob,
who may not be perfect,
but is perfect for me.

Prologue

Hertfordshire, England — 1796

Many a man has been inspired by a great father or a noble brother, and young six-year-old Lord Trent Hawthorne had been blessed with both. Standing by his father atop a hill that looked out over a large portion of their country estate, he didn't bother asking why he, a younger son, had been brought out to talk about the estate. Ever since he was three Father had included him in lessons, saying, "Life is unpredictable and you have to be ready. I hope you both live to see your grandchildren, but God may decide He'd rather have you as duke one day."

Trent didn't understand all that, but he liked spending time with his father and brother, so he didn't complain.

On the other side of the large man stood Trent's older brother, Griffith. Even at ten years old Griffith was showing signs that he would be as big as their father, if not taller. Trent stretched his back as straight as it would go, even lifted a bit onto his toes to see if he too could make his head reach Father's shoulder. The highest he could get was a little below the man's elbow.

"What do you think, boys?"

Trent gave off trying to stretch his spine and looked out over the land below. The vine-covered walls of an old stone keep rose from the hillside across the way, beneath a crumbling stone watchtower. The valley below boasted scraggly trees and patches of grass scattered amongst large puddles of water. More tufts of grass stuck up through the shallow water, giving it an eerie, dangerous look. Maybe they should dig out the field and make the puddles deeper so they could swim in them. But of course, there was already a perfectly good lake closer to the house.

Griffith tilted his head and looked up at their father. "Sheep."

Father squinted his eyes as he looked over the land, considering. "Sheep, you say?"

This was what Trent loved about his father. Most of the world would have been afraid to answer him. They'd have waited to see what he was thinking and then agreed with whatever it was. After all, the big man was a powerful duke. The only people in England more prestigious than he was had royal blood in their veins. But the truth was — at least when it came to his family — John, Duke of Riverton, was the most approachable man in the kingdom. Even if the idea involved throwing sheep into a boggy mess.

Trent had no idea whether sheep liked to swim. If they did, Griffith was smart to want to bring them here instead of having them dirty up the lake. It was probably a good thing he was the older son. Even though the title would never pass to Trent, he wanted to make his father glad that both sons were included in this discussion. He racked his little brain for anything he knew about sheep. "Won't the wool shrink if we let them swim in that? Nanny said that's why my coat shrank after I wore it into the lake last year."

Father beamed at his younger son and ruffled Trent's blond hair. Bright green eyes smiled down at him, making Trent feel six feet tall, even if he never would be. "I don't think it works that way, son. It is a lot of water, though. Do you think the sheep like to swim, Griffith?"

Griffith looked from Trent back to his father with a hint of uneasiness that he quickly covered up. Griffith would be leaving for school soon, and their father had lately been pressing him more and more to start voicing his thoughts and opinions. He shifted his feet, almost tripping over the gangly legs of a tall ten-year-old. "I've been reading about the drainage ditches they're doing in Scotland. We could build some and turn most of the area into pasture for the sheep. Then plant crops in their current pasture."

Father bent down to be at eye level with Griffith. "Drainage ditches?"

Griffith's throat shuddered with his heavy swallow. "Yes, sir. We dig them out and put rocks in to keep the mud out. Then the water runs down to the river."

"Where did you read about these ditches?"

Trent tried to copy Father's impressed demeanor, but the wind kept pulling the hair from the short queue at the nape of his neck, sending a blond curtain into his eyes. It was hard to look composed, much less impressed, with hair blocking his face. He pushed the hair back with both hands to see Griffith gathering his words. Griffith always liked to think about what he was going to say. It took too much time as far as Trent was concerned.

After a deep breath, Griffith squared his shoulders and spoke without any of his earlier hesitancy. "When we visited Mr. Stroud several years ago, all he had were those peat bogs. But when he came to us last month he brought those excellent cabbages. I asked him what changed. He gave me a book about the new methods."

Father straightened back to his full height with a wide smile. His shoulders pressed back, and he put his fists on his hips. Trent poked at one of the jacket seams that looked a bit stretched by his father's proud stance. Had he worn his jacket into the lake too?

"As sure as I was blessed in birth, I've been blessed in progeny." Father wrapped one strong arm around Griffith's shoulders and pulled him in tight. "God knew what He was doing when He gave you to me. Let the Lord guide you, boy, and you'll be a better duke than I ever was. In some ways, I think you already are."

They tromped back through the fields toward home, talking about drainage ditches and throwing stones.

Four days later, the duke died.

CHAPTER 1

Hertfordshire, England, 1814

Lord Trent Hawthorne was convinced that breakfast was one of God's greatest gifts to humanity. What better way to celebrate the Lord's new mercies and fresh beginnings than rejoicing in the day's opportunities by eating a crispy rasher of bacon? Even after his father had passed, the morning meal had been a source of consolation for Trent, a reminder that God still had a reason for him to be in this world. Yes, for most of his life, Trent had awoken every day secure in the knowledge that nothing could ruin breakfast.

It took a wedding to prove him wrong.

Specifically, it took his wedding.

To a woman he barely knew.

Trent frowned at his plate, and the sweet roll plopped in the center of it frowned back. For the first time he could remember, the eggs looked unappealing, the bacon appeared dry and brittle, and the toast tasted like dust bound together by spoiled butter. He simply couldn't see a positive side to the way this day was beginning — and he'd been searching for the past three weeks.

Three weeks of listening to the banns read in church, bearing the speculative glances and thinly veiled curiosity alone while his bride-to-be spent the weeks in Birmingham acquiring a new wardrobe, since clothes fit for an unmarried young lady apparently disintegrated into dusty rags when she finished reciting her marriage vows. He didn't remember such a thing happening to his sisters' clothing when they'd married last year, but Lady Crampton must have witnessed it at some point because she'd been adamant that her daughter be outfitted in an entirely new wardrobe.

Of course, she'd also been adamant that they not wait any longer than the required three weeks between the reading of the banns and the actual wedding, so Trent wasn't inclined to think her the most logical of decision-makers.

Not that he'd ever cared much for Lady Crampton. Or her daughter — at least not the daughter he'd known about. As he'd probably known at some point in his life but had rediscovered only three weeks ago,

Lady Crampton had a second daughter. A second daughter with no debility or problem aside from the fact that she'd been born second — and that Lady Crampton was already focused solely on devoting her time to raising a spoiled, selfish, scheming, socially ambitious viper in her own image and hadn't found the time or inclination to raise a second one.

Of course, the countess was more than happy to claim that daughter today. She was marrying into the Duke of Riverton's family, after all, and what more could a mother want for her daughter? In Lady Crampton's case, she probably preferred that her daughter be marrying the duke himself instead of the duke's younger brother, but all in all it was still a rather nice match for a girl who knew all the best places in the district to gather mushrooms — including the depths of an old stone keep on a neighboring estate beneath a half-fallen roof and a partially collapsed floor.

Trent poked at his eggs before letting the fork clatter to the plate. "I'm going to rip those ruins down with my bare hands."

"Hardly necessary now that you've spent a whole day and night clearing the vines from one of the windows with a rock. An endeavor that did enough damage to your hands that I think you should reconsider using them on the stone wall."

Trent turned his head to glare at his older brother, seated next to him and having no issue with the meal whatsoever if the dents he was making in mounds of food on his plate were any indication. Griffith, Duke of Riverton, was a mountain of a man, but Trent had trained with the best pugilists in the country. He was pretty sure he could take his older brother down.

Griffith shrugged as he cut a perfect square of ham. "Well, you did. How are they doing, by the way?"

Trent flexed the appendages in question, pleased to note that the pain in both had subsided to a tolerable level. A few faint lines remained from the cuts he'd sustained while hacking away at a dense covering of thorny vines with nothing but a sharp stone for assistance. The knuckles he'd smashed in the near futile task could finally bend enough to curl into a fist. "My hands are fine, though I'm going to be much more conscientious about having a knife on me in the future."

A single golden eyebrow climbed Griffith's forehead. "You intend to make getting trapped in old ruins a regular occurrence? I suggest you make sure the next one isn't being occupied by a young lady. You can only propose once, you know."

Trent groaned and rubbed his hands over his face before letting his gaze crawl across the room in search of his new wife. Her slender form was rather easy to spot in a group of well-fed aristocrats — and was likely the reason she'd been able to walk back and forth across the floor that had crumbled beneath him. Once the floor had given way, the stair joist holes she'd used to climb down to the bottom of the ruins had become a useless ladder to nowhere, and they'd been trapped.

And not just for the night. Trapped for the rest of their lives by the bounds of propriety that demanded Trent salvage her threatened reputation by marrying her. Never mind the fact that no one knew they'd been there. Regardless of the fact that they'd managed to free themselves by breaking through the vines as the sun crested the horizon the next morning. As a gentleman, Trent could not leave her reputation to chance when he was the one who caused the problem in the first place. "Actually, you can propose as many times as you like. You can only be accepted once."

A spurt of laughter had Griffith lunging for his serviette as he tried to avoid choking while still keeping his bite of food in his mouth. He swallowed and dabbed at the corners of his lips. "Nice to see a bit of your humor coming back. For a while I thought you'd broken it along with your ankle."

"I didn't break my ankle." Though he should have, given the way he'd fallen through the rotten floor of the old stone keep. "The surgeon said it was simply a bad sprain. Made worse by the fact that I left my boot on all night and then proceeded to ride without removing it the next day."

Not that he'd had any choice. Escorting Lady Adelaide home from their adventure had been a necessity, as had discussing a wedding settlement with her father, the Earl of Crampton. Unfortunately the conversation had also included the sickening cloying of the socially ambitious Lady Crampton. That awkward meeting had also taken place over breakfast.

Griffith snagged the sweet roll from Trent's plate. "If you're only going to frown at this, I'm going to eat it. You might want to consider not looking so tortured, you know. People are starting to stare."

Trent grunted but adjusted his posture and tried to smooth his facial features. "They've been looking since I sat down.

Why do you think they're avoiding this table?"

"Because they've all stopped by to congratulate you, and you've done nothing but nod in acknowledgment?"

Trent grunted again and shoved the rest of his plate in his brother's direction. A somewhat familiar-looking brown disk lay on the edge of Griffith's plate. "What is that?"

"Mushroom." Griffith grinned. "I think your new wife might be a bit of a wit. They're quite tasty. Would you like to try one now that it's been properly prepared?"

"No, thank you." Trent tried not to gag at the thought of eating the mushroom. During that interminable night, they'd had nothing to eat other than the flat, brown winter mushrooms Lady Adelaide had climbed down to collect. And while they were rather good even when raw, he wasn't sure he'd ever be able to eat a mushroom again without thinking about being trapped, sitting in the dirt of a partially crumbled stone castle, watching his life plans slowly fade with the setting sun.

Trent picked up his napkin and ran the edge through his fingers. "I've never paid much attention to etiquette at these things. When do you think I can leave?"

"You do intend to take Lady Adelaide with you, don't you?" A canyon of concern formed between Griffith's thick blond brows as they lowered over deep green eyes. It wasn't a look Trent saw very often, but it was the one that proved Griffith was going to make an excellent father someday.

"Of course." Trent balled up the square of fabric and tossed it onto the table. "It's no gentleman's trick to leave his wife in her father's house. Especially when it's inhabited by a woman like Lady Crampton. I'm still not thoroughly convinced Lady Adelaide was raised by that woman. She's far too sweet."

"And you've spent how much time in her company?"

Trent frowned. "A day and a night. But we spent those sitting in the dirt, and she didn't turn into a shrew. That has to count for something."

At least he hoped it did.

Lady Crampton and her elder daughter, Lady Helena, were two of the most irritating people Trent had ever met. And he'd met all of London's aristocracy and a good portion of the gentry. If the second daughter turned out to be cut from the same cloth, Trent's life was going to become difficult indeed. "I'm sure we've run into her at gatherings over the years, given that we live near the same village and all. The very fact that I don't remember her when I so clearly remember her mother must be a good sign."

"Looking at her now you wouldn't think she'd be so forgettable. She's rather unconventional."

Trent followed Griffith's gaze and had to acknowledge the truth in his comment. Lady Adelaide was rather unique in appearance, with thick hair so dark it was nearly black and enormous blue eyes that would have appeared even larger if she had been wearing her spectacles. Several locks of hair — too short to curl or smooth back into her coiffure — fell across her forehead. Without the black-framed spectacles, a few wisps of hair threatened to droop into her eyelashes. She'd accidentally burned the hair along her forehead while trying to use curling tongs one morning, and it was taking a long time to grow back.

That was one of the things he'd learned while sitting next to her in the dirt eating mushrooms. In the quiet darkness between short snatches of sleep and attempts to hack through the vines, they'd talked. It was the one thing that made Trent not completely terrified of this marriage. If they could find their way back to the way it had been before they'd admitted their fate, it was possible this marriage could at least be tolerable.

"I'm surprised Mother didn't make it back for this. You received a letter from her yesterday, didn't you? Did she say why she wasn't coming?" Griffith sliced through the sweet roll, releasing a waft of steam from the still-warm pastry that simultaneously made Trent's mouth water and his stomach roll over.

Although the queasiness in his stomach probably had more to do with the fact that the reason his mother hadn't made it to the wedding was because he hadn't told her. He'd tried. Sort of. He wanted to believe there was a way out of this situation, though, and putting it down on paper made it seem so permanent.

Rather like the parish register they'd signed a mere hour ago.

Trent cleared his throat and avoided Griffith's gaze. "Er, no. She didn't mention the wedding."

Griffith's eyes widened in surprise. "Really? I had no idea she disliked Lady Crampton that much."

"I am certain I once heard her say that one of the best things about getting remarried was that she didn't have to live next to the countess anymore."

The countess, Trent's new mother-in-law, didn't appear to be having any of the discomfort that the bride and groom were experiencing. She stood next to her daughter, smiling and talking, while Lady Adelaide's serene smile tightened and her unfocused eyes began to look panicked. Trent looked a little closer, trying to see if there was a problem or if the attention was simply getting to her. As she stumbled to the side it became clear the heel of her slipper had somehow gotten snagged in the hem of her dress and she was trying to free it without anyone noticing. She wasn't being very successful, if her mother's warning looks were anything to go by.

This was something Trent could save her from. If nothing else good came of this wedding, at least Trent would be removing Lady Adelaide from her mother's influence — and perhaps save London from one more vapid attention seeker.

"I'd like to make London tonight." He had a closer estate, a small one his brother had sold him for a pittance, but the bedchambers had been damaged in a recent storm and were still under repairs. Besides, going to London meant they had to leave right now, and even then it would be a hard ride.

"It's quite a large party, and you are the guest of honor." Griffith dabbed at his mouth with a serviette, but Trent was fairly certain it was with the intention of hiding a forming smile.

"You're enjoying this, aren't you." Griffith had always warned Trent that one of his schemes would one day blow up in his face, but this hadn't been a scheme. This had simply been him coming across a lone horse tied up by the ruins and investigating out of curiosity. Regardless, consequences like this were a bit much for even a brother to revel in.

"No. Though I have done a bit better job resigning myself to it in the past few weeks." Griffith set down his fork, and the smile fell from his face, leaving it solemn and thoughtful. "I'd take your place if I could. I considered it. Lord Crampton wouldn't have protested such a switch."

"As if I would have let you make such a ridiculous proposal." Trent closed his eyes and sighed at the idea of Griffith stomping his way into Moonacre Park with his younger brother dragging at his heels. It was a funny picture, and this situation could certainly use a bit of humor. "In all honesty, Lord Crampton would have fallen down and kissed your feet. After he shoved Lady

Crampton out of the way, of course."

Griffith's answering smile was small and a bit sad, still tight with a look of regret as he shifted in his chair. Since boyhood Trent had marveled at his brother's size, wondering why God had chosen to make a man with such incredibly broad shoulders. Now it was obvious. Without them, Griffith wouldn't have been able to carry the abundance of responsibilities he'd claimed for himself. Responsibilities Trent had been unwilling to help with as he'd gotten older.

Watching his older brother rub his forefinger against his thumb like a world-weary old man instead of a young fellow of twenty-eight, it occurred to Trent that his own twenty-four years meant it was time for him to shoulder a bit of the manhood himself. As much as he wanted to avoid the consequences of his circumstances, he would never have been able to abide Griffith suffering in his place.

"God doesn't make mistakes." Trent's declaration cut through Griffith's guilt-ridden pondering.

"What?"

"God doesn't make mistakes. You told me that. When I was starting school and I said it was wrong that Father wasn't there with me." Trent swallowed hard at the memories.

He hadn't cried over his father in years. Now was not the time to renew the old habit. "You said God doesn't make mistakes and He had something planned for our lives even though we didn't understand."

"Well, I . . ." Griffith eased back into his chair, looking once more like the sophisticated duke. "That's true."

"Then we trust Him in this. Yes, they'd love to have married a daughter off to the duke. But they got me instead." God willing, it was a title he'd never hold. "So I've married Lady Adelaide. And we're going to see what He has planned for that."

Griffith smiled. His proud, fatherly smile. The one that puffed up Trent's chest even as it broke his heart. "When did you become so wise?"

Trent grinned back, doing his best to look boyish, trying to bring Griffith back to being a still-young older brother. "Must have been when I was trying to be you."

Chapter 2

Lady Adelaide Bell — now Lady Adelaide Hawthorne, she supposed — had always thought the day her mother was finally proud of her would be a very happy day.

It wasn't.

She'd rather go back to the days of listening to her mother complain about how horribly average her second daughter was. As far as insults went, it wasn't such a bad one. Weren't most people in the world average? Wasn't that the very definition of the word? Honestly, being lumped in with the bulk of the populace wasn't such a bad thing. It meant you blended in better and were quickly forgotten.

Being forgotten was a mixed blessing, though. It was nice that the dressmaker, haberdasher, and various other local merchants forgot that her mother had at one point or another left her at each of their shops and she'd had to walk several miles back home. Of course, if her mother hadn't forgotten her in the first place, it wouldn't have been necessary to be thankful for the shopkeepers' lack of memory.

Today, though, Mother was determined to make up for all the years she'd ignored Adelaide. When Adelaide had woken this morning, her mother had been watching her from the foot of the bed, ready to impart wisdom upon wisdom on how to make the most of this day. Adelaide hadn't been out of her sight since. Thankfully, Mother had stopped speaking during the actual ceremony, but she'd been making up for lost time since they'd arrived at the wedding breakfast.

Adelaide smiled at Mrs. Guthrey. At least she thought it was Mrs. Guthrey. Without her spectacles — which her mother had insisted she not wear today — everything beyond the length of her arm was a complete blur. Not that it really mattered who was speaking to her. She'd done nothing but smile and nod all morning, unsure what to do with all of the attention being sent her way. Until three weeks ago most of these people wouldn't have even been able to remember her name. She doubted it'd been very far from their lips lately though. A hasty marriage to one of the favorite local bachelors tended to make for fine gossip, especially when the woman in question abruptly left town until the day before the wedding.

There was a break in the conversation, and she tried to nod and say her good-byes so she could move on to another group, but she had to free her slipper first. And she had to free it without being able to see what was actually caught. She was going to have to bend down to rectify the problem. And her mother was going to be mad.

She took two shuffling steps out of the conversation circle and knelt down to free her shoe. Sure enough, as soon as she rose, her mother was there, a smile on her lips but not in her eyes. "What are you doing?"

Adelaide blinked. Wasn't it obvious? She'd felt she was rather quick about the entire business, but it had taken her a moment or two to free her slipper. "My shoe —"

"Mrs. Guthrey was telling you how delightful she thought you'd find the Blossom Festival this year, and you simply dropped out of the conversation." The disappointed whisper in her ear was considerably more familiar than the praises her mother had been heaping on her since her engagement to the son of a duke.

"But you hate the Blossom Festival. You always say you wouldn't set foot in it even if they did give you an invitation."

Mother frowned, more a flattening of the lips than an actual turning down of the corners. She wouldn't want to cause wrinkles, after all. "That was before I understood what the event really was. Now that Mrs. Guthrey has expounded upon its virtues, I am anticipating her invitation with considerable excitement."

Adelaide resisted the urge to roll her eyes. She wished her brother, Bernard, had been in the vicinity so they could exchange knowing glances. The saddest part was that Mother actually believed the reason she'd disliked the Blossom Festival was because she didn't understand it and not the fact that she'd never received an invitation to the house party. Because that was what the "festival" really was — a prettily named house party to show off Mr. Guthrey's impressive collection of tropical plants residing in his conservatory. And now she was going to have to go so that her mother could go as well. "I'm sure it will be delightful."

With a small smile and a nod, the same combination she'd been doing for the past three weeks, Adelaide turned to walk across the room only to have her mother catch her arm.

"Where are you going?"

"Over there." Adelaide gestured toward a table in the general direction of away. She couldn't see what was on it, but there was a high probability it contained food. "I'm hungry."

She took another step, only to trip on her hem again and have to take two quick steps to keep from falling. The bottom seam must have come loose.

Lady Crampton sighed the beleaguered sigh of a countess doomed with incapable children before leaning down and snapping the loose thread Adelaide kept stepping on. "I've never known you to be so clumsy. This is the third time I've had to fix your clothing today."

And that was the truest indication of how much attention had been paid to Adelaide in the last few years, because her maid was constantly pointing out various things amiss with her clothing.

As the middle child of a very busy family, Adelaide had shifted back and forth between her parents and the governess, doing and being whatever she needed to in order to make everyone around her happy. And they always seemed happiest when they forgot she was there. She became the quiet daughter who smiled at the guests and then trotted up to the nursery or softly played the piano while everyone else visited or played cards. Adelaide played the piano as passably average as she did everything else.

Mother sighed. "I suppose we should at least be thankful that trains are no longer in fashion. They made all the gowns so elegant during Helena's first year in Town."

Adelaide tried not to wince at the mention of her beautiful, blond, spectacle-less elder sister. For as long as Adelaide could remember, Mother had been preparing Helena for a great future, molding her to be the most sought-after woman in the land. A future princess or at the very least a duchess. The fact that she'd ended up a mere viscountess still gave their mother fits of vapors. And now, somehow, Adelaide had stumbled into the position Mother had always wanted for Helena — well, nearly the position she'd wanted — and the expectations were heavy indeed. It was enough to make a girl long to be forgotten at the modiste again.

Not that she'd been forgotten recently. And she'd spent the better part of the last three weeks at three different modistes, selecting dresses, getting fitted, and hearing her mother badger the poor seamstresses into making the dresses in a ridiculously short amount of time. Didn't they know Adelaide was to marry the Duke of Riverton's brother? It had been awful, but at least they'd traveled to another town to do it. Adelaide was never setting foot in Birmingham again.

"And it wouldn't hurt you to smile. People are watching, you know. This is your wedding. Never again will you be able to command so much attention, and you're more interested in the food. No wonder you weren't able to catch the right brother."

Adelaide stopped trying to squint at the table to determine what type of food was laid out on it and turned wide eyes to her mother. "I wasn't trying to catch one at all. I was hunting mushrooms."

"And that, my dear, is the problem. How difficult would it have been to ask the duke to help you? You were on his property, after all." Mother brushed invisible dust from her skirt. "I was hoping you'd realized what a boon your unfettered access to his property was. Why else would I have left you down there all night?"

"Given how often I used to get mushrooms from the old keep, I could hardly ask him to . . . Wait. What do you mean you left us down there? There *was* a wagon!"

A stinging burn pricked Adelaide's eyes,

and she blinked rapidly to keep the tears from forming. Once during that long afternoon they'd thought they heard someone driving by the old ruins so they'd shouted as loudly as they could. The lack of response led them to believe that they'd only heard their horses shifting around, moving from the patch of grass to the nearby creek. Only they hadn't been hearing things, and her mother had deliberately left her abandoned.

"Please do not call my visiting chaise a wagon. And yes, I was coming back from visiting Mrs. Pearson and I cut through Riverton lands. I thought you'd landed the duke, but I should have known not to get my hopes up that you would make such a lofty connection. Still, the younger son of a duke is a sight better than you were likely to attract during a summer in London."

Adelaide blinked while her mouth dropped open and snapped shut as if she were a fish. She wanted to say something, should say something, but what was there to say? The knowledge that they could have been saved or at least had a witness to their proper behavior changed everything and nothing at the same time. They were still married, would still have to be married, because if her mother had been planning to save her from the potential loss of reputation she'd have done so already . . . but what would Lord Trent do when he found out? Would he think they'd somehow planned the encounter, despite the fact that he'd climbed into the ruins out of his own curiosity?

"Pardon me, but may I claim my wife for a moment?"

The deep voice broke into Adelaide's thoughts, and she let out a squeak as she spun around to find her new husband less than a foot away.

"It's not my fault," she blurted.

"I'm aware of that." His lips curved into a crooked, dimpled smile. The brilliant green eyes didn't convey the same joy and charm of the smile, but she really couldn't blame him for that. She was certainly gaining more by this marriage than he was.

"Of course you can steal her away, my lord." Mother put on her most gracious smile and curtsied. "After all, you are family now."

His smile lost some of the little radiance it had, and his eyes flinched in a quickly disguised wince.

"Yes." He cleared his throat. "Thank you. My lady?" Lord Trent extended his arm in Adelaide's direction, and she took it numbly. Were they going to dance? Mother had hired a string quartet, but they were hardly playing anything lively at the moment. She clutched his arm tightly enough to feel the tensed muscles beneath. He might look like a relaxed gentleman, but the day was obviously wearing on his control. Not that she could blame him.

He led her up the short flight of stairs at the end of the room and paused in the open double doorway.

"Where are we going?" Adelaide whispered.

"To London," Lord Trent whispered back.

While she blinked repeatedly in an attempt to comprehend his statement, he turned them to the gathered crowd. "I want to thank you all for joining us today."

His voice carried over the room without sounding like he was shouting. One by one the conversations stopped until everyone faced the newly married couple. Even at this distance she could sense the expectation from some of the revelers, though she didn't know what they were hoping for. As far as scandals went, this one wasn't very interesting, and Lord Trent wasn't about to reveal what few details there were. Perhaps the crowd was hoping for something worth writing to their friends about. She found herself rather glad that she couldn't make out any faces at this distance.

Lord Trent smiled down at Adelaide. "My wife and I couldn't have asked for a better celebration, and I want you all to enjoy the hospitality of Lord and Lady Crampton for as long as you like."

Adelaide bit her lip to keep from laughing. Her mother had driven the servants to distraction preparing for a morning full of people, counting on all of them to have left by noon because her father refused to provide the funds to keep them happy longer than that.

"The time has come, however, for us to bid you farewell." Lord Trent's voice carried over the rush of gasps. "I've a new life in front of me, and I'm afraid staying here won't let me start it." He patted the hand Adelaide had wrapped around his arm.

The crowd melted in a unified sigh. Adelaide tried to smile because people were looking at her and it wouldn't do to look terrified as her new husband led her away, but she was. Oh, she was. His speech contained all the right words, and his demeanor would make even the most skeptical people question what they'd heard about this hasty marriage, but they couldn't see his eyes or feel the tension that ran through his body until his muscles quivered under her hand.

He escorted her from the room, and every step away from the gathering brought another measure of relaxation to the man at her side.

Neither of them said a word as he handed her into a waiting carriage and climbed in after her. The door closed, and he rested his head against the red velvet cushion, letting his eyes drift shut as his mouth flattened into a grim line.

Silence still reigned as they rolled down the drive. She pressed her head to the window and watched the already blurry house grow smaller and smaller until it disappeared behind a small rise in the drive.

She'd never loved that house. More than one afternoon had been spent with her nose in a book so she could escape to somewhere else, anywhere else. The sadness that crept in as they turned onto the main road surprised her. She might never have cared for Moonacre Park, but it was all she knew. And it wasn't home anymore.

So what was?

CHAPTER 3

He was married.

It was difficult to move beyond the undeniable fact that the rest of his life would now include the woman sitting across from him.

From the time Trent was old enough to realize the freedom granted to second sons, he'd known that his eventual marriage would be one of the most significant decisions he ever made. Without giving it any conscious thought or particular care, an expectation had developed. He'd assumed it would be a happy occasion, filled with friends and family thankful for an excuse to gather together in the middle of the year. He'd anticipated loving his bride and sharing small smiles fraught with hidden meanings, like he'd seen his sisters exchange with their husbands.

Instead he had a wife who hadn't met his gaze once, not even during the ceremony.

She'd spoken her vows to his cravat, so he hoped she wouldn't mind the fact that he didn't wear the same one every day.

It was his own joke, formed only in his head, but he couldn't resist the smile it inspired.

She didn't smile back, but that could have had something to do with the fact that her attention had drifted all the way down to his toes. Did that mean she would soon circle back around to the top and finally look him in the face?

"I hope you don't mind leaving a bit early. I thought we might be more comfortable in our own home."

"Our home?" Lady Adelaide blinked at him, or at least her gaze was directed in his general vicinity when her thick black lashes fluttered up and down over her crystal blue eyes.

The owlish blinks reminded him that her mother had insisted she not wear her spectacles during the wedding. He'd retrieved them from her maid, intending to give them to her at the breakfast, but she'd been pulled away as soon as they walked in the doors and he hadn't been near her since. Hopefully the lenses would make a nice peace offering now, a tiny gesture to set the tone he wanted for the marriage.

It was the one they were both stuck with, after all.

He pulled the spectacles from his pocket and extended them across the carriage. "Here. I obtained them from your maid earlier today."

"Thank you." She slid the frames onto her nose and looked him in the eye for the first time since that disastrous night in the old stone keep. "Isn't London a bit far to travel in one day?"

"I've arranged for fresh horses halfway along the route. If we push hard, we can make it." Trent shifted in his seat, wondering not for the first time if he'd made the right decision.

She nodded. "I'm sure we can. Perhaps one of the inns along the way will pack us a meal we can bring with us."

It was Trent's turn to blink. He'd expected a little bit of resistance, had even been reconsidering his options on places to stay the night. Now he couldn't help but wonder if her ready acceptance of his pushing to London meant she was in agreement with his thinking or that she expected him to be a harsh husband. Why hadn't it occurred to him before now that she might be just as wary of this marriage as he was? "I think we can take the time to eat properly."

"Oh. I'm sorry I misunderstood, Lord Trent." She blinked again and her gaze fell once more to his toes.

If this was an indication of how the rest of their lives was going to be, it was a sad sign indeed. With a sigh, Trent switched to her side of the carriage. Perhaps they could start over and find better footing before they made it to London.

Sitting shoulder to shoulder with her unsettled his insides, though. He couldn't recall ever sitting alone in the same carriage as a woman he wasn't related to, much less in the same seat. The sensation was far from unpleasant. He cleared his throat and reached for her hand. "I believe it would be proper for you to call me Trent, as my family does."

"If that is what you wish."

The silence pressed in as Trent waited for her to reciprocate the offer of a less formal name. When it didn't come he decided to press for it. "May I call you Adelaide?"

She turned and blinked those confused owlish eyes again. "Of course."

The carriage rolled easily along, but the conversation was mired in the deepest mud he had ever encountered. They'd found things to talk about when the sun had been high in the sky, beating down on them as they tried to find a way out through the vines. It was only as the moon had risen, and its silvery glow had sealed their fate, that the conversation had withered. Three weeks apart in anticipation of the wedding hadn't done anything to revitalize it.

The miles that had separated them while growing up seemed shorter than the distance between them in this carriage.

"I went down to the creek you mentioned. The one by the sheep fields that curves around and almost makes an island." When they'd talked about their favorite places to walk in the area, Adelaide had mentioned how she liked to go there and read because no one else ever disturbed the natural beauty.

"Did you take a book with you and sit in the gnarled tree?" She shifted her shoulders until she faced him more fully.

He grinned and turned his body to face hers as well. "I'm afraid I was a little too big for your reading nook. I had to sit on the ground and lean against it."

"Oh."

And the topic of the almost island was over as soon as it had begun. Adelaide turned back to the window, seemingly unperturbed by the lack of conversation and the high tension. It made Trent wonder what she was expecting of this union. If it wasn't interaction with him, what was it? Social connections? Managing the house?

Trent bit back a groan. His house. He'd been so focused on getting away from the prying eyes, so desperate to return to what was familiar, that he hadn't thought through all the ramifications of taking her home to London. "I should probably warn you."

She turned from the window, eyebrows lifted until they were completely lost behind the short hairs over her forehead. "About what?"

"Our home. In London." Trent smiled through the stabbing pain in his chest at using the word *our.* "It's a bit unconventional."

That was putting it lightly. He'd inherited half the staff when he moved in after Amelia, a family friend abandoned by her guardian in London, had moved into Hawthorne House as Griffith's ward. The staff had all but raised Amelia, which meant they acted more like family than servants. It had taken him a few weeks to adjust — and he'd known what he was walking into. How much worse would it be for Adelaide? He should probably try to ease into explaining the bizarre world she was about to walk into. Any woman who knew the extent of the strange way his household functioned would run in the other direction.

Not that Adelaide had that option anymore.

A small crease appeared above the center of her glasses as she tilted her head in thought. "You have been living in bachelor quarters, so I would assume things have been done a certain way. I can change that."

"No!" The word came out sharper than he'd intended, but Adelaide needed to know that she was not going to dismiss anyone from Trent's household staff. She could hire more if she wished, but he couldn't let go of the ones that were there. That would upset Amelia and all the other women in his family by extension.

"No?" More of that blinking. Did her eyes not get tired?

He rolled his shoulders and tried to look relaxed as he leaned against the cushioned seat back. "What I mean is that I'd prefer you not let anyone go who is currently employed. They do good work. It's just that the house is run a bit . . . differently."

"Oh." Her eyes widened in surprise. Long black lashes rimmed the large expanse of white with the clear blue lakes in the middle. The pupils were extremely small. That probably wasn't a good thing. "I'm sure I can adjust." She shifted farther into the corner of the seat. "Mother woke me quite early this morning. Do you mind if I take a nap?"

"Of course not." What else could he say? No, you may not fake sleep just to avoid an awkward conversation? With parents like hers — or rather a mother like hers, because Lord Crampton wasn't the worst sort of fellow — she had to have encountered more than her fair share of discord. Had she simply taken herself off to bed when things got difficult? Maybe that explained her constant state of mild dishevelment.

He watched his wife pretend to fall asleep. If he didn't keep calling her that, he was afraid he'd forget that he was married. Despite the uncomfortable morning, part of him wasn't convinced it had actually happened. Yet he'd stood before the priest and claimed her as his own, said the vows before God and man, and signed his name to the church register. What more did he need to do to convince himself the deed had been done? That he was now in possession of a wife?

He frowned. That probably wasn't the best way to think of her, even in the privacy of his own mind.

A light snore drifted across the carriage, surprising him enough to pull the beginnings of a smile from the corners of his lips.

She'd either been truly tired or she was the most accomplished fake sleeper he'd ever encountered. Not that he'd encountered that many. There wasn't much call for pretending to sleep at social functions.

Trent settled into his own corner. He could have moved back across the carriage, but that was what couples did when they were courting. Even if he did not feel married, he needed to start acting like he was. Farce had become truth for Adelaide's sleep. Maybe the same thing could happen in their marriage.

Chapter 4

The race to London — for it could be called little else — left Adelaide confused, with a dull ache over her whole body and stabbing pain in the back of her head. In the last vestiges of sunlight, London was still busy as they pulled into the city, allowing Adelaide to marvel at the hugeness of it all.

She tried not to gawk as they rolled through, but it was fascinating to a girl who'd never seen anything larger than Birmingham. The columned façade of St. George's of Hanover Square jutted into the road, just as it did in the Ackerman prints. It was a wonder that Mother hadn't been willing to wait and have the wedding there.

It wasn't as if delaying would have given Lord Trent an opportunity to back out, would it? If that had been an option, Adelaide wished they'd taken it. She'd read enough books to know that loveless arranged marriages, where the parties barely knew each other, were quite plentiful throughout history, particularly amongst the aristocracy. But she was a modern woman, and being foisted off onto a man she barely knew felt wrong. Besides, there was no political gain, no great joining of estates or assets. Nothing but the societal requirement that Lord Trent's freedom be sacrificed on the altar of her reputation. At least women who had stumbled into truly compromising situations would know the man in question, would have chosen him in some way. All she knew about Lord Trent was he enjoyed reading novels.

And he had an affinity for punching things. The fact that he trained to be able to punch things better made her a little uneasy. She'd heard the stories before, whispers about the women who wore an extra shawl in the village marketplace even in the summer heat. She tore her gaze from the city scenery outside the window and took in the way his shoulders took up a large portion of the seat and stretched the seams of his well-tailored coat. A shawl might not be enough for Adelaide if he wasn't the man she hoped he was.

She snapped her head back around to face the window once more. The houses they now passed were beautiful and well-appointed, with large numbers of windows testifying to the wealth of the area. Was he taking her to Hawthorne House? That would explain his cautioning her about not having much say over the hiring of servants. She'd heard quite a bit about the splendor of the mansion on Grosvenor Square and looked forward to seeing it, but she hoped they weren't going to live with his family. "Where do you live?"

"*We* live in Mount Street."

The emphasis he placed on the word *we* brought a swift blush to Adelaide's cheeks.

"And here we are." Trent smiled as the carriage slowed.

Adelaide pressed her face to the window, anxious to see her new home in spite of the sudden trepidation that made her dinner shift uncomfortably in her stomach.

She'd heard enough about London to recognize that the homes in front of her were modest by aristocracy standards but were certainly better than many others in Town. Bay windows curved out from the light brown building, adding a sense of division to the attached houses. They were too small to house ballrooms, which suited her nicely. A small dinner party would be easy enough to handle, but were the drawing rooms in this house large enough to hold more sizeable gatherings?

"Do you host things?" She winced at the blurted question. Her tongue was really going to have to learn to phrase things better before letting them out.

"As a bachelor? I haven't hosted anything, aside from the occasional family meal."

He opened the door himself and jumped from the coach, leaving Adelaide to fret over whether or not that meant he expected her to arrange a lot of social gatherings now. Would a younger son have reason to host such things? She took the hand Trent extended back into the carriage and stepped down to the pavement, willing her shaky legs to hold her steady.

The door in front of them swung open to reveal a tall man with a large pointed nose and a shockingly bald head. Light from nearby candles actually reflected off of the man's scalp. Did he polish it?

"Welcome home, my lord."

"Good evening, Fenton. Is the household assembled?" Trent reached back for Adelaide's hand and pulled her arm through his before escorting her into the house. *Escorting* might be a misleading word to use. He nearly had to drag her into the house because her feet had somehow become disconnected from her brain and refused to walk next to him without inducement.

There was a household gathered beyond that door waiting to meet her. What if they didn't like her? What if they wouldn't listen to her? What if she didn't know what to say to them? There was no *what if* about that one. She hadn't the first idea what to say to them.

"Yes, my lord." The tall man swung his arm wide to indicate the line of servants along the hall wall. The hall wasn't large, but the staff wasn't either, leaving plenty of room for all of them to stare openly at the woman beside their master.

Had Lord Trent sent word? Did they know who she was?

"Everyone, I would like you to meet Lady Adelaide . . . my wife." Trent dropped her hand and stepped to the side, throwing his arm out with a flourish, as if he were presenting a prize mare at the market.

"Oh, how exciting!" A tall, thin woman with nearly nonexistent hips and tight grey curls framing her face stepped forward from the front of the line. The housekeeper, Adelaide assumed. She looked like a friendly woman. An overly friendly woman if the hug Adelaide found herself wrapped in was any indication.

The embrace was brief and the housekeeper soon stepped back to more fully address Trent. Her fists plopped on her hips, or rather the narrow section of her body where hips could normally be found. The woman looked like a tall, skinny column. "You didn't drive all the way from Hertfordshire today, did you?"

Trent ducked his head and shifted his feet like a little boy caught stealing biscuits from the kitchen. "Well, I . . ."

"Hmmph." The housekeeper sniffed at Trent before turning her smile back to Adelaide. "I'm Mrs. Harris, the housekeeper. Would you like tea in the drawing room? I'm afraid he told us only that someone important was coming, so I didn't air out the proper bedroom. It will take me a bit to set things to rights. Did you bring a maid?"

Why hadn't Adelaide considered her maid and her trunks? Their mad dash for London didn't seem to include an abundance of luggage. "I don't —"

Trent cleared his throat. "My apologies for the misinformation."

Adelaide blinked. He was apologizing to his housekeeper?

"Her maid and Finch will be arriving Monday or Tuesday with the remainder of our luggage. Lady Adelaide has a small trunk in the carriage. I was hoping Lydia could see to her needs for the next few days."

Would anyone notice if Adelaide simply sat on the floor? She hoped not because she was actually becoming dizzy. There was so much to take in. She assumed Finch was Trent's valet, which meant both of them were now here without their personal servants. Rushing to London was seeming more and more a bizarre decision with every passing moment.

"I'd be delighted."

Adelaide swung her gaze down the short line of servants until it landed on a blond moppet. Wild yellow corkscrews of hair jutted out from various places beneath her cap. At first glance, Adelaide thought the young woman was a child, but closer inspection revealed otherwise. Where Mrs. Harris was lacking any curves, this young lady had them aplenty. Including one in the front that gave her skirt a slight flare. Adelaide couldn't stop herself from going a bit slack-jawed. That maid was with child!

Trent slid her arm through his once more and leaned in until his lips brushed her ear. "Not a word. I'll explain later."

She was still shaking off the shivers his whispering breath had induced when the housekeeper shooed them toward a drawing room off the hall. "You two rest, and I'll see to the tea. There's no reason she can't meet the rest of them in the morning."

The staff scattered by some unspoken command, leaving Trent and Adelaide alone in the once elegant drawing room. She'd barely had time to take in the green-and-white-striped settee that had certainly seen better days when the butler entered. "Will you be requiring anything else, my lord?"

Trent smirked. "Besides refreshment and a proper bedroom for my wife?"

"Er, yes sir. I see your point. I suppose you'll need me to stand in for Finch as well."

"Indeed. It will give you a chance to tell me the latest news."

Adelaide looked from her husband to the bald butler. They were going to exchange gossip? She groped for the arm of the worn sofa and lowered herself onto the seat. She couldn't remember the last time anyone in her home — well, her old home — had conversed with a servant beyond what was essential to get a particular job accomplished. So far tonight she'd been hugged by the housekeeper, been assigned a pregnant lady's maid, and watched her husband set up a chat session with the butler. Unconventional was putting it mildly.

After the butler left the room, she looked

up to find Trent observing her from beneath lowered lashes, almost as if he were waiting for her to pass judgment on her new home. His insecurity looked out of place on a face that had seemed confident and composed for as long as she could remember.

He rubbed his hand across the back of his neck and looked away from her before pacing to the window and back again. She might have worried about him wearing a track in the rug, but the floor covering already bore signs of more than one line of regular traffic. The room didn't look too out of fashion, but it had certainly been well used since it was decorated. It probably looked exactly as it had when he moved in. A bachelor wouldn't have much reason to redecorate the drawing room, after all.

She'd almost worked up the nerve to say something when a footman entered with a laden tea tray. He set the load on a tea table and left, closing the door quietly behind him.

Leaving her alone in a room with an unrelated man.

Yet another reminder that she'd gotten married that morning.

Was everything in her life destined to become unfamiliar because of that one event?

Porcelain clinked and she jerked her attention to the tea service only to find Trent taking care of the pouring duties. The teapot looked strange in a man's hands. "How do you take it?"

"The same way you do," Adelaide said quietly, cringing a bit as he dropped five lumps of sugar and a splash of milk into her cup. How did the man drink something that sweet?

She sipped at her tea before selecting a biscuit just to be polite. The biscuit was surprisingly bland, a perfect complement to the overly sweet tea. Someone knew the master of the house well. Afraid she was about to drop both, she set the teacup on the table and slid the half-eaten biscuit onto the saucer before folding her hands in her lap. Things were happening too fast for her to keep up so she latched on to the one thing she could demand an explanation for. "The maid. Explain."

Trent sat back with his own cup and a handful of biscuits. "She's married to my valet."

Adelaide was very glad she'd put her tea down or she would have certainly dropped it in shock. "I beg your pardon?"

"Lydia. She's married to Finch. It's worked out nicely so far. I only keep a couple of horses here so have need for only the one groom. Lydia and Finch live in the second groom's room above the stable. The baby's due sometime in summer, though, so they're going to take positions at my Hertfordshire estate after this Season. Well, he is. I doubt she'll be doing much of anything other than mothering for a while. They've talked of eventually opening an inn."

Trent stuffed his mouth with half a biscuit but still avoided her gaze.

"I see." Although she didn't. Who had a married valet and let the man live separate from the actual house? Didn't men need their valets close by? "Are there any other special cases I should know about?"

Trent shrugged. "Lydia, Fenton, and Mrs. Harris came with the house. Finch too, in a rather roundabout way. Oswyn, Digby, Mabel, and Eve have all joined the staff within the past two years. There was another scullery maid but she had trouble adjusting to Mrs. Harris's . . . uh, familiarity, so she went to work elsewhere. Everyone else seems to thrive on the environment."

"She hugged me." Adelaide couldn't help the flat tone of her voice. She couldn't remember the last time her parents had hugged her, much less a servant.

"I know. She usually eats dinner with me. Fenton too. We've also been known to share a glass of port in the evenings." Trent blushed and looked into his teacup.

Adelaide didn't know what to say. Or think. Or do. She'd spent every spare moment the last three weeks poring over any home management book she could find, lamenting the fact that she'd never really learned how to run a household. Helena's lessons had always come first, and there never seemed to be any time left to teach Adelaide anything. Not that any knowledge she might have gained would be useful here.

While it was nice to know life wasn't going to be like the dry and discouraging situations mentioned in the book she'd pulled from her father's study, she wished she wasn't quite so lost as to what to expect. The constant surprises weren't helping the pain in her head any. "Well. I'm sure everything will settle in nicely."

Trent smiled at her. A wide, genuine smile that made her breath catch. Did he often go around smiling at women like that? If so, she was sure to run into more than one lady who had been hoping for her position.

A brisk knock preceded Mrs. Harris popping her head into the drawing room. "My lady, your room is prepared. Feel free to finish your tea. Lydia's waiting for you when you're ready."

Ah yes, the pregnant lady's maid. It boggled the mind, really, and gave her a better understanding of the social rule that servants never married. It was awkward knowing the person waiting on you was in a delicate condition.

More important, though, the fact that her room was ready meant that her bed was ready. She peeked at Trent through her lashes. A bed that her husband had the right to visit. After tonight there could be children. She had never even danced with the man, much less kissed him, and they could be having children together.

It was enough to make her want to order another pot of tea.

Chapter 5

There was a surprisingly large amount of tea in the cup Adelaide slid onto the table, considering the fact that she'd tilted the cup to her lips nine times. Trent knew. He'd been counting.

She smoothed her skirts and cleared her throat. "I suppose I'll go up to my room."

Trent nodded, but Adelaide didn't move from her perch on the edge of the settee. He looked up from his teacup and frowned. Was her glove inside out? He was sure it hadn't been that way during the wedding.

Adelaide shifted on the settee and wrapped her arms around her middle as if she were trying to shrink into the very fabric of the furniture.

What was wrong? Trent's gaze flew over the tea service. It wasn't the most elaborate spread, but given that they'd been traveling all day it seemed adequate. On days when Trent had been boxing or riding all afternoon Mrs. Harris brought out cold meat and bread with the evening tea. Perhaps traveling was more strenuous for a woman than it was for him. "Are you still hungry? I can have something more substantial sent up from the kitchens."

"What? Oh, no. It's not that. I . . . well, I don't know where my room is."

Her voice was so quiet he almost couldn't hear what she said, and then he wished he hadn't because her words made him feel like the veriest dolt. Of course she didn't know where her room was. She'd barely seen more than the front hall.

He cleared his throat and set his teacup back on the tray. "It's not that late, yet. Would you like a tour of the —"

"Yes, please."

Trent chuckled at how fast she'd jumped at his offer. It reminded him of the day he'd taken up residence in the house two years prior. He'd spent the entire first day wandering room to room, trying to adjust to the fact that it was all his now. Granted some of the furniture was shabby and very little of the decor was in the current fashions, but it was his, and that had made him feel like a proper adult for the first time. He'd even set up a study. Not that he did much more than answer correspondence in it, but still, he had one.

He rose, surprised to find his hands were a bit sweaty at the prospect of showing his new bride around the house. What if she didn't like it? Perhaps he should have spent the last three weeks in London fixing up the house. No, she'd probably want to decorate everything herself anyway. His mother always did. Not to mention there wasn't much he'd have been able to do sitting on a sofa with his ankle propped up.

"Obviously, this is the drawing room." He swung his arm in a wide arc, indicating the room they were occupying. As her head swiveled to take in the faded green silk wall coverings, he tried to surreptitiously wipe his hands on his trousers before offering her his arm.

"It's very . . . green."

Trent laughed. "It's at least a decade past needing redecorating. You can take care of that, if you wish. I've never had much use for the room before, so I've left it as it was when I acquired the house."

"It's a very nice place for a bachelor." She stood and slid her hand into his elbow.

"I know. Griffith inherited it, and since he didn't need two homes in London, he gave this one to me." There was more to the story than that, of course, but it all seemed like a bit much to get into with Adelaide right now, so he left it alone.

His wife blinked up at him. "That was very . . . nice . . . of him."

Wasn't that the kind of things families did for each other? In his experience it was, but the older he got the more he realized that his family might not fit in with the aristocratic norm. Or any norm for that matter. "Yes, it was."

He cleared his throat, wondering how to explain his family to Adelaide or if he even needed to. She'd discover it on her own soon enough. His mother and sisters would shower her with more affection than she could handle. Once he got around to telling them he'd gotten married. "The dining room is through here."

On and on the tour went. It wasn't an especially large house, but many of the upper rooms had been closed up for several years. "I'm not sure what this set of rooms is supposed to be, but you can turn it into whatever you wish."

Adelaide, who had been smiling softly through most of the tour, suddenly dropped her gaze to the floor and turned bright red. "I believe it's the nursery."

Trent looked around. This couldn't be the nursery. It was too stark. Not a single thing about the room looked like a child had ever lived in it. "We'll have to do some extensive renovations up here, then. I remember the Hawthorne nursery as a bright and cheerful place. I'll want the same for my children." He darted a quick look at the woman who was now destined to bear those children. "I mean, our children."

"Perhaps we could find my room now?"

The small, quiet voice was back. She'd almost begun to joke with him as the tour progressed, and one awkward conversation had her pulling back into herself. Trent didn't know how to handle that, having grown up around women who were more than willing to make their presence and their opinions known. Of course, they'd done so in the most polite and ladylike way possible. His mother would have had it no other way.

His mother would also not have him staring stupidly at his wife after she'd made a request.

"Of course. Your room." He took her down a flight of steps and escorted her into the small parlor shared by their bedrooms.

"My room is through there." Trent pointed to his door. "Yours is here."

"Thank you." She paused at the door to her room. "Is there, I mean, I . . . . good night, er, for now . . . that is . . . I . . .”

Before Trent could make sense of the jumbled words spilling from her mouth, she’d jerked the door open and slipped inside, shutting it just as quickly.

Even if Gentleman Jack himself beat him to a bloody pulp, Trent still wouldn’t admit it out loud . . . but he’d been looking forward to marriage for a long time. He leaned back in the leather wingback in his study and crossed his extended legs at the booted ankles, wondering how things had gotten so messed up and what on earth he was supposed to do to put them right again. True, he’d never sat around with other men at the club chatting about what he hoped his future wife would be like, but he’d spent more than one evening in the same position he was in now, imagining her. Not necessarily of her appearance — he’d never been infatuated with one woman enough to picture her in the role — but of their life together.

Never did those imaginings begin with his wife being a stranger from a family he could barely tolerate. They had never included the uncertainty of whether he would ever learn to like his wife, much less love her. His wildest scenarios had never included him wondering if people would think it anything other than a love match, or if anyone would have the gall to ask him how he felt about the pairing.

And they had certainly never included him sitting restlessly in his study on his wedding night.

He shifted his shoulders against the dark leather, trying to find a more comfortable position in the massive Chippendale wing-back. His best thinking was usually done in his father's old bergère chair, but he hadn't lasted five minutes in that chair before retreating to this one. His father's chair, situated as it was in Trent's bedchamber, was entirely too close to the problem to allow for proper consideration of the issue. A mere six steps from the door connecting his room directly to Adelaide's. He'd counted, twice, before bursting through the door to the sitting room and retreating to his study.

This was the real reason he'd wanted to get to London tonight. Here, in his own home, with servants he trusted and surroundings he was comfortable with, he could acknowledge something he'd been worrying about since the engagement had been officially announced. Upstairs, in a room that hadn't been used since he took up residence, slept a woman. Well, he assumed she slept. He didn't really know because she was up there and he was down here. It had been more than two hours since she'd closed her bedroom door. He really hoped she wasn't still waiting on him.

Unlike a lot of the boys he'd gone to school with and the men he encountered at his athletic clubs, Trent hadn't yet participated in the physical side of romantic relations. Griffith had always frowned at the boys swaggering into the room with smug smiles on their faces, getting congratulatory elbow nudges and knowing laughs. His opinion had been that he had no right to expect something of his wife that he didn't expect of himself, and if waiting weren't a feasible thing for a man to do, the Bible would never have indicated they should. Trent thought those rather profound and true statements, so he waited. It hadn't always been easy, but he'd waited.

And now he was married.

He had the wife upstairs to prove it. Well, legally anyway.

But he didn't feel married, and that was the thing that had driven him downstairs when his normal place of pondering was in direct view of the door connecting his room to hers. After years of building walls around his natural urges and convincing himself to ignore conversations that exhibited the difference of popular opinion, he'd finally gotten his body to align with his mind on the subject. But now they were in a state of disagreement again. His mind knew there was a wife upstairs, one who'd been raised to see marriage as a duty. She wouldn't understand why he was down here swirling a glass of untouched brandy instead of knocking on her door in his dressing gown.

Part of him didn't understand it either.

But the fact remained that he'd convinced himself to wait until he was married, to have his wife be the only woman he ever touched. And he'd always pictured that wife as someone he chose, someone he loved, someone he was eager to start a family and build a life with. Instead he was married to Adelaide Bell, and he didn't love her. He didn't even know her aside from the fact that she wore spectacles and didn't like carrots.

He'd always thought he'd know his wife a bit better than that.

What if she wasn't asleep? Should he send word? What would he even say? There wasn't a way to word such a message that wasn't cold, insulting, or both. He'd been counting on her to quietly fall asleep while waiting for him in the bed.

That would save all of the awkwardness for the morning breakfast table.

Trent frowned. Was this marriage going to ruin every breakfast for the rest of his life?

Nothing could be done about tomorrow's breakfast, but something had to be done to salvage the rest of them.

Tomorrow they would do whatever married people did — well, whatever they did during the day. He'd been fairly young when his father died, so his remembrances of his mother and father together were dim and colored by the mind of a child. Adelaide's parents, however, were still alive. And while it irked him to model anything in his life after something Lady Crampton did, the truth was that she and Lord Crampton seemed to rub along well enough. Adelaide would know what married people did. He could simply follow her lead.

Once they acted like a married couple, he'd feel like part of a married couple, and then the idea of knocking on the connecting door wouldn't make him feel so guilty. The whole process shouldn't take more than a few days, a couple of weeks at the most.

Trent lifted the glass to his lips but never tipped it to drink. There was only one problem with his plan of action. How in the

world was he going to explain it to Adelaide?

CHAPTER 6

She debated pleading a headache. Didn't some women require a day of rest after traveling? She could become one of those women. Or maybe she could become one of those women who took their breakfast on a tray in their room. As the lady of the house it was her prerogative to do so, if she wished. She was really ready to do anything that meant she didn't have to finish dressing and face the man she'd married.

Never had she been so embarrassed. What must he think of her? Once she'd entered her room last night, the events of the day had finally caught up with her and she'd become extraordinarily tired. Lydia had been very competent, if a little rough with the hairbrush, and within twenty minutes Adelaide had been tucked into bed wearing the new negligee her mother had insisted she purchase.

Even now Adelaide's face flamed as she

considered the flimsy garment now draped across the back of a chair. She'd hated being measured for the thing, disliked even more the conversation with her mother insisting she get it. Never had she dreamed that her maid — her temporary, increasing maid — would be the only one to see it.

What had he thought when he came to her room and found her sleeping with the blankets pulled all the way to her chin? She must have appeared the most unwilling wife in England. The poor man had already been trapped into marriage to her. And now he would think she was a . . . a . . . Adelaide didn't actually know what to call such a woman, but she was certain a man would know the right word. And now she was one.

There was no choice but to go down to breakfast and somehow tell him that she was open to his visiting her room. She considered leaving the connecting door between their rooms open, but that might embarrass the maid. Of course, her current maid was married so the regular rules of decorum might not apply in this case. Still, she couldn't impose upon Trent's privacy like that.

"I pressed this lovely blue gown last night. Will it do for the morning? I'll see to the rest of your garments while you eat." Lydia bustled out of the dressing room showing only the slightest waddle in her walk. Being with child certainly didn't slow the girl down as she herded Adelaide into the dressing room and whipped the gown over her head almost before she could blink. Within moments Adelaide found herself sitting on the stool in front of the dressing table with Lydia undoing the loose plait she'd created the night before.

Her mother had always admonished her to never talk to the servants about anything other than their duties, but Adelaide had a feeling that wasn't the way things were done in this house. She was going to have to learn some new rules if she wanted to meet her husband's expectations. "Do you know . . . Has my husband risen yet?"

"Oh yes, my lady." Lydia ran a comb through Adelaide's hair, drawing forth a wince. A good night's rest hadn't made the maid any gentler when it came to hair ministrations. "He's gone riding in Hyde Park, though I expect he'll be home any time now. He never misses breakfast."

Adelaide started forming a mental list of all the things she knew about her husband. There wasn't much to work with yet.

- Enjoys morning rides

- Likes breakfast
- Writes with his right hand but fences better with his left

That last thing was one of the few pieces of information she remembered from their conversation on That Night, as she'd taken to thinking of their time in the stone prison that had started this whole business. Despite the fact that she knew for certain there had been no way out of those ruins, the whole story felt a bit pathetic. Trapped into marriage by a mound of vines and stones. And one opportunistic mother.

"Does he ride every morning?" Adelaide fiddled with a pile of hairpins on the dressing table in front of her, trying to ignore the gouges Lydia was making in her scalp. Honestly, Rebecca couldn't get there fast enough.

"Yes, my lady."

Perfect. She'd have Father send her mount to London and she could ride with her husband in the mornings. If he wanted her to. Oh, bother. Figuring out what Trent expected husbands and wives to do together was going to be quite difficult.

Or maybe not. Breakfast was already going to be unpleasant enough with the whole conversation about nighttime visits. She might as well throw in a discussion about other marital duties while she was at it. Maybe that would make the whole thing less unpleasant. It certainly couldn't make it any worse.

Half an hour later Adelaide was frustrated as well as embarrassed.

The problem with conversations is that someone had to speak in order to start them. A cordial "Good morning" from one person followed by an equally polite "Good morning" from the other person didn't create much of a verbal foundation. Obviously he wasn't willing to ask the other frequent morning question of "Did you sleep well?" and she didn't really blame him. She wasn't willing to ask it either.

The sideboard of the breakfast room was piled with platters of food. Eggs, toast, bacon, and a large assortment of pastries made her mouth water. He gestured for her to go ahead of him to fix her plate. As she took more than she would probably be able to eat, she tried desperately to find something to say. Anything that didn't sound as if she was mocking him with the previous night's events.

When she turned from the sideboard, her mind was absorbed with another problem.

Where was she supposed to sit? The small breakfast table was round, so she didn't know where the foot was. Normally she'd choose the seat with the best view out the window, but what if he did that as well? Not that it was a very spectacular view, as it mostly overlooked the kitchen yard and small stable, but it did let in a bit of sunlight.

A footman relieved her of the decision by sliding a chair out and bowing her into it. Adelaide gratefully settled in, almost missing the servant's inquiry as to whether she would like tea, coffee, or chocolate to drink.

"Oh, coffee!" Adelaide couldn't contain her excitement. She'd had coffee at her aunt's house and adored the drink. Her mother considered it too plebeian for an aristocratic household, so Adelaide never got to drink it at home. The fact that as a married woman she would now get to start every day with the hot, bitter beverage made her happy enough to try to start a conversation with her husband.

Unfortunately, her glee also took over her thought processes because the next words out of her mouth were "Did you sleep well?"

Adelaide froze with her cup of steaming coffee still an inch above the saucer. The very thing she'd wanted to avoid was now floating between them, waiting to choke them like the infamous London haze.

What were the chances that he would notice if she excused herself now and didn't show her face again for a while? A month or two ought to be long enough for the fierce heat in her cheeks to subside. She lifted her lashes enough to peek at him. His green gaze was aimed directly at her, proof he would notice if she attempted to slink away. The only saving grace was that he, too, was in possession of a rather alarmingly red face. He ran a hand through his hair, sending his blond locks tumbling over his forehead, but that did nothing to hide the two spots of color riding his cheekbones.

If they were both embarrassed by the reference, they should be able to move on to a new topic of discussion without the other one complaining about it.

As soon as one of them found something else to say.

"I have a horse." Adelaide nearly followed her bumbling spill of words with a groan at how desperately abrupt they sounded, but she managed to restrain the sound by stuffing her mouth so full she nearly choked on her eggs.

"Ah," Trent stammered before taking a delaying sip of tea. "As do I. Were you intending on having your horse sent to

Town? We could send her to one of the estates if you'd rather."

Adelaide gulped down her half-chewed mouthful. "Will we visit the Hertfordshire estate soon? You mentioned repairs?"

Trent nodded. "The bedchamber wing suffered considerable damage during a recent storm or I'd have taken you there last night. The journey wouldn't have been as grueling."

Both of them blushed again. If this kept up they would be able to save a bundle of money on heating the house. Even now she was giving serious consideration to throwing some coffee onto the small fire that had been built to ward off the early morning chill. It was a bit ridiculous to blame her current discomfort on the flames burning so low in the grate they could really only be described as smoldering, but it made her feel better to do so.

Adelaide determined it was best to finish eating in silence. It seemed safer that way. Surely tomorrow things would be less awkward since the delay, for lack of a better word, wouldn't be between them anymore.

Would it?

What if her falling asleep wasn't the reason he hadn't visited her room? What if he had no intentions of truly making her his wife? He was a second son. He had no real need for heirs. He could ignore her, ship her off to one of his estates, and continue living life as he pleased. It had never occurred to her before now that she might not even get children out of this forced marriage.

Her toast stuck in her throat. Not even a large gulp of her quickly cooling coffee could wash it down.

Trent cleared his throat and stood. Adelaide looked up at him, not trusting her legs to hold her as she convinced herself this new fear was ridiculous and unfounded. Traveling was exhausting. Surely they weren't the only couple to wait a night.

"I usually go over to Grosvenor Chapel for Sunday services. I'm afraid I haven't rented my own pew yet. I can look into obtaining one at St. George if you'd rather not use the family pew at the Chapel."

Adelaide had completely forgotten that today was Sunday. They would attend church together. She would enter on his arm and sit in his pew. Their marriage would be efficiently announced by such an event without her having to suffer through personal introductions and less than subtle questions and skeptical looks at her midsection. "The family pew sounds wonderful."

"Can you be ready in half an hour? Most of the servants attend St. George, so I take the curricle over to Hawthorne House and then walk to Grosvenor Chapel."

"That sounds splendid." It did, actually. By the name it sounded like a smaller, cozier place to attend worship. Perhaps even similar to the village church at home. She'd spent a lot of time in that church, visiting with the rector and his wife when Mother would accidentally leave her behind on Sunday mornings, particularly once her brother, Bernard, was born. An even number made such a more elegant picture walking down the lane, after all. The rector had an affinity for jacks, and he and Adelaide would play the game while discussing the sermon.

She doubted that she would be playing jacks at any point today, but the distraction of attending services and actually having something to do caused the shaking of her legs to cease. She was fairly certain she could walk now, and she needed to if she was to have any hope of being ready to leave in a mere half an hour.

"May I escort you back upstairs?" Trent gave a half bow, unstyled hair flopping against his forehead once more, making her want to reach out and brush the strands back into place even though they wouldn't stay there.

She slid her hand into his arm with a smile of agreement. As she thrilled at the warmth she felt holding a man's arm with an ungloved hand, it suddenly became real to her. She was married. This man was her husband.

And for the first time in three weeks, she thought maybe that was a going to be a good thing.

He could have waited a week. They'd only been married yesterday. Most people wouldn't expect to see them out and about for several days, if not several weeks. The complete disconnection from everything he was familiar with left him craving a return to his normal routine. Though with Adelaide perched next to him in the curricle, the routine felt nothing like it used to. Her blue skirts draped against the dark brown of his trousers, a stark contrast that he'd never looked down and seen before.

Taking women for rides in his curricle wasn't something he did. Unless they were related, he confined his social encounters to more public venues. When he decided to court a woman it was going to be special, as exciting for him as it was for her.

At least, that had been the plan.

But now he was riding with his wife, and though he'd expected the worst after they'd bumbled through the morning's breakfast, there was something thrilling about looking over and seeing the morning sun glinting off her bonnet, highlighting the chin ribbon that had come untied and blown away from her face to tangle in the feathers on the side of the bonnet.

He smiled. A beautiful woman was riding down the street with him, and he was bemoaning the fact that the relationship was already a guaranteed success? At least guaranteed to reach matrimony. What would he do if he were courting Adelaide? If he'd gone to her house and picked her up like other gentlemen did when they went courting?

"Have you a favorite color?"

She blinked at him. "Color?"

"Yes. Color. Blue, green, brown. That sort of thing."

"Oh." She faced forward again, scrunching her nose until small wrinkles formed between her eyes. "I like blue. At least, I tend to buy a lot of blue dresses. I get to choose bolder blues now, which was a delightful change when Mother took me to the modiste a few weeks ago."

This was hardly the first time a woman of his acquaintance had brought up fashion in his presence. He'd even been known to carry his weight in a conversation or two on the subject. But it felt different talking about her dresses. Perhaps because he would now be buying them. "Did you get everything you needed? I don't expect you were able to outfit yourself for an entire Season in a mere three weeks."

"Oh, well, not for a normal Season, no, but as a married woman I'm sure what I have will be sufficient."

They fell into silence for the rest of the short ride. Where was the glib tongue that had gotten him invited to every society function in the vicinity since he was fifteen years old? He was the fellow who had talked his way around every bad mark in school, convinced the Earl of Egleshurst's heir to set up a desk and work on his Latin conjugations in the middle of the Eton athletic field, and very nearly came close to actually convincing one of the patronesses to let him into Almack's at five minutes past eleven.

With all of that experience he should be able to find *something* to talk to his wife about.

They left the curricle with the grooms at Hawthorne House and walked the short distance to Grosvenor Chapel, stumbling their way through a stilted discussion on tree leaves. Even that topic deserted them as they climbed the chapel steps.

How many times had he walked through these doors without thought for who else had passed through before him? For the most part he saw these people at various other events he attended. And while many of them viewed church as another place to see and be seen, his family had always been more interested in the service itself, part of the reason they elected to attend Grosvenor Chapel instead of St. George's.

Today, however, Trent was aware of every person they were escorted past. As the Duke of Riverton, Griffith had rented a pew at the very front of the sanctuary, and Trent and Adelaide had to walk past everyone to get there.

And everyone was very interested.

The door of the box pew clicked shut, putting a period on the statement that Adelaide was now a member of the Hawthorne family.

Hundreds of whispers created a low murmur right up until the first strains of organ music echoed through the chapel. As a boy, Trent had always prayed for a short and succinct sermon. Today he found himself hoping the message droned on. Not that he was interested in it — he had barely heard a word, highly distracted by the small shifts Adelaide made every few minutes.

She wasn't the first spouse to have sat in this box. Both of his sisters' husbands had sat here a time or two. Colin and Georgina still used the box when they were in London, though Ryland and Miranda now rented the one across the aisle. Adelaide was, however, the first of Trent's spouses to sit here. The only spouse. Because if this awkwardness was what other marriages were like, he had to call into question the sanity of the men he'd heard about who took more than one wife.

All too soon the service concluded, and Trent faced the difficult decision of when to leave the pew. Behind them, feet shuffled along the worn floorboards and pew boxes opened and shut in their own form of familiar benediction. It was the sounds of people, and people meant questions. He should have waited a week. Next week Griffith was supposed to be in town. With the duke at his side, no one would have dared approach him. Griffith was simply too intimidating. Never before had Trent considered his innate personable friendliness to be a disadvantage.

"Shall we get this over and done then?" Trent asked the fretting, dark-haired, unconventional beauty by his side.

She blinked up at him. He was becoming addicted to those blinks, crazy as it sounded. Her eyes were mesmerizing, capturing his attention even without the help of the slow blinks or the enhancement of her spectacles that made them appear even larger.

Trent cleared his throat. "There will be introductions, I'm sure. Are you prepared for them?"

Adelaide nodded. "Oh, yes. I'm rather good with names, I think."

"Once more into the breach, then." Trent reached across her to release them from the pew enclosure.

Her soft giggle caressed his ear as he pulled his arm back.

An answering grin slid across his face. He was glad she found his reference to *Henry V* amusing, even if Shakespeare would probably scoff at Trent's comparison of running the gauntlet of church members to a near-hopeless war invasion.

If the wide-eyed looks sent in their direction were any indication, news of their nuptials had yet to spread through London. He had half expected Lady Crampton to do everything shy of take out a column in the newspaper to let all of the aristocracy know she'd married off her second daughter to the son of a duke. Everyone he introduced Adelaide to seemed thoroughly shocked, as if they'd tried to convince themselves she was a visiting cousin or some such thing, even though all of the Hawthornes' cousins were considerably fairer in coloring. One young lady even seemed to be fighting to hold back tears.

That one seemed to bother Adelaide as they broke free of the throng and made their way back to Hawthorne House.

"Did you know her well?" The hand at his elbow tightened momentarily before the fingers smoothed along his forearm once more.

"Who?"

"Miss Elizabeth. The one who cried when you introduced me. Were you courting her?"

Trent stopped and turned to face her on the street. "I was not nor have I ever courted anyone. I go to gatherings because I have to. Occasionally I even want to. I dance. I smile. But I do not court. I'm certain she was upset about something else."

"Hmm." Adelaide glanced him up and down and then looked back over her shoulder at the church.

"Regardless," Trent said as they resumed

walking. “I’m married to you.”

“Yes. I suppose you are.”

And with that, any hope they’d had for maintaining a pleasant conversation on the way home disappeared.

Chapter 7

Trent's customary morning stretch was hindered by the sofa arm above his head and the upholstered back pushing against his right shoulder. With a groan, he rolled himself to the side and swung his legs up until he could lower his knees to the floor and stretch his arms out along the couch. A night of sitting up in a chair followed by a few hours of tossing and turning on a narrow sofa had left his muscles screaming in agony.

He rolled his head back and forth, hoping a good stretch would alleviate some of the tension and the headache that had come with it.

It didn't.

Marriage certainly wasn't doing him any favors yet, though he didn't know why it really should. He'd done it because he had to, because there'd been no other way around it. It'd been a gentlemanly duty, like dancing with wallflowers and holding the door open. Yes, this duty had more far-reaching consequences than doffing his hat in deference to a passing lady, but did it really have to change his entire life? He hadn't been courting a woman before, hadn't even been interested in one, so in a large way, nothing had changed.

He could continue on as he had been and it would almost be like the marriage had never happened in the first place.

One mighty push propelled him up from the sofa, ripping a groan from his chest as all the kinks rolled through his body in protest. He'd be good as new after a few hours of his customary morning exercise though.

The house was still quiet as he slipped up the stairs to his room, making a point not to look at the door across the upstairs parlor. More often than not, Trent readied himself for his morning ride, so he could easily avoid looking too closely at why he didn't want to ring for Fenton to come fill in for his valet. Though thinking about the fact that he didn't have to think about it diminished the benefit.

Digby's eyes widened and cut to the clock on the wall to note the early hour, but he didn't say anything as he readied Trent's horse. The sun was barely forcing its way through the clouds and smog when Trent trotted off in the direction of Hyde Park. A good run down the bridle path would set his mind back on track, and he could set about putting his life back the way he'd had it. So now there was a wife at home. That didn't really have to change anything.

The horse danced sideways as a leaf blew across the path. Apparently even Bartholomew wasn't buying that lie. Trent patted him on the neck and gave him the signal to stretch his legs into a near gallop. The wind blew Trent's hair off his face and cut through the seams of his coat, bringing with it the sharp chill of morning and the feeling of being alive.

A few other men were spaced along the path, some running their horses as he was, while others rode at a more leisurely pace. Seeing a black gelding with foam drying on his haunches as his rider walked him back toward the main road reminded Trent that he couldn't take out his need to escape on his horse. An easy pull on the reins slowed the horse to a jog. A good move for the health of the horse, but one that left him accessible to any other riders who were feeling a bit chatty. A rare occurrence this early in the morning, but when the news was interesting enough, people would ignore an inconvenience.

"Ho there, Hawthorne!" A gorgeous brown horse pranced over and fell into step beside Trent's. "There's talk that you had a wife sitting next to you at church yesterday."

Trent glanced at Mr. Bancroft over his shoulder and made himself grin. "Well, I'd hardly make her sit in the free seats."

Bancroft chuckled. "Made my own wife cry into her tea, you know. She'd had hopes for our Hannah. Didn't think you'd marry for years."

That made two of them, not that Trent had ever thought such things about Bancroft's daughter. He wasn't even sure he'd ever met Hannah, was fairly certain she wasn't yet sixteen. Still, it wouldn't do to insult the other man's wife. Or his own wife for that matter. "What can I say? I fell into the match when I wasn't looking."

"Ah, yes, love will get you like that. Happened that way with my own wife. Yes, sir, we're the lucky ones, you and I. The good Lord saw fit to bless us in spite of ourselves." Bancroft patted his horse on the neck. "Ulysses is getting restless. See you around, Hawthorne."

Trent could do no more than lift a hand before Bancroft's horse had taken off down the path.

One of the lucky ones. Trent didn't feel lucky. He felt the exact opposite. The conflict between reality and people's assumptions crawled under his cravat and shot an itch down his back, effectively ruining what freedom he'd found in the morning's rough gallop.

He turned the plodding horse toward home, resisting the urge to restrain the beast when his pace picked up the closer they got to the small stable.

The uncomfortable irritation had spread across his entire back by the time he walked in the house for breakfast. It wasn't helped any by the fierce scowl on Mrs. Harris's face when she met him at the door.

"I took a tray up this morning."

Trent rubbed a hand along the back of his neck. "I'm sorry to put you out. I always take breakfast down here after my ride though."

She crossed her arms over her chest, the dark frown on her round face looking out of place on his normally doting housekeeper. "I didn't make it for you."

"Oh, yes, Adelaide. Good." Trent pulled off his riding gloves. "Just so we're all clear here, why, exactly, is that a problem?"

"Because the sofa in your study wasn't

made for sleeping." She sniffed. "I've half a mind to serve you gruel this morning."

And he'd half a mind to get a new housekeeper. Not that he'd tell her that. Or follow through on the threat if he ever did get up the nerve to say it aloud. The other half of his mind knew that he was quite stuck with the woman until she chose to retire, unless he wanted to suffer the wrath of at least half of his family. "I'd really rather you didn't. If I had to start the day without your cinnamon butter and perfectly turned bacon I'd never manage to get anything accomplished. If I'm to function at all I can't be pining away for your inspiring breakfasts."

One side of her mouth ticked up. "Go on with you, then. Upstairs to freshen up. I'll tell Fenton you've returned."

Crisis averted and breakfast salvaged, Trent made his way upstairs, treading carefully, so as not to announce his return to the entire house. Talking his way past Mrs. Harris was one thing. Talking his way past his wife, whom he'd abandoned . . . again . . . was another thing entirely. He was more likely to stammer and blush his way into oblivion.

He ate breakfast with an eye on the door, fearing that despite having had a tray sent upstairs she intended to make an appearance downstairs as well. But she never showed, and he was left sitting in front of an empty plate, staring at the walls and wondering where he could go in his house that he could be assured of not running into her.

The pickings were slim, so he made the next logical choice.

He left the house.

Another breakfast tray, another harsh reminder that yet another day and night had gone by without any significant interaction with her husband. Adelaide frowned at her coddled eggs. Forget significant. She would have been happy with something as simple as "Good morning" or even a nod of acknowledgment. That, however, would require they be in the same room, and aside from a brief discussion about where to store her trunks, she hadn't seen him since her maid and clothing arrived from Hertfordshire.

She plucked the rose off the tray and spun it in her fingers. Mrs. Harris always added the flower — probably her attempt to make them both forget the reason she'd taken to having a tray sent up. After lifting the flower to her nose for a brief sniff, she slid it into the vase on the writing table she'd taken to eating at. Four roses. One for each day she'd avoided her husband in the morning. Monday's rose was starting to brown on the petal edges, yet another sign of how much time had passed since she'd spoken with Lord Trent.

Beneath the roses was a small pile of folded papers, the only type of communication she'd had with her husband in days. He sent a message every afternoon, delivered by Fenton, each more inane than the last. On the first day it had been a reminder that he'd instructed Oswyn, the footman, to make himself available should she wish to go anywhere, something that was already part of the man's job.

The following days had been even more ridiculous, telling her things such as where he'd left the newspapers if she wanted to read them and reminding her to tell Mrs. Harris what her favorite foods were. As if Mrs. Harris wouldn't track her down to find out that information on her own. Adelaide spent a great deal more time with the housekeeper than her husband, a fact that wouldn't have bothered her overmuch if she'd been spending any time with her husband at all.

The corner of her toast fell against her eggs and she nudged one side of the browned bread until it poked a hole in the pile of eggs. How many times had she wished for breakfast on a tray while growing up? It meant she wouldn't have to sit at the breakfast table, listening to everyone else plan a thrilling day while she contemplated which tree she was going to sit beneath while reading. Unless, of course, her mother needed her for something such as dancing lessons. That was the real reason Adelaide had always made an appearance at breakfast. If Helena's lessons required a partner, Adelaide was required to be present.

But now Adelaide was married, and she wasn't required to be anywhere.

Adelaide blinked, straightening her spine as the implications rushed through her. She didn't have to be anywhere, do anything, or help anyone if she didn't want to. While there might not be children in her future — a possibility she hoped to one day to rectify — there could at least be life in her future, and she was going to take control of it.

Rebecca, her lady's maid, gave a startled shriek when Adelaide all but pounced on her as she entered the room with a freshly pressed gown over her arm. After taking a deep, calming breath, the maid went about preparing Adelaide for the day in quiet efficiency, as any normal servant would do.

Except this morning she was humming.

Ever since Rebecca had arrived late Monday afternoon — along with the rest of Adelaide's trunks and Finch, Trent's valet and Lydia's husband — Adelaide had been fighting the urge to question Rebecca, speak to her, indulge in conversations she'd never dreamed of having with a servant before. After three days of Lydia's constant prattle and scalp abrasions, Adelaide expected to nearly wallow in Rebecca's more demure behavior. Instead she chafed against it, though her scalp found considerable solace in it.

The humming was the final push, though. Adelaide looked out the window, but the low grey clouds appeared to be ushering in the most dismal day they'd had since coming to London. It wasn't a beautiful day that inspired the maid's apparent good mood.

"Are you having a good morning, Rebecca?"

The maid smiled and moved toward the small dressing room at the back of Adelaide's bedchambers.

Adelaide followed with narrowed eyes. The dressing room was small, forming more of a large closet, so Adelaide had been getting ready out in the main room. Why was

Rebecca changing things this morning?

"Of course I am, my lady. Why do you ask?"

Could she possibly not know that she was practically singing as she worked? "The humming."

"Oh, yes." Her gaze darted down to the left before swinging back around to Adelaide's. An overly bright smile curved the maid's lips. "Do you like it? We thought it might brighten up the morning."

A perfunctory agreement had been poised on Adelaide's lips — after all, what did she care if the maid hummed while she worked — but the phrasing of Rebecca's answer gave her pause. "We?"

"Er, myself, Mrs. Harris, and Lydia. And Finch, of course." Rebecca began tugging at Adelaide's nightclothes. "It's a bit strange, really. Of course there's always talk in the servants' quarters, but this is well beyond the usual gossip. They actually want to help you, and . . . Oh dear. I'm saying the wrong things, aren't I? I told them I wasn't going to be any good at this. I haven't the slightest idea how to be so familiar."

Adelaide's eyes were wide. She thought her mouth might even be hanging open.

Rebecca slid the dress over Adelaide's head and walked behind her to work the fastenings. "Don't worry, Lady Adelaide. As of this moment I'll go back to being quiet, like a proper servant. We'll both be more comfortable that way."

Adelaide said nothing as silence fell in the room. Near silence, anyway. A bump and rustle echoed through the door connecting her room to her husband's, causing her to snap her head around in that direction. "Is he in there?"

Rebecca looked down, seeming to busy herself with Adelaide's slippers. "Yes, m'lady. Finch said he was running a bit behind his normal schedule this morning so you might hear when he came up to dress for the day. Mrs. Harris and Lydia said I should hum so you wouldn't notice."

The staff at this house was beyond Adelaide's understanding. Still, her earlier resolve remained — to do something with her day other than stare at the walls of her bedchamber or tiptoe around the house as if afraid she'd run into anyone, even though she was supposedly the mistress of the house. She hadn't the first notion of where she could possibly go beyond the house, so that left the house itself to serve as the focus for her industriousness.

And she intended to start with the drawing room.

After she finished her coffee. That should give her husband enough time to finish dressing and go to wherever it was he spent each day.

Trent adjusted the sleeve on his jacket and turned to Finch so he could put the finishing touches on Trent's cravat.

"Will that be all, my lord?" Finch turned to gather Trent's discarded riding clothes, once again avoiding looking Trent in the eye.

"You're mad at me too, are you?" Trent shoved his hand through the hair Finch had just finished styling. "Mrs. Harris stands in the front hall and glares at me any time I leave the house or come home. Fenton hasn't shared a single piece of gossip since Tuesday. And now you're acting like the world's most exemplary valet. I could only imagine what sorts of things your wife is saying about me."

Finch cleared his throat. "They're not very complimentary, my lord."

Trent grunted and dropped into his father's bergère chair.

"Will you be leaving for the club now, my lord?"

"No." Even that pleasure had been stolen from him. Trent couldn't go anywhere anymore without someone wanting to talk to him about his wife. With new people arriving back in London every day, it was remaining the fresh and favorite topic of conversation. He hadn't even been able to pick up a foil at his fencing club yesterday, given the number of congratulations and condolences he'd received as soon as he'd stepped in the door. "I'm staying home today."

Finch's entire body seemed to lighten. His shoulders popped back, and a smile stretched across his face. "That's fabulous, my lord."

Trent closed his eyes and sighed. The valet obviously thought Trent intended to do something with his wife. He didn't. There were weeks' worth of correspondence piled up in his study that he had yet to get to, despite the fact that he'd spent every night this week sleeping in that room. But he didn't tell Finch that. It wouldn't hurt for one of them to hold on to his dreams for a little longer.

CHAPTER 8

As the most public room, and quite possibly the shabbiest, the drawing room was in desperate need of an overhaul. The only problem was that desire and intent did not guarantee ability. Adelaide didn't have the first notion regarding what to do to redecorate a room. Change the drapes, certainly. That couldn't be too difficult. They were merely fabric hanging from rods.

Adelaide pulled back the heavy green brocade to look up at the fixture to see if it would need replacing as well. From what she could see, the rod and hooks were fairly simple in design. Something more elaborate would have been nice, but the existing ones were sufficient.

A movement on the other side of the windowpane caught Adelaide's eye, and she found herself staring into the faces of two women. One was young, likely around Adelaide's own age. Her eyes widened as she took in Adelaide's presence in the window. When the young woman wrapped her hand around the elbow of the older woman, gesturing toward Adelaide with her free hand, Adelaide's instincts took over and she jerked away from the window.

Unfortunately she still held the curtain she'd been inspecting.

Her foot landed on the fabric, sending it sliding across the floor and Adelaide tumbling backward onto her bottom.

With the curtain on her head — rod, hooks, and all.

So much for not replacing the curtain fixtures.

Had the clumsy accident caused enough noise to bring one of the servants running? She rather hoped not, as she wanted to stay down on the floor until the two women outside had been given more than enough time to finish gawking and move along.

No hurried steps echoed through the house, indicating that at least one thing was going in her favor today. After waiting a few more minutes, she extricated herself from the old brocade and left the entire mess in a pile behind the settee.

If the drawing room hadn't topped her list of rooms to redecorate before, it certainly did now.

■ ■ ■ ■

Trent requested that his breakfast tray be delivered to his study the next morning. He'd even given instructions for Oswyn, arguably the most deferential of the staff, to deliver the tray. As familiar as they were, his staff had never gone against a direct request before, so when the knock came he had every confidence that Oswyn was on the other side of the door.

And he was, tray in hand and frown in place. And ranging behind him in a half circle of disparagement stood the rest of his staff. His goal had been to avoid their disapproving frowns, but he clearly was doomed to disappointment. Only Adelaide's lady's maid seemed to be missing. Even Digby had come in from the stables for the confrontation.

With a groan Trent ripped the tray from Oswyn's hands and kicked the door closed in their faces.

He'd taken care of his correspondence the day before, so after finishing his breakfast he settled into the wingback chair with a book. He considered stretching out on the sofa, but the sofa was getting enough of his attention lately.

The last thing he expected as he turned another page without really knowing what he'd read was for Mrs. Harris to burst into the study unannounced.

She stomped across the room to collect his breakfast tray but didn't pick it up from the desk where he'd left it. "I've never taken you for a coward, my lord. I'm not sure that I cotton to working for such a man."

The book fell from Trent's stunned fingers and lay open, forgotten in his lap, page lost.

"She's such a lovely young lady." Mrs. Harris picked up the tray. "An utter pleasure to work with."

Trent frowned. A pleasure to work with? Doing what? As near as he could tell, Adelaide never left her room. Not that he'd know because he so rarely left his study, but he knew what his house had looked like before, and it didn't look a bit different now. Even the food was the same, so she wasn't having much effect on the menus either.

"Having a woman in the house again is so nice. Not since Amelia was here have I had reason to pull out the fine china."

A laugh, born of equal parts despair and humor, threatened to bust through Trent's lips. The only difference between the fine china and the plates Trent had been served on before he got married was that the fine china had four matching place settings. On the rare occasion that he'd had the family over, he'd borrowed dishes from Hawthorne House.

Mrs. Harris walked toward the door but turned back before leaving the room. "Hiding in here, reading a book. When's the last time you read in the middle of the day, my lord? You think about that and what you're hiding from. I think you'll agree with my assessment of your recreant tendencies."

Trent coughed. "Recreant?"

"I read it in one of Lady Adelaide's books. She said it meant to give in to a trial. More than applies in this case, if you ask me."

And then she was gone, leaving Trent to stare at his unread book and wonder if she was right.

After wrecking the drawing room, Adelaide had retreated back to her solitude, finding comfort, as she always had, in books, both novel and academic. By Sunday morning, she had abandoned her plans to cry off going to church, because she simply couldn't stand to be in the house any longer. She was waiting in the front hall, pressed and coiffed and ready to go when he came trotting down the stairs. He paused in the middle of the staircase when he caught sight of her by the door but did no more than nod and say a quiet "Good" before ushering her out the door to the curricle.

Church was little better than it had been the first week. They arrived just before the beginning of the service, and Trent ushered her out before most of the other people had a chance to open their pew doors.

Back home they'd stood awkwardly in the hall, facing each other but staring at points on either side. Adelaide chose a strange still-life painting to inspect, noting that all the fruit in the bowl appeared to have faces. Her humiliation was being witnessed by a painting of sentient fruit. She'd truly reached the bottom of her ladder.

Perhaps that sensation of having nowhere to go but up was what gave her a spurt of gumption when the sun rose Monday morning. So what if she'd pulled the curtains from the wall in the drawing room? It was simply another sign that they needed to be replaced. Eventually someone — her mother, if no one else — was going to come for a visit, and she would have to use the drawing room. It might as well look presentable.

All she had to do was pick new curtains and she would be off to a great start.

Reality splashed a bucket of cold water on

her plans for the day, however. She could practically hear the shopkeepers laughing at her trying to buy things under Trent's name with no proof that she was at all connected to him. Church-fueled rumors weren't likely to be enough to make them part with their goods. And she had no idea how much money she had to spend. That would require talking to her husband, which would mean spending actual time together in the same room — something he didn't seem inclined to do.

Perhaps she should send a note through Fenton? Perhaps ask to have an appointment in his schedule? Did he even have a schedule? Her father did. It was managed by the secretary who came by the house twice a week to assist her father in correspondence and other paper-related things. Being a second son, would Trent have need for such a thing?

With her hands on her hips, Adelaide stood in the middle of the front hall, unwilling to give up yet another week to melancholy. Where else could she stake a claim in the house? The door to the servants' domain caught her eye. As the lady of the house, she should know the kitchen — shouldn't she? What sort of food stocks did they have?

Simply walking through the door to the

lower floor made her giddy. There weren't many servants in the house, but at least half of them were likely working belowstairs at the moment, and Adelaide was going to go spend some time with them. She might not have any interaction her husband, but she could certainly embrace her bizarre new household.

After Mrs. Harris's admonishment, Trent had moved back to his desk. As days passed, he'd gone over every account book, every estate report, until his eyes had nearly crossed. His poor sleep habits had caught up with him, and he found himself nodding off at the desk more than once. And finally, he'd exhausted even the remotest account-related work. For a man who had always taken as little interest as possible in the business of his estate, Trent was finding an awful lot of reasons to hide away.

Desperate for something that could be deemed productive while still keeping him in the study, Trent yanked open the bottom drawer of the cabinet behind his desk. A pile of papers and a discarded cravat were on top, but he shoved them aside to pull out the farm management book he'd stashed there a few months prior. When he'd come across the book he had flipped through it, thinking it would be something interesting to pass along to his brother. But soon he found himself actually reading it. He'd been fascinated by the discussion of how to grow pineapples in less-than-tropical weather. He even caught himself pondering ways to make the process better as he rode his horse through Hyde Park in the morning.

That was when he buried the book. The thoughts and ambitions running through his head scared him. They were thoughts of a responsible, take-charge man, not a carefree, athletics-obsessed boy. And he wasn't ready to be a man, appearances to the contrary. Just because he had his own house and now his own wife didn't mean he wanted to show God how capable he could be in other areas of his life.

If he wanted to remain in his study, though, this book was all that was left. All of his correspondence was up to date, even those he'd originally had no intention of answering. He'd had Fenton deliver any and all invitations to Adelaide, but she had yet to tell him which events they were to attend. Granted there weren't that many to choose from so early in the Season, and the attending crowds would be small — which made it harder to avoid speculative questions — so he wasn't really bothered by their lack of activity. No one else would think a thing of it either, since the few people who were already in Town wouldn't expect a newly married couple to spend all of their evenings out and about. They probably didn't even expect them to stay in Town.

He should have taken her on a trip.

But then he wouldn't have an entire town house in which to avoid her.

He should ask her to sort through the invitations and accept one or two, to give them something to do.

But that would mean seeking her out. And the mere thought of doing such a thing caused his cravat to feel too tight. Mrs. Harris was right. He was a coward.

Since he already was one, it wouldn't hurt to bear the title one more day. Holding on to the topic would give them something to actually discuss, should they find themselves in the same room. If he sought her out he wouldn't have anything to fall back on when they accidentally encountered each other again.

Apparently he was pathetic as well as a coward.

He plopped the farming book onto his desk, and it fell open to the page he'd marked with a tattered scrap of parchment.

Trent grabbed a clean sheet of paper and a pencil and began sketching out his idea for growing the pineapples in tiers, thereby saving more of the heat. Though it was rather disgusting to think about, he'd need a steady supply of horse deposits if he wanted to actually implement this process. Trust the Dutch to figure out that the stuff would generate enough heat to keep a glass enclosure tropically warm.

Adelaide's dowry estate was in Suffolk, very near to Newmarket, with its abundance of horse farms and racetracks. Getting a steady supply of the necessary product would actually be feasible.

Not that he had any intention of actually implementing any of this. It was simply something to do while his wife . . . He laid the pencil on the table and sat back in his chair, brows lowered in thought. What was his wife doing? Some of the people she knew from the country had to be arriving in Town. Was she going to visit them? Letting them know of her changed status by leaving cards around the city?

He jerked upright, bumping his hand against the pencil and sending it rolling across the desk and clattering to the floor.

Cards. He'd forgotten to have new cards made up for her. She couldn't visit anyone without them. And if she couldn't visit anyone, she couldn't leave the house, which meant Trent could bump into her at any moment.

Clearly his wife needed calling cards. Today, if at all possible.

Pleased to have a mission, Trent threw the book back into the drawer and slammed it shut with his booted foot.

He nearly ran down the stairs to the front hall. "Fenton! My hat and coat, please."

His hand twitched with impatience, beating his thumb against his thigh as he waited for the butler to bring the requested items. When had the man gotten so slow? Granted he was on the older side, but he'd always seemed quite spry, despite his lack of hair. It had taken Trent six months to convince the man to stop wearing the ghastly powdered wig and just embrace the natural look. It shocked a few people, of course, but it wasn't anywhere near as bad as his brother-in-law Ryland's butler. Those wishing to visit the Duke and Duchess of Marshington had to get past a hulking man with no neck and a rather prominent scar on his face. In comparison, a bald butler was nearly normal.

Mrs. Harris came bustling into the hall with Trent's coat thrown over her arm.

Fenton was on her heels with the hat, his lips pressed into a thin line of displeasure. Sometimes Trent wondered if his butler and housekeeper weren't a married couple as well. They certainly acted like one at times.

"And where do you think you're going?" Mrs. Harris crossed her arms over her chest, effectively holding Trent's coat captive.

Trent grinned, knowing he had an answer the woman would approve of. "To get my wife calling cards. She needs to be able to tell the world of her new status, doesn't she?"

The motherly housekeeper looked torn as she held out the garment. "I suppose. Maybe being able to get out and about will lift her spirits."

The triumph he'd felt at getting his busybody of a housekeeper to relinquish the coat dimmed. "She is unwell?"

Mrs. Harris shrugged. "Don't know what else you expect when you haul a woman into an unknown house and leave her to her own devices. Poor Lydia's taken to working in the kitchen because she feels so terrible. Her ladyship cries whenever Lydia enters the room. Makes it awfully hard for a maid to do her work that way."

"Lydia shouldn't be working anymore, anyway," Trent grumbled. Weren't pregnant women supposed to be delicate?

It bothered him, though, that Adelaide was so unhappy. During their night in the ruins she'd told him that she spent most of her time reading and going for walks unless one parent or another wished her to do something else. Trent's library wasn't large, but it was respectable. And if her maid wasn't willing to go out he had other maids and a footman who could escort her wherever she wanted to walk in London. He thought she'd be happy.

Apparently not.

Hardly more than a week into his marriage, and he'd already broken his wife.

"Calling cards." His voice was thin, like a man taking his last gasping breath before drowning. "She needs calling cards so she can get out more. That's all."

Mrs. Harris frowned. "It's a start."

Trent grabbed his hat from Fenton and restrained himself from running out the front door as if he were a convict escaping from prison.

Chapter 9

He took a hack to the print shop, where the helpful man told him he could have a batch of cards delivered tomorrow and send a larger box within a week. Unwilling to return home so soon, he convinced the man to do a small batch right away and have them delivered to Trent's club. That he was willing to pay for such an extravagance was a true sign of his desperation.

It was as good an excuse as any to spend the remainder of the day within the walls of Boodle's. Perhaps now that he was actually doing something for his marriage, no matter how small, he wouldn't feel so pinned down by the questions and stares. Besides, it had been over a week. Surely it was old news by now. He certainly hoped so, anyway. He couldn't figure out what to say to his wife, much less what to say about her.

Trent wasn't sure what all the fuss was about anyway. Yes, the marriage was a surprise, but it had taken place in the country during the late winter. There was no reason for anyone in London to think it had been anything less than planned. Unexpected, yes, but not scandalous. Unless, of course, someone from Hertfordshire had decided it was interesting enough news to write their cousin about.

Trent sank into one of the tufted leather club chairs, a book open on his lap that he hoped would be a deterrent to those looking for a casual chat — even if he wasn't reading it. All he wanted was to breathe. And to not be married. But since the second wish wasn't about to come true unless God decided to dabble in time travel, the first one was increasingly difficult.

It was obvious that he'd failed at the one thing he thought this marriage would accomplish. While it was entirely possible Adelaide cringed every time her manipulative overbearing mother entered the room, he was fairly certain no one at Moonacre Park could cause her to cry with their mere existence. So why Lydia? The girl wasn't always the sharpest mind in the room, but she was very sweet and incredibly loyal. She would never have said or done anything to Adelaide, at least not on purpose. One never knew when a person had hidden issues waiting to be stumbled upon by an unsuspecting person, though. That was why Trent was careful to keep his social interactions as light as possible. He had close friends, but they were carefully selected.

"How is married life treating you?"

Trent looked up to find someone who decidedly didn't make the list of close friends. Mr. Givendale would be one of those who would ignore the unspoken signal of the book.

"Splendid," Trent lied. "I happen to be waiting here for a delivery to take back to surprise my wife."

Givendale smirked and adjusted the sleeve of his almost too closely tailored blue coat. "Why not have it sent to the house so you wouldn't have to leave your new bride?"

Trent turned the page in his book, making a point of looking at the pages. "I didn't want to risk her coming across the delivery without me. I wish to give it to her myself."

"I hear she's quite striking. You'd think someone that memorable would have been recognized by someone, but no one knows who she is." As rude as he was loud, the obnoxious man settled into the chair to Trent's left.

"She's my wife." Trent tried actually reading the book to see if the movement of his eyes would convince the other man to leave. It wasn't that Trent wasn't willing to talk to anybody today, he just didn't particularly want to talk to Givendale. Perhaps he could abandon the book and make his way into the billiard room. If Givendale followed, Trent could accidentally skewer him with a cue stick.

"Is she a lady?"

"Of course she is. She's married to me." Trent snapped his book shut in a rare show of irritation and rose. "I'm going to get a drink."

Givendale raised his light brown eyebrows toward the edge of his carefully waved and waxed dark blond hair, looking at the porter who had just passed them and could easily have gotten Trent's drink. But the man didn't say anything and he didn't rise, so Trent left him there to go in search of a drink he really didn't want.

Was this what life was going to be? A series of doing things he didn't want to do in order to keep himself from thinking about the fact that he didn't know how to do what he needed to do?

He got a glass of port and joined a casual game of whist. The conversation was general with no mention of his home or his wife. It was exactly what he'd thought he wanted, yet he found himself having to make a conscious effort to go through the proper motions. Obviously he wanted to be elsewhere — he just didn't know where that was.

Mixed feelings shot through him when the package finally arrived with the setting sun. Part of him was eager to get home and see if Adelaide liked the gift, but the rest of him still wanted to avoid his wife. Some delusional part of him believed if he pretended she wasn't there, he would wake up and discover he was still a bachelor.

He took out one of the calling cards. *Lady Trent Hawthorne* strode across the stiff card in black script. It was there. Undeniable. Real.

It was time for him to grow up and make the best of it, become a man in at least a few aspects of the word. Life wasn't going to change, and he really missed enjoying his breakfast. He would like his wife to feel as if she could leave her room for breakfast. Not that he blamed her for not coming down anymore. As he had yet to appear at her bedroom door at night, it stood to reason she wouldn't want to see him in the morning.

With renewed if shaky resolve, Trent stabbed his arms into his greatcoat and strode home, unwilling to wait around for a hack to be called. Energy spilled through him, lengthening his stride until he was nearly running toward home, though he had no idea what to do when he got there.

The thought pulled him to a stop at the corner of Berkeley Street and Bruton Place. Intention was all well and good, but what was he actually going to do?

A wagon rolled down the street next to him, rattling over the cobbles and jarring him from his introspection. He continued strolling home, though with less power than before. God had put him into this situation, so Trent was just going to have to trust that God was going to tell him what to do next.

Adelaide's afternoon in the kitchens had gone better than she'd expected. The staff had welcomed her with smiles and pulled a chair up to the worn worktable for her. She'd stayed to visit with them after eating the snack they put in front of her, even helping Mrs. Harris knead bread. The time had been very educational. Aside from learning the proper way to punch a pile of dough, she learned that Digby, the groom, had started his working life as a chimney sweep before moving to the considerably cleaner and less hazardous job of mucking stalls.

She also learned that Lydia and Finch had grown up near each other before going into domestic service. They'd occasionally bumped into each other when they visited with their mothers and that was how their romance was born. It was all very sweet, but she still couldn't bring herself to look at Lydia's extended front. The idea that her maid was going to have a child and Adelaide wasn't was depressing.

Adelaide even learned more about her own maid, having had no idea that Rebecca had an affinity for licorice candy. It was an insignificant detail, but it made her feel connected to the weird little group that had formed a strange sort of family in the servants' quarters of the town house.

She would probably have to look into hiring a cook soon, and it would be an added difficulty finding one that would work well with the existing staff. Mrs. Harris had been overseeing the meal preparation for Trent since he moved in, a simple enough task when the man frequently ate dinner at his club or one social engagement or another. But they were married now and more meals would be taken at home, and eventually they might even have guests. Assuming she ever saw her husband again, of course. She wasn't about to invite anyone over so they could see that she'd been exiled in her own home.

As the afternoon wore into evening, she waited expectantly for Fenton to relay the day's message from Lord Trent.

Today, however, there had been no message for her. Nor had Mrs. Harris received word that he was planning to dine elsewhere, which meant that he would likely be coming home for dinner. Determined not to miss him, Adelaide plopped herself in the dining room to await her husband.

The servants hadn't let her wait alone.

She'd started out playing Patience since it could be played on her own, spreading the cards out along the table so that it didn't feel quite so empty. Before long Mabel, the parlormaid, asked to join her, followed by Oswyn, the footman, and they'd started a simple game of Maw, using the silver utensils from the sideboard as markers. After the first round, Fenton joined in, and before long most of the staff were seated around the dining room table. It was somewhat amusing to see a pile of gleaming flatware in the middle of the table. And since none of it represented real money, they were making the most ridiculous wagers and taking outlandish risks with their card play. She hadn't had so much fun in weeks. Maybe even years.

"Hullo?" a voice called from the main hall.

Adelaide jerked at the sound of her husband's voice and darted a look at Fenton. The butler was in the dining room playing cards instead of manning his post, and it was her fault. Trent had said she wasn't allowed to fire any of them, but that didn't mean that he couldn't.

"We're in here, my lord!" Fenton called, never taking his eyes from his cards while he decided which one to play.

Trent entered the room and didn't even blink at the scene he found. "Ah, Silver Maw. Who's winning?"

Adelaide blinked. They'd done this before? No wonder Oswyn had been so quick to suggest they pull out the silver.

Fenton glanced up. "My lady is rather good at this, my lord. You'll definitely want to partner with her at your mother's card party in a few weeks."

Adelaide blinked again. She was going to a card party? But she'd already exhausted her entire repertoire of card games.

"Mother's having a card party? I didn't even know they'd arrived in Town." Trent shrugged his coat off and draped it over the back of a dining chair before settling into the seat next to her. He placed his arm along the back of her chair, leaned in to look at her cards, and grinned at the rest of the players. "I'm afraid all of you are doomed."

Adelaide looked at her cards. They were rubbish. She had nothing worth playing and expected to lose every trick.

Fenton narrowed his eyes in Trent's direction before looking at Adelaide, obviously trying to discern her hand from Trent's statement. "Your mother has not yet arrived, but she sent word to her staff in Town to prepare for a gathering and that invitations have been delivered to the most essential guests."

Essential guests? Adelaide had never been considered essential anywhere. Convenient, yes, but never essential. The idea caused panic to curl her toes in her slippers. That was easily ignored, though, as her brain was entirely taken up by the confusing man who was her husband. Fortunately her cards were nothing of note, and as long as she made sure to follow suit, no one would notice that she wasn't applying anything anyone could remotely call a strategy to her playing choices.

What was Trent thinking? He'd ignored her for days, essentially acting as if he didn't have a wife, and now he wanted to watch her play a simple game of cards? Looking over her shoulder as if this were a leisurely family evening?

Her fingers curled tighter around the cards, and the worn edges bit into her palm. She leaned away from the warmth emanating from Trent's body and sucked slow, steady breaths between her teeth. She'd been ignored a lot growing up, and more often than not she'd found comfort in assuring herself that as long as she was being ignored she at least wasn't disappointing anyone. Her parents had hoped for a boy when anticipating her birth, so she'd never really blamed them for not having much use for her.

This man was her husband, though. He didn't have a single viable reason for ignoring her until her presence was convenient, yet that appeared to be his intention.

She slid her card carefully onto the table so as not to display the desire to chuck the whole hand — along with the mass of silver in the middle of the table — at her husband's head.

The hand finished and the servants rose to return the silver to the cabinet, moving back to their jobs as if they'd often taken this kind of interlude. Maybe they did. They seemed to know their place in the house, know what they were to do, where they were to go. She never thought she'd be even the slightest bit jealous of anything a maid had, but there was no denying that she was jealous of the servants' comfort and security.

"I got you something." Trent pulled a small package from his pocket and set it on the table in front of her.

Her heart pounded as the muscles in her middle relaxed. What did it mean? Was it an apology gift? Was he regretting the distance of the past week? Perhaps she'd been too hard on him in her mind. This wasn't the marriage he'd grown up expecting, after all. Unlike her. She'd always expected her marriage would be little more than a business arrangement. Such a thing would be convenient for her father, after all. She hadn't even been all that surprised when her mother had played an underhanded part in the situation.

The string tying the package closed slid away easily and she was soon staring at a small stack of stiff cream-colored cards.

Lady Trent Hawthorne.

It was the correct form of formal address, she knew. It was what everyone expected. It was what she'd expected. It didn't make any sense to resent the fact that the new calling cards he'd gotten her looked more his than hers. Not only did she not have a husband in anything beyond a legal sense, but now she didn't even have her own name.

Adelaide was no more.

The anger that had simmered in her chest since his arrival spewed forth in a volcano of hurt and frustration she'd never experienced before and certainly never come close to unleashing before. He dared to bring her this. After leaving her to wander the rooms of this house for days with only his staff for company, he expected her to be delighted over the fact that she now got to use his name.

Delight was not what she felt.

"They're lovely." Adelaide pushed the stack of cards back at him. "When you have a wife, I'm sure she'll be happy to use them."

Chapter 10

He didn't leave the dining room for hours. Eventually he rose from his seat and paced to the window and back. He leaned on the back of the abandoned chair, the wall, the sideboard — anything in the room that was capable of holding his weight — but always, always his eyes strayed back to the stack of cards still sitting on the table. The servants were worried about him, finding any and every excuse to walk past the open dining room door. Even Mrs. Harris refused to take the opportunity to admonish his choices.

And his choices were definitely at fault here.

With the sun long gone and the single candle Fenton had left him threatening to gutter out, Trent finally left the room to meander toward the leather chair he'd already spent too much time in. He didn't know what to do. Though they'd been little more than strangers before, somehow they had managed to grow even further apart. He was still adjusting to the fact that this marriage was real, that nothing was going to come and magically take it away — that this was his life now, and he couldn't go back.

He'd finally accepted the truth, but how was he going to convince Adelaide of that fact? Would anything he did now be seen as genuine effort instead of simply a reaction to her cutting outburst?

As he passed through the hall on the way to the stairs, a collection of calling cards on the silver platter by the door caught his eye. When he had been a bachelor, people rarely felt the need to drop their cards by to let him know that they'd arrived back in Town. Word of his marriage must be spreading for people to start the formal observance with him now. That or they were hoping to be among the first to receive a visit from his wife.

His wife who hadn't been able to do any calling of her own because he'd been so busy trying to pretend she didn't need to.

And now that she was trying to pretend the same thing, he realized just how badly he'd handled the entire situation.

Longing for a distraction, and perhaps even a miracle, he flipped through the cards to see who had stopped by.

One familiar name caught his eye and made him groan and laugh at the same time. His Grace, the Duke of Riverton. With a handwritten note along the bottom that said he wanted to let Trent know he was back in town but didn't want to disturb the newly married bliss.

If only he knew.

The fact that Griffith was now only a brief walk instead of a grueling daylong ride away started an itch under Trent's skin. For as long as he could remember, when Trent hadn't known what to do he'd asked Griffith. Trent knew his brother wasn't God and that, despite his steadfast personality and rock-solid presence, the man had made a mistake or two in his life, but his advice was rarely wrong. Griffith had a way of cutting to the heart of the matter, simplifying an issue until a person knew exactly what he needed to do.

If ever an issue needed simplifying, it was this one. In a matter of days Trent had made one complicated mess of his life and marriage, and it needed to get sorted out. Tonight, if possible.

His hat still hung where he'd placed it on the hooks by the front door when entering. Someone, likely Fenton, had retrieved

Trent's greatcoat from the dining room and hung it beside his hat. A tall clock stood next to the hooks, the hands pointing to an hour somewhere between ridiculously late and insanely early, depending upon one's perspective. Waiting until true morning wouldn't hurt anything, but the restlessness and desperation that had driven him to pace the confines of the dining room for hours were now pushing him out the door. He'd reached the edges of Grosvenor Square before he even knew he'd made up his mind to go.

The imposing yet familiar front of Hawthorne House was unsurprisingly dark when Trent bounded his way up the steps. His knock was still answered promptly, though by a footman instead of Gibson, the butler — further proof that Trent had lost his grip on what was considered polite and appropriate at this hour.

"My lord?" The footman stepped back to allow Trent to enter, but he looked poised to run around waking the house for what he probably assumed was an emergency.

"My brother is back in Town, is he not?" Trent shucked his hat and coat and handed them to the anxious footman, whose name he couldn't quite remember. Odd that he knew everyone on his own staff but not here. It really wasn't home for him anymore.

"Yes, my lord, but I'm afraid he's already retired for the evening. Shall I wake him for you?"

Trent rolled his shoulders, trying to ease the desperate tension. "Don't bother. I believe I'll stay here for the night. Please leave a message for Cook that there will be another for breakfast." When only one Hawthorne was in residence, the staff didn't lay out a spread on the sideboard, instead fixing a plentiful plate of the family member's favorites. Trent had been beyond lucky to have avoided the notice of footpads on the way over here. He wasn't chancing a walk back to his own house tonight. And since he had high hopes of finding the solution to his problem within the next hour, he wanted breakfast in the morning.

A good breakfast to welcome the promise of a new day.

"Very good, sir. Can I get you anything?" The footman looked confused. Griffith liked to have someone manning the door at all hours of the night in case urgent news arrived, but whatever footman drew the duty rarely had to do more than polish a few extra pieces of silver.

"No. I can see to myself." Trent ran up the stairs before the servant could respond.

He walked right past the door to his old room and down the passage to his brother's. The elegance and grandeur of the corridor caught his attention like it never had before. Growing up this had simply been home. The gilded frames, spotlessly polished wall sconces, and gleaming floors were things to walk past, not be admired at length.

But Trent now stopped in front of a tall vase on a narrow table. The artful arrangement of flowers and branches nearly reached the ceiling. Why hadn't he put such beautiful things in his own home? Trent had made an effort in a few rooms because his mother and sisters had insisted, but by and large he'd left the place in its semi-neglected state of genteel poverty. Hawthorne House might not feel like home anymore, but he wasn't all that certain his place in Mount Street felt like home either. If he'd been waiting until he found the person to share his future before he made his home, where did that leave him? Sitting on threadbare sofas until he settled things with Adelaide? Sipping from mismatched teacups for the rest of his life because she would never forgive him for ignoring her the week after they were married?

Trent pushed open the door at the end of the corridor. He needed to talk to Griffith, and it wasn't going to wait the seven hours until proper morning visits commenced.

A large lump lay under the simple blue bed coverings. It looked like a mountain in the middle of the room. A light snore reached Trent's ears, proving that Griffith had more than gone to his room for the night. He'd actually gone to bed.

The kind thing to do would be to slip quietly back out of the room and let the man sleep. Fortunately, loving brothers didn't always have to be kind to each other.

Trent took two quick steps and launched himself into the air, landing on the mattress and sending the slumbering mountain bouncing across the bed while the bindings holding the mattress up creaked in protest.

Snuffles and snorts accompanied muttered half words as Griffith grappled with sudden wakefulness. Trent turned on his side and propped his head in his hand, taking care to plaster an enormous grin on his face.

Griffith pushed the covers down and ran his large hands over his face, blinking in the dim light coming through the not-quite-closed curtains. His voice was rough and thick, and it took two attempts to get a single word out. "Trent?"

"Last time I looked in a mirror, yes."

The deliberate blinks Griffith used to focus himself and complete the waking-up process reminded Trent of Adelaide's blinks. Those infernal, distracting blinks that did strange things to his insides that he was going to have to live with for the rest of his life. He flopped down onto his back and covered his own face with his hands.

Griffith's groan as he sat up in the bed sounded like rocks tumbling over each other. "What are you doing in my bed?"

Trent uncovered his face and turned to look at his brother. "I need to talk to you."

"And it couldn't wait until morning?"

"I'm afraid not." Trent sat up as well until he was shoulder to shoulder with his brother, a man who'd stepped in to fill the role of father, though he couldn't even grow whiskers at the time. "I've created a bit of a tragedy, Griffith."

Griffith's face lost all signs of sleepiness as he snapped his head around to frown in Trent's direction. "Are you well? Mother? Georgina? Miranda?"

"No, no, nothing like that. I'm well." Trent raised his hands to calm Griffith's sudden worry. "Last I heard our family is all healthy as well."

A grunt that bordered on a sigh was Griffith's only response as he turned to drop his feet over the side of the bed. “Well, if we are going to have a conversation, let’s have it elsewhere. I find having you in my bed rather awkward.”

Trent bounced up from the mattress. “Agreed. Would you like me to wait in the upstairs parlor?”

Griffith shrugged into his dressing gown and shook his head. “The study. I prefer to surround myself with manliness when I converse in my dressing gown.”

“You do this frequently?” Trent’s eyes widened. He knew he hadn’t kept up with all the demands on his brother after their father died, but did dukes truly have many middle-of-the-night conversations in their dressing gowns?

“No,” Griffith muttered, “but I have decided that manly surroundings will be a rule for any future occasions.”

Trent grinned — a real grin born of a spark of good humor. Coming to Griffith had been the right thing to do. “Very well. I shall meet you in the study.”

Griffith’s study was almost as familiar to Trent as his own. More so, in some ways. Griffith had inherited the room at ten years old. Since then the brothers had spent many a day sitting in the old leather chairs, mulling over the important things in life like frogs and puddings while pretending to be adults. Then they'd actually become adults and the mullings over life had gotten more serious.

Theological debates aside, though, Trent didn't think they'd ever discussed something as personal as this.

Griffith tightened the sash on his dressing gown as he entered the study and collapsed into a chair. With one hand he rubbed the last of the sleep from his green eyes and with the other pushed his dark blond hair back off his forehead. "Talk."

The urge to pace was tough to quell, but Trent made himself sit in the matching chair and face his failure like a man. "I've ruined my marriage."

"I couldn't have even traveled to Scotland and back in the amount of time you've been married. What on earth happened?"

"Well, if you had taken the mail coach and turned right back at the border you could probably have gone to Scotland and back. It would be close." Trent plucked at a piece of grass that had gotten stuck to his trouser leg when he cut across Grosvenor Square.

"Trent."

There was no sigh, no rolling of the eyes, nothing to mark Griffith's frustration over Trent's delay. The simple utterance of his name was all it took to convey the sentiment that had become something of a mantra for their family. Their mother had said it first after quietly telling them their father had died, his heart simply stopping while he slept. Griffith had repeated it before getting in their uncle's carriage to hie off to Eton. He'd said it again when Trent took the same ride to join him. It had been Trent's turn to remind Griffith the first time he took his seat in the House of Lords. The admonishment had always been the same — that they would face reality with God at their side and England beneath their feet and do what they could to make the world better.

Right now Trent didn't find it very comforting. He dug his fingers into the arms of the chair, watching the skin around his fingernails whiten as he pressed the wooden trim. "I don't know what I did. I think it's more what I didn't do."

"Which is?" Griffith rubbed his forefinger up and down along the edge of his thumb, the only sign that Trent's slow answers were perturbing his older brother.

"Nothing. I've done nothing." Trent gave in to the desire to pace and strolled over to the desk and picked up a large, round paperweight. The black marble ball was cold and heavy, grounding Trent in the moment. "I've ignored her."

Griffith cleared his throat. "Completely?"

"Yes." Trent rolled the ball from hand to hand and leaned one hip against the desk. "I didn't want to believe I was married. Still don't, for that matter."

One thick blond eyebrow climbed, and Trent knew he was about to be handed the Word of God in such a way that he was going to feel ridiculous for not having turned to it himself. " 'The lip of truth shall be established for ever: but a lying tongue is but for a moment.' "

Griffith had always liked the book of Proverbs. Trent placed the weight back on the desk, knowing the time for lying was over, even if he'd only been lying to himself. "Well, when you put it like that."

Trent crossed back to the chairs. He placed his forearms on the back of the old upholstered wingback and stared into the cold fireplace. "I suppose my moment caught up with me today, then. The thing is, this isn't what I thought my marriage would be. I always pictured myself taking my time, courting my wife through the Season, maybe even longer."

Griffith sighed and leaned his head against

the back of the chair. "What's stopping you?"

Trent really should have let Griffith sleep, because apparently his mind was addled by the middle-of-the-night interruption despite his ability to quote Scripture. "I've already got a wife, Griffith."

The raising of a single eyebrow called Trent's intelligence into question and made him want to plop down in the chair and sulk. The words that followed knocked the breath from his lungs. "I guess you can take your time courting her, then, can't you."

CHAPTER 11

Adelaide wallowed deeper into the mattress and tucked the covers in around her shoulders, determined to stay abed until morning. She had no idea what time it was, and the drapes had been pulled tightly together, blocking out any attempts the rising sun might be making to light the room. It had to be morning, though. She'd been staring at the ceiling so long that time must have passed.

Still, she was going to stay in bed until Rebecca arrived. The maid had been wide-eyed but silent during Adelaide's nightly routine, not saying a word about the fact that the numerous negligees Adelaide had continued to wear in an effort to pretend her marriage was normal had been replaced by the oldest, softest cotton night rail Adelaide owned. The comfortable sleeping gown should have made it easier to stay in bed, but instead it only served as a reminder of the pique she'd been in the night before.

She'd begun to regret her outspoken behavior before Rebecca had even left the room. Regretting the words didn't mean she knew what to do, however. She'd had plenty of time to consider her options, though, since she wasn't about to seek him out in the dark, quiet house. She would wait until breakfast, when they were seated in a nearly public room, to make things right.

Her fingers curled around the edge of the coverlet, and she moved it aside to stare across the room at the dark shadow that was the door connecting her room with his. Was he sleeping? Watching his windows for the sun's permission to rise, as she was? Had he sat up last night, waiting for her to come apologize? He had to know she'd never seek him out in his bedroom. If she'd been willing to do such a thing she'd have done it days ago. Then they might not have had last night's incident at all.

A light sleep finally overtook her tired brain, but Rebecca's quiet early morning movements had her flying from the bed like a freed raven. She dressed quickly but sat still long enough for Rebecca to take extra care with her hair.

Adelaide's mother had never let anyone, including her husband, see her at anything less than her best. Adelaide had never taken quite so much pride in her appearance — mostly because it never lasted past the door of her dressing room — but it couldn't hurt to show a bit more consideration for her position as the wife of a duke's son.

Rebecca tried to curl the short hairs falling over Adelaide's forehead and brushing the edges of her eyebrows, but the short hairs only sprang into a strange band of loops around her face. She considered leaving her spectacles off but decided tripping down the stairs wouldn't make an advantageous impression, so she left them on as she hurried from the room.

She hadn't been down to breakfast since their first morning in the house. Hopefully he would see her presence this morning as a sort of peace offering.

The first sight to greet her was a trunk.

Her feet stumbled to a halt three steps from the hall floor, eyes glued to the traveling trunk. The rather large traveling trunk.

She took the last three steps slowly, swallowing hard at the evidence before her. A rather large traveling trunk that she recognized as belonging to her husband.

A slight burn preceded the pool of wetness across her lower eyelid. She blinked it away, sinking her teeth into her lower lip in hopes that the sharp bite would grant her some composure. Until yesterday he'd been willing to ignore her from underneath the same roof. If she'd ever needed more proof that life was easier if you just let everyone else have their way, this was it. A single moment of standing up for herself and she was doomed to be a married widow. Or would she be a married spinster? Surely they had a term for women whose husbands deserted them after hardly more than a week, and Adelaide was sure to learn it, even if she only heard it whispered behind nearby fans.

In her hurry to get to the breakfast room and try to rectify the situation, she tripped over her own feet and caught herself on a nearby table, knocking over a candle that had been guttered out but still contained a pool of melted wax in the top. Wax that now graced the hem of Adelaide's morning dress. With a sigh, Adelaide righted the candle and continued at a more sedate pace to the breakfast room. At least the wax was a translucent white. No one was likely to notice, particularly once she was seated and the smudged hemline was safely hidden beneath the table.

He was standing at the window, much as he had been their first morning in London. In some ways it seemed like years had passed in hardly more than a week, and at other times it felt like mere hours. Despite his presence, there were no place settings waiting on the table, no food on the sideboard. Only him, standing at the window, outlined by the early morning light, and looking as handsome and athletic as a young woman could ever hope her husband to be.

Adelaide would have traded all of that handsomeness for a bit of direction on what type of marriage they were to have. Or rather a different direction than the trunk in the hall seemed to be pointing them.

His head turned toward her as his body stayed angled toward the window. A thick lock of hair fell across his forehead as his green eyes met hers and he smiled.

The dimples appeared in his cheeks as his lips curled and displayed straight, white teeth. She swallowed hard. Perhaps she wouldn't trade all of the handsomeness.

Mrs. Harris bustled in with a frown before Trent could say anything. A grimace crossed Trent's face before he turned back toward the window.

Adelaide turned questioning eyes back to the housekeeper. "Good morning?"

The housekeeper plopped her hands on her narrow hips and sniffed. "If it is, it won't be on account of Lord Trent. Thinking like a man today, he is."

Adelaide blinked. "Well, I should hope so."

Trent's laughter burst across the room, effectively cutting off any tirade Mrs. Harris had been planning. A small, indulgent tilt of the housekeeper's lips was followed by a shrug. "I suppose that's true. We can't expect anything else of them, can we? He probably even had another man agree that this preposterous idea was a good one. Will you be taking breakfast down here then, my lady? Would you like me to fix you something particular?"

Adelaide hated not knowing what was going on. Had she been in a normal house, with servants who at least pretended to mind their own business, she wouldn't have any notion that her husband had cooked up a potentially preposterous scheme. But now she did. And she had no idea how long she would have to wait until learning what it was. Her gaze tripped from the housekeeper to her husband and back again. "I'm not very particular. Whatever Lord Trent is having will suit me."

"Well, I wouldn't know what he's having, seeing as he felt the need to have breakfast elsewhere this morning." She sniffed in Trent's direction before turning a smile back to Adelaide. "I'll fix you my specialty."

Mrs. Harris strode toward the door with purpose.

Leaving Adelaide alone with her husband. A husband who had apparently eaten breakfast elsewhere this morning. She wasn't sure what to do with that information.

Trent stepped forward and pulled out a chair for Adelaide, even as he frowned at the door Mrs. Harris had walked through. "There's no law against a man eating two breakfasts," he grumbled.

A giggle threatened to climb up Adelaide's throat, but it was squashed by the reminder that she still didn't know where the man had eaten that morning.

Adelaide cleared her throat and waited as Oswyn set a cup of coffee down in front of her. Once he'd left the room, she turned to her husband, who had settled in the seat to her left. "Where . . . That is, er, um . . ." She swallowed and blinked at her coffee. "You've already had breakfast?"

Trent nodded, taking a sip of the tea the footman had brought him. "At Hawthorne House. I stayed there after talking to Griffith last night."

Tension Adelaide hadn't fully realized she'd been holding seeped away. It was perfectly acceptable to have breakfast with his brother, if a bit odd. It had been rather late when Adelaide left him in the dining room last night, and he'd given no indication that he had any intention of leaving the house again.

Adelaide ran a finger on the curve of her coffee cup handle. "Was it business?"

"No. Our discussion was of a considerably more personal nature."

"Oh."

Had she really wished to spend more time with her husband? If this morning was any indication, they were better off apart. Yet they'd had such a nice time in the ruins before they were, well, ruined. And the ride to church their first morning in London had been awkward but pleasant. For the most part, anyway. Why couldn't they get back to that?

Trent cleared his throat. "The thing is, Adelaide, I've decided to eat breakfast there for a while."

That explained the traveling trunk in the front hall. Adelaide took a gulp of coffee, wishing her food had arrived so she'd have something more substantial to focus on. "I see."

"You've never had a Season, Adelaide."

And now she wouldn't even have a marriage. Not a real one. She nodded, not knowing what to say. She'd spoken her mind last night and he'd moved out. What would he do if she said anything this morning?

He cleared his throat again, and Adelaide tilted her head so she could watch him fidget with his coat sleeves out of the corner of her eye. "Well, I'd like to give you that."

Her head jerked up so fast that her spectacles tumbled off her nose. Trent's arm jerked forward to catch them before they could clatter to the table. Gentle hands slid them back onto her face, smoothing the loose tendrils of hair away from the earpieces. Adelaide's heart thundered in her chest, the blood making a crackling noise in her ears as too many thoughts crossed her mind, the implications of his statement making no sense to her. "You want me to have a Season?"

Trent wanted, desperately, to examine the swirls in his teacup. Or perhaps the play of light across the back wall of the breakfast room. Truthfully he wanted to look anywhere besides Adelaide's face, but he had been enough of a coward in this relationship already and he forced his gaze to remain on hers, where he could watch the rapidly changing emotions as she took in his declaration.

He couldn't blame her for any of them, even though she was too composed for him to decipher the flickers of emotion with any sort of confidence.

Oswyn delivered a plate piled high with Mrs. Harris's best breakfast offerings. The dark frown as he looked back and forth between them let Trent know what the servants thought of his plan. He'd tried to keep it quiet this morning, but in a household such as his, no one was going to let Finch pack Trent's trunk without learning exactly where the master of the house was intending to go.

Not that Trent felt much like the master of anything right now, much less his own household.

Adelaide looked down at her plate, blinking as if she couldn't imagine where the food would have come from. Eventually she picked up a fork and poked at a piece of ham. "Are we talking about a proper Season?"

"Yes. No. Well, after a fashion." Trent rubbed a hand along the back of his neck. Somehow his decision that seemed so brilliant at dawn now felt weak and foolish as he tried to find the words to explain his plan. "You'll still be married to me."

She glanced up at him without lifting her

face. "Comforting."

The dry comment had Trent choking on a chuckle. Now wasn't the time to laugh, but it was nice to know that there was some wit buried inside his quiet wife, though he'd had little doubt of that after her cutting remark the evening before.

Part of him wanted to tell her she was safe, that she was free to unleash the woman he saw glimpses of when she was caught off guard by the unexpected. What if the hidden woman was like her mother, though? He'd take sullen solitude over living with a power-hungry she-wolf any day.

He cleared his throat and gave in to the desire to look down into his tea, afraid she would look up and see disdain on his face and think it was meant for her instead of her family — if she was indeed different than the other women in her family. Pain stabbed behind his ears as he clenched his jaw together. No matter her parentage, they were married and he needed to accept that. "What I mean is that I'd like to get to know you."

She cut the ham with slow, steady swipes of her knife. "And you feel the best way to do that is to move out of the house?"

A burning sensation touched his ears, and he struggled against the urge to shift his hair so that it covered the tips, which were likely reddening. His heart beat faster, as if he were in the boxing ring instead of his breakfast room. Her breakfast room? If he was moving out, even temporarily, should he think of the things in the house as hers instead of his?

He shook his head and leaned forward to brace his forearms on the tables, clasping his hands loosely together, hoping he looked sincere and earnest instead of desperate. "I would like to court you."

She froze, the precise square of ham dangling from her fork halfway between the plate and her lips. Her head lifted and she blinked at him. Blinks that were as slow and steady as her knife had been moments before. Blinks that seemed to cut through his simple statement to the fear beneath. Fear that this plan wouldn't work. Because if it didn't, he was out of ideas.

"If that is how you wish to do it." She gave a slight nod and turned back to her breakfast.

Trent stared at her, watching her eat until his eyes began to burn. That was it? That was all she was going to say? What did she think of the idea? Had she already given up hope that they could have a good marriage?

Had she ever had that hope in the first place?

"How —" He snapped his teeth shut. If he asked her how she felt about it, he would look insecure. And he didn't want to. As much as he wanted to fall in love with his wife, he needed her to fall in love with him as well. Part of him was more concerned about her feelings than his. If she loved him, she'd care more about the marriage than their social standing and she wouldn't push him to try to be more than the happy-go-lucky man everyone thought him to be.

Whereas if he loved her more than she loved him, what would that drive him to do? Take a greater interest in his estates? Apply himself to improving their standing? Would he do things that were better suited to a duke than a second son? Would he prove himself capable and put Griffith in danger?

Not that there was much danger of Trent being a better duke than his brother, given that God had chosen Griffith to take over the dukedom at the tender age of ten, but Trent knew God saw things men did not, and if He saw greater potential in Trent, what would happen to Griffith?

No, it was more important that Adelaide become at least infatuated quickly, before

Trent became too emotionally invested and hatched more foolish plans in order to win her heart.

She was watching him. How long had she been watching him? Had she said anything?

"I'm sorry. Did you say something?" Trent winced. Ignoring her at the breakfast table was not a good beginning to their courtship.

Her face remained stoic. "I said if you aren't sure of the *how,* you could borrow my deportment book. It was Helena's, but mother gave it to me when Helena married. Left it on my bed one night, actually."

"Your deportment book?"

She shrugged and looked down at her plate. "The instructions would be from the female's perspective obviously, but it would stand to reason that you could deduce the male side of the interactions from the descriptions."

They wrote books telling women how to be courted? "I'll remember your offer. Thank you."

The words came out stilted, but what else could he say? One side of her mouth tilted up a bit and he felt considerably less regret over the awkward exchange. Much better to leave her with a smile, even a minuscule one, than a perplexed frown.

"I'll pick you up this afternoon to go riding then, shall I?" Trent could make this romantic. He would sweep her off her feet and give her the experiences and attention she would have gotten if she'd had a Season. Should have gotten many years before now, given the standing of her family.

She nodded but didn't look up from her plate. "If you wish."

Trent stood and adjusted his coat sleeves, wishing there was something he could do now, but courtship rules didn't include breakfast for very obvious reasons. "Yes. Well, then. I'll just . . . be off. I suppose."

The walk through the house felt strange. He hadn't thought the shabby rooms felt like home before, but now he was second-guessing his decision to move his residence, even temporarily. Mrs. Harris was standing by his trunk, frowning.

Her disapproval strengthened his weakening resolve. "I'll be back this afternoon."

"See that you are."

"You will support me in this, Mrs. Harris."

Her eyes widened, and one hand went to her throat before falling to her side. Her posture straightened and she looked more like a servant than he'd ever seen her. "Yes, my lord."

Trent had never felt the need or desire to

exert his position in this house, and the fact that he'd done so now surprised him. He'd taken comfort in his unconventional servants, knowing that any man who ran his house thusly wasn't fit to be a duke.

He didn't want to lose that comfort now, so he stepped forward and wrapped the thin housekeeper in a hug, leaving her open-mouthed in shock as he fled out the door. His plan was going to work. It had to.

Chapter 12

Six hours later, Trent was practically shaking as he stared at his front door. He hadn't been this nervous on his wedding day. Somehow that hadn't felt quite as life changing as this moment standing before his own front door.

Trent smoothed his cravat and glanced back at the curricle he'd had Griffith's grooms polish to a high gleam. The horses were brushed until every hair shone in the sun. Even the harness buckles twinkled in the afternoon light. This courtship was a guaranteed success — he was already married to the woman, after all — but right now it didn't feel like a sure thing.

The normal goal of a courtship was to win the lady's hand in marriage, but Trent needed to win her heart and, in some weird way, try to give away his own. Neither of those things was a foregone conclusion. All of the ways this endeavor could fail suddenly punched their way into his mind. She'd seemed to be in agreement when he left this morning, even if it was a resigned sort of agreement. What would he do if she rejected him? Move back into the house? By living at Hawthorne House he hoped to give this courtship as authentic a feel as possible, but did that leave too much room for failure?

He knocked on the door.

It swung open to reveal Fenton looking as unsure as Trent felt. Was that because Adelaide had some sudden hesitation or because Trent was visiting his own house?

"Er, please come in, my lord. My lady has bid you await her in the drawing room as she's not quite ready yet." Fenton opened the door wide and gestured Trent in with a sweep of his hand.

Relief sagged Trent's shoulders as he crossed the threshold. She was coming. That was good.

He walked into the drawing room as if he owned the place — which he did, but that wasn't how he'd intended to play this game. Not that it mattered unless Adelaide was in the room.

"Can I get you anything, my lord?" Fenton asked from the doorway.

Trent declined without much thought. His

focus was on the pile of fabric that looked like his drapes and the warped metal rod that had once held them on the wall. What had happened? When had it happened? He'd been avoiding his wife with such diligence that he hadn't stepped foot in this room all week. He'd heard that some women went into frenzies when they were upset, hitting people, throwing things, destroying furniture. Had she done this in a fit of pique? If so, why start in the front rooms, where any visitor would see the damage right off? He had to admit that the room was better off for the loss of the old and faded drapes, but there had to have been a simpler way to remove them.

The click of the door latch opening distracted him from the window dressings, and he whirled around to see Adelaide standing in the door, her hair swept up into a simple knot on her head, those thick locks still hanging over her forehead, curling against the tops of her spectacles and framing her eyes. Trent knew it was highly out of fashion, but he rather hoped she kept the look. It suited her. Her dress was light blue with darker blue embroidery across the bodice. The skirt was sheer over a dark blue underskirt. Her eyes looked wide behind their lenses, brightened by the matching blue of her unbuttoned spencer.

Trent tried to speak, but his mouth had gone dry. Why hadn't he asked Fenton for some tea? He could certainly use it now. It took a bit of work, but eventually his tongue freed itself and he blurted out, "You're lovely."

The inelegance of the compliment made him wince, but the light blush that ran up her neck to her cheeks proved she found nothing wrong with his delivery. Maybe the lack of charm had leant it a note of sincerity. Still, he was going to endeavor to show a bit more sophistication.

"Would you care to go for a ride?"

Her brows drew together, and she blinked at him. "Isn't that the purpose of this . . . visit? Are you visiting?"

"Yes, I rather thought I was. I mean, I suppose I could court you from the next room over, but that loses a bit of the intent, I would think." Trent shifted his weight and adjusted his hold on his hat. Last night he'd thought his plan brilliant. This morning he'd still been convinced of its cleverness. Now, faced with the actual execution of his plan, it looked like the plot of a mad man. He'd be lucky if she didn't try to have him committed.

"I know you said you've never courted

anyone, but is this how it's truly done? I've never heard of such a thing. We're already married. Doesn't that defeat the purpose?" Adelaide settled her bonnet on her head, knocking her spectacles slightly askew. She fixed them, but not before the earpiece pulled a lock of hair out of her bun and left it curling against her shoulder.

The errant curl made him smile and returned to him a modicum of confidence. "I . . . well, frankly I've never heard of such a thing either, but it seemed the thing to do since we missed it the first time around."

Dear God, please let her find the entire concept the slightest bit romantic or at least appealing. He couldn't live with Griffith forever, and he really wanted to return home as the husband and leader of the house. Even if it meant he had to actually take charge of something. He hated to think of having to slink back in simply because his plan had failed.

"I see." Adelaide seemed to consider his words for a while, and then a slow smile spread across her face.

That smile hit Trent in the gut, stealing his ability to speak all over again — along with his ability to breathe. Her smile was wide, her teeth just peeking out from between slightly parted lips, one of the front ones just the slightest bit crooked. And for the first time he was grateful she was his wife. He would never have considered courting someone related to Lady Crampton on his own, but God had allowed the decision to be taken out of his hands, and now this gorgeous creature before him was going to be his for the rest of his life. And if he could make that smile appear more often, it'd be a sign that he was succeeding in his ultimate goal of having a happy wife.

It was a good goal to have in life. One worthy of a husband who hadn't another care in the world other than seeing to the well-being of his family. He offered her his arm. "Shall we go for a ride, then?"

Adelaide slid her small hand into the crook of his elbow. "Yes, I believe we shall."

Adelaide felt a little absurd as Trent handed her up into the shiny yellow curricle. In all the time spent in the same house they hadn't even managed a good-morning greeting, and now they were going to spend upwards of an hour within the confines of a small vehicle. What were they going to say to each other?

She'd been in his curricle before, on their two trips to church. Her focus, then, had been on her husband and all the people she was soon to meet. Those worries had distracted her from the strangeness of riding in something so high and open. Before coming to London she'd never ridden in anything other than a coach or a landau, safely tucked away with cushioned seats and closed doors. Now she could reach out and touch the wheel while they rolled down the street if she were so inclined.

Not that she could imagine a single scenario in which she'd feel the need to deliberately stick her hand on a moving wheel. The fact that she could, though, made her a little nervous, and she took a moment to make sure her dress was securely tucked underneath her leg. It was the best she could do, though it didn't make her trust the safety of the shiny yellow wheel. With her luck she'd somehow catch her bonnet ribbon in the spokes.

The vehicle dipped and swayed as Trent climbed in on the other side. Adelaide clenched her fingers together to keep from grabbing the side and launching herself out to the pavement.

"Are you comfortable? There's a lap blanket under the seat, if you'd like it." Trent picked up the reins and smoothly directed the horses down the road behind a high-perched phaeton.

Adelaide was suddenly thankful for Trent's more sedate curricle. The wheels on the phaeton were nearly as tall as her head while seated in the curricle. And then to be seated on top of that would be unthinkable.

"No, this is pleasant." And it was. Once the curricle was moving it wasn't so scary. Trent kept the horses at a slow trot, enough to create a soft breeze but not so much to make her uncomfortable.

At least not physically.

The painful silence was another thing altogether, though. The steady clop of the horse hooves was worse than a ticking clock, counting off the moments until one of them broke the silence. The longer it lasted, the more desperate she was to say something but the more profound she felt it needed to be. Breaking such a long silence with a mundane comment on the weather would only draw attention to the fact that they had nothing to talk about.

"Have you ever eaten a tomato?" Trent's words pulled Adelaide's attention from the various buildings they were passing.

She blinked at him. Did the man start every conversation with food? That night in the ruins they'd discussed their least favorite dishes. He declared favorite dishes too common a conversation choice. On the way to

London their only conversation of any significant length had debated the merits of the different meat pies and pastries they'd gotten from an inn along the way. Once again he was turning to food to start a conversation.

He glanced at her with a small smile. "Ryland sent Griffith a few, and I had one with breakfast this morning. Mrs. Harris refuses to touch the things, but I'll bring one over if you'd like to try it."

Adelaide ducked her head to hide her silent laughter. She'd read once that the way to an Englishman's heart was through his stomach, but she'd never seen evidence to support that notion before. Her father was certainly more interested in the land that grew the food than the food itself, whereas Trent seemed nearly obsessed with it. At least he seemed obsessed with anything eaten before noon. He'd yet to discuss a single brace of roasted pheasant or bowl of turtle soup. "Why haven't you hired a cook?"

The shifting of his shoulders could have been a shrug or an adjustment of his coat, but there was no question that the rush of red appearing over his cravat was the beginnings of a blush. "Mrs. Harris has been cooking in that house for years. She suits my needs well enough. I brought in a chef to help with a small dinner party I had last year."

Given what little Adelaide knew of the protective housekeeper, another cook in her kitchen might not have gone over well. "How did that go?"

Trent grinned. "He quit before the end of the soup."

They fell into silence, and Adelaide went back to watching London slide by. She recognized some things from her sister's frequent descriptions, but it was soon obvious that Helena had left out many of the more interesting aspects of London architecture. If it didn't have to do with social interactions, it hadn't been worth discussing. A wide, tree-lined dirt path angled off the road in front of them, and Adelaide's heart beat faster, though she wasn't sure if it was trying to hurry the horses along or run in the other direction. This was Rotten Row. Even if she hadn't seen a drawing in a magazine last year she'd have known it from her mother and Helena's excited discussions of who they'd seen and talked to while riding along the popular path.

Tension broke into the easy silence. Even though London wasn't packed for the Season yet, there were still enough of the *ton* in town that the path was scattered with carriages and riders. People were going to see her. They were going to see that while she and Trent were riding together, they weren't having much to do with each other. It was bad enough that the outing didn't feel like one between a husband and wife. She didn't need everyone else knowing it too.

She turned her head and opened her mouth, but nothing came out. She had nothing to say. They could talk about food again. Now that she thought about it, it was a fairly genius contingency topic. After all, everyone ate. "They had tomatoes at the fair last year, but Mother wouldn't let me eat one. She said they were poisonous."

Trent tilted his head to the side, appearing deep in thought. His hair slid out of its slicked-back style to flop boyishly against his temple. As his wife she should feel free to reach up and brush the lock of hair back into place. But there were quite a few things she should feel free to do as his wife that she hadn't been able to do yet.

He turned his face back toward her with a self-assured grin that made her fidget in her seat. "If they are, they're rather slow acting. I had my first one at least ten months ago and haven't felt an adverse effect yet." He pursed his lips together, looking to the sky for answers to the deep questions he appeared to be pondering. "Although I did have a nasty head cold this winter. Do you think I could blame that on the tomatoes?"

Her smile arrived before she realized it was coming. "I'm afraid not. While some scientists believe that the stomach essentially ferments what we eat, I don't think anyone believes the process takes months. We eat too often for that."

Trent's laughter drew the attention of what few people weren't already looking their way. "Do I even want to know why you know about the fermenting theory of digestion?"

Unfortunately her bonnet did not have a very wide brim on the sides, leaving nothing to hide the blush she was very afraid was encroaching. She knew better than to share her collection of strange facts with anyone other than her brother. He found them fascinating, while her mother despaired of the amount of intellectual reading Adelaide had to do to collect them. Her father simply shook his head, knowing he'd started her off on the bizarre hobby and regretting it ever since. Now Trent would know her mind was full of useless information instead of social niceties.

"I must have read it somewhere," she mumbled.

His eyebrows rose as he settled back in the curricle seat, angling himself into the corner and holding the reins in one hand. "So I would assume. My only question is why?"

Adelaide sighed and let her eyelids fall closed over her burning cheeks. "My father despaired of the number of novels I was reading. He admonished me to choose something from the library that would feed my intellect instead of rotting it away." She swallowed before continuing. What if he thought less of her for trying to outwit her own father? "It took me two days of looking through every title in the library before I found something that would suit my purposes. I read *Observations on Digestion* and proceeded to share everything I learned with him. He looked at his food strangely for a month. I'm still not sure why he owned a copy."

Laughter escaped Trent's chest again, though this time it was more like a low chuckle. "I assume you've been able to read whatever you wish since?"

"Yes. Though I found myself picking up many of the other educational books I'd come across during my search. Some of the information out there is fascinating."

"What else did you learn?"

She watched him for a moment, searching his words and face for any sense of condescension or derision. There was none. He looked at ease, comfortable, even interested in what she had to say. She liked him this way. It made her want to join him, to be as comfortable as he was with this courtship idea. Her shoulder brushed against his as she made herself stop clinging to the edge of the curricle. "The French are measuring things in meters now."

"We'll have to get you some more current books to study." Trent guided the curricle around a horse and rider that had stopped against the fence. "They stopped doing that two years ago."

Adelaide couldn't stop her own lips from curving into an answering smile. The moment was intimate. They were a *we,* sharing and planning for the future as if they were forging ahead together. Yet when this ride was over he'd be leaving her behind, alone in the house with the servants. Who knew what they thought of this entire situation?

Well, she probably would know by the time she went to bed tonight. Mrs. Harris wasn't exactly known for keeping her opinions to herself.

A couple drove by on the other side of Rotten Row, not even hiding their curiosity as they stared into Trent's curricle. She hadn't thought much about the implications of Trent's claim that he'd never courted a woman before. Had he never even taken one for a drive? The curiosity aimed in their direction indicated that this was a very unexpected sighting. A sudden thought stole the glimmer of pleasure that had been blooming inside her middle during their brief conversation. What if there had been another young lady — one he'd taken riding on a regular basis — and that was why people were staring. Despite his claims otherwise, had she stolen him away from the love of his life? It would certainly explain his distance over the past week.

"Have you been into our library yet? I don't think we've any books detailing the functions of the human body, but there is a volume somewhere with a chapter on the molting patterns of tropical birds."

She didn't miss his use of *our.* That flicker of hope ignited once more, that awkward sense of unity that didn't sit well with their current situation. While part of her still worried about who she might have taken him from, she liked the idea of them being a unit. Being able to use *our.*

"I did peruse the library a few days ago. You — we — have several books I hadn't heard of before. I took both volumes of *Don Quixote* up to my room. It's an incredibly long book."

A look of pain flashed across Trent's face. It was so sudden she looked to see if he'd pinched his hand in the reins or somehow bumped his leg against the edge of the wheel, though he'd have had to dangle his leg over the side to accomplish that. "You've probably finished it by now," he said in a low voice. "Did you like it? I've never managed to get through it myself. It was one of Father's favorites so I borrowed the volumes from the Hawthorne House library and forgot to return them."

How nice it must be to be so comfortable with not caring for something a parent was fond of. The fact that he was at odds with his father's opinion gave her more courage to share her own. "I'm not sure what to think of it. Some parts of it are entertaining, but at times it seems to belittle the man. I would not want to be written about in such a way."

He tilted his head, as if she'd made a point he had not thought of before but that merited consideration. "Our library isn't that large, but the one at Hawthorne House is quite extensive. You can borrow anything you'd like from there. Griffith keeps his particular favorites on a set of shelves in his study, so you don't have to worry about borrowing something he'll need or want later. Of course, if there's something in his private collection that you wish to read, I can make arrangements for that as well."

Adelaide blinked and stared straight ahead at the horses' heads swaying slightly back and forth. She was going to be able to casually borrow books from the Duke of Riverton whenever she wished, had access to his house, even. Her mother was going to be incredibly jealous. "I would like that."

They fell into silence once more, but this time it wasn't uncomfortable. It was actually pleasant to ride alongside him and watch the scenery go by. She looked around and realized this was her first time in Hyde Park and she'd spent every moment thus far looking at the curricle or the backside of a horse. She was missing all of the beauty around her. "This is lovely."

A masculine arm crossed in front of her vision, distracting her from the scenery. "Over there is the Serpentine. We'll have to come here on foot one day so you can get a better look at it. It isn't a bad walk from the house if the weather is nice."

"Do people swim in it?" The only body of water she'd seen like that was the lake in Hertfordshire, where her father had taught her brother to swim. After much cajoling from her, he'd taught Adelaide as well, though only after she'd sworn to never tell her mother he'd let her out of the house in her brother's clothes.

Trent smiled again. She could easily get addicted to those smiles. "Not intentionally. More than one person has taken an accidental swim or been dropped in by their friends after a night of overzealous drinking."

They continued down the path with Trent pointing out different features of Hyde Park or occasionally another member of the *ton* making their way down the fashionable riding path. Adelaide couldn't remember a more pleasant outing. Not once did she find herself wishing she could reach for the book she'd tucked into her reticule. The weight of it rested in her lap, all but ignored as she found herself responding more and more freely to Trent's comments.

As they approached the exit to the park, she couldn't help but hope that the rosy glow of the curricle ride would follow them home. For surely he meant to return home now that they were speaking pleasantly again. It didn't fit with the plan he'd outlined this morning, but if they were getting along, was there any reason to stay at Hawthorne House? Unless he meant to quietly make the move permanent. What if this ride was only for show? To make everyone think they had a happy marriage when he still wanted nothing to do with her? The Hawthorne family marriages were rather notorious for being happy ones. Was he afraid to break the pattern?

The traffic on the path thickened, and the horses had to slow to a plodding walk. Trent reached one hand across the bench to wrap his gloved fingers around her own. The touch was brief, and then he squeezed her hand and returned his grip to the reins.

No one could have seen that. It wasn't meant for anyone but her. She straightened her shoulders and didn't bother to hide the smile on her face. In fact, it wouldn't surprise her if she was still smiling when she went to bed that evening. The attentions of a man such as Trent were heady indeed.

Her smile suffered a blow much sooner than she anticipated however, for another carriage passed them as they crept toward the exit. Inside it was her mother.

Chapter 13

And this was the fly in the ointment of his potentially, hopefully, one-day-to-be-happy marriage. That he would have to spend the rest of his life knowing that the most socially aggressive and annoying woman he knew could show up in his life at any time.

He was too much of a gentleman to allow his aggravation to show as he smiled politely and nodded his head in Lady Crampton's direction.

She wasn't satisfied with a simple acknowledgment, though. "What unexpected fortune to see my daughter and new son! Such a shame we're traveling in opposite ways. We must catch up at the Ferrington ball tonight. I am quite looking forward to it!"

Her voice carried across the park until there wasn't a soul in sight that didn't know of the countess's plans.

It was enough to make Trent want to

schedule a very prominent appearance somewhere else. Anywhere else. Even if it meant making a scene at Vauxhall Gardens to make sure everyone knew they'd gone somewhere other than where Lady Crampton expected them to.

Unfortunately it wasn't up to him. The mere sight of her mother seemed to crumble all of the confidence and camaraderie he'd been building with Adelaide for the past hour. Her shoulders fell into a slight slump as she nodded her head slowly. "Of course, Mother. I'm looking forward to the ball as well."

Adelaide's voice didn't carry nearly as far, but it wouldn't matter if no one else had heard her but him. They were now committed to the ball. Trent didn't even know if they'd received an invitation, though it was highly likely that they had. There weren't many events that Trent didn't receive an invitation to, and the one time he'd gone somewhere without one he hadn't been turned away. Of course, he wasn't an eligible bachelor anymore.

The ride back to the house was even more painful than the ride to the park had been. He had half a mind to turn around and go through the park again to try to reclaim the feeling of fragile connection. Neither of them needed or wanted the speculation a thing like that would cause, though. Trent was all too aware of the unconventionality of his plan and that it was probably in his best interest to let everyone else think the marriage was progressing normally.

Assuming anyone else had a clue what normal entailed. If they did, he'd like to know about it.

Still, they were probably better off if no one knew he was currently living in Hawthorne House. He bit back a groan as the wheels clacked over the cobblestone street. This was getting much more complicated than he had anticipated.

The house came into view, inspiring relief and dread. The ride was certainly uncomfortable and he'd be glad to get back to familiar ground, but he hated that their first outing was ending on such a note. He wove desperately through his memory as he helped Adelaide from the carriage, trying to think of some interesting fact he could share since minutiae seemed to be the most common ground they could meet on. As Adelaide steadied her footing on the pavement, he noticed the sleeve of her spencer jacket was tucked into her short glove. How had she managed such a thing while sitting in the curricle?

He found it adorable. With a gentle touch he slid one finger between the glove and the sleeve, moving it in a circle around her wrist to dislodge the garment. He didn't let go of her hand, even when the sleeve hung free once more. It was like a game he got to play every time he saw her, looking for the hidden flaw in her appearance. It was never the same thing twice. It filled him with a sudden urge to pull her close and kiss her.

The urge stunned him even as it shot an arrow of heat down his spine.

He wanted to kiss his wife.

It wasn't a bizarre concept, of course. Men did it every day. But he hadn't done it every day. Hadn't done it all. He hadn't even wanted to, which was part of the problem in the first place. But he wanted to kiss the woman who had ridden through Hyde Park with him, not the shy creature asking his boots if he planned on attending the ball with her that evening.

As if he would leave his wife to attend her first social gathering in London alone. It would be like feeding a lamb to the wolves. "Of course I shall escort you." They should probably dine together. But the thought of sitting in their dining room, just the two of them, while Mrs. Harris frowned in the doorway wasn't the least bit appealing.

"Would you like to go to dinner beforehand? There are some lovely restaurants in London."

"Of course." She swallowed visibly and blinked up at him. "Wherever you wish to go. I've seen so little of London that I'll not be particular."

And just that quickly Trent felt like a brute once more. How long had his wife been in London and she'd seen little more than the Great North Road and Rotten Row.

There was a lot to love about social gatherings, but Trent had never quite caught on to the appeal of balls. No one really got to know anyone there, and the constant dancing was rather exhausting. Of course he wasn't a bachelor anymore. He didn't have to feel duty bound to take to the dance floor every time he saw a young lady look longingly at the swirling couples. He would, however, get to swirl his wife onto the dance floor. Anticipating that moment as he'd helped her down from the curricle when they returned from their afternoon ride, he couldn't help but pray that she knew how to waltz.

He would really like to waltz with his wife.

For the first time in years he also wouldn't have an unmarried female to look after.

He'd married off both sisters last year, leaving him free to enjoy Society without any chaperone duties.

If it weren't for the promise of Lady Crampton's presence he might actually get excited about the coming evening, despite the crushing crowd and pandering that always accompanied the bad punch and subtle maneuvering for partners.

Griffith was attending the same ball, so Trent rode with his brother over to the town home to pick up Adelaide.

It was a bit strange to stand in the front hall beside his brother like visitors. Fortunately, Griffith was taking it all in stride, acting like any other gentleman arriving to pick up a lady for an event, though where he'd gotten the practice Trent couldn't begin to guess. While Trent had been careful to never connect himself too closely to any one female, Griffith had perfected the art of keeping all of Society at a distance.

The town house was too narrow for a grand stairway, and instead had a straight staircase cutting down through an opening in the ceiling. Trent watched the break in the ceiling above him, waiting for his wife, praying that this night would go well. Everything that could go wrong went through his head. His mother and sisters weren't in town yet, so he had no guarantee that any of the other women in attendance tonight would welcome Adelaide. He wouldn't put it past her own mother to give her the cut direct if the woman thought it would boost her popularity.

All the worries and concerns fled his mind at the first appearance of deep blue velvet. Slowly the rest of the dress appeared, a silky white gown with a blue velvet overdress that fit Adelaide perfectly. One more slow, steady step and she was fully revealed. Her dark hair pulled into an intricate arrangement of curls with the short strands still falling over her forehead to skim the top of her eyebrows. Her spectacles didn't detract from the image at all, instead seeming to magnify the blue of her eyes, highlighted even more by the blue velvet hugging her shoulders.

Perhaps Trent should have waited in the drawing room instead. At least then he'd have somewhere to sit if his legs followed through on their threat to give way underneath him.

She hadn't had time to mess up her outfit yet, so she looked flawless. The belt of the vest-style velvet ensured that the gown would be flattering from every angle. Trent had a feeling he'd be seeing each of those angles, because there was no way he was taking his eyes off of her for the entirety of the evening. One gloved hand reached up to sweep the short hairs to the side, though a lock or two immediately fell back into place. Trent liked it, liked the softness it brought that the most perfectly formed curls could not. Perhaps he could pay Rebecca to burn them again after they grew out a bit more.

Gold embroidery danced along the open edges of the blue velvet, and a large gold medallion kept the exposed white bodice from being plain against the decorative vest. A scalloped lace trimmed the neckline of the bodice, keeping the low cut from being immodest.

"I do believe worse things have happened to you than having that woman as your wife," Griffith whispered.

Trent couldn't answer. His mouth had gone dry. For the first time since his forced betrothal, Trent thought he just might have gotten very lucky in this arrangement. If they could manage to make every moment half as magical as this one, they'd have a marriage to be envious of. Griffith's large hand planted against Trent's back and gave him a light push, knocking Trent out of his trance so that he could cross the floor and offer Adelaide his arm.

"You are beautiful." His gaze became snared in hers as he offered the compliment in an almost reverent fashion. Her eyes seemed to widen until they were all he could see, glistening pools of fear and excitement surrounded by the black frames of her spectacles. How had he forgotten that this wasn't just her first ball of the Season? It was her first ball ever.

Horrid mother or no, he was going to make sure this night was the best she'd ever had.

Trent didn't realize that they'd been standing in the hall simply staring at each other until Griffith cleared his throat. "I can send the carriage back for you if you aren't ready to depart yet."

"We're ready." He reached up to brush a stray hair from her cheek, grinning at the light blush that stained her cheeks in response. "Aren't we?"

She nodded and reached for the wrap and reticule waiting by the front door. The reticule was enormous. He knew Georgina always carried a slightly larger than average reticule in order to have spare slippers and a small sewing repair kit with her at all times, but even hers wasn't as large as Adelaide's. Nor was it as heavy, if the way it pulled down Adelaide's wrist was any indication.

"Do you have everything you need?" It was the closest he was going to be able to come to asking her what was in the bag. One day though, he promised himself, one day he'd be in a position to know because he'd see her pack it. He'd never dare ask a woman he wasn't related to what was in her reticule, so he couldn't ask Adelaide. Not if he were going to commit to actually courting her as he should. He had to treat her as if they weren't married. Two days ago he'd have thought that the easiest thing in the world. Now he wasn't so sure.

Chapter 14

On her fifth birthday Adelaide got a pony. Her baby brother wasn't old enough to ride the estate with their father yet, but she was, and he took her out riding to every corner of land he owned. She'd felt so important on that pony, one step below the queen herself. For the rest of her life she'd wished she could feel that way again.

Tonight she did.

Entering the ballroom on Trent's arm and hearing the bailiff cry out "Lord and Lady Trent Hawthorne" had given her an even bigger thrill. She'd felt as if she could rule this ballroom, that there was no one in the crush who could touch her. She knew the feeling wouldn't last, not with her mother and dozens of other women like her in attendance, but for the moment none of those women meant a thing because Trent had walked her straight onto the dance floor as the first notes of a waltz drifted through the room.

She thought she'd be nervous about her first dance. How many times had she thought about making her first bow in a London ballroom? She'd begun to think her mother never intended to give her a chance, and she certainly hadn't expected to do it as her dance partner's wife.

Never in all her imaginings had so many eyes been trained her direction, though. But it didn't seem to matter. The rustle of silk and satin that filled the floor around them faded into the background as Adelaide felt the heavy weight of Trent's arm curl around her waist. Her gaze fixed on his cravat, the strong jawline above it edging into her field of vision.

It felt different, dancing with Trent. Bernard was still a young boy — his dancing skills reflected as such — and the few times she'd taken lessons with Helena, Adelaide had been placed into the man's position. There was something comforting about Trent's steady guidance across the floor. It felt like a promise of support as she faced the women of London for the first time. It was fanciful thinking, of course, because he was likely to disappear once this first set had completed. For the moment, though, she would allow herself to believe it and enjoy the blissful sensation of dancing, trusting Trent not to twirl them into any of the other dancers.

The dance set ended before she was ready. Not that she would ever be ready. Leaving the dance floor meant facing the elite of London from an approachable place. A church pew and a moving curricle were rather protected locations, but at a ball, she was utterly exposed. Helena had told her what a cruel lot they were, lying to each other until no one knew what truth was anymore. Having spent enough time sorting Helena's lies from her truths led Adelaide to believe the other women weren't the entire problem. Still, it didn't take much to believe that aristocratic women were a difficult bunch to impress. Her mother certainly was. They couldn't all be like that though, could they?

Trent escorted her to the side of the floor, stumbling to a halt at the edge of the dancing area. He glanced around and then back down at her before pulling her into the edge of the gathering people. After looking around once more, he slid her hand from his elbow and ran one hand across the back of his neck. What could possibly be wrong? Was he trying to find a way to tell her he was going to wherever the men went when they didn't want to dance? She didn't mind, honestly. It wasn't as if she expected him to remain in her company all evening. Her mother was going to be there, after all, even if Adelaide wasn't quite ready to see her.

And that, of course, was part of his issue. If Trent had truly been courting Adelaide he'd have taken her to her mother at the conclusion of the dance, but her mother was nowhere to be seen. A rather mixed blessing at that moment, but one that left them with an awkward situation. What did they do now? Did they simply part ways and go about their own business for the rest of the evening? Stand together until they came across someone they both wanted to talk to? Would he introduce her around until she knew enough people for him to leave her to her own devices?

The awkwardness shifted into a burning sensation that ran from her middle to her chest as other attendees took the question of what to do next out of their hands. People swarmed to their side and Trent began introducing them as quickly as politeness would allow. Adelaide smiled and nodded at all of them, keeping her gaze firmly on everyone's chin so they would hopefully miss the heat crawling up her neck and the aching tension creeping across her shoulders. The introductions began blending together, and she knew she'd never remember everyone's name.

No one seemed to care, though. In fact, the conversations were easier than she would have dreamed if she'd ever dreamed of conversing with this many people in a single night. Years of practice at saying whatever her mother and father expected her to say gave her a natural ability to allow the other person to lead the conversation. Sometimes she had no idea what or whom they were talking about, but her noncommittal answers seemed to please most people, and they moved on from the encounter with a satisfied nod or even a smile.

And thus went the next hour of her evening. It wasn't unpleasant. If she hadn't felt like such a charlatan she might have even enjoyed it. But every time Trent appeared at her side with a cup of lemonade or simply to share in the conversation, women around her would enthuse over her luck and fortune. While some seemed envious of her new position, most simply wanted to gossip on her newly married life. When she wasn't forthcoming enough, they began to speculate. She let them. She wasn't about to share the truth of her situation or how the marriage came about. It was reasonable for people to assume they'd had a quiet romance in the country, so she felt no need to contradict them.

In her experience, people would believe whatever they wished to anyway.

"Married life seems to suit you well, Adelaide." Mother approached and hooked her arm with Adelaide's during a rare lull in the attentions.

Adelaide murmured something between a yes and a groan because she wasn't really sure how to answer that statement. Nothing good ever came from being the solitary focus of her mother's attention. It inevitably ended with Mother lamenting the fact that Adelaide wasn't Helena and Adelaide wishing her parents' second child hadn't been born to wear skirts.

Mother pulled Adelaide along as they started a slow walk along the edge of the ballroom. "Now that you've settled in so well, you should have Helena around for dinner. With her husband, of course. Did you know that Lord Edgewick has been trying to get an introduction into Alverly's fencing club?"

Adelaide let her sigh puff her cheeks out before silently sliding out between her teeth. Even now it was about what Helena needed, what leant her the most social advantage. Perhaps Adelaide should be thanking God for her unconventional marriage instead of sending questioning glances to the sky. Who knew how Mother would have tried to manipulate Adelaide's potential suitors if she'd come for her Season as planned.

"He's been trying for a sponsorship to White's, you know," the countess continued. "But Boodle's would be nearly as good. His current club has no influential connections to speak of."

Adelaide sighed, knowing she had to crush her mother's dreams before they grew to unfathomable proportions. "I'm afraid I won't be able to help him with those."

Mother laughed.

Adelaide winced. Had her mother's laugh always been so grating and false? Or was this something she saved for London because she thought it made her look more sophisticated?

"Dear Adelaide, you've only to mention it to your husband a time or two. It's obvious he dotes on you. I knew he would. The family is notoriously obnoxious about their marriages."

Perhaps because they notoriously married for love, which Trent had not been able to do. No wonder he didn't want to live under the same roof as her. "I'm afraid you're mistaken, Mother. Lord Trent feels nothing but obligation for me. We aren't even living in the same house anymore."

Mother froze, the flattering, false smile dropping from her face. "What?"

Adelaide shifted her weight from foot to foot. She should not have brought this up in public, despite the fact that it felt like an enormous relief to finally admit the problem to someone. Her voice dropped to a whisper in the attempt to keep her secret. "He's staying at Hawthorne House."

"Useless," her mother hissed.

"I beg your pardon?" Adelaide's eyebrows drew together as she leaned forward to better hear her mother's quiet words.

"You. You are useless. All you had to do was keep him happy and then you could have helped Helena rise to her rightful place in society." Mother dropped her arm from Adelaide's elbow and smoothed her skirts. "I should have known this wouldn't work out when you merely managed to catch the younger son. The duke would have been so much better. I blame myself. I should have looked over the wall to make sure it was the duke, not simply assumed you'd gotten it right."

Adelaide blinked at her mother, trying to

bring the words into focus, but it didn't work. Mother had never been complimentary, but *useless* was a good bit harsher than her normal declarations. "I . . . didn't . . . I mean . . . what?"

Mother looked around the room and pasted her smile back on her face. "We can fix this. Come along."

Adelaide trailed after her mother, trying not to trip over the hem of her gown. "What are we doing?"

"Jealousy, my dear. It's time you learned how to use it. A smile here, a little flirting there. Nothing grabs a man's attention faster." Mother's sharp blue eyes cut through the crowd. What was she looking for? Who was she looking for?

The implications of her mother's plan finally formulated in Adelaide's confused brain. Obviously her mother had gone mad, because the last thing Adelaide wanted to do was flirt with a man who wasn't her husband. There were so many reasons to avoid doing such a thing — not the least of which was the fact that Adelaide hadn't the foggiest notion how to flirt. If she did she'd have certainly been using her skills on Trent and not some other man of her mother's choosing. "Mother, this won't work."

Mother rolled her eyes. "Of course it will,

darling. How do you think I got that new diamond necklace last year? A solid month of dancing with the Viscount of Strenwhite at every possible function. Believe me. This is the fastest way into a man's attentions."

A month didn't seem very fast, but what did Adelaide know about marriage? Perhaps a month was a veritable blink in marital relations.

And then the introductions began. Adelaide had already been afraid of forgetting the women she'd met tonight, but now she was being inundated with men as well. Most of the gentlemen were polite, even as they sent puzzled looks her way when her mother tried to rather obviously manipulate them into asking her daughter to dance. Did married women dance at these gatherings? Adelaide had rather thought the dancing was mostly for the unmarried young ladies — a classification she was feeling an increasingly urgent need to remind her mother she did not possess any longer.

Her mother finally achieved her goal, and as Adelaide danced with a man named Mr. Givendale, she tried to come to grips with this new look at her mother. She'd always known there wasn't an abundance of affection between her parents, but she'd assumed that was the fault of both parties. What if it wasn't? What if her father had simply grown tired of her mother's scheming and trickery? Her need to constantly push for more? It didn't make any sense, really. The woman was a countess. She outranked over three quarters of the ladies in the room, and still she worried, still it wasn't enough. Of course, Helena was only a viscountess and hadn't been invited to tonight's ball. And it was always about Helena.

"Are you enjoying living in Town?" Mr. Givendale asked.

Adelaide tried to bring her thoughts back to the dance at hand. No matter how uncomfortable she was with her mother's maneuverings, there was no cause to be rude to a man who had asked her to dance. The dancing was something she'd been particularly looking forward to before she'd gotten married.

"Town is lovely," Adelaide answered. And it was. The beauty of London, despite the smog and crowdedness, was about the only positive thing she could say about her current living arrangements.

"You make it lovelier."

A flush burned up Adelaide's neck to her ears as she turned to follow the dance pattern. She might not know how to flirt but it seemed at least some of the gentlemen could more than make up for her lack of competency. What was she supposed to say to that? Should she say anything? Nearly half a minute had passed before they were shoulder to shoulder once more.

"Have you been to the opera yet? I've a box there you're welcome to use any time." He paused as another couple passed between them. "Your husband too, of course."

Adelaide didn't have to feign her sudden difficulty breathing. As much as she craved the oxygen she was suddenly deprived of, she was more than grateful for the excuse to leave the dance floor. "I beg your pardon, Mr. Givendale, but I don't think I'm feeling quite up to finishing the set."

"Of course."

He pulled them from the formation and escorted her to the side of the dance floor, where she immediately dropped his arm and kept walking. With every step she took her chest seemed to loosen until she could finally breathe properly again. Was this what Trent had wanted for her? He'd said he wanted to give her the experience of the Season she'd missed out on, but it didn't seem right to include any other men in that experience. Now she just had to convince her mother of that.

"Whatever did you do that for?"

Mother appeared at Adelaide's elbow, but Adelaide didn't stop. She kept going, even as her mother began yet another tirade on Adelaide's inability to see a plan through properly. As they rounded a large pillar at the side of the ballroom, Adelaide collided with an older man coming from the other direction.

"Oh, pardon me!" Adelaide took a quick step back, almost tripping over the velvet train of her ball gown. The dress was gorgeous, but maneuvering in it was proving exceptionally difficult. Trent had shown her how to hold the trailing skirt when she was dancing, and as long as she moved forward while walking she did all right, but backward was a tricky endeavor. The older man reached for her hand, giving her support until she was steady on her feet.

"All right, then?"

She nodded. "Yes, thank you."

The man was obviously important. Some men just held themselves with power. Given that his clothing was also very fine, she assumed him to be an important personage indeed. She waited for her mother to introduce them.

A glance to her side showed that her mother had disappeared. She twisted her head, looking for the dark orange of her dress, but the vicinity was full of pastels and whites with the occasional deep purple or blue.

She turned back to the old man and gave him a small smile before moving to walk past him. Without an introduction she could do no more, but she was burning to know who he was. Whoever he was, her mother wanted nothing to do with him. Which might make him one of her favorite people in London.

Lady Crampton wasn't to be avoided for long, however. Once Adelaide was out of sight of the old man, her mother reappeared at her elbow seemingly out of nowhere.

She turned her head to see if the old man was still visible, but he'd gone on his way and was nowhere to be found. Trent's brother, however, also occupied the fringes of the crowd on this side of the ballroom, and he stepped forward with a frown of concern that made Adelaide worry that her panic was starting to show on her face. The entire evening had been a series of questions that left her second-guessing her every move.

"Would you care to dance?" The duke took Adelaide's hand and bowed over their connected fingers.

"Of . . . of course."

Adelaide had a feeling the man didn't really want to dance. If the speculative glances in his direction were any indication, he didn't do it all that frequently. She soon understood why. Even though he showed a greater than average amount of grace, he took up a considerably larger than average amount of space on the dance floor, leaving him bumping shoulders with the other people in the quadrille formation.

"What am I to call you?" Adelaide asked as they linked elbows and circled another couple.

"The family calls me Griffith. You are welcome to do the same. Or Riverton, if that is more comfortable for you." He angled his shoulder to avoid another couple.

Adelaide noticed they were garnering more than a few whispers and stares as they went through the dance.

"They are trying to verify with each other that you are indeed Trent's new wife," Griffith murmured in her ear.

Adelaide looked up at him to see if he too was noticing the many people paying attention to him, but his gaze seemed to rest solely on her. It was unnerving. His eyes were nearly identical to Trent's in color, and his features were similar enough to declare them related at a glance, but Griffith's gaze held solidity, a strength that Trent's lacked. The marked power of duke versus the comfort of the second son had never been so evident to her, and she found herself thankful that Trent had come to the ruins that day instead of Griffith.

"How do they know?" she whispered back.

"I'm dancing with you." Griffith took her arm and led her down the line, having to fold nearly in half to go under the raised arms of the other couples.

"Do you usually avoid dancing, then?" Adelaide asked as they came to the end of the line and added their arms to the tunnel of dancers.

"I avoid anything that requires singling out a specific female. The speculation is too great. I only dance with family. I always seem to have a cousin or two in London for the Season."

Adelaide blinked. What a lonely existence. How would Griffith ever find a wife if he didn't participate in one of the hallmarks of aristocratic courtship? Not everyone could expect a floor to give way and make the decision for them.

Nervous laughter lodged in her throat, but thankfully the dance separated them for a moment to allow her to regain control before needing to speak again.

As the set continued, Adelaide tried to subtly steer the conversation to his brother, though she had a feeling he knew exactly what she was doing and she wasn't gaining any knowledge he didn't specifically want her to have — which wasn't anything Trent hadn't already told her. When the dance set ended, Griffith escorted her to Trent's side on the opposite side of the room from her mother.

Wondering if she was actually free of her mother for a while, Adelaide looked around as Trent talked with a man she'd met earlier but whose name she had forgotten . . . and her gaze connected with her mother's, and she actually wasn't frowning for once. Perhaps the reminder that Adelaide was now solidly connected to a duke had softened her disapproval. She was, however, headed in Adelaide's direction. Adelaide's shoulders sagged.

Then her mother's eyes cut to the left and she changed direction, veering off to the door leading to the women's retiring room.

Adelaide glanced over, wondering what had caused her mother's change of mind. The old man from earlier stood a few feet away, drinking a glass of lemonade and talking to a younger man who was most definitely related to him, given the shape of the nose and chin.

She waited for a break in Trent's conversation before leaning in. "Who is that man?"

Trent followed her gaze. "The Duke of Spindlewood. Why? Would you like an introduction?"

"Yes." Adelaide wound her arm into his. "I believe I would."

Chapter 15

Sweat ran down Trent's face, stinging his eyes and threatening to impede his vision, a dangerous thing when a man was in the ring with Gentleman Jack himself. He feinted left and threw another punch that was easily blocked by the seasoned boxer who immediately threw a punch of his own. Trent managed to block it, though without the finesse of the other man.

Finally the prizefighter stepped back, declaring they'd had enough. "You're a bit heavy on your feet today, Lord Trent."

Trent grunted as he climbed out of the ring and joined the mass of men milling about the exclusive boxing club.

"Feeling a bit off today, Hawthorne?" Lord Worthorp slapped Trent on the back and handed him a linen towel to mop off the sweat. "Not surprising, considering you haven't been in for weeks. I think even I'd be willing to have a go at you after that long of an absence."

Trent had no idea what to say to the man, so he buried his face in the towel. Bringing up his marriage would only lead to questions or worse, comments and jokes he had to pretend to go along with even though he hadn't a clue what they were talking about. He had no idea what it was like to have his wife change his regular menu or throw the servants into chaos. He could only hope another man would inform Lord Worthorp and they could find their teasing hilarious and leave him to shrug in silence.

As he'd hoped, another man, whose voice he didn't recognize, decided to join in the good-natured ribbing. From the sounds of shuffling feet, the conversation was drawing the attention of more than one other man.

"Haven't you heard, Worthorp? The infamous Lord Trent is no longer on the market."

Worthorp laughed and slapped Trent on the back, forcing him to pull the towel from his face or look like an idiot. "I had no idea you were married."

"Neither does Hawthorne." Mr. Givendale pinched a bit of snuff from his tin before grinning like a man who was betting on a race he knew was rigged.

Trent did his best to look like Griffith at

his haughtiest and didn't grant Givendale an answer.

Worthorp looked from Givendale to Trent and back again. Obviously debating the merits of friendship versus good gossip. "What do you mean?"

Trent bit back a sigh. This was London. Good gossip always won.

Givendale leaned against the wall. "Lord Trent here is residing over on Grosvenor Square these days. I doubt he's even seen his wife since he left her in Mount Street yesterday afternoon."

How could Givendale know Trent had returned to Hawthorne House after taking Adelaide riding yesterday? He'd had the servants take his curricle around back and then he'd ridden his horse over to Hawthorne House.

Worthorp looked at Trent with surprise. "No — you're not."

"I had business with Griffith last night, and we didn't finish until late. It made sense to stay at the house last night. Contrary to what Givendale seems to think, it is not a change of residence."

The other man in the group, whom Trent still didn't recognize even after seeing his face, clapped a strong hand on Trent's shoulder. "Good. I'd never believe it if you couldn't talk your way around your wife. You've always been able to charm the ladies."

Trent winced at the suggestive look in the man's eyes that implied Trent had done much more than pull a smile from a nervous wallflower or two. How was a man supposed to correct an image like that? There was no evidence, no reason for anyone to make such a claim, when he hadn't ever done so much as pull a lady into an alcove to steal a kiss. He supposed he should just let people think what they were going to think. He and God knew the truth, and one day soon Adelaide would as well. Those were the only people who mattered. Weren't they?

"Have you met the lady yet, Stapleton? She's quite charming herself." Givendale lowered his face to look at his snuff box before tilting his eyes back in Trent's direction.

Trent shrugged out of his sweat-soaked linen shirt and dropped a clean one over his head, trying not to look concerned. Givendale had never been one of Trent's favorite people, but they'd never had a row. So why did the man seem determined to bedevil Trent at every opportunity? And why was he so interested in Trent's marriage? Whatever the reason, it was time to put a stop to it.

The boyish grin Trent plastered onto his face might have been a bit overdone, and it certainly felt silly, but then again wouldn't a man who was happily married be likely to grin in just such a way? "She is rather charming, isn't she? Why else do you think I married her before any of you lot got the chance to meet her? There's not another one like her in all of England, boys. You'll have to settle for who's left."

Stapleton snorted. "Another Hawthorne beset by love. It's like a curse with your family."

Yet one more stone on the monument to Trent's unsuitability to ever take over as head of the family. He'd be grateful if it didn't come with a life sentence to a woman he didn't love.

"Have you looked into the horses racing about this year?" Givendale asked. "I've been thinking about investing in a stable. Rumor is you've just acquired one along with your wife. We should discuss it sometime."

Had he? He knew her dowry included an estate in Suffolk, but he'd thought it just that, an estate. Did it have horses on it? Was this something he should know? "Of course.

Any time."

With a final nod to the group of men, Trent left the building, doing his best to avoid the knowing smile still on Givendale's face — and the niggling idea that holding his wife's hand was quite a bit different than holding her heart.

Two days later Trent was still mulling over the thought as he leaned against the billiard table in Hawthorne House, idly rolling the balls across the smooth green surface with no real rhyme or reason. How long did a courtship take? What did people even do when they were courting? The clacking of the balls against the bumpers and each other was somewhat satisfying, but it didn't answer any of his questions.

He knew couples went riding together, and they'd done that every day for the past four days. Rotten Row was becoming more and more crowded as London's aristocratic population settled in for the Season. People barely glanced at them now as they rode along, Trent pointing out the same sites over and over again because he didn't have anything else to say. Neither of his sisters had taken conventional routes to marriage, but they'd had some suitors before finding their husbands. Trent had just never paid much attention to what they did.

Flowers were obvious, and he'd taken a large bouquet of them to the house when he took her riding the day after the ball. Sweets were often mentioned by the women in his family as well, so he'd asked Griffith's chef to create one of his famous sugar confections. That too had drawn a serene smile and a thank-you from Adelaide, though Mrs. Harris had sniffed and frowned even as she gave the elaborate creation an intent examination. He hadn't taken any gift yesterday and yet he'd still been granted the same greeting, the same smile, the same everything. He wasn't accomplishing anything other than becoming adept at maneuvering his curricle in a crowd, and he'd already been a rather better driver than most of London.

There were couples that announced their engagements mere days after meeting each other. Shouldn't Trent at least feel like he was making ground? It wasn't as if he had to convince Adelaide to marry him. He simply had to convince himself they were actually married. Why was that so difficult?

He'd driven his curricle over to Hawthorne House last night, hoping that it looked less suspicious than him simply riding his horse. The grooms were shining the vehicle, readying it for his afternoon ride, but he considered borrowing Griffith's carriage, since the sky looked a bit heavy. How desperate was he if he took her riding in a closed carriage that he couldn't even drive himself? Where was his famed charm and creativity that he could think of nothing else to do with his wife besides ride down an old dirt lane in the middle of a park?

The smirk that had been on Givendale's face two days ago sliced through Trent's memory, firming his resolve to do something special to court his wife today. He would not let a day go by that they didn't do something together in an effort to create some sort of affection or at least connection between them. He would take the carriage and they could go for a walk if the weather held out. That was at least a bit different than going for a drive. If it rained, though, they would have to visit in the drawing room. With nothing to look at but each other and the curtainless window.

He still hadn't asked about that window covering, though he probably should. Surely she was planning on replacing it soon. Didn't all women yearn to redecorate? Claim a space as their own? Maybe Adelaide was having as much trouble accepting the situation as he was.

He wouldn't know unless he talked to her about it.

And if the conversation went nowhere? If they ended up staring at each other with nothing to say? Trent rolled a billiard ball around with his flattened hand. There was a fine chess set in his study. Surely the precious progress they'd made, little though it may be, could withstand a bit of intellectual competition on a chessboard. It wouldn't be at all strange to play a friendly game of chess without an inkling of conversation.

He gave the ivory ball a particularly hard shove, sending it ricocheting across the table, scattering the balls until the entire table appeared to be in motion.

They could do dinner. He had taken her riding and now he would take her to dinner. At least then they could blame any lack of communication on being too polite to speak with their mouths full.

Her mother had arrived.

To be honest, Adelaide was rather surprised it had taken the woman four days to make an appearance — assuming she'd taken the ride on Rotten Row the day she'd returned to London. She might have been in Town upwards of a week.

And now she was in Adelaide's drawing room.

The one without a curtain on the window.

The one that had borne up well under more than two decades of use but was still showing the age of the decor.

The one that Trent picked her up in every day so they could ride through the park like near strangers.

Adelaide supposed she should be grateful for those rides. They were certainly the highlight of her day, as she spent most of the remaining hours wandering the rooms trying to avoid the staff while she worked her way through the books in Trent's — no, their — small library. Still, she'd thought he'd have moved home by now. She'd been peaceful and serene. Nothing like the irate woman that had sent him packing in the first place. There was nothing else she could do to convince him that she would be a proper, meek wife. The small smile and soft words had always been enough to appease her mother.

The mother who was even now sitting in the drawing room.

Alone.

Probably making a list of all the ways Helena would have handled this situation better.

Mrs. Harris was waiting at the bottom of the stairs. "Tea, my lady?"

Adelaide nodded, wanting to smack herself for not thinking to request a tray. She had never liked the stuff, but everyone else seemed to consider it a social necessity.

Taking one last deep breath, Adelaide pushed the door open and entered the room.

"I don't know how you expect to make the most of your new position if you don't take advantage of everyone's current curiosity. You've been seen in the park so often that hardly anyone talks about you in the shops anymore."

Adelaide stumbled to a stop three feet into the room and blinked at her mother. "Good afternoon, Mother. I've ordered tea."

Mother huffed out a breath and lowered herself to the sofa. "Of course you've ordered tea. I've taught you to always do so even if the guest claims not to want it."

Confusion drew Adelaide's eyebrows together. When had her mother taught her anything about tea? Perhaps she assumed that teaching Helena was as good as teaching both of them, but Adelaide had never been allowed to sit in on the lessons unless they needed another person. Still, it wasn't worth bringing up now. There was nothing to be gained from it, since Adelaide didn't think she'd need to know much more than how to keep her skirt out of the carriage wheel and not embarrass herself in a ballroom. Both of those she could manage nicely. "Of course, Mother."

"Have you been by to see Helena yet? She got into Town three days ago."

Adelaide had left a card, the only calling card she'd actually left anyone, but at that time Helena hadn't yet arrived. "No, she wasn't there when I went by. I didn't know she'd returned to Town."

Fenton entered with the tea tray, setting it lightly on the low table before bowing his way out of the room. Mother picked up the teapot before Adelaide could say anything. It was impossible to tell if the slight had been deliberate, but Adelaide let it pass. Even if it were, what did it matter if her mother thought she had the upper hand? It was simple enough to smile and nod and then ignore her wishes.

Adelaide didn't really care for pouring tea anyway. She accepted the cup of tea with a splash of milk, noticing that the delicate white tea service trimmed in gold was more elegant than the service she saw when Trent had tea delivered. The fact that she hadn't known they had two complete tea services bothered her.

"I saw her the day before yesterday. She's doing well but is anxious to establish herself a bit more. They're sure to have children soon, and she's worried she'll lose some of her status during her confinement."

Adelaide tilted her head as she watched her mother sip tea, wondering if the older woman even realized the implications of what she'd just said. Helena had barely had a chance to shake the country dust from her hems before Mother had gone to visit. And yet this was her first time coming to Mount Street.

"I'm sure Helena will have a fine Season."

"Of course she will." Mother set her teacup down. "With your new connections it shouldn't be difficult to secure her a few more coveted invitations."

Adelaide seriously doubted that she had more pull than her mother. Mother was a countess, after all. Adelaide was just married. "My position is merely circumstantial. Trent isn't due to inherit a title."

"Hmm, yes, not unless something happens to his brother. The duke is still unmarried, so your husband would be the next in line should something unfortunate occur."

"Mother!" Adelaide fumbled her cup to the table, cold shivers making small bumps rise from the skin of her arm. "That's a horrible thing to say."

Mother sighed, lowering her chin to spear Adelaide with a chiding glare. "Really, Adelaide, accidents happen. The duke wouldn't be the first man to die conveniently."

Memories of the large man dancing with her, welcoming her to the family, contrasted with the callousness of her mother's statements, making Adelaide shudder. "Perhaps we could discuss something else?"

Mother sighed. "Very well. But you would do well to take advantage of people's curiosity. Right now you're a novelty. You could get invited anywhere and easily request that Helena and I come with you. Everyone would understand your desire for a friendly face."

Adelaide rather thought everyone would expect her husband to be the only comforting presence she needed, but she knew better than to say anything. Smile and nod. Smile and nod. Most of the time Mother would forget what she'd asked of Adelaide in the first place.

Dear God, don't let this time be the exception.

CHAPTER 16

Trent dropped to the pavement and sent an anxious look at the sky. They weren't going to be able to go for a walk. The weather was entirely too unpredictable to risk taking Adelaide out in it. Still, he didn't want to forgo his visit. He was trying to shove weeks if not months of courting into as short a time as possible. He couldn't afford to miss a day because of the threat of rain. This was England, after all. He'd never get anywhere if he limited himself to blue skies and sunshine.

Having to do something other than go for a drive, however, made him sweat. For all of his reputed charm and grace, he didn't have much practice in one-on-one situations with females. Particularly ones who weren't his sisters.

Perhaps he should treat Adelaide like he did one of his sisters.

No. No. He shook his head fiercely to

shake free any vestiges of that thought. Adelaide was most certainly not his sister, and he didn't even need to consider trying to see her as such. It was much too disturbing.

The door opened behind him, and he turned to ask Fenton if he thought the weather would hold long enough for him to take Adelaide to Gunter's for ices.

It wasn't Fenton in the doorway, though.

It was Lady Crampton and her maid.

Trent cleared his throat and shifted his weight. "Good afternoon."

Lady Crampton looked from him to the carriage and back again. Trent could only imagine the thoughts that would be running through her head. It must look strange, him standing by the road in front of his house with a carriage that wasn't his own. Had Adelaide told her mother about their circumstances? What they were attempting? He rather hoped not. He hadn't told his own mother. Of course, he still hadn't gotten around to telling his own mother that he'd gotten married either. She was going to be beyond cross with him, but he couldn't figure out what to say. He started the letter three times a day and always ended up chucking the thing in the fire. She was going to have questions. And he didn't want to answer them, was afraid he wouldn't know how to answer them. She was sure to be arriving in Town soon, and it wasn't going to be pretty when she learned his unintentional secret.

Very well, his intentional secret. He was going to have to take total responsibility for keeping it from her, but at least then he'd know why she was disappointed in him. That was far better than having her be disappointed and him be left wondering why. And after going against the norm and raising her family to marry for love, she was certain to be disappointed in Trent's situation.

He bit his cheek to stave off the urge to defend the carriage on the street. It was much better if he pretended there was nothing curious about the situation.

"What are you doing?"

Of course, pretending was so much easier if the other party went along with it.

Trent went with the simplest answer. "Taking Adelaide to dinner."

Her eyebrows lifted. "At half past three in the afternoon?"

Hair flopped against his forehead as he tilted his head to the side and tried for a boyish grin. He hated playing the idiot, but sometimes it was the easiest way out of a conversation. "Is it that early? I must have gotten anxious."

"To eat dinner." She adjusted her spencer jacket.

He shrugged. "I'd be eating dinner anyway. It's the company I'm looking forward to."

A frown pulled the countess's lips into a wrinkled pink slash across her face. "One would assume you could have the company regardless of whether or not you were eating."

Maintaining his smile and relaxed posture grew difficult. Perhaps he'd bought into this courtship ruse a bit too much and he'd forgotten that the rest of London assumed he was still living under the same roof as his wife. And while it shouldn't matter if Lady Crampton knew the truth or not, Trent didn't feel it was in his best interests to let her know. Especially with some people already suspecting. "There's something satisfying about letting the rest of London know how lucky I am."

And while Lady Crampton made noncommittal noises, Trent looked over her shoulder to find the luck in question standing in the doorway.

Adelaide brushed the hair off her forehead and attempted a smile, though the corners of her mouth pulled down and her lips poked out the way they do when a person clenches their jaw. Her gaze kept flitting from him to her mother and then around the entire area, taking in the number of people witnessing the strange meeting in front of a house he supposedly lived in.

Nothing about this tableau looked like a man returning home. It looked like exactly what it was — a man coming to visit a woman.

Trent bit back a sigh as he wished Lady Crampton a good afternoon and pushed past her into the house. He had a feeling life had just gotten a bit more complicated.

Even though the visit had gone horribly, Adelaide wished her mother had stayed. As uncomfortable and embarrassing as the ensuing conversation would have been, it had to be better than the awkwardness now covering the dilapidated drawing room. She'd just choked down tea with her mother so she wasn't about to suggest Fenton bring another loaded tray, but without the sights of London to focus on, she and Trent were left without a common distraction.

The fact that they apparently needed a common distraction was possibly proof that Trent's courtship plan wasn't having the effect that he'd planned. Assuming he planned for them to actually become closer — perhaps even find love — during this time. He'd said that was his objective, but then again he'd also moved out of the house, thereby limiting the amount of time they spent in each other's presence.

Adelaide didn't know what to think anymore.

Trent shifted, causing the settee to creak. His eyes widened as he cast a worried glance toward the thin, curved legs. He rolled his shoulders and sat up a bit straighter. "Did you have a pleasant visit with your mother?"

Did anyone have pleasant interactions with the countess? Well, perhaps Helena did. The two saw the world in much the same way, after all. "My sister has returned to Town."

"Oh. Do let me know if you'd like to visit her one afternoon. I can easily adjust our ride." He coughed and looked at the holes in the plaster where the curtain rod had once hung. "Assuming you wish to continue our rides, of course."

"Oh yes," Adelaide rushed to assure him.

Silence fell once more. Should she suggest he take some time to catch up on things in his study? Didn't men need to spend time on their business things every day? Her father always spent the majority of his time in his study. And Trent had been essentially blocked from his for several days. But if she suggested that, would it start a pattern? Would he keep coming by only to seclude himself in his study?

He cleared his throat.

She sniffed.

He shifted in his seat, causing another ominous creak to cut through the room.

But none of those sounds could lift the weight of silence caused by two people in a room who didn't know what to say to each other. If the furniture bore the weight of the silent expectation as heavily as she did, Trent had reason to be concerned about the stability of his seat.

"You can't hum while holding your nose."

Trent startled, his mouth dropping open slightly as if he, too, had been about to break the silence. Adelaide wished he had. Whatever he'd been about to say couldn't be as inane as her blurting out a random fact she'd come across in a book one day.

"Seriously?" he asked.

And before she could find a way to extricate herself from his embarrassing scrutiny, he lifted one hand and pinched his nose while pressing his lips together. No noise emerged until he released his nose and opened his lips to let a gush of air out. "Fascinating."

She blinked at him. Fascinating? While it was true he'd seemed to enjoy her bits of trivia on their rides, she'd never pulled out something so obscure before.

He leaned forward, bracing one elbow on his knee. "Did you know that you cannot lick your own elbow?"

Adelaide looked down at her arm. "Why on earth would anyone want to do that?"

Trent shrugged. His eyes crinkled slightly at the corners and a small smile tilted his lips. "Who knows? But I won two pence from Griffith once by telling him he couldn't accomplish it."

"How old were you?" The words tumbled out along with Adelaide's laughter.

"Six. I'd just lost one pence to Henry Durham because he'd challenged me to the same thing."

Adelaide's laughter eased into a quiet smile. "I once dared my sister to climb onto the gardener's tool shed to get our kite so we wouldn't get in trouble."

"And . . . ?" Trent's even, white teeth split his face in anticipation of a good story, making Adelaide realize this hadn't been the best continuation of the topic.

"She told my mother I'd gotten it snagged

up there deliberately and tried to make her bribe one of the stableboys to retrieve it."

One hand clamped over Trent's mouth as he tried not to laugh but it sputtered out anyway. "How old were you?"

Heat crept up Adelaide's neck. "Fifteen."

A loud crack of thunder cut through their shared laughter. Trent rose and crossed to the window, sighing as the rain began to pelt the glass panels.

Adelaide stood beside him, watching the rain. Did this mean he would leave? His time in the drawing room had been as long as most men stayed to visit with ladies when they were courting. At least, as far as she understood it. Right now she would have been more than happy to forfeit half her knowledge of various trivia for the chance to have witnessed one of Helena's Seasons. Any insight would be better than the darkness she now found herself in.

"I had planned on taking you to the Clarendon to dine tonight."

Adelaide blinked. He wasn't going home? They'd spent a mere hour in each other's company while they rode the last several days and now he wanted to spend the entire evening with her? In the confines of a dining arrangement? That seemed like considerable progress to her. "Is the food good there?"

Trent nodded. "French. I had been hoping the rain would hold off long enough for us to enjoy the outing."

Did that mean that now that the skies had opened up they weren't going? If that was what he wanted, why had he mentioned it to her in the first place? Unless that wasn't what he wanted. "We could dine here."

Her voice had been so quiet, she wasn't sure he'd heard her. Wasn't even sure the words had gone anywhere outside her head, until he turned his face from the window and smiled at her. The smile was tight and his eyes looked a bit wide and fearful, but her suggestion was rather terrifying. They were going to spend an evening together. Alone. Without a single distraction or activity to refocus their attention on.

He stared at her, holding her gaze with his own until her eyes started to dry out, and she blinked to break the connection.

"You would do that?" he asked. "Forgo an evening at the Clarendon to stay here?"

She blinked at him, partly to relieve the burn from her eyes but also hoping she could somehow find the question he was really asking, because it felt like his words were weighted. By agreeing to this change in plans, was she setting them in an entirely new direction? If she was, she could only hope it was a good one, because she found herself nodding and leaving the room to see to the arrangements.

They were deviating from the courtship plan, veering into waters no courting couple would dare to go. If it failed, their fledgling relationship would take a while to recover, but if it succeeded . . . Adelaide floated off to find Mrs. Harris, dreams of a real marriage filling her head and raising her hopes.

Dinner was simple, with Mrs. Harris being torn between grumbling about the late notice and rejoicing over the fact that they were dining together at home. Where no one could see them. It hadn't stopped Adelaide from dressing for dinner, though, and Trent's breath had been stolen all over again as he waited for her at the bottom of the stairs.

Just as she had when he picked her up for the ball, she'd stolen his wits for a few moments, and for the briefest time he'd been inclined to whisk her out onto the Town despite the rain. To show her off in her finery and splendidness.

But he didn't. They'd chosen to stay in for the night, and he marveled at the decision too much to take it away from her.

Sliced roast in their own dining room was of no benefit to Adelaide's social status. There was no gain from it outside of their own personal connection. It was hard to imagine the daughter of Lady Crampton being willing to eat a simple, private meal when they could have been prominently seated at one of the best restaurants in London.

But when she tossed a grape at him, daring him to catch it with his mouth, he had no choice but to believe it was true. She was untainted by the desperate measures of the *ton* debutantes, never having had to weigh a friend's happiness against her own future well-being, never having had to betray herself or someone else in order to gain social standing. While he didn't fully understand her view on life, he was willing to admit it wasn't as tarnished as he had feared.

She was a different person in the privacy of their dining room. Different than she'd been on their rides, and certainly different than she'd been at the ball, where she'd tried to fade into the background. She hadn't been successful, of course, with her unique eyes, gorgeous dress, and well-trimmed figure, but he'd seen her try.

While Mrs. Harris fixed dinner, they'd played chess. During dinner, she entertained him by retelling the story from one of the novels she'd read lately, complete with commentary on the foolishness of the hero and heroine. She never volunteered her opinions, but he soon found all he had to do was ask and she would tell him what she thought. For a woman so inclined to keep her opinions to herself, she had formed surprisingly decisive ones.

The rain tapered off while they ate, and eventually Trent could put it off no longer. The evening had been splendid, more than he had hoped for. But he was still committed to his plan. After all, wasn't tonight an indication that it was working?

She walked with him to the darkened front hall, saying nothing, both of them barely breathing as Fenton saw to having Trent's coach brought around front. Her hands felt small in his, and he clasped them lightly. In the dim light of a single lantern, he could make out the glint of gold in her necklace. The chain had gotten twisted during the evening and now the brilliant dangling sapphire was trapped near her collarbone, pointing somewhere beyond her shoulder, the clasp twisted against it.

Somehow the flaw made her even lovelier

than she'd been when she'd stolen his breath earlier in the evening.

"I enjoyed dinner." He kept his voice low, afraid that anything above the gravelly near whisper would break the peaceful bubble they seemed encased in.

"As did I." She must have felt the same as he did, that the glow around them was delicate and needed to be cared for. Her words escaped on a breathy sigh, quiet and deep with meaning.

He wanted more. She'd been so much more than he'd expected today. He hated that he'd wasted the past weeks, setting their marriage off on the wrong foot because he feared she would be too much like her shrewish mother. It was clear now that Adelaide was nothing like Lady Crampton, and Trent couldn't wait to start them back on the path they should have been on before he messed everything up.

Slowly he released his grip on her hands and trailed his fingers up her arms, past the edge of the gloves that draped away from her elbows after the busyness of the evening. Past the puffed blue sleeves of her dress, and over the embroidery dancing across her shoulders. Finally he slid his hands up her neck until they softly framed her face. Fingers that spent most of their time gripping a foil or curled tightly into a fist now trembled in an effort to cradle her head gently. One thumb traced the side of her jaw as he looked into her eyes, wondering, hoping, praying she wanted him to kiss her as badly as he wanted to.

Her lips parted on a gentle sigh, and he lowered his head to touch his lips to hers.

It was a mere brush of flesh on flesh. Intellectually he knew this, knew that this meeting of skin couldn't be all that physiologically different than the holding of hands, but it felt like so much more. It felt like that moment of beauty when the morning sun hits the glass just right, showering the room with tiny crystals of light.

He brushed his lips against hers again, unwilling, unable, to leave it at a single touch. It felt like the special, stolen moments as a child when he curled up in front of the Yule log on Christmas Eve and fell asleep on the settee, waking in the morning to find his mother had simply draped a blanket over him and left him there so he could enjoy the magic.

Finally he pressed his lips harder against hers, taking her sigh as his own and sliding his hands deeper into her hair until he fully supported her head.

It felt like home.

He didn't know how long they stood there, trading breath and sharing space. When he finally lifted his head, her wide eyes blinked up at him slowly, glazed and unfocused, the large, dark centers threatening to take over the blue he was always tempted to drown in. He could stay here tonight, he knew. The barriers keeping him from knocking on her bedchamber door had been obliterated the moment his hand had grazed the bare skin of her arm. And if the way her tongue darted out to catch his taste from her lips was any indication, she would open the door when he knocked.

But he wanted more.

What had seemed like a desperate and almost ridiculous notion a few days ago was now the battle plan that was going to get him what he wanted more than anything in his life.

Because he didn't simply want his wife anymore.

Now he wanted Adelaide.

CHAPTER 17

By morning Adelaide was beginning to understand why she'd never completely understood how God worked. Given that He had made the bewildering, maddening, incomprehensible species that was man from His own image, it stood to reason that the Creator would be a complicated mass of logic never meant to be understood by the female mind. That, or the fall of man in the Garden of Eden had taken them even further off the path than she'd ever realized. Because the fact was, despite a night of tossing and turning and deep contemplation, Adelaide was no closer to understanding her husband than she'd been the day before. And while she was considerably more hopeful this morning — she had that kiss to think about, after all — she was still confused by the fact that she was going to eat breakfast on her own.

She rose with the sun, tired of lying in a

bed that wasn't granting her any sleep. Again. Rebecca hadn't come to the room yet, but Adelaide didn't feel like ringing for her. There was something peaceful about wandering her room in solitude until she ended up by the window, amazed at the view of the city while it was still sleeping.

A few clouds drifted across the sky, making shadows dance down the back alley and across the buildings. Occasionally an industrious ray of early sunshine broke through and highlighted a window or lamppost.

The growling of her stomach reminded her that she hadn't eaten much dinner the night before, too focused on keeping the conversation flowing with Trent. As if it were only awaiting the acknowledgment, her stomach cramped in hunger, making her dread having to wait for Rebecca to come and spend the appropriate amount of time preparing her to go downstairs.

Letting the drape she'd been clutching slip through her fingers, she realized she didn't have to wait. This was her home, and it was past time she start living like it.

It didn't take long to go through her dressing room and find her older dresses. She wasn't sure they'd be there, since her mother had seen to her packing, but at least three of her favorites were tucked away in the corner. Back home — or in the country, rather, since she needed to remember that this was now her home — she'd grown accustomed to dressing herself in the morning, only requiring her maid for the more elaborate afternoon and evening clothes.

Her braid from the night before wasn't as destroyed as she'd expected, given the amount of tossing and turning she'd done through the night. She coiled it into a knot on her head, securing it with more pins than Rebecca would have required, but no one would know that but her.

A glance in the mirror above her dressing table showed that she was woefully out of fashion, but that didn't matter. She wasn't going to see anyone but the servants this morning. Her husband wouldn't arrive until afternoon, and no one was going to come calling this early. Except maybe her mother. She hadn't been happy with Adelaide's lack of agreement in helping Helena and her husband, so she might return for another go at it.

The thought of her mother stopping by again made Adelaide reconsider leaving the room in her comfortable, worn gown. While it was highly doubtful that the woman had even woken yet, and she wouldn't dare step out of the house without the full attention of her lady's maid, her mother was also very adept at catching Adelaide at her absolute worst.

But this was her home, and if she wanted to walk around in near rags she should be able to.

Adelaide's moment of disgruntlement faded into delight. She had a butler. Her own butler. She could ban her mother from entering her home until a more appropriate visiting hour or even a more convenient day. What a freeing realization.

She threw open the door, sending a *whoosh* of air to ruffle her skirt. As she skipped down the corridor, the frayed hem of her old morning dress flipped about her ankles in a manner that she could never have gotten away with in front of anyone. Helena had written Adelaide three times since getting married, but never once had she mentioned how wonderful it was to be in control of one's own home. Adelaide completely understood the point of dowager houses now. If Trent were the duke, she would definitely be grateful that his mother had remarried and lived elsewhere. The more she thought about it, the more grateful she was that Trent wasn't the duke. A duchess probably didn't have the luxury of running about in old clothes and banning people from the door.

Adelaide's feet hit the floor in the main hall, reveling in the freedom of being able to go downstairs in nothing but her dressing gown, if she was so inclined. That would draw the notice of the servants, of course, but Adelaide had a feeling her staff wasn't prone to gossiping about their employers the way other servants did.

With a twirl through the hall and another bout of skipping, Adelaide danced her way to the breakfast room before her joyful scamper came to a stumbling halt in the doorway. Nothing was laid out in the breakfast room yet. Despite the realization that this was her house and she could do whatever she wished, she was still at the mercy of what she told the servants to do. They couldn't be expected to know that she was going to rise hours earlier than normal today.

She could, however, go down to the kitchens and get something herself, because they were, after all, her kitchens.

A giggle escaped, and she felt like a child venturing into places she'd never dared go before, despite the fact that she'd been down to the kitchens already. It had felt like Mrs. Harris's space then. But now, now it was Adelaide's. Though she wasn't quite brave enough to say as much to Mrs. Harris yet. Maybe she'd ask the housekeeper for cooking lessons.

She paused at the top of the stairs heading down into the servants' domain, thinking this must be what Evelina felt like in Fanny Burney's novel before she took those first steps into Society. Once Adelaide crossed that threshold, life would never be the same. There would be no area of her house that she hadn't claimed. It would be well and truly hers.

Her foot looked small as she extended it onto the first step. The rough planked wood, worn smooth in the middle, was unlike any set of steps she'd descended before. Somehow the frayed hem lying against her leg made it seem right though. The worn dress matched the worn steps. She'd clearly dressed appropriately for this morning.

Easing down the steps, she relished each moment of this freedom, this declaration of ownership. What would she find when she reached the kitchens? Mrs. Harris rolling out more of that splendid cinnamon biscuit dough? Fenton, Lydia, and the others taking their breakfast? What happened in the kitchens before the rest of the house awoke?

Her mind danced with all the options of what she might find belowstairs. By the time she reached the opening to the kitchens at the bottom of the stairs she was half expecting to find them feeding a tame monkey or spinning each other in an impromptu dance. No matter how fanciful her imagination, however, she'd have never guessed that there would be another lady present amongst the servants.

Yet there she was, seated at the worktable, cutting out biscuits with an apron thrown over her pink-and-brown morning gown. Her dress was certainly not from a previous Season. In fact, Adelaide remembered seeing that exact dress in an Ackermann's Repository last month, though not in pink, of course. She didn't know anyone who bought morning dresses in pink.

She also didn't know anyone who visited someone else's kitchens without being announced to the people who actually lived in the house, so that probably said something about the type of lady that bought pink morning dresses. Assuming, of course, that the woman at the worktable was indeed a lady. She certainly had money and taste, but why would she be up at dawn and in Adelaide's kitchen? She appeared very comfortable. As if she'd been there many times before.

Air got trapped in her chest and she had

to force it through a throat that was suddenly thick with a heavy heartbeat. A woman. A refined and elegant woman was comfortable in Trent's kitchen. Why? What was his relation to her? She wasn't a sister. The brown hair coiled into a neat bun and framed with perfect curls was enough to declare her a nonmember of the Hawthorne family. But what if she'd thought she would become one? Trent had said he wasn't courting a lady, and Adelaide believed him, but that didn't mean feelings hadn't existed for another woman. What if this was her? What if she'd returned to Town and hadn't yet heard that Trent had gotten married? Worse yet, what if she didn't care?

Between the tight, shallow breathing, the slow thudding heartbeats, and the massive race of questions, Adelaide was beginning to lose her steadiness. The room was out of focus, and her legs were threatening to give way at any moment. No one had noticed her yet, so it would be a simple matter to slip back up the stairs and pretend she didn't know of this woman's existence. She'd pretended not to notice all kinds of things growing up. Namely anything her mother and sister did. It couldn't be that much harder to ignore a strange woman who may or may not be connected to her husband.

With one hand on the plain wooden newel post at the base of the stairs, Adelaide stepped backward, thinking that if she could just keep her eye on everyone, she'd be able to will them into not looking at her.

She'd forgotten about the buckets of water that had been set near the stairs, ready to be hauled up to prepare the house for the day. They'd been conveniently placed for Oswyn to take them upstairs. Which also made them inconvenient for a quick escape by a woman who wasn't looking at them. Adelaide knocked the bucket sideways, her grip on the newel post making her swing around and land on the stairs instead of splashing into the river of water now gushing across the kitchen floor. If that wasn't enough to attract everyone's attention, the bucket rolled into a collection of brooms, sending them crashing down on Adelaide's head.

It was safe to assume that everyone was now aware of her presence.

Several concerned voices called out as a rush of feet clattered over the stone floor of the kitchen. "My lady!" There were several gasps and another crash or two as they slipped in the spilled water. Adelaide squeezed her eyes shut before admitting the brooms weren't going to hide her existence and she might as well pull herself up from the stair tread jabbing her in the back. As she hauled herself upright, she mumbled a quiet prayer for strength and perhaps a shred of regained dignity. There was no evading it now. She was going to have to be polite to her husband's . . . someone.

Mrs. Harris reached her first, grasping Adelaide's arm tightly until it was clear she wasn't going to do something horrible like topple into the oven or knock down the bread rack.

Easing one eye open at a time, Adelaide took in the concerned circle of servants, the lady in pink right in the middle of them and not even trying to hide. There was no sense in putting it off. The hope Adelaide had woken with was shattered right along with a bowl the scullery maid, Eve, had dropped when she slipped in the newly installed kitchen brook.

Adelaide looked straight at the kitchen inhabitant she didn't employ. The nerve and resolve straightening her back were foreign but not entirely unwelcome. "Who are you?"

It took a moment for the lady in pink to realize Adelaide was talking to her, and then a blush stole across her cheeks. Now that everyone was standing, Adelaide could see that the other woman was incredibly tiny, with dark brown eyes that matched the perfect curls framing her fine-featured face. There was a delicate grace in the way she moved, even when she'd made her way across the slippery kitchen floor. She probably didn't trip over buckets or accidentally turn her gloves inside out.

Mrs. Harris wiped her hands on her apron. "Oh dear, Lord Trent must have forgotten to mention Miss Amelia's visits. She's only just arrived in Town, you know."

No, she didn't know. The last shred of hope that this woman wasn't connected to Trent froze into a lump of ice that dropped into the pit of Adelaide's stomach and radiated cold down her legs until she thought her knees might give way. Again.

"Yes, he must have forgotten." Even though they'd talked for hours last night, and he'd had more than one opportunity to mention this Miss Amelia.

With an exasperated glance at the housekeeper, the woman in pink pushed through to the front of the group. "I'm afraid I didn't realize that Trent had gotten married until Mrs. Harris told me a few moments ago. Had I known, I would never have presumed to visit without speaking with you first. I'm Lady Raebourne."

Adelaide blinked. She was fairly certain her mouth was hanging open. As all her emotions shifted into a massive, undefinable pile, her brain struggled to comprehend this new information. This tiny, smiling woman was Lady Raebourne? This was the harridan her mother and sister claimed had ruined Helena's chance at an advantageous marriage? For the past two years Adelaide's ears had been filled with so many vile diatribes against this woman that Adelaide had expected Lady Raebourne to be nothing short of an utter virago. Instead she looked rather like a woodland fairy.

Adelaide curtsied. "H-how do you do?"

Lady Raebourne's smile was wide and caused her eyes to crinkle at the corners. "I am well. I hope you don't mind if I come visit the kitchens. Trent told me to come whenever I wished as long as I didn't venture upstairs without someone warning him first. Since I was coming to visit the servants, that wasn't a problem."

Placing her feet carefully on the slick stones, Lady Raebourne made her way back to the worktable. Slowly everyone else followed suit, returning to the jobs they'd been doing before Adelaide's inelegant arrival.

"No, no, I don't mind." Adelaide stumbled over to a stool. There was a marchioness cutting out biscuits in her kitchen. She was wearing an apron and everything. Why was a marchioness visiting Adelaide's servants? What sort of person did something like that?

"Good." Lady Raebourne began placing rows of dough on the pan. "I can't believe Trent got married and didn't tell us. Where did you meet?"

"In Hertfordshire." Adelaide took a deep breath and plunged on. Despite Lord Raebourne's country seat being in Hertfordshire and, in fact, bordering Lord Crampton's estate, Adelaide's family had nothing to do with him. Or rather the women didn't. Her father still went over to visit, and on a couple occasions Adelaide had seen the marquis as he was leaving her father's study, but given Mother and Helena's animosity toward the man's wife, they never saw the family socially. "I'm Lord Crampton's daughter."

Lady Raebourne's brows scrunched together while she tried to place Adelaide. It wasn't a surprise when she failed. No one ever remembered Adelaide.

"I didn't know Lady Helena had a sister." The confusion cleared from her face, replaced once again by the sweet, welcoming smile. "I'm pleased to meet you."

She handed the filled pan to Mrs. Harris

and took off the apron. "Why don't we go upstairs and get to know one another?"

Adelaide pressed a hand over her stomach, afraid it was going to loudly protest the prolonged wait for food. "Well, I came down to ask about breakfast."

Mrs. Harris herded the two women toward the stairs. "I'll have Oswyn bring some up to you. Go on now. Coffee and chocolate will be following you up to the breakfast room."

"Thank you, Mrs. Harris." Lady Raebourne kissed the old housekeeper's cheek before climbing the stairs without a bit of the hesitation Adelaide had felt on her way down. Her familiarity with the house disturbed Adelaide, who had only yesterday tracked down where they kept the flint in the drawing room.

They settled into the breakfast room, the promised beverages sending fragrant steam up from their cups, Adelaide's bitter while Lady Raebourne's was sweet. Adelaide truly hoped there wasn't anything symbolic in that. Lady Raebourne's marriage had been a love match by all accounts so Adelaide was no longer worried about the woman's connection to Trent, but that didn't stop her from thinking about all the other things that could go wrong given the bad feelings between the lady and Adelaide's family.

"I grew up in this house." Lady Raebourne looked fondly around the shabby breakfast room. "Mrs. Harris and Fenton practically raised me."

"Here?" Adelaide choked on her coffee. She remembered the story, or at least Helena's version of it, where the eligible Marquis of Raebourne had fallen in love with the Duke of Riverton's newly acquired ward. She just hadn't realized that prior to the duke's patronage Lady Raebourne had been left in the care of servants. It made the story much more romantic than Helena's rantings made it sound.

Lady Raebourne nodded. "For ten years. Then everything changed quite suddenly."

Adelaide couldn't even begin to imagine how different being married to a marquis would be than living in a home with only the servants for company. It must have been like family if Lady Raebourne still visited. More like a family than Adelaide's. It had taken her mother nearly a week to visit her, and here Lady Raebourne was visiting the housekeeper who had raised her after being in Town a mere day.

"You're welcome any time. I didn't mean to cut your visit short." Adelaide fiddled with the handle of her cup before lifting it to take a long drink of coffee. She'd nearly finished the cup but didn't think it would be enough to help her gain any equilibrium. There'd been too many ups and downs already this morning.

"Thank you, but I'll try to arrange a more regular schedule now. When it was only Trent here it didn't matter much, as he left the running of the house to Mrs. Harris." Lady Raebourne took a delicate sip of her chocolate. "Will Trent be joining us soon?"

Heat flushed across Adelaide's chest and up her neck. She hadn't wanted anyone to find out that Trent wasn't living with her, yet there was no hiding the fact that he wasn't home from Lady Raebourne. "He's not here."

"Has he gone riding already, then? Would you like to wait and eat when he returns?"

Adelaide forced herself to look unworried, though she wasn't quite sure what that entailed. A choked laugh and a flip of her hand would have to do. "Oh, no. We don't need to wait on him. It could be hours before he returns."

Oswyn entered and set a plate piled high with all of her favorite breakfast foods in front of Adelaide. A similar plate was set in front of Lady Raebourne. As they ate, they talked.

It was surprisingly easy to talk to Lady Raebourne. They discussed the village of Riverton, comparing thoughts on which of the two teahouses served better cakes. The topic of books came up and they chatted about their favorites until both women were contemplating the crumbs on their plates. Finally the conversation rolled around to social engagements.

"Have you been out anywhere yet? Anthony and I only arrived into Town yesterday morning and wanted to take the day to settle in, but I would be happy to suggest a few things. You simply must see the opera. I've heard the new one is fabulous. What else have you put on your agenda?" Lady Raebourne leaned back in her seat, abandoning the proper ladylike posture she'd held while she was eating. She closed her eyes and inhaled the steam off the cup of chocolate that had just been poured.

Adelaide fiddled with her discarded serviette, poking at its corners until it stood up like a tent on the table. "I don't know. We haven't really discussed it. Trent told me I should go through the invitations and let him know what I wanted to attend, but I don't know where he left them."

Lady Raebourne tilted her head to the side. "Fenton usually piles them on the desk in Trent's study. I've come over with Miranda a time or two to sort through them for him. He neglects them terribly, sometimes shoving them in the bottom drawer of his cabinet and ignoring them completely. For so long he was at the whims of his sisters since he had to escort them. I think he just goes to whatever event he hears people talking about at one of his clubs. I'm surprised Miranda hasn't been by to coordinate your schedules yet. She arrived in Town two days ago."

Adelaide said nothing. What could she say? She'd seen nothing of Trent's family, other than his brother. She was beginning to think the reputed closeness of the Hawthorne family was a very elaborate ruse to fool society.

The other woman suddenly sat up, sloshing the light brown drink over the edge of her cup. "Oh my! Miranda doesn't know, does she? I would have expected her to write me if she knew, but I can't imagine Trent not telling her he got married."

"I . . . well, that is, it was all very sudden and . . . I'm not sure." Adelaide blinked nervous tears away, hoping the spectacles hid the telltale sheen, not magnified it. She had tried not to let it bother her that Trent hadn't seemed very anxious for her to meet his family as his wife instead of the neighbor, not even ensuring his mother attended the wedding. It was as if he were trying to pretend the marriage had never even happened. But his sisters were sure to be coming to London with their spouses for the Season and his mother usually returned with her second husband, the Earl of Blackstone, as well, so Trent couldn't expect to hide Adelaide forever. Especially not now that he'd introduced her to a good portion of the *ton* at the ball and with their subsequent rides in the park.

Lady Raebourne clapped her hands together. "Oh, this is going to be fabulous. You must send me word on what engagements you plan to attend next. I'll make sure to be there in a show of support. The rest of the family should be in Town within the week. I'll have everyone over for dinner if Lady Blackstone doesn't take care of that first."

CHAPTER 18

No matter how old a man got, there was something decidedly uncomfortable about being in trouble with his mother. And if the thin line of tightly pressed lips as she stared at Trent across the expanse of Griffith's study was any indication, Lady Blackstone was decidedly not happy with her son.

"You got married."

Trent ran a hand through his hair. He should have written sooner. He'd finally drafted a letter last night and sent it off to the post this morning, but that wasn't likely to appease the woman in front of him. "Yes, Mother, I did."

"And you knew about it." Mother turned her icy blue eyes to the Duke of Riverton, staring him down the way only a mother could — for no one else would dare to glare at such a powerful man that way.

"Yes, Mother, I did." Griffith didn't squirm under their mother's scrutiny and his voice was calm and steady, but he rubbed his forefinger against his thumb.

Trent cleared his throat and shifted in the chair beside Griffith's desk. They'd been talking about the upcoming horse races when their mother had arrived, storming through the house without waiting to be announced. One of these days she was going to regret that habit. This was now a bachelor's residence, after all. "And how did you find out? The letter couldn't possibly have reached you yet. I sent it to the country."

One of Griffith's eyebrows shot up in inquiry at Trent's claim that he'd sent a letter. It was an affectation Trent found annoying and arrogant. Mostly because he'd never been able to do it.

Their mother could, though. She held a similar expression of skepticism, proving that not all of Griffith's imperious habits had come from their father. "You wrote?"

"Yes." Trent swallowed hard enough to make his ears crackle. Hopefully it wasn't as obvious to the rest of the room's inhabitants.

"Your pen seems to be a bit tardy, as I had to hear about it from my lady's maid, who heard it from the housekeeper next door, who learned about it from reading the scandal sheets after her mistress discarded them." Mother folded her hands in her lap and gave Trent the look that always had him squirming as a child. It was still effective on the twenty-four-year-old man. "I have many questions, but the first of which is why you are here instead of home with your wife."

Trent tapped his fingers on the arm of the chair. "How did you know to come here?"

She sniffed and folded her hands tightly in her lap. Trent thought she might prefer them about his neck at the moment. "I didn't. I was coming to ask Griffith if he knew more about your situation. I've already been by to see Miranda and Georgina. Both of them were as surprised as I was. Surely your wife wondered why I wasn't at the wedding. I didn't want to walk into your home without knowing what else I should expect. I'm rather glad I took the precaution."

"Oh." What else could he say? He could claim to simply be visiting Griffith, but that lie wouldn't hold up long. The family was a stalwart fortress when it came to keeping their business out of the public eye, but within the walls of family, keeping a secret was a difficult endeavor. A glance at Griffith proved he wasn't going to be of any help, as he'd opened one of his ledgers and appeared intent on ignoring the entire conversation.

"Why. Are. You. Not. At. Home?"

He had been hoping she would move on to another line of questioning, but it had been a fairly weak hope. His mother wasn't very distractible. He looked at her, wondering how to phrase the situation in a way that would cause him the least amount of trouble. Age had added a few lines to her face, but her hair was still mostly blond and her posture still perfect.

Not that the former Duchess of Riverton and current Countess of Blackstone would have it any other way. For as long as Trent could remember, his mother had been the definition of a well-bred lady. She would never have gone about town with her glove inside out or even a crooked hem. Adelaide couldn't seem to help it, which Trent found endearing, and it brought a smile to his face even as he worried about what his mother would think of her.

"I'm courting her," he finally mumbled.

"I beg your pardon?" Mother's reticule slipped from her hand and rolled down her lap before landing on the floor with a light *plop.*

He swallowed again and resisted the urge to adjust his cravat, feeling a bit irritated at himself. A grown man shouldn't feel like he needed to cower when he explained himself to his mother. Of course, he so rarely had to explain himself to his mother. Whatever trouble he'd gotten into at school had been handled with a self-deprecating grin and a well-timed joke. By the time he'd outgrown that, Griffith had come into his own, and more often than not people deferred problems to Trent's brother instead of his mother. He could only hope this situation felt as strange to her as it did to him and she wouldn't be willing to drag it out much longer.

"I am courting my wife." With some effort, Trent straightened his shoulders and looked his mother in the eye. It wasn't as if he should be ashamed of his plan. It was a good plan.

"That is a terrible plan." She frowned before picking her reticule up and slamming it into her lap.

No, it wasn't. "She's never had a Season, Mother. Lady Crampton robbed her of her chance, and I'm restoring it the only way I know how."

Trent and his mother stared each other down. The only sound in the room was the occasional scrape of Griffith's quill against his ledger. Trent had sat in this room more than once while Griffith worked in his ledgers, and the duke was writing considerably slower than normal. He wasn't going to wade into the conversation, but he was apparently not above watching with fascination as it played out.

Mother blinked first, but it was a short-lived victory for Trent. "While you will get no argument from me that Lady Crampton is a poor example of motherly devotion, it is not your job to fix it. Do you think you can keep your living conditions secret? What do you think will happen when everyone finds out you are not living with your wife?"

Trent hadn't thought much about it. He'd instinctively been discreet, but he'd never had to think much about gossip and scandal rags. His life was far and away less interesting than those of other young aristocrats. While he'd taken care to never show too much affection toward any particular woman, he hadn't had to watch much else. His well-known skills in the pugilist ring kept him out of other non-exercise-related confrontations.

His mother was right — people might start talking — but the past week had proven that his idea had merit. He and Adelaide were forming a relationship, and all of London thought them adorable. "It's been working quite well for the past week. Much better than the week before, if I'm being honest."

Narrowed blue eyes conveyed the mistake in Trent's statement. "How long have you been married?"

The scritching of the quill ceased. Even the clock on the mantel seemed to fall into silence. That or it simply couldn't be heard over the blood rushing through Trent's head. He couldn't resist the urge to adjust his cravat this time. "About two weeks."

"Two weeks. And the banns were properly read, I assume?"

Trent cleared his throat. "Yes, Mother."

"Five weeks. Five weeks and you've only recently seen fit to write to me?" She pushed up from her seat and swept toward the door of the room. "Here is what will happen. While I'm certainly not through talking to the pair of you about how this possibly came about, I'm not going to let another day go by without welcoming your wife to the family. We will be there for tea. See to it that she is aware and your staff prepared."

Trent stumbled to his feet, knocking his knee against a table and making a lamp jump. "We?"

"But of course. You don't think Georgina

and Miranda are going to wait to meet her, do you?"

"But you've already met her. All of you. Surely you all know her better than I do."

Mother smiled, that indulgent smile only women seem to be able to perfect — the one that told Trent he obviously didn't understand and that he was rather pitiful and adorable at the same time. He hated that smile. "My dear son, I'm not coming to your house to have tea with a neighbor. I'm going to meet my new daughter."

Bravado can only carry a woman so far before reality intrudes with crushing abruptness. In this case, it came in the form of a door. More specifically, it came in the form of the room on the other side of the door.

Adelaide had seen Lady Raebourne off with a smile a few moments ago, but she wasn't really sure how she felt about the tiny woman who knew more about the workings of Adelaide's home than Adelaide did. That jumble of feelings could be sorted out later. Of considerably more pressing concern was what to do about her social calendar.

If she were going to build a life in London, she needed to go out. Meet people. See and be seen. It stood to reason that the sooner people got used to seeing her around the sooner they'd stop whispering behind their fans every time she walked by. Besides, she was tired of cowering in the house.

She could ask Fenton about the invitations Trent had said he'd put aside for her, but that felt like something she should know or should have learned from her husband. Asking the servant meant admitting that she and Trent weren't communicating. Not that there was any real reason to hide it from the servants. Still, she couldn't bring herself to admit it out loud. Especially not when Lady Raebourne knew more about where her husband kept his correspondence than she did.

Which was why she was standing at the door of his study, facing the realization that this wasn't really her house at all. She could ban her mother from the premises — and in a fit of power-declaring pique had done so by giving Fenton instructions to keep the woman away for the entire day — but at the end of the day the house was Trent's. He could truly go anywhere he wished, while there were rooms that were nearly impossible for her to enter.

His study, for instance.

But if that was where the invitations were, then that was where she needed to be, and it was his own fault that she was going to have to invade his territory to get them. If he'd been home like he should have been, this wouldn't be happening.

She built up a large well of irritation at the situation and used it to open the door and propel her way into the room. Once over the threshold, it didn't seem so scary. It was a masculine room — one of the few in the house that seemed to have had some attention recently — but it wasn't overly imposing. Trent probably had no need to appear imposing, unlike her father, who had actually set his desk up on a dais so he could always look down on his visitors.

The desk surface was clear, which meant she would need to go digging in the drawers as Lady Raebourne mentioned. Adelaide's heart threatened to beat its way through her stomach and down to her toes. It was one thing to enter his room, but quite another to go through his drawers.

As fascinating as she was finding the strange little group of people living under her roof, though, they all still had jobs to do and trying to have social interactions with a person holding a cleaning rag left her feeling a bit lazy. Useless. In the end it was the thought of spending another week with nothing to look at but the house and no one to speak to but the servants that had her yanking open drawers and looking for cream and white squares of parchment.

Instead she found drawings.

In a drawer behind the desk sat sketch after sketch of a greenhouse. It was laid out differently than any other greenhouse she'd ever seen. It didn't appear to be for growing flowers, though. It looked as if Trent was planning to grow crops inside the greenhouse. Actually, just one crop. She adjusted her glasses and squinted at the words scrawled across the top of the page.

Pineapple growth plan, adjustments to Dutch method, version 5.

Trent was planning to grow pineapples? A pineapple was something that grew? She'd read about carvings of them but had never seen a picture. With spikes all around the body and huge leaves sprouting off the top, the pineapple looked nothing like any apple she'd ever seen. How did one go about eating something so . . . prickly?

"My lady?" Fenton's voice drifted down the upper corridor.

Adelaide squeaked and dropped the drawings back into the drawer, slamming it shut with her foot and scampering around to the front of the desk. "What is it, Fenton?"

Fenton's eyebrows rose as he stood in the

open door to the study. Wrinkles formed, making him look like a pug dog she'd seen one of her mother's friends carry around. "What are you doing in here, my lady?"

The curse of Trent's unusual household. Where else would a servant question the intentions of the lady of the house? Adelaide considered lying and saying that Trent had asked her to get something, but the potential mess such a lie could cause wasn't worth it, so she opted for the truth. "Lady Raebourne mentioned that this was where you usually placed the invitations. I wanted to go through them."

The pug wrinkles dropped into a wide smile. "I've been placing those on your desk now, my lady."

Her desk? She had a desk? Why didn't she know she had a desk? And where in the world was it? Unfortunately none of these were questions she could ask the butler. It was embarrassing for a lady not to know where her own desk was. There weren't that many rooms in the house. She'd be able to find it on her own. "Thank you, Fenton. I'll just go look at those now then."

She stepped forward, but Fenton didn't shift away from the doorway. "I beg your pardon, but Lord Trent is looking for you. He said his mother is coming for tea."

Chapter 19

Her drawing room was full of blond heads. Three of them to be precise, each more elegantly coiffed than the last. And the women attached to the heads were equally elegant. Peering at the women through the crack in the partially closed door, Adelaide took a moment to compose herself.

Would she ever not feel like an intruder wandering around someone else's home without permission? Her early morning burst of confidence and optimism had lost a good bit of its strength. Even Lady Rae-bourne knew more about Adelaide's hus-band and house than Adelaide did, proving that Adelaide was certainly not the most important lady in Trent's life.

And now her shabby drawing room, com-plete with broken curtain rod, was occupied by the other three women in Trent's life. She'd met all of them at one point or another, though they may not remember it.

If the gossip columns were to be believed, few people in London had even realized Lord and Lady Crampton had two daughters. Being overlooked by her mother and the second choice of her father had never bothered her before, possibly because it was all she'd ever known, but she was beginning to wonder what was so wrong with her that they'd all but hidden her existence from the world.

There was no hiding anymore, though. Three of the most popular women in London were in her drawing room, and they'd come for the sole purpose of seeing her.

At least she'd had warning and was now wearing her nicest afternoon dress. Trent had offered to stay, but she'd foolishly insisted he leave. How would it look if she wasn't even willing to sit down with her mother-in-law for tea without her husband at her side?

Lady Blackstone was going to expect her son to have married a composed, elegant young woman. And while no one was going to confuse Adelaide with the more gregarious ladies, she could probably manage to appear a bit more put together than normal for the sake of a good impression.

With one last deep breath and a quick smoothing of her skirts, she pushed her way into the drawing room.

Three heads turned. Three faces smiled.

No words emerged from Adelaide's mouth.

"It is nice to see you again, Lady Adelaide." The cultured voice cut through the air, almost drawing a wince from Adelaide. The power had been claimed by the eldest lady in the room, though she didn't appear nearly as old as she had to be, given that all four of her children had reached adulthood already.

The countess's presence nearly knocked aside Adelaide's plans for composure and poise, but she gave a regal nod. "Lady Blackstone. It has been a while."

Lady Blackstone was sitting neatly on a settee next to the most gorgeous woman Adelaide had ever seen. It had been some years since she'd seen Lady Georgina, but it was obvious why Helena had been so determined to marry before the young woman made her debut bow in Society. That Lady Georgina had married a businessman so far beneath her on the social ladder was a testament to how much love matches meant to the Hawthorne family.

The welcoming, humor-touched smile on the beautiful young woman's face did nothing to quell the clenching of Adelaide's heart even as she refused to let herself fret, at least not outwardly. She and Trent weren't a love match. They weren't even a marriage of convenience. They were the product of bad luck and a conniving, status-hungry woman.

"Would any of you care for tea?" Adelaide asked as she looked toward the third lady in the room.

The Duchess of Marshington, the older of Trent's sisters, stood by the window. She didn't fidget or move about but she still projected a nervous energy, as if she were too agitated to sit until she absolutely had to. It had to be her eyes. For while Her Grace's posture remained perfect and calm, her eyes immediately flitted in Adelaide's direction and assessed her in one long, sweeping gaze before tightening at the corners. "Tea would be lovely."

Grateful for any excuse to step from the room, Adelaide turned back to the door to give instructions to the waiting footman. She shouldn't have been surprised to see Fenton already making his way through the house with a loaded tea service. Of course the servants would know what Trent's family members liked and see to it as soon as they arrived. Like Lady Raebourne, the three ladies in the drawing room probably knew more about the house than Adelaide did.

At least the prompt arrival of tea would give her something to do with her hands.

She just hoped they didn't shake. Nothing gave away nerves like a clattering teacup.

With Fenton on her heels, she walked back into the room. "Here we are."

Another several minutes were spent arranging the tea service and pouring tea. Lady Blackstone waited until her daughters had been served to request hers with a light splash of milk. Adelaide handed the cup to Lady Blackstone before giving her tea the same treatment.

"I hear you married my son." Lady Blackstone's voice wasn't cold, but Adelaide didn't think the woman was particularly happy about the statement she'd just made either.

"Mother, kindly remember that Lady Adelaide is your daughter by marriage, not birth. There's no need to lecture her." The Duchess of Marshington dropped back in the chair to Adelaide's right, saluting Adelaide with her teacup before bringing it to her smiling lips. "Welcome to the family."

"Miranda, a lady never slumps in a chair, particularly not in public." Lady Blackstone frowned at her oldest daughter, but it looked like nothing more than habit, her eyes conveying loving indulgence.

Her Grace sighed but righted her posture. The smile on her face tilted a bit higher on one side, making it look impish. "I'm not in public. You know, I outrank you now. If I wanted to I could make slumping in drawing room chairs the *de rigueur* thing to do. Particularly if I got Georgina to join me."

"I'll thank you to leave me out of this." Lady Georgina cut her hand through the air. "Besides I don't know how you can abide sitting like that. It makes it very uncomfortable to drink your tea."

"She knows." Lady Blackstone lifted an eyebrow in the duchess's direction even as a smile teased the corner of her mouth. "And regardless of your rank, I am your mother. And since, as you reminded me, we are not in public, it means that at this moment, I outrank you."

Adelaide swung her gaze back and forth among the ladies, marveling at the banter. She couldn't imagine having such a conversation with her own mother and sister. Was this what all families were like, or was it Trent's family that was different than normal? Her eyes were threatening to dry out with her wide-eyed staring, so she blinked a few times and took a sip of tea, hoping the women would continue to talk amongst themselves until they decided they'd stayed the proper amount of time.

She was not to be so lucky.

The duchess grinned at her mother before turning the wide smile in Adelaide's direction. "You may call me Miranda. There are too many dukes and duchesses in the room when the family gets together to go around Your Grace-ing everyone. Besides, it makes Georgina feel left out."

"Hmm, yes, quite. That's why I've started going by Mrs. McCrae in more informal situations. I crave the ranking."

Adelaide wanted to shift in her seat as all three women turned in her direction, but she forced herself to remain still — with the proper ladylike posture, of course — and asked Georgina, "What should I call you?"

"Georgina will suffice when it is family. I do still go by Lady Georgina in London, though. It makes things a bit easier for Colin if people remember he married the daughter of a duke."

Miranda snorted. "It makes things easier for Colin when people remember how much money he helps them acquire."

Lady Blackstone set her cup in the saucer and sighed. "Miranda, a lady never discusses money with anyone except her husband.

And even that should be avoided whenever possible."

Adelaide was fairly sure she could slip out of the room and none of the three ladies would miss her.

Georgina looked from her mother to her older sister. "Kindly remember we came to visit Lady Adelaide, not discuss your ongoing difference of opinion on proper behavior for a lady." Her green eyes speared into Adelaide, proving she could be as lethal as her mother if she decided Adelaide wasn't good for Trent.

Not that there was anything they could do about it. The marriage had already occurred. The worst that could happen now was Adelaide being banished to the country and Trent continuing on as if she didn't exist. He wouldn't be able to marry again, but he'd at least have his home back.

"So we are." Lady Blackstone slid her cup onto the table and folded her hands in her lap. "I apologize for not visiting sooner. I'm afraid I didn't learn of your marriage until yesterday. I know I haven't been to Riverton much since my marriage, but I wasn't aware that you and Trent were even acquainted."

"We aren't," Adelaide stammered before she had a chance to think it through. That probably wasn't the best thing to have said. Trent had told them the circumstances, hadn't he? He could hardly hide his presence in Griffith's house from his family. Still, she tried to lessen the shock her words seemed to have brought to the other ladies' faces. "Or rather we weren't. It's a bit complicated."

"I see," Lady Blackstone — who had not invited Adelaide to call her anything else — said quietly. Adelaide was rather afraid that she did.

Three pair of eyes stared her down. Despite the fact that Lady Blackstone was the scariest woman in the room at the moment, Adelaide chose to meet her light blue gaze. The other two were a green much too similar to Trent's for her comfort.

Moments passed. Adelaide's heart couldn't decide if it wanted to beat uncontrollably or stop altogether.

Despite the earlier banter, the daughters seemed to be waiting on some signal from their mother. Adelaide didn't know what she could do to satisfy the countess beyond what she'd already done, so she simply sat there and focused all of her energy on not breaking eye contact, though she probably blinked a few more times than was absolutely necessary.

Finally, Lady Blackstone spoke. "I don't know what happened, and at this moment it bares little significance, as the deed is done. But regardless of the situation my son's happiness is of great importance to me. So I have one question, if you don't mind my asking it."

Adelaide swallowed and nodded. There was truly no other possible response.

"Do you love my son?"

"I barely know him, my lady," Adelaide whispered, stunned at the truth that popped out of her mouth. She spoke again before she could really think about it. "But I'd like to. It seems like it would be a nice thing to love one's husband."

The answer seemed to satisfy the countess because she nodded and broke their connection. "I'm positively thrilled that Lady Yensworth has decided not to do a particular theme for her ball this year. Last year's masquerade was tedious."

Miranda groaned while Georgina tried not to cough into her teacup. She took a hasty swallow before looking up. "Yes. Quite tedious."

"Are you and Trent attending the ball?" Miranda slid her cup to the table and folded her hands in her lap.

Adelaide blinked. "I . . . that is . . ."

"Of course she is going." Lady Blackstone rose to her feet and extracted a paper from her reticule. "Since Trent is determined to give you the Season you never had, I've taken the liberty of making a list of events you shouldn't miss over the next few weeks." She handed the paper to Adelaide.

"Thank you." And Adelaide was thankful. Without guidance, determining their social engagements had been daunting at best, but more often than not the task terrified her. It wasn't lost on her that Lady Blackstone was providing more assistance and care than her own mother. Did Trent know how fortunate he was?

Lady Blackstone's lips curled into a smile a bit broader than the polite smile she'd been wearing earlier. "Now for the fun part. We must get you ready."

Georgina clapped her hands together with glee. "I love spending other people's money."

Miranda frowned. "Do I have to go? I hate shopping."

Lady Blackstone lifted an eyebrow again. "We are showing solidarity for your new sister. As the Duchess of Marshington you will participate."

"Shopping?" Adelaide's knees shook as she rose to her feet. "I don't think that's necessary, Lady Blackstone. I haven't discussed pin money or anything with Trent yet."

"I know how many bills my son can manage. Just because a lady never talks of money doesn't mean she shouldn't know a thing or two about it." Lady Blackstone swept across the room toward the door. "And do call me Caroline."

Chapter 20

"I assured your lovely wife that you would not be upset at her missing your ride this afternoon. While I'll endeavor not to interfere in your plans in the future, I'm afraid it was unavoidable today."

Trent stared wide-eyed at the mother who only that morning had informed him that his courtship plan was nonsense. "Of course I don't mind. But, er, what were you doing?"

"Spending a great deal of your money, which you should have seen to already. Also, I was making sure no harm would come from your ridiculous plot. You may thank me later."

She handed Trent a piece of paper. "These are the events I recommend you attend if you want to give her a complete social experience as quickly as possible. I assume once you've done that you'll move back home and stop this nonsense?"

Trent took the paper with numb fingers as he nodded.

"Good." Mother folded her hands in front of her. "Until that happens I suggest you spend as much time at your clubs as possible. People must see you out and about, not gathering dust here in your brother's home. You will send Adelaide a note each morning, detailing where you expect to be so that she will not be caught off guard by any visitors looking for you."

Trent hadn't thought about that, though his experience with Givendale at the boxing ring had made him a bit concerned. Trust his mother to come up with a solution before he'd even realized the full problem. Because it was better than being shamed by his mother's accusatory glare, Trent looked at the list of events. Nearly every day had something, and some days even listed two events. They were going to be a very busy couple, which he had no problem with. A bit of excitement unfurled within him at the thought, proof that his courtship plan was working. "It's not nonsense."

Mother sighed. "It is. But somehow you've convinced her it's romantic. Miranda seems to agree with her."

Trent knew there was a reason he liked Miranda. Less than a year apart in age, the two of them had always been especially close growing up. He knew he should have expected her to see what he was trying to do. Still, something about the way his mother was talking about the entire thing made him uneasy. "What do you mean you were making sure no harm would come from my plan?"

Mother tilted her head and sighed, making Trent feel like a foolish child instead of a grown man. "You have left your wife, a woman unknown to most of London, alone. She has no established friends, no history. My son, you are the brother of a duke. A duke with a reputation for actually caring what happens to his family. Do you honestly think no one will try to use her to get to you and by extension, Griffith?"

Apparently there was very good reason for Trent to feel like a foolish child. Had he missed this sort of subtle political manipulation before or had he been left alone, seen as the careless younger brother not yet worth the effort? Funny how marriage suddenly matured a man in the eyes of society. "I hadn't thought of that." He swallowed. "I'll move home."

"While I would obviously think that wise, it goes against the course of action you have chosen. Your situation is ridiculous enough without your adding bitterness or some other such notion to the mix. You've nothing to worry about. We have set up a visiting rotation. As her new family we will be able to chaperone Adelaide without raising suspicion among anyone. And as much as I've never understood the familiarity you have with your staff, in this case it is a boon, because they will look out for any mischief as well. Whenever you go out, you will escort her home and send the carriage away. After thirty minutes you will come out the back, where Griffith's driver will be waiting in a simple hack. There's no need for all of London to know about this foolishness."

If Trent had ever wondered how his mother managed to raise a duke after the death of his father, all of his questions would now have been answered. In less than twelve hours his mother had concocted and put into motion a plan that was more thought out than his simple idea had ever been. She'd looked at every angle and effectively planned against potential pitfalls. No wonder his father had always looked at her with such awe on his face.

Trent smiled and leaned forward to kiss his mother on the cheek in a show of affection he hadn't given her since he'd been a boy. A hint of pink brushed her cheeks.

She cleared her throat and clasped her hands together at her waist. "Now. We've a few minutes yet before I need to return home and ready myself for the evening. I hadn't planned on going out much this Season but that has obviously changed for the foreseeable future. We will be out in full force to show support for your new wife. Speculation about the marriage is already rampant, and that foolish woman Lady Crampton is only fueling it. I've always thought that woman would throw her own daughter to the wolves if it achieved greater popularity." Mother pressed her lips together in irritation. There weren't many people who bothered his mother enough for her to show it, and even then she only released the emotion in private, but Lady Crampton had always been one of them. The two women had known each other since their own London Seasons, and more than once Trent had wondered if something had happened then to cause the lingering animosity.

Unfortunately, Mother's irritation was now redirected at him. "In these remaining moments, you are going to sit down and explain to me exactly how you ended up in this situation. And you" — she pointed to somewhere over Trent's shoulder — "are going to tell me why you didn't stop it."

Trent turned to see Griffith coming down the stairs with a stack of papers in his hands. He'd obviously been headed toward his study and looked confused by his mother's interruption. Though he couldn't possibly have known what was going on, the confusion soon cleared from his face. "My study, then?"

"No. The drawing room. The white one with all the spindly furniture you both despise. I have a feeling I am not going to like this conversation, and so you are not going to like it either." Mother sniffed and turned toward the formal drawing room off the main hall.

Trent groaned and followed. He was convinced there wasn't a man alive who didn't hate this room, though none of them had ever complained when they came to visit Miranda or Georgina. Done almost entirely in white, it made a man feel like an awkward, bumbling schoolboy. It had been decorated for his sisters to receive callers in during their Seasons, and both of the brothers were convinced it had been intentionally designed to make men feel ill at ease in order to give their sisters every possible advantage.

Now it was their mother holding the

advantage. The brothers walked to the drawing room like men headed for the gallows.

The glaring white of the room was broken only by the occasional accent of gold. From the gold-veined white marble fireplace to the thin gold stripes on the white settee and the lightly gilded frames that dotted the white silk-covered walls, there wasn't an inch that would forgive the slightest bit of dirt on a man's clothing or boots. The room was famous across London, and Trent guessed that many a man had made sure to come calling straight from his rooms so as not to be the one to mar the white perfection.

Mother preceded them into the room, but instead of sitting to the side on the gold-striped settee she'd occupied through her daughters' Seasons, she settled into a white-on-white-brocade armchair, gesturing for the two men to share the sofa across from her.

Trent eyed the thin curving legs before easing onto the seat. Griffith plopped his massive frame down with more force than normal, his feet actually lifting from the floor as his back landed against the back of the seat. Trent wished he'd had the foresight to join him. If they'd broken the sofa, their mother couldn't make them sit on it, might not have even wanted to stay in the same room as the splintered furniture.

But the spindly legs held, and there was nothing left to do but face their mother and smile.

She didn't smile back.

"I was staying at Riverton," Trent began.

"Because he didn't want to stay at his own house while the construction was going on." Griffith settled farther into his corner of the sofa, trying to look as confident as a large man on a delicate piece of furniture could.

Trent glared at his older brother. "The entire bedchamber wing was in shambles. I'd have been sleeping on the drawing room sofa."

"But you wouldn't be married."

Trent couldn't think of a single remark cutting enough to be a proper response to that low blow.

"Boys." The quiet word brought them both to a halt the way it always had. Trent and Griffith never came to actual blows, but when the matter was personal, they could verbally spar with the best of them. It didn't happen often, but when it did the only one with the nerve to come between them was their mother.

Trent turned back to face her. "I was cutting across the west fields by the ruins — the small keep built into the hill beside the old watchtower — and I heard singing and saw a lone horse. I climbed in to investigate."

Mother closed her eyes and sighed. "The mushrooms."

Trent looked at Griffith, who appeared as surprised as he was. "How did you know?"

"She walked out there with me ages ago and asked if she could collect them. It must be nearly ten years ago now. She walked across that old wooden floor, confident as you please, and then climbed down the holes from the old stair supports. But she was a child then. Surely she wasn't still scampering up and down the wall as a grown woman."

Mother had always kept strict rules for her girls on what ladylike behavior consisted of. Trent couldn't imagine her ever letting Miranda or Georgina climb into ruins to collect mushrooms, even when they were children.

Trent shifted in his seat, wondering if he should feel embarrassed on Adelaide's behalf. "Er . . . yes. She was."

"But that floor could give way any day now."

Griffith coughed. "Not anymore."

Trent frowned at Griffith. "And you wouldn't have allowed curiosity to trump your good sense for a few moments? I'll have you know —"

"Boys." Mother cleared her throat. "I surmise you were the reason the floor finally fell?"

Trent nodded his head. "And it took all night to cut through the vines and find another way out."

He left off the story there, deciding it was best to keep to as many cold facts as possible. No one else needed to know how scared he'd been or how the miserable pain in his ankle and hands had prevented him from finding a moment's sleep. It wasn't necessary to share the despair he'd felt when the moon broke through the clouds, sealing his gentlemanly fate.

"And then he proposed," Griffith muttered.

"You proposed?" Mother asked with clear surprise. She hadn't been surprised by the rest of it, knowing that something outrageous had to have happened to force Trent's unexpected nuptials. But his unforced proposal seemed to knock her off guard.

Trent really didn't understand why that was the part of the story that seemed to shock everyone instead of the ridiculousness of falling through an obviously rotten floor.

"Yes, I proposed. It seemed the thing to do since we were spending the night together — alone." How could he explain to them how despondent he'd felt when Adelaide's ruination became a done thing? When her reputation was lost to the stars and lack of proper chaperone? Within miles of their respective homes, they'd been condemned by circumstances. He knew at that moment he would never get the chance to propose to anyone else. And it had bothered him. Looking back, part of him had wanted to feel like he wasn't just a victim in the whole mess.

He'd pulled up one of the early blooming violets and twined it into a circle before offering it to Adelaide and asking her to marry him. It was a moment that had been just for the two of them. A moment they'd claimed before the world condemned them. That way, when they finally climbed out of that stone prison, they would be able to declare their fate instead of having it declared for them.

But he didn't know how to explain that to his mother.

So he didn't.

Mother's brow creased. "And in all that

time, no one came looking for her? No one came by? I can't believe no one knew she was going out there."

"There was a wagon of some sort, or we thought we heard one. We shouted as loud as we could but no one answered." Trent rubbed his hand along the back of his neck. "Her mother knew she was headed to the ruins, but Adelaide said it wouldn't be the first time the countess had forgotten about her."

Griffith shifted in his seat. "And you believe her?"

Trent and Mother both frowned at Griffith, but it was Mother who finally spoke. "Why shouldn't he? You've met Lady Crampton."

Trent wanted to jump to his wife's defense, but he couldn't. Griffith had always been able to see the bigger picture, to know what was going on beyond the portrait's frame. What was he seeing now?

"Consider for a moment if you did actually hear a wagon. How often does one of us ride through there alone? What if she wasn't simply down there for mushrooms? It's an incredibly risky gamble and highly unlikely to pay off, but did it really cost them anything? I can't put it past Lady Crampton to leave her daughter there as potential bait and then come back to help her out of the ruins later. Only this time she kept driving because she'd actually been successful."

They all sat in silence for a moment until Mother broke it with a rough laugh. "That's rather farfetched. Even for one of those Minerva Press novels."

But Trent couldn't completely shake the idea. They'd been so certain they heard someone drive by. And if someone had, Trent knew they'd heard the shouting. Trent had been able to hear Adelaide's singing clearly as he approached.

Not that it mattered. Trap or not, he was married, and no amount of plot discovery now would change that fact. "The deed is done. This is the last time we speak of how it came about. Adelaide is now my wife, and there's nothing I can do about it." He bit his tongue before he could spout the rest of his bitter thoughts. Things like telling the rest of them to go on and enjoy their love-filled marriages, or chance at a love-filled marriage in Griffith's case. For whatever reason, God had chosen this trial for Trent to bear, and it didn't matter how much he'd wanted to court a woman and fall in love, this was his life and that was all there was to it.

He didn't say any of those things because he didn't know how. There wasn't a way to phrase them that didn't sound pitiful and pathetic. And he already felt plenty of that for being forced into marriage in the first place.

He stood and looked at his brother and then his mother. "If you'll excuse me, I need to go dress for whatever event you've arranged for me tonight."

"A card party at Lady Lyndley's," Mother said quietly.

"Very good, then. An evening of whist awaits. I will see you all there." Trent left the room without looking back and tried very hard not to think about the discussion they'd just had. Because if he didn't think about it, it wouldn't hurt.

Chapter 21

Rebecca finished dressing Adelaide's hair, *tsk*ing over the strands that insisted on nearly falling into her eyes but refused to lie in a reasonable-length curl. Tonight she'd tried pinning them straight back off Adelaide's forehead. It looked a bit odd to Adelaide, who'd gotten used to not seeing her forehead, but it was considerably closer to the modern hairstyles.

As the lady's maid hooked a simple gold chain around Adelaide's neck so that the small stone cross dangled just above the edge of her dress, Adelaide looked at the maid in the mirror. "Are you settling in well enough, Rebecca?"

"Er, yes, my lady. I believe I am." The maid looked a bit startled by the question. Understandable given the fact that such a question would never have entered their conversation before coming to live in this house. What a difference a few weeks could make.

What a difference a day could make, for that matter. This morning, she'd arisen alone and confused by her husband's departure, but now she felt as if she had friends, or at least the beginnings of what could become friendships, and she was actually excited for her husband to arrive. It was sweet of him, really, to try to give her what she'd lost. Miranda had pointed out that all he was doing was giving their marriage the foundation that most normal marriages got, although they had the added benefit of being allowed to wander off by themselves if they wished.

Adelaide had flushed bright red at that comment, as it brought forth the memory of his sweet, gentle kiss the night before as well as inspiring the hope that he might give her another one tonight.

"I believe that should hold, my lady."

Which was the maid's way of saying she'd done her best to put together an ensemble that could withstand Adelaide's unique way of, well, living. She never knew how she managed to get so disheveled, but it never seemed to fail. Rebecca had been working for her since Adelaide's eighteenth birthday, and in those three years the maid had never once admitted defeat, constantly trying to find new ways to ensure Adelaide remained presentable.

"Thank you, Rebecca." Adelaide rose from the dressing table bench and then stopped. What was she supposed to do now? Georgina had made her promise not to be waiting in the drawing room when Trent arrived, assuring her that descending down the staircase provided the most impactful entrance a woman could make. "I'll wait here. Have someone come get me when my husband arrives."

"Very well, my lady." The momentary twist of Rebecca's lips let Adelaide know the maid thought this entire scenario was a bit silly, but she didn't say a word as she left the room.

And now Adelaide had nothing to do but wait. She paced the room, wondering how long it would be, wishing she could go downstairs even though the only difference would be that her pacing had an audience. She'd promised Georgina, though, and since the younger lady had been the talk of the Town during her Season, she probably knew what she was talking about.

It was difficult, though, as the view from her room did not include the front of the house, and so she couldn't see when Trent arrived. The anticipation was threatening to make her start sweating, something she did not want to do in the bright blue evening gown. If she wanted to preserve her sanity she was going to have to change rooms. The house was very narrow, meaning only one room on each floor faced the road. That left Trent's study, Trent's bedchamber, or the nursery.

Her eyes strayed to the door leading to Trent's bedroom. Of all the rooms she could go to, it was the most logical. Whoever came for her would be coming to this floor and she'd be able to hear them, and who did she think she was fooling? Ever since she saw the study she'd been looking for an excuse to enter Trent's bedchamber. If any room in the house could tell her more about her husband it would be that one, wouldn't it?

Before she could talk herself out of it, she threw open the connecting door and barreled through it, stumbling into a room that mirrored hers in layout, but boasted much more masculine decor, with clean lines and the most beautiful bed she'd ever seen. The wooden headboard reached to the ceiling before curving out and forming a half-tester wooden canopy over the top portion of the bed. The vertical portion of the headboard boasted an elaborate carving of a hunting party. It was an exquisite piece of art, so detailed she expected to feel the wind that whipped through the horses' manes or hear the cacophonous bark of the dogs mingling with the melody of the horns. The base of the bed was simpler, squared off below the mattress and covered with elaborate carved vines and flowers.

The bedding was a rich swirl of blue cut velvet, the darker blue giving way to the light blue base. It looked so inviting she couldn't resist running her hand along the edge of the fabric.

What kind of man chose a bed like this? For it was obvious he'd chosen it. Nothing else in the house was like this. She stood in the middle of the room, turning circles on the golden-edged Persian rug that took up most of the floor space in the room. Unlike the house she'd grown up in, the room wasn't crammed with as many expensive things as possible. Every item in the room was splendid and placed in a way that proved it had been chosen with care. Each piece was there because Trent liked it, wanted to see it when he awoke each day. The art on the walls wasn't chosen because it was expensive, though a glance at the signatures proved the paintings hadn't been chosen for economical reasons.

A collection of antique swords hung from one wall, with an oversized bergère wing-back chair underneath them. The chair was old and well-worn. More worn than Trent alone could have made it. Next to the elegant chair sat an old military drum instead of a matching side table. A Bible lay on the drum along with a pocket watch and a pair of emerald-jeweled shirt-cuff studs.

Somehow it was the jeweled studs that made her realize what she was doing.

Trent had gone so far as to move out of the house in an attempt to give their marriage a semblance of normalcy and she was repaying him by invading his most personal of spaces.

She rushed back to her own room, pulling the door closed with a quiet click. In comparison to the handpicked beauty behind her, the room in front of her looked cold and uninviting. It looked like an Ackermann print, with coordinating furniture and bed linens. A beautiful room, but containing not a lick of the charm and warmth of Trent's room.

They were going to have to find time to discuss a redecorating budget. Any man who put that much thought into his bedchamber deserved an equally thought-out house.

In the meantime she'd give him what she could. She resumed her pacing, this time with a book in hand. Something in this extensive tome on bridge building had to be interesting enough to share.

Trent covered Adelaide's hand and gave it a gentle squeeze as they walked into the drawing room, where a scattering of tables and chairs held groups of men and women and piles of fish-shaped tokens. The shuffling of cards meshed with the murmur of voices, broken by an occasional laugh and accompanied by a young woman softly playing on the pianoforte in the corner.

In return she hugged his elbow tighter, bringing her body closer to his side. He liked her there. Niggling doubts from Griffith's theory had plagued Trent all afternoon, but now, looking at Adelaide's wide-eyed wonder at everything that surrounded her, he felt absolute confidence that she was as much a victim of coincidental fate as he had been.

Wide doors stood open on all sides of the drawing room, inviting the guests to wander through the library, another smaller drawing room, and the dining room. Trent led

Adelaide on a casual stroll through the rooms. “Let’s see who’s here, shall we, before we settle down to a game?”

Adelaide nodded. “I’ve no strong desire to play, my lord. If you’ve a group you wish to make a game with, I’m happy to sit by and watch as those young ladies are doing.”

She leaned her head to the side to indicate a table with four gentlemen deep in play. Two young ladies sat at the table watching the card play and occasionally joining in the conversation. It looked supremely boring to Trent. “Nonsense. I’d much rather you enjoy the game.”

“I’m not very good.” She reached up and adjusted her spectacles. In the carriage, she’d confessed to having considered leaving them at home, but worried she wouldn’t be able to see the cards clearly if she did that. Trent had made a mental note to have an extra pair made and keep them in the coach in case she ever followed through on the foolish notion. He would rather she be able to see than conform to some silly inclination of fashion that required women deprive themselves in order to look a certain way. Even Georgina had briefly worn spectacles at the end of last Season, and the world hadn’t ended. Fashions were entirely nebulous anyway, changing on the whim of who even knew.

He, for one, was supremely grateful that heavily boned corsets had gone the way of the powdered wig. Some of the ladies had worn the contraptions to a masquerade ball last year, and he'd felt as if he were dancing with a chair. He dearly hoped that whoever was in charge of naming the next fashionable affectation wouldn't return to those monstrosities.

As they moved through the rooms, it was clear his mother hadn't been jesting about sending support for Adelaide in force. Family friends who normally only attended smaller, more intimate gatherings stopped them to exchange pleasantries and offer congratulations. By the time they made it to the dining room he was fighting to keep his grin at an acceptable size. Their poor hostess had likely been overrun with considerably more attendees than she'd anticipated after his mother finished convincing people to accept the invitation or even talk their way into the party without one.

In the dining room, however, he lost the fight for decorum and laughed out loud. Standing disgruntled in the corner was Miranda's husband. Since their marriage, the Duke of Marshington only went out socially when his wife forced him to. After spending a decade as a spy for the English Crown, he found the constraints of social gatherings exhausting. Yet here he was.

Trent had never felt so blessed. He didn't know why God had plunked him down in the middle of such a family, but he was ever so grateful for it.

He smiled down at his wife, who didn't seem to be sharing his enjoyment of the surrounding cohorts. If anything, she looked overwhelmed. She'd already met Miranda, though, so perhaps a moment in discussion with her husband would calm Adelaide's nerves. He patted the hand trying to press permanent wrinkles into his coat sleeve. "Come. Meet Miranda's husband. I'm sure she talked about him while you were shopping today. She's annoyingly obsessed with the man."

Trent led the way, but for the first time all evening Adelaide pulled against his arm. He turned to her with an inquiring look.

"Is that him? In the corner?" She blinked her eyes twice. "He looks mean."

"He only does that so no one will come talk to him."

"An excellent idea. Let's accommodate him."

"He's not actually going to do anything. Not here, anyway." Trent grinned, remembering the time Ryland had snuck into Trent's house and rearranged everything in his study in exchange for Trent's trapping him into spending an evening discussing the merits of the latest opera. There was still a log book Trent hadn't found.

"No, really. I think I've a mind to indulge his preference." Adelaide stopped walking entirely, forcing Trent to stop as well unless he wanted to bodily drag her across the floor.

"We'll simply greet Miranda, then, shall we?" Not that he was going to pass up an opportunity to try to haul Ryland into a conversation. It was so rare for Miranda to force him out to large parties that Trent couldn't resist having a little fun whenever it happened.

Miranda was talking to Amelia, which meant Anthony, Marquis of Raebourne, was around here somewhere as well. The gossip papers would certainly have something to say about the attendees of this party tomorrow.

As Trent rounded the refreshment table, he noticed that three large curls were about to escape Adelaide's coiffure. He gave them a gentle tug, freeing them the rest of the way and draping them over her shoulder. Fortunately he'd left his gloves with his coat and he could feel the soft slide of the dark strands across his fingers, the weight and length making them feel so different from his own hair.

She looked at the black tresses lying in stunning contrast to the bright blue of her gown before blinking up at him.

"I like it," Trent said with a small shrug of one shoulder. "You're beautiful. I don't know if I remembered to tell you that earlier. I think I forgot to speak at all."

A soft pink touched her cheeks, and she looked a little flustered by his statement. He'd meant every word he'd said, but he'd wanted her that slightest bit distracted as well so she wouldn't notice when he pulled her to Ryland's corner.

"Your Grace, may I present my wife? Lady Adelaide, the Duke of Marshington."

Her momentary glare was more welcome than she would have believed. Over the years Trent had learned that women only showed their ire to people they felt safe with, close to. If Adelaide was willing to glare at him, even for a moment, it meant they were getting to know each other, that she cared about him and felt she could trust him. Of course, he'd just betrayed that trust a little bit, but not enough to damage it.

He hoped.

Ryland pushed off from the wall and executed a perfect bow, causing Adelaide to rush into her curtsy. This was a notorious and powerful duke after all. Probably someone she'd never expected to meet even though she was the daughter of an earl. "Your Grace."

"Please call me Marshington, or Ryland as the rest of the family does, or Duke in public, if you prefer." The scowl lifted from Ryland's face, proving it was a habitual affectation more than true irritation. "And may I offer felicitations on the union?"

His grey eyes swept toward Trent, making him wish he hadn't insisted on coming over here after all. With his connections, Ryland probably knew more about the marriage circumstances than Trent did. "Thank you."

The three of them fell silent, all trying to figure out how to get around the unspoken topic Ryland had just dropped into the circle. How was it that they had graciously accepted numerous congratulations already tonight, but the way Ryland said it made it obvious he knew the marriage had not been planned? And there was nothing Trent could say. He certainly couldn't address the unspoken question, and he knew he couldn't broach another topic without receiving smug looks from Ryland for the rest of the evening.

In the end it was Ryland who came to the rescue, though Trent had no doubt it was more for Adelaide's sake than for his. "Have you played a game yet this evening?"

Trent shifted his shoulders so that his coat would settle more comfortably across them as he relaxed. There was no doubt Ryland would eventually pin him down and make him share the story, but at least it wouldn't be tonight. "No. We were making the rounds before sitting down to a table."

"Well, then, shall we play? It's why my wife chooses card parties. I grumble less because there's actually something to do." Ryland, nearly as tall as Griffith but not quite as broad, cut through the small gathering of people next to them to collect his wife. Miranda left her conversation with a smile, and the four of them made their way into the drawing room to find an empty table.

"Shall we take on our men, Adelaide?" Miranda asked as she took one of the seats at a table set up near the front-facing windows. The noise of the horses and carriage drivers could be heard from the other side of the window, but it wasn't loud enough to make conversation difficult.

Trent was more than happy to partner

with Ryland since it meant Adelaide sat to his left instead of across the table. He already missed the weight of her hand on his arm and shifted his leg under the table until his knee rested against hers. That light contact seemed to settle something in his chest, something that was beginning to accept that he and this woman were united.

Ryland shuffled the deck of cards while Trent distributed the pile of fish.

"Shall we play for dinner?" the duke asked.

Adelaide blinked at him, the candlelight from a nearby candelabra reflecting off her spectacles and framing her eyes in light. "Dinner?"

Trent shook himself from his fanciful thoughts and looked at the cards he'd been dealt. "Yes. Whoever loses has to have the entire family over for dinner. It's not the actual hosting that's an issue — it's the fact that the winner usually spends the evening taunting the loser."

"But if I'm partnering with Miranda, who will host the dinner when we lose?"

Miranda coughed. "I have no intention of losing."

Adelaide fingered the cards she had yet to pick up from the table. "I'm afraid I'm not very good."

Trent thought of everything Adelaide had missed out on in life. He couldn't recall ever seeing her at gatherings, even as children. Her sister Helena had always been there, decked out in bows and curls and other frippery that a child should never be subjected to. In later years he recalled seeing her brother, Bernard, though he was quite a bit younger than Trent and they'd never spent any time together. But he'd never seen Adelaide.

Adelaide, who hadn't been brought to London for a Season even after her oldest sister was married off.

Trent tapped his cards into a stack and leaned toward his wife. "Adelaide, do you know how to play whist?"

Her eyes darted around the table, her gaze flitting from person to person but never landing on anyone long enough for her vision to actually focus. "I've read about it."

Without a word, Ryland and Miranda began laying their cards face up on the table, sorting them by suit and rank. Trent helped Adelaide lay hers out before doing the same with his own.

They played three hands with the cards down, Miranda calmly explaining the rules and basic strategies that went along with the game. By the fourth hand, Adelaide felt confident enough to try it on her own.

Trent smiled almost as wide as she did when she took her first trick, even though she'd thrown a low trump on top of one of his kings.

"Well done, Adelaide." Miranda smiled and gathered up the cards. "We really should circulate a bit more. No one is seeing you together in this corner."

Ryland grunted. "Is that why we had to come tonight? Then let's plop them on top of the table and be done with it."

Trent sat back in his chair, still pressing his knee to Adelaide's. When his leg had followed hers the first few times she'd shifted, she'd finally relented and stopped moving it. "I thought the point of these outings was for Adelaide and me to get to know each other."

Ryland sighed. "How is it I understand Society better than you do?"

"Because I haven't spent the past ten years dissecting it for weaknesses," Trent grumbled. He'd never had to think about the consequences of his actions that deeply. Until a few months ago, he'd only had to consider the immediate ramifications of a deed upon himself. His reputation was nearly untouchable because he never did anything to endanger it, but he didn't think about it like that. He tried to do what was right and then moved on with his life.

The fact that everyone else seemed to know how to see life beyond that made him feel like a child.

Miranda frowned with indulgence at her husband and then turned her annoyance to her brother. "Courtship is as much about declaring yourselves a couple to everyone else as it is about getting to know each other. It's possibly even more important in your case, as . . . well, the men who like to get to know unhappily married women aren't very principled."

Adelaide's face lost all signs of victory. "I don't have to play whist with someone else now, do I?"

Trent shook his head and covered her hand with his. "No. There's enough people standing about that we can move around without much notice." He stopped and turned to his sister and her husband. "We can do that, can't we?"

Ryland bent his head in a poor attempt to hide his ensuing laughter. Miranda jerked and Ryland's laughter only got worse, a clear indication she'd attempted to kick him beneath the table. "Of course you can. Only take care not to stay in one room too long.

People might start to notice you aren't playing."

With four rooms to wander through, that shouldn't be too difficult. Trent rose and offered Adelaide his arm again. They worked their way from conversation to conversation until Adelaide asked for a moment to collect herself. They stepped to the side of the library, sipping at glasses of punch and discussing some of the books on the nearby shelf. Actually, it was more like Adelaide discussed them and Trent tried to come up with questions to keep her talking. Was there anything the woman hadn't read?

The crowd around them began to thin, but Trent didn't think about what it meant beyond the fact that he could hear Adelaide better.

It took Amelia's husband, Anthony, tapping him on the shoulder to break him free of the conversation.

"Were you planning on spending the night? I'm sure it wouldn't put out Lady Lyndley too much to make up a guest room for you." The marquis leaned against the library shelves and crossed his ankles. "Although this is a splendid library as well. She might just let you stay in here all night."

Amelia didn't say anything as she stepped forward to place a hand lightly on Adelaide's shoulder. "I'm going to come by tomorrow, if that's all right. Caroline arranged for several pattern books to be brought by so you could be making plans for the drawing room. I thought I'd take a look at them as well, since I'm thinking of redoing our upstairs parlor."

One dark brow lifted over one of Anthony's blue eyes. If Trent needed any more convincing that he would make a horrible titled aristocrat, the fact that he couldn't do the arrogant single brow thing solidified it.

Anthony cleared his throat. "We're redecorating the parlor?"

"Yes. We are." Amelia looked over her shoulder, and the marquis and marchioness stared at each other for a long moment, communicating in the way that only people completely connected to each other could do.

Jealousy churned in Trent's gut. That was what he wanted, what he'd always wanted in a marriage. And while he was coming to respect and even enjoy his growing relationship with Adelaide, he didn't know if it would ever become what he saw in the couple before him or what his sisters had found. He'd spent the past hour listening to Adelaide talk about educational books, something he'd avoided as much as possible. He didn't want to be any better at numbers than he had to be, and philosophy made his head spin. He enjoyed certain scientific texts, but he always felt guilty for reading them. Fiction hadn't been something emphasized as he was growing up, but he'd turned to it in order to stay away from the more learned texts. After hearing about Adelaide's favorite titles he was willing to consider the practice for its own merit.

At the very least it would give them something in common, because what else did they have? That they took their tea the same way? It was hardly the kind of connection that built the unspoken communication before him.

Finally Anthony shook his head and gave Trent a bland look. "We're redecorating the parlor. I hope you enjoy it."

Trent gave Anthony a quizzical look. "Why would I —"

"Our parlor windows face the same way your drawing room does," Amelia broke in. "So the lighting will be the same. And it's ever so much more fun discussing decor with someone else instead of debating with yourself over everything."

Adelaide looked as if she didn't know what to say, but she agreed to have Amelia come to the house.

Trent didn't know if he liked his mother being so high-handed about the decorating, but he did feel better knowing that Amelia would be there if anyone else decided to come calling.

Chapter 22

A low grunt ripped from Trent's chest as he felt the pressure of Anthony's blunted foil tip press against his shoulder.

Again.

The marquis laughed as he pulled off his protective mask and grinned at Trent. "Either I've gotten exceptionally better at this in the last few months or you're a bit distracted."

Another, deeper laugh came from the door to the terrace. "I believe even I could beat him today."

Trent glared at his brother from behind the shield of protective mesh. "I'm sure Anthony would let you borrow his sword."

"And have to trust you to avoid taking advantage of my lack of protective clothing? I think not."

How much would it take to bribe Griffith's valet into shaving off that irritating eyebrow? Just the image of Griffith walking around with only one eyebrow drew a grin to Trent's face. He pulled the mask from his head, feeling the flop of sweat-soaked hair against his forehead. "Scared?"

Griffith scoffed in big-brotherly disbelief. "Smart."

Trent stacked his gear on the table on the terrace and began pulling the protective arm and chest pads from his body. "Weren't you planning on fencing this morning when you invited Anthony over?"

Anthony inspected the tip of his foil before jabbing it in the duke's direction. "You did tell me to bring my gear."

"Foresight on my part, I'm sure. I wanted the two of you to be able to entertain yourselves should I be delayed for our meeting."

Trent narrowed his eyes at his older brother. Had he noticed that Trent had been avoiding his fencing club? Every time he went he ran into Mr. Givendale or Sir Durbin, who couldn't seem to stop themselves from making snide comments about the state of Trent's marriage. Blunted tip or not he was ready to run the both of them through with his foil. It didn't help matters any that Givendale had dropped his card by the house yesterday. Trent had wanted to give Adelaide a Season, but he wasn't about to let her entertain other gentleman callers.

"Did your wife mention if anything unusual happened while she was visiting Adelaide yesterday?" Trent's attempt at nonchalance didn't fool either of the other men.

"As a matter of fact, yes." Anthony began peeling off his own protective shirt. "Your housekeeper sat down to tea with them, and the entire household took luncheon together in your dining room."

Trent frowned. "I said unusual, not odd. That happens all the time when Amelia comes to my house."

"Something that is considerably more acceptable for her to do now that it is no longer a bachelor residence."

The men fell silent as a footman carried out a tray of lemonade and biscuits to the terrace. Trent wasn't particularly hungry, but he wasn't about to turn down the lemonade.

Griffith contemplated one of the biscuits while he waited for the servant to depart. "You know, it's still a bachelor residence. Just one of the female variety."

"She's not unmarried." Trent gripped his glass tighter.

His brother shrugged. "Might as well be."

Anthony stepped between the brothers but couldn't contain his laughter. "Griffith, I'm going to have to step in for Trent here. Until you've treaded the waters of love yourself, you should avoid throwing stones at those who are." He glanced at Trent. "Even if they are drowning."

"I hope Amelia redoes your entire house in shades of puce," Trent grumbled.

"She won't." Anthony crossed his arms over his chest, the picture of male confidence. "She's never liked that color much."

Did Adelaide like the color puce? Did anyone? Was Trent going to return home to discover his drawing room covered in drab linen? These were the moments Trent hated the most when it became so glaringly obvious how little he had connected with his wife. "What is Amelia's favorite color?"

Anthony thought for a moment. "Pink? I think? Although she used a good bit of yellow when she redecorated her bedchambers." Then he shrugged and bit into a biscuit.

Trent tried to look casual as he fell into a nearby chair. Anthony and Amelia were as in love as anyone Trent had ever seen. They'd braved the displeasure of Society to be together, and while there were many who still whispered about them behind their fans, everyone enjoyed a good love story. But Anthony wasn't sure of his wife's favorite color?

The other men sat in chairs around the table as well.

Trent wished he had a better relationship with Anthony at that moment. In the four years they'd known each other they'd become friends, but friends of the athletic variety — fencing often with both foils and words, but never going much deeper than that. He and Griffith were closer . . . but he was unmarried. Right then, more than anything, Trent would have liked to feel comfortable enough to ask, if love wasn't knowing and appreciating all the little things about a person, what was it?

After three days it became very obvious what the ladies Hawthorne, or formerly Hawthorne, were doing. Each day a different one came up with an excuse to spend the bulk of the afternoon in Adelaide's drawing room. They would stay until Trent arrived to take her for a ride, which he did at the end of each afternoon. After Trent brought her back, she'd prepare herself for the evening's activities and then await his return.

It was helpful to have someone else there when the visitors started coming. Adelaide was going to have to decide which days she was going to be at home because the constant flow of callers was making her feel frantic. What did all of these people want from her anyway?

Today Miranda was sitting with her, and if Adelaide hadn't already figured out what the Hawthornes were doing, Miranda's arrival would have tipped her off. She didn't have an excuse to be there. She'd simply come.

Miranda had come armed with several decks of cards and even a container of dice, determined to teach Adelaide all the latest games so she wouldn't feel out of place at her next gathering. Between visitors, they went through the rules of faro, basset, and a new game called skat that Miranda had learned from some visiting German dignitaries.

After one particularly long conversation with a caller, they had tea brought to the drawing room before returning to their practice game of piquet. Adelaide had just finished dropping three lumps of sugar into Miranda's tea and an equal number into her own when Fenton announced that she had another visitor.

Adelaide was thankful she'd been practicing her smile all morning, because it threatened to droop when he announced the visitor was her mother.

They'd seen each other at two of the places Trent had taken her that week, but their encounters had been blessedly brief. She spent enough time fretting over the progress of Trent's strange courtship, and she didn't need her mother's constant advice on how to hurry it along. She'd yet to hear anything that didn't sound more detrimental than helpful. Small wonder her father tended to stay in the card room all night.

Miranda took a large swallow of tea. "Show her in, Fenton, but if she's still here in twenty minutes have Mrs. Harris invent an emergency."

Adelaide blinked. Why hadn't she thought of such a thing? Mother would catch on if it happened every time, but for days when she really didn't want to see someone, the method was genius.

"As you wish, Your Grace." Fenton bowed and left to collect Adelaide's mother.

Adelaide and Miranda moved the tea service away from the card table and over to the grouping of seats upholstered in the outdated green-and-white stripe. Adelaide had finally decided the room really needed new furniture and had chosen not to reupholster the pieces that were here. Determining what furniture she wanted was delaying the entire process, though.

Miranda sat herself next to Adelaide on the sofa, not leaving room for a third person to join them. Mother would have to sit in one of the chairs facing the settee.

Mother's lip curled as she came into the room and took in the faded wall coverings and drapery-less window. Adelaide had finally had the pile of curtains removed, but she hadn't yet replaced them. Choosing room decor was turning out to be much more difficult than she'd thought it would be, though that was possibly because she was trying to make every room as special for Trent as his bedroom was, and that was difficult when she was only just now getting to know the man.

"Haven't you done anything with this place yet, Adelaide? The duke has plenty of money, you know."

Did her mother not realize that Miranda was in the room? Did she care? Adelaide was torn between simply letting her mother prattle on like she normally did, or exerting herself and her wishes the way Miranda did. Since she couldn't let the reference to the duke pass with Miranda in the room, she tried to find a response that fell somewhere in between. "I didn't marry the duke,

Mother. I married Lord Trent."

"Yes, yes, but he's the duke's brother, so I'm sure you could get him to give you enough to redo this room. Probably even enough to move to a nicer location." Mother sat on the chair and gave a pointed look at the tea service before looking at Adelaide. It was the first time she'd actually looked her daughter's way since entering the room, which might explain why she hadn't noticed the presence of another person. Miranda had been sitting unusually still for the entire exchange.

Mother had the tact to look a bit embarrassed. "Your Grace, my deepest apologies. I should not have spoken so boldly."

Adelaide poured her mother a cup of tea with a liberal amount of milk and passed it across the low tea table, trying not to cringe as she waited for Miranda to berate Lady Crampton with the bluntness Adelaide was coming to expect from the duchess. It never came.

"Perhaps not," Miranda said calmly, "but I shall overlook it. The room is in rather desperate need of refreshing. It was in need of it when Lady Raebourne lived here as well, though she didn't have access to any funds at the time. Now she does, of course, since she married the marquis, but the house had already passed on to Trent by then. Rest assured we have no intention of letting anyone in the family retain such shabby accommodations. We've been trying to trap Trent into agreeing to redecorate it since he moved in, but you know bachelors. They can be so elusive about such things."

Miranda gave a smile that projected camaraderie before lifting her teacup to her lips.

Adelaide looked down into her own cup. So that's how it was done, then. In a single minute Miranda had put Adelaide's mother in a very uncomfortable position without saying anything overtly rude or cutting. In fact the words themselves were congenial and even friendly. Yet her mother's tight face proved she hadn't missed the underlying meaning. The reminder that a nobody like Amelia had stolen the marquis away from Helena, that everyone in the family knew Adelaide and Trent had been forced to marry, and even that they knew Lady Crampton intended to use the marriage for her own gain. There had even been the subtle hint that Adelaide was part of their family now and they had every intention of protecting her. All of that without stepping a foot from the parameters of cordial, ladylike behavior.

Adelaide gaped at Miranda in a bit of awe,

thankful now that she'd been given Miranda's blunt observations instead of being subjected to this polite warfare.

Still, whether awed or not, she'd rather not have her new relations battle her old relations in her drawing room. "Mother, have you settled in? What are your plans for the Season?"

"What are my plans? Honestly, Adelaide, what else does a woman plan for during the Season?" Mother frowned into her tea and set the half-full cup on the table. "You must convince your husband to let you purchase a better quality of tea, Adelaide. This is terrible."

Given that Adelaide hated all versions of tea, she hadn't noticed whether or not this one was particularly worse than the others. She nodded though, the same as she'd done all her life, already making plans to ask Mother's London housekeeper what type of tea Mother took so that she could keep some on hand. If Trent liked their current tea, Adelaide wasn't about to change it, but she would make sure her mother didn't complain about it next time.

Miranda sighed and smiled into her own cup with a sort of reverence for the tea within. "My deepest apologies. I brought over my own special blend. I'm afraid I've become rather accustomed to it, and Adelaide was indulging me. We didn't know you'd be joining us."

It was enough to make Adelaide smile. Almost enough to make her laugh. Until that moment Miranda had been disturbingly honest, so she did have to wonder if Miranda had actually brought over her own tea. "I'll be sure I have different tea next time, Mother."

"Yes, well, I'm sure this is one I could become accustomed to. It's just an unusual blend."

The trio fell into silence. Mother was obviously expecting Miranda to leave soon, assuming the duchess was here on a normal call. They exchanged pleasantries about the weather and complaints about the pollution. Mother must have decided she was tired of being there because she finally came to the point of her visit. "I do hope you are planning to attend the Sutherland ball tomorrow night."

"As a matter of fact, I am. Will you be there as well?" The idea of being pulled around another ball by her mother made her want to come down with a sudden debilitating headache.

Mother shifted in her seat, looking extremely uncomfortable as she perched on the edge of the chair, as if she were afraid the worn upholstery might contaminate her new gown. "Of course I will. Your father is even going to be there."

It would be nice to see her father again. Adelaide hadn't seen him since the wedding, though she had received a letter from him telling her when they could be expected to arrive in London.

Mother turned to Miranda. "Will you be in attendance, Your Grace?"

"Oh, yes, we never miss the Sutherland ball."

Adelaide's eyebrows drew together. The duke and duchess had been married a mere year. How could they have anything they never missed yet?

"Yes, well, I'm sure we'll all see each other, then. If you have time, Adelaide, do see if you could mention your brother-in-law to your husband. He's having a difficult time locating a sponsor for Boodle's. Good afternoon." Her mother gifted Miranda only with a curtsy before taking her leave, apparently unwilling to completely snub a duchess.

Silence fell until the thud of the front door echoed into the drawing room.

"Sweet mercy, how did you not turn into a shrew?" Miranda plunked the teacup she'd been sipping at down onto the table. She'd been working on the same cup the entire visit, taking a small drink after every sentence she spoke.

Adelaide gathered up the rest of the tea things so that the tray could be returned to the kitchen. "I never saw much of her growing up. She was too focused on Helena. It was always her turn to go first since she was the oldest."

"Did she think you were just going to stay a baby until she had time to raise you? Well, I wouldn't normally say this, but I think you're better off for the negligence." Miranda frowned at the tea. "But she is right about the tea. I can't believe you're still drinking it."

Adelaide stood to ring for Fenton to come get the tray. "You didn't like the tea either?"

"No. It's a wretched blend. That's why I brought it over to Trent. He drinks anything. Half the time he lets it sit and get cold. I thought he'd have used it up by now. Didn't you notice it was awful?"

"I assumed Trent liked it." Adelaide frowned down at the tea. Had they been serving this same blend to everyone for the past few days? Why hadn't anyone else said something?

Miranda stuck out her tongue and made a

strange coughing noise. "He wouldn't know good tea if it hit him in the face. We'll go by my favorite tea house tomorrow, and you can give the rest of this away."

"But isn't tea expensive? There can't be that much of it left to use up."

"Trent still hasn't talked about household budgets with you, has he. You can buy some new tea. But to make you feel better, we'll tell Mrs. Harris to keep serving Trent this horrid stuff."

It didn't sit right with Adelaide to deliberately tell the housekeeper to serve Trent disgusting tea, but it didn't seem right to get rid of it either. She supposed she could forgo her coffee for a while until the rest of this tea was used. How much of it could they possibly have?

Masculine voices drifted into the drawing room from the front hall, drawing the attention of both Adelaide and Miranda. One belonged to Fenton, but Adelaide couldn't place the other one.

Miranda frowned. "That's not Trent."

Adelaide crept to the door, but she couldn't see anything. Curiosity was making her shake, though, or perhaps it was Miranda's bold nosiness that was motivating her. All afternoon Adelaide had been doing her best to keep up with Miranda's energy and enthusiasm. Regardless of the initial spark of motivation, Adelaide was devoured by curiosity to know who had come by the house.

Her house.

In which she was free to walk through the front hall, if she so wished.

"Miranda, would you care to see what I'm thinking of doing in the bedchamber?" Adelaide gestured Miranda toward the drawing room door.

The duchess sauntered forward with a grin. "You mean the bedchamber we would have to climb the stairs in the front hall to go see?"

Adelaide's mouth curved into an answering smile. "The very one."

"I'd be delighted."

The two women strolled into the front hall to see Fenton in discussion with a handsome young man who seemed very disappointed until he saw them over Fenton's shoulder. "Your Grace, my lady."

Miranda looked as if she might be ill, but she made the introductions anyway. "Lady Adelaide, this is Mr. Givendale. Mr. Givendale, Lady Trent Hawthorne."

Adelaide wondered at Miranda's use of the more formal name, but she stepped forward to greet the man with a smile anyway. "Yes, we've met. Good afternoon, Mr. Givendale. Is there a problem?"

"Not at all, my lady." Fenton took a side step toward the door. "The gentleman was seeking an audience with Lord Trent, who I'm afraid is unavailable."

The man held up a calling card with Trent's name printed on it and a date and time scrawled underneath the name. Adelaide glanced at the clock. The current date and time. "Were you to meet him here?"

Mr. Givendale nodded, his dark blond waves barely moving with the motion. "Yes, I am certain. It was a rather pressing business discussion about his estate in Suffolk. Are you sure he's unavailable?"

"Quite." Adelaide felt badly for the man to have made the point of coming to an appointment that the other party hadn't seen fit to be in residence for. That alone was enough to make her irritated with her husband. The fact that he was doing business with the estate she'd brought him and yet was still unable to bring himself to live under the same roof simply firmed up the feeling.

Whenever gentlemen left her father's study disappointed with the results of the meeting, her mother had consoled them with tea saying it was bad for a family's reputation for anyone to leave the house unhappy. Knowing the currently brewed tea blend was bad almost made her send the man on his way regardless, but if her mother was right it would mar her already fragile public opinion. "I'm afraid we've just finished taking tea, but there is probably some left if you wish to have some before you leave."

"You're too kind, my lady. I do so hate to impose, but the dust is quite dreadful today."

He was already moving toward the drawing room Miranda and Adelaide had just left. The ladies returned to the drawing room with him to partake of yet another awkward cup of tea. To his credit he didn't stay long, but the conversation flowed with incredible ease, even with Miranda's unusual silence.

Adelaide couldn't help wishing that — despite the banal nature of her conversation with Mr. Givendale — she and Trent could sit and talk in the same easy manner. While she and her husband generally talked of things other than the weather and the beauty of some of the local architecture, it always seemed to take them a while to get going. Perhaps they should start with the same inane conversation Mr. Givendale had.

As the man took his leave, Miranda stood, crossing her arms over her chest and tapping her foot until the closing of the front door echoed through the house once more.

"Do be careful with that man, Adelaide."

Adelaide paused in the act of cleaning up the tea tray for a second time. "Why? Mother always said not to let anyone leave your house unhappy because it was bad for your reputation."

Miranda scoffed. "Well, my mother says ladies should always be on guard for a scheming man, and this, my new dear sister" — Miranda held up the calling card Mr. Givendale had left behind — "is not Trent's handwriting."

Chapter 23

Adelaide couldn't keep the smug little grin off her face as she hopped into the curricle with the barest amount of assistance from Trent. Thanks to their nearly daily rides, she was growing quite comfortable with the vehicle. She was even considering asking him to teach her how to drive it.

Not that she'd have anywhere to drive to while they lived in the city. But perhaps later, when there were children — and she was beginning to believe that one day there would be children — they would spend more time in the country. Then she could drive herself places, perhaps even get her own wagon, like her mother used.

But for now, she was satisfied with the fact that she no longer gripped the seat in abject terror or spent the whole ride worrying about falling out or catching her skirt in the wheel.

She didn't even blink at the curricle's

rocking and swaying when Trent climbed in the other side.

As the wheels began to roll, though, the comfortable familiarity disappeared. Every day they'd gone to Hyde Park, rolling down Rotten Row to see and be seen. Adelaide knew every inch of the road to the legendary pathway, and this most certainly wasn't it. "Where are we going?"

Trent grinned like a little boy, cheeks creasing into deep dimples as his nose crinkled in obvious glee. "Somewhere new. I truly can't believe we haven't done this yet. I can only blame my nervousness over the entire courting situation."

Adelaide blinked at him, forgetting all about watching for clues as to their new destination in favor of examining her husband for signs that their relationship was changing. Never before had he said anything so personal, so closely connected to something relating to feelings. "You've been nervous?"

His eyes were wide as they glanced her way before returning to the traffic. "Haven't you been?"

"Well, of course, but I didn't think you were. I assumed this marriage was a mere inconvenience that you were trying to decide what to do with."

One hand twisted to take both reins, freeing his other hand to run through his hair and across the back of his neck. "I suppose it was, at first. I can't deny that I wished more than once that it would simply go away."

"That I would go away." Adelaide dropped her gaze to her lap, where her fingers were tightly laced together.

They were silent for a while as Trent maneuvered the horses under a cluster of trees in one of the open Mayfair squares. He hopped down and walked around the curricle but didn't help her down. Instead he stood, arms braced on either side of the opening on her side of the carriage. She'd never seen his green eyes so dark and serious, his mouth relaxed but straight without an inkling of either smile or frown. "I thought I did, for a while. Want you to go away, that is. But I'm truly coming to believe that God doesn't make mistakes and He had something planned for our lives even though we didn't understand" — his wide grin returned — "and so I'm going to treat you to something no other woman has ever had."

Resisting the answering joyful grin that tugged at her lips was impossible, so she gave in to it, throwing herself into whatever experience he was so excited to share with her.

A man in plain, black clothing stepped over to the curricle. "Good afternoon, my lord."

"Ah, yes." Trent rubbed his hands together and bounced on his toes. "Two Hawthorne Special Concoctions, if you please."

The man nodded and then turned to dart through the traffic and into a shop on the corner of the square. From his drawings, she recognized an elaborate pineapple on the shop sign, and that made her wonder if their outing had anything to do with Trent's pineapple-growing aspirations, but then another plainly clothed man darted through the traffic, this time with a pink confection in one hand and a yellow one in the other. He took them to another couple in another carriage positioned much like Adelaide and Trent's curricle was.

"We're at Gunter's!" Adelaide clasped her hands to her chest and met Trent's excited gaze with her own. She'd heard of the famous confectioner, popular not only for his cakes but for his delicious ices. "I've never been here."

Trent laughed. "I know. I can't believe I haven't brought you here before now."

Adelaide looked at him with narrowed

eyes, waiting to speak until a particularly loud wagon and a large, noisy carriage passed on the street behind them. "But what, exactly, is a Hawthorne Special Concoction?"

"The only way to eat an ice at Gunter's, my lady." He leaned one shoulder against the curricle, rocking the vehicle slightly as he crossed one ankle over the other and folded his arms over his chest. "James Gunter himself worked it up for me after I spent half an hour trying to decide upon a flavor one day."

"And what did you do to deserve such special attention?" Adelaide was a bit awed that Trent had received such personalized service that he could order the confection by simply giving his name. Everyone in the aristocracy came to Gunter's and there were plenty of people more important and powerful than Trent.

He gave a one-shouldered shrug. "I pay my bill on time."

Adelaide was still laughing when their waiter ran back across the street with two of the most ridiculous-looking desserts she'd ever seen. Shaped like a pineapple, each ice was a mottled collection of at least a dozen different colors, each pineapple segment bearing a different shade. Coming out of the top was a delicate, lacy biscuit.

She held the dish in one hand and a spoon in the other without the faintest idea how to start eating such a concoction. "What is this?"

"Fifteen flavors of ambrosia and a sprinkled sugar biscuit." He scraped a spoon across the top of the ice and slid the bite into his mouth with a sigh of contentment.

Adelaide stabbed her spoon into her own frozen treat, drawing a groan from her companion.

"No, no, don't do it that way." He thrust his dish toward her. "Here. Hold this."

She stuck her spoon in her mouth and let it dangle inelegantly from her lips so that her second hand could be free to balance his ice as well as hers. The utensil was nearly a lost cause at least three times as Adelaide couldn't stop laughing at Trent racing around the curricle to climb back up into the seat.

He took his ice back from her, his fingers feeling even warmer than usual against her chilled hand.

"This is a delicate combination of flavors and you must eat it a certain way to obtain as much enjoyment from them as possible."

"You've put a lot of thought into this."

He leaned toward her until his nose was a

mere three inches from her own. Adelaide blinked, trying to bring him into focus as her spectacles caused him to blur in such close proximity. His breath was already sweetened by the few bites of dessert he'd eaten, and it washed over her like a comforting autumn wind. "I take my frivolity very seriously."

She saluted him with her spoon. "Then, as your wife, I consider it my duty to give proper consideration to it as well."

"Quite right." His gaze dropped from the spoon to her lips and then back to his own confection. "Pay attention then, wife, and learn the only proper way to enjoy the best that Gunter's has to offer."

Trent was certain that one day he'd be able to look at his wife all dressed up for an evening out and not lose his breath. One day his heart wouldn't forget its job for a moment and would maintain a steady rhythm in her presence. One day. But today was not that day. Especially not after sharing his treasured ice combination with her that afternoon. She'd applied herself with gusto, diligently copying every movement he made with his spoon until he began making some up. He'd discovered that, while swooping up a dollop of lemon and chocolate in the same bite was positively blissful, the lemon and the rose should never be mixed.

She'd coughed through that combination with a smile on her face, though, and once she'd regained her composure, waited patiently with spoon poised for his next instruction. The memory of her anticipatory grin had him smiling even now. At that moment she'd been the most riveting woman he'd ever seen, and he was baffled as to why. Why she'd pulled at him so much then — and even more so as he stood in the hall watching the top of the stairs.

It wasn't that she was exceptionally beautiful, though he supposed he saw her as such now. If he had seen her for the first time in a crowded ballroom, he would certainly have noticed her unusual looks, but she wouldn't have called to him like she did now. There was something about the knowledge that she was his, that he had the permission of God and man to look at her with appreciation, to hold her in his arms and kiss her each evening when he brought her home.

The fact that he was the only person who ever saw her this way left him feeling protective, special. By the time they reached their destination, a slipper would be smudged or a jewel knocked askew. He hadn't quite figured out how she managed it when she always came down the stairs looking like utter perfection, but it never lasted beyond the carriage. He wondered sometimes if she even knew when she became disheveled. It didn't stop her from doing anything.

As was becoming common, he saw the hem of her dress first as she descended the stairs. Gold satin slippers peeped out from beneath the white-and-gold gown. This one, too, was cut like a belted vest, with pearls lining the white dress beneath as well as the gold satin overdress and belt. The rest of her emerged as she slowly descended the steps, giving Trent time to admire her grace and form. Even when he moved back into the house, he was going to make a habit of waiting for her in the front hall. Watching her come down the steps was turning into one of his favorite moments of the day.

Until her face appeared.

Instead of her normal shy, welcoming smile, she wore an anxious frown. Obviously something about this evening's plans didn't thrill her.

"We don't have to go." Trent rushed forward to meet her at the bottom of the steps, taking her hands in his.

She clasped his fingers tightly enough to

cause wrinkles in her white gloves. "Your mother —"

"Isn't here." Trent lifted a hand to Adelaide's cheek. Whatever had caused the apprehensive look in her eyes, Trent wanted to vanquish it. If the world beyond the front door was causing her grief, he was more than happy to turn her around and escort her back up the stairs until it no longer bothered her. Anything to bring back the happy woman who'd gone to Gunter's with him that afternoon.

How could he care this much about someone he hardly knew, someone he hadn't bonded with, couldn't tell what she was thinking with a single look? Every married couple he knew that was also in love had that. Georgina once said she heard her husband, Colin, in her head even when he wasn't there. His relationship with Adelaide didn't look anything like what Trent knew love to be, so why did it bother him so much that she wasn't happy? "Please tell me what's wrong."

"We should go." She tilted her head into his hand with a soft, sad smile. "Everyone is expecting us."

Trent bent his knees and ducked his head to look Adelaide in the eyes. They were still large, still a pure, clear blue, still framed by thick black lashes, but something was wrong. "Where are your spectacles?"

She held up her oversized reticule. "In here. Mother's going to be there tonight, and she fusses when I wear them to balls."

Trent frowned and wanted to hit something. All the work he'd done over the past few weeks — getting her to smile and talk and laugh with his friends and family — and her mother had broken it with the mere promise of her presence. He kept his touch gentle as he pulled the reticule from her wrist.

His mother would swat him with her fan if she saw him opening a woman's reticule, but this was his wife, and these were extenuating circumstances.

The slim novel tucked in the bag made him smile as he dug around for her spectacles. He found them wrapped in a soft cloth and tucked into her spare pair of slippers. Georgina must have taught her that trick when she'd been here two days ago. After unwrapping the frames, he slid them carefully onto Adelaide's face. He shifted his hands until his palms cupped her cheeks, his thumbs grazing right below the spectacle frames. As her eyes drifted shut he leaned down and brushed a light kiss across her lips. "Mother or no mother, I want you to be able to see when I dance with you."

As she blinked up at him, her eyes adjusting to the lenses once more, he vowed that no matter what her life had been before, he was going to make her future one better. Starting tonight.

Chapter 24

As had become his habit when they entered a venue where dancing was available, Trent pulled Adelaide to the dance floor immediately. He always seemed to time it so that they walked into a waltz. Whether or not he was that knowledgeable of song order at balls or he actually arranged it with the different hostesses and orchestras, Adelaide didn't know. And she didn't care. She simply enjoyed starting the evening wrapped in her husband's arms.

He smiled down at her, almost making her forget that she had another night of uncomfortable interactions ahead of her. One day, God willing, these social functions wouldn't make her want to run screaming into the night. The number of people crowding the ballroom meant that the *ton* had arrived in London full force, and there was sure to be someone more interesting than her for the masses to focus on very soon.

Unless her mother did something to change that.

The pressure of Trent's arm at her back pulled her back to the present. The warmth of his hand through her glove reassured her. She enjoyed dancing with Trent.

She knew he was a superb athlete, spending a great deal of his time at athletic clubs, boxing, fencing, or even playing cricket. He'd mentioned once that he liked rowing, as well, but hadn't had much chance to do it since school. The Thames was a bit too crowded for a rowing team in London. All of those athletic pursuits made him strong and graceful and he led her around the floor with confidence.

Secure that he would lead her the way she needed to go, she let her mind drift. They'd had fun the past few days. Their outings had seemed less like obligations and more like excursions. They'd had such fun eating their ices that they'd been unable to contain their laughter, and more than one person crossed the square to chat with them. Well, him, mostly. Everyone had been very polite to her, but it was becoming obvious that nearly the entire aristocracy loved Trent.

Did she love him too? What did that mean? Love. Years ago, an aunt assured Adelaide her mother loved her, but if that was love, what was this she felt with Trent? Was it love that she hoped one day very soon he'd stop leaving her at the foot of the stairs in the evening? Was it love that she looked forward to seeing him smile and scoured the obscure texts in the library looking for strange facts to make him laugh, that she was spending each morning with Mrs. Harris learning to cook a perfect rasher of bacon? Was it love that she couldn't move forward with the drawing room because she so desperately wanted him to like it?

Did he like the green that was currently in the room? Did he want it designed for large gatherings or merely intimate visits? Those things seemed like something someone in love would know. Wouldn't they? Could it be love if she didn't know his preferences?

All too soon the song was ending and Trent was bowing. Adelaide dropped into a hasty curtsy before laying her hand on his arm to be escorted from the floor.

As soon as they cleared the dance floor, her mother appeared from seemingly nowhere. "You two simply look divine together. Fate is certainly kind, isn't she?"

Adelaide's tongue felt thick and swollen. What was the proper response to something like that? Stating that fate was considerably kinder than her own mother didn't seem like the correct response. If for no other reason that Trent was unaware of the fact that fate had next to nothing to do with their marriage, and they could have been rescued.

"You look lovely tonight, Mother." When in doubt, compliment — at least when it came to her mother. Acknowledging her superior taste in fashion always put the countess in a good mood.

"Have you met Mrs. Seyton yet, darling?" Mother fluttered her fan lightly as she sidled up to Adelaide's free arm and looped her own through it.

"I'm afraid I haven't had the pleasure," Adelaide mumbled. How ridiculous she must look with her husband on one arm and her mother on the other. As if they were about to begin a strange country reel.

Mother tugged lightly at Adelaide's arm. "You simply must meet her. She has the most splendid little house in Brighton. They don't use it much, so she's always willing to let me stay there when I need to visit the coast. Sea-bathing is very beneficial for the constitution, you know."

"I would love to meet Mrs. Seyton, Mother." To be honest, she was just grateful that her mother wished to introduce her to another woman instead of making more suggestions about which men she could use to make her husband jealous. She pulled her arm from Trent's. If meeting Mrs. Seyton would placate her mother, she'd be more than happy to get it over with.

"Yes. Well, perhaps I can introduce you later."

Adelaide's mouth dropped open a bit as her mother faded into the surrounding crowd.

"I see you made it," a male voice sounded from behind her. "We had to take a very circuitous route to avoid the mess on Bruton Street. It was a wagon full of lumber, so there's fortunately no loss, but it's taking them a dreadfully long time to clean it up."

Adelaide turned to find Lord and Lady Raebourne smiling at them. Was that why her mother had left? "You're my new favorite people."

The stunned silence was the first indication that the words had actually come out of her mouth instead of staying safely locked in her head.

Trent looked from her to Lady Raebourne and then out over the crowd before he tilted his head and smiled at the marchioness. "You might be mine as well. Anthony, we'd be more than happy to visit with your wife for a while if you have anyone you need to speak with. Or punch you need to fetch."

The other couple looked from Trent to Adelaide with equally confused expressions.

Lord Raebourne scratched behind his ear. "I was going to speak to —"

"Wonderful!" Trent rocked back on his heels. "You take care of that while we stay with your wife."

Lady Raebourne hooked her arm securely into her husband's. "I'm not sure that's a good idea."

Trent laughed. "Nothing nefarious, I assure you. Simply trying to help Adelaide become more comfortable with a few people in Town. She had to leave all her friends behind in the country, you know."

Lady Raebourne's expression turned more than a little skeptical. Adelaide was fairly certain hers had as well. Trent hadn't shown the least interest in her personal friendships since they'd gotten married and now he wanted to encourage her friendship with the one person they'd come across that her mother was afraid of? It wasn't very subtle of him. Sweet, but not subtle.

After staring at Trent for a few tense moments, Lady Raebourne released her husband's arm. "If you wish."

"Oh, I wish." Trent's actions didn't match

his words as he was once more looking around the room. Finally he found what he was looking for, but they didn't set off across the room again. Instead he simply smiled.

With another questioning look in Trent's direction, Lord Raebourne slipped off to take care of his business, leaving the three remaining people to stand around staring at each other. As much as Adelaide enjoyed the fact that Lady Raebourne's presence kept the countess away, they couldn't stand like this all evening.

Trent apparently had other plans. "How is the redecorating going?"

"Hmm. Slowly. I'm having trouble selecting the right fabric." Lady Raebourne cut her eyes in Adelaide's direction, making her want to squirm. "Anthony won't tell me what he wants."

Trent tried to hold back a laugh, but it sputtered out anyway. "Anthony doesn't care what your parlor looks like."

Lady Raebourne sighed. "I know. But I still want him to like it."

"Then put furniture he's not afraid to sit on in there. As long as it's comfortable and you're happy he won't care what it looks like."

Adelaide blinked, looking from Lady Raebourne to Trent and back again. How was it that all of these women were more clever with words than she would ever be? She struggled just to say what she meant, never mind layering it into a conversation in such a way that it either portrayed an unsaid second meaning or unearthed answers no one was willing to ask for. With a silent thank-you to Lady Raebourne, Adelaide began thinking through the furniture she'd seen in some of the galleries, mentally discarding anything with spindle legs or delicately carved backs.

"Might I have the next dance?"

Adelaide blinked out of her contemplation to find Mr. Givendale standing in front of her, and Trent gritting his teeth. Adelaide had enjoyed dancing with the man before — as much as she could enjoy dancing with anyone other than her husband, anyway — and would have accepted without much thought if it hadn't been for Trent's apparent dislike of the idea. Yes, the man had feigned a scheduled meeting with Trent, but she'd heard her father complain of men doing the same thing in an attempt to gain an audience, so was that really such an awful thing? Even with the card he'd been stopped at the door by Fenton. Was there more going on here than Adelaide realized?

"I'm afraid I was planning to dance the next two with Lady Adelaide."

Beneath Adelaide's fingers, Trent's arm relaxed as they both turned to Griffith, who had come up behind them as Mr. Givendale spoke. It was obvious Mr. Givendale wanted to object, but there was nothing he could do except acquiesce. Having a duke in the family did have certain advantages.

She let go of Trent's arm a bit reluctantly but was happy to be going back to the dance floor, where she had at least some idea of what she was doing and could avoid a great deal of conversation if she wished to. Griffith's wide chest expanded and released on a sigh as the music began, his expression almost grim as he took the first steps in the dance.

"Thank you for dancing with me." Adelaide knew singling her out to dance had gone a long way toward getting her accepted by people she still didn't feel like she fit in with. She'd been in London mere weeks and already missed the freedom of the country. She supposed she should get used to it though. Trent lived year round in the city, only taking short trips to his country estates.

"Has he been coming around?" Griffith whispered in her ear as they passed each other in the dance.

Adelaide looked back to where she'd come from. Mr. Givendale was in a low conversation with Trent. With similar coloring and height, the two men made a handsome picture. Mr. Givendale's hair was a touch darker, and his high cheekbones gave his face a bit more starkness, but there was no denying his good looks. The appealing picture stopped, however, when one looked closer at the men's faces. Mr. Givendale looked almost smug, while Trent's face remained as devoid of expression as she'd ever seen it. She came to Griffith's side as they circled. "He's been by to see Trent, though he obviously missed him."

Griffith nodded, a thoughtful look on his face. "Does Trent know?"

"I believe Mr. Givendale left a message with Fenton yesterday afternoon, but I don't know if Trent has received it yet."

Silence fell as they went through the next formation of the dance. They approached the end of the line of dancers before Griffith spoke again. "Trent has a tendency to assume the best of people. He's never had a need to do otherwise."

Where was Griffith going with this? Adelaide didn't for one moment believe that Griffith would share information like this without a reason. "I've noticed."

They stopped at the end of the line, facing each other while the next formation was executed. "Do you? Assume the best, I mean?"

Did she? It wasn't something she'd ever thought about. She never assumed the best of her mother — experience had taught her otherwise — but her father often got a bit more lenience from her. "I think it depends upon the person."

He nodded before letting all expression fall from his face as he saw something over her shoulder.

The ballroom was crowded, and the line of dancers pushed up against the people milling around beside the dance floor, leaving them very accessible to anyone who wished to speak to them. For instance, someone like her mother.

"You are such a dear, Duke," she said from the edge of the dance floor. "I'm so thankful you've accepted our girl like a sister. We must have you to dinner next week in gratitude."

Adelaide counted the music, praying it would speed up so they could leave the edge of the group and move their way across the floor once more. How could her mother try to finagle her way into the duke's inner circles like this? Very well, she knew how, but it was still a bit tiresome that Mother was trying to use her this way. Had Helena had this problem? Probably not. Helena had likely been just as bad.

Griffith nodded. "The whole family has accepted her. She is one of our own."

Mother tittered. She actually tittered. "Of course, we'd love to have all of you, including the Duke of Marshington."

Griffith nodded again. Adelaide couldn't believe he was actually agreeing to this. He was a duke. Politeness only had to go so far. "I'm sure he would be delighted, along with Lord and Lady Raebourne. Even though she's married now, after her time as my ward, I still consider her family."

Adelaide looked to the side in time to see her mother turn pale. "Of . . . of course. I shouldn't have disrupted your dance. We'll discuss a date at a later time."

Griffith gave her one more nod before taking Adelaide's arm and rejoining the dance.

"She's never going to have you to dinner now," Adelaide whispered. "She simply cannot abide Lady Raebourne."

The grin Griffith sent her way made him look so much like Trent her heart turned over a bit. "I know."

Trent's heart pounded in his chest, and his

fingers relaxed their fists as he saw Lady Crampton slink away from the dance floor without taking Adelaide's smile with her. Whatever Griffith was saying had actually drawn a laugh from his wife, something he'd thought impossible given her sullen mood in the carriage on the way to the ball.

Though he'd never cared for Lady Crampton, the more he saw her interact with her daughter, the more baffled he became. It made him want to find his own mother and write sonnets to what a wonderful parent she'd been. Part of him wished there was a way to eradicate the countess from Adelaide's life, but the woman was her mother. A certain amount of respect had to be granted to her because of that.

Respect, yes, but not free access. He could respectfully limit their interaction if he was clever. There hadn't been much cause for him to be deliberately clever in his life. Charming, yes, but never clever. He could only hope he was up to the challenge.

As the dance ended, Lady Crampton found the couple again, all but dragging Adelaide off with her, disappearing into the crush. Trent worked his way around the ballroom until he found them again, only to wish he hadn't. The two women were talking to Mr. Givendale. What was the man up to?

There was nothing he could do about it in the middle of a ballroom, though. Neither his wife nor his mother would thank him for making a scene. Especially simply on the basis of not liking the way the man smiled at Trent's wife.

He tore himself away from the torture of watching Adelaide speak to Mr. Givendale. Amelia was still standing near him though her husband had rejoined their little group. "I don't suppose you'd like to move into my house for a while?" he asked.

Anthony frowned. "You mean the one you aren't even living in at the moment?"

The marquis jerked as his wife nudged him with her elbow without a thought to being gentle about it. "Keep your voice down. And I don't think he was talking to you."

"Well, you're certainly not living anywhere without me."

Trent wished he could go back and change things so that he'd never asked the question in the first place. It was rather ridiculous. He needed other options. "Who other than your wife does Lady Crampton avoid?"

Anthony frowned. "You're asking the wrong man. I make a point of not noticing anything Lady Crampton does. Lord Crampton too, if I can manage it." Anthony took Amelia's arm, preparing to escort her to the floor for the next dance. "Georgina's on the floor now, which means Colin is around here somewhere. If anyone would know, it would be him."

Trent glanced over the dancers, and sure enough there was Georgina. Despite being married, she still dressed in white, though it was broken by a wide emerald-green sash and covered with so many embroidered flowers the white was more of a suggestion than an actual color on the dress. But Georgina never attended an event like this without her husband. Trent and Colin had met at the club for billiards earlier this week but hadn't really talked about how Trent had ended up married. Still, the man knew everything about everyone in London. If anyone could suggest who Trent needed to use to make this plan work, it would be Colin.

Once the dance was over, he followed Georgina to a nearby window where he not only found the Scotsman, but Lady Blackstone as well. He greeted his mother before turning to Colin. "I need information."

Colin took a sip of lemonade and leaned one shoulder against the window casing.

"The price of corn has gone down now that the war is over. You're better off investing in oats."

"You handle my investments, so I trust that's already been taken care of." Trent shifted to lean against the wall next to Colin, trying to keep the conversation looking casual. "Who does Lady Crampton avoid?"

"Why would I know that?" Colin coughed on the lemonade he'd sucked in on his surprised gasp.

"Because you always know who doesn't like each other."

"Only as it applies to business, and Lady Crampton's inclinations don't have all that much to do with Lord Crampton's." Colin looked toward the ceiling as he thought. "Now, he tends to avoid Anthony and Amelia and never seems to have much to do with Mr. Burges. Oh, and he refuses to have anything to do with Spindlewood."

Georgina shook her head in surprise. "As in the Duke of?"

Colin nodded.

Trent's mother flicked her fan open. "That is hardly surprising."

Trent, Colin, and Georgina all looked at her with wide eyes. Mother never indulged in malicious gossip, but it sounded as if she was about to jump right into something London would think was rather significant.

When she didn't say anything else, Georgina finally let out an exasperated "Why?"

Mother looked at them as if she simply expected them to know, but Trent couldn't think of a thing he'd ever heard about Spindlewood. Other than the fact that the man's mustache was most unfortunately shaped, the old man didn't do much of anything interesting.

"The Duke of Spindlewood has a son."

"Three, if we're being particular," Colin murmured.

Mother waved her fan in Colin's direction as if brushing off his words. "Only one who will one day be the duke. And Isabel very much wanted to one day be his duchess."

Trent felt himself pulled into the drama of the short tale. Lady Crampton was a countess, so it was sometimes difficult to remember that she'd started off aiming higher than that. "What happened? Obviously she's not waiting to become a duchess right now."

"The Duke accused her of being after the money and the title and threatened to cut his son off from anything that wasn't entailed unless he married someone other than Isabel. Embarrassed her thoroughly by bringing forward one of her friends, who verified all the times the woman had plotted and planned to encounter Spindlewood's heir. She then tried to trap the son in a compromising position so they would be forced to marry — only she ended up snaring the old duke instead of the son. She couldn't show her face in a ballroom for the rest of the year."

Trent gave a low whistle. Was that why Adelaide requested an introduction to him at the Ferrington ball? That scandal would certainly be enough to make a woman such as Lady Crampton avoid a man for the rest of his life. It was rather amazing that she'd been able to land an earl after the scandal that had probably ensued from seemingly propositioning a married duke.

After thanking his family profusely, Trent went off in search of his wife, hoping against hope that he wouldn't find her in Givendale's arms on the dance floor. As he went he kept an eye out for the Duke of Spindlewood.

With any luck, the old man was feeling chatty this evening and Trent and Adelaide could spend the next half hour at his side.

CHAPTER 25

Adelaide climbed into the carriage with a small sigh of relief. Had an evening ever been so exhausting? She'd done her best to make everyone happy, but what was she supposed to do when they wanted different things from her? Her mother obviously wanted Adelaide to be vivacious and personable, and she had truly tried to be those things. While she had absolutely no intention of following through on her mother's less-than-veiled suggestions that, with just the slightest bit of effort and coercion, Adelaide could use her new status as a member of the Hawthorne family to improve her mother's and sister's social positions, there didn't seem to be a reason not to at least try to be nice to the people Mother introduced her to.

That was until she saw Trent waiting for her to come off the dance floor after sharing a quadrille with Mr. Givendale. Her husband hadn't frowned or even looked unhappy, but he'd been stiff as he took her arm. Adelaide let her head fall back on the carriage seat and roll to the side so she could watch Trent adjust his coat and situate himself on the seat beside her. Had a man ever spent so much effort on a woman?

After collecting her from Mr. Givendale, Trent had spent the rest of the evening at her side, engaging them in conversation with the Duke of Spindlewood and his grandson and sharing dance formations with Lord and Lady Raebourne. He was obviously trying to keep her away from her mother and having a great deal of success in doing so.

Which meant no matter what she did, one of them was going to be disappointed. Never before had Adelaide been faced with such a decision. Her parents rarely had strong opinions about the same thing, so it was easy enough to please both of them. And Helena was happy as long as everything in the room revolved around her. But now there was a battle going on for Adelaide's attention and someone was going to have to lose.

As Trent's laugh rolled softly across her ears, Adelaide was afraid that the loser was going to have to be her mother. And she was more than a little afraid of what the repercussions would be when that happened.

If Trent's objective with this courtship had been to make her feel like someone worth winning, he was succeeding. What she'd thought would be a dreadful evening had turned into one of the most delightful nights she'd ever had in her life. And it was all due to the man beside her.

What did that leave her with? Gratitude? Certainly. He was an answer to a prayer she hadn't known how to phrase. Love? Maybe. She still wasn't certain she knew what love was, but if it meant wanting to spend the rest of her life making someone else's life better, then yes, she loved him.

The horses broke free from the crush in front of the house and trotted easily though Mayfair, leaving the two of them snug in the darkness of the carriage. It had become a habit to take the long way home, knowing their time would be limited once they got there.

Trent reached through the darkness and took her hand. "Did you enjoy this evening?"

It was his standard question, and she'd never thought to wonder why before. Was he concerned? Did he feel responsible for her? Was it possible he was coming to view her happiness as essential as she was coming to view his? Or was it a safe inquiry, relying on the commonality of a shared event to start a conversation? Rather like his discussions on food. The questions and uncertainty swam through her head and made her dizzy. "It was a very pleasant evening. Did you win your fencing match today?"

He settled closer to her until their shoulders brushed and began talking to her about the fencing club. He had won his match, but he found plenty else to tell her about as well. The other people he'd talked to, a funny story about the lady's dog that had run into the club leaving his mistress shrieking on the pavement outside.

Adelaide listened, but she also wondered why she felt so unsettled. They'd spent several evenings this way now, and it was always nice, but it bothered her too. They were married, yet they weren't, courting but not. She didn't know wifely things such as household budgets and where they got their tea, or even what he liked for breakfast, but she knew what his kiss tasted like. Their courtship lacked the restraints a normal relationship would have, allowing them to do things such as ride through Mayfair in a darkened carriage to spend half an hour alone in a dimly lit hall. But their marriage lacked the security that normally came with the institution. She didn't know where he spent his days or even his nights. There was a constant need to look her best whenever he saw her, despite the fact that she'd somehow managed to end this evening without her fan.

She had so many questions about him but no answers. If he enjoyed physical activity so much, why wasn't he taking a more particular interest in his estates? Why was he sketching plans for pineapples and then stuffing them into a drawer? Why did he treat her like the most precious thing in the world when they went out together and then drop her at their doorstep? Which Trent was she really married to?

A public marriage in name only wasn't going to be enough for her much longer. The better she got to know Trent the more she wanted to make this marriage work, only she didn't know what to do next.

"Have you ever had a dog?" Trent asked as the carriage pulled up in front of their house.

"Once. One of the foxhounds had puppies, and the smallest one wasn't doing well. So I cared for it, and soon it was following me all over the house." Adelaide gathered up her skirts.

"What happened to him?"

"He got older and stronger. And one day we were out for a walk and he saw the other dogs training. I didn't have the heart to keep him with me all the time after that. I still visited him every now and then. He turned into a decent hunting dog."

She took his hand and let him help her out of the carriage. She hadn't thought about Milkweed in years. It had been a ridiculous name for a dog, but she'd been a lonely six-year-old girl, and sometimes six-years-olds were ridiculous. The truth hadn't gone quite like Adelaide had told Trent and the look of near pity on his face told her he guessed at the truth.

The truth was they'd been out walking and he'd naturally snuffed out a bevy of quail and sent them soaring into the heavens. Her father had asked her if she thought Milkweed would like to come with him on his next hunt. From then on she'd only seen him when she snuck down past the barn to the kennel where they kept the dogs. Eventually she stopped even doing that.

As usual, Fenton was waiting at the door. After letting them in, he locked the front door and left them in the hall, a single lantern burning on a side table to hold away the blanket of darkness.

"Where did you learn to dance?" Trent asked.

Adelaide flushed, knowing the question was born of the other things she'd shared about her time growing up — how her mother had continued to treat her like a child even as she reached the age when other girls were thinking of who and when they would marry. It had always been Helena's turn first, as if Mother only had enough energy for one child at a time. "Dancing lessons are easier with additional couples. I was partnered with my brother, Bernard. He didn't like it much, but he suffered through it because father said he had to. I sometimes wonder if Father made him do it for my benefit as much as Helena's."

"Adelaide, I . . ." Trent's voice trailed off, not as if he didn't know what he wanted to say but as if he didn't have the words to say it. She knew how he felt. She felt like that almost all the time these days. Like life was throwing so much at her and she knew how she wanted to respond but didn't know how to express it or motivate herself to actually do it.

But she knew what she wanted now. She didn't want his gentle platitudes about how he was going to take care of her — he'd proven that with more than words tonight. She didn't want him to say that she should have had more as a child — there was no gaining it back, and after seeing how Helena turned out she wasn't sure she wanted to have gotten it anyway. Right now Adelaide wanted the unvarnished truth that came when he kissed her, when he couldn't hide the harshened breathing and the unsteady hands, when he didn't rely on his charming words or winning smile. She wanted what only she received.

As if he could read her mind, he slid his hands up her arms. His gloves had been discarded in the carriage. One of the few wifely things she knew about him. He couldn't stand the feeling of evening gloves and shed them as soon as he was out of public.

Small calluses covered his hands from years spent rowing and fencing, and she felt every one of them as his hands slid off her gloves and onto her upper arms, pausing below the cut sleeves of her ball gown. He held her steady as he stepped closer and lowered his head. She loved this moment each night, lived for it when the evening grew tedious.

One hand released her arm and slid along

the back of her neck, dislodging the pins that had already worked loose at the bottom of her coiffure.

And then his lips were on hers. There was no fumbling hesitancy now, as she felt the familiar warmth of his lips brush gently against hers before returning again with more pressure. She felt his teeth, his tongue, things she never would have thought a woman would enjoy, but she did.

She took her own step forward, pressing into the kiss in a way she hadn't done before. More than his hands bore evidence of his athletic pursuits and she rested her hands on his shoulders, wishing she dared to wrap them around him, to hold him to her the way she wanted to.

A small cry escaped her lips as he pulled away, and he returned immediately, giving her the second kiss he'd always denied her before.

But the kiss was brief, and before she was ready he was pulling back once more, farther this time until her fingertips fell from his shoulders.

"Don't go."

She didn't realize she'd said the words out loud until he sucked a harsh breath in through his teeth, but she wasn't upset that she'd said it. Thank goodness her subconscious had more courage than she did. But she didn't want it to be her subconscious that kept him here. She wanted to have the nerve to say it deliberately, to ask him to stay and mean it.

A deep breath filled her lungs and pushed her shoulders straight. She licked her lips and said it again.

"Don't go."

Curls he'd knocked from their moorings draped over her shoulder, emphasizing the fast rise and fall of her chest. The form he'd so admired as it came down the stairs draped in utter perfection was even more enticing in its altered state. The ensemble, naturally mussed and broken by simple virtue of Adelaide being in it, drew him in the way perfection could not. Because it was her. No one else lived in their clothes like she did, without guile or concern for appearance.

She blinked at him, her spectacles magnifying what little moonlight made it into the room and highlighting her clear blue eyes until he wanted to drown in them. That wasn't possible, so he did the next best thing.

He decided to drown in her.

She'd asked for so little since they'd married, had gone along with everything he'd declared. And when she finally asked for something, all she seemed to want was him.

Could anything be more humbling?

There was also a part of him that wanted to stake his claim, to prove to her and all of the men like Givendale that he was her husband and no one else. He hadn't liked watching her smile at another man. Perhaps if he did this, if he took that last step in making their marriage real, her most special of smiles would be only for him.

He stepped forward again, throwing caution to the wind and wrapping his arms around her. She pressed against him, already lifting her head for his kiss, wanting it as much as he wanted to give it.

For weeks now, he'd been wrestling with how to love her, how to get her to love him. Maybe it wasn't so important that he figure it out. Maybe it was more important that he be with her. It wasn't as if he was going to get to change his mind at the end of this courtship. The awkwardness they'd brought home with them was gone, and maybe that was enough. Maybe it would have to be.

The kiss was different this time, tinged with nerves and excitement as he realized this time he didn't have to pull back. This time he wasn't going to slip out the back door to meet the carriage in the alley. This time he could enjoy everything about his wife. Not just could, but should.

Her arms crept around his sides, pressing into his back as she went up on her toes in an effort to get closer.

He broke the kiss, grinning like a fool. He hoped she could sense it in the dark, knew how happy he was to be staying tonight. One arm was already tucked around her shoulders, holding her close. He bent and slid the other hand behind her knees, lifting her high against his chest as she squealed and wrapped her arms around his neck.

The motion pressed his face into the place where her neck and shoulder met. He kissed her there before lowering her enough that she could snag the lantern with one hand while keeping the other wrapped over his shoulder. He climbed the stairs, holding her tighter with each step. He'd never been so glad for the relatively small house that allowed him to reach the bedchamber without hiking down long corridors.

They didn't call for her maid, and his valet was across town, so they fumbled with each other's fastenings, falling into fits of giggles when her dress confounded Trent to the point that he threatened to fetch a knife. She was fascinated by the unfolding of his cravat, even taking a moment to try to re-create the folds herself. He'd thought that once they finally got to this point there'd be a rush, driven by the same sense of urgency that had nibbled at his nerves when he kissed her each night. But now that they were here, steps away from the bed he hadn't been able to sleep in since he married this woman, a calm sense of rightness took away the need to hurry.

She looked right in this room, the room that was more his than anywhere else in the house. It was one of the few rooms he'd taken the time to refurbish when he moved in. Much to the dismay of Mrs. Harris, the rest of the house hadn't been necessary to him. But this room was his private sanctuary, the place where only he went, and now his wife would be there as well.

The soft light from the lantern flickered over the bed, creating its own sense of magic as he pulled back the covers before taking her hand and guiding her the last few steps across the floor. He didn't know what Adelaide knew about tonight, and what he knew was limited at best, but that didn't matter. They would take it slow and discover it together. It had taken them nearly a month to get there, but tonight would finally be their wedding night. It was a natural act, designed by God to bring a man and woman into perfect union.

Trent kept that in mind as his heart raced and his lungs filled with the intoxicating combination of heat and roses. He gathered her in his arms and kissed her, savoring the freedom to enjoy his wife, even if there were moments of awkwardness where he could only guess at what he was doing. If her smiles and sighs were any indication, she didn't mind his fumbling. The way her hands brushed his shoulders and back proved that she reveled in the new freedom as well.

Trent pulled her close, wondering what he'd been so afraid of, but knowing that they'd been right to wait. This moment should be the most easy, natural thing in the world. All of the reservations he'd had about this marriage were about to disappear. He grazed his fingers over her cheek, knowing the morning light would bring them a whole and splendid new marriage.

Chapter 26

A few hours ago Trent had been sure he was done with sitting in chairs, waiting for the sun to rise. He'd thought his nights of sleepless contemplation were over.

He was afraid they were just beginning.

If anything, this night, this moment was worse than all the sleepless nights that had come before. This time he wasn't waiting for the first rays of sunlight to bring him new opportunities and fresh hope. No, on this morning, on which he wasn't going to be able to bring himself to even attempt to eat breakfast, he was waiting for daybreak to give him permission to flee the scene of his atrocity and seek advice from the only person he could.

His Bible sat forgotten on his leg. The answers were probably in there somewhere, but in his agitated state he hadn't been able to find anything but genealogies, proof that what men had been accomplishing for centuries either came at a great cost to their wives or Trent was a dismal failure.

On the other side of the connecting door, Adelaide slept. He knew she slept because he'd gone to check on her every half hour since he'd carried her to her own room. He was glad she slept, but he couldn't. Couldn't even bring himself to return to the bed. He'd hurt his wife. He hadn't meant to, hadn't even known that he could, but somehow the moment had gone from blissful and beautiful to tragic in a single instant. Her squeal of pain still echoed in his ears, refusing to give him peace.

So he sat in his father's chair and waited for the sun.

How often had his father sat in that very chair, contemplating the questions of life? While Trent was fairly certain his father had never had to come to terms with this particular question, he knew the man had struggled with more than one life decision in this chair. He was a duke, after all. Making life-changing decisions seemed to be all they ever did. But his father had been lucky enough to know and love his wife before their marriage. The story of how his father had pursued his mother was almost famous among the *ton*. Courting her for over a year. Buying an estate next to her father's so he could continue courting after the Season was over.

Was that what Trent had wanted? Was it the reason he'd been so hesitant to focus on one woman before now? Or had it been that he'd instinctively known there was something wrong with him? That any woman who married him would be getting a bitter life sentence of pain. Since he had obviously done something wrong, did that mean there couldn't even be children?

He left his curtains open, watching the building across the street so he could know the moment the sun's rays hit it. He could have gone to the breakfast room, where the sun would shine through the glass, but he had no idea what time she rose. What if he ran into her? He wasn't sure he'd ever be able to look her in the face again. Not after he'd turned her sweet request into such an abomination.

The sun streaked the sky, lighting on the rooftops across the street. He waited until the attic windows of the house across the street glinted in the sun before he rose from the chair to dress. The muscles in his legs protested, stiff after their prolonged time in one position. He didn't ring for Fenton, choosing instead to dress himself. He didn't even know if the butler knew Trent had spent the night at the house.

His tying of the cravat wasn't anything to speak of, but otherwise he looked like any other aristocratic gentleman going for a morning ride. He hoped his household thought so, anyway. They had no need to know he was riding but one street over and not to Regent's Park or even Hyde Park.

Mrs. Harris was coming out of the breakfast room as Trent made his way toward the small stable at the back of the property. "May I say how nice it is to see you this morning, my lord?"

The twinkle in the housekeeper's eyes nearly choked Trent. He had to get out of there. "Yes, well, let's not mention it, shall we? We don't want to embarrass anyone."

For once he hoped his staff would act like staff and not make any comments like that to Adelaide. While she'd initially seemed to accept the marriage more easily than he had, she was probably regretting it now. There was no need to constantly remind her of the regret they couldn't change.

Knowing he didn't have far to go, Trent made himself think of his horse and walked him the short distance to Anthony's house. The butler threatened to throw him out, but since Trent had charmed his way through the kitchens and was already at

Anthony's study door before the butler saw him, Trent was able to convince him not to. He'd already asked one of the footmen downstairs to tell Anthony he was here because he didn't trust the stiff-necked butler to do it.

Trent tried to settle into a chair in Anthony's study, but he couldn't do it. Lots of men had books in their study, but Anthony's walls were lined with floor-to-ceiling bookshelves. So many books made him think of how much Adelaide would enjoy looking through the shelves for unusual titles. She probably wouldn't hunt down obscure facts for him anymore. She probably wouldn't even speak to him.

He paced. From window to door and bookshelf to bookshelf, but he didn't have long to wait before Anthony came busting in still tying his dressing gown. "What's wrong?"

"I need . . . I don't . . . I can't . . ." Trent fell into a chair, elbows on his knees and head in his hands, as words, the one thing that had always saved him before, failed him. "I've botched everything."

Anthony stopped in the middle of the floor. "And you came to me?"

Trent looked up, wondering if his despair

was evident. "I didn't know where else to go."

Shock drifted across Anthony's face, but he contained it quickly. Trent didn't blame him. While he and Anthony had always gotten on well enough, often fencing or going riding together, Anthony had always been more Griffith's friend than Trent's. But Trent was counting on that friendship being extended to him now.

"Is anyone hurt?" Anthony asked slowly as he lowered himself onto the edge of the chair next to Trent's.

"No." Trent fell back to slump into his own chair. "At least she said she isn't. Well, not anymore, anyway."

"Ah." Confusion and even worry dropped from Anthony's face to be replaced by a ghost of a smile as he sat deeper into the chair.

"I shouldn't have come here." Trent wanted to stomp out of the room, but the truth was he really didn't have anywhere else he could go.

"I'm sorry, I'm sorry." Anthony wiped a hand over his face and did his best to erase the smile. "What happened?"

"I stayed the night."

"I gathered as much."

Trent popped back up to resume pacing.

"She asked me to stay. I wanted to stay."

Anthony leaned back, watching Trent go back and forth across the room as if he were watching a tennis match. "That's a good start."

Once more words failed him as he didn't begin to know how to tell Anthony what had happened next.

"I'm assuming there was kissing at that point." Anthony couldn't quite hide the humor in his voice, even though he managed to keep from smiling. He was intently studying his fingernails in order to keep from laughing.

"Yes," Trent growled. "There was kissing."

More silence. Finally Anthony looked up. "Was it good?"

Trent groaned at the memory. "The best."

"So it was everything else that was the problem, then?" Anthony wasn't even trying to keep the smile off his face anymore, and Trent couldn't bring himself to care.

He braced his hands on the desk and leaned forward, hunching his shoulders and dropping his head. "It didn't work."

Anthony barked in laughter before taking huge breaths to try to contain it. "I'm sorry, I'm sorry. What didn't work? Er, was it you?"

Finally the other man seemed to realize

the awkwardness of their conversation as two high spots of red formed along his cheekbones.

Trent glared at the marquis. "No. I worked just fine. It was the . . . Well, the process didn't work. I bungled it, Anthony. I thought I knew what to do. I've certainly heard about it plenty of times, but then it didn't . . . go right. And then I hurt her. I hurt my wife, and I don't know how to fix it."

He rubbed his hands over his face hard, as if he could wipe away the events of a few hours prior, surprised when they came away wet. When was the last time he'd cried? His father's funeral? Maybe the first day he'd gone off to school and his father hadn't been there? But if ever there was anything to cry over as an adult, failing at one of the prime responsibilities as a man was certainly a good one.

Anthony rose and crossed the room. He took Trent's shoulders in his hands. "Trent, it happens. There are plenty of men who bungle their wedding night. Though most of them do it on their actual wedding night."

"I'm sure you didn't bungle your wedding night," Trent muttered before breaking away from Anthony and throwing himself back into the chair. The tufted club chair rocked back on its legs with the force of his weight.

Anthony's good humor disappeared as he slowly sat in the other chair, looking every inch the powerful marquis that he was. "I think Amelia would have happily accepted some bungling on my part if it meant I came with a purer past, but that's not of consequence here. Is my experience the reason you came to me, Trent?"

"No." Trent hated himself this morning. First he'd hurt his wife, and now he'd hurt his friend by unintentionally bringing up his dark past. "Griffith isn't married, so what does he know about it? Colin and Ryland are married to my sisters, so I'd really rather not have this conversation with them."

Anthony relaxed and held his hand out, palm up. "Point taken. The thing is, Trent, if you got your information about how last night should have gone from the boys at school, it's not a wonder that it didn't go as planned. As for hurting your wife, I'm afraid the first time is difficult for a woman no matter what — a man too, for that matter. How was she this morning?"

Trent didn't answer, couldn't answer. He avoided Anthony's gaze but couldn't bring himself to actually get up out of the chair, as that would be too obvious an avoidance of the question.

"You didn't see her this morning?"

"I saw her." He had. He'd slipped in to make sure she was still sleeping peacefully before he left.

"Did you talk to her? Kiss her? I can already tell you didn't try again."

"Try again? Are you crazy? I broke my wife last night. She cried out in pain, and I caused it."

Anthony sighed. "Didn't your father ever . . ."

"No. I was so young when Father died. I don't know if he ever even talked to Griffith. It's not a subject that comes up on a regular basis with us."

"No, it wouldn't." Anthony scrubbed his hands over his face. "Awkward though it will be, I promise you I will talk to Griffith before he marries."

"He won't have this problem." Trent grunted.

Anthony lifted that annoying single brow. "He won't?"

"Do you think Griffith would be foolish enough to be trapped into a marriage? No, he'll know and love his wife before it ever becomes an issue. I have to think if I'd known Adelaide better, if we'd fallen in love like we were supposed to, last night would have gone better."

"Maybe." Anthony shrugged. "But probably not. You aren't the first man to fudge his wedding night and somehow the human race continues. Which means people get past it. You just have to take your time and learn together. Next time will be easier."

"Not if she hates me. I should have waited. What if what we've built isn't strong enough to withstand this?"

Anthony sighed. "Do you love her?"

Trent stared at the other man, feeling like the life had drained out of him. "I don't know."

Chapter 27

There's a moment of bliss when the morning arrives, when sleep still clings to the brain and all of the bad memories have yet to awaken.

Then there's the moment when everything crashes into reality with a heartrending wrench and sleeping until sometime next week sounds like a fabulous prospect.

Adelaide rode through both of those moments before daring to open her eyes. A quick glance revealed she'd somehow gotten back to her room, even though she'd fallen asleep in Trent's bed the night before. *Fallen asleep* was probably not the correct term. Cried herself into unconsciousness while he held her and stroked her hair would be a much more accurate description. She wiggled and twisted, verifying for herself that the pain indeed had been momentary and didn't return with the cold light of morning. The pain had in fact been gone before she'd fallen asleep, but part of her feared it would return.

A frown touched her face as she pushed back the covers and fought her way into a seated position. She had told him there was no more pain before she fell asleep, hadn't she? It had been uncomfortable and scary, but not as painful as she feared Trent thought. She'd been startled more than anything. And rather disappointed in the whole event, or rather the end of it. Trent had obviously not enjoyed it, and she knew she hadn't, so the only reason to do it would be in order to gain children. Unless, of course, it wasn't always like it was last night.

She dressed and then took fifteen minutes to decide if she wanted to have breakfast downstairs or in her room. On the one hand, she was hoping to catch Trent — if he had not already left the house. On the other, she would rather avoid the knowing looks the staff was probably giving each other this morning. As much as she wished she had someone to talk to, this wasn't the kind of thing she could discuss with her housekeeper. All of her new friends, if they could even be considered as such, were related to Trent, and she didn't want them to know that she had failed at being a proper wife.

Her mother was out of the question, as she would probably say it was the perfect time for Adelaide to make some sort of outlandish request of her husband. As if Adelaide would use his sense of guilt as shop credit. No wonder her father rarely spoke to her mother.

She could try her sister. Helena had been out from under their mother's thumb for well over a year now. And they were sisters. That would count for something, wouldn't it? Adelaide knew it was a foolish hope even as she thought it, but desperate people had been known to cling to slimmer hopes. Unfortunately even an absurdly early call to visit family would have to wait a couple of hours.

She had Rebecca fetch a breakfast tray, but after that her room felt stifling. If she wanted to preserve her sanity, she was going to have to find something to do.

Books had always been a source of solace for her, and the small library Trent had created from the old music room had become her favorite retreat.

She stumbled through the door, making the unpleasant discovery that the library was being cleaned by Lydia. A pregnant Lydia. Proof that the maid and the valet had managed to muddle through what Adelaide and

Trent had not.

Of all the servants to receive that knowing smile from, Lydia was probably the worst.

"Good morning, my lady." Lydia smiled, but any veiled suggestion behind it could only be put there by Adelaide's imagination. She hadn't expected the young woman to be that discreet. Surely everyone knew Trent had stayed the night last night.

Assuming he had stayed the night. What if he'd retreated back to Hawthorne House after taking her back to her room?

"I can finish later, if you'd like." Lydia packed up her dustcloth and cleaning supplies in a small bucket. "No one normally uses the room this early."

"No, no. Now is fine. I'm simply getting a book." Adelaide grabbed for the closest shelf and pulled off the first volume her fingers could find. "This book."

Now came the smile that said Lydia knew too much. And given her current situation, she probably did know too much. She certainly knew more than Adelaide. If things didn't go well with Helena, would Adelaide possibly be desperate enough to seek advice from the parlormaid?

"That's an interesting choice, my lady."

Adelaide glanced down to discover herself holding a book on animal husbandry. She slammed it back onto the shelf as if it were made of burning coals. Why was such a book even in a library in Town? That sort of thing belonged in the country.

"There's several novels over there." Lydia pointed to the larger bookcase on the other side of the room from Adelaide.

That would certainly be better than a manual on mating animals. Adelaide tried to hurry across the room without looking like she was hurrying. She was tempted to simply grab a book and run but that hadn't worked well for her a few moments ago, so she made herself look long enough to at least be sure she wasn't picking up a volume of love poems or the latest romantic gothic novel.

Out of the corner of her eye she saw Lydia squatting down to dust the bottom shelf.

"When is the baby coming?" Adelaide really didn't want to know, but at the same time she did. It was rather fascinating, having a servant with child who was not trying to hide it, as she'd heard of other servants doing. Besides, asking after the baby seemed to be one more way to immerse herself in this household where everyone else seemed to know each other's business.

Lydia stood and stretched her back. "This summer." She ran a hand over her belly.

"We're hoping to be settled in Hertfordshire before then. We were going to go next month, but Lord Trent asked if we could stay a bit longer. I think he wants to be a bit more settled before finding a new valet."

A wash of pink touched the maid's cheeks, as if she realized she might have said a bit too much. Did all the servants talk about them like that? Had Lydia simply forgotten she was talking to Adelaide and not Mabel or Eve?

Adelaide snatched an innocent-looking book from the shelf. "I'll take this one."

Lydia said nothing but gave a tight smile as Adelaide scurried out the door.

The morning crawled by until Adelaide couldn't take it anymore. Even though most of London's inhabitants were probably still in their dressing gowns, she dressed for the afternoon, gathered Rebecca, and departed from the house within the hour. The ride to Marylebone didn't take long, though they had to take more than one detour to avoid some of the areas under heavy construction. Soon Adelaide was marching to her sister's door, new calling card in hand. She ran her thumb over the name.

Lady Trent Hawthorne.

It was strange to think of the aversion she'd felt when first seeing these cards.

Nothing could be further removed from her current sense of pride.

The butler took her card and admitted her to the hall but had her wait there while he went to see if Lady Edgewick was home.

Adelaide prayed Helena was home. They'd never been particularly close, but who else could Adelaide turn to?

The butler returned, showing her into a drawing room and showing Rebecca to the kitchen, but it was another fifteen minutes before Helena arrived.

"Sister!" She entered the room with her deep red skirt billowing around her, arms extended as if she were greeting a long-lost friend. In a way she was. Adelaide and Helena hadn't really spoken since Helena's wedding. Nothing beyond a handful of increasingly brief letters.

Adelaide stepped into the hug with some confusion and not a little bit of relief. She'd been afraid her sister wouldn't want anything to do with her. Was it possible that marriage to a viscount had settled her?

Helena led them over to a sofa and sat, still clasping Adelaide's hands in hers. "Have you come to extend an invitation to the Duchess of Marshington's ball?"

Adelaide blinked. "Miranda is throwing a ball? I had no idea."

The sour turn of Helena's mouth killed Adelaide's budding hope that her sister was going to be of any comfort. "The paper this morning said she was undergoing preparations for such. Some even assumed it was in honor of you."

Adelaide sighed. She didn't think Trent's sister would be honoring her anytime soon. Not if he had anything to do with it. "I haven't heard anything."

Helena's shoulders slumped a bit. "Do remember us if she asks you about the guest list. Oh, and Mother told me she asked you to give a hint or two about sponsoring Lord Edgewick for your husband's fencing club. He's simply dying to get in there."

"I don't think I have any say in who Trent sponsors."

A frown marred Helena's smooth, pale face. "Why did you come, then?"

Sudden anger flashed through Adelaide. Her chest actually warmed with the emotion, her fingers curled in to her palms, nearly cramping as they threatened to poke a hole in her gloves. She had done everything ever asked of her growing up. She'd worn Helena's castoffs. She'd been Helena's dance partner, even learning the male steps for a dance or two. She'd waited quietly while every other girl her age took their bows and started finding husbands. But never, not once, had Helena thanked her for it or considered that maybe it hadn't been what Adelaide wanted to do. The bitterness of it all felt thick on her tongue as it coated her words with sarcasm. "I don't know. Perhaps I thought I'd come see my sister since we were in the same county for the first time in a year."

Helena waved a hand in the air. "We barely saw each other when we lived in the same house. Sentiment is for fools, Adelaide. Though I must congratulate you on having the nerve to trap the duke's brother. Such a shame you weren't able to land the duke himself."

The smirk on Helena's face indicated she didn't think it was a shame at all. Adelaide guessed that if it had been the duke who tumbled through the old wooden floor, Helena would have been beside herself with anger that her younger sister now outranked her. The truth was Adelaide still outranked her, but not by a significant amount.

Now, however, the only question that remained was how soon Adelaide could leave without being rude. Any notion of confiding in Helena had been obliterated by the unshakable feeling that her older sister would gladly trade the personal gossip for a voucher to Almack's.

The conversation fell flat then, though they did each manage to say a few things about the weather and the traffic. Even that topic brought another sour turn to Helena's lips because it only served to remind her that Adelaide was living in Mayfair while Helena was in the very respectable but not as exclusive Marylebone.

Helena plucked a stray thread from Adelaide's skirt. "You are going to get me an invitation to that ball, aren't you? We are family, after all."

And with that Adelaide didn't care about being rude anymore. She stood to her feet. "Sentiment is for fools, Helena." Nothing was going to mend the rift between the sisters, at least not anytime soon. Helena's mouth dropped open as Adelaide pushed past her and left the drawing room.

Her grand exit was spoiled a bit by having to wait in the front hall for her maid to be collected from the kitchen, and her sister did nothing but glare as she left the drawing room and stomped off.

Despite the indignation, which Adelaide decided she had every right to wallow in, sadness threatened to overwhelm her as she watched her sister's bold red skirts disappear. The difference between her relationship with Helena and Georgina's relationship with Miranda was stark and revealing. And it made Adelaide feel too many things at once, particularly on top of the confusing tumult of emotions from the night before.

Restless and tense, she didn't want to return to the house on Mount Street. When she was in the country, she'd taken long walks to sort things out in her mind. There weren't any rolling hills or rambling forests in London so she went for the next best thing.

She went to Hyde Park.

CHAPTER 28

Despite Anthony's assurances, Trent retreated to Hawthorne House instead of returning to his own lodgings.

Griffith looked up from his desk and grinned before looking back at the ledger in front of him. "Someone didn't come home last night. Or should I say someone finally went home last night."

Trent grunted and walked to the dart board to pick up the handful of darts. Griffith had installed the board several years ago, after he and Anthony became friends. No matter how much Griffith practiced, though, Anthony could still beat him soundly. Trent wouldn't admit to any aspirations of beating the marquis — at least not until he was considerably more proficient than he was now — but it was nice to have something to do when he came round to bother his older brother.

Juggling the darts in his hands, Trent

walked across the room until he was even with Griffith's desk. The heavy fragrance of Griffith's preferred morning tea still hung in the air, letting Trent know he really was disturbing the normal way of things with these morning visits.

He couldn't bring himself to care.

He let the first dart fly, frowning when it embedded in the outermost ring of the board. "I saw Anthony this morning."

Griffith glanced at the clock. "You've been busy. Rough night?"

Only a brother would dare to give a duke the look Trent gave Griffith. Even then it probably wasn't as scathing at Trent wanted it to be. His experience at giving strong, harsh looks to people was rather limited. "You could say that. Anthony's decided you're probably as woefully uneducated as I was so he intends to have a talk with you before you marry."

"Sounds delightful. Why are you here, then?" Griffith ran a finger down a column of numbers in the ledger before dipping his quill in the inkpot and jotting the sum at the bottom of the page.

One more reason Trent would make a terrible duke. Numbers took him forever to deal with. Though they might not if he spent as much time with them as Griffith did. He wasn't willing to find out.

He threw another dart, pleased when this one landed a bit closer to center. "I'm here because I think he's wrong."

"And you're basing this on . . . ?"

Trent threw two more darts in quick succession, one of them pinging off the metal hanger and the other one smacking into the wooden wall below the dart board. "He thinks I love my wife."

Slowly, ever so slowly, Griffith set the quill down on the desk. "And you don't?"

The remaining two darts clattered across Griffith's desk as Trent dropped them so he could pace. Considering the frequency with which he had been indulging in the habit lately, he was going to need new boots by the end of the week. "I don't know. How can I? I'm not even sure I knew she existed two months ago. And now she's here and she reads and hates carrots and would rather be living in the country. And I can't believe I'm saying this but I've actually considered taking her there. I don't know if that's love or a sense of obligation because I've muddled the only marriage either of us will ever have."

Griffith sat back in his chair, folded his hands over his middle, and stared at his thumbs.

Trent stopped pacing and braced his hands on his brother's desk, leaning over until he could skewer the larger man to the chair with his gaze. "Why haven't you married yet?"

That one infuriating eyebrow winged upward. "Why do you think?"

"Because you're an exacting perfectionist and there isn't a woman alive who would put up with having to keep her teacup three inches from the edge of the table at all times?" Trent pushed off the desk and resumed pacing.

Griffith tried to frown, but the edges of a grin crept through. "I don't make anyone else place their cup that way."

"Ah, yes, but we aren't married to you. We can ignore all your little personal rules. She'll have to live with them." It was well known in the family that Griffith liked things a certain way. He thought through everything, even the order in which he ate his meal. Trent had made the mistake of asking him about that once and had to sit through a bewildering discussion on how the flavors of different foods interacted and how some tastes lingered on the tongue, altering the experience of future bites.

"In a way, that's true." Griffith picked up the quill and ran his finger along the edge of the feather. "I have a plan for selecting a wife. It will happen soon enough, but I've already decided that when I marry her, I'll love her."

Trent scoffed. "It's not as easy as it sounds. Believe me, I'd be eternally grateful if I could just point to Adelaide and say 'I love her' and have everything fall into place. But I don't know how she thinks or what makes her happy. We're not connected like Ryland and Miranda or Colin and Georgina. Even Mother and Lord Blackstone have that certain thing about them when you look at them. That look that tells you they know each other inside and out. Isn't that what love is? It's what I always imagined I'd have. I remember Father quoting bad poetry to Mother and making her laugh all day long as she remembered it. I wanted that. I was going to take my time like Father did and have the next epic love story."

He collapsed against the wall, his voice growing small as he acknowledged out loud for the first time the death of the only dream he'd ever allowed himself to have. "That was the plan."

Griffith sighed and set his arms on the edge of the desk, one thumb rubbing along his forefinger. "Trent, you didn't give your life to Jesus to follow your own plan. You have to follow His plan, and for whatever reason He gave you Adelaide and you accepted her. Now what are you going to do about it?"

"How do you make yourself love someone, Griffith? And I'm not talking about the good Christian kind of love, where we extend charity and grace and forgiveness. That's the kind of love that keeps us from using our social clout to shun people like Lady Crampton." Trent placed his hands on Griffith's desk and leaned forward, this time pleading for help instead of glaring him into submission. "Griffith, how do I love my wife?"

Adelaide had enjoyed Hyde Park from the seat of Trent's curricle, but she adored it on foot. The Serpentine sparkled like a sea of jewels, and this far from Rotten Row she could hear the birds instead of the clatter of carriage wheels and snorts of horses. She lifted her face so the sun could reach past the rim of her bonnet, enjoying the heat on her skin when she felt chilled to the bone. It wasn't the kind of cold that came from the wind or wearing a dress that was too thin. The chill seemed to actually be coming from her bones, making her numb to everything.

She stepped on a rock, the sharp point digging through the thin sole of her slipper and proving at least one part of her could still feel something. With a yelp she danced sideways off the rock, stepping on her hem and nearly tossing herself nose first into the water she'd recently been admiring.

"My lady!" Her maid rushed forward, but Adelaide righted herself first, though not without smudging the bottom of her dress in the dirt and grass.

She frowned at the stain, knowing it wasn't the first dress she accidentally marked. As she walked away from the Serpentine she watched the smudged fabric dance above the toe of her slipper. A slipper she suddenly realized had lost its decorative bow somewhere along the way.

"Rebecca?"

"Yes, my lady?" The maid scurried from three paces back to Adelaide's side. Trent's unorthodox staff must be rubbing off on Adelaide since it even crossed her mind to suggest her maid stop walking so far behind her.

"How many dresses have I ruined since we came to London?"

"Completely ruined? Only two, my lady. I was able to fashion repairs on all the others." The maid sounded almost proud of

Adelaide for ruining only two dresses. There was something rather ridiculous in that, considering Rebecca likely didn't have more than four or five dresses in her entire wardrobe.

Adelaide restrained the urge to sigh. "And how many shoes?"

Rebecca beamed at her. "Oh, I've been able to fix all but one of those. I remembered to request extra ribbons from the cobbler this time."

Adelaide reached the top of a small rise and stopped to look around the park at all the people who seemed to have their life under control. "Hats?"

"I rearrange the feathers and ribbons sometimes, but we haven't lost a hat yet." The maid bit her lip. "Please don't ask about the gloves."

Adelaide knew better than to ask about the gloves. Her mother had started buying gloves in mass quantities almost as soon as Adelaide had gotten old enough to wear them.

No wonder things had gone so badly last night. Adelaide was a klutz. She'd never really had to admit it before, though she was fairly certain everyone knew it. They'd been wealthy enough and her mother had liked to shop enough that her wardrobe destructions were never that noticeable. There was always another dress, another pair of shoes, another hat, fifteen more pairs of gloves.

But there wasn't another Trent. She couldn't shove her husband into the ragbag and get another because she'd messed this one up. It was time for Adelaide to grow up and stop blaming her upbringing for everything.

Perhaps it was even time to stop trying to make everyone happy.

Her mother wanted her to be socially ambitious and popular. And to be honest, the skills she'd acquired growing up — of doing whatever was expected of her and disappearing whenever she wished — would probably stand in her in good stead if she wanted to pursue such a life. But she had only to look at her parents to see the cost of living life that way, a cost she wasn't willing to pay.

But what did Trent need her to be? Despite his claim to the contrary, he enjoyed being social. He spent time at the clubs, taking her out for rides and meals and ice treats. He needed someone poised, capable, and polished who could attend the horse race with him one day and the opera the next with a sophisticated soiree in between.

She knew now that she could handle herself in all of those situations, could interact with numerous people as long as she didn't have to start the conversation. The only problem was that she did so while looking like an oafish simpleton.

Trent hadn't asked for this marriage. The least she could do was give him a wife who was a real lady. A wife who rose to the expectations created by the women who'd already filled his life.

She strolled along, trying to figure out what ladies did that she needed to learn. Elegance and poise such as Georgina possessed was a necessity. It was doubtful that young lady ever returned to the house less presentable than when she left it. Wit, such as Miranda and Lady Raebourne utilized, would certainly be an asset. The way both of them and even Griffith were able to turn conversations and politely handle people with a turn of phrase was a skill she desperately wanted to learn. Could such a thing be learned? Could any of them teach her?

With renewed purpose, Adelaide trod across the park and hailed a hack to take her and Rebecca back across Mayfair. There was only one thing, one person, all of those women had in common. And the very thought scared her until her mouth turned dry.

At least three times she raised her fist to stop the driver and have him turn around. Each time she took a deep breath and whispered a pleading prayer for strength before letting the driver continue. Rebecca sat in the other seat in wide-eyed silence, occasionally glancing out the window as if to discern where they were going.

Finally the carriage stopped at another town house, and Adelaide was presenting her card to another butler. Her entrance this time was immediate and welcoming.

Adelaide waited in the drawing room, determined not to run. Less than five minutes passed before she heard someone enter behind her. She whirled around, pasting a smile on her face that she hoped looked confident and friendly instead of reflecting the ill feeling that was growing in her midsection. "Good afternoon, Lady Blackstone. I need your help."

Chapter 29

Trent should have known better than to ask his brother a question. Griffith didn't do things like a normal man, speculating and pulling from his prior knowledge to answer a question. No, when Griffith needed answers, he researched.

"Can I leave now?" Trent tilted his head back over the edge of the club chair he'd sprawled in. It had been an hour since Trent asked his question, and Griffith had responded by summoning a footman and sending out three letters. Then he'd gone back to work and told Trent to make himself comfortable.

"No."

That was it. No explanation, no reassurances. And yet, Trent waited. It wasn't as if Griffith was going to come after him and bodily restrain him if he tried to leave. At least he didn't think Griffith would do such a thing. But he'd asked a question, and Griffith seemed to think the answer was coming, so Trent waited. His older brother had never let him down before.

A loud *thunk* drew Trent's attention, and he rose, waiting for Griffith to stop him from leaving the room. When no objection came, Trent wandered out of the study and toward the front hall. Finch stood next to Trent's traveling trunk, discussing with Griffith's butler how to transport the trunk back to Mount Street.

"Finch?"

"Yes, my lord?"

Trent cleared his throat. "What are you doing?"

Finch looked at the trunk and then back at Trent, a hint of worry creeping across his face. "Packing us to return home, sir? His Grace informed me that you had decided to move back."

Trent stared at the trunk. Part of Trent wanted to resist, to send the trunk back upstairs and return things to the way they'd been yesterday.

But things weren't the same as they'd been yesterday. And while Trent didn't regret his courtship plan, it was time to move on. There was no reason to stay in Hawthorne House any longer.

"Should I take it back upstairs, my lord?"

Finch shifted his weight from foot to foot, casting anxious looks at the trunk, the butler, and the corridor that led to Griffith's open study door.

"No." Trent swallowed. "No, Griffith is correct. It's time for us to go home."

And it really was. Was this what Griffith had been keeping him here for? Had he been giving Trent the time needed to come to his own conclusions and understand that it was time to move on?

A forceful knock echoed through the front hall and Gibson, the butler, strode calmly to the door to answer it.

"I had a feeling such a summons would be forthcoming," Anthony said as he patted Gibson on the shoulder and strolled into the house, looking exceptionally more put together than he had when Trent invaded his home early that morning.

Trent's mouth dropped open a bit as Anthony turned him toward the back of the house and gave him a light shove in the direction of Griffith's study.

Trent stomped into the room and glared at his brother. "You called in the cavalry?"

Griffith shrugged. "I don't know the answer, and you've already established that what you've learned from books and rumor is wrong, so the obvious choice is to ask someone trustworthy with firsthand experience."

"Griffith, I'm touched." Anthony placed a hand over his heart and pretended to swoon into the club chair across from the one Trent had been occupying.

"Don't be." Griffith grunted and began stacking his ledgers and clearing his desk. "I hear there's going to be a lecture before I marry."

Trapped in what was sure to be life's most awkward conversation ever, Trent fell back into his chair and draped his arms over the sides before sticking his legs out to cross them at the ankles.

Anthony's grin was unrepentant. "Would you rather get it from Trent? I'm assuming he'll have time to figure everything out by then, unless you've got something in the works you're not telling us."

"He has a plan," Trent muttered, happy to see someone else under scrutiny, if only for a little while.

Griffith didn't even blink or bother raising his arrogant eyebrow. He also didn't hesitate as he continued putting his things in order. "I always have a plan."

The next knock interrupted the conversation, and Colin entered with Ryland on his heels. Trent's brief reprieve was over. The assembling crowd would give him helpful, godly advice, but he had no doubt that they were going to humiliate him first.

"Gentlemen," Griffith said, rising from his position behind his desk once everyone had claimed seats around the room. "The question I'd like to put to you today — more for Trent's benefit than my own, though I do find myself curious as well — is what you mean when you say you love your wife. And how one is supposed to go about attaining that emotion."

Three powerful men stared. Not a word was spoken, leaving the tick of the mantel clock the only noise in the room. Griffith waited them out. Trent tried to do the same but found himself fidgeting under the weight of silence.

"Well, that was not what I expected," Anthony said at last.

Colin ran a hand behind his neck and cast a look over at Ryland before addressing Griffith once more. "You realize that's a bit of a tricky question, don't you?"

That drew forth the arrogant eyebrow. Trent was really going to have to discover an exercise of some kind to learn how to do that. "If the question were simple I wouldn't need to assemble all of you, would I?"

"I think what he means," Ryland said

dryly, "is that he and I are married to your sisters, and this discussion has the potential to get more personal than you might like."

Griffith nodded in understanding before leaning back against his desk and crossing his arms over his wide chest. "Trent informed me that Anthony has already covered a discussion of the more physical aspect."

Trent groaned and closed his eyes, praying for the Lord's return. Any moment now would be nice and then he wouldn't have to deal with the problem or this conversation.

Ryland's smirk was evident in his voice. "That must have been interesting."

"You have no idea." Anthony kicked Trent's extended legs. "Pay attention, pup. We're only assembling for this conversation once, so take notes."

"First, know you aren't going to change her." Colin held up a single finger. "You love her as she is, flaws and all, because you've got flaws of your own that she's going to have to embrace."

A laugh burst from Griffith before he could attempt to contain it to a series of snorts and coughs. "Please tell me you've mentioned that part to Georgina."

That mental image took the edge off of Trent's anxiety. Georgina was exceptionally good at presenting a picture of perfection to the world.

Anthony nodded. "But at the same time, you are going to change each other. The closer you get to her, the more you'll adapt to each other. It's hard to explain, but it happens. One day you're making yourself wade through acres of flowers because she likes them, and before you know it, instead you're just having to accept a ridiculous number of vases filled with fresh flowers all over your house."

"Sounds fragrant," Griffith muttered.

Anthony grimaced and shrugged.

Ryland sat forward and stretched one long arm toward Griffith's desk, where a Bible sat on the corner. "You really want to love your wife? Let's talk Isaac and Rebekah."

"I'd think Ephesians would be a better place to start." Colin leaned an elbow on the arm of his chair in order to better see the Bible in Ryland's lap.

Anthony crossed the room to lean over Ryland's shoulder. "What about First Peter?"

Griffith remained leaning against his desk with his arms over his chest, but he turned his head and caught Trent's eye with a self-satisfied smile on his face. Trent had to concede to his older brother once more. As much as he hated to admit it, calling these men in had been the right thing to do. One could never go wrong with advice from the Bible.

"I need you to teach me how to be a lady." Adelaide sat in her mother-in-law's drawing room wishing there was another way to describe what she wanted. Also wishing that she'd decided to go to Miranda, Georgina, or even Lady Raebourne first. But this new idea of taking charge of things hadn't had much time to grow a logical side yet, so she'd gone straight to the person who'd taught her daughters the skills she wanted to know.

"Nonsense." Caroline waved a hand through the air. "All you lack is a bit of grace. You've the tact of an angel and there's absolutely nothing wrong with that, though perhaps a bit more gumption is in order."

Adelaide blinked at the matter-of-fact compliment. "Oh."

"Now. Let's start with how to sit." Caroline led Adelaide over to a grouping of chairs.

Sitting seemed like a strange thing to teach. Adelaide had been successfully getting in and out of chairs for as long as she could remember. Had she been doing it wrong? How could there be a wrong way to do it? Adelaide lowered herself into the chair. Once seated she tried to fold her hands gently into her lap, but the dress pulled at her shoulder. Her skirt was folded underneath her in a way that severely limited how much she could move without wriggling her clothing into a better position.

She turned wide eyes to Caroline in time to see her nearly float into her own chair, skirts delicately spread on the seat to allow adequate movement in all directions.

Adelaide couldn't even sit in a chair correctly. This was going to take considerably more than a single afternoon.

She was late. Caroline had made her rise and sit so many times that her legs were burning by the time she'd gotten home. Dressing for the night had taken twice as long as normal, and now she stood at the top of the stairs, terrified to take the first step.

There were no polished black evening shoes visible in the hall at the bottom of the stairs. Was it possible he wasn't here yet? Could she still await him in the drawing room so that she wouldn't have to notice if he'd lost that look of wonder he always wore when she came down the stairs?

"You're lovely."

The deep, quiet voice at her side made her jump and clutch for the top of the stair railing.

With a firm hand gripping her elbow, she knew she was in no danger of tumbling headfirst down the stairs, but it still took her a moment to pull her gaze from the treacherous stairs.

To her right, in the corner of her vision were the shoes she'd been expecting down below, the polished leather catching the light of the stairway candelabra. Her gaze climbed up, across buff-colored trousers and then the blue stripes of his waistcoat before giving way to the deeper blue of his cutaway coat. One hand clasped her elbow while the other rested at the small of his back, emphasizing his broad shoulders and making her middle jump in a way she'd thought it never would again.

But it was his face that truly robbed her breath. The wonder was still there, thank God. But it was veiled now, with some other undefinable emotion. Fear? Worry? Was he as nervous to see her again as she was to see him?

"You're home."

"Yes."

She didn't know what to say to that. She'd

wondered if, even dared to hope, he would be returning. Was it possible they could move forward and she could stop worrying if he ever meant them to be more than only a public couple?

"Shall we?" He let go of her elbow and offered his arm. For the first time in their wedded life they walked down the stairs together. It was an important moment, Adelaide knew, and she did her best to follow Caroline's hasty instructions so she didn't muss the elegant picture they surely made.

They didn't say anything as they crossed the hall, but he pulled her to a stop before they reached the door.

"Adelaide." He cleared his throat and turned her to take both of her hands in his own. "I need you to know I'm going to be a good husband."

Thick emotions she couldn't begin to name choked her throat.

His gloved hand lifted and smoothed his bent knuckles across her cheek. "You don't have to say anything, but I do. I want to make things right with you, and I think, from here on, we move forward without a plan or a scheme. Could we do that? Can you give me one more clean slate, Adelaide?"

"My mother knew." The words tumbled

out of her mouth, as if her tongue were racing to get her own confession out of the way so they could claim a new start together.

Trent opened his mouth and then shut it with a click of teeth. He blinked at her. "Knew what?"

"That we were there. In the ruins. She was the one we heard drive by."

"And she left you there to force our marriage?"

Adelaide winced, knowing she needed to come completely clean but not wanting to. "She thought you were Griffith."

Silence pressed in for a moment, and then Trent threw his head back and laughed. "No one can accuse us of being normal, Adelaide, that is for certain."

An answering smile stretched across her face, and giddy freedom bubbled into her own laughter.

He leaned over and skimmed a gentle kiss along her lips. "No more secrets, no more schemes. I promise not to hurt you again, Adelaide. I will be a good husband."

The little memory of her snooping through his study drawers ran through her mind, but she pushed it away. That wasn't a secret, not really. It was the type of thing people learned when they lived together. As long as she never brought it up it would never be an issue.

The tightness around his green eyes lessened as his laughter faded into a brilliant smile complete with a deep dimple in his left cheek. As he escorted her out the door, Adelaide thought about her feet, made sure her head was held steady so she wouldn't dislodge her feathers or her curls, and maintained a respectable distance between her body and Trent's so as not to accidentally trod on his foot the way she had a few nights ago on their way in to a musicale.

The ache that hit her legs as she tried to climb into the carriage almost made her turn back and decide the opera wasn't worth going to after all. Only the knowledge that she'd still have to climb stairs to get back into the house propelled her forward. After meticulously adjusting her skirts so that she wouldn't pull off any ribbons or stress any seams, she folded her hands in her lap, keeping her average-sized reticule secure so it wouldn't lose any of the fringe circling the base. Without a book inside, the bag felt light, and she worried that she would swing it around indiscriminately because of that.

Trent climbed in after her, easing into the seat with the same unconscious care that he always did. He wasn't pretending to be a consummate gentleman. It had been bred into him while he was still in short pants.

"Did you know," she said as the carriage began rolling, "that one of the first operas in the United Kingdom was performed on a covered tennis court?"

Laughter immediately filled the carriage. Trent reached over and took Adelaide's hand, pressing it between his own. That alone made her mad dash through the library at Lady Blackstone's house worth it. She'd wanted something to break the potential tension of the evening, and the book on the history of the theater had provided exactly what she needed.

He didn't say anything as the laughter faded away but he wrapped his hand around hers and stared at it, running one finger along the seam of her glove, following it from finger to finger, sending shivers from her hand, along her spine, to the tips of her toes curling in her slippers. "There's one more thing I need to say, Adelaide. I want to apologize. Last night I —"

"Please don't." Adelaide lifted her free hand and pressed her fingers over his lips, causing surprise to break through whatever thoughts had been focused on setting things right. "We're starting over, remember? Clean slate. I'm well. Honestly, I am. So I think the best thing we could do now is enjoy the opera."

He looked at her for a moment, long enough that she began to wonder if they were going to discuss it after all. But then his smile returned, his even, white teeth barely visible through the curved lips. "Agreed. We'll enjoy our evening. Have you ever been to the opera?"

She shook her head. "No, but once Father took me to Birmingham with him, and we went to the theater."

"How old were you?"

How old had she been? It had been several years. Before Helena had started coming to London. "I think I was twelve. Perhaps thirteen."

"And that was the last time you went to a theater?" His voice was quiet as London rolled by the carriage window.

"I always caught the traveling shows when they came through Riverton." She knew that wasn't what he meant but she didn't want his pity tonight. She wanted to be a lady, worthy of respect and perhaps even a little bit of love. If they were going to start anew, that seemed like as good a goal to work for as anything.

They climbed out of the carriage, and Adelaide was so distracted she almost snagged her trim on the carriage door. She sucked her breath in between her teeth as she carefully leaned back to dislodge the trim from the door hinge. Perhaps tomorrow she could make it an hour without mussing up her outfit. She at least needed to make it for the hour she was going to spend at Caroline's house practicing how to sit and learning how to walk. Perhaps they could adjust the lesson to include climbing into carriages properly.

She curled her fingers around Trent's offered arm, giving it a light squeeze that drew another one of his dimple-inducing, heart-stopping smiles, making her remember his passionate kisses before everything had gone wrong. She smiled to herself as they entered the opera house. Maybe she didn't want to forget everything about the past twenty-four hours after all.

CHAPTER 30

Trent was supposed to be responding to something Colin was saying — that was a person's normal role in a conversation, after all — but instead he was staring at his wife on the other side of the conversation circle in Griffith's opera box. Something was different, and Trent had no idea what it was. He couldn't say for sure what it was about his wife, but she was not the same young woman he'd become accustomed to taking about town.

They'd arrived at the opera with barely enough time to greet the other occupants of the box before settling in for the first act of the performance, which meant intermission was the first opportunity they'd actually had to converse with Colin and Georgina, who had decided to join them tonight. The current conversation was mostly between Georgina and Adelaide, though Colin threw in an observation or two along the way.

They stood in a circle behind the chairs, stretching their legs and avoiding some of the curious eyes that always watched the aristocratic boxes for interesting gossip.

Not that there was much of interest to be seen with two married couples as the only occupants of the box, but Trent was starting to crave his privacy in ways he never had before. It could possibly have something to do with having had his life dissected earlier that day by a group of men he highly respected.

They were discussing the costumes of the first act now, something Trent really didn't have an opinion on because he hadn't paid much attention. He'd been too busy making sure Adelaide was enjoying her evening. If they hadn't had their vague but cleansing conversation in the carriage, he would have counted the change as awkwardness or even worry, but he truly felt they'd moved on. Moved on to what he wasn't sure, but they'd moved beyond whatever limbo he'd put them in with his courtship idea. Still there was something more, something missing. His eyes ran the length of her, wondering if she needed to stretch her legs more than they were already doing. He'd brave the crowds in the outer corridors if she needed to walk.

But she wasn't fidgeting. She was hardly moving at all, which was very unlike the Adelaide he'd come to know. Normally she exuded a quiet but bubbly sort of life, which was probably how she always ended up with her ensemble in disarray. Trent's lips quirked up as he took in his wife once more, this time searching for some adorable flaw in her appearance.

"Don't you agree, Trent?" Colin smirked as he aimed the question Trent's way.

He wasn't about to admit that he hadn't been listening, so he took the risk of agreeing. "Of course."

"There, you see, Adelaide? Trent agrees that it would be ridiculous to stay in London during the summer heat. Now you've only to decide which of the estates you want to go to."

Trent wanted to glare at Colin — he really did — but there was such hope in Adelaide's face that he couldn't look away from it. He didn't know when or how the topic had veered away from the bizarre costumes of the opera, but did it matter?

Scripture from his afternoon at Hawthorne House drifted through his mind.

". . . she became his wife, and he loved her . . ."

"Husbands, love your wives, even as Christ

also loved the church, and gave himself for it."

". . . giving honour unto the wife . . ."

Trent looked at the joy on Adelaide's face at the mere thought of returning to the country, and his decision was made. What was keeping him in the city year-round, anyway? Just because he stayed on one of his estates for a while didn't mean he had to get involved in the day-to-day running of things. His estate managers could carry on as if he weren't there, and he'd be taking care of his wife, giving of himself for her. It wasn't easy and it didn't feel like love yet, but it felt right and that was a start.

"Why don't we go to Suffolk?" Trent asked, unable to resist running one knuckle down her cheek when it was lit by such a wide smile. "I've yet to see it. You spent time there as a child, didn't you?"

Adelaide nodded. "Father always stayed there when he went to the races. He usually took me with him. We stopped going about five years ago."

When Helena had come to London. Had life stopped for her with her sister's societal debut? Trent gave serious consideration to calling her parents on the carpet for their favoritism and negligence, but that would require spending time in their presence, and he was becoming more and more determined to avoid that unless absolutely necessary — and to keep Adelaide as far away from them as possible as well.

"It's settled, then. We summer in Suffolk. Maybe Colin and Georgina will even come visit."

Now he was volunteering to host country house parties? Was there anything he wasn't willing to do if it meant making Adelaide happy?

Colin rubbed his chin in thought. "I've never really looked into horses. They're a rather unpredictable investment, but it could be fun."

Georgina sighed. "You don't need another project." Her nose wrinkled. "And horses smell."

Colin frowned. "But I've already stepped away from the shipping, and now I'm putting less in corn. I need something to do."

"Be glad you didn't marry a businessman, Adelaide. I spend half my life competing with profit shares and stock exchanges." Georgina tempered the complaint with a small smile.

No one had been more surprised than Trent when Georgina had declared herself in love with Colin. Perhaps because he'd seen them at the beginning of their acquaintance when the mere sight of the man made Georgina flush with irritation.

That volatile emotion had transformed over time, making them one of the most devoted couples Trent had ever known. The way they helped and supported each other was a thing of beauty.

Servants began dousing some of the candles, signaling an end to the intermission. Colin wound an arm around his wife's waist as he led her back to her chair. "You know, if you want me to put down the newspapers, all you have to do is ask."

His sister's cheeks pinked slightly, and Trent hurriedly escorted Adelaide to their seats at the front of the box.

Sometimes Trent really hated being such good friends with his sisters' husbands.

She wouldn't have thought one small change could cause such a disturbance in her morning routine, but the knowledge that Trent would be in the house seemed to change every pattern she'd formed over the last few weeks. Adelaide had gotten in the habit of dressing herself in the mornings and only requiring Rebecca's services when she dressed for the afternoon.

But now Trent was home. Would he expect her to come down properly dressed and coiffed? She stared at the ceiling, wondering if she should ring for Rebecca or simply keep to her normal routine. Whatever she chose couldn't be as awkward as their return from the opera.

He'd escorted her in, but it seemed strange somehow for him to lean in for a kiss as had been their custom before . . . well, before. Especially since he hadn't stopped at the bottom of the stairs but had escorted her all the way up to their shared parlor. The enjoyment from the evening made the unusual end feel all the stranger. He'd darted in and given her a quick kiss before exchanging a stilted good-night and retreating to his room.

Now knowing he was on the other side of that door, that she'd be seeing him at breakfast, that she was going to have to watch every move she made for the entire day and not just the evening, all of those things made her terrified to get out of bed.

The soft knock at her door made her jump. At first she thought it came from Trent's room but then the door from the parlor opened and Rebecca came in. "Good morning, my lady."

Adelaide sat up in bed. "How did you know to come this morning?"

Her maid pulled back the curtains, letting

in the morning light before bustling to the dressing room. "Lord Trent will be at breakfast this morning." She paused at the door and tossed Adelaide a smile that could almost be termed cheeky. "I'm starting to learn how this house functions, my lady. It takes a bit of getting used to."

"I know what you mean." Adelaide threw the covers back and submitted herself to Rebecca's ministrations, already missing the comfort of her old morning dresses and braided hair. Lady Blackstone's rules had been firm, though, that she was never to let her appearance put her at a disadvantage. Adelaide assumed that included when she was dealing with her husband.

The sacrifice was worth it though, when Trent's eyes followed her across the breakfast room to the sideboard. She fixed her plate, carrying it to the table carefully. Rebecca had stared openly when Adelaide returned from the opera last night looking nearly as put together as when she'd left. It had been a difficult thing and she had nearly broken her fan, but overall she'd been impressed with herself, if a bit uncomfortable. There was candle wax on her glove and she'd apparently bumped her toe against a soot-stained wall at some point, but the dress was intact, her hair still perfect

— or as perfect as it could be with hair that now occasionally got trapped in her eyelashes — and her reticule unblemished.

She intended to continue her appearance-maintaining habits this morning, even if they took more thought than she liked to give her clothing. So much thought that last night she often had trouble following the conversation and giving adequate attention to her gloves at the same time. Eventually she hoped the careful movements would become second nature and she wouldn't have to think about them all the time. Being a proper lady was exhausting.

Her plate made it to the table without incident, but it unnerved her to try to sit correctly with Trent's eyes glued to her. He waited until she was situated to resume his seat.

"I'll be out for a while, but I'll be back in time for our ride this afternoon." He cleared his throat and ran his napkin through his fingers. "Assuming you still wish to go for a ride."

She nodded. "That would be nice. I don't have any other particular plans."

And so their morning went.

And every morning after for the next two weeks.

From what little Adelaide knew of marriages, the Hawthorne ones notwithstanding, theirs was a better than average existence. They talked. She continued to look up interesting facts to share on their afternoon rides. Cooking was turning out to be something she enjoyed and was actually good at. After Adelaide mastered the cooking of bacon, Mrs. Harris had moved her on to more complicated dishes.

It wasn't the most ladylike of pursuits, but even Caroline had been forced to admit that Adelaide would never be a normal lady. Though she still gave Adelaide suggestions on how not to ruin slippers and hemlines, she'd given up on the gloves and simply suggested Adelaide keep an extra pair in her reticule now that a book no longer took up most of the space.

Mr. Givendale came by to visit Trent twice more, always when he wasn't home and always when another visitor had just left, leaving Adelaide stuck in the front hall when he tried to gain entrance. She never invited him in for tea again, but they always seemed to stand in the front hall chatting for a few moments without her ever intending to enter into a conversation. Fenton would clear his throat and Adelaide would wish the man a good afternoon. It had been odd but never concerning.

They went to his mother's card party and let everyone in the family believe that everything had worked out between them, and in a way she supposed it had. It hadn't become the marriage she'd been hoping for when he first proposed his courtship idea, but it was better than she'd actually thought she'd have.

She did want children though, and she didn't know how to broach the topic.

Now sitting at the breakfast table two weeks after Trent had moved back in, her fork poking holes in her ham, she admonished herself to keep giving it time.

"Mr. Lowick is coming by today. I don't know if you know him. He manages the Suffolk estate."

Adelaide nodded as she carefully chewed and swallowed her toast, taking care that not a single crumb escaped. Caroline's lessons had gotten easier to apply but she still had to be very conscious of everything she did. "Oh, yes, I remember him. Would it be a terrible imposition of me to greet him while he's here? He used to sneak me candies when I was a child."

"Of course. I'll have someone let you know when he's been shown to my study, and you may come in at your leisure. I haven't met him yet, though we've exchanged letters a few times." Trent's plate was empty, but he didn't leave the table. "Have you any other plans for the day?"

Adelaide sighed. Was this what they were to become, then? Polite strangers sharing a house? Little more than housemates? A rather lonely existence stretched out before her and the pressing need to establish a connection — any connection — made her heart race. "Your mother is coming by this afternoon."

Trent choked on his tea. "My mother?"

Adelaide nodded. She hadn't told Trent of her lessons because she didn't know what he'd think about them. Despite his declaration that they were to have no more secrets between them, the intimacy of that moment before the opera had disappeared, and she felt compelled to maintain the idea that everything was perfect. That she was perfect. "She's going to show me how to address invitations."

"How to address . . . I see. Good. I'm glad." He took another sip of tea and adjusted the fork he'd put down on his empty plate moments before. "Are we having a gathering?"

Panic tightened Adelaide's grip on her own fork. Should she have cleared her plans with Trent beforehand? It had been a spur-of-the-moment decision at Lady Blackstone's the day before, an act of near desperation in her attempt to be a better wife. "I thought we might have your family over for dinner, a sort of trial gathering, if you will. The house isn't really ready for much entertaining. Your mother and I thought about three weeks from now would be good timing."

Trent smiled, easing Adelaide's unease. "That's a splendid idea. Be sure to include Anthony and Amelia." His smiled dropped a bit at the corners. "Is it . . . ? Are we only inviting *my* family?"

The thought of having her mother and Helena in the same room as two dukes and a marquis made Adelaide want to push the rest of her breakfast aside. "Yes. I think my family might wait for another time."

Or never, given that she couldn't remember the last time her mother and father had attended an intimate gathering at the same time. They rarely even sat down to dinner together at home in the country.

She was beginning to have an idea as to why.

"I think that might be wise." Trent fiddled with his fork a bit more, seeming about to say something else before changing his mind. Instead he stood and started to lean over her chair as if he were going to give her a kiss before starting his day. She rather hoped he would follow through on the motion, but he righted himself instead. "I'll be in my study if you need anything. Mr. Lowick should be here in a couple of hours."

"All right." She watched him walk from the room before turning back to her plate.

They were making progress, weren't they? He'd stayed after finishing his food and had almost kissed her good morning. There was no need to wallow in self-pity simply because things weren't moving as fast as she'd like.

She stabbed at her breakfast until it turned cold and then abandoned the unappetizing mess to retreat to her small study to take care of what little correspondence she had before Lady Blackstone arrived. At the top of the pile was a note from her mother inviting her to tea that afternoon. Who invited someone for tea? Did her mother think she'd be so rude as to not return the exceedingly brief visit she'd made earlier that week? While it was true Adelaide had contemplated doing such a thing, she didn't think she'd have had the nerve to follow through on the notion.

The three other items on her desk were easily taken care of, and then she had nothing to do but wait and stare at the peeling wall coverings and compare their sad state to that of her own life until Lady Blackstone was announced.

Chapter 31

There were fewer than ten people in Trent's family. Invitations to a simple dinner should not have taken very long — at least Adelaide hadn't expected them to. She hadn't counted on Lady Blackstone's exacting measures on proper penmanship and address. By the time the countess was satisfied, Adelaide had done four complete sets of invitations. They had then pulled Mrs. Harris in to discuss the menu, which took another half an hour but thankfully didn't leave Adelaide with a cramp in her wrist.

By the time Lady Blackstone took her leave, Mr. Lowick had been in Trent's office for two hours, and Adelaide was afraid she'd missed him. Not that it would be that devastating. Trent had promised they would go to Suffolk this summer, so she would see the man then. It wasn't even that she'd been all that close to him. He'd been employed by her father, after all. Adelaide thought maybe it was a desire to establish the connection between her past and her present, to remind herself and Trent that something good had come of their union.

She knocked softly at Trent's study door.

"Enter."

With a proper ladylike smile that even Lady Blackstone would approve of, Adelaide pushed her way into the room. "Pardon the interruption — a little later than expected, but I'm afraid my morning went a little differently than planned."

Trent grinned without restraint. "My mother made you write everything six times, didn't she."

"Well, four, but the invitations look stunning."

Surprise and something that might have been pride flickered across her husband's face. "Four? Your penmanship must be exquisite. I dare you to send out the first set and see if she notices."

Such a thing had never crossed her mind — would never cross her mind, as she'd never been brave enough to step outside of expectations before. Marrying Trent had been enough out of the normal way of things to make her the subject of speculation for another three years, at least. Still, the invitations were only going to family members, and the playful gleam in his eyes was so tempting that she found herself drawn in. "Perhaps the second set. I spelled your sister Georgina's name incorrectly on the first set."

The approval in his smile made her want to send the first set out even with the incorrectly spelled name.

Trent stood and came around his desk, sweeping an arm toward the country gentleman standing in front of one of the chairs in the study. "You remember Mr. Lowick, don't you, Lady Adelaide?"

Adelaide had completely forgotten the man was in the room, but she tried to cover it with a gracious smile and a tilted head, berating herself for having forgotten her manners and determined to be perfection for the rest of the meeting. "Of course. I'm glad I was able to see you before you left. I remember walking the estate with you and my father as a child."

"Oh, yes," the older man said. "I used to sneak you pieces of peppermint as we walked." He pulled a small tin from his pocket. "I still carry some everywhere. Would you care for a piece?"

As she smiled and took a piece, it was nice to be reminded that not all of her growing-up moments were dark and dismal.

The sweet flavor of the peppermint brought back images of sunrises on dew-dampened fields and horse rides across flowery meadows. Summer couldn't come soon enough for her country sensibilities.

"Your timing is perfect, Adelaide. Mr. Lowick and I were just finishing up." Trent crossed the floor to stand next to her, as if they were a single unit sending off one of their guests. Would they stand like this when they greeted his family at their dinner party? Stand together as the couples filed out? She was suddenly looking forward to an evening that had seemed more of a chore or a rite of passage a few hours earlier. Of course, once everyone was gone they would probably coldly part ways and go to their separate rooms unless she could take the time between now and then to convince him that she was a perfect wife despite their earlier stumbles.

Mr. Lowick slid a stack of papers into his leather satchel. "I'll take the mail coach Monday morning and start implementing these crop plans as soon as possible. It's still early enough in the spring that the changes should be easy enough to make."

"Oh, wonderful. Are we going to do the pineapples, then?"

Silence met Adelaide's question. Tense

silence. Adelaide bit her lip. She wasn't supposed to know about the pineapples, had only come across the plans because she'd been going through Trent's drawers, but she'd still been dreaming of them as a unified, sharing couple, and she'd been unable to let the opportunity to prove she knew something about him slide by.

The stunned curiosity on Mr. Lowick's face proved that pineapples had not been discussed in that meeting. She was almost afraid to look at Trent, but she told herself that being a coward would only make it worse to deal with later.

His easy smile was gone, replaced with a dark frown. Irritation narrowed his green eyes, devoid of any trace of laughter. All the softness she'd grown accustomed to seeing in his face disappeared. She'd never seen him mad, wasn't sure many people had, but there was no doubting that he was feeling the emotion now.

"What do you know of pineapples?"

A glance away from Trent's angry scowl revealed that Mr. Lowick really wanted to leave. Only Adelaide and Trent were blocking the door, and she didn't think Trent would take kindly to a suggestion that they move out of the way. "I was looking for the invitations Fenton set aside for me. Lady

Raebourne said sometimes you stuff them in a drawer. I saw the drawing and was curious. I'm so sorry. I shouldn't have looked, I know, but it was fascinating. And I thought maybe, since Suffolk had so many horse farms you would be able to get the . . . well . . . the necessary elements for your plan. I never meant . . . ." Adelaide swallowed, her mouth dry after her rushed explanation. "I never meant any harm."

Trent rubbed his hands over his face and pushed his fingers into his blond hair, sending it flopping around his head in a tangled mess that only made him look more fashionable and handsome. It really wasn't fair that the man wore dishevelment so well.

"Begging your pardon, sir, but I've heard about pineapples. They're very precious, but I don't know that they can be grown in England." Mr. Lowick held his satchel in one hand and scratched his head with the other.

The sigh that drug its way out of Trent's chest sounded painful. As if he knew he were about to say something he would later regret.

"The Dutch." Trent stopped and cleared his throat. "The Dutch have come up with a method for growing them in greenhouses. I sketched out a few modifications to make it more efficient, but I hadn't planned on doing anything with it."

"And it involves horse, er, byproduct?"

"Yes." Trent nodded, his lips pressed tight and his eyes sad as he fought some inner battle. Adelaide couldn't believe she'd done this to him. After all of her intentions, all her plans to be the best wife she could possibly be, she'd gone and done this. Exposed something he'd never meant to show anyone. Though her limited knowledge recognized the plans were well thought out and rather remarkable, he obviously thought they weren't and had meant them to remain private.

When nothing more was said, Mr. Lowick finally cleared his throat. "Well, I'll be off, then. I'm staying at the Clarendon if you need me, my lord."

"Of course, Mr. Lowick." Trent nodded and pulled Adelaide away from the door with a gentle hand on her arm. Even in his anger he still treated her gently. Adelaide's admiration for the man grew.

If only she hadn't wrecked whatever remained of his admiration for her.

They stood there, waiting in silence until they could no longer hear the manager's footsteps.

Then they waited a few moments more.

Adelaide wasn't about to be the one to break the silence. She didn't know what Trent was thinking or what she should do, so she fell back on the habits of childhood and waited.

When Adelaide was twelve she'd worked for months to learn how to scoop an uprooted shrub from the ground as she rode by, the way she saw them do in one of the trick-rider shows that had come through the village. Of course, that rider had picked up a handkerchief, but he'd been male, considerably taller than Adelaide, and able to ride astride. She decided picking up a tangle of branches was enough of a feat for her to master.

She'd shown no one, though, afraid they would laugh at the amount of time she'd spent on such a ridiculous feat. Her brother had seen her practicing one day and brought her father out to see the spectacle. He'd beamed at her and shown all his friends who came to the house until she turned thirteen. After that he deemed it unseemly to show off such tricks to his friends, but Adelaide never forgot how much he'd encouraged her for those few months.

"You've known about the pineapples for a while, I gather." Trent's voice was quiet, and he looked tired, as if all the righteous anger had slid through him, leaving him drained and exhausted.

Adelaide blinked, trying to reconcile the man in front of her with the vibrant, athletic man she normally saw, but she couldn't do it. Everyone had secrets, and it seemed she'd somehow stumbled onto Trent's, but she didn't know what it meant or why. Why would such a confident man be unwilling to share such innovative ideas? Was it possible that when it came to things of the mind he doubted his abilities in ways he didn't when it involved physical exertion? "Yes. Since, well, a long while."

He took a deep breath and blew it out slowly between pressed lips. "I'm going for a walk." His gaze found hers, and her heart broke over the torturous look in his eyes. "I need to walk when I'm upset. It isn't you. I want you to know that. We'll talk later."

"Are we still going to the Bellingham ball tonight?" Adelaide wanted to go to him, wrap her arms around him, and offer comfort for a wound she still couldn't identify. But she knew that it hurt, and that knowledge was enough for her to want to make it better.

"Yes. I . . . Yes. We're still going. If you want to."

Adelaide nodded, not sure what to do but

trying to trust him when he said they would talk later.

Trent looked at her, and already she could see him pushing the sadness down to wherever he normally stored it. The light was coming back to his eyes and the anger was nowhere to be seen. But it wasn't enough to erase her memory of his earlier emotion.

"It's just a walk to clear my head. I'll be back." He came forward and tipped one knuckle under her chin, forcing her to look into the green eyes she found herself avoiding. "We're going to make this work, you and I. In time, we'll learn how to rub along well." He brushed a light kiss over her lips and walked out the door.

Leaving her alone in his study. After what he'd just learned, how could he trust her?

Her eyes drifted to the bottom drawer of the desk, where the pineapple papers probably still resided. It would be so easy. She could get them now, send them to Mr. Lowick at the Clarendon. She could play the role her brother had played for her all those years ago.

Indecision glued her feet to the wool rug. While the revelation of her horse riding escapades had ended well, the initial feeling of betrayal had driven a wedge between her and her brother for a while. She'd forgiven him, of course, and until now she never thought of the bad part of the story when she looked back and remembered.

Her familial relationship had weathered the betrayal without any lasting damage.

But would her marriage? Trent had promised they'd talk later, that they'd learn how to rub along well together, which was all she'd ever thought she'd get in a marriage. So why was she suffering disappointment that she was going to get what she'd expected?

The walls of the house seemed to press in until she couldn't stand them anymore. So she did the one thing she'd planned on putting off for as long as possible.

She went to visit her mother.

Chapter 32

Trent walked all the way to his fencing club and spent half an hour stabbing a straw-filled dummy with his sword because he didn't trust himself to spar with an actual person. The long walk home still didn't free him from the agitation crawling under his skin, so he took his horse to the less crowded Regent's Park, but at that time of the afternoon the bridal paths were still too crowded for him to lose his frustrations in the wind of a hard gallop.

Which was how he ended up back at Hawthorne House, throwing darts in Griffith's study.

"It occurs to me," Griffith murmured as he sliced open the seal on a letter, "that I've seen more of you since you married than I did when we lived under the same roof."

"Nothing works, Griffith." Trent threw another dart into the dead center of the board. At least his irritation was improving his aim this time. "I've done everything a man does to court a woman."

Griffith didn't say anything but rose to take three of the darts from Trent's hand. He tossed them toward the board with an easy grace that still sent the tips sinking deep into the cork — proof that while his older brother lacked most of Trent's athleticism, it wasn't due to lack of strength.

Trent leaned his hip against Griffith's desk and watched the darts fly. "I know it's only been a matter of weeks, but things should be accelerated for us, shouldn't they? There are couples who met at the Season's first ball who are now announcing their betrothals. I thought it was working, but today all those soft feelings disappeared in a single moment. I didn't want her anywhere near me. I failed, Griffith. I failed at courting my wife."

Griffith crossed the room to collect the darts from the board. "I've been thinking about this, and I have a question. Have you tried being married?"

The pressures of the dukedom had finally addled Griffith's brain. Didn't he realize that being married is what had gotten Trent into this situation in the first place? "I am."

"No, you're not." Griffith tossed a dart and then handed one to Trent. "You're trying to conduct a courtship that has no rules or order to it."

"It seemed like a good idea at the time." Trent's dart landed three inches right of center. He'd be off the board again by the time Griffith finished imparting his wisdom.

Griffith considered the dart in his hand, weighing it like he appeared to be weighing his words. Trent wasn't going to like whatever came next because it usually made too much sense to refute.

"Obviously," Griffith said, "something happened this morning. You don't want to talk about it, and I respect that, but the fact is you've run from it. You're here. Again. Leaving your marriage to be picked up and pieced back together by one person, which as we learned in here not too long ago, is never what God intended marriage to be."

Trent crossed his arms over his chest, trying his best to look imposing so Griffith wouldn't continue. It was hard to scare a mountain. "I didn't ask for this marriage, Griffith."

"And yet it's the one that God gave you. If you don't protect it, who will?"

He'd never thought of it that way. Oh, he'd told Griffith he trusted God's plan and that this must have happened for a reason, but he wasn't sure he'd actually believed any of it. At what point had he stopped trying to do things to fix the situation and let God handle it for him? Never. In fact he'd run from being in the one place God needed him to be in order to make what Trent had promised he would make: a God-honoring marriage. One couldn't be married from across town or even across the room if he didn't accept that the woman involved was well and truly forevermore the woman he had to protect and cherish above all others.

Including himself.

"I haven't married," Griffith said quietly.

Trent pulled himself from his thoughts to find that Griffith had finished throwing the darts and was now simply watching him. "So I've seen."

"I've seen a lot of marriages though, and there's one thing I've noticed. They have good days and they have bad days. But at the end of the day they're still married and that makes them deal with the situation."

Trent frowned. He'd been mad at Adelaide, but she was still his wife. He couldn't walk away from her like a man in a normal courtship could. Tonight he was going to walk back into that house and take her out for the evening. And at the end of the evening he would take her back home. To his house. Their house.

And there was nothing he could do about it.

Which made him even more angry than he'd been about Adelaide snooping through his papers.

Griffith pried the last dart from Trent's hand and tossed it at the board, giving a small smile as it landed in the center ring. "God gave you this marriage, Trent. Now what are you going to do about it?"

Adelaide gave a bemused smile as she looked around her mother's large drawing room. The invitation to tea had not been the close family gathering Adelaide had assumed it would be. The gathering of people sitting on sofas or talking in corners could almost be considered a midafternoon party.

The mix of people was strange. About half of them were married, the ages ranging from hers to possibly a little older than her mother. Most of them were ladies, but a handful of gentlemen were scattered about the room as well. She'd met all of them at one time or another at her mother's urging, but hadn't realized that they were actually all friends of a sort. Including Mr. Givendale. It probably shouldn't surprise her that the man who made Adelaide the most wary she'd ever been was apparently good friends with her mother.

He sat beside Adelaide on the rose-colored sofa, his leg pressed scandalously close to hers while they sipped their tea and talked to the other people seated in the cozy circle. Mrs. Seyton sat on his other side, meaning no one looking would think twice about Mr. Givendale's nearness, but Adelaide knew there was no need for his knee to bump against hers.

"May I take a moment to compliment your appearance this afternoon, Lady Adelaide? That dress is very becoming on you."

"Oh yes, it is." Lady Ferrington leaned forward in her chair to more closely inspect Adelaide's skirt. "Is that muslin? Wherever did you find it in such a lovely blue? And the cut is divine."

"A beautiful dress is meaningless if it doesn't grace a most becoming woman." Mr. Givendale saluted her with his teacup, drawing giggles from the rest of the people in the circle.

Adelaide buried her face in her teacup. Did none of these people think it odd that the man was complimenting a married woman?

"There is something different about you today, though, Lady Adelaide." Mrs. Seyton narrowed her gaze. "Have you always worn spectacles?"

There was still tea in her mouth when Adelaide gave a slight gasp, drawing forth a short set of coughs. "Ah, yes. I've always worn spectacles."

"It's the hair." Mr. Givendale leaned toward Mrs. Seyton, effectively pressing his leg more tightly against Adelaide's. "She's pinned it back."

Not even Trent had noticed that her hair had finally grown long enough to be pinned back in a fashion that more closely resembled the current style. But no matter how easy and charming Mr. Givendale's conversation was, she couldn't seem to quell the notion that he wasn't simply being friendly. His leg bumped hers once more, and she set her cup on the nearby tea table. "Please excuse me. I need to speak to my mother for a moment."

She rose, tugging the edge of her skirt from underneath Mr. Givendale's leg, and crossed the room to where her mother stood, near a corner, alone for the first time all afternoon. "Quite the gathering you have here, Mother."

Wide blue eyes blinked slowly in Adelaide's direction. It was obvious now where Adelaide had picked up the affectation, but she dearly hoped she didn't look like that when she did it. "Of course it is. People get bored during the afternoon, Adelaide. Especially if they don't have unmarried daughters to take about. I discovered that last year."

Last year. While Adelaide had been home in the country with an outgrown governess acting as companion.

"And Father doesn't mind?"

"Your father doesn't know, and I expect you to keep it that way. He only allows me to plan one social event a month, but he's never limited my use of tea and biscuits." Mother looked across her casual gathering. "You are being careful with Givendale, aren't you?"

Adelaide's eyebrows shot up, and she looked from her mother to the man who'd been plaguing her since she arrived. "Careful?"

"Yes, darling." Mother finished her tea and set the cup on the table. "A flirtation is all well and good, but things get rather uncomfortable if you take it any farther than that. He's quite amusing, though, so I keep him around."

Adelaide didn't know what to say, so she stood there, gaping like a landed fish.

"He'll marry one day, though I don't see his behavior changing much. Marriage vows have never been sacred to him. Still, he has his uses. If you're going to continue flirting with him, you might see if he would be willing to sponsor Edgewick, since you haven't seen fit to ask your husband."

"Why not simply have Helena do it?"

Mother's mouth screwed up in a frown. "Edgewick is the wrong coloring. Givendale only pursues women with fair-colored husbands. In case there's a baby."

"In case there's a . . . Mother!" How had Adelaide reached the age of one-and-twenty and never truly known her mother? She should have seen it. All the signs had been there but she'd always thought that somehow, at the end of the day, her mother would do what was right.

"Well, you haven't a title to worry about. And no one is saying you have to do anything with Givendale, but if your marriage isn't making you happy, you'll have to make your own happiness elsewhere." Mother shrugged. "It's a fact of life. I found my happiness in doing what I could to raise Helena's stake in life."

Adelaide thought she might be sick.

Especially when a green-wool-covered masculine arm reached into her field of vision holding a plate with three small sandwiches on it. "Did you try one of these yet?"

"Those are wonderful, aren't they?" Mother reached out a hand, her long, tapered fingers lifting a sandwich from the plate.

"I think I need to get out of here," Adelaide whispered through a throat tight with she didn't even know what. Amazement? Revulsion? Horror?

"It is a bit crowded." Mr. Givendale set the plate down. "Would you like to walk through the conservatory? I've never been there, but I hear the roses are already starting to bloom."

Adelaide blinked at him, his blue eyes much closer to her than they should be, and a dozen realizations occurred to her.

She couldn't walk with him in the conservatory, even if she'd wanted to, because she didn't know where it was. She'd never been in her family's London home because she didn't belong in this world. She didn't want this world, her mother's world. God had saved her from her mother's attentions and from being raised to accept this as normal, and she wasn't going to waste that gift to earn the approval of someone who hadn't affirmed her in twenty-one years.

And whatever mess she and Trent had made of their marriage, they'd still been honest with each other. She knew he was trying, and she dearly hoped he knew she was as well. Even if she never had a happy marriage like she saw in the rest of the Hawthorne family, she could at least have an honorable one. She owed Trent, owed God, that much. She owed herself that much.

Mr. Givendale took her hand in his own. "Are you feeling well? There's a smaller drawing room across the way if you need to sit for a while."

Adelaide was definitely going to be ill.

"Good-bye," she muttered before pushing her way past him and all but running from the madness of the drawing room. She found her pelisse by the door but didn't see her bonnet, and she wasn't going to wait around for it to be fetched. It went against her new efforts of ladylike appearance, but the *ton* was just going to have to forgive her for an afternoon of wind-ravaged hair because she wasn't staying in this house a moment longer.

Chapter 33

He'd never hated balls before. Well, that wasn't true. He'd always thought he hated balls. Nowhere was the courtship dance of the *ton* more evident than inside a ballroom. Even those who were in London to simply enjoy the camaraderie and festivities of the Season could turn obnoxious in a ballroom. If they didn't have anyone of marriageable age in their own family, they took delight in gossiping about those who did.

But tonight he came to the realization that until now he had only found balls annoying.

Because he truly hated this one, and they'd barely stepped foot in the door.

Had his mother not brought the entire family out in a show of support he'd have skipped the evening entirely, but he respected her efforts and what she was trying to do. She didn't know that what Trent really needed was to be home with his wife, having a long discussion about what had happened this afternoon. Since he'd returned home too late for them to talk, he'd gotten dressed and hurried down to the drawing room. She'd seemed a bit confused at first, coming down the stairs with a bit of hesitance in each step, but as her face came into view he knew it had been the right thing. There was something exciting about waiting for his wife, watching her come down the stairs, getting the chance to admire her in a way he didn't get to for the rest of the evening.

This moment of grandeur was the least he could give her. He'd known better than to dabble in things best left to his brother, but he'd thought no one would ever know. As long as he didn't show his thoughts to anyone, didn't put anything into action, nothing would ever come of it and he would go through life as the carefree pugilist without anyone the wiser.

His illusion of protection had shattered today with one innocent question.

And in return he'd shattered her.

He swept her into their customary waltz, but she felt stiff tonight, stiffer than their current strained emotions would have justified. At least in his opinion. He was quickly learning that he had to remember his view of things wasn't the only one that mattered anymore.

"Are you well?" he asked softly in her ear.

She blinked up at him. "Of course. Why do you ask?"

Why had he started this conversation on the dance floor? He cleared his throat. "You seem . . . different tonight."

Her eyes widened and then narrowed. "Different?"

He tried to smile through the looming panic. "Different. You don't look quite like yourself. And it isn't only the pinned-back hair."

"You noticed?" A small smile touched her lips and her shoulders relaxed a fraction. "I didn't think anyone besides Mr. Givendale was going to notice."

The muscles in Trent's shoulders seized and he pulled her closer. "When did Givendale notice?"

She winced, and he immediately relaxed his hold. "At Mother's. I stopped over there for tea this afternoon."

"Did he . . ." Trent swallowed and guided her around the end of the circle of dancers. "Are you all right?"

Her eyes widened as she realized what he was really asking. "I left. I mean, I didn't do anything. Not that he wouldn't have or didn't . . . I'm not really sure, because I don't really know about such things, but even my mother warned me to be careful."

They stumbled through the rest of the dance, and Trent couldn't help but see all the places he'd mishandled their situation. His worry that he would hold her hand but not her heart was proving more than valid. And all because he hadn't been willing to risk his own heart. As Griffith said, he hadn't been willing to be truly married.

He escorted her to the side of the dance floor, but her grip on the inside of his elbow lacked its usual strength.

He couldn't feel his feet. They were numb, as if his custom boots had suddenly shrunk to the size of a child's foot. The sensation was also threatening to overtake his hands. The only thing he was sure he could feel was his heart, and it wasn't beating in any kind of steady rhythm. Was he dying? He'd never heard of someone's heart giving out at the age of twenty-four, but stranger things had happened. Maybe if he died Adelaide would go on to find happiness.

Perhaps even with Mr. Givendale.

Trent scowled into the crowd in general since he didn't know where the wife-stealer was at that particular moment. She'd link her future to that man over his dead body.

"I should probably greet my mother at some point this evening."

The blood drained into his too-small boots. She would rather be with her mother than him?

"Of course. Would you like me to help you find her?"

Her eyes looked somewhere in the vicinity of his left elbow. He'd thought they'd moved past her talking to various parts of his person instead of his face. "No, I think I see her."

He feared she was lying, but there was nothing he could do about it, so he nodded and let her disappear into the crowd of people around them.

A wall of windows looked over Piccadilly Street, and he positioned himself between two of them so he could watch her. It took him a while to find her, but once he did he didn't let the crowd take her from his gaze again. She did find her mother, or rather her mother found her. He couldn't resist the small smile that formed as he then watched her seek solace at the side of Amelia or Anthony or, once, in a discussion with the Duke of Spindlewood.

Trent stayed in his spot. Watching her. Wishing he were somewhere else. Anywhere else. Somewhere totally devoid of people.

Well, not all people. He needed to talk to Adelaide. The emotion boiling in his gut was unfamiliar, and he didn't know what to call it, but it was fast taking over every part of his mind and body.

Thirty more minutes of torture and they would have stayed long enough to satisfy his mother's sensibilities and avoid a lecture from an annoyed Ryland that he'd drug himself out in society for nothing. Thirty minutes should be plenty of time for him to find some control over himself and think of the right words to say that would convince Adelaide she wanted to leave. Thirty more minutes and he could be on his way home, where he could rip off his cravat and jacket and be comfortable.

The crowd shifted, and he lost Adelaide for a few moments. He told himself not to worry. She was managing herself with aplomb even though he knew she didn't like being the focus of so much attention — and she was probably feeling a bit torn up inside as well. At least he hoped she was, though at the same time he didn't want her to be suffering the agony he was at the moment.

People shifted once more, and Adelaide's profile came back into view. Her smile was stiff now, as if she didn't want to talk to whomever she was talking to but couldn't find a polite way out of the conversation. Trent couldn't see who she was conversing with, even when he stood to his full height. What he wouldn't have given for Griffith's height at that moment.

A look around the ballroom revealed the rest of his family was engaged in other conversations or pursuits, leaving no one to rescue his wife but him. Which was as it should be, really. It was cowardly of him to park himself on the side of the ballroom and leave her to fend for herself, but pleasant inane conversation was beyond him tonight. Even his closest friends had deserted him after a brief conversation.

Trent cut his way through the crowd, twisting and turning as if he were in the ring instead of the ballroom.

He broke around a tight knot of gossiping mothers to see Adelaide's own mother at her side. Lady Crampton was smiling and Adelaide was frowning. A dark, intense frown he'd never seen on her face before. Whatever was happening she didn't like it, and the fire in Trent's gut finally found a focus. Whatever was causing his wife distress was about to be vanquished by sheer determination if nothing else.

Especially when he identified the third person in the conversation.

Mr. Givendale was ignoring Adelaide's frown, using the charm that had gotten him into more than one party without an invitation.

"You really should check with Lord Trent for when an acceptable time would be to meet with him." Adelaide's voice finally reached Trent as he veered around one last grouping of people. "You've wasted two afternoons this week alone coming by when he wasn't there."

Trent stumbled to a halt. Givendale had been coming by the house? On the pretense of having business with Trent? The only time Trent ever saw the man was in one of his sporting clubs. Trent would never trust him enough to have anything to do with him elsewhere. Didn't really trust him at the clubs since the time he'd tried to hide weights on his opponent's fencing foil.

Lady Crampton tittered as if there were something funny about the encounter. "You'll have to excuse Adelaide, Mr. Givendale. She's only been in London a short while. Have you met my son-in-law, Lord Edgewick? He's quite the fencer and would be a welcome addition to your club."

"I can hardly recommend a man I've never fenced with before, Lady Crampton. Perhaps Lord and Lady Edgewick could meet me at your house one afternoon. Lady Adelaide, you should come as well and visit with your sister while the match is taking place."

While Adelaide might not have been sure of Givendale's intentions, Trent certainly was. Everything about him reflected a man on a mission. Heat surged through him, bringing feeling back to his fingers and toes as he shouldered his way to his wife's side. "That won't be necessary."

While his very skin seemed to burn with heightened emotion, his heart calmed into a steady beat as Adelaide's shoulders relaxed and her gloved fingers wound tightly around his hand.

Mr. Givendale smiled. "Oh, you intend to be home this week, do you?"

Trent's eyes narrowed. "I do. I've found my home quite pleasant to be at for several weeks now."

The other man nodded. "Perhaps, Lady Crampton, we can schedule this meet-up in a few weeks?"

This was going to end right now. Trent might have an almost insurmountable obstacle between him and his wife, but he was going to take care of it. Somehow. And this man wasn't going to get in his way. "Perhaps you can," Trent said, "but rest assured that

Adelaide will never be a part of it."

"Strong words." Givendale lifted Adelaide's other hand and kissed the knuckles before she had the presence of mind to yank her hand back to her side. "Until we meet again, Lady Adelaide. Perhaps over tea?"

Lady Crampton tried to laugh, but it came out a nervous squeak. Trent had never had such a desire to punch a woman in his life. "Stay away from my wife, Givendale."

"Oh, she's your wife now, is she? A couple of months ago she was the woman who ran you out of your own home. I'll just wait until you take up residence at Hawthorne House again. How long will that be? One week? Two?"

He couldn't hit Lady Crampton, but Givendale was another matter entirely.

The screams that echoed off the ballroom walls brought the first conscious realization that he had followed through on his desires. He shook the haze from his eyes to see Givendale rising from the chalked dance floor, touching his nose to see if Trent's punch had drawn blood. Adelaide's hand was still clenched in Trent's left, and he pried his fingers free so he could step fully in front of her.

Givendale stepped forward, clenching and releasing his fists. "That was unwise."

Trent grinned, feeling in control and like himself again, even if that strong emotion still rolled through him. "But satisfying."

A few giggles scattered through the crowd that was growing around them.

"You think you're better than me, *Lord* Trent? I may not have the honorific yet, but at least I'll come into a title one day. You're simply going to fade away."

"God willing." Trent rolled his own shoulders, trying to ease the tension and make it look like a careless shrug. "The Lord knows I'd make a horrible duke."

"You don't make a much better pugilist."

Trent's grin was true and wide. There wasn't much Trent knew in this life, but he knew he could box and fence with the best of them. If it came down to it, he could have Givendale carried out of here in need of a surgeon and not even break a sweat. Trent boxed for the enjoyment of it though, and this wasn't a war that could be won with fists anyway. He'd started it too publicly. The winner of this battle wouldn't be the one who hit the other hardest, but the one who won the crowd over to his side. He'd seen too many public confrontations to think it would go any other way.

Fortunately Trent was almost as good with words as he was with his fists.

"How about we find you someone else to fight, if you don't feel I'm up to your standards. Perhaps one of the other men you've pretended to visit under the guise of business? I have a feeling I'm not the only man whose house you've watched to know when he's in residence."

It was a shot in the dark but one Trent felt was likely to land somewhere. Givendale's method was too polished, his expectations too clear, for it not to be something he'd done many times before.

Gasps rolled through the crowd at Trent's accusation.

The other man sneered. "You've no proof."

Trent crossed his arms and settled into the most arrogant stance he could muster. He thought he might have even managed to lift his right eyebrow a little. "I've no need of any. You just gave it by not denying the accusation outright."

The appearance of arrogance clearly riled Givendale, so Trent took it one step further, turning to address the crowd and taking his eyes off his opponent. He kept himself between Givendale and Adelaide but tried to look unconcerned. "If you care about your wives, men, take care in doing business with this man. Not only is he without principles, but he is also without discretion."

"You dare?" Givendale spit out. "I could see you at dawn for that."

Trent narrowed his gaze at Givendale. "Did you or did you not tell at least three people at Gentleman Jack's that you knew more about my private business than you should?"

Murmurs ran through the crowd as men worked their way to the edges with anger in their clenched jaws. He didn't see his brother or his friends among them, but he was counting on them to have moved in to flank Adelaide, offering her protection should this crowd get unruly.

"Frankly, Givendale, I don't care what you do. There will always be those who turn a blind eye to the life you like to lead. I, however, am not one of them. So I say it again. Stay away from my wife."

"While you're staying away from my daughter, you can avoid *my* wife as well." Lord Crampton stepped up and crossed his arms at the edge of the circle. If the venom in his glare was anything to go by, he wouldn't be one of the ones carrying Givendale out if things turned ugly. He'd likely help in the beating.

Trent felt his neck heat up, knowing Adelaide's father was witnessing this. At the same time he was glad that at least one of her parents seemed to care about her.

Givendale spit at Trent's feet. "You've humiliated me."

Trent crossed his arms over his chest and gave his head a sad shake. "No, you've humiliated yourself."

Then Givendale attacked.

CHAPTER 34

If there'd been anyone in London who hadn't heard about his marriage before, there wasn't one now. Nor would there by any more rumors that the marriage had been anything other than a love match. Starting a fight in the middle of a ballroom tended to quell that sort of thing.

As Givendale slammed into Trent, sending him down to the floor where his shoulder drilled into the wooden surface with the force of both men's weight, it was almost enough to convince himself.

The strength of Givendale's hit sent the pair sliding across the floor, making finely dressed men and women scatter and squeal. A fist barreled into Trent's ribs as he scrambled to his feet. Fists flew as Trent adjusted to Givendale's movements. He took two more punches before taking control of the fight and making sure the weasel wouldn't be stealing kisses from anyone anytime soon. In return Givendale connected his knee to Trent's side. Evening clothes with seams, buttons, and other accoutrements weren't as forgiving as the linen shirt and breeches he normally boxed in. He wasn't sure if it was the seam of his waistcoat or his flesh tearing, but the pain that lashed through him gave him a pretty good guess.

Trent's rebuttal was a swift punch to the breadbasket that sent Givendale doubling over, making it simple work to send him to the floor with a less than gentle nudge of Trent's knee.

A few men came forward to assist Givendale from the premises with less than helpful intentions. Trent winced as more than one foot trod on Givendale's toes and a couple of fists connected with ribs Trent had already bruised. There would probably be a few butlers getting new instructions when it came to Mr. Givendale. It was well known that at least half the *ton* marriages were little more than a sham, but woe be to the person who actually got publicly caught, particularly if he was caught by the very man he was making a fool of. Givendale wouldn't be doing much of anything in the near future, which was a good thing, since that meant he couldn't call for pistols at dawn.

The fight would be old news before Givendale could call for retribution. Oh, it wouldn't soon be forgotten, and Trent was sure to be infamous for a long time to come, but Givendale's suffering would probably be short-lived.

Unless he tried something with Trent's wife again.

Noise exploded through the ballroom as Givendale and his escorts cleared the door. Trent's chest heaved with breaths so harsh he thought he might actually be breathing in the noise along with the smell of sweat and blood. He looked down at his still-clenched fist to find a smear of red across his hand. The burning emotional monster still rode him, and he knew he needed to leave.

He looked back at Adelaide for the first time since the confrontation began. She was still where he'd left her, supported on either side by Miranda and Amelia. The fight had moved him halfway across the ballroom, and people were quickly filling in the gap, but he could still make out the stunned face and pale features that hit him harder than anything Givendale had managed to land. What would she think of his forceful answer to the problem of Givendale? If she actually cared for the man, he'd probably just given her the final push that would send her to his side.

She might even go to him tonight to nurse his wounds. It wouldn't change the fact that she was married to Trent, but it could change everything else.

And to think he'd wanted a courtship. What would he have done if Adelaide had been free to walk away? He could hardly have punched every man who tried to win her heart.

Her horrified blue gaze met his tortured green one through the glare of her spectacles.

He didn't know what to do. He couldn't go to her, covered in sweat and the blood of the man she might care for more than him.

So he did the only thing he felt he could do.

He looked for Griffith.

He didn't have to look far. His mountain of a brother was cutting through the crowd to Trent's side, Ryland immediately behind him. "Get her home for me. Or wherever else she wants to go if she doesn't want to be there. Just get her out of here safely."

Ryland placed a hand on Trent's shoulder. "Consider it done."

The Duke of Marshington looked across the crowd to his wife and jerked his head toward the side door opposite of where Givendale had been taken out. After a brief nod, Miranda began ushering Adelaide through the crowd, slipping quietly along the edge so as not to draw attention to their departure.

Ryland looked at Griffith. "You've got him?"

"As long as he can walk."

Trent scowled at the pair of them, but as long as Adelaide was taken care of, he didn't care what they did with him. Someone bumped into his back, and fire shot across his shoulder, nearly sending him to his knees.

"Off we go, then." Griffith wrapped a hand around Trent's arm and guided him outside with more speed than skill. "My carriage is around the corner."

Breathing harshly through his teeth, Trent nodded and turned the way Griffith had pointed, his forceful stride eating up the pavement at a pace that actually exceeded that of Griffith's normal long stride.

The footman saw them coming and jumped to open the door. It wasn't until Trent was faced with climbing into the vehicle that every hit Givendale had managed to land made itself known. A groan vibrated through his gritted teeth as he climbed in and threw himself onto one of the seats.

Griffith unhurriedly climbed in after him, carrying one of the carriage lanterns. As the conveyance began to roll, he set the lantern on the floor. "How bad is it?"

Trent undid the buttons on his waistcoat and pulled the linen shirt from the waist of his trousers. Every move was agony, and he was soon breathing harder from the effort to move sore muscles than he had been after the exertion of the actual fight. His side had a definite, distinct pain.

Air hissed through Griffith's teeth as Trent pulled the shirt up. "You need a surgeon."

Trent looked at his side. In the light of the lantern it did look bad. The blood wasn't running freely though, so he guessed it was more of a scrape than anything else. "I'll clean it up at home."

He looked up at his brother's stern expression. "I promise if it's worse than a scratch I'll send for the surgeon myself."

Griffith crossed his arms over his chest.

Trent flopped onto the seat, leaving his ruined clothes in their state of disarray. "Honestly, Griffith, do you think Mrs. Harris would let me do anything less?"

His brother grunted but said nothing else on the fifteen-minute ride to Trent's house.

He started to get out and help Trent inside, but Trent held up a hand to stop him. "I can make it inside on my own. I won the fight, remember?"

"Did you?" Griffith lifted an eyebrow as he let the question sink in.

Yes, he had won the physical fight with Givendale, but whether or not he'd won the prize remained to be seen. "I'll see you tomorrow."

Trent didn't wait for a response as he walked into the house with as much grace as possible. His legs weren't damaged or even very sore, so it was mostly his back and side causing him to walk like an overworked laundress. His hands also hurt, but that didn't affect his walk any.

When Fenton opened the door, Trent simply held up a hand in a bid for silence as he walked past and stumbled up to his room, shucking his cravat, jacket, and waistcoat as he went.

Trent rolled his shoulder, trying to ease the discomfort as he achieved the sanctuary of his bedchamber. He pulled his shirt over his head and turned to look at his back in the mirror. The light from the lamp played over his skin, picking up the darker colors that were starting to discolor along his ribs.

He washed the blood off, revealing that

the wound on his side was indeed a long scrape with a shallow cut near the front that had caused most of the smeared blood. Considering his own stiff movements, he was fairly certain that Givendale wasn't cleaning himself up tonight.

Trent couldn't find a lot of sympathy for his opponent. He'd probably be begging God's forgiveness for that in the morning, but tonight he was caught in the mire of his human fallibility and couldn't help but be glad he'd gotten the best of the man who seemed intent on ruining his chances for a happy marriage. Not that Trent hadn't done at least as much damage himself. He clearly didn't need outside help in that effort.

He stretched his arm once more, wincing at the pain but knowing that he couldn't let the muscle tense up — that would make the pain much worse.

Despite the energy still flowing through his veins, he tried to convince himself to go to bed. Wandering the room wasn't helping his sore body, and any moment the pulsing frenzy would leave his system and his energy would fade into nothingness.

He leaned toward the mirror to check his face one more time to make sure the small cut along his cheekbone wasn't bleeding again.

A soft sound jerked his gaze from his face to the reflected area beyond his right shoulder. He spun around, desperate to see it with his own eyes, but the truth was there in a white cotton gown with a bright blue wrapper.

She hadn't gone to Givendale.

She had come to him.

She'd told herself not to come, that the day had been too full of emotions and it would be best to save any conversations for the light of a new day. But as she'd lain in bed, waiting for sleep that refused to come, all she could think about was how slowly he'd been moving when he left the ballroom. How stiffly he'd held his body when he met her gaze across the heads of circling bystanders.

Once Miranda had gotten her clear of the ballroom she'd tried to rush around the side of the house to find him, but the crush of curious people had been more than she could stand. Everywhere she went people pressed in, trying to get her to tell them why Trent had felt the need for such a public altercation with Givendale. As if she wanted to talk about something so personal with people who were still near strangers. Ryland put an end to the questions with a glare and ushered her into his carriage, offering to take her wherever she wanted to go for the night.

The offer had broken her heart because she knew that the order had come from Trent. After everything that happened, he was giving her a choice, as much of a choice as he could. Somehow she knew that no matter what she did he would always choose their marriage. He'd proven as much tonight.

So she'd come home and gotten in bed, trying not to listen for the sounds of his groans in the next room, racking her brain for anything she could do that would ease his suffering. Suffering he'd picked up on her behalf.

One of the medical texts she'd glanced through when looking for interesting facts to share with Trent explained that smoothing and manipulating the muscles could ease soreness from the body. She hadn't read the whole text and so had no idea what methods the book actually called for, but if she could help him, she wanted to try. No one had ever stood up for her, implicitly believed in her like he did. As much as she was coming to crave a deeper affection from him, she would be satisfied if his protection and confidence were all she ever had.

Afraid she'd lose her nerve if she waited for him to answer a knock, and knowing that it was possible he was already asleep, she'd eased the connecting door open.

She expected him to be collapsed into his faded wingback or sprawled across the bed. She wasn't expecting to see lantern light playing across his muscled and bruised torso. Suddenly offering to rub the soreness from his muscles didn't seem like such a good idea. Or perhaps it was the most inspired idea she ever had.

"Adelaide?" He crossed the room in three long strides and took her shoulders in his hands. "Adelaide, are you well?"

He'd been knocked so hard that he slid at least six feet across a ballroom floor and he was concerned about her well-being?

"I thought I might . . . That is, I wanted to see if I could help you. I've read that massage can ease the pain after, em, after physical altercations."

Trent's eyebrows shot up as he smoothed his hands up and down her arms. The silk wrapper and cotton nightgown were no match for the warmth of his hands, and she wanted to sink in to it, suddenly feeling chilled at all the ups and downs she'd experienced today.

His voice was rough, and he had to clear

his throat before the words came out clearly. "It can. There's a surgeon that comes by the fencing club sometimes. He sees to the occasional sore muscle in exchange for free membership."

"Oh." Adelaide's eyes widened, and she blinked. If it was normally performed by a doctor, could she do it wrong and actually end up hurting him more? "Should I call for a surgeon, then?"

"No, no, that's not what I meant." He ran his gaze over her, brows pulled in as if he couldn't decide what he wanted to do next. He glanced over his shoulder at the bed before closing his eyes and whispering something she couldn't quite understand. When he opened them again she caught her breath at the intensity she saw in his emerald eyes. It had to be a trick of the lantern light, but for a few moments all of the sentiments of the day seemed to be swirling in his gaze. "If you want to help, I won't turn you away. But know you don't have to do this."

She was surprised to find herself smiling. Even her bones seemed to be shaking inside her from a combination of nerves and the memory of the last time she'd been in this room. Yet somehow, she still wanted to smile. "I want to help."

He nodded before going to the bed to lie

down on his stomach. "Most of the tension seems to be in the left shoulder."

"Okay. Do I just . . . push on it?" Adelaide moved the lantern to the table beside the bed and found herself wishing she hadn't. Even scraped and discolored his back was a thing of beauty. And she had volunteered to touch it.

He turned his head to grin at her. "I'm not sure. I've never been on that side of it to see what he does. Just try something. I'll let you know if it hurts."

"All right, then." Adelaide rubbed her hands together, her fingers so cold she didn't dare place them against his skin. She blew on them to warm them up, contemplating his back and trying to decide the best place to start.

"You don't have to do this, Adelaide. I've been punched before. My body will recover."

"No," Adelaide said softly, then repeated the word with more conviction. She decided to start at the top and work her way down. Her first touches were so light they barely made an impression in the skin, but as the heat from his body melted the ice in her fingers she began to press harder, running her hands along his shoulders and down his spine.

His first groan had her snatching her hands back as if she'd been burned. She knew she should have called a physician. It was foolish to practice medicine with only a few paragraphs of a medical text for guidance.

"Noooo," he groaned. "Feels good."

That was a good groan, then? Pleased, she set her hands to the task once more, almost forgetting that the beneficiary of the exercise was supposed to be him. She was getting such enjoyment out of running her hands along his skin that she stopped thinking and trusted her instincts on where to go next.

After a while his groans were replaced by a soft snore.

She smoothed her hands over his skin one more time, enjoying the texture and avoiding the long scrape. Then she took the lantern back to her room with a smile.

Chapter 35

Adelaide was certain that one day she would walk down this church aisle and not be the subject of everyone's speculative stares. It didn't help much that she knew the stares were more for Trent than for herself — she was still in the line of everyone's vision, still part of the story on everyone's lips, and still uncomfortable with the whole thing.

But if that was the price she had to pay for walking the aisle on Trent's arm, she'd accept it. She'd sat up most of the night thinking about her life and come to the very difficult conclusion that if she had to choose between pleasing her mother and pleasing Trent, her mother was going to lose. She was fairly certain that decision was even biblical.

Griffith was already in the family pew when Trent and Adelaide slid into the box.

The duke looked his brother over before lifting one side of his lips. "You're looking well. Considering."

Trent straightened the sleeves of his coat. "He barely touched me."

Since Adelaide knew how much he'd moaned while climbing into the curricle that morning, she was impressed by his façade of painless movement. She was also honored that he had allowed her to see his suffering and trusted her to keep it secret now. She smiled. Perhaps he would need another massage later.

Heat immediately flushed her cheeks. She shouldn't be having thoughts like that. Especially not in church. She yanked her fan from her wrist and waved it rapidly in a furious bid to cool her cheeks.

"I'd love to know what you're thinking right now," Trent whispered in her ear.

She blushed harder. At this rate God wouldn't need to strike her with lightning. She was going to catch fire all on her own.

"Thank you for the massage last night."

Really. If the man did not stop whispering in her ear, she would not be held responsible for the spontaneous combustion of the church.

"Last time I felt that sore I couldn't get out of bed the next morning. I felt almost normal this morning."

She turned her face to find his less than

an inch away. Anyone looking at them would think they were about to kiss. For a moment even she thought they were about to kiss. "I am glad to hear that. Truly I am."

"Perhaps I could return the favor."

His gaze bore into hers, making her think of all the things he wasn't saying. Was it possible that they could still enjoy some of the other things like kissing even though the rest of it hadn't worked for them? She'd certainly enjoyed those other things, and she'd enjoyed giving him a massage last night. And she really couldn't handle this conversation and expect the skin not to burn off her face. "Trent, we're in church!"

"Adelaide, we're married!"

She screwed up her face in confusion. "What has that to do with anything?"

Griffith leaned toward them. "You do know it's considered rude to whisper."

Trent grinned back at his brother. "We're in church. One should always speak in reverent tones in church."

"One should also speak of reverent subjects," Adelaide murmured.

The deep, low laugh that reached her ears shivered down her spine to land in her middle with a tightening thud. "What could be more holy than the union of two people in the eyes of God?"

Adelaide lifted a brow, almost giddy to learn she had the skill when Trent had once confessed how much it bothered him that he couldn't do it. "Perhaps the union of a man's soul with the risen Savior."

"Touché." Trent didn't seem overly concerned that he'd conceded her the conversational point, and why should he? Her cheeks still flamed at the implications of his earlier conversation. It would be a miracle if she heard a thing the rector said this morning.

They dined at home that night. Throughout the quiet dinner and when they'd later retired to the upstairs parlor, Trent found himself searching his brain for topics that would make her laugh, make her smile. He couldn't get their banter at church out of his mind. It fed the craving he had for more talks like that one. Adelaide didn't often rise to his baiting statements, but when she did, he sat in awe of her quick wit. When he thought back to their wedding day, when she'd been unwilling to even look him in the eye, he never would have guessed that she would blossom into the woman sitting across the parlor from him.

Well, sort of the woman across from him. For those few moments when her blush had threatened to overtake her senses, she'd seemed like the Adelaide he married instead of the one that had been so distant for the past few weeks. But even though their relationship had turned some invisible corner last night, she still seemed different. So what was causing it?

The parlor was quiet and comfortable, the perfect place to relax on a quiet Sunday evening. She read while he pretended to. The book he'd brought up was boring, but he kept turning the pages, counting to ten each time she turned one so he wouldn't give away his inattention to his book.

"You've got it upside down," she said quietly.

Trent knew that trick, so he ignored her and turned another page, gathering his wits before he looked down at his book . . . and discovered that it was, indeed, upside down. He snapped it shut and threw it onto the seat of the chair across from him. "No wonder it was boring."

She grinned at him over the top of her own book, and he looked at her, really looked at her. Her hair was neat, looking almost normal with the hair pulled out of her face. That wasn't all it was though. Her dress was in perfect fashion — just as the rest of her new clothes were — the feathers on her slippers nothing out of the ordinary.

Everything looked just as it should.

Everything looked just as it should.

That was it. She'd looked perfect for weeks now. What had happened to his Adelaide?

With a frown he reached out and pulled a pin from her hair, sending two curls cascading over her shoulder. Then he bent down and snagged her slipper off her foot, tossing it in the direction of her bedchamber.

He sat back, satisfied with the changes. "Much better."

"Was that really necessary?" Her exasperated sigh delighted him.

"Yes. You looked too perfect."

She blinked at him — perfect, adorable blinks. "Too perfect?"

"Hmm, yes. It's taken me a while to place it, but yes, you looked too perfect."

She set her book to the side, confusion stamped across her face. "Are you saying you'd rather I walk around with mismatched gloves, smudged slippers, and ripped hems?"

"Not all at once." He shrugged. "You never did all of those at once. I just rather liked that I was the only person who ever saw you when everything was perfect."

She tucked one leg underneath her and leaned over the arm of her chair to look him in the face, eager curiosity molding all of her features into a blend of wide-eyed inquisition. "But your mother gave me very specific instructions on how to keep everything in order. I must admit it's difficult to think about every move I make all the time, and I take a full inventory every time I visit the retiring room. It's very frustrating to find that even with all the care I find little things wrong."

"While I fully respect my mother, I didn't ask to marry her." Trent stopped and shook his head. "That came out entirely wrong."

Adelaide stared at him for a moment. "You didn't ask to marry me, either."

"Actually, if you'll recall, I did." Trent smiled as Adelaide blinked at him once more.

He leaned across the gap between their chairs and captured her lips in a kiss.

What he'd meant to be a sweet meeting of the lips soon grew as he cupped her face in his hands and drove his fingers into her curls, setting more pins free and sending more tendrils dancing around her shoulders.

"Adelaide." Trent swallowed as the word came out too rough to be understood. "Adelaide, do you think we could try again?"

She glanced at the door to his room and then back to his eyes before leaning forward and capturing his lips in a kiss of her own.

Their days fell into a pattern once more, and while it wasn't all that different than what they'd done before, it felt like everything had changed. They would breakfast together in the morning. She would then curl up in the chair in his study and read while he worked for an hour. Then he would go off to one of his clubs while she met with Mrs. Harris or went to see Lady Blackstone. Unless she was in the presence of the countess, she stopped worrying so much about her appearance. It was incredibly freeing to finally relax again.

Sometimes she even deliberately set part of her ensemble wrong just so Trent could find it. He had started gently and quietly correcting the mishap. If they were alone when he did it he followed it with a kiss.

Trent would return home in the late afternoon and take her for a ride before bringing her back home to dress for dinner. They'd only gone out once in the past three days and that was to a small gathering a friend of Trent's from school was having. Otherwise they dined in and then retired to the parlor.

Trent taught her how to play chess. She read to him from some of her Minerva Press novels, using funny voices for the different characters, like she would if reading to a child. Once they even played a silly game of jacks, though they spent more time chasing the errantly bouncing ball than scooping up knucklebones.

Then they retired to his bedchamber, and sometime in the night she would come half awake while he carried her to her own bed.

On the surface everything looked wonderful. Anyone looking in would think they'd finally embraced their marriage and were as in love as any young couple who'd gone about it in a more conventional way would be.

But Adelaide knew differently.

She knew the balance they had was incredibly delicate. The unspoken-of incident with the pineapple papers stood between them, an ignored barrier to finally moving forward. She wasn't careful of her shoes anymore, but she feared taking another wrong step with Trent, and it kept their conversations superficial.

And she didn't like it.

Darkness pressed around them, as comfortable as the heavy blankets on top of her and the warm, hard shoulder she was using as a pillow. She loved this part of the day, when she was warm and happy and as close to her husband as any person could be to another. Sometimes they exchanged whispered stories about their childhood, other times they lay in silence.

She snuggled closer to his side and traced a looping design across his chest. "It's so warm here. The cold always wakes me up when you take me back to bed. Maybe I'll just stay here tonight."

Trent laughed, causing her head to shake on his vibrating shoulder. "And send Rebecca and Finch into scandalous despair?"

"Finch is married," Adelaide muttered. "I think he could handle it."

He brushed her hair away from her face. "You know I could come to your bed instead. Then you wouldn't have to get cold when I move you."

She pouted. She felt ridiculous doing it, but she didn't want to be deprived of his bed. "But I like your bed. It's the most beautiful piece of furniture I've ever seen."

He kissed her gently on the lips. "Then we'll have one made for you just like it. Though I can think of several things you would rather have carved into the headboard than a hunt."

"A bed like this is too expensive, Trent. I'll redecorate my room eventually, and I'll find a lovely bed, but I'll always love yours more."

One finger tipped her chin up, and she could see Trent searching for her eyes in the pale moonlight that crept around the edges of the curtains. "You really don't know how much money I have, do you?"

"Trent, stop it. You're a younger son. I know we'll always be comfortable, but I can't expect you to be able to live like your brother."

Trent tilted his head back. "No, not like my brother. But probably similarly to your father."

Adelaide sat upright and twisted in the bed to stare at him. There was no way that he was as rich as her titled father. He was a younger son whose brother had already inherited. "It's not necessary to go into debt to impress me, you know."

Trent laughed and pulled her back into his arms. "My father left me a generous sum, and Colin's been managing that for years, even before I knew he was managing it. Interfering brothers are sometimes beneficial."

"Oh." Adelaide went back to tracing designs across Trent's chest, wondering if she dared ask what had been bothering her all day. For several days really. She knew their delicate idyll couldn't last forever, but did she really want to be the one to break it?

"Trent?"

"Yes, my dear?"

"Will you please tell me about the pineapples?"

Chapter 36

He tensed, and it actually pulled her closer to his chest until he was hugging her to him. That more than anything convinced him it was time. It was time to let down his guard, time to let her in.

Time to be married.

"I don't know if I can explain it." He took a deep breath. "But I'll try."

She smoothed his hair back with soft fingers but didn't say anything, patience lacing her content expression. A part of him wanted to lash out, though, tell her it wasn't her business, tell her that, if she hadn't looked into his private papers, she'd never have known about the pineapples and they could have gone happily on in their current bliss.

"It's foolish," he whispered.

She propped her head up on her hand and gave him an encouraging smile. "I thought the plans looked quite brilliant, actually. A remarkably efficient use of space."

Trent laughed, surprised that he could, given what he was about to tell her. She was going to think he was touched in the head. "Not the plans themselves. The reason they've stayed in that drawer."

"Oh."

He sat up and ran his hands through his hair. It helped that he couldn't see her face now. "Planning crops and making changes to the way things run is something a duke does."

She frowned. He couldn't see it, but he could feel it. Adelaide expressed herself with her whole body. "No, that's what estate owners do."

He shrugged. "And when I was growing up, the estate owner was a duke. And I learned about estates because I sat in on lessons with my brother, the future duke. So those things . . . Those are ducal things. And I don't want to be good at them."

The blankets rustled as she sat up and then shifted to her knees in front of him. "Trent, just because you weren't born to the title and don't make plans for half the country doesn't make your abilities any less than Griffith's."

"No, you misunderstood me. It's not that I don't think I'm any good at it — it's that I don't want to be. I don't want God to look down and think that I might be a better duke than Griffith."

Trent swallowed hard, knowing what he was about to say was absurd, was not logical, that it was a bit of nonsense implanted in the mind of a young boy. And yet he couldn't get past it. "That's how I lost my father."

Adelaide crawled into his lap and wound her arms around his neck, laying her head on his chest. He could feel her breath, thought maybe he could feel her heart, unless that was his own pounding hard enough for two. It made it easier, holding her but not having to see her face. He could accept her comfort without worrying about her censure. "God saw that Griffith would be an amazing duke, and He made it so. Father even said it was going to happen. I just don't think he thought it would happen so soon."

There was quiet for a long time. Trent wanted to fill it but he didn't know what else to say.

Eventually she broke the silence for him. "Trent, growing pineapples won't make you any more fit to be a duke."

"It's not the actual growing of the pineapples. It's the act of getting involved in things like that."

Adelaide sat up and took his face in her hands. "May I be blunt, Trent?"

Trent froze at the sternness of her words. He'd been expecting gentle understanding, maybe even some platitudes and comforts. "Of course."

"You would make a terrible duke."

The tension eased out of Trent, and he laughed. "I would, would I?"

"Yes. There is so much more to having a title than seeing that your estates are profitable. You also have to manage people. And you, my dear husband, would be terrible at that."

Trent looped his arms around her waist. "I beg your pardon. People love me."

"Exactly. People love you. You set them at ease. Before your altercation with Mr. Givendale, when have you ever seen the bad in someone? Trent, you are a fabulous person, and the world is better off because you're in it, but I'm afraid you would have a very difficult time foreseeing potential problems if you were a duke."

Adelaide's observation didn't cure his irrational fear right away, but it did help put it in perspective. It gave him a tool to combat the insecurities and fears. It gave him the courage to consider doing some things without constantly looking over his shoulder to make sure Griffith was all right.

He pulled Adelaide into his arms and kissed her. He wasn't sure what he was putting into this kiss, but it was something more, something different than he'd given her before, and she kissed him back as if she realized it.

Then he held her and kissed her on top of the head. "Have you ever eaten a pineapple?"

Adelaide's happiness rose with the sun. All was right with her world . . . until Fenton announced that her mother and sister had arrived for a visit. Then the happy bubble burst into a dozen pieces, still recognizable and probably even fixable, but broken nonetheless. How did her mother always seem to know when Adelaide was finally feeling happy? Did Adelaide's happiness somehow siphon off some of her mother's own joy? Did the world really shift that much just because Adelaide smiled? It had been over a week since the altercation in the ballroom, and Mother had been doing a very good job of avoiding her or keeping their public encounters polite and brief.

Apparently it was too much to ask that they settle into that routine for the foreseeable future.

She had Fenton take them to the drawing room, even though it was a bit sparse. Workers were coming tomorrow to re-cover the walls and hang new curtains. Adelaide hadn't decided the furniture she wanted yet, unable to find something both sturdy and feminine to fill the space, but she didn't see that as a reason to continue looking at shabby walls. Particularly since one of the windows was already bare.

With a glance in the mirror to ensure that she wasn't too disheveled, Adelaide went downstairs to greet her guests, reminding herself they were, indeed, her guests and this was her home. She asked Mabel to have tea sent to the drawing room. There was no reason to dawdle over things and prolong the visit unnecessarily.

She felt a bit guilty, wishing her family hadn't come for a visit while at the same time busily planning for an extended visit with Trent's. But the truth was, her family wasn't as nice as his. And while she truly wanted to honor her mother the way the Bible told her to, she was having a hard time reconciling it with the verses that told her to stay away from fools.

If she took a little longer going down the stairs than normal, no one would know but her. And if she made a face at the drawing room door before pushing it open with a smile, that too remained her little secret.

"Darling." Mother rushed forward with her hands extended in a show of affection Adelaide hadn't even seen her bestow on Helena. "I've been so worried about you. I haven't really been able to speak with you since The Incident."

Adelaide hadn't known someone could actually talk in capital letters, but her mother had managed to do so. An awkward pat from Adelaide brought an end to the uncomfortable hug.

"I don't think it's as dramatic as you're making it out to be, Mother. Certainly not an occurrence that needs to be referred to with its own name." Adelaide perched on one of the faded chairs just as Lady Blackstone had taught her. She could easily rise if need be but didn't look as if she were trying to rush her guests out the door.

"Even I heard about it." Helena's eyes were wide as she gave her head a solemn nod.

Adelaide's eyes narrowed at her sister. "You subscribe to every gossip rag in London, Helena. Of course you heard about it."

Helena dropped the false innocence. "And your husband's altercation was written up in every single one of them."

"So was your exchange with Lady Raebourne two years ago, but we didn't give that occurrence its own name and speak of it in hushed tones." Adelaide couldn't believe she was calling forth the biggest scandal her family had ever had — or ever been caught in, as Adelaide was beginning to believe was the case. She felt a twinge of guilt at bringing up the past, but if Helena was going to attack Adelaide's husband, everything was fair game. "If I recall, you wrote me that the entire thing was being exaggerated and shouldn't have been worth more than a few drawing room giggles."

Adelaide paused while Fenton brought in the tea service. Once he departed, she looked back at her sister. "Do you still wish to use the number of articles as a gauge for an event's level of scandal?"

"Really, Adelaide, the two events hardly compare." Mother folded her hands in her lap and pursed her lips.

Adelaide didn't know why they'd come, but it seemed she'd somehow managed to put a crack in their intentions.

Her moment of satisfaction died when her mother took the teapot and began pouring Helena's cup. This was Adelaide's home. She should be serving the tea. For her mother to take up the pot was an establishment of power that went beyond rude to insulting. As Adelaide debated whether or not to wrestle it from her just to prove a point, the drawing room door opened.

Expecting a servant but hoping for one of her new sisters-in-law, Adelaide turned to see who was entering. She was very glad she wasn't holding the teapot when Trent walked in. Shock would have probably had her dropping the thing.

"Sorry I'm late, darling." Trent crossed the room and sat on the settee with her as if it were perfectly normal for a husband to take visitors with his wife. It was amazing how different the word *darling* sounded on his lips than her mother's. "Oh good, I'm glad I didn't miss tea. Five sugars and a splash of cream, if you will."

Mother frowned as she prepared the cup, but the tight compression of her lips she passed off as a smile was back by the time she handed the cup to his waiting hands. She then proceed to make Adelaide a tea nearly white with cream before making one for herself.

Adelaide took a closer look at Trent. She thought he'd said he was going to be fencing with Anthony today. As he leaned forward to accept his tea she noticed his pulse jumping in his neck. His hair, tousled in the current fashion, looked damp at the temples and a little more rumpled than it had when he left the house that morning. Had the man run from Anthony's house to be here with her so she wouldn't face her mother alone? Fenton would have had to send Oswyn even before he'd come upstairs to talk to her.

What man made those kind of arrangements if he didn't care about his wife? No one. They hadn't gotten there through any conventional means, but no one would be able to convince her there wasn't at least a little love in their relationship.

She took a sip of her tea and found Trent frowning at her cup. She gave a tiny shrug, trying to tell him that she didn't care overmuch that her mother had poured. Whether the message was conveyed or not, Trent decided to move on.

"I trust I'm not interrupting anything." Trent settled deeper into the settee and sipped his tea. It was more than obvious that he didn't care if he was interrupting or not — he wasn't going anywhere.

"Of course not, my lord," Mother said behind her teacup.

Adelaide bit her lip to keep from grinning. Trent, being a younger son set to inherit nothing beyond some money and family connections, was all but worthless in Mother's eyes. As a countess she outranked Trent in her own opinion, and it must rankle to have to appease him, even a little bit.

Helena, however, had no such problems.

"Were you part of the horse race last week, my lord?" She fluttered her eyelashes in Trent's direction. His eyes widened and he made a hasty swallow of tea before coughing lightly.

"I don't believe I was. I do sometimes gallop through the park in the mornings, though, so I may have inadvertently joined a pursuit in action."

Adelaide gave him a little grin. "Do you often join races accidentally?"

"It's been known to happen." Trent grinned back at her, ignoring the other two women in the room.

"And do you win?"

"Of course." Trent saluted her with his teacup. "Why play if you've no intention of winning?"

"Even when you had no intention of playing."

He winked at her. "Sometimes those wins are the most satisfactory."

Adelaide ducked her head in a blush, having a sudden feeling they weren't talking about horse races anymore.

Mother set her cup down with a rattle. "I hear your sister is giving a ball next week."

And thus the true purpose of the visit was revealed. They still hadn't received invitations to the ball. Knowing how Miranda felt about Adelaide's family, that slight had probably been intentional. And brazen in a way that only a famously eccentric duchess could get away with.

"Is she? I wouldn't know. I don't handle the invitations. Particularly not hers." Trent sipped his tea again.

Adelaide tried not to smirk. She really did.

Helena smiled and fanned the room with her lashes once more. "I'd be happy to help you learn how to organize your social calendar, Adelaide. You've never really had to do such a thing before."

"Yes, I know. Such skills are certainly easier to practice when one comes to London for a Season." Only the fact that she held a cup of hot tea kept Adelaide from clamping her hands over her mouth. Where had such an impertinent statement come from?

She glanced at her husband, expecting stunned censure in his face — instead he looked almost proud.

The silence that fell over the drawing room was thick enough to swim in. The only person who looked comfortable was Trent. He drank his tea and smiled at everyone as if he had no idea of the undercurrents that had been stirred up.

"I've heard that Montgomery House has a lovely ballroom." Helena ran a finger along the edge of the saucer. "I've heard the floor is inlaid with the image of a peacock."

"Is it?" Trent lifted his brows in Adelaide's direction. "Won't that be exciting to see? Of course, I don't know that we'll be able to see it with the crush of people Miranda's invited. We'll have to go by another day to look at it properly."

"That sounds lovely," Adelaide murmured, wondering how long it would be before her mother and sister asked outright for an invitation or gave up hope. She was almost embarrassed for her family and desperate to change the subject to something they wouldn't feel humiliated by. "How is Father doing?"

Mother waved a hand in dismissal. "He's doing acceptably well. Bernard is down from school for a while, and your father's been taking him around to some of the clubs and such. Not that he can join yet, of course, but it's so important to teach young men the proper social interactions early. I was able to do much the same with Helena."

Adelaide saw her cup shaking in her hand, heard the rattle of china. Part of her knew she'd eventually drop the thing if she didn't put it down, but that part of her didn't seem to be in control of any of her motions. Her mouth worked, however, though without her normal discretion. "Bernard is in London?"

"Of course. What else would we do — leave him in Hertfordshire with the nanny?"

"That's what you did with me."

Gentle fingers pried the rattling cup from her hands before wrapping her icy fingers in warmth.

Mother looked stunned, as if she suddenly realized her faux pas. "Your father has only Bernard to deal with. I couldn't very well teach you and Helena the same things at the same time. You were too young back then. Besides, things are different for gentlemen."

"Yes, they are." Trent squeezed Adelaide's hands and then stood. "For instance, a gentleman is perfectly within his rights to remove people from his home when they upset his wife."

"My lord —"

Trent crossed his arms over his chest and glared at the countess.

Mother turned her attention to Adelaide.

"Adelaide, I —"

"Before you say anything, you should know I have no intention of asking Miranda to adjust her invitation list." Adelaide was still shaking, the quakes coming from somewhere deep inside her and causing her voice to tremble slightly. There was no misunderstanding her words though.

Helena shifted to the edge of her seat. "I can't tell you how upset it always made me when Mother insisted we leave you behind. I tried, Adelaide. Truly I did. Perhaps now that we're both on our own we can finally be sisters."

Adelaide frowned, still focused on her mother. "Nor will I ask Trent to stand up for Helena's husband. He owes you no such thing."

Mother looked as if her head were about to explode, making Adelaide very glad the workers hadn't come by to replace the wall coverings yet.

Adelaide stood and wound her arm around Trent's, clinging to him to keep herself upright. "This has been a lovely visit. But I'm sure you'll understand that I have a pressing engagement to prepare for. I'll have Fenton see you out."

Trent smiled at her. A full-blown smile, complete with dimples and teeth and a light dancing in his eyes. "Shall we, my dear? I believe we're scheduled for dinner with the Duke of Spindlewood."

They left the room, but Trent pulled her to the side after they left the room, tilting his head to listen. Angry whispers lashed from the room, too indistinct to hear clearly, but it was easy enough to grasp that they were arguing.

Trent patted Adelaide's hand and led her away. She kept glancing at the drawing room door as they started up the stairs. "Aren't you worried they'll destroy something? They sound very angry."

"Aren't we gutting the room tomorrow?" Trent looked at the door and then glanced around the hall. "Fenton!"

"Yes, my lord?"

"When our guests decide to take their leave, make sure they go straight to the door without any detours. Have Oswyn help you, if need be."

"Of course, sir." The bald butler bowed before pulling the bellpull to summon Oswyn. Then he stood in the hall like a sentinel.

Trent sent Adelaide a questioning glance. "Satisfied?"

Traces of dried sweat were still visible at his temples, proof that he cared more than he'd put into words. "Yes, I believe I am."

"Good." They continued up the stairs to the parlor. Before they parted ways to dress for the evening, he took her hands. "It's possible that honoring your mother is sometimes accomplished simply by not telling the world what a heartless person she can be."

Adelaide thought about how broken she felt after every encounter with her mother and how long it took to put herself back together afterward. She hadn't noticed the pattern when she lived at home, but now that the instances were farther apart, it was obvious. "I think you might be right. Are we really dining with Spindlewood tonight?"

Trent squinted and tilted his head. "Well, I did hear he was dining at Vauxhall Gardens tonight, and we're meeting Georgina and Colin there, so in a very broad sense of the word, yes. Yes, we are."

Delight bubbled up and burst forth as laughter from her lips. "Oh, Trent Hawthorne, I love you."

He looked like she'd hit him with a fire screen. She didn't want to wait to hear him spout gentle platitudes. "Vauxhall Gardens, you said? I'd best go see what Rebecca has laid out for me to wear."

Then she fled into her room, her pounding heart leading the way.

Chapter 37

Sleep was a blissful escape where questions and confusion took a holiday, allowing a person momentary peace, even if they weren't awake to enjoy it. It was an escape denied to Trent that evening. He sat in his chair, watching the light from his candle flicker to the corners of the room. Shadows played over the figure huddled beneath the covers in the center of his bed. He didn't know what to do, but he knew he had to do something. They couldn't avoid it forever. He just had to find the courage to ask her about what she'd said, the same way she'd mustered up the courage to ask him about the pineapples.

He didn't know how long he'd stood in the parlor after she left. Finch found him there, staring at a wooden door as if it could answer all the deepest questions in life. But it couldn't. She probably couldn't even answer them. Not that he would ask. How could he ask the questions that had swirled through his mind without hurting her with his lack of ability to say the words back?

What did "I love you" mean anyway?

They'd certainly sorted out the physical issues of their marriage relationship, but that couldn't have been more than a small part of loving his wife as God had called him to do. Caring for her, putting her needs above his. He was trying to do all these things, committing himself to her well-being.

Did that mean he loved her?

He slid the Bible from the drum he used as a table next to his father's old chair, flipping to the verses in First Corinthians that Anthony had mentioned all those weeks ago. A lifetime seemed to have passed since then, leaving him feeling older and wiser and befuddled all at the same time.

When he'd looked at them before, the verses had seemed like a condemning mass of things he lacked. They also hadn't said anything specific about husbands and wives so he'd used that as an excuse to ignore them. Now they looked more like a checklist, a map to what it took to love a person.

Suffereth long.

Kind.

Envieth not.

Is not puffed up.

He wasn't perfect — no man was — but he could see all those things when he looked at his life with Adelaide. It had never occurred to him that she was flattered by Givendale's attentions or encouraged them in any way. What was that but kindness and lack of envy? Not to mention trust.

Doth not behave itself unseemly.

Well, he had punched a man in the middle of a ballroom, but he didn't think that was what God meant.

Rejoiceth in the truth.

Like confrontations over pineapple plans and interfering mothers?

Beareth all things.

Believeth all things.

Hopeth all things.

Endureth all things.

That was a lot to ask of someone. The candle sent licks of light across the page, highlighting the truth of God. If this was love, this was what he needed to do. Because God had commanded him to love his wife as Christ loved the church. Which meant he had to love her above himself, with everything in him, even unto death. *Beareth, believeth, hopeth, endureth.* What did that look like in a marriage?

He considered her problems his own. To

the extent that he'd told Fenton to send word if Lady Crampton ever came calling. Then he'd run the entire way from Anthony's house. A short distance to be sure, but he'd still run.

He had every confidence that she would rise above her upbringing. That the glimmers of strength he saw would only grow if he nurtured them properly.

And above all else he knew that she was the only woman for him. Not because of some fanciful poetic look but because God had given her to him and he trusted the Lord's judgment.

But did all of that mean he'd learned to love his wife? If there was one thing the passage in front of him made clear, it was that love was considerably more than the emotion that drove men to write poetry and subject themselves to societal events they would otherwise avoid. In fact nowhere in the passage did it say anything about knowing what the other person was thinking or feeling as if you couldn't live without them. Love seemed to be more about what you did and gave for the other person than about what they brought to you.

He slid the Bible back onto the large Army drum and blew out the candle before making his way across the room. It might shock

Finch, but tonight Trent was going to hold his wife. And tomorrow he was going to start examining his life, looking for anything that was keeping him from fulfilling this most sacred of jobs: loving his wife.

Adelaide stood in the corridor outside the parlor, trying to decide if she really wanted to go in. Trent had asked her to have tea with him this afternoon. She'd accepted before thinking it through, but now she wondered if it would be best to limit their interaction until they'd both had a chance to move past her instinctive statement the night before.

Breakfast had been more strained than it had been since the first morning after they'd married. Every time he took a breath she expected him to say something about what she'd said. To either ask her about it or give her some watered-down platitudes in return.

He did neither. Instead he acted just as he'd been doing for the past several days. He asked after her plans, shared funny stories about something that had happened at the club the day before. And then invited her to take tea with him.

They'd gone their separate ways after she'd agreed, but now the time was here and she wished she'd been able to come up with an excuse.

"I beg your pardon, my lady." Fenton appeared behind her with the laden tea tray, effectively forcing her to walk into the room.

Fenton set the tray on the low tea table and then sent a significant look toward Trent. He nodded, and Fenton left the room quietly.

What had that been about?

"Would you pour?" Trent asked.

"Of course." Adelaide sat, trying to remember how he took his tea.

"Cream and five lumps of sugar."

"Oh, yes." Adelaide poured a bit of cream into his cup and then dropped sugar in it before giving hers the same treatment. She lifted it to her lips and sipped, hating the taste as it hit her tongue but ignoring it as she'd trained herself to do.

"How do you take your tea, Adelaide?"

She blinked. "Same as you."

"Hmm. And the same as Miranda? The same as your mother?"

She opened her mouth to answer but snapped it shut with a click of teeth. With a calm she didn't really feel, she slid her cup onto the table.

Trent's cup joined hers as he leaned forward to look her in the face. "How do you like your tea?"

"I don't."

He jerked back with a stunned expression on his face. "I beg your pardon."

Adelaide swallowed and rubbed her hands over her legs. "I don't like tea."

Fenton entered again with another tray. This one filled with teacups. He set in on the table and left.

"You don't like it at all?"

She shrugged. "Not really. It's just simpler to fix it the same way I fix someone else's. I've yet to find a combination I like."

Trent plucked a cup from the tray. "Then let's find out, shall we?"

An hour and two more pots of tea later, Adelaide sat back and folded her hands in her lap. "I think we could put an official seal on this declaration now. I don't care for tea. Although it is more palatable with a significant amount of milk and the slightest bit of sugar."

Trent leaned back in his chair, enjoying his own cup of tea. "We'll have to keep it our secret. They might kick you out of England if it becomes public knowledge. What do you like, then?"

"Coffee. Mrs. Harris brews wonderful coffee. I always have two or three cups at breakfast."

His face showed surprise. "That's coffee?

I thought it was chocolate. My sisters insist the day can't begin without a hot mug of chocolate."

She shook her head. "Chocolate is good but coffee is wonderful."

He settled back in his chair and crossed his booted feet at the ankles. "Tell me something else about you that no one else knows."

Adelaide looked over the scattered cups, the dregs of tea long forgotten in a quest to discover what she liked. She didn't need the words. This was proof enough for any woman.

She leaned back in her chair and copied his pose. "I've been stuffing a strip of linen into my dancing slippers in case I have to partner your uncle Charles again. He steps on my toes."

Trent roared with laughter and drank another sip of tea.

Neither left the room for another hour.

Trent paced the study wondering why on earth he thought this would be a good idea. It was a terrible idea, he was going to bungle it horribly, and he'd spend the rest of his life making it up to Adelaide.

"Your brother has arrived, my lord."

Trent nodded at Fenton. "Thank you."

It was time to go downstairs. He should have already been downstairs. This was Adelaide's first time as hostess, and he should be there to support her. Instead he was upstairs fretting like a girl before her first ball. Why had he done this to himself? Two weeks ago Adelaide had told him she loved him. She'd said it again four days later as she drifted off to sleep. Each day he saw it in the way she spoke to him, looked at him.

After examining himself for a week he'd come to one conclusion. Somewhere along the way he'd learned to love his wife. And he'd learned to embrace her belief in him. He'd sent copies of the pineapple plans to Mr. Lowick two days ago. He'd thought of telling Adelaide everything last night, but then he'd had this idea. At the time he'd thought it brilliant. Now he knew he was insane.

He ran down the stairs and into the newly decorated drawing room. She'd insisted it be done in time for her dinner, scouring London to find the appropriate furniture. She'd done a fabulous job. Upholstered in red and gold, the sofa reminded him a bit of the wingback chair in his room, with elaborate curves along the top of the back. It still had the thin curving legs that were so popular, but it had eight of them, joined together with a grid of wooden bars underneath, providing a strong appearance, so he wasn't afraid to sit on it.

Griffith was taking in the room, kicking lightly at the legs on the sofa. He looked up at Trent. "You'll have to tell me where she found this. I'm going to get one for the white drawing room."

Trent walked to the new walnut cabinet and poured Griffith a glass of water from the decanter he'd had Mrs. Harris prepare in preparation for this evening. He poured himself a sherry before taking the water to his brother. "Are you going to get one in white?"

"Not a chance. I'm leaning toward a peacock-colored cut velvet."

Trent nearly choked on his sherry while Griffith calmly drank his water.

The rest of the family arrived, and Adelaide bustled about, eyes wide with nerves and excitement as she greeted everyone, making sure they had drinks and running out of the room every ten minutes to check on Mrs. Harris.

It was a relief when Fenton finally called them to dinner.

As was always the case when the family got together, everyone stood for a moment looking around and doing mental calculations of rank to see who was supposed to go first. Two dukes, a marquis, and an earl tended to have that effect on a social situation.

"Would everyone simply go to the dining room," Trent grumbled. "And sit wherever you please? It's family."

Adelaide gasped next to him and paled a bit. "But the place cards," she whispered. "I've been studying days on the proper position of the place cards."

"Wait!" Trent sighed and gestured the group back into the drawing room. "Mother, if you please?"

In short order, Mother had everyone properly lined up for the short walk to the dining room, where she beamed at Adelaide after a glance at the place cards.

It felt strange to sit at the head of the table when every man in the room save one outranked him. But it filled him with happiness to look down the table and see Adelaide beaming in success as everyone began to eat. Especially since she'd had a part in creating several of the dishes on the table, including the platter of bacon set directly in front of him.

Before the dessert could be brought out, Trent rose to his feet. "If I may have your attention. As you all know, this year did not start out as expected for me. I had no plans to marry and certainly no plans to marry so quickly. Yet our God is a God who knows more than we do, though we frequently act otherwise. And in His infinite wisdom, He brought me a wife who suits me more than anyone else ever could."

He walked around the table and knelt beside Adelaide's chair. He thought he heard Georgina sigh but didn't look her way. His eyes were only for Adelaide, locked to the light blue eyes that brought her face to life, even though it was a trifle pale at that moment.

"Adelaide, you read some of the strangest things I've ever heard of, your taste in food is somewhat questionable, and you can't keep an ensemble together for more than half an hour."

Griffith coughed. "Ahem, brother, I know I'm the only unmarried man in the room, but I don't think this is the kind of thing a woman wants you to tell her in front of other people."

Trent ignored Griffith, pushing on. He was trusting that he knew Adelaide, that this public declaration would give her confidence in his love. Dear God, he prayed he was right.

"But, Adelaide, all of those things only

make you, you. And I wouldn't change one single thing about you. If I had it to do all over again, I'd happily crash through that floor and sit in the ruins with you all night. And I'd ask you to marry me all over again, but this time it wouldn't be because I had no choice."

Trent swallowed, hoping he could get through the next part without having his tense throat steal his voice. "Adelaide, I know it's not normal, but we threw normal out the window a long time ago. I'd like to take this opportunity to ask you to marry me all over again, because I love you. And I can't wait to grow pineapples with you."

More than one person sniffled behind him as the sentimentality of the moment washed over everyone. But he also heard a few murmurs about pineapples, letting him know a bit of confusion had leaked into the moment as well. And he wouldn't have had it any other way.

Adelaide, looking not at all confused, sniffed and let the tears course down her cheeks to get lost in her wide smile. "I love you too," she whispered, "and I'd love to marry you again and grow lots of pineapples."

Epilogue

Suffolk, England, 1816

"You could have warned me that it took two years to grow these things," Adelaide grumbled as she waddled into her husband's specially constructed greenhouse. Layers of carefully made shelves filled with dirt and whatever else it took to grow the tropical fruit lined the room, and at the far end, where the first plants had been planted two years ago, were lovely green-and-brown spike-covered lumps.

Adelaide poked at them, having to fully extend her arm since her belly kept her from getting too close to the shelf. "They're rather ugly, aren't they?"

Trent laughed, as she'd intended him to. He'd been beside himself for months, as it became apparent that it was a toss-up which would come first — the harvesting of his first pineapple or the birth of his first child. Adelaide was rather glad it was the pineapple so she could be here for the moment. She would have hated to be confined to her room, recovering from childbirth when he pulled the first plant.

"Shall we?" He held a wicked-looking long knife in one hand, and a gleam of anticipation lit his face. His cheeks were going to hurt later from all the smiling he was doing, but it would be worth it.

"Yes, please." As much as she wanted to be here for this moment, she also really wanted to sit down. Her back was aching like never before, and her feet were so swollen she'd had to wear her dancing slippers with the extra padding removed.

Trent hacked the first pineapple free from its plant and took it to the worktable at the end of the greenhouse. They'd brought a large platter out with them so they wouldn't have to wait to taste it.

He cut off a section and held a dripping chunk of yellow fruit out to her. She took it between her fingers and waited while he cut his own. Years of work came down to this moment. Soon after he'd begun his plans in earnest, Trent had offered to buy her a pineapple so she could taste one, but she'd told him she'd wait and let his pineapples be the first she ever tasted. At the time she didn't know how long they took to grow.

Now she just hoped she liked it and didn't cast up her accounts the moment it hit her tongue.

"Shall we?"

Trent tapped his piece of pineapple against hers, and they both took a large bite.

Adelaide didn't know what she'd expected, but that wasn't it. The tart-and-sweet flavor hit her tongue and then seemed to swell through her whole head. "That's fabulous," she cried before popping the rest of the chunk into her mouth.

Trent laughed and cut the rest of the fruit up to share with the staff who had gathered for the occasion. It was the first taste of the exotic fruit for more than one person, and it was fun to watch the looks that ran across their faces.

Before long though, she really needed that chair.

And perhaps the midwife.

"Trent."

"Yes, my love?"

"I think I need to go to the house. And for the last time, we are not naming this child Pineapple."

ACKNOWLEDGMENTS

Dear Reader, you have no idea the small but intense village required to put this book into your hands. It would absolutely never have happened without the blessing of the Lord and the support of my husband and kids. The shout-outs to them may get repetitive, but they fall short of the acknowledgments my family deserves. Seriously. I could write this entire section on that small group of people, but then you wouldn't read it and all the other important people wouldn't get thanked.

Another constant in my writing is my amazing beta readers, who really worked for their thanks on this book. Your honest feedback made all the difference, even when it made me grumble. Your willingness to read the second draft after the train wreck of the first draft continues to humble and amaze me.

To my Aunt Delana, who feeds and shares

my obsession with Rolos, thank you for providing fuel for the editing process.

To Trent's fan club, I hope his story lived up to your expectations. If not, well, they were a little daunting to begin with. I love you all, though, and you are the reason I get up every day and write. You are also the reason I don't go to bed so that I can meet my deadlines.

Take a moment to marvel over the artistic talents of the Bethany House cover art team. Thank you all so much for bringing Adelaide and Trent to life in a way I never thought possible, right down to Adelaide's unfashionable bangs. I'm convinced you all are truly magicians. Hugs to the rest of the Bethany House team as well, for believing in me and this book and walking through the process with me.

Finally, I'd like to thank HP, for making a laptop sturdy enough to handle everything I've thrown at it. This book was written in about fifteen different locations and would never have gotten finished without the ability to write anywhere with a laptop that has held up to dance class, car lines, and being stepped on by a five-year-old.

ABOUT THE AUTHOR

Kristi Ann Hunter graduated from Georgia Tech with a degree in computer science but always knew she wanted to write. Kristi is an RWA Rita® Award winning author and a finalist for the Christy Award and the Georgia Romance Writers Maggie Award for Excellence. She lives with her husband and three children in Georgia. Find her online at www.KristiAnnHunter.com.

The employees of Thorndike Press hope you have enjoyed this Large Print book. All our Thorndike, Wheeler, and Kennebec Large Print titles are designed for easy reading, and all our books are made to last. Other Thorndike Press Large Print books are available at your library, through selected bookstores, or directly from us.

For information about titles, please call:

(800) 223-1244

or visit our Web site at:

http://gale.cengage.com/thorndike

To share your comments, please write:

Publisher
Thorndike Press
10 Water St., Suite 310
Waterville, ME 04901

MEXICO'S SPLASHY NEW RESORT
'TEEN
GIANT SURFARI ISSUE
57 WILD WILD SWIM SUITS
THE BEACH BOYS
THE TURTLES
BEAUTY WAYVES
HOW TO SURF ANYWHERE
HOW TO BE A BEACH BUM
BRIDE
THE MOST BEAUTIFUL BRIDE IN THE WORLD YOU!
SEXUAL ADVICE
HOW TO BE ATTENTIVE WITHOUT REALLY TRYING
HOW TO CREATE A BEDROOM
"THE FIRST MEAL I COOKED FOR MY HUSBAND..."
VEDETTES EN VEDETTE
SPORTS ILLUSTRATED
CHIEFS HEAD FOR SUPER BOWL
us
Why she's America's top model
When it comes to selling products, nobody does it better than Cheryl Tiegs
The unlovable side of lovable Ed Asner
Why more women aren't managers
An Osmond family album
L.L. Bean: the camping king
'TEEN
Noel Harrison Spies Fall Fashions
17 Ways To Catch Boys and keep them!
REDBOOK
Luscious desserts for dieters
SPY NOVEL OF THE YEAR!
THE SALZBURG CONNECTION BY HELEN MACINNES
plus a complete novel by Sonya Dorman
DUSTIN HOFFMAN THE MAN BEHIND THE SMILE
Brigitte
heitsplan
THE JACKIE O. YOU NEVER KNEW!
A bold new book tells it like it is
GREAT NEW FASHIONS FROM TOP DESIGNERS
Journal
HOW GOOD A FRIEND ARE YOU?
Take our quiz and find out
PHIL DONAHUE, MIKE DOUGLAS, DAVID HARTMAN
The men who love women
"LASSIE" PUP WINNER!
NEW APPLE PIE IDEAS
plus hearty Fall dinners
Don't just lie there: TALK BACK TO YOUR GYNECOLOGIST
LIZA MINNELLI
Is she burning out like Judy Garland?
WORKING MOTHERS
How to give your kids more "loving time"
GLAMOUR
SEPT. $1.25
THE BEST OF THE NEW FALL LOOKS
THE BIG BEAUTY CHANGES
3 GREAT HAIRCUTS
SEPTEMBER 1978
BAZAAR
A COMPLETE GUIDE
YOU & YOUR HEALTH
HOW TO GET YOURSELF IN PERFECT CONDITION FOR SUMMER
3 SIMPLE NEW DIETS
TO REVITALIZE YOUR HAIR, SKIN, SEX LIFE
THE $45 EVENING DRESS EVERYBODY WANTS
CHERYL TIEGS LOVING THE GREAT OUTDOORS
TOO MUCH WOMAN TO BE A WIDOW
YET AFRAID TO LOVE AGAIN
SECRETS
GLAMOUR
YOUR SUMMER MAKE-OVER IN 2 STEPS
FASHION:
BEAUTY:
BAZAAR
SEPT 1976
THIS ENTIRE ISSUE
AMERICA'S CONTEMPORARY WOMAN:
WHAT TO DO ABOUT THE KILLER FLU
SPECIAL SECTION
HOW TO HAVE FIRM, BEAUTIFUL, HEALTHY BODY FOREVER
NO-WORK DIET: LOSE 10 POUNDS
NEW YOUNG DRESSES UNDER $65
THE NEW FALL COLLECTIONS
BAZAAR PICKS THE WINNERS
AT THE PRICES YOU WANT
Woman's own
WAYS WITH A SHILLING

Cheryl Tiegs

THE WAY TO NATURAL BEAUTY

WITH VICKI LINDNER

SIMON AND SCHUSTER
NEW YORK

Published by Simon and Schuster
A Division of Gulf & Western Corporation
Simon & Schuster Building / Rockefeller Center
1230 Avenue of the Americas / New York, New York 10020
SIMON AND SCHUSTER and colophon are trademarks of Simon & Schuster

Manufactured in the United States of America

3 4 5 6 7 8 9 10

Library of Congress Cataloging in Publication Data
Tiegs, Cheryl.
The way to natural beauty.
1. Beauty, Personal. 2. Women—Health and hygiene. 3. Tiegs, Cheryl. 4. Models, Fashion—United States—Biography. I. Title.
RA778.T552 646.7'2 80-13719
ISBN 0-671-24894-4

Grateful acknowledgment is made to:
The Condé Nast Publications Inc. for permission to reproduce six photos from VOGUE, thirty-six from GLAMOUR, three from BRIDE'S, Copyright © each year, 1963 through 1979, by The Condé Nast Publications Inc. All rights reserved.
The Condé Nast Publications LTD. for permission to reproduce two photos from British VOGUE. Copyright © each year, 1963 through 1979, by The Condé Nast Publications LTD.
Bernard Leser Publications PTY, LTD. for pemission to reproduce two photos from VOGUE AUSTRALIA. Copyright © each year, 1963 through 1979, by Bernard Leser Publications PTY, LTD.
The Hearst Corporation for permission to reproduce fifteen photos from HARPER'S BAZAAR, and two from GOOD HOUSEKEEPING. Copyright © The Hearst Corporation 1968 through 1980.
Additional picture credits appear on page 288.

FOR MY PARENTS
AND
FOR STAN

Contents

9

ACKNOWLEDGMENTS

I would like to thank my best friend Christy for the original idea; Peter Beard for his enthusiasm, inspiration and photography; Barbara Shapiro for her patience and good cheer; Marvin Israel for the look of the book; Russell Goldsmith for years of creative counsel; Ray Cave for being a believer; Tony Mazzola for his help from the beginning; Michael Korda of Simon & Schuster; Charles Schulz; Bill Connors; Bill King; Ellen Bernie; Paula Greif; Mary Giatas; Phil Pessoni; Betty Thompkins; Gary Simmons; and Jack of Kenneth's Salon.

I am grateful to my friend Steven Aronson for his crisp editorial overview; and to my sister Vernette, for always being there.

A "Natural Beauty" Who Me?

I can't count the number of times I've heard or seen myself described in print as a "Natural Beauty." And every time, I think to myself, "They should only know what it takes to be 'Naturally Beautiful.' " The term conjures up a woman who has been born beautiful and who, without any effort at all, remains beautiful. Well, there's no such creature in life—there never was, and there never will be.

Famous models are often thought to be possessed of some kind of magic—fortunate, gorgeous, remote creatures, strangers to blemishes and telltale wrinkles, circles under the eyes, extra pounds, blasted "cellulite," bulging thighs, and such mundane worries as which shoes to wear with which dress and whether or not a certain dress is smart or out of date. All a model has to do is enlist the hired help of a famous hair stylist or makeup artist to put the final touch, the coronet of perfection, on her inborn glamour and aside from that, she never has to fret over her appearance the way other women do—right?

Wrong. A thousand times wrong. Twenty push-ups, fifty sit-ups, and one hundred leg raises a day wrong.

So people think I look the way I do because I'm "lucky," because, like Beatrice in *Much Ado*, I was "born under a star that danced." When I work out at the gym, for instance, many of the women there come up and ask me, "What in the world are *you* doing here?" Or else they don't say anything and just sneak looks at me to see how I do the exercises. Or else they can't look at me at all! (The implication being that exercise is strictly for that accursed race: the overweight and out of shape.)

What was Cheryl Tiegs doing there? Listen my children and you shall hear. . . . At the beginning of my modeling career I ate my way up to a gross 155 pounds; I had a double chin (*two* double chins), and when I lay down I couldn't find my hipbones, and I was only twenty. My egregious eating habits almost destroyed not only my figure but my skin, and no ad in the lost and found was going to get my hipbones back. I had made the near fatal mistake of believing that I *was* a "Natural Beauty" and of taking my looks—my slim figure and good skin—totally for granted. But I was caught in that mistake—by Nature, which was there to remind me, quickly and unsparingly, that the gate-

Minnesota — 1955.

way to good looks is good health, plain and simple. I should say plain but *not* so simple, because I had to be remade, to remake myself, to start over again at the beginning: I had to study nutrition to learn what foods would keep me slender without depleting my energy. And, reflecting one day on my reflection in the mirror, I determined to learn how to exercise, so I could get my shape back *and keep it*. No makeup artist, no hair stylist in the world, no cosmetician, can supply a woman with the essentials of beauty: a good figure, good skin, and eyes and hair that shine (Oh, these magicians can see to it that she glitters for an evening, but then the glitter fades like fairy gold). The essentials are *her* job—*your* job, *my* job—and, as I was to discover, it requires self-discipline, knowledge, and a heavy bundle of work.

When I went into modeling, I was like any other girl just starting out—insecure. When you're that young, you think that everyone else is super-confident about themselves and that you're the only one who's weak in the knees and a little white about the lips. What I didn't realize is that there's a side to insecurity called vulnerability and it's very sympathetic, at least at the moment when a person is on the verge of accepting full responsibility for herself. It's true that love and even admiration can be killed dead by cockiness. My point is that there's more than one kind of self-assurance just as there's more than one kind of vanity and more than one kind of love.

In those days, I knew next to nothing about fashion. I didn't have a clue about how to style my hair—I don't even think they had hot rollers back then—or about how to apply makeup. (I remember sneaking into the gym in high school and putting on mascara, which we were forbidden to wear till we turned sweet sixteen, putting it on illicitly in front of the mirrors with all the other girls—it was almost as wicked as running off to the bathroom to smoke. My sixteenth birthday present was a tube of lipstick—baby pink, what else? I can almost taste it now. I had that tube of lipstick for a whole year, I had so little occasion to use it. But it made me feel quite the little lady. As for mascara, my first time out I went and did a really stupid thing—I got it in my hair. One of my girlfriends said, "What's that in your hair?" I ran to the bathroom, feeling I'd touched the rock bottom of the sea. She hadn't even noticed my lush lashes that I'd used the mascara to accentuate. Anyway, those were the days.) I didn't know the first thing about putting a "look" together or anything about the tricks of our trade: perfumes, accessories, shampoos, skin-care products. I was very fortunate to be working with the top makeup artists and hair stylists and they gave me advice, for which I was extremely grateful (at times their advice amounted to a life line). But I also had to learn for and by myself just when their advice was not for me. I had to find—by trial and error, hit and miss—the look that expressed *my* personality, that made *me* feel comfortable with myself and that in turn attracted others to me. My experience was not by any means unique or exotic; in fact, if anything it was representative. Every girl who believes in the life of her looks has to learn the exact same things about beauty that I did.

A "Natural Beauty," then, is not some lucky girl who can keep her looks without having to work hard at it; nor is she a butterfly of fashion whose appearance is contrived, self-conscious, and quite lacking in *sincerity*. Natural beauty, to the extent that it can be achieved at all, must embody a contemporary attitude toward life, energy, incorrigible vitality, and, at one and the same time, self-awareness and a wholly delightful forgetfulness of self. No so-called natural anything would dream of erecting a wall of artifice between herself and her beholder—such as wigs, excess makeup, the falsest of false eyelashes, untouchable bouffants teased into man-o'-war hair helmets, and ferociously flamboyant clothes; if she resorts to *any* of these things, she won't stay "natural" for long, will she? Some women can manage an elaborate facade better than others; occasionally it even becomes the hallmark of their style, but sooner or later this artificial look comes unglued, and then the big picture drops out along with the frame.

I usually feel too made-up after a single modeling assignment. My feeling is my makeup's had its brief heyday before the cameras, and I can't wait to get home and wash it all off. Too much makeup has the air of a premeditated device and the look of a barrier, and a barrier is a bar or obstacle, something that restrains or obstructs or limits access—in this case to none other than y-o-u. You should want other people to feel as if they could touch you. A natural look, the look that should be coveted, lets you and others relax and communicate.

Not that a natural look should be *so* laid back, so once-over-lightly, that it's drab and eminently ignorable. Too little attention paid to hair, makeup, and wardrobe, too little awareness of and sense of style,

DECEMBER 22 FRIDAY

ke NOON
BC for
n footage
no + ele charge
E PB
Xmas shop
ad. Ave
rs to look......
LD—
t for Xmas
decorations
E for bath
5:00
arrives
d with

tletoe
setta's
ath
Ribbon
s books
tc. etc.
D
ecorated

Barbara
or
oj + Vodka

om Nix.....
emory of
who ran

her way
w Wyeth")
B.
ele HERD

HOME
ervice:
chyssoise, steak tartar, etc, etc.
IEAU de la GRAVE red wine

will definitely not advance the good fortunes of a woman. The modern beauty industry has provided us with so many aids that there is no reason for any woman's doubts about her physical appearance to remain unanswered. Today every woman can look her best, and none of us need actually see the work that went into the enterprise. Vanity can be innocent of trivial or corrosive self-regard; it can be healthy, positive—"I am proud of who it is I am! I deserve some attention and I hope I get it!" The dictionary opposite for "vain" is "useful," but vanity can be a very useful quality. All of us, to one degree or another, are vain. And so we should be. Let us, then, contrive to be vain of our good figures and fine clothes.

The natural look, once you know how to bring it off, should take relatively little of your time. I hate spending even an hour fussing in front of a mirror in the morning, and even if I didn't mind it as much as I do, my schedule doesn't permit it. (Whose does these days? Nothing could be more alien to the spirit of our times than spending most of one's spare moments working on your face and body and thinking about the way you look; the world today makes wider claims on all of us.) And yet, an attractive appearance is always going to help make a woman more effective in both her career and her personal life—not least of all by giving her the self-confidence she needs. But if she becomes obsessed with being and staying attractive, if that becomes the sole focus of her life and she works ceaselessly and unremittingly at it, it may pay her back by consuming her at the expense of her spontaneity and spirit.

During the two years at the beginning of the seventies, when I took "early retirement" from modeling, I went into a decline. The most glaring manifestation of this decline was that I was spending much too much time on my appearance, scrutinizing every infinitesimal wrinkle and pore and examining my hair twenty times a day for split ends—I'd clearly lost all perspective. At the age of twenty-two, there I was anticipating and dreading the signs of old age. The narcissistic impulse that we are all born with and that, with a little luck, fades into the background around about puberty, was reasserting itself—but in a sadly disproportionate way. When I returned to work, however, I began consorting again with my active, unself-regarding self—there were so many things to do, so many places to go every day that the unhealthy concern over my appearance just phased itself out. And do you know something? I looked much the better for it. I was once more focusing on the worthwhile things, and though achieving and maintaining good looks was still important to me (and a major part of my work as well), I was doing it with far less pettiness and drudgery.

Now once again I found that there was joy to be had in preparing myself for a special evening—a leisurely bath, a facial, a little experimentation with a glittery new makeup, and the *pièce de résistance*—the selection of some fabulous outfit to wear. I was doing it again with great *désinvolture*, offhandedness. Before these special occasions I enjoy toying with new makeup products, hair colorings, conditioners, and other gadgetry. But the rest of the time I want my beauty regimen to be convenient and easy to accomplish.

Every woman needs and wants a system of health and grooming habits that will both insure she'll look her best most of the time and also take as little as possible of her time. No woman need feel "desperate" about her appearance every time she's faced with an important event in her social or professional life. Good looks are looks that wear well—they don't disintegrate under pressure. But they do require maintenance; the woman who cultivates her physical qualities instead of nagging at and worrying over them will never "suddenly" discover that she is fifteen pounds overweight or that her hair is a dull, drab mass or mess or that her skin is dry or that she has nothing stylish in her wardrobe. She's learned the basics of a good appearance, and the first basic is that she must conscientiously follow an everyday regimen, including a low-calorie, nutritious diet, exercise, and a program of skin care to keep her figure and skin in good, humming condition. Just add to this a good haircut, a well-thought-out wardrobe, and a practical selection of cosmetics, and her most elegant self will always be available to her.

No system should be rigid, it should always leave room for the growth and change and experimentation that are so important to a contemporary look.

Experiments, however, must be undertaken with some caution and mitigated by self-knowledge. Once, during my fallow housewife period, I was going to a theater première in Los Angeles and I wanted to look special, so I took a long silk scarf and swirled it around my head a few times and knotted it in a fanciful way and let it droop. When I presented myself to my husband, he suggested as politely as possible under the

—my first cover

dire circumstances that maybe I didn't *need* that special creative touch. I undid the wild scarf, and went out to meet the world on my own terms, posing as nobody but myself. And that's who I've remained.

The chapters that follow are full of tips (many of them drawn from the professionals I've worked with for so long) for health and beauty that I've learned in my fourteen years of modeling and my thirty-two years of living. Reading them should help you come up with a look that expresses your personality and attracts others to you. I'm going to ask you a lot of questions about yourself and if you take the time and trouble to answer them honestly, I think you'll be able to pick out the areas where you need help the most.

Throughout the book I'll be coming back again and again to the crucial relationship between the body and the mind. How you think and feel is related in a thousand ways to how you look. I'll be suggesting methods for you to enhance your positive points and make light of, or disguise, your less good ones—by means of regular exercise, carefully applied makeup, and practical wardrobe selection. The time-saving things I've learned to do throughout the day to maintain my appearance in the face of a murderously busy schedule, you'll learn to do, too. And, to give the complete picture, there's a list of the most common mistakes women make when it comes to diet, exercise, makeup, skin care, and wardrobe.

It is no unattainable ideal to which I would have you aspire. It's your own originality that I hope to help you find—an active, healthy attitude. I want you to cultivate or develop your own humor and sympathy. The rest is icing on a really good cake.

—the wave of the future...

When I was a teenager in Alhambra, California, my best friend was always running across the street to show me her latest copies of *Seventeen* and *Glamour*. "Cheryl," she would say, "you should be a model!" And I thought that she must see something in my round face and tall, skinny body that I couldn't see. I took in what she was saying, but I didn't believe it.

I studied the faces of the beauties in those magazines as if they were lessons I had to learn for school —Jean Shrimpton, Colleen Corby, Twiggy. I remember some of the individual pictures—the perfect profiles, pixie noses, lustrous, long, beautiful hair, and snazzy clothes. I wanted so badly to order a neat plastic raincoat in one of the photo spreads; it was the most weightless adornment I had ever seen, and underneath it there was a heavenly blue sweater and a deep blue skirt. Luckily I didn't have the money. I say luckily because the coat just wouldn't have looked right on me—for one thing, I didn't have the wardrobe to wear underneath all that see-through plastic. The world of the models in all those photo spreads seemed about as unattainable as that raincoat. I planned to go on to college and become a teacher or a nurse.

But then a representative from a modeling agency came to speak to a girls' club at my high school; he talked about the experience and meaning of being a model, from every perspective, and he brought the modeling world a little closer—at least it ceased to belong simply to the province of the magazines. After his talk, he took three or four of us aside and invited us to come to Pasadena for an interview.

I remember I put on a little pink dress—with a pink bow on top of my hair—and my mother and I went up to his office. He accepted me on the spot as a student in his modeling class—along with a thousand other girls, as I would discover—for a fee of three hundred dollars. We were given lessons in etiquette by a woman who would always enter the classroom in white gloves and tell us things like to be sure and eat our ice cream at dinner parties before it melted; and there were lessons in commercials conducted by a woman who had never done a commercial but who would hold up an eraser with the greatest authority and show us how to say meaningfully, "this is the *best* eraser"—and we believed her.

I modeled in department store fashion shows for free, and occasionally I would get up at dawn and report as an extra for *Beach Blanket Bingo*-type movies for twenty-five dollars a day (once, I was cut from the final picture because I didn't have enough "personality"; you were supposed to dance wildly, with complete abandon—I guess they wanted a real bimbo and I wasn't it). So many times my mother and I would drive in for interviews after school and they'd say "thanks but no thanks, you're beautiful, but don't call *us*." Sometimes I posed for snapshots to be used by illustrators of fictional magazine stories; for this I received the princely sum of five dollars an hour. On one occasion I modeled at a nursing home; I paraded around in the fashions I'd brought with me, and I chatted with each and every patient. The patients would then judge me on my "charm, personality, and fashion appeal" —which seems kind of funny, when I think about it now. The head of the modeling school always encouraged us to try out for contests like "Miss Army" and "Miss Navy." My best friend in the school won Miss Navy and I was one of the runners-up. I remember the little army hats—honest-to-God official ones—that they'd stick on you if you placed. Who voted I don't remember. I actually won one of those contests once; for a few hours I got to hold the awe-inspiring title of "Miss Rocket Tower." Somebody'd needed a girl to get up at five in the morning and go to the beach and stand by a rocket tower. It was in the papers and that was it, that was the end of my reign.

Meanwhile, some of the other girls had been talking to other modeling agencies, and I began to get the drift that ours was the smallest of small-time. It was about then that I made the switch to the Nina Blanchard agency, and that's when my career—if you'll forgive the rocket tower imagery—really took off.

I was determined from the start to work as hard as I could and to go as far as hard work could take me. This often entailed giving up social functions or even just being quietly with my friends. I found myself rushing to modeling interviews right after school. I had to go to a lot more interviews than I care to remember before landing a single job. My hair wasn't long enough, I was too tall—there were at least a million things wrong with me, but everyone was very nice—what they said, in effect, was "Don't give up."

With Ali MacGraw in St. Thomas

MARINELAND SKY TOWER — Model Cheryl Tiegs shows model of new California landmark under construction at Marineland of the Pacific. The Swiss - built tower is scheduled to be opened by July 4. Taller than the Statue of Liberty, it is equipped with a two - tier rotating elevator that will whisk visitors skyward for a panoramic view. Sixty persons can ride at a time, 30 to each tier.

My family and friends supported me in my career choice, although my father was always uneasy about the "types" he was afraid I would meet in the fashion world. "Of course you can model," he told me, "but I'd feel better if you didn't date anybody in the business." Naturally, within a month I disobeyed him. I dated a very cute male model who took to wearing boots with two-inch heels because he was shorter than I was. My father had very little to fear; my date from the wild, wicked world of modeling would always take me to the local donut shop after the movies—it was all very innocent, really.

When I was seventeen I entered California State College in Los Angeles, planning to major in English. I continued modeling on the side. My big break came when I was featured in a Cole of California bathing suit ad, a dreamed-of double-page spread, that appeared in national magazines. The fashion editor of *Glamour*, Julie Britt, saw me in the ad and booked me sight unseen to model *Glamour*'s spring fashions for a week in St. Thomas in the Virgin Islands. Julie's call had come at four, and the flight to St. Thomas was at seven. I was half in shock as I packed, and I did what you do when you pack half in shock—I packed all the wrong things: it was winter in L.A., so I took care to include all my little wool dresses and I forgot to bring my bathing suit. The other model on the trip was Ali MacGraw; we shared a room, and that first night she unpacked all these beautiful summer dresses from Paraphernalia. She kept apologizing for having so many. When she got an eyeful of what I'd brought with me, she threw me a dress across the room and said, with thoughtfulness and tact I'll never forget, "Maybe you'd like to try something like this?" I'd never seen clothes like Ali's. In Pasadena you didn't have Paraphernalia. For the first time ever, I felt I looked really fabulous: I had on the latest, hottest little numbers, and don't forget, I was in the tropics. (Would St. Thomas ever be the same?)

This assignment resulted in my first *Glamour* cover, and then *Glamour* started booking me regularly. Usually they came out to California and photographed me there, but once they flew me to Fort Lauderdale during Easter when the college kids were there *en masse* for their vacation (talk about density!)—the famous hairdresser Kenneth was along and he introduced me to the more sophisticated look of big fat braids down my back. And I got to go to New York several times. During all this, I was still very much the college En-

— the Cole Scandal

The Great Cole Scandal Suit

glish major, but frankly, it's the real world that's always taught me the most.

I knew that for any aspiring model, New York was the place, the "Big Time," the ultimate challenge, and that in order to "make it" I would have to make it there; New York was the one and only place to be validated, or at least the one and only place where the validating counted. I decided to try my luck there. With a model friend from California, Kelly Harmon, I moved into a suite on the first floor of the Shoreham Hotel on West Fifty-fifth Street just off Fifth Avenue. Every morning at four the garbage was collected right in front of our windows, and that included the discarded bottles from the Shoreham restaurant. It was all a little much for Kelly and after about a month she moved back to L.A. I was on my own now.

With Kelly in L.A.

I didn't understand the labyrinthine bus and subway systems, so getting myself to job interviews was a real ordeal, weighted down as I was with a heavy shoulder bag full of hairpieces, falls, makeup, hot rollers, lingerie, and other atrocities as well as my newly purchased appointment book. It was August, and the heat was coming down out of the sky and up out of the pavements, annihilating whatever was foolhardy enough to be in between them; by the end of a day like that, I was drained and limp, and my feet had blisters.

And whenever I felt confident that I had conquered the bus system, my uptown bus would turn a corner on me long before my stop and I'd have to get off and start all over again—that is, if I'd been lucky and been observant enough to notice in time.

One shooting that summer was scheduled for Bridgehampton in the outer reaches of Long Island. Our first stop was Cartier's where we picked up thousands of dollars' worth of jewelry, which was to be our lavish and light-hearted companion on the trip out. So far so good. But then it began to pour, and then, an hour out of New York we had a flat tire. The fashion editor swerved over to the right lane and told me to stay in the car with the Cartier family jewels while she went to get help. Presently she reappeared with a tow truck in hand or rather, in tow. And soon we were on our way again. By the time we arrived at this beautifully restored old barn, it seemed a true haven. And suddenly I just felt that things were going to work out for me.

Thanks to the exposure I'd had in *Glamour*, I was booked fairly solid from the beginning. I accepted every job I was offered except lingerie, which I didn't think was dignified.

"Big Time" in N.Y.C.

Aside from lingerie, though, there was practically nothing I didn't model. I modeled for newspaper advertisements, women's magazines, catalogs, you name it. I had as many as five bookings in a single day. Often on a job they ask you to work "just a little overtime," so then you're late for the next place, and you have to work "just a little overtime" there to make up for it—so it's a bit of a vicious circle till you arrive home late at night, practically good for nothing but sleep.

I soon discovered that those etiquette classes at the modeling school back home weren't going to come in all that handy and that if I let the ice cream melt at a dinner party in New York, the harlequin sky wouldn't fall in. I watched how the other models did their hair. I knew next to nothing about the high-fashion look. I remember Lauren Hutton patiently sitting in the studio—she'd just finished putting her makeup on and now she was taking the trouble to show me how to put mine on. I had always admired her. She was just beginning to make it really big with *Vogue* covers. That day, when she went out in front of the cameras, she looked *incredibly* sexy—she kind of pushed her breasts up. Then I went out, feeling like a little girl with lots of makeup on but, thanks to Lauren, looking pretty good. I've always found that the top models are the most helpful as well as the most down-to-earth.

Many of my first assignments were for modeling junior fashions. I must say I rarely met an unpleasant client or editor, and I never encountered the legendary lecherous photographer who chases models around the studio and worse.

Particularly wearing on my nerves were the "go-sees" or tryouts, where there were usually ten or twenty girls waiting to be called for their interviews for a given commercial. These were sometimes referred to as "cattle-calls," a cruel but accurate word for them. One day I saw a girl I particularly looked up to come out and I thought, well, that's that, she'll get the job, and the next day when I was told that in fact *I* was the one who'd gotten it, I realized the quick turnover there could be.

Modeling is a mercurial profession as well as a very demanding one. Yesterday's sensation is today's has-been. Also, modeling, like everything else in life, can be lonely. The girls are young; usually it's the first time in their lives they've been alone in a big city, and they're making unrealistic amounts of money to boot. They are criticized by some clients; glorified, even apotheosized by others. I don't need to tell you that this can be confusing psychologically, and it's not hard to lose perspective. There was one beautiful but temperamental girl who burst into tears—for no reason I could ever fathom—at every shooting. I went on a trip with her to Hawaii with Helmut Newton for *Vogue*, and every single day she cried. If she didn't like how she'd been made up, she would go into the bathroom and wipe off the makeup and throw it at the mirror or something equally insulting to the makeup artist, who would then have to start all over. In Hawaii you have these tropical showers for half an hour every so often —they're no big deal, but every time we had one, she would go stalking off somewhere to cry. At first everyone had quite naturally sympathized with her, but by the end of the trip nobody but nobody was speaking to her. It was clearly only a matter of time before clients and photographers were going to refuse to accommodate her. There are just too many lovely young girls —emotionally stable ones—competing for the same jobs. I considered myself lucky to be a model. I was grateful for the opportunity to make so much money per hour, and I wanted to give the clients what they were paying for—not only efficiently but as graciously as I could manage. I made it my policy to be businesslike and, once I got the gist of the bus and subway systems, prompt.

Julie Britt, Barbara Stone (my first New York agent), and many of the photographers and magazine editors I had worked with helped me adjust to New York, whose ways are wonderful but also sometimes very mysterious. They helped me move into empty, cold apartments—I had about seven apartments in one year, I think. I finally found one I really liked, on Seventy-second Street between Second and Third avenues—a nice brownstone. I was working so hard I didn't have time to furnish it, but a photographer I knew brought over a table and some chairs he had, and on Christmas day, with my apartment as "spacious and sparse as an autumn wood," another photographer friend appeared at my door with a tree, so I would at least have the smell of Christmas.

And Julie Britt would make sure I got out of the city from time to time. She invited me to her weekend house in Water Mill on Long Island where, with the sea on one side and the potato fields stretching, it seems, into infinity on the other, I always had the somehow comforting feeling of being at land's end. So little by little I got used to New York. I'll say one thing for it: never for a moment was it boring.

Twiggy + me . . .

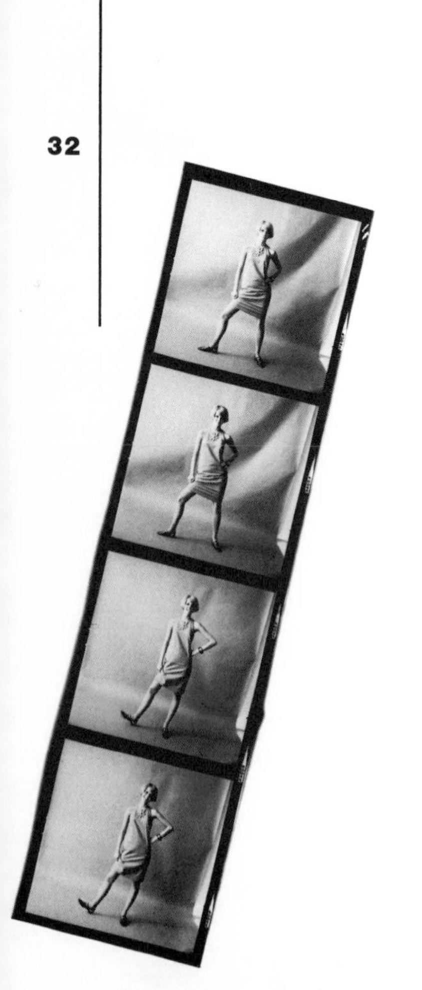

I discovered that most of the top models had never even gone to modeling school but had learned what models need to know the same way I had learned it—through practical experience and through a careful examination of the clothes, makeup, and hairstyles featured in the fashion magazines. One of the first things I noticed was how much these styles changed within a single issue even, and I realized that the most interesting models were the ones I could look at page after page and they would have a different look every time, which of course is how you last as a model. I also learned to analyze the work of the well-known photographers, how they used different kinds of lighting and the different ways they liked their models to pose for them. I remember studying the way my idol Jean Shrimpton flew across a room in *Vogue* (with the uncramped confidence of a bird!). In the privacy of my own bedroom I tried to fly—like Icarus, I was prepared to try anything once!—and what I looked like was ever so hopelessly earthbound. I also admired Twiggy, and in front of my mirror I imitated *her* bird-like pose, but my feet seemed to be made of clay or something, leaving me to wonder how *they* did it. In time I came to understand that your hips and shoulders, arms, hands, and even facial expression all have to work together in a split second of camera time. With practice and knowledge, I became quite a credible flier across rooms.

Another thing I did was buy the European fashion magazines so I could study how the European models ("mannequins" they call them over there) achieved their svelte (*soignée* they call it over there) look. I was my own guinea pig, I tried everything out on myself, and sometimes it worked, and often it didn't. Because I was a model I got to see the new fashions before other people did. I developed an eye for which styles would flatter me the most, and soon I was able to put together a look that expressed my own personality and struggling sense of style. Above all, I was no longer timid. You might not be able to see anything exactly courageous in this but one day I went out and bought a bizarre antique snake ring; I was somehow sure it would look right on me, and probably the reason it did look right on me was because I felt it would. A little thing called mind over matter, I guess.

When I first came to New York, in the late sixties, models were a lot thinner and much more dramatically made-up and stylized than they are today. They wore hairpieces, falls, and three or four false eyelashes all stuck together and then, to my astonishment, *glued* to their eyelids. I loved wearing the falls—all that hair cascading down my back made me feel as if something unbelievably romantic was just about to happen to me. (Luckily, I didn't hold my breath.) But when it came to wearing the heavy makeup, I upped and rebelled. "Go back in the dressing room, Cheryl, and put on a little more," the stylists all kept telling me, but I could never bring myself to paint my face to the degree that they wanted me to. I was new and unknown and very eager to please, but I just was convinced that exaggerated heavy makeup was all wrong for me, that it would destroy rather than enhance my looks.

I used liner, shadow, and mascara, but I drew the proverbial line at the false eyelashes—besides making my eyes tear and itch, they gave me the queasy feeling I was assuming a false identity by masking the natural expression in my eyes. When I had them on, it was like I was wearing a hat over my eyeballs.

Then, just as my modeling career began going strong, I started putting on unwanted weight—a traumatic enough thing for anyone, to be sure, but for a model a public as well as a private event. For a long time the extra weight hardly affected my bookings. Julie Britt would just mock-groan and mock-huff and puff as she zipped me into the outfit I was to wear, and as for the stylists, they would just have to remember to order a size ten for me from the designer instead of my former size eight. But then the day came when I began bursting out of the size ten!

The stylists began having to cut my dresses and pants up the back seams to make room for my hippy hips. And the final photographs now had to be retouched; my thighs and midriff had to be thinned down, not to mention the sum total of my two double chins. Everyone was very tactful and I shall always be grateful for their understanding during this difficult time. Barbara Stone especially, who would defend me by saying that I was "just a great big healthy California girl."

But the day of reckoning was near at hand, and like most days of reckoning it would turn out not to be without value. It was a cold, dreary day to begin with; perhaps all days of reckoning are cold, dreary days to begin with. I'd been booked by a photographer I had long admired but never before worked with. When I got to his studio, I went right into the dressing room to change. None of the clothes fit me, but I wasn't worried; I just assumed the stylists would make them work for me, as they had always done before. But when the phone rang in the studio (what made me so agonizingly sure it would be for me?), it was my agent calling to say she'd just been called by the client, etc., etc., "Cheryl," she said, in a very embarrassed voice, "You can go home now." I gathered up my belongings with a false smile pasted to my face and left the studio, completely and utterly humiliated. Everyone there—the photographer, the other models, the stylists—knew that I was having to leave because I was just too fat for the job. The first thing I did when I got home was put on my baggy jogging suit and, in the forlorn hope of reversing reality, run around the block several times. But the second I got in the door I hit the refrigerator for a Sara Lee fix, as if fulfillment were to be found only there.

When I was twenty-two, I got married to Stan Dragoti, the brilliant "creative director" of the innovative agency Wells, Rich, Greene. We moved back to L.A., and I decided to retire from modeling—I'd worked hard in New York and I felt I needed some time for myself. Stan said, "You'll be sorry," but that's always something you have to find out for yourself—as I did, watching my self-esteem slip through the net of leisure. At first I read a great deal, took cooking lessons, tried gardening—all the sacred little tokens of domestic happiness. But, as Stan had predicted, it just wasn't enough. When people asked me how I was, I found myself talking about Stan and all the exciting things *he* was doing. I no longer had goals or any real purpose in life; soon I began to feel that I was of little or no account. But then, on a day when I had nothing more to do than peel and chop a couple of bunches of carrots for a soup, I got a call from one of my former clients asking me to consider modeling for them again. I immediately said yes, and I know that whatever the future may bring, I'll never take early retirement again.

"You've come a long way, baby."

It was during my so-called "retirement," though, that I regained my slender figure. One night Stan and I were at the movies; as usual I had one hand in the buttered popcorn and the other on a candy bar. But when a beautiful actress in a bikini appeared on the screen, the lump of dough I then was groaned inwardly, "If only *I* could look like *that* again." I was on the verge of making some Faustian pact with the devil when it occurred to me that maybe the only difference between her and me was one of will power. My fat, eating self immediately went on strike. (Well, maybe not immediately—I think I finished the buttered popcorn.) In a year of quite serious dieting I plummeted from 155 to under 120 pounds. My face and figure came back to me, but with a new maturity, my face having acquired more definition, my body more muscularity. In modeling circles I'd been known for my young, innocent look, but no more—after the trauma of these cookie-jar years (everything is the result of something, right?), my looks were at last appropriate for sophisticated, high-fashion modeling. And my exterior circumstances weren't the only thing that had changed; my whole attitude was fresher, thanks to the sheer discipline involved in exercising properly and losing weight.

Now that my "junior" days in fashion were behind me, I had access to a greater range of magazines. I traveled all over the world; I was deliciously torn in all different directions. I posed for *Sports Illustrated*, *Harper's Bazaar*, and not only for American *Vogue* but for English, French, Italian, and Australian *Vogue* as well. Some of these magazines used my name so that I began to exist a little in the public eye.

I was thrilled when the Virginia Slims people called to ask me to do a series of ads for them. I'd always thought theirs were the classiest ads. And what's more, they were going to let *me* choose the clothes I thought suited me best. For one ad I would select very sporty fisherman's gear and for another a very elegant dress that I'd wear with my hair pointing up, in the direction of the twinkling stars. When you're having a good time, the pictures turn out the best. On the night of the famous blackout in New York, I was at a friend's high-rise apartment on Gramercy Park, and I had to walk down all twenty-five flights of stairs because I was booked for a Virginia Slims ad the first thing the next morning. When I arrived at the studio, there was of course neither electricity nor running water. But there were plenty of candles and everyone was laughing and running around opening bottles of champagne. What better way to get a shooting started than with laughter and champagne? No, those were some of my best pictures.

As a lifelong sports fan, I was pleased to be asked to take part in the annual *Sports Illustrated* bathing-suit feature. We went down to Manaus, the oldest city in Brazil, to shoot. On our last day there, we went out for about two hours on a river in a canoe. I had on a thick fishnet bathing suit which I promise you the naked eye could not see through. They asked me to go

into the water, and I did. It was sunset and the water was the color of tea. When that shot was developed, you could see right through my thick suit—it must have been the combination of the light, the wetness, and the filters on the cameras. People still ask me how I feel about that fishnet bathing-suit shot. I'm not embarrassed because it was natural. I've seen plenty of photos in which the models were all covered up that were much more provocative—deliberately so. I got thousands of letters, most of them favorable, to say the least.

I was still living in Los Angeles but I was spending a lot of my time now traveling around the world. It was on these trips that I learned the difference between looking and seeing.

Travel of course has its light side, but even light sides have their dark sides. When I was asked to model a bikini in Acapulco, I accepted at once because what could be more glamorous. The photographer took me out to this huge rock in a boat, literally deposited me there like a castaway, then sped back to shore to shoot me with a telephoto lens. I noticed that the tide was rising and the rock area shrinking. Huge crabs crawled up from the waterline—closer and closer to me. I actually screamed at them, trying vainly to scare them into going back to their element. And meanwhile the water, naturally, kept rising. By now I was yelling and signaling wildly to the photographer but he either couldn't hear me or else thought I was getting all happily carried away with the job. I thought of the English poet Stevie Smith's great two-line poem, "I was much further out than you thought/And not waving but drowning." Finally the photographer got the message that his star model *was* about to be carried away—not with the job but with the tides; and rescue was at hand.

It is also possible to feel stranded in a speedboat—to this I can attest. We were on the wide, free, open seas off Honolulu; Helmut Newton, the photographer, likes the real thing, so when he discovered that we were behind an atomic submarine heading off to Alaska he was hell-bent on overtaking it. Picture me stretched out on the edge of the transom decked in white with Helmut filming all the while and me pretending I wasn't the least bit terrified I was going to be sucked into the wake of the monstrous sub. The final shot looks casual, but believe me, it was panic city all the way!

I vividly recall another colorful assignment in the tropics, where another model and I would spend hours

VOGUE

American VOGUE

Brazil—1974

GUE

1973 Hawaii Resort scene '73

maillot,

shirt

Sun, sand, water, and these—what else is there? . . . The supplest little black maillots on Waikiki beach, left, and on you—absolutely no construction to them whatever. They feel like part of you . . . and show of all the rest. The cross-strappe one by Maidenform; Antron nyl and Lycra. $28. At Lord & Tayl Filene's; Burdine's. Plunge-y one Cole of California; of Antron lon and Lycra. $20. Saks Fifth nue. Sharp, shirty way to shore bandeau and trim, tight shorts —a crisp white blouson no than a baseball jacket, b here on all that unclutter that stretches for miles Honolulu. Blouson (about shorts (about $18) by Re for Jones New York; W Monsanto polyester an cotton (Greenwood M February, Franklin Sim el's, Washington, D.C

Malibu—Australian VOGUE

and hours having our hair and makeup expertly done, after which we'd dress up in the most fabulous evening clothes and lay on the accessories. And *then*, dressed to the nines, we were directed to fall backwards into the pool! It took the photographer a while to get the right moment. I think we had to fall backwards into the pool twice a night for seven days running. And each time everything had to be *just right*—the champagne asparkle in our glasses, our hair, the expressions on our faces, the slits in our dresses, our shoes, necklaces, bracelets. Such was life in the higher reaches—and lower depths.

I went to Rome to model collections for Italian *Vogue*. David Bailey was the photographer. We stayed at the famous Hotel Hassler on the Piazza di Spagna—a dreamlike setting. The collections were photographed at night, so I had to work from eight in the evening till four in the morning. Around dawn, after our "workday" was over, we'd go off to some wonderful little café on the Via Veneto for eggs and champagne. It was like something out of *La Dolce Vita*. Then back I'd go to the Hassler to sleep all day. I loved having my usual schedule completed reversed for a change.

But after a while the novelty wore off and I felt like I was living out of a suitcase. I'm not saying I was a captive to my career; I don't think I was ever that. I always felt that the rewards and excitement involved in modeling were worth a little sacrifice. And anyway, for me security was not specifically synonymous with home; I had trained myself to find security wherever I happened to be (or find myself). Many models complain a lot about the stress. The amount of stress *is* great; striking poses on different continents month after month isn't all "champagne, sunglasses, and autographs." But I learned to enjoy the variety and to see the necessary travel as an often delightful extension of my inner home.

Thousands of girls have written asking me to advise them on how to embark on a modeling career. For photographic modeling, also called "print" work, there are very definite physical requirements. "Print" models are almost always taller than average (5′7″ to 5′10″ in bare feet), seldom weigh more than 120 pounds, and have long torsos, long legs, and long necks. Hips should measure approximately 34″–36″, waist 24″–26″, and bust 32″–36″. They must be able to wear a size eight, the size that most fashion samples come in. Contrary to the common belief, today you can be *too* thin to model. (I have a friend who has a

—falling for Helmut Newton.

perfectly exquisite face, but eventually clients stopped booking her because she couldn't fill out their clothes.) Hands and feet should be shapely, skin clear, teeth white and in line, hair shining and healthy. Circles or bags under the eyes are a disqualifying feature if they're beyond the pale of the retoucher's talents.

The most important qualification for a "print" model is, naturally, a photogenic face, because it is not the model herself the client hires to advertise his product so much as it's her two-dimensional image. "Photogenic," however, does not necessarily have to mean "conventionally pretty." There are plenty of beautiful faces that happen not to photograph well, and other, more ordinary faces that do.

It's not possible to define the qualities of a photogenic face. Like a successful painting that can't easily be described, it could be summed up as something that—simply and mysteriously—"works." I think it's helped me to have small features, since the camera increases their size, and wide-set eyes, but there are many successful models who have large features and close-set eyes. There just aren't any rules.

For showroom, ramp and fitting models, who work for designers or fashion shows, the requirements are pretty much the same, they're just not as strict. But for any kind of modeling, the younger you start (after sixteen), the better your chances for success.

One of the most important things is to be able to work spontaneously, unself-consciously, without a morbid awareness of your every gesture and expression. This takes years of practice, of both learning and then learning how to put what you've learned into the back of your mind. This holds true for the photographer as well; he can be dragged down by techniques, filters, lenses, exposure meters—and miss the main drift of the occasion, lose his sense of its aesthetic as he pursues a more accurate f-stop. The more accomplished the model, the more naturally she will be able to work with the photographer. Some photographers operate in deadly silence like surgeons or scientists; others coax, flatter, and cajole; some work with music on; some prefer to have clients, art directors, and complex sets; others prefer to work alone and with just the bare no-scene paper. Flexibility is essential.

Beauty, youth, and a photogenic quality, however, do not automatically make for a successful model. Success comes with learning such things as changing hair and makeup to match the clothes you're wearing, and projecting a personality to suit the mood of the photograph. You must be able to put on a dress you don't even especially like and make it look like it was made for you, like you were just on this earth to wear it. I was lucky: most of the clothes I modeled were gorgeous, but there were times when I had to invent a way to make them appealing. A laugh can help—or an amusing gesture, perhaps wrinkling the dress up a bit —*anything* to make you look like you're at ease with what you're wearing.

A good model knows how to make a photograph come alive. She can't just stand there like a doll or a wax effigy, one hand on her hip and the other on her hair. Successful models, even if they're stiffly posed with accessories and pins and wires holding everything in place, have and use an innate sense of timing. They have a rapport, or at least a communication, with the photographer, and know instinctively when he's going to take the picture. Every photographer has his own particular rhythm. At the moment his shutter snaps, the model's whole body—hands, feet, smile, glance, and outfit—should fall into place.

Modeling is for the most part an exciting and a broadening profession, but this doesn't mean there aren't going to be frustrations and disappointments—slow periods, delays, postponements. You may have to invest money in photographic composites and transportation and hair salons and clothes before you earn anything to speak of. And you don't get to keep the clothes you model, which are valuable samples belonging to the designer. You will be rejected not once but often, and you will have to learn not to take this too personally. Once you are established, your career will demand grueling work and self-discipline. If you regularly stay out till dawn, dissipation will inevitably register in your face. I've always loved staying out late, but I often had to sacrifice my social life to my early-morning bookings. A model's working day is long and arduous. Few people outside the profession realize the pressures, the numbers of collaborators with different ideas, the patience it takes to stand in position while hairdressers, stylists, editors, makeup artists, clients, and photographers fuss and fiddle with you.

Frequently a shooting session lasts eight hours, and can stretch to ten. There have been moments when I didn't think I could stand one more brushing by the hairdresser. You'll need stamina and, above all, *patience* to survive as a model. And a good business sense, too. Having a pretty face is only part of the job.

2

Getting It Together

Appearances are not all-important, but they are definitely important. The first thing we perceive about other people is how they look. Psychologists have done studies that indicate that in general people find physically attractive men and women kinder, stronger, more intelligent and more outgoing than others. And there can be no denying that good-looking people have an easier time of it getting jobs and making social contacts. If they happen to be smart and have a pleasing personality as well, then the world is not only an open door for them, it's their "oyster, their champagne, their caviar."

We're all of us more confident about ourselves when we know we're looking good. Others in turn are persuaded by our fine display of self-esteem (one reason it works like a charm is that we have very often first had to persuade *ourselves!*). The more we get out of ourselves, the better able we are to relate to others. But sadly, there are those who do not feel as attractive as they actually are, and others who don't take the time and make the effort necessary to look their best.

I believe that just about anyone can be attractive. There are no absolute standards of beauty. Women who seem beautiful to us have often simply learned the art of making themselves alluring. They have learned to express the positive aspects of their personalities in the way they dress, wear their hair and makeup, and carry themselves. They have the glamour of their own identity.

Growing up, I often had those old chestnuts "Beauty is only skin deep" and "Pretty is as pretty does" flung willy-nilly at me. But when I stopped dodging them and actually thought about them, I realized they were true. And certainly, the way a woman looks is not the *most* important thing about her. God knows, great beauties can be calculating, manipulative, dissembling, or just plain dishwater-dull; and when they are, their beauty is diminished, the gilt peels off the statue (going, going, gone!). A less-than-perfect nose, slightly crooked teeth, a higher-than-high forehead, when they are those of someone we love, can be beautiful to us. We no longer look at them critically, for the spell of love is everywhere.

Physical beauty can be something of a double-edged sword. It is often the mother of complacency and the

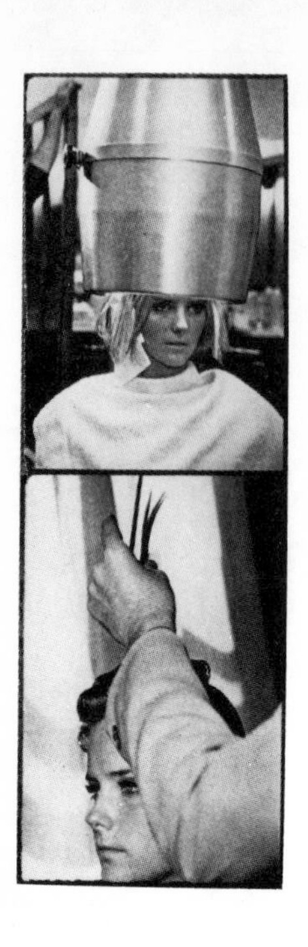

sire of lack-of-development: enter the living doll who just sits around attracting jocks like flies while her tongue melts and her brain atrophies. Sure she has an edge over the rest of the field, but there are dangers lying in wait for her—half-hidden, implicit, often unrecognized until too late. Don't get me wrong, I'm all for good looks but not when they're used as a shield or crutch or short-term weapon.

The landscape of a woman's face is composed of many things—her smile, the light in her eyes, the way she holds her head: in a word, her *character*. That makes every woman responsible for her own face. Classic features, a great figure, and even youth, with the grace *it* confers, can all spell emptiness. Soon enough we'll all be old—wrinkles will inevitably develop and muscle tone go—and unless there is an ever-developing brain, what will we have left?

A couple of years ago, *Harper's Bazaar* came out with a list of the "Ten Most Beautiful Women." They were: Lauren Hutton, Elizabeth Taylor, Faye Dunaway, Diahann Carroll, Candice Bergen, Princess Grace of Monaco, Ali MacGraw, Cheryl Tiegs, Lena Horne, and Farrah Fawcett. I was very gratified to be included because the women were all individuals who had built on what they had in order to make the most of themselves and their lives; it wasn't the symmetry of their faces and bodies that made them beautiful and alive—it was what was going on inside them.

Some women have just the knack for creating a style that expresses their nature in a very *contemporary* way. Others have unconsciously formed habits and attitudes and fixed patterns of living and looking that all but bury them alive. Often the mistakes they make—again and again, in many cases—are ones that some honest self-analysis could help win a victory over.

MISTAKES PEOPLE MAKE

Overfocusing on Flaws

Don't become obsessed with a feature or a part of your body you dislike. A beautiful model I know used to go around claiming she had a "droopy eye," that it was ruining the symmetry of her face. No matter how hard I looked, I could never discover which eye it was she was talking about.

Try transferring your gaze and attention to whatever *assets* you possess in the most natural setting on earth—your own person.

Projecting an "Uncomfortable" Look

Any look that requires a lot of extra effort to carry off—be it in the hair, eye shadow, lipstick, or wardrobe department—is ultimately going to catch you out. Every woman has found herself in this predicament; the moment comes when she can't imagine what she could have been imagining when she got herself together in the first place. Recently, because they were in style, I went and bought some "gathered" skirts, the kind I've always disliked. When I actually put one of them on, I felt completely lost in it—and it served me right. Once, I said okay when a hairdresser asked to tease and spray my hair before a party; he promised I would never regret it, never look back. I looked like a spider's web, a sparrow's nest, a pumpkinhead—all that hair just wasn't me, I couldn't relax and be myself. Following fads takes a toll, and you can't always be sure of applause, either.

There's a big difference, though, between forcing yourself to accommodate to a look and adapting to a positive change of style in hair, makeup, or wardrobe.

Changes, even when you know you need them, may make you feel uncomfortable right off. Only time will tell you whether you just need to adjust to your new look, or whether you really did make a mistake. We're all entitled to a few mistakes. The thing is not to make a fine art out of making them.

Resisting Change

Yes, you always run the risk of bungling the job when you attempt to change your basic look, but the biggest mistake, in my opinion, is not changing your look at all, ever. Your appearance should reflect both the changes for the better going on inside you and the changes in taste in the world at large. Few of us feel the same way we felt a decade ago—so why should we stand still and be a walking advertisement for interchangeability? Taste has many provinces, and some of them are difficult to reconcile: how, for instance, can you keep abreast of current styles and also preserve your individual taste? The first step is not to typecast yourself unfairly by modeling yourself on a figure from the past, even your own past. I'm not telling you to rush out and in a confused moment acquire every cosmetic and accessory mentioned in the latest fashion magazine you happen to have read. On the other hand, you really do want to try to avoid looking like a dinosaur.

Neglecting the Basics of Good Health

Extra fat usually goes hand in hand with less than perfect skin, unhealthy color, dreary hair and a crying lack of mobility and animation. These are the signs—and there are no mistaking them—of poor nutrition and lack of exercise: ignore them at your peril. Only in a fairy tale does fat disappear by itself. In real life, it glaringly points out that you have somewhere along the line lost your belief in your own attractiveness.

Overweight and other problems caused by bad nutrition and lack of exercise are less "mistakes" than they are the result of a sometimes criminal neglect, lack of discipline, and lack of knowledge about health practices. What extra pounds say to me (and I know—remember, I carried more than my share of them around with me for a couple of years) is, "I don't care enough! I don't know enough!" And it follows that if *you* neglect the way you look, you're extending an invitation to others to neglect you, too. It might help to bear in mind that the biggest essential of natural beauty is good health.

Not Spending Enough on Your Appearance

Enough what? Not money. Time and attention. Throughout this book I'll be suggesting different ways for you to approach the problem of your appearance: by studying and analyzing yourself, by experimenting, and finally, by getting professional advice when necessary. But nothing I say is going to make a whit of difference unless you program yourself to spend the time it takes to work on the ideas I throw out. But once you decide to invest the time to work out the general look that's most becoming to you, putting yourself together on a day-to-day basis should take only a few minutes. My point is, you can't just close your eyes and open them again and find yourself transformed.

Spending a lot of money to look your best is not necessary. We all know women who manage to put themselves together brilliantly on a shoestring (and some divine inspiration), and we also know their opposites, women who have obviously spent hard, cold cash—and lots of it—to make themselves alluring, and who have failed ignominiously. Conspicuous consumption is out these days; what's in is taking the measure of what's available and using it to make the most of what you have to offer.

Women sometimes change their look at random, without adequate thought or preparation—sometimes out of reaction to a bad day or a low mood; the change itself will generally repay the compliment by making them look not better but worse. So don't let yourself be a sandwich board for your inner confusions and private disasters.

Instead, imagine yourself in the most positive terms. Coming up with a look to express your personality is going to be a bit tricky if you have never fully understood yourself or if you tend to think of yourself in terms of your faults, failings, and faux pas. When you think of yourself, don't think "No! No! No!" but rather, "Yes! Yes! Yes!" I used to think of myself as a shy person, and "shy" to me had a negative, thwarted connotation. Now I think of it as meaning cautious, not pushy, etc. If I'd attuned myself to hear only the negative implications of "shy," I might be wearing drab clothes and dull makeup today, all the better to recede into the woodwork. As it is, I prefer somewhat conservative styles, muted colors, and soft, understated fabrics, but I know full well the value of an occasional splash of color and of wearing what I call "energy clothes."

So: don't run yourself down and don't drag yourself down to where you can't get up and walk on. Consider how you would represent yourself on a job interview. Would you describe yourself as aggressive? Aren't dynamic and vivacious more positive terms, connoting the sort of attitude an employer would want you to bring to the job? And wouldn't you describe yourself as calm and relaxed instead of introverted? If you think of yourself as uncreative, ask why you're so confident of your own uncreativity. And maybe you're zany instead of scatterbrained, thoughtful instead of aloof, honest and direct instead of tactless and brash. Describe yourself as you would describe someone you loved and you may just find out that you *are* describing someone you love: yourself.

Now ask yourself which of your physical characteristics you're happiest with. Do you have eyes that are a nice color? A slender waist? Long legs? A clear skin with smooth coloration? Full lips? A beautiful bosom? Lustrous long hair? Whatever . . .

Dwell on the parts of yourself that you may have been ignoring and work back from there. Forget about the flaws—for *now*. There are bound to be things you don't like about yourself—try to redefine them in positive terms. Place them at your service: try to see yourself as voluptuous instead of fat (remember Rubens!), petite instead of too small, slender instead of skinny. Find flattering adjectives to describe your face, and then your body. Now is the time to be generous to yourself—so you'll be in a better position psychologically later on to deal with the parts of yourself that even a switch in adjectives can't make you like.

Believing That Beauty Is Unattainable

Don't rule out something because you've convinced yourself you can't achieve it. Don't allow some mythical distance to be built up between you and a far-off end product. A human being is by definition a "living contradiction of rules and prejudices, and everything that is human is a special case." I urge you to consider that beauty and glamour are like almost everything else in that they require a step-by-step process that is *not*—I repeat *not*—beyond your reach. Don't feel bound by what *you've* decided are your limitations. Most of those glamorous magazine cover girls came from Kansas and Kalamazoo; they struggled from the word "go," and absorbed—through hard work and concentration—the details of the beauty industry. My advice is to follow up your dreams to the point where they become reality. It was Lillian Hellman, I think, who said the things in this world belong to the people who want them the most.

Once you've focused on your good points and are beginning to feel like someone who can set out to do something and then actually get it done, begin scrutinizing the women you know whose looks and clothes you admire, as well as fashion models, actresses, and strangers you see on the street or at parties. What is it about them that traps your attention, pleases your eye, and in rare cases even lays claim to your imagination? Is it the way they wear their makeup, clothes, or hair, or something more elusive—the way they speak, the gestures they use? And above all, notice how what they wear complements their personality. Do they strike you as being able to live up to their trimmings?

One difficulty is that most people have preconceived notions of how they look and have little or no idea how others see them. Many of us simply think of ourselves the way our parents and friends have "seen" us all our lives. If we were made to feel awkward and unattractive during our formative years, we may go on feeling awkward and unattractive, however unblemished the rest of our lives has been. Some of us continue to see ourselves in terms of a beauty problem that afflicted us long ago. For example, long after I lost all those extra pounds, I saw myself as overweight. And I think that many other women look in the mirror and see a self that no longer exists except insofar as it prevents them from seeing their real and better selves. To compound matters, since they can't see themselves as they are, they can't make the right changes—or even discern good advice when they hear it, as I've noticed from when giving out beauty tips every Thursday morning on *Good Morning America*. I might say something like, "If you have a round face, don't wear a round hat." And the next day someone with a round face will come up to me and tell me how much they enjoyed the day before's program—*wearing a round hat!* They just don't see themselves realistically enough to realize that the recommendation applied to *them*.

But how can you possibly see yourself as others see you? One way is to use your acting potential and glance into the mirror (the best critic there is, the only truly honest friend) and pretend that you're a stranger to yourself. Then act out various scenarios in front of the mirror: imagine you're walking into a room, or sitting down, or talking to someone you've just met by chance, or looking at a painting in a museum, or waiting for a bus. Smile, grimace, laugh, frown—how do you look? Run the gamut from clown to tragedian. The old mirror won't betray you, and your perception of yourself may become more realistic.

Now you can stop play-acting, theater-time's up. You're you again, your one-true-first-last-only self. Move closer to the mirror and examine yourself for areas that you *know* could use improvement. A close look at your body may reveal the beginnings of problems that just aren't visible when you have layers of clothes on. Chances are those specters will indicate that you could use a good diet, some more exercise, and some good old "R and R." Now look very closely at your face. It should be clean and without makeup. Don't get depressed—we all need work, and not everything in life is as pleasant as licking ice cream.

Studying a photograph of yourself is yet another way of learning something about the visual impression you make on others. You may see you have your mouth open or a false smile, a mannerism of one kind or another you never realized was yours. "Surprise" photographs are the most useful—the ones that have been taken without your having had time to “pose.” Are your shoulders slumped down? Are you sitting up straight? Is your belt halfway up to your neck? Is your stomach sticking out? A photo that has caught you animatedly talking to someone may reveal in capsule form the way you look to others.

Also, criticism—although you may not always delight in it—when you are trying to work out a look for yourself, is indispensable and should be taken seriously. I’m talking about constructive criticism from your friends, something as far from idle flattery as it is from insult and injury. Photographers, stylists, fellow models, makeup artists, hairdressers, and other professionals in the fashion world have given me great ideas. And my husband also happens to have a good sense of fashion and has always been quick to point out if I had anything on that would take away from my kind of casualness. Close friends have an eerie way of knowing if you really want to know what they think or are just fishing for compliments. Cosmeticians and salesgirls often have good ideas but since they don’t know you, they may recommend some weirdo fashion slant that will start you on the road to becoming a great big phony.

Keep an open mind. Embrace the suggestions that seem right to you and discard those that you don’t feel comfortable with. In order to please others, you have to please yourself. And pleasing yourself entails knowing exactly who and what you are. Then and only then will you be ready to act on this understanding.

Now what was that last thing I wanted to remember...

East Africa — 1979

ONE FOR ME..
AND ONE FOR
CHERYL...

3

Food Therapy and Eating Strategy: Advice to the Food-lorn

Is there a woman alive who would rather be fat than thin? I doubt it. A body without extra padding is the most pleasing to look at; it also gives off an aura of health and dynamic vitality that makes people want to be around you. A slender form may be a thing of beauty but it doesn't happen all by itself; rather, it is the result of exercise and a low-calorie diet.

A good diet, however, is not just one that keeps you thin, but one that is also nutritious and provides you with the energy that today's super-active women need. Many women suffer (*and need not suffer*) not only from overweight but from its grim accompaniments as well: frayed nerves, assorted digestive problems, poor skin, weak nails, lifeless hair, and so on. Diet-related health and beauty problems are often caused by lack of knowledge as to just what food *does* in your body. But it doesn't have to be this way.

HOW MUCH DO *YOU* KNOW ABOUT YOUR DIET?

■ *Allow 100 pounds for the first five feet of your height. Add three pounds for each additional inch. This is your ideal weight. Now: How far do you exceed it?*

■ *Does your weight vacillate by ten or more pounds several times in the course of a year?*

■ *Do you shed a lot of weight in a short, concentrated period of time with some "miracle diet"—only to regain it?*

■ *Do you know how many calories there are in a hamburger on a roll? In an average serving of fish? In an apple? In a doughnut? In a cup of sweetened breakfast cereal?*

■ *Do you know approximately how many calories there are in the total amount of food you consume (including liquids) in an average day?*

■ *Do you know which foods contain Vitamin A? Fiber? All the B vitamins? Calcium?*

■ *Do you suffer frequently from heartburn? Constipation? Headaches?*

■ *Are you often irritable? Depressed? Lethargic?*

■ *Are you apt to overeat when you're feeling lonely or bored?*

I have a lot of suggestions on how to turn around your behavior patterns. First of all, if your weight is not "ideal" and you were unable to give the total calorie count of the food you eat, you've probably already discovered one very big reason why you're overweight: You are eating a lot more calories than you think you are.

If you are slender and feel great you must be doing something right, or else your lack of knowledge hasn't caught up with you—yet. This chapter should provide you with some of what you need to know in order to *stay* thin and healthy. A new awareness of the food you eat can only improve the way you look and feel. The rest of the package is motivation, discipline, and sheer old-fashioned guts.

MY VERY OWN BATTLE OF THE BULGE

When I was overweight I would have flunked the preceding questionnaire gloriously. I ate whatever and whenever I wanted to, and as not too much else was going on in my lazy life, most of what I did was eat. But my worst sins lay in not knowing about nutrition and in never considering how what I was and wasn't eating would make me feel.

My binge-eating syndrome came into its own in college. I started each day with a huge, satisfying breakfast—the only problem was it didn't even begin to satisfy me. Between every morning class I would pay a little visit to the handy candy machine. I could hardly wait till lunchtime. First, I would demolish whatever I'd brought from home, then I'd repair to the snack bar for some hot-buttered popcorn or ice cream—I needed that extra incentive to go back to class with its routine of note-taking and lecture-listening. The good thing about candy bars was they could easily be transported from English Lit. to Psychology 1A and so on. I was still pretty skinny—I guess I was burning up most of the calories with the flame of youthful energy or something—and I never gave a thought to how much I was consuming.

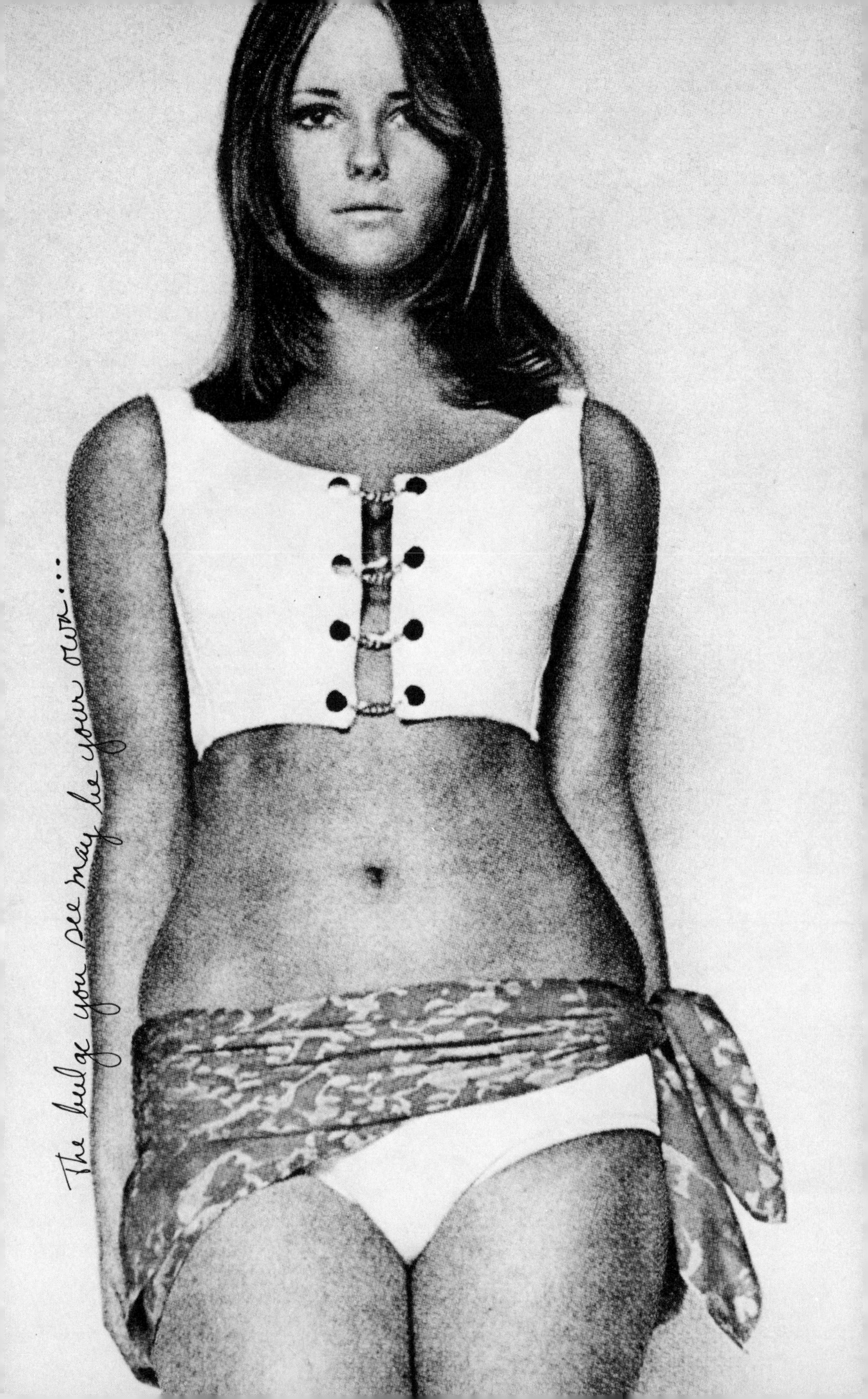
The bulge you see may be your own...

DREAM PIE

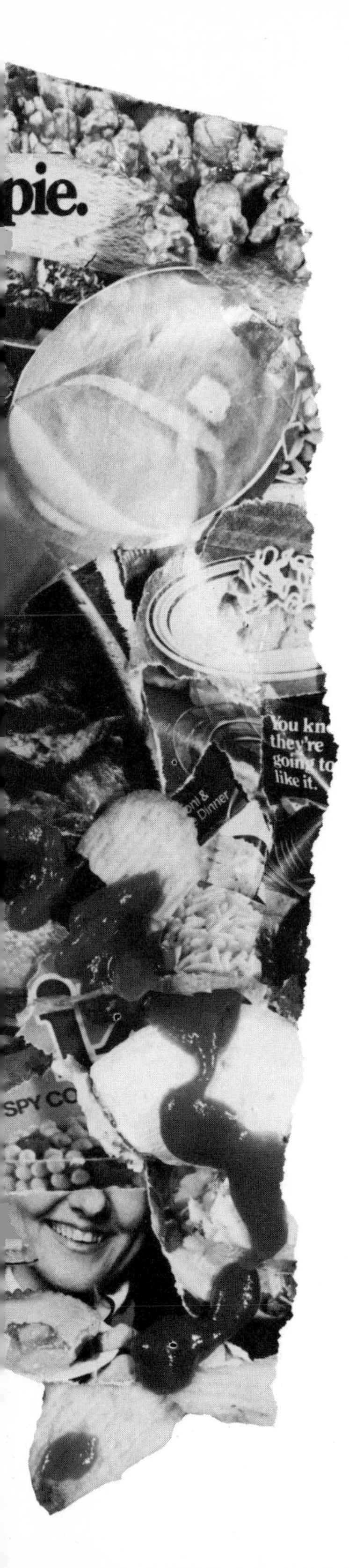

When I went to live and model in New York at the age of nineteen, however, the tons of junk I was forever eating began to catch up with me. My body had reached its full growth and now I could no longer burn off the inordinate number of calories I was shoveling in. The extra pounds that had congregated around my midriff and thighs didn't stop me—I naïvely thought it must be my metabolism. And as for any anxiety I felt, I simply fed it—literally as well as figuratively!

Thinking back on these tales of the Burger Princess, I'm amazed at the amount of food I managed to choke down. I loved veal parmesan, breaded, with lots of cheese and sauce. And I loved noshing on combination pizzas and double-decker Big Macs with ketchup and mayonnaise. I never thought about the difference in calories between steak and fish, between potatoes and broccoli (with plenty of hollandaise, naturally—I mean, *unnaturally!*), or between tomato and orange juice: to me it was all the same—it was, in a word, *food!* I loved banana splits, butterscotch sundaes, hot-fudge sundaes with whipped cream, nuts, and, topping it all off, the maraschino cherry, which sometimes I ate and sometimes I didn't (I'd already concluded that almost anything anyone does with a maraschino cherry is symbolic). I loved doughnuts and I ordered them pumped full of whipped cream and dipped in deep, dark chocolate. But most of all I loved cherry pie à la mode. I wasn't fussy, though. When they didn't have my favorites on hand, I'd order at random and in bulk and often quite wildly—cookies with peanut butter, Ritz Crackers with Hellmann's Mayonnaise and bread-and-butter pickles. As long as there was a *lot* of it, I loved it. I remember visiting a friend for the weekend and asking for double helpings of every single course at both lunch and dinner. "*Cheryl*," my friend said, leaving it at that. Later that night, I felt the old urge and sneaked downstairs in the deep dark of the unfamiliar house, longing for the feel of the icebox door, the pulling of the handle and the clicking on of the inside light—it would be like coming home. The range of possibilities was disappointingly limited: jars of mustard, pots of margarine, vegetable trays of zucchini and rhubarb—nothing that could be immediately eaten. If only there had been a potato, I could have peeled and devoured it with salt. Way in the back was an old box of after-dinner mints. They must have been in there for about a year because the chocolate was starting to turn moldy. I ate one and then another and another of the tasteless sweets until I saw that more than half the wrappers were empty; I nervously arranged them so they'd look as much as possible like the same old mess I'd happened upon. Then, I quietly shut the fridge and in total darkness crept upstairs to bed, thinking of course of the remaining sweets which I had a feeling I would meet again.

with Liz Landis — 1968

After I was married, I continued to overeat. I was a bad influence on my slim husband and he gained, too. We'd spend weekends lounging around our apartment ordering in sundaes, pastries, pizzas. I guess you could have called ours "The Catered Affair." Or else "Getting Fat Together."

By now I had begun to worry about the extra pounds, but worrying only made me hungry, even while I was gorging. Unlike most binge eaters, I had an economic reason to fear those pounds. They were threatening to blight my budding career. In retrospect, I think that I ate to try to fill up an empty space —not in my stomach but in my soul, because whenever I felt anxious, depressed, or insecure, I ate: speed eating—food on the run, food on the fly (toy food on planes), and, going overboard, bulk food on ships.

One Christmas I went home to visit my family in California. My older sister, Vernette, had always been a bit heavier than I, but that year, when she giddily tried on my skirts, they were swimming on her. With my heart in my mouth, I went into the bathroom and stepped on the scale for the first time in months (binge eaters for obvious reasons don't like to weigh themselves) and, my God, I saw the needle hover at and come to rest on the 150 mark. I burst into tears! Then, not unnaturally, I marched into the kitchen and ate everything in sight, including an entire box of See's candy. It was like I was officiating at my own funeral.

Sometimes I actually scare myself by recalling things like how on a trip to Puerto Rico for a bathing suit issue I raided the cupboards of a house we had rented in the old section of the island; no one human had been living there for a while and insects were hatching inside the boxes of crackers on the shelf. And what did *I* do? I ate around them! Ugh!!

My roommate of those days in New York, Liz Landis, can vouch for my abilities as a disposal unit. Somebody once sent her a box of cookies from Paris and she ate out their gooey insides and threw the crusts into the garbage can. When I got home that night, I caught a glimpse of these castaways and one by one extracted them from the garbage and finished them off. Some had the flavor of orange peels, others of coffee grind, but soon they were gone, and I remember standing there afterwards feeling thoroughly ashamed of myself—as if I'd just committed some form of gustatory rape.

During this time, I was afflicted by migraine headaches. I spent a lot of time in agony in bed, and was constantly having to refill prescriptions for painkillers. I had the idea that hearty eating would make the violent headaches disappear; so, whenever I felt one coming on, I'd order up a hamburger smothered in onions.

Then my mother confided that every time she ate ice cream she got a headache. I looked at her and thought, maybe that's it—or part of it, anyway. I've since realized that my body simply couldn't handle all the sugar I'd sent flooding through it. When I changed my eating habits, my migraines all but vanished. Now, when I feel a headache coming on, I stop eating altogether, take a single aspirin, and nip it in the bud.

My binging habits also blemished my skin and made me feel tired. My remedy for lethargy was my old familiar one—a candy bar or a sundae.

So now you know how I know what it feels like to be a foodaholic. But don't despair, there is light at the end of the tunnel—your days as an obsessive muncher in public and a compulsive muncher in private can definitely be put behind you (instead of on your behind).

When I first tried to diet, I failed, because my diet was based on as little knowledge of nutrition as my abnormal eating habits had been. For breakfast I would have "only" a corn muffin (plastered with butter and jelly) and I would take care to eat "only" one or two desserts a day. When this "diet" didn't produce results, I devised others. Sometimes I just skipped breakfast altogether and went as long as I could without eating anything at all. But total abstinence made me feel tired and irritable, and, needless to say, very, very hungry, so that when I finally did eat, I ate as though I was starving, which in fact I was. Once I tried a "no-meat diet," because some self-styled expert had told me that meat was fattening. So whenever I ordered Eggs Benedict—a super-rich concoction of English Muffins, ham, poached eggs, and hollandaise sauce, I virtuously stripped away the little piece of ham—content in the sure knowledge that it was this torn flesh of pig that was causing the trouble.

The next mistake I made was "diet-hopping." I went

my elephant cookie jar.

out and bought every diet book on the market and read them all. (I used to joke that my real problem was always what to eat while reading the latest diet book.) Name a diet, and I've been on it: the grapefruit diet, the all-meat-and-water diet, the all-fat diet, the all-juice diet, the yogurt diet. But after a few days of rigorous self-denial, I'd be right back where I started—in the refrigerator, cleaning out the leftovers. By the law of averages, *some* of the diets I tried, such as the Weight Watcher's diet, were quite sensible, but I never lost weight on any of them because I supplemented them with the "Cheryl Tiegs Diet"—*lots* of junk food and multiple snacks. At one point I even went to a "diet doctor," who prescribed diet pills containing the dangerous stimulant, amphetamine. In this post-Doctor-Feelgood decade, most people know that the diet pill syndrome can be addictive, but in the sixties, few realized this. Most models took amphetamines, not to mention Vitamin B-12 shots. My mistake was thinking that since I was taking diet pills, I didn't have to diet. So I continued eating as before. I lost a bit of weight, yes—but not nearly enough. It was ludicrous. The doctor could see that the boxes of multi-colored amphetamines he'd prescribed for me had all been consumed, and he must have been wondering why my face and body were still blubbery.

Finally I reached the point of total desperation. None of the diets I'd attempted on my own had worked; if anything, I was getting fatter. I would contemplate my hips and thighs and chins and just cry. I felt really terrible about myself. I resolved to take the matter (meaning me) in hand, and I enrolled in a diet clinic in New York—determined to eat *only* what the doctor told me I could.

The clinic weighed me in every day and gave me a shot of special vitamins and nutrients (no amphetamine). Every noon I received a bag of food, containing my lunch and dinner—a total of 400 nutritious calories. Lunch was a small piece of fish or meat, a tiny whole-wheat cracker, and a little side dish of vegetables. Ditto dinner, with two pieces of fruit thrown in. I stuck to that diet for an entire month. Nothing—and I *mean* nothing—that wasn't in my bag passed my lips. When I went to parties, I didn't drink a thing, and when I went to restaurants I carted along my little bag. At the end of just one month I'd lost twenty pounds. After that I gradually increased my intake of calories. I won't easily forget how terrified I was that I'd gain weight again, when I sipped my first glass of

wine and tasted my first morsel that didn't come from my clinical feedbag. But I never did regain that weight. I was so happy to be thin again I never returned to binging. The pattern was broken, the neurotic cycle destroyed.

I don't think it's necessary for everyone to enroll in a diet clinic in order to lose weight. I now see that it was my determination to become thin again, my sheer need to overcome, that made me stop overeating. Without that desperate need, the clinic's diet would have been as useless to me as all the other diets I'd tried. I think I might even have lost those first twenty pounds a little too quickly for my own good. Nutritionists consider it safest for dieters to lose weight slowly, two pounds a week at most, over a long period of time, to avoid the risk of depleting nutritional reserves. Fortunately, the shots the clinic gave me preserved the delicate balance of vitamins and nutrients in my system. Also, I was young. I suffered no ill effects from this sudden weight loss—such as sagging skin and dry, brittle hair.

What was invaluable about the clinic is that it taught me the type and amount of food that was both nutritious and low in calories. I have continued with my study of nutrition, and find the subject endlessly fascinating. I am far too aware of what the quantities of junk food I'd been eating had done to me—physiologically and psychologically—to ever eat that way again. I consider myself one of the lucky ones.

THE MATHEMATICS OF A GOOD DIET

Arithmetic has never been my forte, but I've discovered that maintaining a slender figure requires some simple math. Calculate the number of pounds you should weigh and the number of calories you should eat to stay thin.

As I suggested in the questionnaire, ideal body weight can be roughly computed by allowing 100 pounds for the first five feet of height and three pounds for each additional inch. Since I am 5′10″, my ideal weight is 130. When you've computed your ideal weight you'll notice that it's considerably less than the weight advocated by the charts in your doctor's office. You should know that those weights are based on insurance company charts, and they tend to be high, insomuch as they reflect the fact that the average American (25,000,000 of him!) is overweight. Of

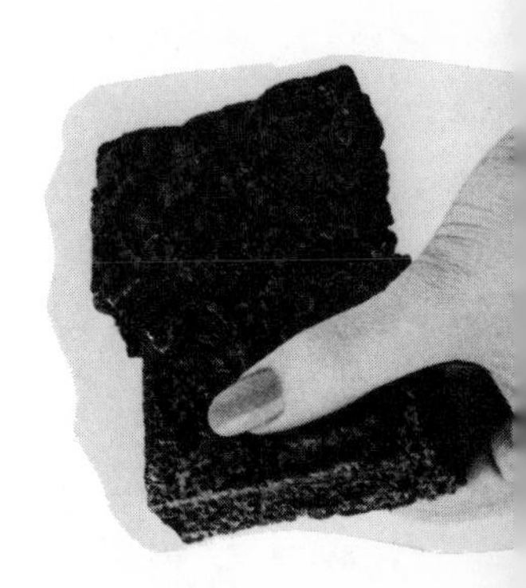

course, if you are large-boned and have very broad shoulders, a large pelvic structure, and big ankles and wrists, you may look better when you do weigh a bit more. But since I am relatively small-boned and spend a lot of my working day in front of a camera, which automatically puts about ten extra pounds on you, I feel more comfortable at 120 pounds. So adjust these "ideal" figures to suit your body build, but don't leave room for fat—we all know a bulge when we see one.

A good diet also calls for some addition and subtraction. Let's imagine you need to lose ten pounds to reach your ideal weight. According to nutritionists, a pound of stored fat contains 3500 calories. For every pound you want to lose, then, you must cut back your present calorie consumption by 3500 calories over a period of time. Only when those calories have *not* been taken in will you drop the pound. For example, if you take in 2000 calories a day and cut them back to 1500 calories a day, you will have eliminated 3500 calories, or shed one pound, in seven days. At this rate it will take you ten weeks to lose ten pounds. You will have cut a total of 35,000 calories out of your diet in two and a half months. You must also get into the habit of counting the calories you eat and estimating the calories you use up. Though we tend to think of a calorie as a little fat-producing demon, what it actually is is a positive unit of energy. Calories supply the fuel our bodies need to move, work, think, and otherwise function; we can't live without them. Calories that are not put to work and burned off, however, do get retained as fat. Different types of calories, such as those in starches and sugar, are more likely to turn to fat than are others; and naturally, different types of activities burn calories at different rates.

In general, sedentary activities (sitting, writing, watching TV, reading) burn about 60 calories per hour; light housework (dusting, sewing, ironing) and walking at a normal pace burn about 160 calories per hour. Moderate activities (walking briskly, golfing, shopping, calisthenics, biking at a slow pace) and heavier housework (sweeping, making beds) burn from 280 to 350 calories per hour. More vigorous activities and sports (disco dancing, fast biking, energetic tennis, chopping wood) burn about 450 calories per hour. The real calorie burners and the ones that aid and abet your dieting are squash, paddleball, swimming (a fast crawl), and serious jogging, all of which burn 600

Don't just sit there — do something.

or more calories per hour. You also burn calories while you sleep, but very few—about 30 per hour.

Therefore, if you sit at a desk eight hours a day, walk home from work, clean the house, cook the dinner, and then collapse in front of the TV, your total calorie expenditure for the day is low. If, on top of this, you nibble Danish pastries at your desk, stop for a hot dog on your way home, munch a bunch of peanuts before dinner, and eat three meals a day, you don't have to be an Einstein to figure out that you will probably be gaining rather than losing weight. A bit of work with a pocket calculator will soon tell you whether or not you're consuming more fuel than you can burn up.

To complicate matters, when your body reaches maximum growth it will burn fewer calories, many calories having been burned up by the growing process itself. Moreover, when you are young, you tend to be active—running, jumping, playing all the time. As you get older and become more sedentary, more set—and seated—in your ways, you need fewer calories to maintain your body weight. Some experts maintain that to keep the slender figure you had at age eighteen, you must eat a third less calories than you did then. Yet most people, as I did, continue to eat as much as they did when they were teenagers—or even more. Some people are blessed with a rapid basal metabolism, which means that their bodies burn calories rapidly, but these are few and far between—exceptions to the rule. Many of the overweight just don't realize that the body naturally needs less fuel as it gets older, and try to blame their extra pounds on their metabolism, an old scapegoat. When I first started gaining weight, I took all sorts of diagnostic tests in an effort to find out what on earth had gone haywire with my metabolism—a waste of money and time! The overwhelming odds are that if you're too fat you're simply consuming more calories than you need for fuel.

A low-calorie diet will allow most people to shed extra pounds. A 1200-calorie-a-day diet is considered a safe and effective reducing plan. Designing a palatable, energy-building 1200 calorie diet, however, requires some mathematical planning as well as some knowledge of food preparation. Not all calories are the same, and to stay healthy and look and feel your best, you must make sure you're burning high-quality fuel, packed with vitamins, minerals, and the other important nutritional elements.

From the frying pan...

COUNT THESE CALORIES

My first advice to dieters is to buy a pocket calorie counter. You may be suprised to learn how many calories foods you imagined were non-fattening contain. A half-pound club steak, for example, contains a walloping 670 calories! A piece of watermelon, which no one would ever dream could be fattening, is riddled with sugar and contains 100 calories per medium slice (and whoever heard of anyone's having a *medium* slice of watermelon?). Vegetables and lettuce, composed largely of water, are not a bit fattening, but the things that make them taste delicious—butter, mayonnaise, oil—are loaded with calories. Nuts, seeds, dates and granolas, which all health food fans celebrate, are positively (or negatively, as the case may be) bursting with calories. In general, there are four calories per gram in proteins and carbohydrates, and nine calories per gram in fats.

Many of the people who are struggling to lose weight already know the foods that are low in calories, but they do not know how much of it to eat. They know, for example, that cake, ice cream, pasta, and french fries are fatteners and therefore to be avoided, and that melon, veal, fish, and vegetables are on the whole slimming, health-giving foods. This is all perfectly true, but to diet successfully you must not only eliminate easily identified high-calorie treats but also measure and weigh low-calorie food. Most diets advise you to eat a quarter of a pound of meat, fish, or cheese with your main meals. A quarter of a pound is only *four tiny ounces*—a mini-mini-portion that no restaurant could ever get away with serving.

On the other hand, the caloric value of food is often disproportionate to its size. Sometimes the tiniest morsels are jam-packed with calories. A mere seven cashew nuts, for example, contain 75 calories (and show me the mortal who can stop at seven!). A strip of bacon contains 33 calories, two tablespoons of peanut butter 200, and a measly candy bar 260!

COMPUTE YOUR WAY TO A SLIM FIGURE: GET READY, SET, GO!

If you really want to lose weight, I fervently recommend that you take the time and trouble to follow the formula below. A mathematical approach to dieting will not leave your extra pounds to luck or fate. With

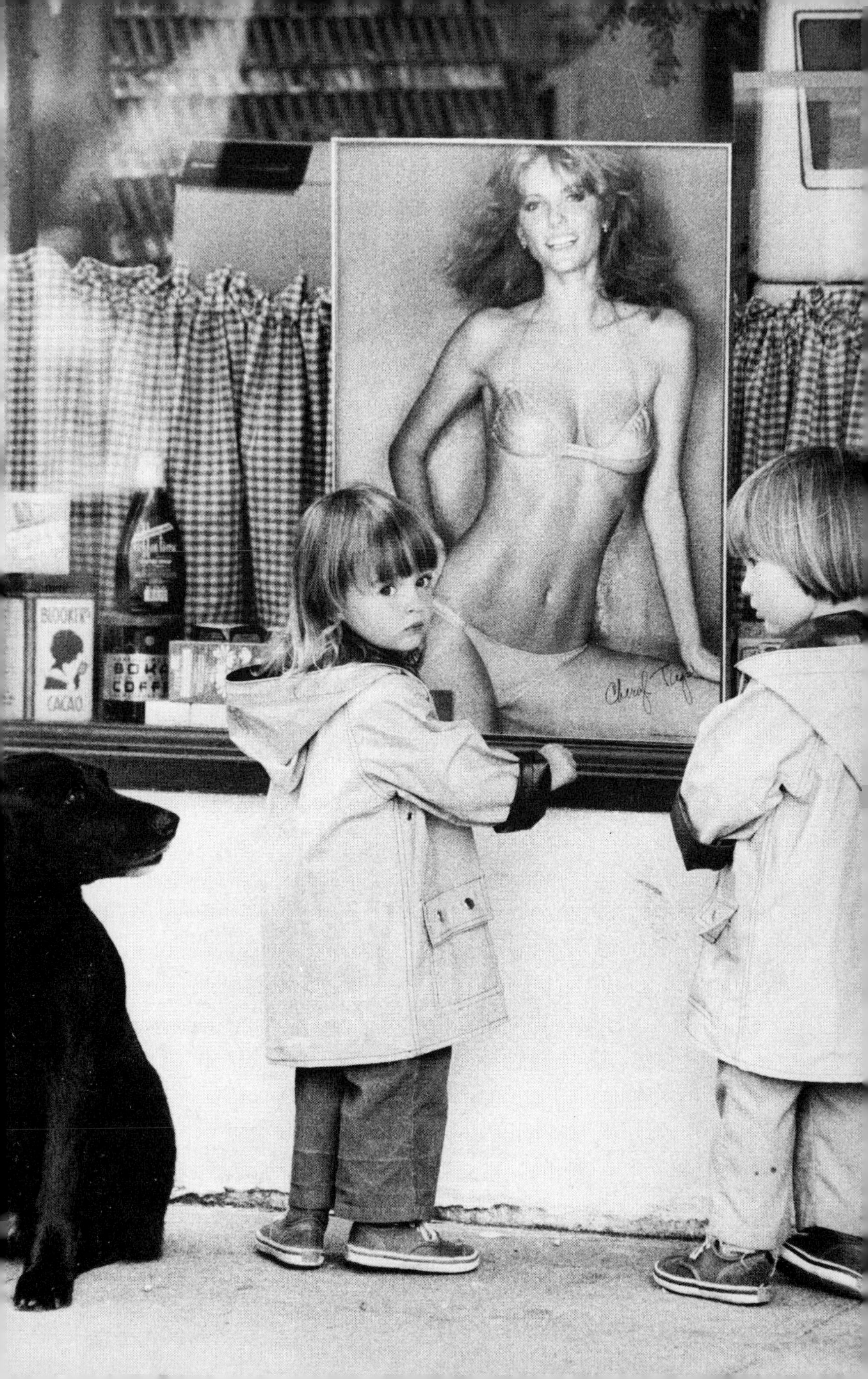
CACAO

this system you will never be able to ignore the extra calories you consume, or the days you skip your exercises. And if you do not succeed in losing as much weight as you'd like, it will be easier to pinpoint the type of food you don't metabolize well and then to eliminate it from your diet.

Having computed your ideal weight according to formula, multiply the pounds you want to lose by 3500 calories. You now know the number of calories you must eliminate from your diet in order to lose your excess pounds.

Keep a record of what you eat for seven days; then, with your calorie counter, compute the number of calories you consumed. You are now in a position to figure out the approximate number of calories you burn in a single day. This is arguably more difficult, since metabolisms differ enormously, and there is a range for each bodily activity, depending on how quickly and vigorously you do it. If you are over twenty-five years old, I advise keeping your figures on the low side; even if they're not completely accurate, they'll give you a good idea of how many more calories you consume per day than you burn. If your food consumption and exercise quotient are likely to change drastically from day to day, compute a weekly average.

On the basis of the figures you now have, you should be able to decide just how many calories a day you can eat and still lose weight. The number of calories you eat per day should be lower than those you expend, but not lower than 1200 calories (the absolute minimum is 1000). Always remember that you must eliminate 3500 calories for each pound of fat you want to lose, and that the longer it takes you to eliminate those calories, the longer it's going to take to lose the unwanted weight. Don't plan on losing more than two pounds per week. A 1400–1500-calorie-a-day diet will enable you to lose weight, especially if you regularly consume more than that number of calories.

Plan a diet for yourself. Make a list of the low-calorie, nutritious foods that you *enjoy*, and of high-calorie junk fatteners that you know you must eliminate.

When you begin your diet, write down the caloric value of every kind of food—and that includes liquids, sauces, and dressings—that finds its way into your mouth. *Everything* you eat contains calories, except water, unsweetened coffee, and tea. You will of course need to know how *much* of a particular food you are eating. This isn't as complicated as it sounds. Note the weight of meat you buy and serve yourself a low-calorie portion. (Calorie counters contain helpful information.) Measure out dressings and fats with a tablespoon. Many breads, cereals, dairy products, and juices feature the caloric content per slice and eight-ounce cup right there on the package. Use a measuring cup. If necessary, buy a food scale.

When the great day comes and you find you've reached your ideal weight, compute the number of calories you can eat in order to maintain it: just multiply the desired number of pounds by twelve. If, for example, you want to stay at 123 pounds, you shouldn't eat more than 1476 (or 123 x 12) calories per day. (Now let's see, did anything historic happen in the year 1476?)

THE LOW-CARBOHYDRATE DIET

Some people will not lose weight on a low-calorie diet if it includes such carbohydrates as bread, rice, pastas, potatoes, sugar, and alcohol. These people tend to retain salt in direct proportion to the amount of carbohydrates they consume, and when you retain salt, you retain water as well. And, as if that weren't enough, the body tends to convert carbohydrates to fat and store them.

If you need a low-carbohydrate diet (and you should let your doctor help you make this decision), lower your salt intake, and swear off sweets and refined starches, substituting unsaturated fats in the form of butterfat, beef, pork, and lamb. Don't make the mistake of eliminating *all* carbohydrates from your diet (they constitute a necessary and life-sustaining nutrient); just lower them to about two ounces a day—preferably complex carbohydrates, found in fruits, some vegetables, and whole grains.

INVENT YOUR OWN!

You're the one who decides what you eat and when you eat it; what your food looks like and how it's seasoned. Every model I know has a scheme for maintaining her weight. Some prefer to skip breakfast and eat a large lunch. Others eat only one meal a day—dinner. Some eat six mini-meals a day. Others fast once a week. To each his own: Your patterns of food consumption *should* reflect your individual nature. If your diet doesn't feel right and also doesn't result in that slim figure you want, then it's obviously wrong for you. So change it.

A good, balanced diet should include a variety of foods. The real test of any diet is how it makes you feel. If you're tired, irritable, and go around the whole time with a "growling" stomach, you are clearly not taking in your fair share of essential nutrients. Ask yourself if you've taken the psychological factors into account. When you begin a diet you're bound to feel deprived, and your mind in turn is bound to communicate that feeling of deprivation to your stomach, making you "crave" the very foods that made you fat in the first place and that are tantalizingly out there waiting to make you fatter. Impatience and fatigue may very well beset you, but they are only temporary symptoms. Eventually your body will adjust to low-calorie food, and as soon as you start to lose weight in earnest, you'll feel happy with your new diet. When I long for a crunchy green salad, I obey my craving; but if it's a cookie I crave, I try to distract myself.

Whether or not you're trying to reduce, your body will tell you if you are eating the right foods. So do yourself a favor and listen to it. Many otherwise intelligent people fail to connect the way they feel with what they eat. The next time *you* feel run down, headachey, queasy, bloated or depressed, think back on the combinations of food you've eaten that day. In fact, don't wait until you're in extremity—check out your body after each meal. Note how sugar, proteins, fats, and heavy starches make you feel. A good diet will supply you with high-quality energy throughout the day.

THE PERILS OF JUNK FOOD

Nutritionists define "junk" as food that contains an inordinate amount of refined sugar or refined grains, or food that has been stripped of its natural coating to make it last longer on the shelf. Unfortunately, the category of "junk food" encompasses most of the foodstuffs overweight people crave: ice cream, pancakes, spaghetti, white rolls, doughnuts, cake, candy, and on and on and on and on. These foods do absolutely nothing to build body tissue, add nothing to your bin of vitamins and nutrients, and convert easily to fat. Even worse, when you eat "junk" instead of nutritious food, you feel as hungry as you did before you indulged yourself. The reason for this is that refined sugars and

starches are digested too rapidly and pour into the blood stream within minutes. Although the body's source of energy comes from sugar, or glucose, the body should be allowed to create glucose itself by slowly converting it from whole foods, and then to filter it gradually into the blood stream. But when you eat a candy bar to satisfy your hunger, the sugar hits your blood in a wave, the blood-sugar level rises rapidly, and you experience an increase of energy known in certain circles as a "high." The minute your pancreas registers this dramatic increase, it sends a flood of insulin, the hormone that controls the level of sugar in the blood, to manage the overdose. But because the pancreas has been overstimulated, it continues to send insulin after the job is done; and the insulin ends up obliterating *all* the sugar in your blood, with the result that you feel let-down, lethargic, and hungrier than ever. You reach for a food that will rapidly raise your blood sugar and restore your feeling of well-being—another candy bar! Is it any wonder that "junk food" is addictive? (Caffeine and alcohol have the same negative effect on blood sugar.)

According to nutritionists, it's a combination of natural, complex carbohydrates such as fruits, brown rice, and whole-wheat breads, and proteins such as meats, eggs, fish, and dairy products, and fats that allows sugar to be slowly absorbed into the blood and a high-energy level to be maintained. When blood sugar stays high, the desperate craving for quick-sugar highs virtually disappears. This is why it's so important for dieters to abstain from sugar totally for a while, and eat satisfying, nutritious foods instead. Once you give up junk food, your sugar addiction will be no more, and if you do succumb every now and again, the junk will taste as false and empty—as well, junky

—as it really is. When I was overweight I indulged in sweets constantly, but now I can confront an entire tray of French pastries and not even be tempted to touch one.

THE BLOOD SUGAR EXPERIMENT

Let's try a simple experiment. The next time you feel starved at three in the afternoon, eat a candy bar. Note how rapidly you feel starved again. The following afternoon, eat a cup of unsweetened yogurt or drink a glass of skim milk. The sugar in milk—known as lactose—digests slowly, making you feel pleasantly full for a longer period of time, as you'll see for yourself.

Beware! Many breakfast cereals, packaged and canned goods, and even such unlikely foods as ketchup are loaded with sugar. A canned peach with a single tablespoon of syrup, for example, contains 3½ teaspoons of sugar. A bottle of Coca-Cola is one of the prime offenders in this department. Aside from minor things like making you tired, hungry, and fat, sugar can cause tooth decay, diabetes, hypoglycemia, and anxiety. Read the labels on the packages and cans and be on the lookout for the ones that contain sugar. Natural sugars such as honey and molasses are whole foods and therefore a little better for you than refined sugar is, but they, too, should be avoided.

MIND OVER FODDER

As you know by now, no one understands better than I do how you lose all vestiges of self-control once that desire to eat overcomes you. You shake, sweat, feel "high." You don't stop to think about *why* you want to eat; you aren't thinking about your health or blood sugar; you're thinking only of how good that box of Mars bars or Mallomars is going to make you feel. Some food bingers inhale, gulp, and grab—they can't even wait till they get home to begin gorging themselves. Diet experts who advise you to "Grab a mate instead of a plate" aren't really allowing for the well-documented fact that the binger usually binges because he *has* no mate to grab (or the mate is ungrabbable).

Other bingers overeat out of habit; they fill the empty spaces in their day with the busy motion of lifting fork to mouth. I often overate because I was bored and had nothing much to think about. I thought about food, and thinking about food made me feel hungry, so I ate—and there we are.

Controlling and curing the binge syndrome isn't going to be easy. Don't underestimate the self-control you will need. It may help if you think of your overeating as a *behavior* problem.

First, I recommend some soul-searching. When the desire to binge has you by the throat (the esophagus?), stop long enough to ask yourself, "Why am I about to eat ten gallons of maple walnut ice cream?" Think about the eating patterns of your childhood. Did your parents give you food as a reward, or when you felt cranky, sick, or sad? Did they used to punish you by sending you to bed without any dinner? Did they deny you dessert when you were "bad?" Most overeaters discover that food is associated for them with feelings of gratification or the lack of it. The main problem with using food to gratify yourself is that it doesn't do the job; you usually feel worse, not better, after consuming all the goodies. And the pounds you gain are guaranteed to take the edge off any pleasure you might feel.

Try substituting other activities for overeating. Many people begin the chow-down the minute they get home from work. I automatically used to head straight for the fridge at 5:00 P.M. I discovered it helped to visit a friend on my way home, or to go shopping, or to attend an exercise class. If you binge mainly at a certain hour every day, plan a regular activity for that time slot. And *concentrate* on that activity, whether it's a course for credit or an escapist movie. If you're spending that time with friends, give all your attention to what they're saying. If food is offered, have only a glass of juice or a cup of tea. If you overeat because you feel lonely, volunteer some of your spare time at a worthwhile organization—hospital, orphanage, school.

There are now many clinics and diet clubs that deal professionally with the problem of overeating. Overeaters Anonymous and the Weight Watchers' organizations have made dieting into a form of group therapy. They encourage their members to speak out about the feelings that led them to overeat, help them develop new habits and attitudes toward food, and provide all-important moral support. Chances are at least one of these organizations has a chapter in your area.

Don't forget that you are you and that the way you

choose to break your binging pattern must suit your personality. In an effort to stop stuffing themselves, some people have gone so far as to fantasize their favorite foods crawling with bugs, or to coat cakes with Tabasco sauce, or to get hypnotized. How you do it is up to you. The first step is to get yourself to do it!

WILL AND WON'T POWER

Special menus, calorie counters, behavior modification plans, and soul-searching will be to no avail without the power to say a simple and emphatic "no" to food. When you're tempted to order a three-dip banana split, no advice, however well meant, will deter you; only the small, firm voice inside you can help. No one can give you that power to say no; you're going to have to find it for yourself and in yourself. You will probably say yes a good many times before you say no, but your desire to become thin, look good, and stay healthy and in control will doubtless win out in the end.

C.T.'S MINUTE-TO-MINUTE GUIDE TO A SLIM FIGURE

I've listed some techniques that can be practiced all day long.

The Morning Weigh-in

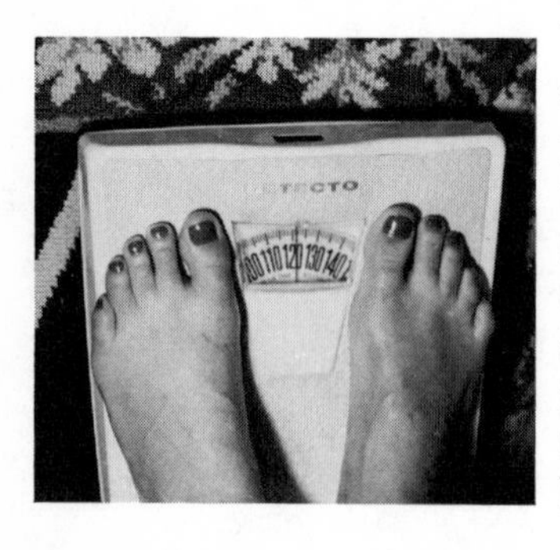

It takes the most courage to step on the dreaded scale the day after you've been particularly self-indulgent, because you may be able to fool yourself but the scale does not lie. As soon as you see that you've gained a pound, cut back on your food consumption. It's easier to get strict with yourself after you've gained a mere sixteen ounces than after you've gained ten pounds and your whole system is out of whack. I've become so aware of my body since I learned about good nutrition that I know when I've gained even before I set foot on the scale. That should be *your* goal, too. Meanwhile, weigh in every morning.

Not Eating After Six

Whenever I feel that I'm gaining, that a pound or two may be gaining on *me*, I have an early supper and that's it, I don't let another morsel pass my lips after 6:00 P.M. This is a fail-proof way of removing extra pounds, because your body has time to burn up its daily calories before you go to sleep. And by not a morsel, I mean *nothing*. If you have plans to join friends for a late meal or if your husband is coming home late and expects dinner, have yours early and drink only a glass of wine at the table.

Lunching with David Hartman— at first he tried to resist...

Keeping a Food Diary

Write down the kind and amount of food you eat, the time of day you eat it, and how you feel. This diary will reveal your eating habits to you at the same time that it forces you to account for every bite you take. Most importantly, it will focus your mind on monitoring—and cutting down on—food consumption.

Keeping It Up in Restaurants

Restaurants offer one tempting treat after another, serve large portions, lots of starches, divine desserts, and, in short, provide a matchless opportunity for you to relinquish—in one fell slurp—your slowly improving habits. Since, like most career women, I have to eat in restaurants fairly often, I've had to learn the art of restaurant resistance.

Sometimes I order a food I'm not particularly crazy about, like smoked salmon or antipasto, so I'm always sure to leave something on my plate. And even when I order my favorite foods, I try never to finish the portion the restaurant heaps onto the plate. If you feel guilty about leaving food on your plate, there is a delightfully unchic, very practical carrier known as the doggie bag. It's also a good idea to order a "healthy" food that you might never be inspired to prepare at home—something in the liver or kidney family, for instance, that's packed with vitamins. I always ask the waiter not to serve me potatoes, rolls, or creamed vegetables if they come with the meal. And if the entrée is served with lots of gravy or a rich sauce, I usually finesse that too. I sometimes order two appetizers and a soup instead of an entrée. I also make it a point to frequent Japanese, Chinese, and seafood restaurants that serve low-calorie fare, instead of Italian, French, and steakhouse restaurants. And when I order lunch from a coffee shop, I make my sandwich serve as instant diet fare by stripping off the top slice of bread—there's no need to eat a hamburger with both buns.

Breakfast Binging

Though I am now just about indifferent to the sweets I craved when I was fat, I sometimes get that old urge for a piece of rich layer cake dripping with frosting. When this happens I try to hold off until breakfast, because if you have to eat something fattening, early morning is the best time to do it. You then have the whole day to burn off all the calories. Eating sweets after a big evening meal is the quickest way to pile on pounds. Cake for breakfast, needless to say, should be an infrequent indulgence for any diet-conscious woman. But then again, it's not every woman who can face a chocolate layer cake early in the morning.

Beginning Your Diet with a Binge

Before you go on a serious diet, I recommend that you eat all the food you can manage for three solid days. The point is to overdo it, knowing that you will never overeat again. While you're stuffing yourself, take note of how your body is reacting, and form a cartoon mental picture of how all that junk that's now inside you is going to make you look. At the end of the three days, I guarantee that you will be looking forward to your diet.

Substituting Quality for Quantity

In my diets at the end of this chapter, I recommend expensive delicacies such as smoked salmon, oysters, and exotic fruits. When you're eating less, you can afford high-quality foods. By cutting out ice cream, cake, soda, and lots of bread and meats, you save all around. If both you and your husband are overweight, buy small quantities of good cuts of filet mignon, instead of the large, cheaper cuts. And when you're lunching out, forget the Coca-Cola, french fries, and —ah!—cherry pie à la mode. Order a single dish such as lobster salad. The check will come to about the same.

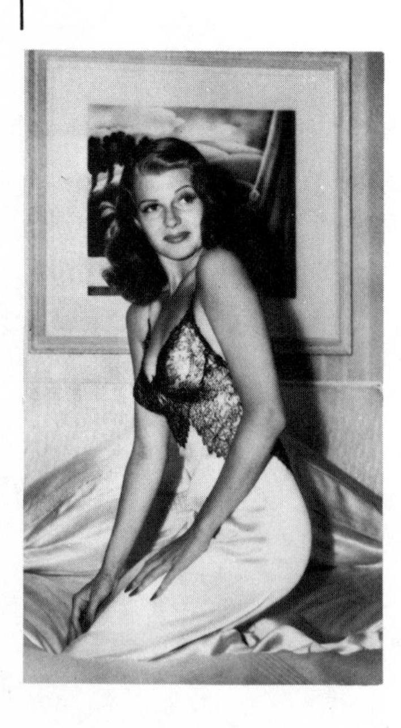

Visual Aides

This is one of the oldest motivational tricks in the book—but a good one. The image of Rita Hayworth on the late show was the inspiration I once needed in order to begin a serious diet. I then went to the magazine stands and found examples of the best-maintained bodies. Overcoming embarrassment, and petty jealousy, I taped up these tear sheets all around my apartment. I was openly admitting to myself—and others—that there was a big discrepancy between me and the clippings I'd chosen to represent my far-off goal. Visual aides can also function as a weapon against temptation. Clip a picture of the figure you'd like to have and tack it up on the icebox door or on a full-length mirror. The mirror itself, of course, is by simple definition your most useful visual aide. Open your eyes and keep looking. Trying on a bikini in front of the mirror once a month is a good tell-me-no-lies way to check your progress.

Packing a Snack

I feel hungry between meals or suffer gnawing hunger pangs whenever I have to miss or put off a meal. My blood sugar drops and I long for a good low-down calorie-loaded junk food orgy. I've learned to carry some low-calorie diversions in my tote bag, which someone, with good reason, once referred to as a snack pack. Oranges are the best—they give quick energy, taste great, and contain vitamins, too. If you pack a snack, make sure it's not some self-defeating and figure-defacing item like fudge brownies or chocolate-chip cookies.

The Twenty-four-Hour Fast

When I need to drop a pound in a big hurry, I skip dinner, breakfast and lunch the next day, and eat a small dinner the following evening. This modified fast, believe it or not, is both safe and effective. Having skipped dinner, you wake up in the morning feeling light and energetic, and by lunchtime you're savoring the evening meal. This is one diet where you never feel "starved."

MISTAKES PEOPLE MAKE

Choosing the Wrong Diet

To maintain a slim figure you must develop sensible attitudes toward food and exercise. Many people recklessly embark on "miracle diets," featuring a small number of foods in odd, even bizarre, combinations, which supposedly help you burn off fat rapidly. A famous nutritionist, Carlton Fredericks, once quipped that the only thing miraculous about "miracle diets" is that people survive them. These diets are dangerous because the limited number of nutrients they provide eventually causes the body to take the nutrients it needs from its own cells. Beware of the following: the Atkins diet, which recommends high-calorie fats and no carbohydrates, is riskily high in cholesterol and

eliminates important nutrients; the Stillman diet, which has you eating an unlimited number of rich proteins and few carbohydrates and drinking eight glasses of water per day, may cause fatigue, nausea, and diarrhea; the macrobiotic diet, consisting mainly of brown rice, a few vegetables and fruits, and reduced fluids, when practiced in the extreme, may actually result in starvation; and the liquid protein diet, possibly the most dangerous of them all, is to be avoided at all costs without close medical supervision.

There are endless variations of these diets which I haven't mentioned. In general, the only really safe and effective way to diet is to eat both fewer calories and as many different foods as you can.

Forgetting Liquids

Most of us on diets forget that liquids are food. Be sure to count the calories in liquids. A single Coca-Cola contains four or five teaspoons of solid sugar. Orange juice is good for quick energy and loaded with Vitamin C, but it's also loaded with calories. Alcohol, too, contains a great many calories. Next time you're at a party or your local bar, order a spritzer (half wine and half Perrier with a twist); it's refreshing and contains half the calories of one glass of wine. Or try two ounces of orange juice mixed with two ounces of mineral water for breakfast. If black coffee is too bitter for you, just add some skim milk. Quite aside from being bitter, it can make you jumpy and nervous—using up a lot of your energy at once, so I often substitute a cup of hot water with lemon juice, which, believe it or not, tastes pretty good. And instead of sweet colas, I usually ask for Perrier water with a slice of lime.

Substituting Sweets

Diet soda is the mainstay of many dieters and I'm all for it. But "diet" sweets should be eaten sparingly if at all. On the whole they add up to more junk. When you're dieting, you should try and stay away from sweets of all kinds. Substitute fruit and low-calorie drinks for confections and soda.

Gulping It Down

Diet experts believe almost to a man that if you eat your food too rapidly, your nervous system won't have time to warn you when you're full. Try to eat slowly. Lay down your fork between each bite, or chew longer, or take smaller bites. Don't read or watch TV while you eat or the amount you consume may get lost in the plot. *Concentrate* on what you're eating and on how good it tastes.

Holding Back and Back and Back

There is a thin line between exercising the will power necessary to stay slim and totally depriving yourself of the foods you enjoy. If you never indulge yourself, life can seem rather grim. Once in a blue moon I treat myself to an enormous stack of pancakes complete with maple syrup, blueberries, bacon, sausages, and butter. Eating a small piece of cake once a week or so won't make you fat and may make you happy. When you're first dieting you should probably give up sweets altogether in order to kick the habit. And even after that, only occasional cravings should be indulged.

Buying Foods You Shouldn't Even Be Thinking About

I refuse to have cakes, cookies, or even peanuts around the house. If you *really* want to avoid temptation, don't buy the stuff. Having to go all the way to the store to buy food that will only make you fat may make you think twice. Don't use children, husbands, or roommates as an excuse for stocking up; the things that pile the pounds on you and undermine your health do the same to them. And when you do buy a treat for your family or friends, buy enough for one time only.

GET YOUR VITAMINS AND MINERALS THE NATURAL WAY

Vitamins stimulate cell growth and aid digestion and nerve function. They also help convert the food you eat into energy. Many people supplement their diets with vitamin and mineral pills in the belief that large random doses of supplements can preserve youth, cure all manner of ailments, and improve hair, skin, and nails. All well and good. But I make sure that the vitamins I take are prescribed by a nutritionist. Vitamin and mineral supplements should be approached with the greatest caution. A daily multi-vitamin pill is definitely a good idea, but no one should prescribe large amounts of vitamins or minerals for herself. Many nutritionists feel that not enough is known about the effect of large doses of vitamins on the human body; they cite that some vitamins in large

doses, such as Vitamins A and D, which are stored in the body, can be toxic. Overdoses of other vitamins can cause gastric disturbances, skin problems, and other damage. In most cases, as with Vitamin C, the body simply eliminates the excess vitamins—but why take a chance?

The best way to get vitamins and minerals is from natural foods. Some excellent sources, which can be taken as supplements, *are* foods and are easily absorbed by the body: brewer's yeast, wheat germ, kelp, raw bran. Here's a list of vitamins and some essential minerals, a description of how they affect your health and your appearance, and the names of some foods that contain them. Your best bet for good nutrition is to make sure that you regularly eat foods that have *all* these vitamins and minerals in them.

Vitamin A

What it does: Improves vision; keeps skin smooth and hair and nails lustrous.

Where to find it: Green vegetables (spinach, broccoli, string beans); yellow vegetables (carrots, squash); apricots.

Vitamin Bs

(There are many vitamins in the B family and few foods contain them all: B_1, B_2, B_6, B_{12}, biotin, choline, folic acid, inositol and PABA, and so on.)

What they do: Aid metabolism, growth, and the functions of internal organs, including the brain; reduce stress; help prevent excess oil in skin as well as skin discolorations.

Where to find them: Liver, brewer's yeast, bran, wheat germ, brown rice, bean curd, watercress, spinach, green leafy vegetables; eggs for Vitamin B_{12}.

Vitamin C

What it does: Helps body resist infection; helps in preventing colds; improves teeth and gums; helps keep skin firm and elastic.

Where to find it: Citrus fruits, watercress, spinach, tomatoes, carrots.

Vitamin D

What it does: Helps build bones and teeth.

Where to find it: Fish and enriched milk.

Vitamin E

What it does: Improves skin; aids healing processes; and helps prevent blood clots.

Where to find it: Unrefined vegetable oils, liver, wheat germ, spinach, celery, watercress.

MINERALS

Calcium

What it does: Helps build bones and teeth; aids blood clotting; reduces fatigue; fosters relaxation; helps prevent insomnia.

Where to find it: Milk (the richest source), watercress, spinach, carrots, salmon.

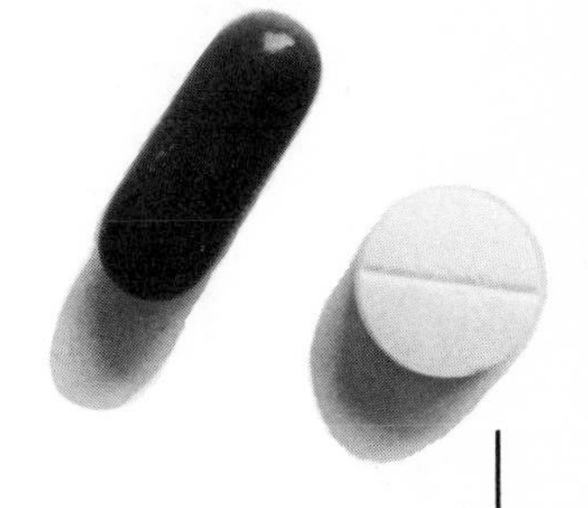

Iodine

What it does: Regulates the functions of the thyroid gland, which regulates the functions of the entire body.

Where to find it: Shellfish, iodized salt, kelp, spinach, cranberries.

Iron

What it does: Builds red blood corpuscles; carries oxygen to various parts of the body (women are often deficient in iron, and need to take a supplement, which works best when taken with Vitamin C).

Where to find it: Liver, eggs, whole grain breads or cereals, wheat germ, dried fruits, spinach, watercress.

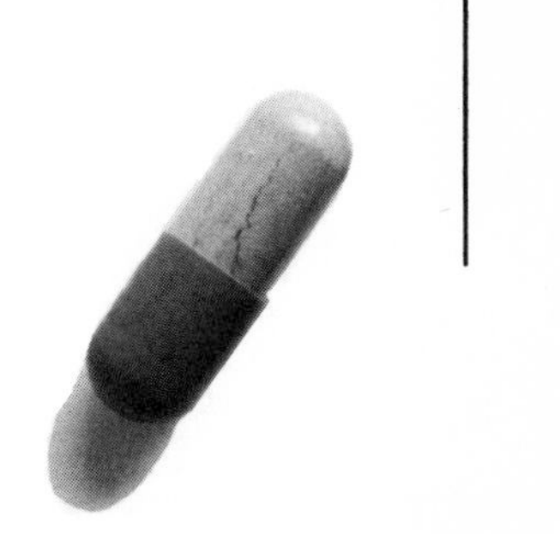

Magnesium

What it does: Synthesizes proteins in the body; protects nerves; prevents cramps.

Where to find it: Whole grains, spinach, green leafy vegetables.

Potassium

What it does: Gives muscles pliancy; aids nervous system, cell and tissue life.

Where to find it: Almost all fruits and vegetables; whole grains and nuts.

Sodium (or salt)

What it does: Spurs digestive juices; helps eliminate carbon dioxide.

Where to find it: Spinach, watercress, whole grains,

seafood. (Too much salt can cause fluid retention, hypertension, and other problems. Try to lower your intake of table salt, and heighten the flavor of food with lemon juice and other condiments.)

Other minerals needed by the body are zinc, fluoride, copper, sulphur, and manganese, to name just a few.

You'll have noticed that I mentioned certain foods several times. Spinach and watercress contain virtually *all* the vitamins and minerals. Carrots, too, are rich in fiber and vitamins. Wheat germ, brewer's yeast, whole grains, and liver also double as nature's vitamin pills.

C.T.'S TIME-SAVING, LIFE-SAVING, MONEY-SAVING DIET

I have never had any ambitions to be a gourmet. Nevertheless, food is very important to me. My career keeps me so busy I have no choice but to go for the most sensible foods, which also happen to be the most nourishing and the easiest to prepare.

The recipes that follow require minimal time in the kitchen. Even the big bow-wow gourmet cooks I know don't want to do it every day of the week.

The foods I've chosen will keep you supplied with all the nutrients you need for health and vitality and at the same time amount to a good basic diet. If you eat a Cheryl Tiegs breakfast, lunch, and dinner (as yet served in no restaurants I've heard of), you will be consuming only 1200 calories a day or thereabouts. If you want to take in fewer calories, just cut down on the margarine, butter, or oils, but never eliminate all the fats in your diet—they nourish the skin and hair with necessary oils and help burn up those calories.

I provide a *selection* of breakfasts, lunches, and dinners, instead of the rigid Monday-through-Sunday calendar of meals. That way you can decide what you want to eat and when. My menus are only suggestions; your eating habits should reflect *your* personality as mine do mine. Maybe that's why these meal suggestions feature some foods and combinations of foods that the regular diets don't include.

BREAKFAST

Nutritional studies have shown that people who eat a high-protein breakfast, in combination with some carbohydrates and fat, work with greater efficiency and feel better throughout the day; their blood sugar level stays high. I wouldn't dream of skipping breakfast.

C.T.'s Favorite

4 oz. unsweetened orange juice (for quick energy) = 55 calories
1 bran muffin (provides a solid carbohydrate for long-lasting energy and fiber) = 106 calories
1 teaspoon margarine (select a margarine made from pure vegetable oil) = 34 calories
1 cup plain yogurt (provides protein, calcium, and bacterial organisms to aid digestion) = 150 calories
1 cup hot water spiked with lemon juice

Total calories = 345

C.T.'s Mock Eggs Benedict

(*A Slimming Version of the Calorific Treat*)

½ grapefruit sprinkled with cinnamon = 50 calories
Tea or coffee
Mock Eggs Benedict = 310 calories

To make C.T.'s M.E.B., top a piece of thin-sliced whole wheat or pumpernickel toast with 1 ounce of boiled ham. Poach or boil an egg and place on top of ham. Top with 1 tablespoon lemon mayonnaise, which you make by beating 2 tablespoons of lemon juice into ¼ cup mayonnaise.

Total calories = 360

C.T.'s Quick Blender Milkshake

My favorite way to quickly fill up on high-quality calories.

1 cup skim milk = 90 calories
1 banana (bananas are particularly rich in potassium) = 100 calories
½ cup orange juice = 55 calories
1 egg = 75 calories
1 teaspoon honey (optional) = 20 calories

Put above ingredients into blender jar and blend till smooth. For fewer calories, you can add just a bit of banana or dispense with it altogether. You can also substitute a vegetable-based protein powder for the egg. You can even drink this breakfast as you're running out the door.

Total calories = 340

C.T.'s "G.M.A." G.C. (or "Good Morning America" Grilled Cheese)

Most people think of a grilled cheese as luncheon fare, but it also makes a quick and nutritious breakfast. For the morning, I prefer one of the lighter cheeses such as mozzarella.

½ grapefruit sprinkled with cinnamon and broiled = 50 calories
1 piece thin-sliced rye or whole wheat bread = 55 calories
2 oz. skim milk mozzarella cheese (¼ of an 8 oz. package) = 160 calories
½ teaspoon margarine = 17 calories

Spread the bread with margarine, top with mozzarella, and broil until the cheese is melted and browned. Broil grapefruit at the same time.

Total calories = 282

C.T.'s Oriental Pudding

Dieters often crave a sweet in the morning but doughnuts and Danishes are taboo, because they provide only useless calories. I've discovered that a bland-tasting Oriental food called tofu, or bean curd, which has few calories and is loaded with protein and the B vitamins, can be transformed into an energizing sweet, with the help of a little honey and flavoring. This breakfast has to be made the night before.

1 block tofu (widely available in health-food or Oriental specialty stores) 120 grams of tofu or about 4 ounces = 86 calories
1 tablespoon honey (add an extra tablespoon if you're not dieting) = 60 calories
¼ cup skim milk = 22 calories

Simmer bean curd in a pan of water for five minutes. Put bean curd, honey, and milk in a blender jar and add vanilla or almond flavoring to taste. Blend till smooth. Pour in a small bowl and sprinkle with cinnamon. Chill. This breakfast sweet is guaranteed to keep you satisfied till lunch.

Total calories = 168

C.T.'s Quick Grab

You may be in too much of a rush to even think of breakfast and make the mistake of settling for a calorific treat from the coffee wagon. But there are nourishing breakfasts you can literally grab on your way out the door that will provide you with far more energy—and fewer calories. Let's grab:

1. *A banana (filling, nutritious, and sweet) = 100 calories*
2. *Two slices of any whole-grain flatbread = approximately 50 calories, depending on brand. If you have time, divide 1 tablespoon peanut butter (rich in protein but very fattening) between them = 100 calories*
3. A handful *of raisins (lots of iron) = 112 calories*
4. *Eight ounces tomato juice = 50 calories, or 6 ounces orange juice = 75 calories; with two heaping tablespoons brewer's yeast mixed in = 60 calories. This is one of the most nutritious breakfasts grabbable. Yeast is one of our best natural sources of protein and the B vitamins. Warning: Many people are put off by the taste, so try different brands (available in health food stores) till you find one you like.*

LUNCH

C.T.'s Scandinavian Smorgasbord

2 ounces Nova Scotia smoked salmon (expensive and delicious) = 200 calories
1 ounce Neufchâtel cheese (less caloric than cream cheese) = 100 calories
2 slices Swedish flatbread = 50 calories
1 raw tomato = 25 calories
3 olives = 25 calories
1 glass of mineral water with 1 slice of lime and/or herbal tea sweetened with cinnamon and orange peel

Total calories = 400

C.T.'s Bunless Burger

The all-American hamburger is fattening to begin with, and when you stuff it between two buns or slices of bread it becomes a big problem. The hamburger is just about everybody's favorite, however, and it's so quick and easy to prepare. I suggest treating it as if it were a mini-steak. Grill a 4-ounce hamburger made of ground round and add ½ teaspoon of a good-quality mustard, a thin strip of Roquefort cheese, and 1 teaspoon chutney for zest. You can also mix chopped onions and parsley into the meat before grilling it.
1 bunless burger = 195 calories
Tomato, celery, and pepper sticks = 50 calories
Unsweetened beverage
1 apple, peach, pear, or nectarine = 100 calories

Total calories = 345

C.T.'s Vitamin Pill

This contains so many vitamins and minerals it amounts to a substitute for a multi-vitamin pill. It's a good lunch to eat before going on that twenty-four-hour fast I suggested. And if you hate liver, no problem—simply substitute a glass of brewer's yeast and tomato juice.

1 cup spinach salad (fresh raw spinach, carefully washed) = 50 calories
1 tablespoon oil and vinegar dressing with ½ teaspoon mustard = 120 calories
2 slices Swedish flatbread = 50 calories
2 ounces sautéed calf's liver = 118 calories
Herbal tea

Total calories = 338

Note: If you want only salad for lunch, increase the amount of spinach and dressing, add a chopped hard-boiled egg, raw mushrooms, and a slice of bacon, and *Violà!*

C.T.'s No-Mayo Fish Salad

There's no rule that says fattening mayonnaise has to be a feature of a fish salad. Substitute yogurt and flavor the salad with chopped scallions or chives, fresh dill or parsley, chopped olives and celery and lemon juice. Come on, use your imagination!

1 cup water-packed crab, tuna, or lobster salad made with yogurt = approximately 130 calories
Cucumber salad (sliced cucumber with 1 tablespoon dressing) = 140 calories
Unsweetened beverage

Total calories = 270

"I Hate Cottage Cheese"

I've always associated bland cottage cheese with a deprivation diet. Instead, I use the Italian cheese ricotta, which looks a little like cottage cheese but has a richer texture and tastes delicious. Ricotta is higher in calories, so you'll just have to eat less. If you are seriously dieting and feel duty-bound to spring for cottage cheese in a restaurant, sprinkle it with chives and fresh ground pepper to make it a bit more exciting.

½ cup skim-milk ricotta = 125 calories
2 slices Swedish flatbread = 50 calories
6 olives = 50 calories
1 slice cantaloupe or honeydew melon = 30 calories per quarter-slice melon
Italian espresso, or tea

Total calories = 255

C.T.'s Instant Satisfaction

My favorite lunch is the one I find waiting for me in the refrigerator already prepared. Among other things, it saves me the expense and temptation of eating in a restaurant. How about:

2 ounces cheese (Mysöst, Edam, or mozzarella, which are lower in calories than the heavier, oily cheeses such as Cheddar and Brie); or *2 small slices cold turkey, chicken, or roast beef;* or *2 hard-boiled eggs = approximately 200 calories*
Celery, carrot, pepper, or cucumber sticks = 50 calories
1 whole tomato = 25 calories
1 small can tomato or vegetable juice = 50 calories
2 slices flatbread = 50 calories
A piece of fruit = 100 calories

Total Calories = 475

DINNER

Who doesn't enjoy relaxing over a home-cooked meal in the evening? Dinner is the most important meal of the day for me, and I like to make it a festive occasion, with good, simple-to-prepare dishes and candlelight. Because I feel wine adds a great deal, I've included it—calories or no calories—in almost all my dinner menus.

Spaghetti Diet-Style

Pasta is not a total write-off for dieters, because small amounts are low in calories.

1 cup tender spaghetti = 155 calories
¼ cup each broccoli and zucchini = 25 calories
2 tablespoons olive oil = 250 calories
Chopped garlic and scallions

Sauté garlic and scallions in oil, then add broccoli and zucchini. Cook only a couple of minutes; the vegetables should be crisp. Spoon over the cooked spaghetti.

1 glass white wine = 70 calories
½ cup raspberries or blueberries topped with 1 tablespoon yogurt = 60 calories

Total calories = 560

Baked Fish

1 average serving baked fish = approximately 250 calories depending on type of fish and size of portion

Buy a whole fish such as trout, bluefish, or flounder, or use a fillet of sole. Melt 1 teaspoon butter in ¼ cup dry vermouth and pour over raw fish. Sprinkle with dill. Bake in 400° oven till fish is tender and white when pierced with a fork (approximately fifteen minutes). Baste once or twice while cooking. Serve with one slice of lemon.

1 cup steamed string beans mixed with ¼ cup mushrooms sautéed in 1 teaspoon margarine = 75 calories
½ cup brown rice = 50 calories
1 glass white wine = 70 calories
½ cup fruit compote flavored with 1 teaspoon sherry = 65 calories

Total calories = 510

Easy-Does-It Vegetarian

This is my adaptation of a lunch served at the "21" Club in New York.

1 cup fresh mushrooms = 15 calories
1 cup spinach = 20 calories
1 cup chopped broccoli = 45 calories
1 cup bean sprouts, optional = 25 calories
1 chopped scallion
1 tablespoon peanut or sesame oil = 100 calories

Heat oil in skillet or Chinese wok. Sauté scallions. Add broccoli, bean sprouts, mushrooms, and spinach, and stir fry for several minutes till tender. You can also steam the vegetables.

Top with a poached egg = 75 calories
Serve with ½ cup brown rice = 50 calories
½ small papaya = 40 calories
Tea

Total calories = 370

Chicken Little

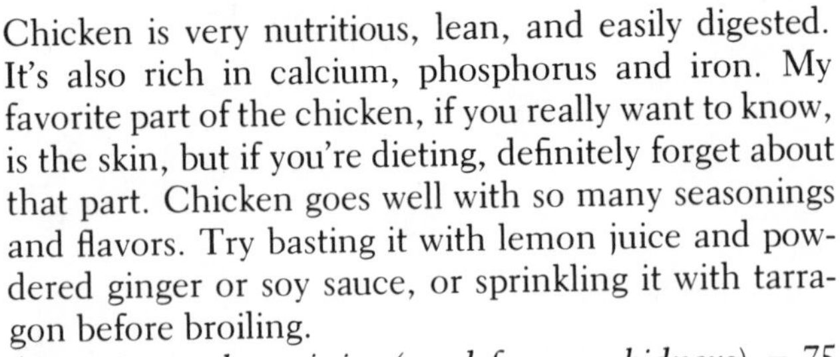

Chicken is very nutritious, lean, and easily digested. It's also rich in calcium, phosphorus and iron. My favorite part of the chicken, if you really want to know, is the skin, but if you're dieting, definitely forget about that part. Chicken goes well with so many seasonings and flavors. Try basting it with lemon juice and powdered ginger or soy sauce, or sprinkling it with tarragon before broiling.

4 ounces cranberry juice (good for your kidneys) = 75 calories
½ small boned chicken or Cornish game hen, which is tenderer and more elegant (3½ ounces of chicken meat contain 171 calories)
Endive, watercress, and sliced water chestnut salad with 1 tablespoon oil and vinegar dressing = 160 calories

1 small baked squash (any variety) with ½ teaspoon butter = 100 calories
Tea

Total calories = approx. 506

Salad à la C.T.

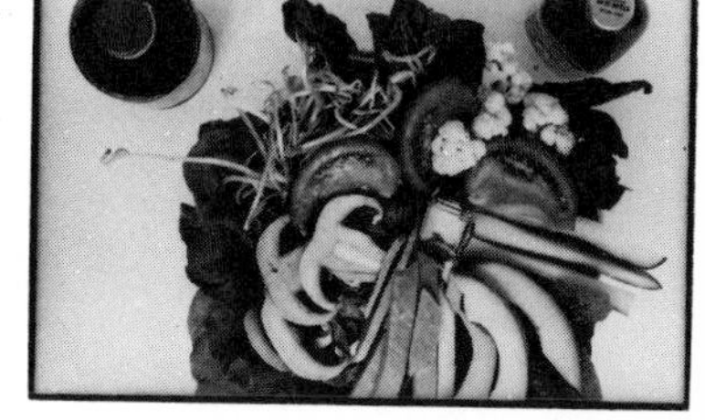

I truly love preparing a giant salad, which brings out whatever dormant and long-buried "gourmet instincts" I may have. Served with flatbread or breadsticks, the following salad makes a very nice light dinner. You can use any or all of the ingredients I've listed below, or improvise as you go along—you can put almost anything in a salad (apart from endangered species!) and it'll still taste good.

1 cup arugula or spinach leaves
1 cup Boston lettuce
Bean sprouts
Thin strips of boiled ham or turkey
Radishes
Tomato
Pepper
Avocado
Thin slices of cucumber or raw zucchini
Sliced raw mushrooms
Raw cauliflower buds
¼ cup sunflower seeds
2 tablespoons dressing of your choice (if you make a large salad for several people, serve dressing in a gravy boat so dieters can measure their portion with a tablespoon)

Food is primarily life-sustaining but we do *not* live by sustenance alone, and food can even be as much a form of therapy as therapy itself. The ritual places for eating range from our own homes to the drive-in and diner, to the restaurant glistening with the apparatus of French cuisine, to the little bistro for the couple just out of college and not yet expense-accounted for, to the high-powered, business-oriented, status-based lunch club. But whatever the ambience, whatever the cost, one's devotion to one's own mouth and stomach is finally relentless.

Since food plays such an important role in our sense of well-being and warm connection to the world, we must try to take advantage of the three opportunities a day we have for food therapy.

4

Push Pull, Push Pull: The High Road to Muscle Tone

10

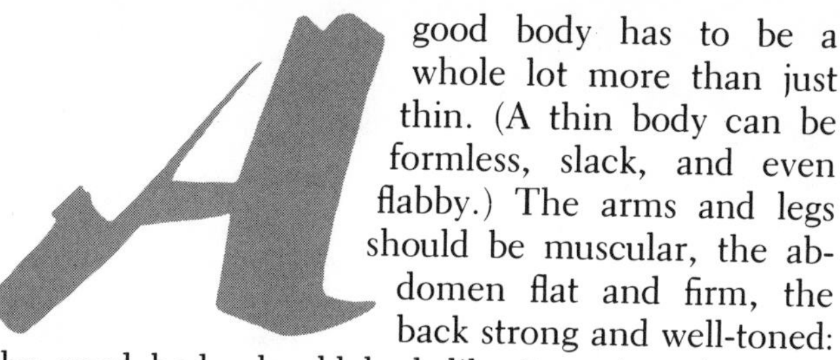

good body has to be a whole lot more than just thin. (A thin body can be formless, slack, and even flabby.) The arms and legs should be muscular, the abdomen flat and firm, the back strong and well-toned: the good body should look like it can't wait to get moving at a good trot, can't wait to run, jump, and bend. A lithe figure makes a terrific impression: the person who possesses it is someone who is obviously on the side of life, someone who has learned how to live the healthy, active way. I say "learned" because it's no trick, and it's not luck.

Few women are born with perfectly proportioned bodies, but every woman, even the roundest of the round, can achieve the best version of the figure she has—by exercising. Being a great big beefy glob is the same as being a parasite; deep down, you have the distinct feeling—and if you don't, there's probably a small, nagging voice that tells you you should—that you're adding nothing to the world but your own weight. And every day, the idea of getting out of yourself becomes harder and harder to contemplate. But take heart: you don't have to be stuck with this indulgent self. You have only one life to live—and none of us gets out of it alive, right?—so you might as well go all the way with it, get the most you can out of it, lift your sights a little higher. All you have to do is make an effort, and if you aren't a natural athlete, what you can do is exercise. Oh I know, everybody has some brisk excuse or other for *not* exercising. It's so easy to wallow around—and just roll down jelly-roll lane—but it's such a waste of precious time.

Exercise alone will not make you fit any more than dieting by itself will make you shapely. So take a good deep breath and decide to do both!

If you're the right weight for your body frame, and still notice sags, bulges, and other gloomy annexes on your silhouette, then your body is clearly famished for exercise.

If you'll get into a bathing suit and be seated, Dr. Tiegs will be with you in a few minutes. Now: with your bathing suit on, stand in front of a full-length mirror. Take a good look at the whole of you. Odds are you are not faultlessly shaped and that your vanity has just been stung, if not demolished. Console your-

self with the thought that none of us looks like her dream picture of herself. And now I'm going to pester you with some questions. Answer them truthfully—if you don't, it's like lying to your shrink, you'll wind up cheating only yourself.

■ *Do your arms have enough muscles in them to form curves? Raise one arm to shoulder height: is there flab on the underside of the upper arm?*

■ *Stretch your leg out in front of you and lift it about a foot off the ground. Now feel the muscles in your upper thighs with your fingers. Or are they non-existent?*

■ *Turn your profile to the mirror. Stand up straight. Now look at your lower abdomen. Does your stomach feel mooshy instead of firm when you press it with your fingers?*

■ *Look closely at your shoulders. Is one of them hunched up, slouched over, or what?*

■ *Stretch up toward the ceiling with your hands. Then, with your knees perfectly straight and your feet a few inches apart, bend down and try to touch your toes. You can't?*

■ *Do you have those glumps of fat jocularly referred to as "riding breeches" on the outside of your thighs even though your weight is close to what it should be? Do you also sport the curdled flesh they call "cellulite?"*

■ *Are your hands and feet usually cold?*

■ *When you run up a flight of stairs, are you breath-less?*

■ *Do you often feel "run down," even after a good night's sleep?*

You've just died a little, because you probably had to answer "yes" to most of these questions. I once had to.

And now back to what you have just seen for yourself in that full-length mirror.

A raised shoulder is often a sign of tension reflected in the alignment of your body. Weak muscles tense up easily, as do any muscles we hold in a distorted position for any length of time. And if we spend many hours at a desk or bent over a typewriter, the area around the shoulders and neck is almost certain to be tense and unaligned. Other obvious signs of body tension are tight, compressed lips and squinty eyes. Exercise creates flexibility in the muscles and joints; and the harder we work at it, the more effectively it relaxes us.

Women tend to pile up fat in the tissue of their buttocks, thighs, and arms. If your weight is near normal and still you are saddled with "riding breeches," your body is probably high in fat. "Cellulite" is the fancy term for fat deposits on those parts of your body that get little circulation—like buttocks and thighs, not to name names. We sit on "cellulite," and it bubbles under the pressure—not audibly but visibly, becoming in time dimpled and rough. Luckily, cellulite responds to the increased circulation that is one of the by-products of exercise.

If your hands and feet feel chilly in reasonably warm weather and icy when it's merely cold out, you are probably not receiving a strong enough flow of blood from your circulatory system. Exercise steps up the circulation, sends a warm greeting to hands and feet. After I've done my calisthenics, I can feel my fingers tingling, and it's an honest-to-God *alive* sensation, a reward for all my exertions.

If you do eat properly and you do get enough rest and you still feel fatigued, not even capable of true relaxation, then you are probably not aware of:

WHAT EXERCISE CAN DO FOR YOU

Improve the Function of Your Cardiovascular System

When you exercise vigorously, you are forcing your heart to work harder, beat faster. The heart is a muscle like any other, and the well-exercised heart can all the more easily cope with unusual exertions, such as shoveling snow after a storm. It pumps more blood—more quickly—through your veins, blood vessels, and arteries, thus toning and burnishing your whole system. In the process, all your internal organs receive a greater supply of nourishing plasma and oxygen at the same time that they are purged of impurities such as carbon dioxide. Before you know it, you're feeling less languid. The color and texture of your skin improve with exercise; blemishes fade out, fade away. Do you know when I look my best? After I've run around a tennis court for about an hour! To me, the natural glow that I feel at that time is more satisfying than any blusher or rouge could ever be. Running, sweating, and working off excess water, I feel as if I'm in ardent pursuit of whoever I have it in me to become.

Improve Your Posture, Balance, and Coordination

Exercise strengthens and stretches the muscles in your back, shoulders, neck, and abdomen. The result is you hold your head higher, your spine straighter; your stomach is flatter, and your shoulders, for once, are sitting back and down. And if that isn't incentive enough, have you ever thought how standing up straight is the best way to reveal the lines of a beautiful outfit? And have you ever considered how—just maybe—slumping around with your feet splayed out is not the very best way to "win friends and influence people?"

Sports, modern dance, and ballet will put you on the road to balance and coordination, a road that from now on you will travel without bulging bags. People who do regular exercise move with more self-assurance and elegance; they have greater linear expression and more grace—because they understand their bodies, and they understand the space *around* their bodies. And moving with confidence is the first step to moving sensually, which as we all know works better than any dress or perfume yet invented.

"Chin up, Feet on the ground, Keep reaching for the stars."

Increase Your Flexibility

A well-toned, flexible body is far less susceptible to accidents. Exercise points up the areas of your body that are stiff and weak. Once when I was doing deep knee bends in an exercise class, I experienced quite a shock: my ankles were about ready to give out—in any case, they gave out a warning crackle from deep within my ankle crust. If I hadn't done that exercise, I would never have thought about my ankles—I mean, why would anyone ever think about their ankles?—until I sprained one! So stand warned: weak, inflexible joints are easy to twist, even easier to break.

If your body is fit and nimble, you can perform physical tasks you might have assumed were way beyond your power of endurance. Last year, when ABC-TV sent me to Africa to host a special on Kenya,

I suddenly found myself on the verge of being overtaken by a demonstrating, rampaging elephant herd (that's twenty thousand pounds I'm talking about!) in the volcanic lava fields of Tsavo National Park. I hesitate to think what might have happened to the special (and, parenthetically, to *me*) if I hadn't been in good enough shape to run for my life. As they say in Nairobi, *Shauri ya naungu*.

Increase Your Mental Energy

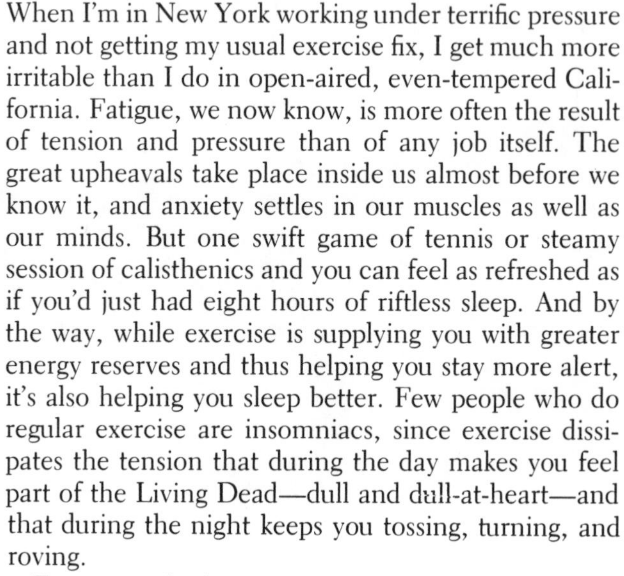

When I'm in New York working under terrific pressure and not getting my usual exercise fix, I get much more irritable than I do in open-aired, even-tempered California. Fatigue, we now know, is more often the result of tension and pressure than of any job itself. The great upheavals take place inside us almost before we know it, and anxiety settles in our muscles as well as our minds. But one swift game of tennis or steamy session of calisthenics and you can feel as refreshed as if you'd just had eight hours of riftless sleep. And by the way, while exercise is supplying you with greater energy reserves and thus helping you stay more alert, it's also helping you sleep better. Few people who do regular exercise are insomniacs, since exercise dissipates the tension that during the day makes you feel part of the Living Dead—dull and dull-at-heart—and that during the night keeps you tossing, turning, and roving.

Everyone who has ever exercised systematically can vouch for the fact that a good run, swim, or game of squash is just about the best antidote for feeling "down." Exercise provides a release for pent-up feelings of depression, restlessness, and boredom. You get that ebullient feeling that, no matter what else, you have a strong, healthy body under your control.

Stifle and Depress an Enlarged Appetite

All the experts agree that nutrition and exercise go hand-in-hand: when you exercise, your body uses nutrients to create muscle cells. Studies have shown that truly vigorous exercise keeps the appetite at bay, especially in chronic overeaters. If you're someone who eats out of boredom or restlessness, why not substitute a little exercise at the times when you are tempted to raid the fridge.

FINDING THE RIGHT EXERCISE

To get all you can out of working out, you will very likely have to take up more than one kind of exercise. If you want to improve the functioning of heart, lungs, and circulatory system, then do an "aerobic" exercise —an activity that makes your heart beat faster and your lungs work harder, such as running, jumping rope, swimming, or playing a hard game of tennis, handball, or squash. While you do any one of these exercises your body will be consuming more oxygen, your blood pressure may well be reduced, and certainly your overall endurance will increase.

Aerobic exercise, however, is not enough to tone and strengthen all the muscles in your body. Any woman who wants a flat stomach and willowly waist will have to practice calisthenic exercises as well—spot-toning exercises, gymnastics, yoga. This stretch-tone-and-relax kind of exercise trims and shapes the parts of your body that aerobic exercise doesn't get to. (The body is a riddle—a very stylish one, to be sure—and riddles take solving.) Jogging, for example, shapes your thighs and calves, but does very little for your arms. The most complete-unto-itself aerobic exercise is swimming; it gives your chest, back, and legs a fine workout. Calisthenics relax your body and make it more flexible. In fact, if you're out of shape, you should limber up with a calisthenic exercise *before* attempting a vigorous sport; otherwise, you're just courting strains and sprains.

Let's say you've never exercised regularly in your life. Then your first job will be to choose an exercise you can stay with and even get to enjoy. This is a lot harder than it sounds, since if you're out of shape, almost any exercise is going to feel like some exotic torture and—at least at first—look like a bad dumbshow. As soon as you come up against all those unfledged, unflexed muscles, each one of which is crying out to you, "Enough already!", you're going to want to abandon whatever exercise you've chosen. But stick with it. I believe in giving anything—from sitting down on up—a serious try.

Which isn't to say that I haven't pulled the plug on various activities I've taken up. I went through a jumping-rope-in-hotel-rooms phase while I was "on the road." I've jogged down more city streets than I can count in more cities than I can name. I've run in place like a little hamster, done sit-ups *beyond* number *before*

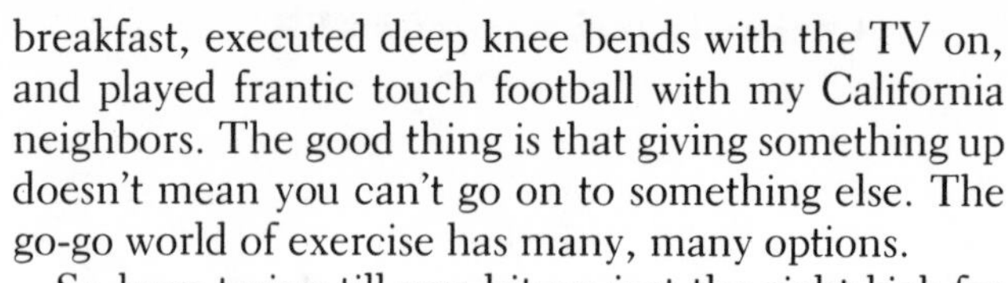

breakfast, executed deep knee bends with the TV on, and played frantic touch football with my California neighbors. The good thing is that giving something up doesn't mean you can't go on to something else. The go-go world of exercise has many, many options.

So keep trying till you hit on just the right kick for you. Waterskiing is exhilarating and phenomenal exercise—you get to cover a lot of ground (well, not ground exactly), see all the sights, splash all your friends, take a few death-defying chances, and benefit from an intense workout at one and the same time. But my heart belongs to tennis. To me there's nothing more delicious than slipping into a T-shirt and a pair of shorts (as opposed to stuffing myself into ski equipment or scuba gear) and getting a chance to utilize my competitive drive and sense of strategy.

Whatever exercise you wind up choosing, just remember that you have to practice it regularly and that it's not a bad idea if you learn to enjoy it. I've put together this list of pros and cons for the most popular types of exercise.

Jogging

What it can do for you: Improve your cardiovascular system and your overall endurance; shape your legs; firm and raise your buttocks. No special equipment needed. A good calorie burner (ten to thirteen calories per minute!).

What it can do to you: Jogging can cause muscle strains, pulls, tendinitis, shin splints and other athletic injuries. If you're over thirty-five or generally out of shape, take it real slow at first. After about twelve minutes, alternate jogging with brisk walking. Jog on grass or dirt, preferably on a low-pollution day, and keep those hands and shoulders relaxed.

Swimming

What it can do for you: Improve your cardiovascular system; exercise every major muscle group in your body, including your back and abdominal muscles; burn off calories at a particularly high rate, especially if the swimming is strenuous (thirty yards or more a minute). Places no stress on any one part of the body. Produces that heady combination of relaxation and invigoration. Particularly beneficial to the elderly and out of shape. But don't just swim, take your swimming seriously, swim energetically, keeping those arms and legs moving. Flutter kick with your legs straight but

relaxed—the kicking motion originating from the hip, not the knee. So good-bye, torpor!

What it can do to you: Swimming in a chlorinated pool may irritate sinuses and dehydrate skin or dry hair, so make sure that afterwards you shower with soap and rinse all the pool water out of your hair. And, by the way, don't go and drown.

Bicycling

What it can do for you: Strengthen your cardiovascular system; firm up your calf, thigh and back muscles. Cycle fast and maintain speed to get the best results; cycling on hilly terrain is ideal.

What it can do to you: Create tension in your neck and shoulders; put extra stress on your knee, hip, and ankle joints. But this is no time to be fastidious. As Tallulah Bankhead used to say, "Press on!"

Jumping Rope

What it can do for you: Same benefits as jogging. A big plus is that you can jump rope indoors in a small area. Begin by jumping fifty times, alternating your feet as if you were running. Gradually work your way up to five hundred skips (at which time you'll explode in an asthmatic puff of dust). You'll need a seven-to-ten-foot cord, a good pair of sneakers, and a good sense of the absurd.

Squash and Racquetball

What they can do for you: Utilize the main muscle group in your body; condition your cardiovascular system (though not quite as much as jogging and swimming can). Competitive sports benefit you the most, because all negative emotions get released in the course of the short, rippling life of the game.

Skiing

What it can do for you: Improve your cardiovascular system (cross-country skiing—not downhill skiing, unless you do it for a long time); burn a fantastic fifteen to seventeen calories per minute.

What it can do to you: Kill you—the end of the day when the light fades and your furious energy uncoils is the time to be extra careful: that's when most accidents happen.

With Bob "Beats" Beattie

Tennis Anyone?

What it can do for you: Strengthen your legs and your cardiovascular system (in a fast match you do about six miles' worth of running); provide an outlet for aggressive emotions; improve your coordination, balance, and overall endurance; uncramp your style.

Calisthenics

What they can do for you: Help flexibility and muscle tone; "burn" fat in those out-of-the-way areas of your body; condition you for demanding aerobic activities and sports. For the best results, don't do calisthenics in fragments, and do them regularly.

Yoga

What it can do for you: Make stiff, out-of-shape bodies flexible by stretching and relaxing your muscles; give you a sense of peace, of calm emotion; improve the function of your internal organs. Should be learned under proper supervision for maximum benefit and minimum strain.

What it cannot do for you: Condition your cardiovascular system.

WHEN? HOW OFTEN? HOW MUCH?

Once is not enough! To see and feel any real results, you should exercise three or four times a week. And don't wait more than thirty-six hours between sessions, or your muscles will contract again and you'll forfeit some of the progress you've made. Do you really want to flatten your stomach and slim down your thighs? Then you've just got to spot exercise these treacherous areas as often as once a day.

Here I am preaching about the benefits of exercise (don't get me wrong, I truly believe in them and live by them), but I often wake up in the morning with a million ready-made reasons why I shouldn't have to move, let alone do calisthenics. I humor myself with, "I was up so late last night," or "I've been working so hard lately I really *deserve* an extra hour in bed," and of course there's always Scarlet O'Hara's inexpungible line about "tomorrow." In that smoked-brown-glassy-gloomy state between sleeping and waking, exercise looms up as an abnormal practice, a downright unnatural act. I've discovered that a few bleary-eyed sit-ups or push-ups while I'm still exquisitely under the covers are enough to get me tumbling out of bed in a rush of ease. If that isn't achieving a kind of oneness with yourself, I'd like to know what is.

HOW TO ENJOY THE TREADMILL

The main thing is to think of whatever exercise you've chosen to practice in bright, spangled terms. Exercise should be a challenging part of your day, not just a time-consuming medicine to keep your body from disintegrating before your very eyes. Here are some suggestions for making exercise more fun.

Wear a Beautiful Exercise Outfit

Leotards and tights are now available in shimmery, synthetic fabrics (Lycra and nylon) and cheerful colors. I have a drawerful, and just looking at them inspires me. Jogging suits also come in a variety of attractive fabrics and designs, and even jogging shoes are now full of life. Dressing as if there were a real pleasure in store for you when you exercise will boost your morale. There's a lot to be said for pleasant associations.

Call for Madder Music

When you're doing calisthenics or yoga, jumping rope, or just jogging in place, it's usually a good idea to play some Baroque Fanfare music, even the radio will do. Listening to music can take your mind off the drudgery part of doing deep knee bends. And the rhythm will help you find a rhythm for whatever you're doing.

Join an Athletic Club

Your local sports club can provide more than a pool and a few courts; it can provide a whole ready-made environment where exercise, far from being the side dish, is the main event. Here you can practice your favorite exercise, learn a new one, and take nourishment from an atmosphere consecrated to physical fitness. Most clubs feature both a sauna and steam and whirlpool baths—just the things for relaxing your muscles and shoring up your shipwrecked attitude. A club membership can be on the expensive side, but it is one of the best health insurance policies you could ever take out. Just be sure you go over your contract with the club carefully, so you understand exactly what rights and privileges are yours once you sign up. Many colleges and universities let you have access to their athletic facilities if you enroll in just a single course.

Sport for Thought

By now, many people have discovered for themselves that meditation is one of the keys to unwinding and thereby to unfolding some extraordinary truths about themselves and their natures (what *they* had always taken for confusion might just turn out to contain a hidden unity!). Meditation is especially beneficial when you practice your aerobic exercise, which is very repetitive. And while you're jogging, try concentrating on your breathing; count your inhalations till you reach the round number ten, then begin all over again. Repetition may not be the spice of life, but it can be awfully relaxing. Think about your breath, where it comes from, where it goes to; clear your mind of all problems, all distractions, all obligations, all entanglements, and in the happy haze that replaces ordered reality, learn to relax.

Variety

Though I'm faithful to tennis and calisthenics in my fashion, I do like to try new exercises and body movements. There are so many new forms of exercise these days. Weightlifting, for one—a very good way to tone up a flabby body. And women don't have to worry about building unwanted muscles, since they lack the male hormone testosterone. And then there's T'ai Chi, a slow, graceful Chinese calisthenic that greatly improves coordination. And gymnnastics, which are especially challenging as they can involve performing stunts. Karate and judo are excellent exercises which can also come in handy. Ice-skating and roller-skating are larky, speedy, and good for your balance and coordination, as are backpacking, fencing, tap-dancing and belly dancing (oooh-la-la, the temperature of the suggested exercises is going up!).

Find a Friend to Do It With

Man is by nature a companionable animal; he doesn't like to do most things by himself. Exercising with a friend can take the sting out of working out. You may even find that your friend brings out in you the spirit of friendly competition and you push yourself even harder. And with him or her running along beside you, you'll be much less inclined to throw in the towel after the first half mile; under the glare of a little friendly peer pressure, you won't want to lag and shuffle.

I found Burt Jones of the Baltimore Colts.

Cardinals
20
USA
Burt Jones
Lou Brock
Shep Messing
Dave Wottle
Vitas Gerulaitis
Bruce Jenner

Professional Help

Any exercise or sport that demands a special physical skill or technique should be embarked upon only with professional instruction. In other words, let the unlimber beware! Errors have a way of compounding—and then perpetuating—themselves. You can injure yourself badly, self-destruct—or simply self-efface. I played tennis off and on for years, loving every heady minute of it. Then one day I decided I just didn't want my game to stay at the same level forever, I wanted to lift myself up into the company of the first-rate. The tactile satisfaction of the game was no longer enough; I had really had it with being mediocre. What I did was take lessons every day for an entire summer. I can't tell you how many times there were when I just couldn't seem to get that serve right, and the quest for the perfect serve was getting me down. But when the frenzy of the lessons had subsided and the strength of my frustrations had grown less, I could see that my technique had improved dramatically. My coach, Bill Regas, was so incredibly patient. At the end of that summer, he wrote me tenderly, in that fierce tennis-hand of his, "I had to sweep a lot of crocodile tears off the court, but I knew that you'd *finally* get it right." Would you call that a backhanded compliment? I would. But at least it wasn't an empty one: He knew I'd never be a Chris Evert but he was pleased that I hadn't settled for mediocrity.

Hang in There

In order to become good at any sport or exercise, the one thing you have to have is patience. The benefits of exercise are often slow showing up, as they are in some other important areas of your life—career and relationships, for instance. But the day will come when you can measure in all-too-real inches the flesh you've lost around the thighs; when you can clock the number of miles you're able to run; when you can actually see the glow and feel the tingle in your cheeks. One of my friends spent six months doing sit-ups without ever feeling anything more uplifting than pain; but she persevered and now she can do a hundred just like that, and for the first time in her adult life her stomach is perfectly flat. Another friend of mine has been swimming religiously for years, and only recently have her narrow shoulders broadened, her pectoral muscles come into their own, and her posture visibly improved. The moral of these two stories is, of course,

"Stick with it—you're not as hopeless as you think you are." And once you see for yourself what exercise can do for you, you'll forget all about the lazy excuses.

TIME-SAVING SHAPE-UP OR SHIP-OUT EXERCISES

Despite the best intentions (and who doesn't start out with those?), there are going to be days (and daze) and even weeks when busy people simply cannot find the time to slavishly jog, play squash, or attend exercise class. When I'm traveling, for example, it's impossible for me to adhere to my regular exercise schedule. But instead of completely abandoning my commitment to physical fitness, I concentrate on the parts of my body that I feel need work the most. My arms have this tendency to become too thin when I neglect them. So, no matter how pressed I am for time, every day I do a few minutes of exercises that add tone and muscle to my arms. The area that most women have to work the hardest on is their stomachs, especially if they sit around a lot. A little work on the stomach every day can make an unbelievable difference—and sit-ups you can do anywhere, even in bed!

With the aid of an expert, Tone Vogt, a Norwegian exercise teacher who's kept a lot of the best bodies in Hollywood together, I've designed a time-saving exercise program for people who think they're too busy to bother. These spot exercises are designed to burn fat cells in particular areas of your body; they'll also activate your muscle cells, and build new ones. There are already plenty of exercises for improving the thighs, stomach, buttocks, and arms, so I've gone and chosen only those that will affect more than one part of your body at the same time. The push-ups I recommend primarily for your arms will also strengthen and tone the muscles of your abdomen, buttocks, shoulders, and chest. Better yet, you can do all these exercises in a small space without any equipment at all. When I travel, I just spread a towel on the floor of my hotel room and . . . press on!

In all of the exercises that follow, keep your stomach muscles flat. And remember to breathe in through your nose and out through your mouth, taking care to exhale at the most strenuous part of each exercise. Don't be afraid to let your breath whoosh out. (Just think of it as energy that's helping to activate and relax each and every muscle in your body.) If you hold your

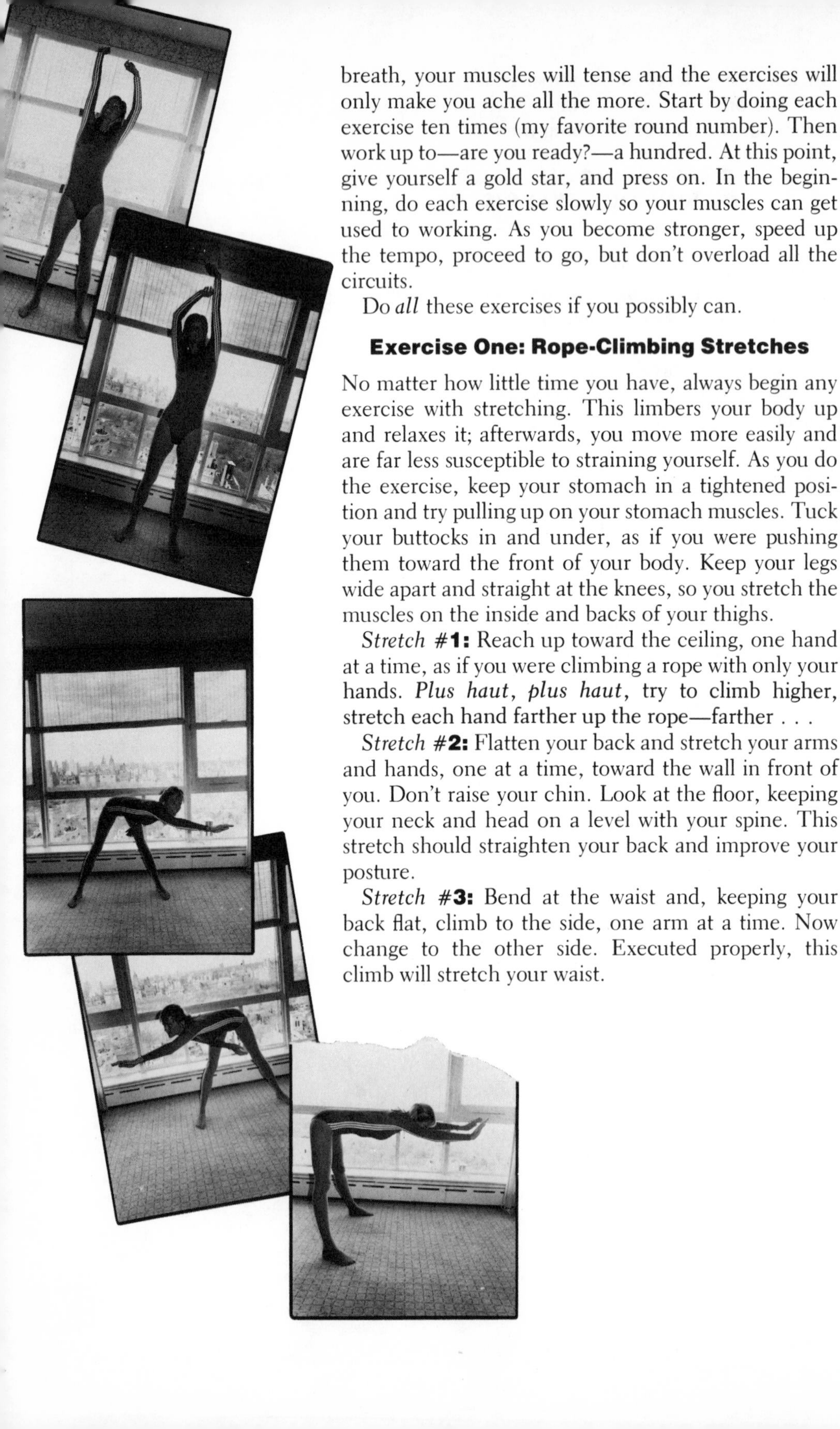

breath, your muscles will tense and the exercises will only make you ache all the more. Start by doing each exercise ten times (my favorite round number). Then work up to—are you ready?—a hundred. At this point, give yourself a gold star, and press on. In the beginning, do each exercise slowly so your muscles can get used to working. As you become stronger, speed up the tempo, proceed to go, but don't overload all the circuits.

Do *all* these exercises if you possibly can.

Exercise One: Rope-Climbing Stretches

No matter how little time you have, always begin any exercise with stretching. This limbers your body up and relaxes it; afterwards, you move more easily and are far less susceptible to straining yourself. As you do the exercise, keep your stomach in a tightened position and try pulling up on your stomach muscles. Tuck your buttocks in and under, as if you were pushing them toward the front of your body. Keep your legs wide apart and straight at the knees, so you stretch the muscles on the inside and backs of your thighs.

Stretch **#1:** Reach up toward the ceiling, one hand at a time, as if you were climbing a rope with only your hands. *Plus haut, plus haut,* try to climb higher, stretch each hand farther up the rope—farther . . .

Stretch **#2:** Flatten your back and stretch your arms and hands, one at a time, toward the wall in front of you. Don't raise your chin. Look at the floor, keeping your neck and head on a level with your spine. This stretch should straighten your back and improve your posture.

Stretch **#3:** Bend at the waist and, keeping your back flat, climb to the side, one arm at a time. Now change to the other side. Executed properly, this climb will stretch your waist.

Exercise Two: Inner Thigh Bounces

Because few of us use our inner thigh muscles in our everyday activities, they get flabby and sag more rapidly than most other parts of our body. I've invented a simple and very effective exercise to activate the inner thigh muscles: the "bounce." Place your legs as wide apart as you can without losing your balance. Turn your toes out. Now, keeping your buttocks tucked under and your stomach tight, bend your knees as much as you can and bounce up and down without ever straightening your knees. If you're doing it right, you should be able to feel your inner thigh muscles tighten. Bounce for at least a minute.

Arm Bounces. Proceed as in the inner thigh bounce, except this time raise your arms to shoulder length. Your palms should be facing the wall in front of you and your hands and fingers should be stretched. Make ten big circles forward with your arms, then ten backward. Then make ten *small* circles forward *and* backward. Keep your fingers stretched, elbows locked, and move your arms and shoulder. What you're doing is firming up the tricep muscles that keep the underside of your upper arms smooth and taut. Combining the two exercises is a real time-saver.

Exercise Three: C.T.'s Friendly Feminine Push-up

Most women don't have enough strength in their arms and shoulders to do push-ups, an old standby if there ever was one for firming and toning arms and shoulders. I've tailored the following exercise especially to women.

Lie on your stomach. Bend your knees and cross your ankles. Place your hands on the floor right next to your shoulders. Your knees should be resting on the carpet. Raise the upper part of your body with your arms. Now lower your body back down till it's almost touching the floor. Raise it up again using your arms. (Don't konk out between push-ups.) Keep your buttocks and stomach tight. The top of your body should be all in a straight line. It's hard work but well worth it —this exercise will firm up not only your buttocks and stomach, but also the muscles in your arms, shoulders, and chest. Remember to exhale when you raise your body, and inhale when you lower it.

Exercise Four: The Cat Stretch (Without Claws)

This exercise will stretch the muscles in your abdomen and neck as well as tone your buttocks, the backs of your legs, and that problem area under your chin. Get down on all fours. Come on, really crouch. Your elbows should be straight, your hands under your shoulders, and your knees six to eight inches apart. Now bring one knee up to your forehead, then stretch the leg through and back, lifting it as high as you can make it go and keeping that knee really straight. Good, that's it. Exhale as you lift your leg, and lift your chin, too, so that you're looking up at the ceiling. When you kick your leg up, you're stretching the muscles in your abdomen, working the area under your buttocks, and firming the buttocks themselves, which are so damn hard to firm. If you have a bad back, don't lift your leg up, just stretch it back toward the wall. Repeat—guess how many times on each side? Ten!

Exercise Five: The Dreaded Hydrant

Unlike most of the other exercises I do, this one activates a part of the body that seldom even moves. It's an exercise guaranteed to trim and tone the fat that invariably, furtively, gathers on the outside of women's thighs and hangs on for dear life even after you've vigorously dieted. It firms the area just *beneath* the buttocks as well.

Get ready, get set . . . Get down on your hands and knees the way you just did in the cat exercise. Put your right leg out to the side and lift it as high as you can. Keep your knee straight and your foot flexed, so you stretch the hamstring muscle on the back of your thigh. Now raise and lower your leg ten times—keeping it straight. Now make ten circles forward with your leg and ten backward. If it hurts, well, it *should* hurt (doesn't everything good hurt a little?). It should hurt right around where all that fat is. Now do the same thing with the left leg. The same number of times. Keep your whole body straight; don't lean away from the extended leg. It's better to lower the leg a little than to lean and go easy on yourself.

Exercise Six: The Half Sit-up

"Ah," you're thinking, "the sit-up—an old, old friend." This version of it, however, won't be all that familiar to you. If it's your lower abdomen you want to tone and strengthen, lie on your back, lift your legs straight up and cross them at the ankles. Then clasp your hands behind your head so your elbows are at right angles to your body. Now, keeping your elbows back and parallel to the floor, lift the upper part of your body toward your knees. Exhale as you come up, inhale as you go back down. You'll probably get your chin only as far as your chest, but even so you'll feel the muscles working in your lower abdomen. If it's the upper part of your abdomen, near the waist, that needs work, bend your elbows toward your knees as you raise the upper part of your body.

Exercise Seven: Lifting Your Legs

This one is hard on the lower back, but give it a chance, it's an excellent stomach flattener. Rest your elbows on the floor, legs straight, lock your knees, and flex your feet to stretch your hamstrings. Raise your legs up and let them down without allowing them to touch the floor. If you can't lift both legs at the same time, scissor them or lift them one at a time, alternating them—but, again, don't let them touch the floor for even a second. Practice control; don't throw them up and down.

RELAXATION EXERCISES OR PARDON MY OXYMORON

Relaxation is not the least important part of exercise. The following exercises will all relax your back and neck.

Relaxation Exercise #1: The Plow

The plow (you're probably imagining the snow crunching under it) is much more beatific than it sounds. What it is is a well-known hatha-yoga exercise, unsurpassable for relaxing and stretching your back and neck muscles. Lie on your back with your hands resting beside your thighs, palms down. Lift your legs slowly (if you've put on snowboots to do The Plow, kick them off), keep them straight, and bring them over your head till your toes touch the floor. Keep your knees straight and together now. Press your chin into your chest. Try to make your breath rush into the parts of your back that feel tense and achy. Hold this position for as long as you humanly can; don't worry, it will get more comfortable as the tension empties out of your back. You get a feeling that's hard to explain.

Relaxation Exercise #2: Head and Spine Stretches

Sit in a cross-legged position. Keep erect (a good way to do this is to imagine that there's an invisible string pulling your head up toward the ceiling). Pull up on your stomach and chest muscles. Now stretch your left ear down toward your shoulder, then your right ear. Then, moving slowly, turn your head to the back and push your chin toward your left shoulder. Do the same now on the right side. Strain to see the wall behind you, and strain hard, because this is what helps prevent a double chin. Now make full circles with your head—to the right, to the back, to the left, and *down*, in a clockwise, then counterclockwise rotation.

Relaxation Exercise #3: Hanging Down

Stand with your legs straight and apart, then let your head drop toward your feet as low as you can go. Think of the upper part of your body as a dead weight: you're an old rag doll, your arms dangle, your head and neck loll. Then roll yourself up slowly to a standing position. This is a good thing to do between exercises, when you're feeling all tuckered out.

C.T.'S MINUTE-TO-MINUTE GUIDE TO KEEPING YOUR SHAPE

Every woman needs to set part of her week aside for vigorous exercise sessions. I also happen to be a great believer in informal exercises you can do throughout the day. These "invisible" exercises involve substituting movement for non-movement at every opportunity, using more muscles to do your ordinary activities, and doing the special isometric "mini" exercises that you can do almost anywhere. These "invisible" exercises can make the difference, the not "invisible," in fact the very, very visible—difference—in your shape.

Walk Briskly

Everybody has to walk. But there's more than one way to do it, that's for sure. You can just shuffle along, barely moving your body, or you can walk exuberantly, exercising as many muscles as possible. When I walk, I keep my shoulders up and back, and pull up on my stomach muscles. As I take each step, I stretch and tighten the backs of my legs. I try to keep up a good pace. All this makes walking a real pleasure. More importantly, it improves my muscle tone and my cardiovascular system. A test conducted by the University of California at Irvine showed that fat women lose approximately twenty-two pounds during their diet programs simply by walking more than half an hour each day. Do yourself a big favor: try it my way—walking instead of riding whenever possible. Prove to yourself that you retain the power of locomotion.

Climb Those Stairs

I'm lucky to live in a two-story house, because climbing stairs does wonders for legs, buttocks, and abdominal muscles. Whenever I can avoid taking an elevator, I do. And when I climb, I pull up on my stomach muscles and take the stairs as quickly as I can. And as for escalators, don't just stand there, nodding or dozing—walk up them!

Use That Beach

The beach is nature's health club and if you're smart, you'll treat it as such. Most people just spread their blankets on the sand, smear themselves with suntan oil, and lie there recklessly exposing their skin to the sun. When I'm at the beach, I run. Running on sand is better for calf muscles and feet than running on dirt or cement. I jog through the surf, lifting my feet high. And back on the beach, I dig my toes deep into the sand to stretch and strengthen my feet. The beach is also a great place for playing frisbee, volleyball, or football. And, in case somebody hasn't noticed it yet, it's not a bad place for swimming.

See C.T. Run

If I'm working out-of-doors and the changing room is a ways away, I jog there. Even when I don't jog regularly, I do try an occasional sprint. (People look at me kind of funny, as if I must be late to something.) Try running to get your newspaper in the morning, run to catch the bus, try outrunning your dog (if he's fifteen and he overtakes you, you've learned a hard truth). Then, if you're ever being chased by a rampaging herd of elephants, you'll be able to run . . . for your life!

Do!

Dance after dinner—it'll help you work off a big meal. Bicycle. Bowl. Play Ping-Pong. Roller-skate. These are all energetic alternatives to an evening spent at home cautiously lashed to your chair.

INVISIBLE ISOMETRIC MINI-EXERCISES

The simple isometric exercises that follow you can do in an office, an uncrowded elevator, or at home. They take almost no time at all. Best of all, you don't even have to change clothes.

Stomach Press

Breathe out all the air in your lungs, then press your stomach with your palms, keeping your elbows at right angles to your body. Continue to breathe deeply, inhaling through your nose and exhaling through your mouth. But keep pressing your stomach as hard as you can with both hands. You want to firm your stomach as well as your upper arms, don't you?

Arm Push

Fold your arms in front of you at chest level, grasping each forearm with the opposite hand. Now push against both arms simultaneously with short, jerking motions. Ahh! This exercise will tone both the muscles that support your breasts and those in your upper arms.

Wall Push

Stand at least an arm's length away from a wall with your feet a few inches apart. Now place your palms on the wall. Lean right into the wall so your elbows bend, then push yourself away. Don't lift your heels. This modified, easy-to-do version of the push-ups you do on the floor will keep your arms and wrists in shape.

Pick-ups/Pick-me-ups/ Pick-me-up-off-the-floor-oops

Are your lower back and the hamstring muscles in the backs of your legs so stiff you can't even touch your toes? Then try keeping your legs and knees straight and bending from the waist whenever you have to pick something up from the floor. That way, you're doing what amounts to a toe touch every time you pick up a fallen pencil or something. As hard as I tried, I couldn't touch my toes till I made this exercise part of my everyday life. You shouldn't try to pick up a two-hundred-pound object this way, though—you don't want to injure your back.

Kick up the Door

This is my invention, a version of a ballet exercise called the *grand battement* that's great for thighs and abdomens. Hold both sides of a door jamb with your hands and kick up a storm, ten times with each leg; then kick to the back ten times. The secret is to pull up on your stomach muscles and keep your posture erect while you kick as high as you can (don't bend to meet your leg as it rises).

Stomach Press

Breathe out all the air in your lungs, then press your stomach with your palms, keeping your elbows at right angles to your body. Continue to breathe deeply, inhaling through your nose and exhaling through your mouth. But keep pressing your stomach as hard as you can with both hands. You want to firm your stomach as well as your upper arms, don't you?

Arm Push

Fold your arms in front of you at chest level, grasping each forearm with the opposite hand. Now push against both arms simultaneously with short, jerking motions. Ahh! This exercise will tone both the muscles that support your breasts and those in your upper arms.

Stretch and Sigh

When I'm feeling restless or lethargic from working really hard, I get up and stretch. When I'm tense, I suck in all the air I can get and then let it all out in a huge, noisy, earthshaking sigh. This habit, which by now is involuntary with me, has produced some weird and worried looks on the faces of those around me, but my accumulated tension sure disappears—and so do some of the weirdos nearby.

Overdoing It

It *is* possible to exercise too much. A couple of summers ago when I was playing tennis regularly and also taking three weekly calisthenic classes, I found I was listless most of the time, and ready to fall into sleep (as if into an open grave) right after an early dinner. My entire system was protesting that it had had too much! If you overswim, overjog, or otherwise overdo, your body will let you know it sooner or later, one way or another. So learn to listen to it. Don't overdo—overdon't.

Giving up too Soon

To get the most out of exercise you have to push yourself a bit beyond the comfortable limit. The best time to do three extra sit-ups or push-ups is at exactly the point when the muscles you're using begin to ache—it's those few extra motions that do the trick. When you're doing an aerobic exercise such as jogging, it's crucial that you go a bit longer and further than you ever thought you could. The line between overdoing it and getting enough is a very thin one. Don't worry about ordinary muscle soreness; treat yourself to a good massage, or a colossal bath with Epsom salts. And don't wait till the soreness has disappeared completely before going back to the exercise. More exercise will, in fact, ease the pain. So keep pushing yourself. It won't kill you; it will do you a lot of good (said she, puffing and panting).

Overeating Before or After Exercising

Don't eat right before you exercise unless you want to feel sick to your stomach. Eat no less than two hours before calisthenics and three hours before a competitive event.

I've known so many people who've used their half-hour exercise session to justify eating a pint of ice cream later on. "I burned up so many calories," they all say, "I can afford to give myself a little treat. In fact," they escalate, "I positively owe it to myself." What's so surprising is how surprised they always are to see the pounds pile up. If you're going to play *that* game, bring a calculator along—I'm not kidding—so that after you've jogged for twenty minutes, you know it's 300 calories you've burned up and not the eight million contained in a pint of ice cream. Fair is fair—and fun is fun (and fun is over).

Crash-Dieting While Exercising

A crash diet and a rigorous exercise regimen combined can throw your whole system out of sync. So, if you are dieting *and* exercising at the same time, make sure that you're eating a varied, nutritious 1200 calories a day. You see, when you exercise, muscle mass increases as fat decreases, so that you may weigh the same even though you look much thinner. If this is the case, only your tape measure will know for sure.

Kid Yourself Not: No-Exercise Exercising

Some people kid themselves that they're exercising when what they're doing is more like play. Machines that jiggle your flesh around are no substitute for exercise, for the simple reason they don't make demands on your muscles. A good game of golf may relax you but, as it involves hardly any muscle activity at all, it does not qualify as a fitness exercise. Walking is naturally far better for you than riding in a car, but walking alone will not keep you in shape. Any exercise that involves a lot of stops and starts and that isn't done strenuously won't give you real and lasting benefits, either. Floating on your back in a lake under an amazing summer sky, for instance, is no more *swimming* than a big icicle is a bed of flowers!

Not Concentrating

When you exercise, you should be thinking of nothing else but how that exercise feels and what it is doing to your body. I've seen women in exercise classes casually throw their arms and legs around while they laugh and yak and live it up. Well, let's see how much good *that* does them! By concentrating, you will very likely find the one way to do each exercise which makes *your* muscles work harder. You become aware of each part of your body, of how the muscles there connect to muscles elsewhere. If you concentrate on your exercise, you become better at it more quickly and enjoy it more. When you do your calisthenics, don't just watch yourself in the mirror (tempting as that might be); instead, think about how the exercises feel. Much of what happens to you is in the brain, after all—so use it!

Crossing Your Legs

Fine, go right ahead, if you want to cut off the circulation in your thighs. Remember, "cellulite" loves a vacuum.

FOOTGEAR FOR RUNNING

As you jog, each of your feet hits the ground approximately eight hundred times per mile. That's a lot of stress on your feet and legs. It is therefore extremely important that you wear good shoes to absorb the shock and protect your legs from injury. Sneakers are not good enough. A good jogging shoe should cup the whole heel and support the arch and toes. And make sure there's one inch between the end of the shoe and the end of your toe, because if you wear short shoes, the constant hitting of the toes against the front of the shoe can damage your foot. Also, buy shoes with a flexible sole.

THE BODY PRESENTABLE VS. THE BODY IMPOSSIBLE

When you exercise, aspire to a realistic version of your present body. No amount of exercise can change your basic proportions or transform your body type from, let's say, soft and round to thin and angular, since exercise is a form neither of magic nor of sorcery. Certain body types, such as those that are heavy from the waist down and slim on top, can be improved, and that's all. What you should look for exercise to do is make the body you already have just as fit and attractive as it was biologically "programmed" to be. And to do that, we have to find out our own rhythm and make our own breakthroughs.

In *A Separate Peace*, one of the most moving books I read in high school, Finny, a fifteen-year-old injured former athlete, coaches his prep-school friend Gene to run the course that he himself can no longer run: "four times around an oval walk which circled the Headmaster's home, a large rambling, doubtfully Colonial white mansion." Here is Gene's account:

. . . After making two circuits of the walk every trace of energy was as usual completely used up, and as I drove myself on all my scattered aches found their usual way to a profound seat of pain in my side. My lungs as usual were fed up with all this work, and from now on would only go rackingly through the motions. My knees were boneless again, ready any minute to let my lower legs telescope up into the thighs. My head felt as though different sections of the cranium were grinding into each other.

Then, for no reason at all, I felt magnificent. It was as though my body until that instant had simply been lazy, as though the aches and exhaustion were all imagined, created from nothing in order to keep me from truly exerting myself. Now my body seemed at last to say, "Well, if you must have it, here!" and an accession of strength came flooding through me. Buoyed up, I forgot my usual feeling of routine self-pity when working out, I lost myself, oppressed mind along with aching body; all entanglements were shed, I broke into the clear.

After the fourth circuit, like sitting in a chair, I pulled up in front of Phineas.

"You're not even winded," he said.

"I know."

"You found your rhythm, didn't you, that third time around. Just as you came into that straight part there."

"Yes, right there."

"You've been pretty lazy all along, haven't you?"

"Yes, I guess I have been."

"You didn't even know anything about yourself."

"I don't guess I did, in a way."

"Well," he gathered the sheepskin collar around his throat, "now you know. . . ."

Yes. As the good book says, so now you know.

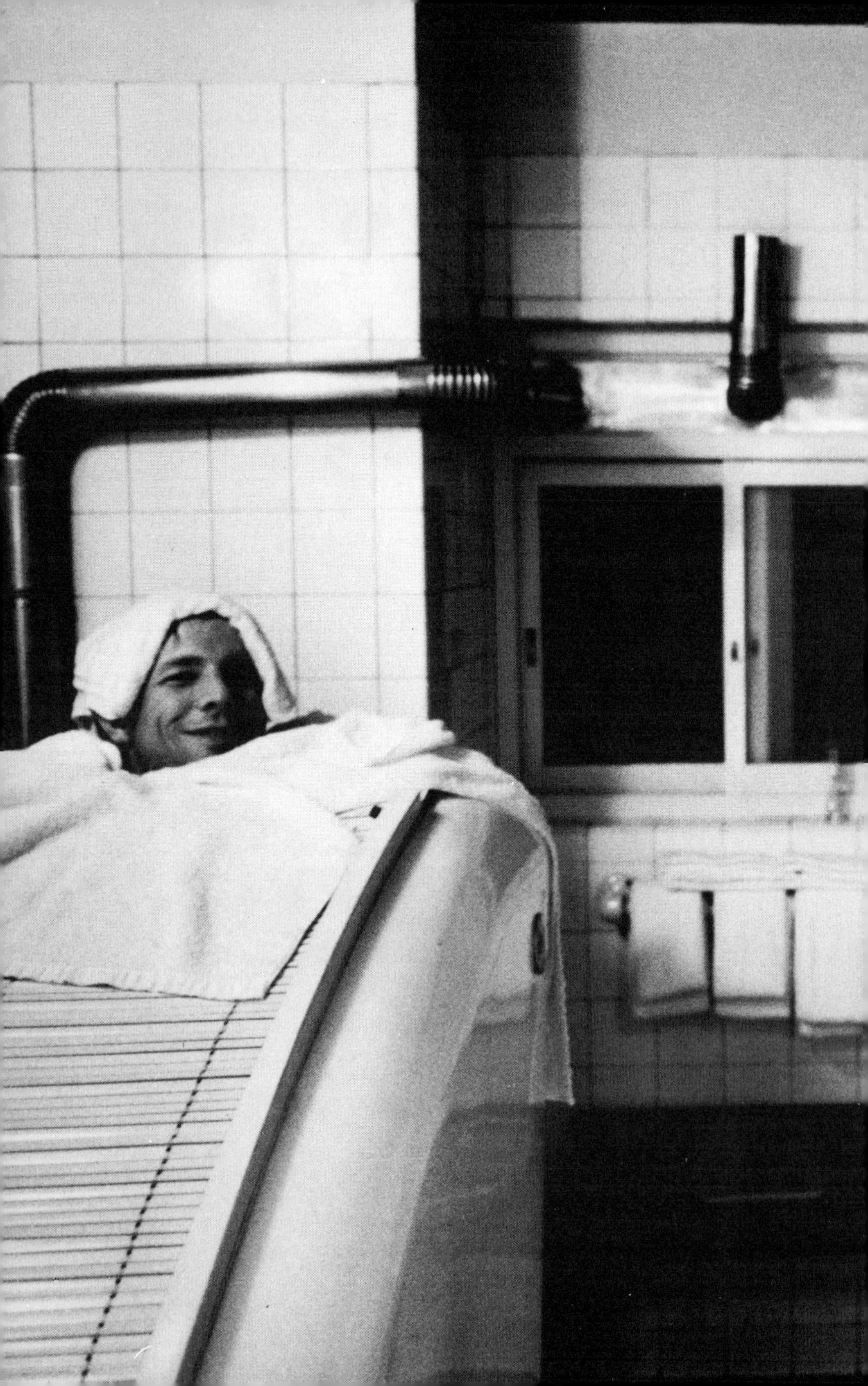

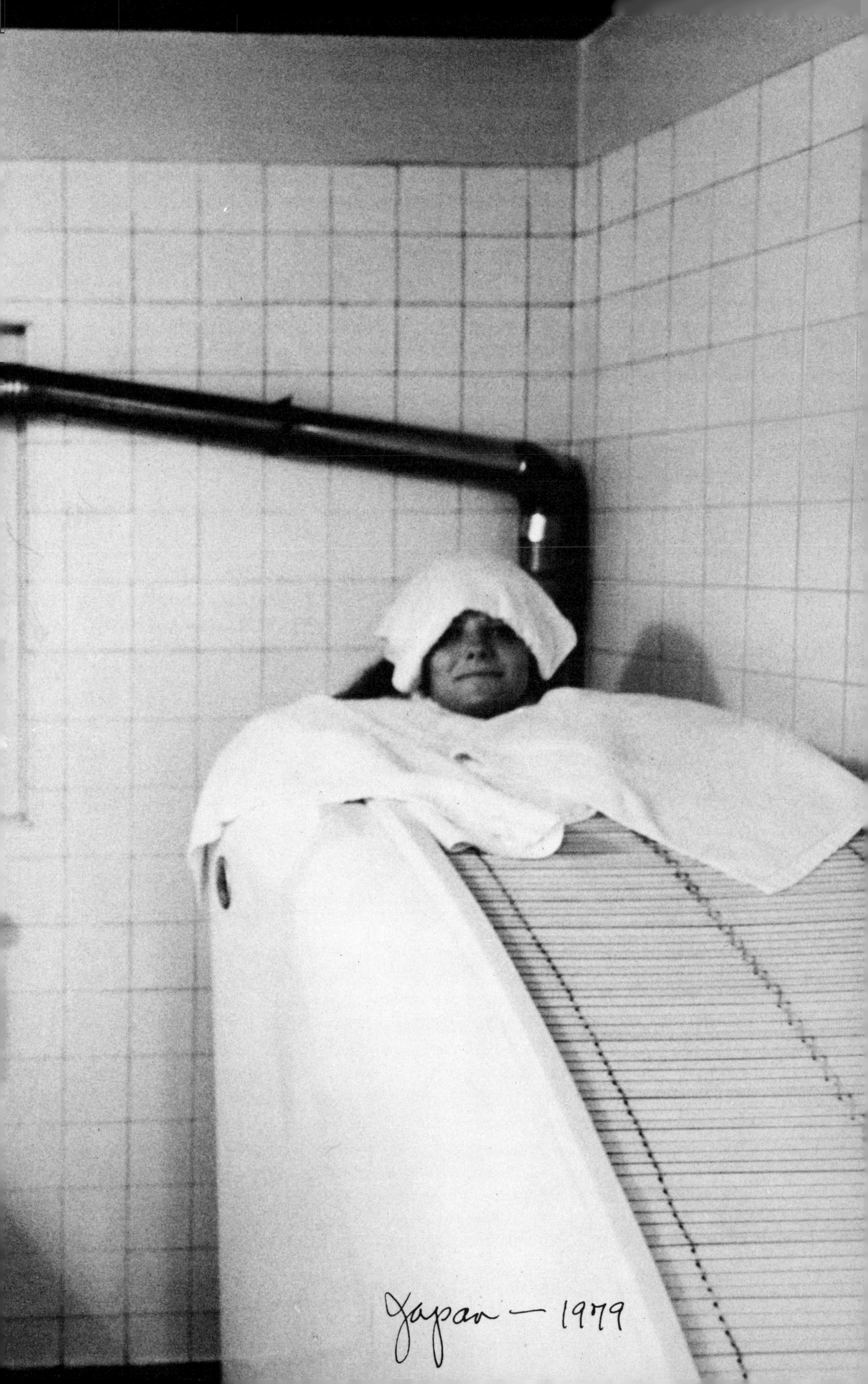
Japan — 1979

5

Hair Today, Hair Tomorrow: Using Your Head

Way back in the eleventh century, Leofric, Earl of Mercia, imposed a burdensome tax on the people of Coventry. And what has this got to do with hair? you're thinking. Well, wait and see. When his wife importuned him to remit the tax, he jestingly promised to do so if she would ride naked through the streets of the town at noonday. She took him at his word, directed the people to keep within doors and close their shutters, and complied with his condition. (Peeping Tom, who looked out, was struck blind.) Her act was not quite so daring as it might have been, because she knew that her entire naked front and back would be covered by her fabulous long blond hair. The lady's name, of course, was Godiva; and that town owes a whole lot to the fact that she had hair to spare, hair that simply would not quit.

And who has not been moved by O. Henry's great short story, "The Gift of the Magi"? The two young people are married and starving, and Christmas is coming up. The woman goes and sells the only possession she has, her extraordinarily long chestnut hair, in order to buy her husband a gold watch chain for his prized family watch, but meanwhile—unbeknownst to her—he has sold the watch in order to buy her combs for her glorious hair.

Hair was the O. Henry heroine's most treasured possession, and it is also one of yours. Shining, healthy hair, attractively cut and styled, is the greatest pleasure, the most tactile satisfaction. It provides a frame for your face, and unlike your figure and your skin, is easy to utterly transform. Within a few hours your hair can have a vivid new coloring, a different texture, or a dramatic new style (as the Clairesse ad says, "Go Glamorous").

But changing your hair color or style takes not only thought but knowledge. In a novel I just read, one of the characters has red hair, and her husband's boss says to him threateningly, "Your wife is a good woman, I'm sure. But that hair . . . there ought to be some way to tone it down." The poor woman probably didn't know how.

Is your hair doing the most it can for you? And are you doing all you can for it? Here are some questions for you to stub your big toe against.

■ *Have you had the same hairstyle for years?*

■ *Do you usually wind up regretting having had your hair cut, or changing the color or style, because the results are not what you'd hoped for?*

■ *If you hair is colored, do you insist on the colors being uniform throughout?*

■ *Do you feel that in order for your hair to look attractive, you have to set it?*

■ *Do you think it's a good idea to give your hair a hundred brushstrokes every day?*

■ *If, after a haircut, you part your hair on either side or in the middle, does it fall evenly and frame your face appealingly?*

■ *Do you wash your hair every day?*

■ *Does your hair become limp and separate into strands shortly after you wash it?*

■ *Do you use deep conditioning treatments for the split ends?*

■ *Do you always have your permanent done by a professional?*

Your answer to the first five questions should be an emphatic "no!"

In this chapter I hope to help you find an exciting hairstyle that reflects the person you are *now*, not someone you were—or think you were—years ago. If you want to look like the ideal picture of yourself, take care that you don't wind up looking like a picture frame out of which the picture has dropped.

Plan your hairstyle realistically, with *your* face and *your* hair type and *your* everyday activities in mind. And don't just hand over the entire responsibility to your stylist—you're going to have to learn to work with him. He'll know how not to make you a slave to your hair; on the contrary, he'll see to it that your hair is easy to care for and that it looks good whether you set it or not. And, yes, Virginia, a good haircut will fall into place no matter where you part it.

There are no hard-and-fast rules for how often you should brush your hair or even wash it. Frequent shampooing won't necessarily harm your hair, as many people believe. And as you will see, it's possible to stop ends from splitting with conditioners. As for hair that's artificially colored, it should contain the same highlights and varied shades as natural hair color does, or it will look lifeless.

WHAT YOUR HAIR HAS TO SAY ABOUT YOU

A woman's hairstyle makes a statement not only about how she sees herself but about how she wants to be seen by others, who she wants them to take her for. Whether your hairstyle is drab and pedestrian, free and flowing, a complete mad raucous mass of wild curls that practically swallows everyone and everything in its path, or so elaborate and baroque that it all but bumps against the ceiling, the truth about how you see yourself will out. If a hairstyle isn't flattering to your face, it won't feel all that comfortable and won't reflect what I hesitate to call "the real you" (which may be somebody you don't even know yet, or have merely a nodding acquaintance with).

When I'm modeling I usually rebel if the stylist tries to overload my hair with flamboyant flips, a pageboy, you name it. I feel totally unconnected to them (and to myself when I'm wearing them). I always encourage the stylist to fluff out my hair so it looks natural and unfettered, and I discourage him from spraying and teasing. I like my hair to look about the same in a photograph as it does in real life, because publicly and privately, I try to stay pretty much the same person. (It's a battle, I can tell you.)

A hairstyle should take into consideration the shape of your face and the type of hair you have, but there's more than one attractive style for every woman. I've often changed hairstyles. And in the process I've noticed that outer changes really do mirror inner ones, so that a hairstyle that's left over from some part of your past is going to look and feel like the most unwieldy anachronism.

I'm always having my hair layered, then letting the layers grow out, or getting a permanent for more body and pizzazz, or highlighting my hair with streaks of color. Like most people, I don't have endless blocks of time to spend on my grooming, so I strive to make my hair look attractive without my having to resort to curling irons, curlers, and a lot of other time-consum-

ing paraphernalia. All I want to have to do is wash it, fluff it, and let it dry—nothing much more esoteric than that, if you please. Of course, for special occasions, I actually enjoy taking the extra time out to curl my hair and maybe even stud it with sparkling combs and barrettes so it'll look . . . well, spectacular!

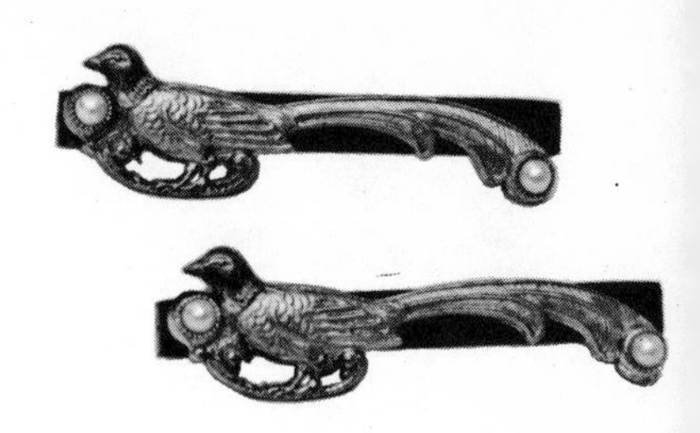

CHOOSING THE RIGHT STYLE

Any hairstylist worth his blow-dryer will take care to emphasize your best features. And so should you. If you have beautiful big eyes, a firm chin line, or sculpted cheekbones, you should choose a hairstyle that makes the most of these assets. Hair pulled back and away from the upper half of your face, for example, will display your eyes and cheekbones to their best advantage. Hair scraped back into a sophisticated chignon, however, may not be very becoming to a long chin, or to a nose that's not as small or well-shaped as you might wish it were. But just a few wisps of bangs can camouflage a wide forehead, and a long chin or jawline can be softened by long hair fluffed and curled on either side of your face. The most important thing to bear in mind is that there are no stiff rules governing the correspondence between a woman's hairstyle and her face. Some of the most attractive styles I've seen on friends are the very ones that, if they'd gone by the book, they would never in a million years have dared to experiment with. (One of my friends, who has a large, slightly crooked nose, looks great with her hair pulled severely back off her face and into a bun on top of her head.) Hairstyles don't exist by themselves, their surroundings are important, to say the least—and their surroundings are none other than *your face*. Every style that works well with a face does so in a mysterious, often totally unpredictable way.

Your body figures into all of this, too. Your hairstyle must balance out the proportions of the body, which is no alien zone as far as hair goes. A very short woman may find that her long straight hair literally buries her underneath it. I have a long, thin body, and a very short cut would be a big mistake on me. Very full, bushy hair on a large woman won't exactly give a slimming illusion—on the contrary: it will make her look hopelessly bulky, as if she could fill the whole back of a taxicab all by herself.

The style you choose should depend not only on the shape of your body and face but on the quality of your

hair as well. Although today chemical processes can alter hair texture, you should never depend on them wholly to maintain your style. If the style you're after necessitates that you drastically change the natural texture, flow, and direction of your hair, and that you constantly set and/or blow-dry it, forget it, it isn't worth it, it won't change your life anyway. Choose a style that's easy to maintain—not some impossible dream from a fashion magazine.

GROWING LONG HAIR

A lot of women truly believe that if they have the patience and hold out, their hair will eventually grow to a length to rival Rapunzel's or our old (eleventh century!) friend Lady Godiva's. But, growth is based not on a wishbone but on a genetic program that allows hair to achieve a certain predetermined length only. According to the *AMA Book of Skin and Hair Care*, hair grows at the rate of about half an inch a month, then takes a little rest. During this siesta, the hairs that have reached their maximum length are shed slowly, and new hair begins growing to replace them. Don't get too frustrated if your hair breaks and splits at the ends. You may just be genetically "programmed" to a relatively short hair-growing span, in which case you're far better off accepting the inevitable and sticking to a shorter, easy-to-maintain style. Salon experts advise women who want long hair to have a quarter of an inch trimmed off the ends every two months to insure sleek, healthy looking hair that will fall smoothly into place.

TRYING NEW STYLES OUT

You should remember, when you up and change hairstyles, that it's going to stay that way for a while. Changing your image, your special imprint, is always a lottery. Careful thought and a bit of experimentation before you take the big plunge will help you make a choice that you know you—and yours—can live with. Never simply surrender yourself to a stylist, because when it's all over you may look into the mirror only to find that, suddenly shorn, the top of your noggin resembles nothing so much as a little guinea pig.

Choose your new hairstyle realistically—bearing in mind not only your face, figure, and hair type, but also your personality—and the amount of time you can afford to spend on maintenance. Fashion magazines

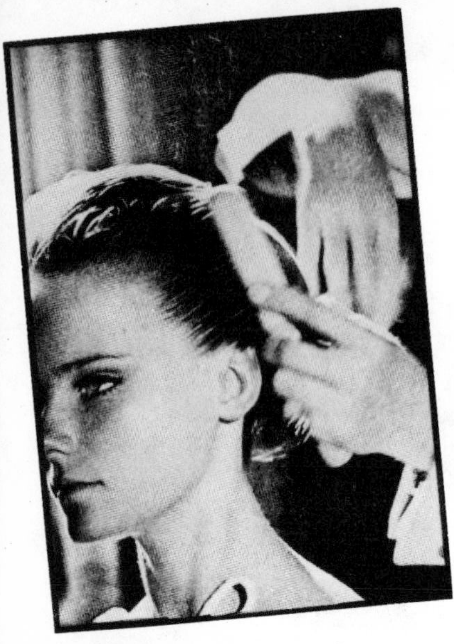

feature fabulous hair styles, concocted by the most inventive stylists. It's all right to be influenced by them, but try not to just copy. Study the type of hair shown in the picture and look carefully at the shape of the model's face. Does it bear more than a passing resemblance to your own hair type and the shape of your own face? Don't go with a style merely because it looks glamorous on someone else! Truth to tell, *you* might be ill-fitted to carry it off.

Wigs and falls can give you some potent clues as to how you're going to look in hair of various lengths and colors. If you're really nervous about changing styles, give a thought to altering the length or color of your hair by degrees. A total change, complete with cut, perm, and new color, may be too extreme for comfort. Consider your nervous system!

CHOOSING A STYLIST

A good stylist will help you decide on a new hairdo or tell you why the one *you* want isn't quite the right one. Unfortunately, not all stylists are equally talented and well-trained. Creating beautiful hair is an art, requiring study, experience, and skill. Some stylists are at their best with certain types of hair; some are better with people than they are with hair—a salon can be a pretty weird place, a hothouse, a tropical aviary. Finding the best stylist requires some real detective work. Don't make the mistake of thinking that anyone who works in a beauty salon, even a celebrated one, is equipped to cut, color, or perm your one and only head of hair!

If you live in or near a large city, the stars of the hairstyling firmament will be available to you. The personnel in the large, better-known salons are for the most part well trained in modern techniques. If you live in a small town, however, there may not be a single salon equipped to give you a top-quality job. Your hair is so vital to your overall appearance that just this once you should indulge yourself in the luxury of getting the best. If none of the stylists in your immediate area live up to your expectations, drive to the nearest city where top professionals *are* available.

In general, when it comes to hair stylists you get what you pay for. Although it is still possible to get a good haircut for a modest price, the best stylists do command top dollars.

If you have to travel to get a good cut, make sure the

stylist understands that you won't be able to come in very often for trims, and that the style he gives you must grow out gracefully. Once you have a good basic cut, your local stylist may be able to trim it for you himself.

The best way to discover the top stylist in your area is, believe it or not, by observing other women's hair. When you see a winner, don't be embarrassed to ask her for the name of the salon she uses. She'll appreciate the compliment and be happy to tell you. If you are still nervous about taking the inexorable step, just poke your head into the salon and take a quick look around. If you don't like what you see, don't make an appointment—it's as simple as that.

HOW TO WORK WITH YOUR STYLIST

Once you have a style in mind and a stylist in hand, make the most of him or her. Hairstylists are artists, and more often than not they have the so-called "artistic temperament." Often the spectacular "new you" they long to create is a you fashioned according to their ideas and inspirations. Years ago one stylist insisted I would look glorious if only I would allow him to tint my hair with henna. He was very persuasive, I must say—to the point where I was projecting how much fun it was going to be to have red hair for a change. Luckily, I had a friend who warned me that I wasn't going to want to confront this color every waking hour for the next six months. Remember, a stylist may have the most original and ingenious ideas for your hair, but *he* doesn't have to live with his brilliant creation—*you do*. Yes, of course, listen to his advice, benefit from his training and experience: but don't be afraid to speak up—and not necessarily in a small voice, either.

When you go to a stylist for the first time, make an effort to get your personality across to him. Also, describe the hairstyle you have in mind in very clear terms. Don't say, "I want it short and curly," but rather, specify whether you want tight curls, or loose waves, and tell him exactly what you mean by "short." And by all means bring any sketches you may have made (he's not going to judge you as if you were Michelangelo) or pictures you may have clipped from magazines. Ask the stylist—tactfully, please!—if he thinks he can create the style you've just shown him or described to him—not all stylists have the talent or

"Peeps into Pepys"

the training to style for magazine layouts where the models' hair looks eternally perfect instead of just about to disintegrate. Ask him also to check the condition of your hair: Is it fragile, damaged, dry? Can it withstand chemical processing, setting, blow-drying? Before he begins to cut, perm, or color, find out *exactly* what he has in mind. Check out how much care and additional servicing, such as trims and color touch-ups, your new hairstyle will demand. Whenever you don't understand what your stylist is talking about, press him for further details. Your new hairstyle should be the result of a collaboration between you and your stylist and not come as a complete surprise. After many a blunder dies the swan.

When the stylist has finished with you, get him to suggest ways to dress up your new hair for the evening, and ways for you to vary it without changing the basic look. Ask him to show you how to work with your hair at home. If the style requires rollers, curling irons, or blow-drying, you'll need very explicit instructions. Try it yourself with him right there.

During your visit to the salon, pay careful attention to what your stylist is doing with your hair. Too often, women concentrate on telling the stylist the story of their lives, or their friends' lives (gush, simper, rasp!!!), or on reading the latest magazines, and as a result they sometimes emerge with a style they hadn't quite imagined. On rare occasions, it's the stylist who gets carried away on the chitchat. Once, I was having my hair done by a ritzy Paris hairdresser who was so busy gossiping madly to one and all as he curled my hair, that when he took out the sizzling curling iron, a large chunk of my hair came out with it. It was actually smoking—skewered to the iron like a piece of shish-kebab. He continued babbling away, reigning in his own salon, and soon he was turning the damage he'd done me into a spectacularly unfunny story. Needless to say, I was not amused.

(I have a wonderfully bizarre artist friend who never ceases to ask me for locks of my hair to paste into his diary or art collages, and occasionally I oblige him and snip off a piece or two—neither smoking nor skewered, thank you—to the horror of the stylists I work with.)

All of us have gone to a hair salon only to emerge thoroughly depressed. A few years ago, on a whim, I sacrificed my long hair to a cute short layer-cut. The result was disappointingly straight and flat, not at all

"Fleetwood Mac"

the fluffy picture I'd clipped from a magazine. A mistake, but not a fatal one, for in a few weeks the layers began to grow out again, and the now not so irregular lengths just began to look quite interesting—or so I kept telling myself.

Few new hairstyles are total disasters. You may be disappointed with a hairstyle only because you haven't yet grown accustomed to your new image, or because the new style doesn't instantly and magically and completely transform you. Also, hair goes into "shock" right after it's been cut, and it may be as long as a week before it accepts its new direction. Or maybe your new style looked terrific when you left the salon and then rapidly drooped at home. It takes time to learn to work with a new style successfully. One spongy, curly permanent I was given made me feel like the Bride of Frankenstein. I desperately tried to get my hair to go back to its sleek, smooth look, but it was obstinate and try as I may—and did—I simply could not bend it to my will. I finally decided to accept the fact that I had a bad permanent, and set out to get it to work *for* me. I had a bit snipped off the ends, which tamed the wild curls, and soon my permanent looked okay.

But, if, when all is said and done, you have to admit that your new style really is a disaster, don't let a single bad experience keep you from changing your hairstyle ever again—that could be the most stunting thing, the biggest mistake of all.

WHEN TO CHANGE STYLISTS

If you find a stylist you like, stay with him for a while. It takes even a professional time to get accustomed to your hair type and learn how to work with it—and with you. On the other hand, every stylist has his limitations. If he's been giving you the same old look time after time, year in and year out, you should consider switching to someone more imaginative.

EXACTLY WHAT IS A GOOD HAIRCUT?

The most important thing in any good hairstyle is the cut.

If your hair is very fine and straight, the best cut for you may be a blunt cut, one the same length all over. This will give your hair body and manageability. The same cut also works well with thick, straight hair.

If your hair is curly or wavy, a slightly layered cut will emphasize the curl without removing too much of it. *Very* curly or frizzy hair should be cut in short layers around the sides and in longer layers in back.

A good stylist will approach the whole problem of your haircut systematically. First he'll divide your hair into sections, and then he'll blunt cut it with scissors. Beware of the stylist who cuts away haphazardly!

Most stylists will wet or dampen your hair before they cut it. When it dries, however, it shrinks and will therefore look shorter than it did when it was wet; your stylist must take this into account when determining your ideal hair length.

A good cut should fall neatly into place after your hair has been washed. You should be able to part it on either side or in the middle and have it fall cleanly. So don't tie yourself down to the same look day after day.

If your hair is layered, it should look even all over, whether it's dry or wet—you shouldn't be able to "see" distinct layers.

ALTERING THE LOOK OF YOUR BASIC LOOK

Once you have a good basic cut and style, there are many ways to change the mood. There are going to be times when the basic style is just not right for an occasion. I've seen photos of myself in evening clothes with my hair still in its casual daytime look and cringed to realize that it did not mesh with the rest of me. Since nothing can transform your entire appearance faster and more fully than your hair, you'll want to experiment with ways to change its look.

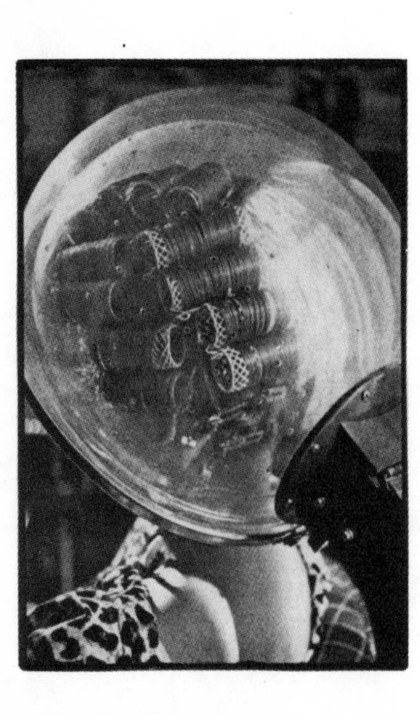

WHAT YOU SHOULD KNOW ABOUT PERMANENTS

For years I was paranoid about permanents, thanks to the home perms I was given as a child. These once-a-year epics always ended badly. Little me would emerge out of the lotions and curlers with a head of short, crimped frizz. I certainly didn't cut much of a figure in junior high. For weeks after each perm, I would try in vain to grease the fuzz away and to make my shortened hair look longer by combing it down and clipping it to my ears with bobby pins. It must have been then that I decided that as soon as I could afford it I would turn myself over to an expert.

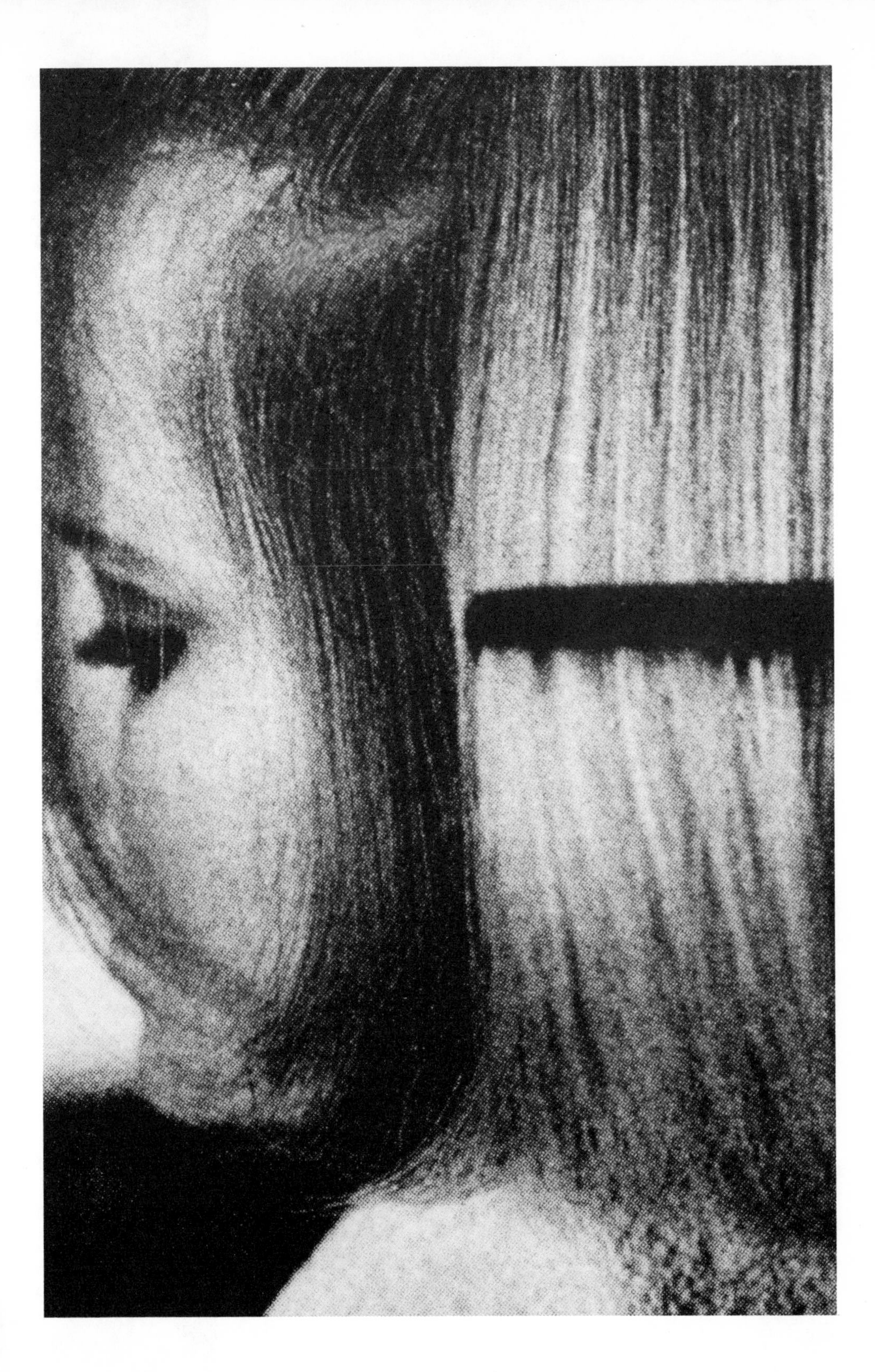

The modern permanent waving process, which is extremely sophisticated, can improve the appearance of many different kinds of hair. A modern perm (also called a "body wave" because of the gentle, relaxed curl it creates) leaves your hair so soft you can step out of the shower and simply shake it dry. The new perms don't leave the sharp indentations between each curl which the old-fashioned perms did; they allow the hair to fall in a natural wave, giving you a style that seems to effortlessly frame your face. Soft, finely textured hair acquires more body with a permanent and holds a set better, while thick, heavy hair acquires a positively beautiful bend. A perm can work a minor miracle on even too-curly hair by removing the topmost frizziness and transforming it into all soft curls.

After a permanent, my hair has shape *and* movement—the same hair that, left to just hang in there, tends to be flat on top and to go limp when I let it grow. A gentle permanent will not produce frizz or fuzz. Sometimes I even forget I have a permanent until I wash or set my hair and realize with grateful amazement how much body and bounce it has.

WHY BOTHER TO GET A PROFESSIONAL PERMANENT?

The permanent wave process is complicated to a degree. If any one of the number of steps it entails is carried out irresponsibly, your permanent will end up frizzy, loose, and limp—a far cry from the shape you'd been counting on it to assume. Perms today are done with a new acid-based type of wave lotion, which breaks the chemical bonds that determine the shape of each hair. These new lotions can't destroy your hair, but it takes an expert to know just what kind of lotion will work best with your hair type and, even more important, how long it should stay on. After the lotion is applied, the hair is set in a curl or wave pattern. Again, it takes a professional to correctly space the curlers and to determine what size they should be to create a particular style. Finally, the hair is neutralized with yet another chemical, which makes it possible for the restructured hair to remain in the shape of a curl. If you can afford it, have your permanent done in a really good salon. However, if you do go ahead and try to give yourself a home permanent, proceed with caution: Read and follow the directions very, very carefully. And if your home perm fails, don't try it again.

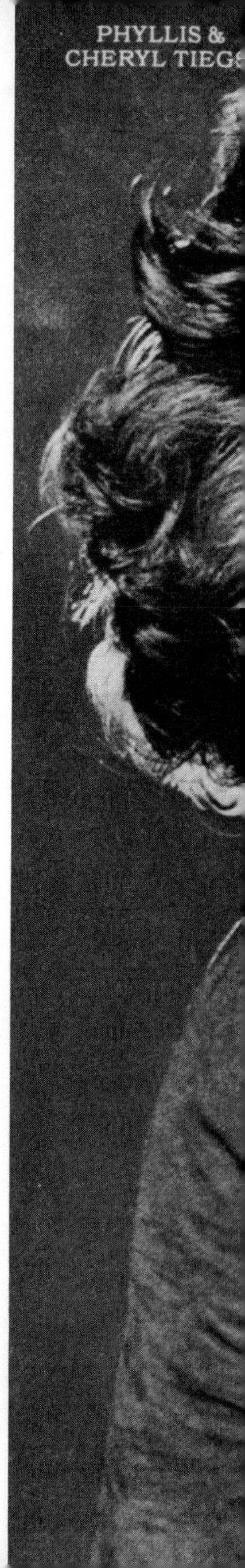

THE AFTER-CARE OF A PERM

A permanent should be trimmed regularly if you want it to continue to look good. A bit of dryness is bound to creep into the last eighth inch of hair that's been permed, but if you just remove those ends the entire perm will get a big lift. If your hair seems too frizzy after a perm, a trim also will tame it down. With frequent trims you can get away with having to have a permanent only every six months or so.

STRAIGHTENING YOUR HAIR: SHOULD YOU DO IT?

Wouldn't you know it: women lucky enough to have naturally curly hair often want to have it straightened. Just why, I always wonder, when curly hair can be brought under control by means of a good cut, and extremely curly hair can be greatly enhanced by a short layered style. If, however, you do decide to have your hair chemically straightened, take your head to a good salon. The chemicals used in reversing a curl are very powerful and should under no circumstances be handled by an amateur. A bad straightening job can cause your hair to break off at the scalp. Try taming any unruly curls by pushing the damp hair into waves, securing them with clips, and letting your hair dry—to use my favorite adverb—*naturally*.

COLORING YOUR HAIR IN: RED, WHITE, BLUE?

A new hair color can pick up glints and flecks in your eyes and tones in your skin, dramatize your hair with deep, rich shades, or cool it down to a subtly sophisticated hue. Streaking can approximate the lightening powers of the summer sun to frame your face with lighter shades. Hair color can also act as a conditioner, thickening each strand for greater body and manageability. Color rinses lightly coat the shaft of your hair till you shampoo them right out, and semi-permanent tints permeate the hair shaft for as long as a month. Both of these techniques are good for temporarily deepening the shade of your hair or adding attractive highlights. If you are intent on actually changing your hair color, a permanent tint that really penetrates the hair shaft is necessary.

Definitely leave any major and drastic color change to a professional colorist. He will have the know-how to select and blend the right tones of the tint with your own hair color, so the hair shade you wind up with is a subtle combination of *natural* tones that is also going to look good with your skin.

Hair coloring can certainly be a success at home. The colors shown on the packages are indications of what the colors would look like on white hair. The packages have a panel showing or telling what the color will look like on different shades of hair. Read and follow the instructions carefully and you can achieve the look you want with the greatest of ease.

Streaking can be natural.

Take the time to analyze your skin tone before you change your hair color. If your complexion is very pale, avoid black or any harsh color. Olive-skinned, dark-eyed women make unconvincing blondes. And women with glowing, ruddy complexions are making a big mistake when they opt for a red or auburn hair color. If you are going gray—extreme hair colors will invariably make you look older than you are. A good rule of thumb is: Select a subtle tone, a shade lighter than your natural color, or one as close to it as possible. If you're a brunette who believes that blondes have more fun, have fun trying it.

If it's a radical color change you're mulling over (from brunette to blond, or black to red, for example), calculate the time and money it's going to take to maintain the new shade. If you can't afford salon touch-ups, either reconsider your decision or get your colorist to give you instructions for retouching your hair yourself.

The front of your hair just near the hairline is usually a bit lighter than the rest. If you want to lighten your hair a shade, try matching the new color to this part of your hair.

Always deep-condition your hair for several weeks before and after a permanent color change.

And this above all: Wait at least four weeks between coloring sessions; and be careful when you use one color dye on top of another that it doesn't produce an unexpected color change.

HENNA

Made from a plant that grows in the Middle East, henna is one of the oldest of hair dyes. The princesses of Egypt and Persia used this organic, nontoxic hair

coloring agent to condition and color their hair, and if it was good enough for *them*. . . . Henna, when used properly, adds a real sheen. It also coats each strand, and gives your hair strength and body. Natural henna adds no color but brings out natural highlights. But, as with most anything, improper use can be damaging. Blondes and those with light-tinted hair should be particularly careful.

HAIR CARE: WHO CARES?

No style will look attractive on you if your hair is bedraggled looking. But if it's well-nourished and looks well-groomed, almost any carefully thought-out style will look flattering.

SHAMPOOING

When I was a little girl I washed my hair once a week only, because my mother put great stock in the old myth that frequent shampooing damages hair by depriving it of needed oils. There are in fact no rules that dictate how often you should shampoo, except the basic one of common sense: If your hair is dirty, wash it. Only oily hair, or hair that tends to become limp and separate a day or so after washing, should be shampooed very often—in some cases, every day. Dry or dull hair requires less shampooing. If you live in a city rather than a suburb or the country, it may be a good idea to shampoo fairly often, given the pollutants in the environment.

WHICH SHAMPOO IS THE ONE FOR YOU?

Try not to cringe, but the best shampoo is a mild, *detergent* shampoo formulated especially for your hair type. "Detergent" is a harsh word, I know, conjuring up as it does sinkfuls of soaking dishes, but it's the best ingredient for cutting through the grease and grime in your hair. Most shampoos contain it. Like many of the other ingredients in shampoo, it passes over your hair shaft ever so briefly, en route to being washed down the drain. Acid, or pH-balanced shampoos, lock moisture into the hair, and are good for normal as well as dry hair. However, they may not be powerful enough to clean oily hair, and might leave it looking dull. Nor will protein, egg, and balsam shampoos do the job for oily hair that they will for fine, thin, or limp

hair. So if your hair is oily, try to choose a shampoo containing *lemon*.

I certainly shopped around a lot before I hit on the shampoo I now use. It's a trial-and-error kind of thing.

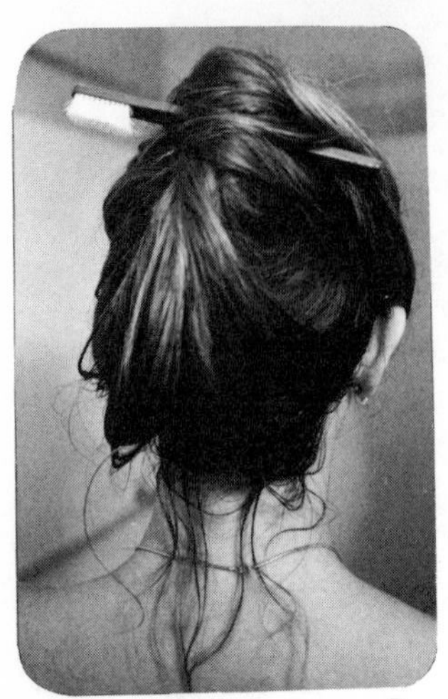

No shower cap? —Use a toothbrush.

HOW TO SHAMPOO: GENTLY, GENTLY DOWN THE DRAIN

Always handle your hair gently. Massaging the soap into your scalp with your fingertips will stimulate the roots of your hair and scalp. And be sure to rinse out every little trace of shampoo, which if you're not careful can leave a dull, drying film on your hair. Don't lather on great gobs of shampoo, because the more of it you use the harder it will be to rinse it all away. At one time in my adult life, I was using shampoo by the handful! Not surprisingly—except, come to think of it, it *was* a big surprise to me—my hair began to dry out. So I decided to be a good girl and obey the instructions on the label for a change, to wit: "Massage one half-teaspoon of shampoo into your hair." I learned the thorny way that a lot is not always better than a little. Also, hot water doesn't necessarily rinse the soap out of your hair effectively. Follow it with a cool rinse that also stimulates scalp circulation. If you shampoo your hair every day, lather once only. But if your hair is really dirty, you may need to give it two separate lathers. Never brush or yank at your hair with a comb when it's wet. And disentangle knots with your fingers before you comb—but gently, gently.

GOOD CONDITIONING

Conditioners help protect your hair from all the factors that never cease conspiring against it—sun, wind, pollution, chlorine, central heating, not to mention blow-dryers, hot curlers, and the alkaline chemicals used in permanent wave and color processing.

No conditioner can actually repair damaged hair, as some of the advertisements would have you believe. Once an end is split or a hair shaft becomes porous and brittle, the only way to cure it is to cut it off and let a new hair replace it.

Conditioners temporarily coat the hair shaft, making it appear thicker. They also fill in the rough surface of the hair cuticle, so the hair seems softer and smoother. The cream conditioners used after shampooing untangle hair, make it easier to comb, and

tame dry, flyaway tresses. But if your hair is oily or damaged, keep clear of cream conditioners; with their alkaline nature, they can make oily hair limp. If you have very oily hair, a home remedy might just do the trick—add a quarter cup of lemon juice or cider vinegar to a quart of water as a final rinse. I use a special conditioner that brings out my blond highlights, which I apply after I wash my hair and let it sink in. If you fail to rinse conditioners out thoroughly, they'll leave a dull film.

DEEP-CONDITIONING TREATMENTS

Dry, damaged, or chemically processed hair should be deep-conditioned often. Protein conditioners, which you should leave on your hair for twenty minutes and/or use with heat, and hot oil treatments penetrate and coat the hair shaft, making it softer and much more pliable. You can make a protein conditioner at home by mixing two egg yolks with one tablespoon of sesame oil (not exactly my idea of a box lunch); work it into your hair, and then cover it with a hot, damp towel. For a homemade oil treatment, heat some plain olive or safflower oil; divide your clean, dry hair into sections; comb the oil through; wrap your hair in a plastic bag; and sit under a bonnet dryer for between twenty and thirty minutes. To get the oil out, apply an undiluted shampoo to your dry hair, lather, then rinse thoroughly.

Oily hair does not benefit from deep-conditioning treatments. But if it's only your scalp that's oily, and the ends of your hair seem dry, deep-condition the ends only. (It makes sense, right?)

BRUSHING

Should you brush your hair the fabled one hundred strokes a day? Yes—if you enjoy a good exercise in futility, and like to live dangerously to boot. Too much brushing can aggravate your hair and scalp and cause your hair to thin right out. If your hair is dry or already damaged in any way, go very lightly with the hairbrush.

If your hair is in generally good condition, however, an occasional brushing will stimulate blood circulation in the scalp, do away with superficial dandruff, and get the natural hair oils moving from the base of the scalp to the ends of the hair shaft, where they're often

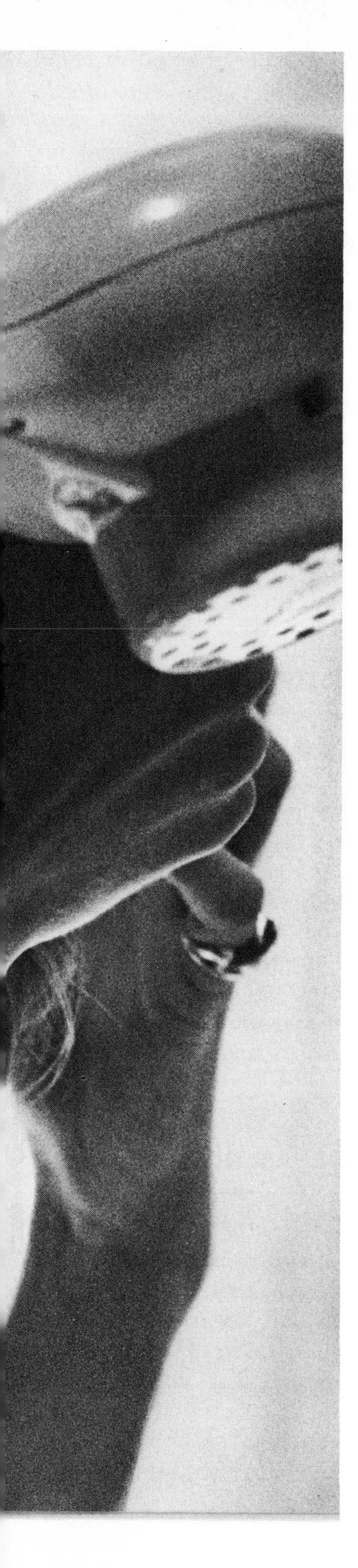

needed more desperately. Since brushing loosens dirt, making it easier to remove, a good time to brush is just before you wash your hair. I brush the underside of my hair by bending over and throwing my hair forward, so it'll look full and flowing. You'll want a good hairbrush, preferably one combining natural boar and soft plastic bristles on a cushioning foam base. Never use a brush with nylon bristles—they tear at the hair and damage it.

DRYERS! HOT ROLLERS! CURLING IRONS!!!

There aren't two opinions: electrical appliances do give hair a glamorous lift but (and it's a pretty big "but"), if you use them too often you may be risking your hair's health. I try to let my hair dry naturally as often as possible. In fact, the only time I resort to hot rollers and curling irons is before special occasions.

Say your hair does look best blow-dried, then go ahead, but set your dryer on "cool" (it's the heat—along with the blast of air—that dries your hair out). The more modern dryers have an adjustable power dial that allows you to control the wattages you send to your hair. For serious drying, a 1,000-watt setting works best, but for styling and touch-ups, 750 or even 500 watts will do. To blow-dry safely and effectively, hold the dryer about six inches away from your head, moving it as you brush continuously, and taking care not to overheat any one section of your hair or scalp.

Hot rollers are wonderful time-savers, yes, but they too can damage your hair if you use them too often. The type that works with steam adds more moisture to hair than the dry-heat types does, but may not be as effective in humid weather, when your hair already contains plenty of moisture. Leave hot rollers in for only three minutes, then let the curls cool before combing them out.

Most modern curling irons are Teflon-coated and have a thermostat so they can't overheat and sear your hair. They should be used only on dry hair; if they're used on wet hair, they may make the curls too tight. Curling irons, like all other forms of heating equipment, must be used in moderation.

HELPING YOUR HAIR FROM THE INSIDE OUT

Truly healthy hair begins beneath the scalp, with the roots you don't see. These roots are nourished through the circulatory system, and just like the rest of your body, they benefit from a good diet and plenty of exercise. The hair shaft is basically composed of a protein substance, so a diet rich (but not too rich) in protein will help form strong, shiny hair. It can be said that good hair, like good skin, is the end result of a balanced diet, one full of vitamins and minerals.

I've made this list of time-saving tips for styling and caring for hair:

SPRAY AND PUFF

To perk up curly hair or a permanent that looks as if it had just been run over, lightly mist your hair with the same spray bottle you use to mist your houseplants. Your curls will spring instantly, abundantly back into shape. Use your fingers to fluff them out.

SUN AND OIL TREATMENT

Not that many people know this but overexposure to the sun can do as much damage to your hair as to your skin. However, if you know how, you can utilize the sun's rays to give your hair what amounts to a deep-conditioning oil treatment. Before you go to the beach, simply comb a conditioner or some sweet almond or coconut oil into your hair. The oil will protect your hair from the sun's drying rays, while the sun helps the oil penetrate your hair shaft. This is the method that women in India and countries with a similar climate have always used to keep their dark hair sleek and shining.

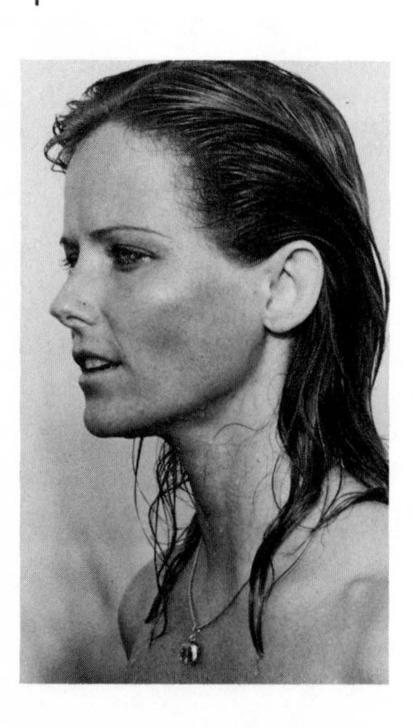

HOMEMADE BALSAM RINSES

An old-fashioned way to bring out the highlights in your hair is to rinse it with a homemade herbal brew. The recipe is anything but elaborate: just steep a quarter cup of rosemary (if your hair is dark; if it's light, substitute camomile flowers) in a quart of boiling water and let it sit till the mixture has a strong color and aroma. Then cool and strain it. Use the aromatic result as the final rinse for your hair. A brew of dried nettles also adds luster and body to hair—improbable as that sounds.

Bows + braids for Anthony Quinn in Italy, 1968

INSTANT PERM

If you'd like to try a curly look without subjecting yourself to processing chemicals, braid your damp hair in about eight braids all over your head just before going to bed. In the morning, undo the braids and marvel at your fluffy, wavy instant perm!

BRUSHING AND SPRAYING

Personally, I hate the look of stiff, sprayed hair that doesn't budge an inch. I've found a good use for hairspray, however, After I remove the hot curlers and brush hair into place, I spray my hair, *then* brush out most of the spray half an hour later. What the spray does is accustom my hair to the shape I want and also adds body, and brushing it out does away with that depressing unnatural look.

RELAXING CURLS

Whenever I set my hair in rollers, I make sure I remove them *before* I get dressed for a night out. That way, I give my curls a chance to relax, and I also get a chance to see the way my hair is actually going to look for the rest of the night: I mean, like can I live with it for five hours?

MISTAKES PEOPLE MAKE

Wearing a Too-Extravagant Hairstyle

Some women persist in making the near-fatal error of sporting a mass of frizzy curls or—every bit as bad—an over-elaborate hairdo, which I jokingly call the

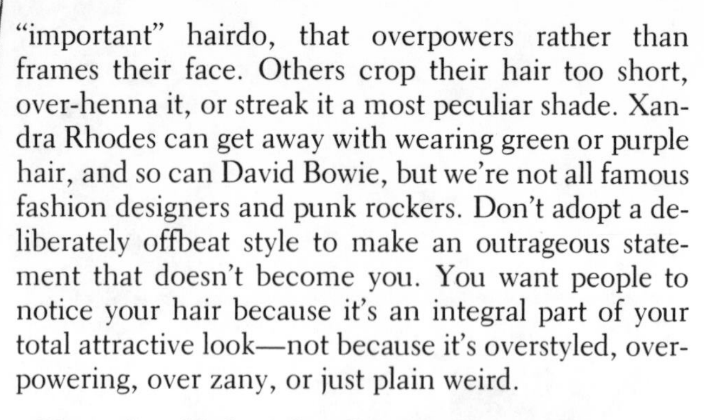

"important" hairdo, that overpowers rather than frames their face. Others crop their hair too short, over-henna it, or streak it a most peculiar shade. Xandra Rhodes can get away with wearing green or purple hair, and so can David Bowie, but we're not all famous fashion designers and punk rockers. Don't adopt a deliberately offbeat style to make an outrageous statement that doesn't become you. You want people to notice your hair because it's an integral part of your total attractive look—not because it's overstyled, overpowering, over zany, or just plain weird.

Changing Hairstyles for the Wrong Reason

It's a mistake to change your hairstyle because you are feeling insecure or depressed. There's a good chance that if you change your hair hoping to improve your state of mind you'll just saddle yourself with another disaster.

I used to go to a lot of trouble to reproduce whatever "latest" hairstyle had caught my fancy or fired my imagination—completely oblivious to how it would look on me. Well, you live and *maybe* you learn. But I do know what I'm talking about when I say: the latest hairstyle should always be the style that looks best on you.

Grooming Your Hair for All the World to See

Nothing can ruin—or, at the very least, tarnish—your image faster than combing or grooming your hair in public. Because I'm always in a rush—with me, it's always one giant step forward and two baby steps backward—I often have to leave the house with my hair still damp from the shower, but I always make sure that the final combing takes place in the privacy of a ladies' room or, failing that, the semi-privacy of a cab. And there's absolutely no excuse to ever be seen in curlers outside your own house—they make everyone look sort of wired-for-sound, and somewhat freakish.

Sleeping on Curlers

Every night during my teens I would set my hair, put out the lights, and lay down to sleep on the bumpy curlers. Had I only seen that great movie *All About Eve*, I could have said the famous Bette Davis line to myself instead of my boring prayers, "Fasten your seatbelts, it's going to be a *bumpy* ride." I shudder to think how fragile and brittle that bad practice must have made my hair. It's amazing how few clangorous nightmares I had.

Butchering Your Own Hair

If you're one of those who must "do it yourself," restrict your cutting efforts to snipping an eighth of an inch from the ends between salon visits. Just about the most frustrating thing to a stylist is having to deal with the ragged ends and holes caused by a bad haircut. Haircutting is not as easy as it looks. It takes a good stylist *years* to learn his trade. And don't entrust your scissors to a well-meaning friend, either.

Crash Dieting

Here's a sure way to damage your hair (as well as the rest of your body): Deprive yourself of the nutrients you need by going on a good crash diet. Each hair on your head has a natural growing and resting phase; it's during the resting phase that it falls out, soon to be replaced by a new hair. If your diet's too poor to provide your hair with the fertilizer it needs in order to grow (about 800 calories per day) your hair will be "hungry," and as many as half the hairs on your head may go into their resting phase at the same time (as opposed to the usual ten percent), with the result that your hair fallout rate will increase dramatically—and visibly!

Styling Hair in Tight Braids, Chignons, Ponytails

Any style that places a disproportionate amount of pressure on one part of your hair will eventually cause it to thin out. So save ponytails, corn-rows, tight chignons for your temporary look. Variety is the answer here as elsewhere.

Fighting Your Hair All the Way

I have a cowlick that I can't lick. It's been the grief of quite a few stylists (and given others an actual sick headache). Over the years my friendly cowlick has eluded all manner of clipping, combing, and nudging. Believe me, the only way to go is *with it*—accept the texture and direction of your hair. By all means, strive to improve the look of it by means of curlers, tints, perms, and new cuts, but don't fight your natural, God-given hair to the death.

Because, take it from me, it's a losing battle.

6

Making Up to Yourself: Facing Up to Your Face

VOGUE
BRITISH EDITION
$1.75
APR 1
40p
the prettiest time of your life
silks chiffons and April flowers
40 best looks in fashion and beauty now

Beauty is never certain, it's highly conditional. Our assets are only lent to us. We *have* to pay attention to them. If only because they are always being assessed—by others as well as ourselves! In Japan recently I picked up a novel called *Snow Country* by Yasunari Kawabata, a Nobel-Prize winner. The heroine, Komako, is a country geisha in a Japanese hot-springs resort. I was impressed by how the author's style communicates "the joy of the knowing eye, of the sensitive skin, of the ear, the nose and the tongue." *I* certainly learned something about the whole procedure of beauty from Kawabata's description of his heroine:

> *The high, thin nose was a little lonely, a little sad, but the bud of her lips opened and closed smoothly, like a beautiful circle of leeches. When she was silent her lips seemed always to be moving. Had they wrinkles or cracks, or had their color been less fresh, they would have struck one as unwholesome, but they were never anything but smooth and shining. The line of her eyelids neither rose nor fell. As if for some special reason, it drew its way straight across her face. There was something faintly comical about the effect, but the short, thick hair of her eyebrows sloped gently down to enfold the line discreetly. There was nothing remarkable about the outline of her round, slightly aquiline face. With her skin like white porcelain coated over a faint pink, and her throat still girlish, not yet filled out, the impression she gave was above all one of cleanness, not quite one of real beauty.*

The inspiration behind the VOGUE cover was — coincidentally — one of my very favorite books — "The Wilder Shores of Love". I imagined myself as Isabelle Burton — entering Mecca — exploring Africa in the 1800's.

Here is a woman who has seen to it that her face mirrors her considerable understanding of the world. Looking into the mirror, she would not be like a character in another novel who said that she felt a stranger to her own face.

At the other extreme, I've just finished Dirk Bogarde's fascinating memoir, *Snakes & Ladders*. He's always been one of my favorite actors, ever since I saw him in *The Servant* in a pokey little art-movie house outside of Alhambra. When Dirk describes the filming of the death scene in Thomas Mann's classic, *Death in Venice*, under the great Italian director Visconti, I couldn't help thinking how the poor pain of all those made-up hours would serve as a cautionary tale, at

least as far as this chapter's concerned—and possibly beyond.

I noticed, casually, one day, that some of the troupe . . . were walking about wearing neat little squares of white paint, no bigger than a postage stamp. I didn't pay very much attention, but after three or four days, and an ever-increasing amount of little white squares . . . I asked. . . . They were testing some kind of make-up.

. . . of all the things which I had to face in the film the thing which frightened me most was the actual, final, death scene . . . Clearly the moment was upon us. They were testing special make-up because the one I would have to use must be a total death mask: it was to crack apart slowly, symbolizing decay, age, ruin . . . But I kept silent, as was my habit, and merely watched with mounting terror the daily proliferation of little white patches among the troupe. Whatever they were using . . . was going to be both unpleasant, and possibly from the amount of care being taken, dangerous.

. . . In the make-up room Visconti was quiet, firm, and very gentle. ". . . you are sick now, and old; remember what Mann has said, you will have lips as ripe as strawberries . . . the dye from your hair will run . . . your poor face will crack, and then you will die . . . I tell you all this because when you have the make-up on your face you will not be able to speak, it will be dead as a mask . . . we only do one take for that reason . . . it is hard like a plaster."

Translated into real life, the moral of Dirk's macabre experience may be that the last thing you want to present to the world is the death mask of makeup.

If you want your appearance to serve you, so that when you look in the mirror it's not an enemy you're facing, you will have to learn the craft of making up. If you apply makeup correctly, it can dramatize your face. Cheek color, eye color, and lip color can all work together to emphasize your best features—adding just the right, sometimes barely perceptible, touch of freshness and get-it-togetherness.

But if you don't take the time to learn how to refurbish yourself, then it's going to be, in Virginia Tiger's clever phrase from her useful book, *Everywoman*, "combat in the cosmetic zone"—and war is war, and "beauty can kill. Yet it is a university as well as a jungle."

We don't have to accept our sallow skin and dank hair. With know-how we can subdue them till we're at the very least, presentable.

So why do many women persist in turning their faces into disaster areas? Too much makeup, coarsely, clumsily, or too thickly plastered on, may make you look garish or artificial. Too little makeup, or none at all, may leave you looking lusterless, definitely on the dull side, just about to be eclipsed by everything and everyone.

Believe me, you don't want to play at making-up. It's a very serious business, and the stakes are high.

If you want your face to come to your aid as you go about your day, the first thing you should do is ask yourself a few hard questions—and not be afraid to answer them. Well, you want to hold up your head and glitter, don't you?

■ *Do you look at your daytime makeup in natural light before you leave the house in the morning?*

■ *Do you apply lipstick with a brush?*

■ *Do you make an effort to use an eyeshadow that matches the color of the clothes you have on?*

■ *Before you buy makeup base, do you test the color on your hand?*

■ *Do you conceal dark shadows under your eyes with a light-colored concealing cream?*

■ *Do you "finish" your evening makeup by applying translucent powder with a brush over your foundation to prevent shine?*

■ *Are you one who believes that makeup base clogs your pores and should be worn only on special occasions?*

■ *How do you keep your eye makeup from slipping? By applying a neutral foundation to your eyelids, or what?*

■ *Do you blend your eyeliner with the tip of your finger?*

■ *Has anyone ever complimented you on your makeup? Were they empty compliments?*

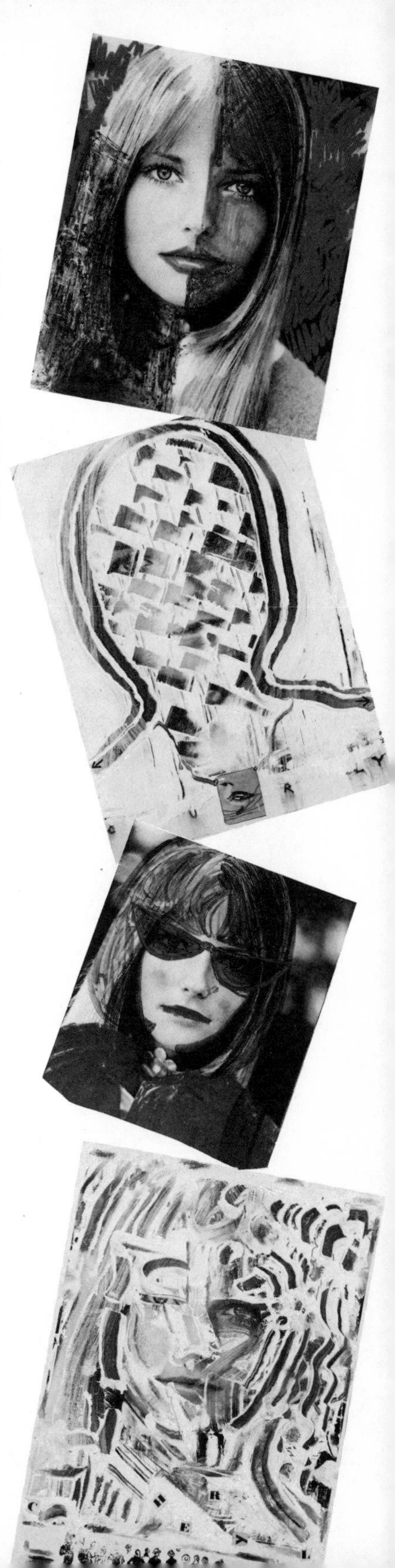

Just show me the face that doesn't need decorating, or doctoring. For models, it's a life and death affair. It's makeup that sets the mood of the clothes we wear, creates a kind of weather for them. It's makeup that heightens the illusion in all those fashion photographs you see. I call it "the art that conceals art" because when it's been done well, you hardly notice it.

In my career I've been very lucky to know and work with some great makeup artists like Way Bandy and François Ilnseher. I've studied the types of makeup they use on my face and the come-and-go of all kinds of powders, shadows, and pastes—and I've studied how they put them on. A lot of this knowledge I save exclusively for the short life of my appearance before the cameras. The makeup that gives my face a vibrant look in a photograph is much too dramatic for real life. I've had to learn patiently how to modify and tone down the makeup techniques used in the studio.

Perhaps the most serious mistake a woman can make in her appearance is to wear too much makeup. Instead of giving her the freshness of whatever age she is, it tends to make her look older and less—rather than more—sophisticated. It's just another form of dishonesty—if you ask me—and one that boomerangs. And *men* don't like it when the makeup gets too thick. In fact, they often complain that they find a heavy cosmetic look unkissable and untouchable. They have to search for the buried treasure: the real girl stirring beneath the plaster. Too much labor, too much *toil*, can actually be the death not only of a woman's looks but of her love life. I'm not saying men don't want and appreciate the transformation—they do, they just don't want to see it, smell it, meet it in your face. They don't want to even hear about the machinery. When they look at you, they want to see a face, and not that fatal mask of cosmetics.

But don't make the opposite mistake of going totally "natural," and not wearing any makeup at all. There are women today who feel that makeup is just too much trouble to put on, or else that it's too "traditional." (Maybe so. But then, so is the whole idea of looking charming!) They fail to take advantage of all that makeup can do for their faces. Oh there are a few women who can get away with not wearing any makeup whatsoever—the ones with the startling coloring, fire-bright eyes, and flawlessly glowing skin—you know them, all five of them, and there comes a time when even they . . . Almost everyone else,

Cover Girl's pressed powder

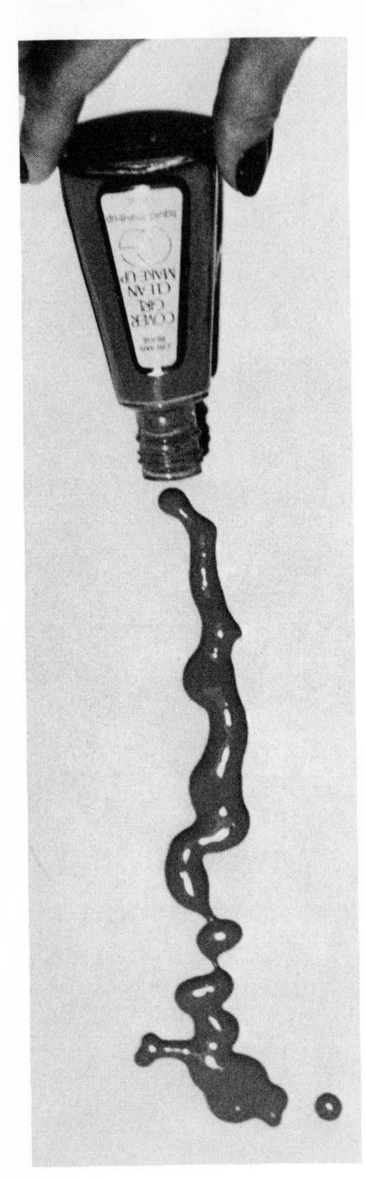

though, can benefit from the addition of color and contrast.

I love a natural look, but it's a rare day when I leave the house without a touch of foundation, blusher, maybe some mascara, and lip gloss. Because I know what even a smidgeon of makeup can do for me: it's the difference between the dog days and the dogwood days. To see a brighter version of my own face in the mirror lifts my spirits and swells my self-confidence when I'm tired or fed up.

BACK TO THE BASICS OR FORWARD TO??

Most people think that models lug a veritable steamer trunk of cosmetics around with them. Not true! I have a battered old striped tote bag containing the most essential makeup products only—and some of these products I've used for years.

Sure it's fun to change makeup colors every now and again, and it's always fun to experiment with new products. The new cosmetics are lighter and sheerer, but I just don't think it's necessary to buy every cosmetic that comes on the market (it's expensive and time-consuming, too).

Whenever you do buy makeup, do yourself a favor and test it first. Most department stores and pharmacies have samples you can try. Many brands of makeup may look the same but they're made from different recipes; once you've applied them to your skin, they diffuse their mystic attributes. And keep it on while you shop, then look in the mirror—hard (you have to be prepared to be self-critical)—and if you *still* like what it's doing for you, *then* buy it.

Another thing I've learned is that the inexpensive brands can be just as effective as the ones that come in those elaborate containers.

Now back to that old striped tote bag. Here are the makeup items I always carry:

MAKEUP BASE OR FOUNDATION

Foundation doesn't clog your pores, as many people mistakenly think. Even when I'm outdoors I usually wear a light coat of makeup base: it protects skin from the sun, wind, and city soot. It also evens out skin tone without camouflaging it. A natural skin tone is never a single, consistent shade. Your foundation—*if* you apply it skillfully—should allow some of your natural skin color to show through. Heavy makeup base tends to accumulate in the creases of your face, so don't use foundation to "conceal" wrinkles.

How to Use It

If you apply moisturizer before foundation, you can spread the base on more evenly. I prefer to let my fingers do the walking—I want to feel where the base is going and work it into all the little out-of-the-way dust-bitten corners. A moist cosmetic sponge is a good tool for applying a super-light coat of base; it wipes some off while some more goes on.

How to Choose It

If your skin is oily, you should probably use a water based or emulsion-type foundation containing little or no oil. But beware: some water-based foundations are so sheer they may not be giving you the cover you need. Dry-skinned women are much better off using an oil-based foundation. Some makeup bases contain moisturizers, special skin medications, and sun screens as well. Foundations also come in gels, in foams that feel practically weightless, and in cake formulations that are too heavy for that sheer natural look I like so much. You should always try a makeup base before buying it; and don't use your hand to test (the skin color of your hand couldn't be more different from that of your face); instead, apply the sample to the skin of your jaw, where you can see easily how the base blends with the skin on both your face and your neck. Most women prefer a base that's close to their natural skin color. An ivory-colored or neutral base is good for removing redness at the base of the nose and for disguising differences in skin tone. But don't hide your ego behind a foundation. You don't want it to completely change your skin color, you just want it to blend with your own skin.

Powder Power

I dust my face with powder to set the makeup and give it a good matte finish. If you don't like the idea of dusting your whole face, do just the forehead, chin, and nose, the "T-zone," which has a tendency to get all shiny. I use one of those big soft sable cosmetic brushes that lightly waft the powder over my face.

Whether you use a pressed cake or a loose powder, choose the kind that won't interfere with the tone of your other makeup.

CHEEK-TO-CHEEK COLOR

In almost every interview I've ever done, I've been asked what's the one cosmetic I would take with me if I knew I was going to be stranded on a desert island, the one cosmetic I would rescue from a burning house. And I always answer that the one thing I'd grab for—vanity of vanities!—is my blusher. To me, the most indispensable item in that old striped bag is cheek color—it adds a real glow to the face that to most of us, alas, doesn't come all that naturally.

Makeup experts haven't been exactly shy in recommending techniques for applying blusher. We've all been inundated and confused by the elaborate crescents, arcs, and circles illustrated in the magazines. For me, the simplest and most effective—not to say, most instinctive—way of applying cheek color is to put it on top of the cheekbone, right where the sun would naturally tinge my face. Most of us don't happen to have very prominent cheekbones. Feel for them with your fingers (just light a candle and pray they're going to be there), or suck in your cheeks to make them stand out like Katharine Hepburn's or Faye Dunaway's. Now blend the blush along the line of the cheekbone out toward your temples. If your cream rouge is stiff and hard to handle, apply it with a damp cosmetic sponge, or with slightly moist fingers. Powdered blusher can be applied with the sable cosmetic brush. Liquid cheek color you can apply just to the cheekbone, or to the whole face for a charged but subtle glow.

How to Choose It

Cheek color comes in cream, rouge, powdered blusher, liquid, gel, and pencil. I prefer a cream-type rouge for day—it adds an extra shine—and powdered blush-on for night. The trouble with powders is they can look obvious and grainy in natural daylight, and shiny creams and gels can look oily under artificial lighting. Powdered blush-on goes better with the powder you use in finishing your evening look. Liquid and gel-type cheek colors are nice for daytime too, because they're light and natural and blend so nicely with your skin.

According to that wizard François, who has done my face for so many modeling assignments, I'm beginning to think he knows it better than I do, there are basically two skin tones: fair skin, with pink overtones, which he calls "cold-toned skin," and skin with a yellow tone to it, such as olive skin, which he calls "warm-toned." (And yes, skin tone can change according to the season.) If your skin is cold-toned, you should choose a shade of cheek color in the pink-to-purple range. If it's warm-toned, a brownish, peach, or taupe cheek color will look best. Most women can get away with wearing more than one color of rouge or blusher. A good time to change your cheek color is summer, when you're tan, or after you've just done some outdoor sport and have one of those healthy pink glows we've all heard so much about. In any case, you'll certainly want to vary it according to your mood and the occasion. François offers a very soothing suggestion: after you've applied your basic cheek color, add a very light pink color. "Only pink," he says, "can *really* warm up the skin." Whatever color rouge or blush-on you select should emphasize rather than be at odds with your natural skin tone. (And if something shouldn't be at odds with something else, then it should be even with it, right?)

EYECOLOR PENCILS

These are just soft crayons made of waxes, pigments, and oils. I have half a dozen of them in different subtle colors. You can use them both as liners and as shadows for the eyes.

How to Use Them

Sharpen the pencil to a blunt point, then line your eyes by drawing a thin, continuous line just above the lashes, and beneath the lashes on the lower lid. Now blend the line by smudging it with your finger. This blending process is essential, because what you want to do is create a shadowy line, not a hard, definite one. Lining the eyes both above and below makes the lashes appear thicker and creates a sultry effect suited to those daydreams that are often the little props of our personalities. You can also use the eyecolor pencil to shade the eyelid.

How to Choose Them

It's important that you select a pencil with the right texture for your skin type. If the pencil is too hard, it's

Make up by Francois Ilnseher...

going to pull on your eyelid and may even damage the delicate skin there; if it's too soft and greasy, it may run, and before you know it you'll be embarrassed at finding the color on other parts of your face. I prefer muted colors for lining my eyes: brown, mauve, navy, and charcoal gray, which create a shadow—not a distinct color—on the eyelid. These colors go well with all eye colors and all skin tones. My guru François says that to make the eyes stand out, the frame of liner around them should be darker than the irises and that the darker your eyes are, the darker the frames should be. Brown-eyed women, then, should line their eyes with a very dark black, blue, purple, or brown pencil, and women with light blue eyes should use a blue or gray or brown.

Eyeliner also comes in a cake form, which you can just brush on with water. This type of liner can create an extremely soft look if you carefully wet the brush, run it over the cake, then brush the liner as close to the base of the lashes as possible, using your finger to smudge before the ink dries.

EYE SHADOW

And God created eye shadow . . . to emphasize the color of your eyes. I believe in keeping it really simple —sticking to one or two shades. Your eyelid isn't a canvas for an abstract expressionist painting, so why pile on a huge eruption of colors that will only call so much attention to your eye shadow that nobody will even notice the shape and color of your eyes?

How to Choose It

Eyeshadow is available in creams, liquids, and creamy, pressed powders. The creams and liquids blend well with the eyelid but might crease with time. Eyeshadows differ markedly in consistency; also, once on, they may look quite different from how they looked in that fancy container—so, again, sample *before* you buy.

Never use a shadow that matches either the color of your eyes or the outfit you're wearing. If you have green eyes and wear a bright green shadow, it's going to be hard to see the true color of your eyes. According to François, whose business it is to know everyone's facial weaknesses, the color of shadow that is most flattering to you is the one *opposite* to your eye color on the color spectrum. The opposite, or contradictory, or complementary color of blue, for example, is

—for Cover Girl. My New York family

yellow, brown, or orange, and François often uses a gold, almost orange shadow on blue eyes. By the same token, brown eyes look great with gray or purple shadow, and green or hazel eyes with purple or pink.

If you take the trouble to examine the iris of your eye closely in a hand mirror, you won't see just one color there, but many—specks of brown, gold, gray, mauve. Select one of these secondary colors and use it as a guide. Eyeshadow was meant to live up to its name, to create a shadow rather than an actual color on your lid. The neutral shades like brown, gray, and mauve, come in a wide variety of colors: gray, for instance, can be gray-mauve, pale silver gray, green-gray, blue-gray, or charcoal gray. And brown can be russet, coppery, or gray-brown.

MASCARA

Mascara is one of the cosmetics that can make the most difference in how you look. It not only emphasizes but deepens the eyes, giving them a dark, expressive quality. I brush-pat on a light coat for daytime and apply extra coats for evening.

How to Use It

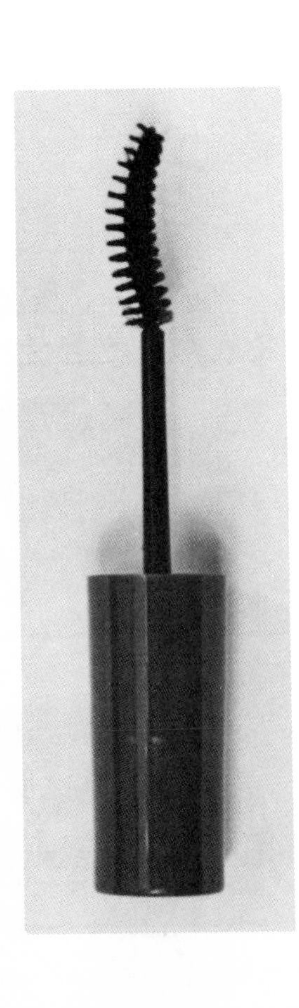

The secret of applying mascara is to brush on a thin coat, from the base of your lashes to the tip, and let it dry completely. Don't "dump" the wand into the applicator, it'll only make it wet and gooey—and be sure it isn't loaded with gobs of mascara that will end up under your eyes. I really prefer a slightly older mascara, because the liquid inside is drier and easier to handle. If you're applying several coats, wait till each one dries before putting on the next. After your mascara is all dry, separate the lashes with a small brush —a child's toothbrush is perfect for this—unless you want your lashes clumped together in artificial-looking, artery-hardening spikes. That look went out of the window with Mary Poppins.

How to Choose It

A good mascara will go on smoothly and won't leave little flakes on your lashes, or clump them together, or go gallivanting to other parts of the eye area. It will come off easily, too. The most modern type is the wand and tube which allows them quantity and consistency control, but some women like the old-fashioned cake and brush. The most natural-looking color is black, or dark brown for a slightly softer look. The colored mascaras can be too obvious and anyway don't add enough depth to the eye. One thing: you have to be prepared to buy a new mascara every six months, because older ones can carry infection-forming bacteria.

EYEBROW PENCIL

Don't look startled when I say that very few women *need* an eyebrow pencil. If you've tweezed your eyebrows into an attractive shape, they shouldn't have to be darkened with any pencil. The experts feel that your brows should be a shade lighter than your hair color, and they recommend bleaching brows that are so dark they overpower face and eyes. I seldom use the pencil. I have pale eyebrows, and occasionally I feather a few light lines into them. If your eyebrows are sparse, buy a soft-colored pencil (never a black one), or a powder, or consider having your brows tweezed by a professional. But easy-does-it, don't tweeze those eyebrows out of existence. And never extend your eyebrow line out toward your temple, Fu-Manchu style, unless you're planning to audition for a part in a Far Eastern flick.

LIPSTICK AND LIP GLOSS

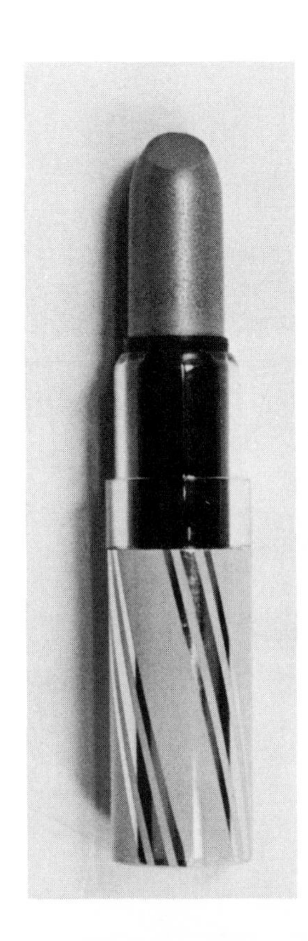

You may think that this is odd coming from a professional model *but:* I hardly ever wear lipstick. Most of the lipstick in my cosmetic kit I use for model assignments only. I use just a touch of natural or pink lipgloss to make my lips shiny and moist and to balance out the colors on my face. A lot of lipstick can look pretty snazzy but you run the risk of overemphasizing your mouth, making it look hard, or painted like a clown's (though probably not as friendly).

How to Use Them

Apply lip color with a lipstick brush, and you can control the density of the color and where it goes—also, the lip color stays on longer. Then blend into your lips. And buy the small, squarish hardibrush, made especially with lipstick in mind. When you smear on lipstick or gloss with a tube or with your finger, you inevitably find it's escaped, gotten outside the contours of your lips. In fact, it's usually all over your fingers, and this is one case where you *don't* want to let your fingers do the talking!

How to Choose Them

Lip color should blend with your skin tone. And unlike eye color and cheek color, it should take its cue partly from the colors you are wearing. Who would ever want to wear mauve or orange lipstick with a bright red blouse? Most women can wear several different shades of lip color. Almost anyone can wear a clear red in a modern sheer lipstick or gloss. Fair-skinned women look good in pink-toned lip colors; women with sallow skin can wear colors in the peach-to-brown range. But always remember, what looks good in the tube or on someone else might not look so good on you, because your skin chemistry changes the color of the lipstick once it's on your lips.

HIGHLIGHTING CREAMS

They're great fun for evening: they emphasize your bones and add some excitement to your face. I apply a pearly white, almost translucent cream to my cheekbones and to the bone beneath my eyebrows. Sometimes I use a mauve, iridescent cream blended right into my skin so I don't get that garish, clown-like effect. Highlighters are available in pencil and in cream and liquid.

THREE TIME-SAVING MAKEUP LOOKS

Once you've selected cosmetics in the colors and textures that become you and, most important, learned how to get the most out of them and make them work for you, the actual application should take only a few minutes. Here are three sure-fire step-by-step formulas for applying makeup. Please follow my instructions in detail.

C.T.'s 10-Minute Natural Makeup Look

1. After you have your moisturizer on, apply a base lightly to your face and neck with your fingertips.
2. Apply an eyeliner just above your upper lashes and below your lower lashes with eyeliner pencil in a soft, muted shade. Blend with your fingertip.
3. Apply one light coat of mascara and let it dry.
4. Apply a cream or liquid cheek color to your cheekbones and blend out toward your temples.
5. Apply a natural or pale lipstick or gloss. Before you leave the house, check your makeup in natural light from the window to make sure your base is on

evenly and the colors you've applied have blended well. This subtle, no-makeup look not only adds a little color to your face, but heightens your natural coloring.

C.T.'s 15-Minute Evening Makeup Look

1. Apply the base as in the 10-minute makeup look. Don't pile on twice as much just because the sun's gone down. Let the sun be always on your cheeks, let your skin show through.
2. Line your eyes with a dark-colored pencil, above the lash line and below the lower lashes.
3. Apply a pressed powder eyeshadow from your eyelashes to beneath your eyebrow. Now shade your eyelid, from corner to corner, with a darker shadow (brown, gray, mauve). You may want to extend the shadow beyond the corner of your eye and blend it into the skin. Blend with a brush or your fingertip, so no line of the powder can be seen. ("The art that conceals art"—remember?)
4. Apply one coat of mascara and let it dry. Then apply another coat.
5. Apply a powdered blusher with a large sable brush, and blend thoroughly.
6. Apply a colored lip gloss or a sheer lipstick.
7. Dust with a translucent powder before you leave the house.

C.T.'s 20-Minute Makeup for Glamorous Nights

1. Apply the makeup base as above.
2. Apply eyeshadow as in the 15-minute makeup exercise, possibly a tad more.
3. Add a bit of gold eyeshadow or a shimmery copper or silver to the middle of your eyelid, lightly around the eye.
4. Apply eyeliner as in 15-minute makeup exercise, using a deep shade of blue or a dark charcoal.
5. Apply two or three coats of mascara. Let each coat dry completely before you apply the next—separating the lashes with a brush if necessary. Be sure to get every lash—the ones at the corner of the eye are important, too.
6. Apply a powdered blusher in a couple of shades; use the more intense color for night lighting.
7. Add just a touch of magenta or white highlighting cream to your eyebone and cheekbone and blend thoroughly. This is the step that really gives you a romantic evening look!

8. Now apply a bright shade of lipstick (clear red, pink, mauve, or coral). Add a clear lip gloss.
9. Dust your whole face with translucent powder.

MAKEUP TECHNIQUES FOR EXTRA GLAMOUR

For the purest, richest glamour—glamour to spare, glamour to bathe in—try the following (but not all of them at once, please—one or two at a time should do the trick).

1. Line the inside of your eye, just above the lashes, with a deep-colored pencil—navy blue, deep purple. This will make the color and shape of your eyes stand out like headlights.
2. If you have any clothes that are electric blue, bright green, or magenta, add a *dot* of the same color eyeshadow to the middle of your eyelid or the corner of your eye, and blend slightly.
3. Shade the center of your lower lip with a deeper color.
4. Add a touch of color glow liquid in pink, mauve, gold, or bronze to your usual base.
5. Instead of ordinary translucent powder, use a fine gold or silver powder to dust your face.

When you apply makeup, if possible use a mirror lighted from both sides. Light coming from above, or from one side only, is going to illuminate only one side of your face, and as a result you may make the mistake of applying more makeup to one half than the other. The key thing to remember about night makeup: don't put it on thicker and darker so that nothing of your real face shines through the cracks and you can't find your way back to it. It's the bits of sparkle that make the difference here.

OUTWITTING YOUR FLAWS

Some say that makeup can successfully conceal flaws. Sorry but I just don't believe that the flaws in a person's face can be blotted out by cosmetics. (*Modified*, yes.) If you opt for elaborate shading to "fix" a crooked nose, or cover your eyes with tons of shadow in the forlorn hope of changing their shape, or line your lips with a vivid pencil trying to change their natural curve, take my word for it—I've been there—you'll only succeed in making yourself—and everyone else! —*more* conscious of the so-called flaw.

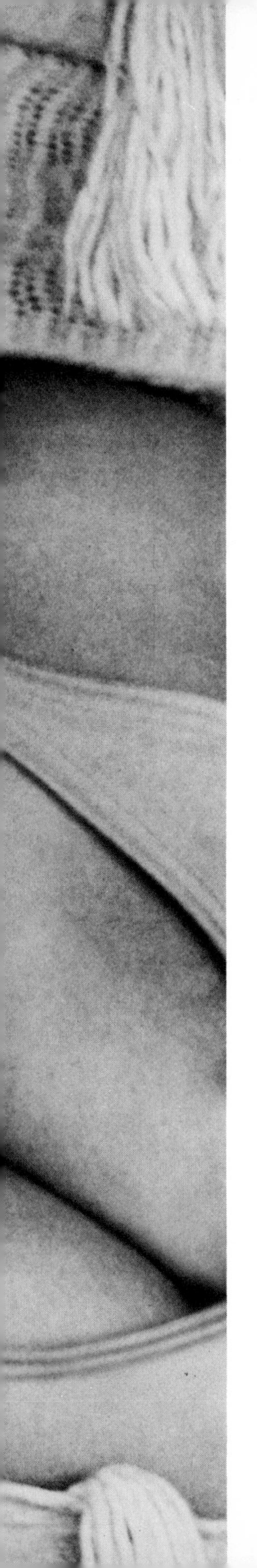

Moreover, you will probably botch the job, and make your skin look all muddy or uneven. I can't say it often enough, here goes: you don't want people to notice your makeup, you want them to notice your face! I confess to having shaded the sides of my nose with brown powder to make it look "stronger" in a photograph, but I've done this in the line of "duty": little sculpting tricks that work for the camera—helping you to create the kind of look you want that feature to have in the final photograph—in real life register loud and clear (and thick) as makeup. I've noticed that women tend to single out a feature on their face and judge it *too* harshly. Often the feature they happen to dislike is not a "flaw," it's just unusual or different (it may even add something to their face). If you think your face has a "flaw," try looking at it in a less trivial and self-conscious light, and from a new perspective —in combination with your other features.

For those who do decide to try a little trick to improve a feature, here's a list of some simple makeup techniques of mine which really do work and better yet, don't involve a great deal of shading, sketching, or contouring. Just keep in mind that dark shading makes an area recede while light shading emphasizes it.

Concealing Dark Shadows Beneath the Eyes

The best shadow-concealing technique I know is also the simplest: apply a light coat of your usual makeup base to the dark area—if you use a lighter concealing stick, make sure you use it subtly, and blend carefully so you don't have an obvious white area. You have to realize that it's impossible to conceal any shadow completely. Lining your eyes beneath the lower lashes with a gray, brown, or steel-dark blue eye pencil, will deflect attention from the circle.

Small Eyes

To make your eyes look bigger, begin your liner in the middle of the upper lid and extend it to the outside corner, and repeat this process below the lower lashes. (The line should be thin and subtle.) Curl your lashes with an eyelash curler. Apply mascara very sparingly; use a smoky shadow in the crease on the lid. Be extra-careful not to load down your eyes with the dead, dead weight of too much makeup, which will hide and annihilate them.

Wide-Set Eyes

If you want to bring them a bit closer together, start your shadow at the corner by your nose and extend it along the crease. Apply mascara most heavily to the lashes closest to your nose. Don't over-emphasize the part of your eyebrow closest to the nose, and don't extend the browline in that direction—leave the eyebrows natural!

Close-Set Eyes

To make close-set eyes look further apart, accent the outer corners by beginning your shadow at the middle of the lid and extending it past the corner of the eye. Now blend. Apply several coats of mascara to the lashes closest to the outside corner of the eye.

A Wide Forehead

I have one, and I minimize it by shading along the hairline (both sides and top).

A Wide Jawline

If your jawline is too wide or "strong," you can minimize it by brushing both sides of your jaw with blush-on and then blending.

A Narrow Jawline

To emphasize your jawline, brush it with a light powder.

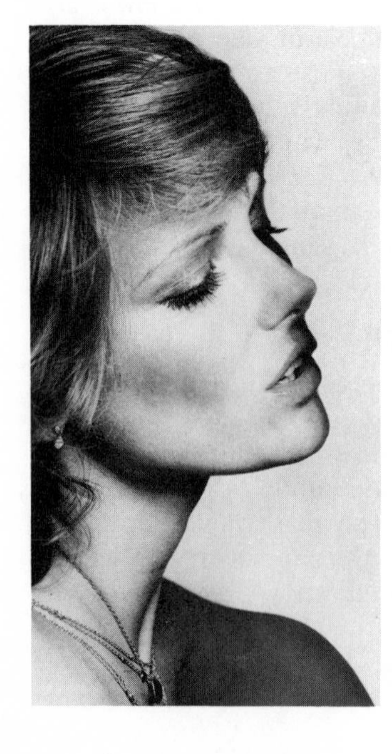

Imperfect Lips

A line drawn around the lips with a pencil can make you look iron-hard. If you do use a pencil, select one that's almost the same color as your lips—and blend carefully so you can't see a line when you're finished. The color of the lipstick or gloss you choose can do a lot for the shape of your lips. If your mouth is wide, use a light, sheer gloss or lipstick, and apply sparingly. Don't emphasize the outer edges of your lips. If they're thin, stay away from frosted shades of lipstick. (Come to think of it, everyone should avoid frosted shades of lipstick.) And too much lipstick, unless it's applied with great skill, can make thin lips look even thinner.

Hidden Cheekbones

If your cheekbones aren't high or prominent enough to suit you, put an accent above the cheekbone with a light highlighting cream, and blend well, then place your blush or rouge just below the bone and extend it out toward the temple.

Blemishes

Don't try to hide a blemish—you'll only arouse suspicion. Just apply your regular makeup base, and dab a little extra on the blemish, along with the tiniest bit of concealing stick or special blemish cream. I've found that powder helps dry up a blemish faster than any liquid base does. Be very careful when you brush the powder on that you don't brush away the base and the concealer.

Sallow, Pale, or Ruddy Skin

If your skin is an unhealthy color, it's trying to tell you something—like go get some fresh air and exercise! You can liven up pale or sallow skin another, less strenuous way. Use a pink-tinted color-glow foundation instead of your usual base, or brush a neutral shade of blusher on the tip of your chin, forehead, and cheekbones. If you're sunburned, or if your skin is on the ruddy side, use an ivory-colored base over an aqua or green-tinted liquid foundation to neutralize your skin tone.

MAKING THE MOST OF YOUR MAKEUP

Keeping Makeup Where It Belongs

If your lipstick has a tendency to disappear or run, apply a light base coat of foundation before you add any lip color. If your eye makeup also tends to slip away or crease on your lid, apply a base coat of foundation and a bit of powder to your eyelids as well. Some cosmetics companies sell a neutral eyelid foundation especially designed to provide a secure base for eye color. Brushing a little translucent powder over your lashes will help keep the mascara in place and make your lashes look thicker.

Refreshing Tired Makeup

If your makeup gets "tired," as it is apt to during a night on the town, you can refresh it with minimal effort and equipment. What I do is blot my base with a damp tissue or cloth to remove some of the shine, then moisten a Q-tip and dab away any specks of mascara or eyeshadow that have landed beneath my eyes; then I freshen the eyeshadow and blush-on, brighten my eyes with eyedrops, add a touch of extra lip gloss, and *presto magico!* I feel and look like new. Unless you have world enough and time, taking all your makeup off and putting it on again can leave your eyes and face red from all the rubbing and pulling. Besides, makeup always looks better when it's had a chance to settle and soak in.

Achieving with the Bare-Minimum Look

If I'm off to the beach or tennis courts and want to add some shine to my face without going to all the trouble of putting on actual makeup, I just apply a sunscreen and a shiny lip protection stick.

Treating Yourself to the Tea-Bag Treatment

If you've over-indulged yourself, or are under a great deal of stress, with the usual accompaniment of sleepless nights, telltale sacks and bags will begin to make an appearance under your eyes. This is, as the Austrians like to say, "serious but not hopeless" (rather than "hopeless but not serious," which the Germans like to say).

I have a good home remedy for the "Puffs." I lie down, put my feet up, and cover my eyes with wet tea bags (any brand will do). The tannic acid in the tea acts as an astringent, has a soothing effect on the eyes, and reduces the swelling. The tea-bag treatment also calms me down, helps me get back onto myself and away from whatever generated those nasty puffs in the first place. (The alternative is getting your personality to conform to the puffs, and I don't think you want to do that.)

Battling the Fluorescent Lights

Many offices and public places are guilty of the bad taste of having fluorescent lighting that drains the color from people's faces and makes them look sickly, if not actually moribund. If you have to spend a lot of time under such lights, use warm colors in cosmetics —red, orange, and golden tones (pinks are out because, surprisingly, they contain blues, as do certain wines and mauves). Experiment with using a foundation in a deeper shade than usual. Also, apply your makeup under a—shudder!—fluorescent light, so you'll know just how it's going to look.

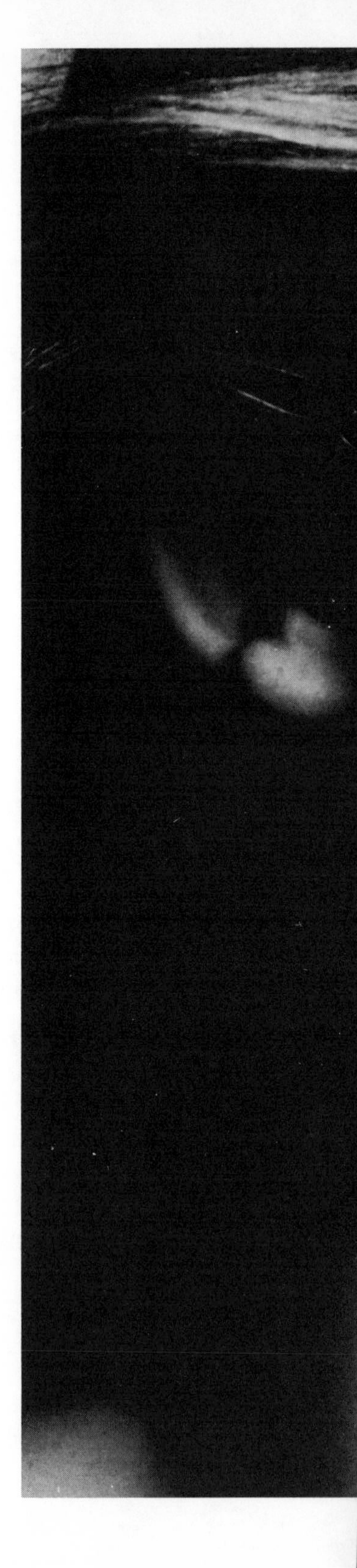

Giving Yourself the Deep Frost

One of the best ways to use a frosted shade of eyeshadow, lipstick, or cheek color is to use it *underneath* a matte shade. This disposition will give the matte some depth and that longed-for sparkle.

MISTAKES PEOPLE MAKE WITH MAKEUP

Not Blending or Checking

The single biggest mistake you can make with makeup is not blending it into your skin. The result is hard lines and great gobs of color that don't look like they belong on your face. Always take that extra second or two to smudge your eyeliner with your fingertip and blend your makeup base, cheek color, and eyeshadow. Also, check your makeup in different kinds of lighting to make sure it still looks natural.

Piling It on Under Glass

Don't put extra makeup on your eyes just because you happen to wear glasses. Make up your eyes as subtly as you do the rest of your face. Overdoing it won't make your glasses disappear or your eyes stand out more.

Over-tweezing Eyebrows

Once upon a time, an over-eager makeup artist tweezed my eyebrows down to a two-hairline. "You'll thank me for this," he said. (He might better have said, "Years from now when you write about this, and you will, be kind.") But when I saw my no-eyebrow look in the mirror, I burst into tears for the first time since I hit the scales at 150. Eyebrows should neither dominate your face nor be totally invisible. The danger of over-tweezing for a long period of time is that the hairs may never grow back. To keep the shape of your eyebrows natural, tweeze only underneath and neaten up the middle between the brows. And pull in the direction the hair grows; this may hurt a little, so you'll want to use a cream, both before and after.

Not Removing Makeup Before Turning in

We all get lazy, but don't worry, we pay for it. Go to bed with your eyes loaded down with shadow and mascara and your skin covered with blusher and base, and you'll wake up looking like the sergeant's mess (eye makeup smeared on cheeks, and puffy swollen eyes, and skin that never even got a chance to breathe).

Applying Bilious Blue and Green Gage Eyeshadow

These outdated bright shades will completely mask the color of your eyes. If you can't bring yourself to toss your blue and green shadows in the wastepaper basket, where they belong, try combining them with charcoal grays or browns, which will at least tone them down, if not neutralize them.

Not Concentrating

When you put on your makeup, concentrate! Forget how late you are for work or what's for breakfast. If your mind is wandering, you may mistakenly use a rouge-covered fingertip to blend your eyeshadow, or smear your lipstick, or brush on your blusher where it doesn't belong. Work carefully: wash or wipe your hands when necessary, use the right tools, do yourself up, do yourself proud. Outdo yourself.

Making Like "The Dragon Lady"

Never draw a slanted line past the corner of your eyes with eyeliner—it will make you look bestial and predatory. It's okay to extend the liner slightly beyond the corner of your eye, but be sure to smudge the line with your finger so there's only a slight shadow.

Experimenting at the Next-to-Last Minute

Get to know your face and makeup before the crucial moment comes when you have to put the two together for the outside world. Your spare time is the time to fool around with new makeup techniques and products. If you do botch your makeup before an important occasion, don't fall apart and try to repair the mistake by applying even more makeup. Just go back to your tried-and-true basic ways.

There's no excuse in this day and age for not looking your best. As the great French writer Colette wrote in *Earthly Paradise:* "Where are those rouges of yesteryear, with their harsh red currant tints, those ungrateful whites, those Virgin Mary blues? We now have a range of tints at our disposal that would go to the head of a painter." Right on!

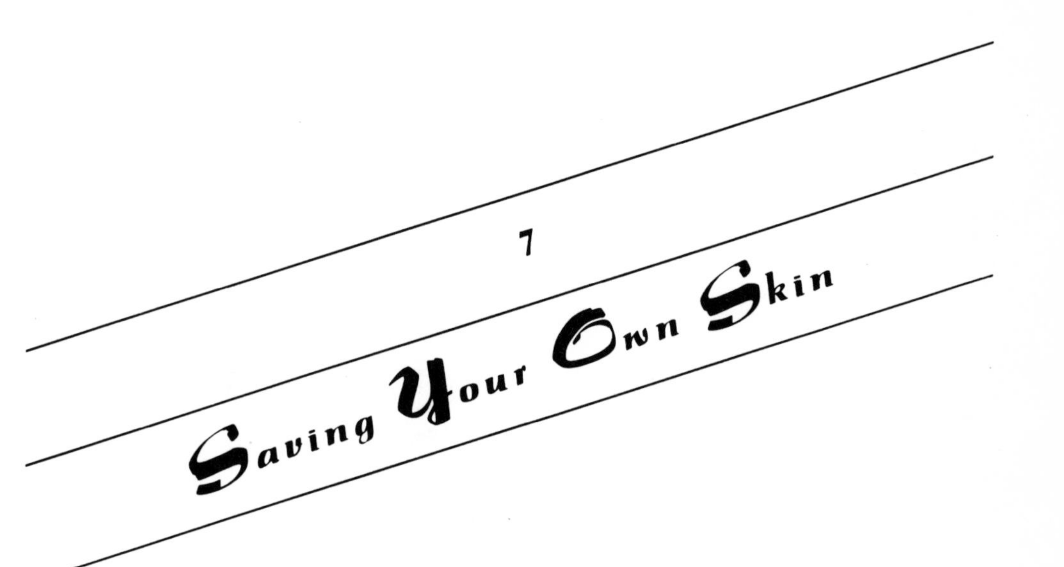

7

Saving Your Own Skin

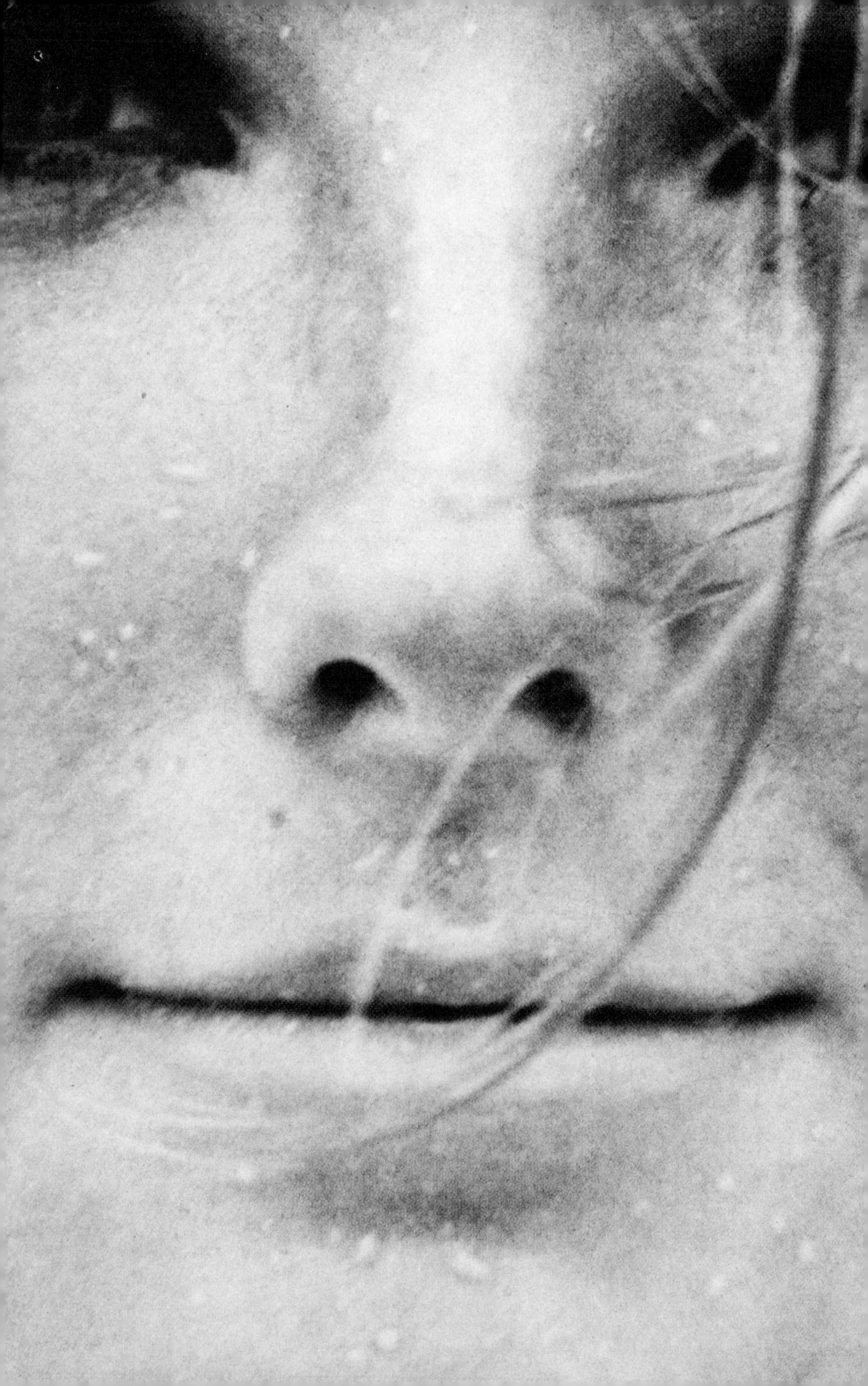

he skin is the only organ we possess that's ever on public display. Among other things, this miraculous envelope regulates body temperature and employs its network of delicate nerves as sentinels for both pleasure and pain. As such, skin can tell us what's happening inside and outside our bodies. It reflects our diet, the amount of exercise we get, our health habits (good and bad), our age, hormonal balance, heredity—and—not least of all—emotional state. In fact, it's the multiplicity of factors influencing the way our skin looks that makes it disobedient to our little tricks and most ardent ministrations. No wonder few of us find ourselves with the skin we would ideally like to have—soft, even-toned, blemish-free, aglow with the color of life. (Some of us aren't very comfortable in our own skins—the French have a wonderful way of expressing this: *On n'est pas bien dans sa peau*," they say. But that's another story.)

Every woman wants a beautiful complexion, but to achieve it she must be prepared to work. She may be more inclined to do so if she recalls that it is her skin that stands between her and the world.

Skin may not be deep, but it *is* sensitive; it needs to be nourished, stimulated, and protected. The first step is to analyze your skin type. Sift through the wealth of information available about skin care, appropriating the facts that apply to you and discarding the others. Then experiment intelligently with the many skin products on the market.

How much *do* you know about your own skin? Mark the following ten statements "true" or "false," and you'll have some idea.

■ *Creams and moisturizers prevent wrinkles.*

■ *Damage to the epidermis caused by excessive sunbathing eventually heals.*

■ *Baby oil helps protect your skin from the sun.*

■ *A woman's skin can be classified as oily, dry, or "normal." More than fifty percent of the female population has "normal" skin.*

■ *Women with oily skin should not use moisturizers.*

■ *There is basically no difference between an astringent and a freshening lotion.*

■ *Acne is not affected by diet.*

■ *"Blackheads" are a sign that you are not washing your face enough.*

■ *The benefits of a skin masque are primarily psychological.*

■ *You should bathe or shower at least once a day.*

Every single one of the above statements is false. Now let's find out why.

THE IMPORTANCE OF SKIN CARE

When I was a formless teenager (or, in the poet Robert Lowell's beautiful phrase, "back in my shaggy throw-away of adolescence"), even when I didn't have actual blemishes, my skin was dry and flaky. As you know by now, I sweetened puberty for myself by means of all kinds of unjust desserts and junk food. It was no big shock to me when I put on weight; what *was* shocking was that the bad food was damaging my skin as well as my figure.

I never really bothered much about my skin. I would spend an entire day in the photographer's studio, piling on acres of makeup, and then go right out to dinner with friends, after which, if it was a typical evening, I'd be far too tired to wash off all the foundation, powder, rouge, etcetera. I'd just fall into bed grateful for the pillow's soft, obliterating white. I would give my face a thorough cleaning once a day only, when I took my morning shower, and I would use the same strong soap on it as I did on the rest of my body. Afterwards, my face would feel taut, dry, and stretched, and I thought that this was exactly how it *should* feel and that *I* didn't need to use a drop of moisturizer. What arrogance! What ignorance! No wonder my skin was dry!!

Sometimes at a party I would notice that my all-day mascara had slipped down beneath my eyes. I'd then try removing the black specks by dabbing at them indiscriminately with a soapy Kleenex; and after this, I wouldn't even bother to rinse the drying soap away. In the years that have passed since then, I have learned that skin is far more vulnerable than ever I imagined —particularly the skin under the eyes.

I never had acne—thank God, because a mere pimple was enough to throw me off balance. When I began posing for magazine covers, I discovered how photographers' close-up lenses and bright lights heartlessly reveal flaws in even the most perfect complexions. "Flaws," I call them—well, I always loved a euphemism. Joseph Conrad called them "grogblossoms" (at least in his great novel, *Youth*, he did). But of course your classmates always called them pimples or, worse, "zits." The photographers assured me that they could retouch the blemishes, and sure enough, they had all been airbrushed away by the final photographic print. However, it was beyond any photographer's power to make them disappear from my face. It never occurred to me that my terrible diet and the lack of attention I was giving my skin (negligence may be a more honest description) had much of anything to do with these flaws. I sort of assumed that the people with forever clear skin were just lucky and that the rest of us, in varying degrees, weren't. It was easy to lay it all on fate, and go back to grimly covering my face with makeup and hoping the spots would fade away.

One day a friend, another model, took me aside and gently—kindly—suggested I see a cosmetician. He in turn gave me special products and worked up a skin-cleaning routine for me to practice at home. Loaded down with special soaps and multicolored lotions, and resenting the expense of the visit, I went sulking back to my apartment. But for the first time in my life I began to give my skin the attention it needed and deserved. Nobody was more surprised than I was when it began to clear. From having been worked on so consistently, my face at first was very dry, but little by little the texture improved and the blemishes disappeared. My whole face felt softer and smoother. It was like a grace.

I remember how, soon after this, I caught sight of my reflection in a store window and doubled back to take a second look. I couldn't believe that this lucky stranger with the clear skin was me. It was about this time that I went on the diet to which I owe my dramatic weight loss. At last I was on the verge of being on good physical terms with myself. Talk about castles in the sky!

Blemished skin, oily skin, dry skin, "muddy" skin with unhealthy-looking shadows, diddy-daddied skin,

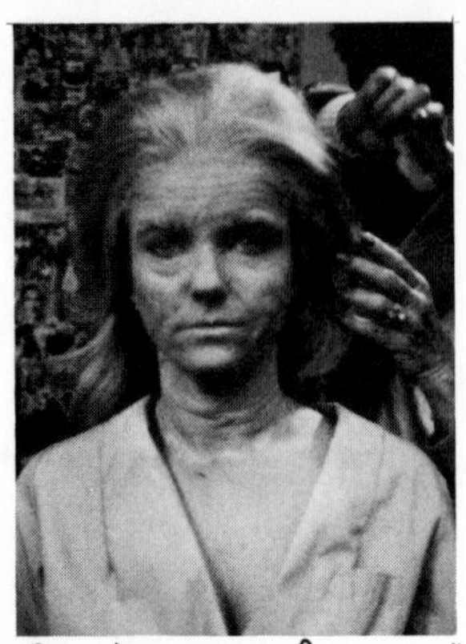

"Good Morning America" ...80 years old in 7½ hours...

and sallow skin all respond very positively to the following *natural* practices:

■ *Proper cleansing, toning, and moisturizing with products designed for your type of skin.*

■ *Treatment of blemishes—with professional help when necessary.*

■ *Deep-cleansing facials.*

■ *Good diet, exercise, and plenty of rest.*

■ *Regulated exposure to the sun.*

But first things first.

DIAGNOSING YOUR SKIN TYPE

This may be more difficult than it sounds, because you can't permanently "typecast" your skin. Oily skin, for example, may become drier in winter when it's exposed to blasts of both central heating and cold air, and even oilier in summer. When I was working in Africa on my ABC-TV special, my ordinarily dry skin got drier and drier. Stress, a change of environment, changes in hormone levels, a new diet, pregnancy, use of medication, menopause, and the whole process of aging (which is, alas, often quite independent of the calendar), can transform your skin for better or worse—it's all something of a lottery, at the mercy of more things than even dermatologists can fathom. I know of practically no one over the age of twelve who has skin that is never tarnished by blemishes, dry flakes, or traces of oil. If your skin looks "normal" most of the time, it's got to be because you are successfully protecting it and keeping it properly nourished.

Now: What skin type *are* you?

Dry skin usually feels "tight" or "taut" for hours after you've washed it. It's also marked by flakes, causing makeup to congeal in the dry areas—to the extent that, if your skin is very dry, it may almost hurt when you smile. (But don't not smile!) Dry skin is usually marked by superficial lines as well. It chaps quickly and may even "crack" in cold weather, and in the sun it burns, baby, burns. On the bright side, it's often so finely textured that you can't even see the pores.

Oily skin generally takes on a greasy shine shortly after being washed; when you touch it with your fin-

gers, it feels all "slick." It also absorbs makeup, sometimes even changing the color of it. Blackheads, whiteheads, and pimples seem to gravitate to oily skin with its enlarged pores. Oily skin can be dull and, above all, flaky (which is great if you're a piecrust but not so great if you're a human). Surprisingly, oily skin is often mistaken for dry skin, and thus incorrectly treated. The flakes, especially if they're accompanied by raised red spots, are sometimes caused by an inflammation called "seborrheic dermatitis." (This condition calls for a dermatologist and plenty of cortisone cream.) A plus factor is that, because oily skin by definition provides its own lubrication, it's not so susceptible to developing fine lines.

Combination skin is just that: oily and dry, or normal in some areas and dry or oily in others. The really oily areas are the nose, forehead and chin.

CLEANSING, TONING, AND MOISTURIZING (OR C.T.'S GUARANTEED C-T-M REGIMEN)

Whatever skin type you have must be cleansed, toned, and moisturized daily. This routine will vary slightly according to skin type, and will take only a few minutes a day. If your skin is still too dry and lifeless, or too oily, or too *anything*, the products you're using are the wrong ones for you—or else your skin has done a number and changed. Most skins, however, will respond to careful handling. Just don't expect the major changes to occur overnight! If you don't have confidence in your own ability to diagnose your skin type or to find the right products, pay a visit to a cosmetician, as I did. The initial investment may be irritatingly high, but you'll ultimately save money you'd otherwise waste on a lot of probably useless experiments with the wrong products.

Cleansing

Dry Skin. Dry skin should be cleansed in the morning to remove the impurities it's accumulated during sleep, and at night to remove those it's accumulated during the day. Many women with dry skin are afraid that cleansing their faces with soap and water will just dry them out more. A mild soap, dermatologists agree, is the best emulsifier of dirt and oil; water is what moisturizes the skin from within and should not be avoided at any cost. Dry-skinned women must be especially careful about choosing the right soap, such as superfatted soap containing olive oil, or a fine oatmeal soap. Transparent soaps with a glycerin base should be avoided, as they may contain drying alcohol and in any case aren't as gentle as they're reputed to be. Like many other women with delicate skin, I prefer to use a special cleansing lotion. Most of these lotions contain a very mild soap (make sure yours doesn't contain alcohol). Some cleansing agents require rinsing with lukewarm water. To avoid irritation, don't wash your face just before you go outside in winter.

How to Wash. Massage the soap or cleansing lotion into your skin with circular motions of your fingertips. The drier and more delicate your skin is, the more gently you should massage.

Oily Skin. Oily skin needs to be washed more often than dry skin—as much as three or four times a day. The best cleanser is a soap containing a small quantity of sulphur, alcohol, or salicylic acid. People with very oily or blemish-prone skin often prefer a cleansing grain, which is a soap composed of tiny, abrasive particles that are very effective in unclogging oily pores. There are also some cleansing lotions on the market that are especially geared to oily skin. Rinse your face thoroughly—some cosmeticians recommend twenty to thirty splashes of water (warm, not hot, as hot water may stimulate oil flow instead of stanching it).

Combination Skin. The cleansing agent you use should depend, naturally, on your particular combination. Many cleansing lotions and soaps were concocted for normal or oily skin, and they might just be your best bet. A cleansing grain, or epidermabrading agent, you'll probably want to save mostly for oily areas.

Toning

A toning lotion will rid your skin of the impurities that are left after you've worked with a cleansing agent or water; it stimulates circulation in your skin, trims the top layer of cells, and tightens your pores (temporarily).

Dry Skin. Dry skin should be toned with a mild skin-freshening lotion that does *not* contain alcohol. Apply with a cotton pad.

Oily Skin. Oily skin is best toned with an astringent lotion with a slight alcohol base. If this proves too harsh, switch to a freshening lotion with no alcohol whatsoever. Wipe the astringent onto the skin firmly with a cotton pad.

Combination Skin. Combination skin can be well served by two toners—one without alcohol for the dry areas, and one with alcohol for the oily T-zone. If you use only one toner, go the teetotalling way: no alcohol!

Moisturizing

Creams and moisturizers don't actually add moisture to your skin; what they do is seal in the skin's natural water so it won't evaporate. They also help the skin retain the oils produced by the skin glands. They lubricate the skin and though they can't prevent wrinkles, they fill in tiny lines and soften the edges; and finally they form a film protecting the skin from harsh pollutants and inclement weather.

Dry Skin. Dry skin all but cries out for a moisturizer. Make it a point to apply a light-textured moisturizer once or twice during the day, and a heavier cream at night.

Oily Skin. To moisturize or not to moisturize: that is the question for cosmeticians. I believe that every skin should be moisturized, if only for protective purposes. If your skin is oily, select your moisturizer with great care—a heavy, oily moisturizer may further block your pores and cause unsightly flare-ups. Some cosmetics companies feature lotions that blot the oil while they soften the skin and protect it from the environment. I certainly don't advise heavy night creams for oily skin.

Combination Skin. This type of skin needs a little extra attention. The dry areas may have to be moisturized more often and with a different product from the one you use on oily areas.

Applying Moisturizer. No matter what type of skin you have, applying too much moisturizer is as bad as applying none at all. There is only so much that even a moisturizer can do, so don't go putting on thick layers in the mistaken belief that "more is better." Tiny dabs, applied with a circular motion, will blend the moisturizer more evenly into your skin.

Moisturizing Your Eyes. The area around the eyes has no oil glands and should therefore definitely be moisturized. I dab a special eye cream around my eyes each night—very carefully, so the cream doesn't ooze into my eyes while I'm sleeping (I don't want to wake up with puffy lids). Don't rub or pull on the very delicate skin around the eyes—wrinkles, sags, and long-term stretches are lying in wait for you.

THE ORIGIN OF ACNE—AND SOME NEW HOPE

Acne (I even hate the *sound* of the word) is the result of the malfunctioning of the thousands of oil glands near the hair follicles, which produce too much oil or "sebum." Oil normally escapes through pores; in acne-prone skin, however, the cells that line the oil ducts build up, stick together, and block the flow of excess oil. The trapped oil then forms a microscopic whitehead below the surface of the skin, where the bacteria in the pores can act on it. When this plug of oil, bacteria, and cells pushes its way to the surface of the skin, it oxidizes in the air and turns black. It's a common belief that "blackheads" are caused by inadequate cleansing, but this just isn't so—they represent a mild form of acne, beginning below the skin surface. Luckily, you can squeeze them out fairly easily or sometimes simply wash them off. If the plug is embedded deep in the pore, it may become enlarged and infected, and eventually break through the wall of the pore to inflame the surrounding tissue. The result is an eye-ravaging "swollen cyst" or blemish that causes so many people such—up till now—*cureless* suffering.

Dermatologists now believe that acne is caused by an excess of androgen, a male hormone that to some extent is also present in women. Androgen enlarges the oil glands, spurring them to overproduce. Which is why blemishes are most common during puberty, the time when hormone levels change. Many women have been known to experience flare-ups during their menstrual period, when their hormones are particularly active, and when they begin taking—or stop taking—birth control pills, which contain hormones. Some people break out when they're under stress or when they travel, or when they don't get enough rest, or, according to at least one school of thought, when they eat certain foods. A tendency toward acne is also thought to be hereditary. Whatever—dermatologists now report that more and more adult women are having problems with it.

Recently scientists from the National Cancer Institute discovered that variations of a synthetic derivative of Vitamin A, called synthetic retinoids, in addition to inhibiting the growth of cancer, are able to "drastically reduce the production of sebum in oil glands." Testing thus far has been extremely encouraging—producing very few side effects. It may be a while yet before a cure for acne is developed and marketed—but stay tuned.

THE ROLE OF DIET

Dermatologists used to single out various foods as causes of acne. They advised patients to stop eating nuts, citrus fruits, shellfish, chocolate, you name it. Recent experiments have proved that diet has little or no effect on acne (with the possible exception of some foods containing iodine). Still, it's a good idea to swear off those foods that you've noticed are directly associated with your breaking out.

Nutritionists, on the other hand, have concluded that a junk-food diet, heavy on sugar and refined foods, will definitely aid and abet bad skin. From experience, I tend to agree. Dermatologists freely (or is that the wrong word to use about these very expensive specialists?) admit that they don't know exactly what causes abnormal hormone activity, or why some people's skins are more sensitive to androgen than other people's. Everybody knows by now that what we eat affects our entire bodies, right down to our glandular and hormonal secretions; in a sense by no means unironic, we *are* what we eat. For example, when we consume too much refined sugar, the pancreas reacts by producing too much of the hormone insulin, and the result can be as drastic as diabetes and hypoglycemia! So when a dermatologist tells you it's okay to eat peanuts and chocolate, that it won't aggravate your acne, you should ask yourself if he's taking into account that you may have been overloading your body with doughnuts, ice cream, white bread, Coca-Cola, and fried chicken since you were *three years old*.

I don't care what the experts say, I still think that if you suffer from bad skin, you owe it to yourself—and to others, who have to look at you—to immediately eliminate as much sugar, refined flour, nuts, fatty meats such as pork and beef, fried foods, and rich dairy products from your diet as you can stand—for at least three months, let's say. If your skin still doesn't improve, at least your figure, digestion, and general health are bound to. But don't be disappointed when you don't wake up the morning after all clear and purified—the toxins from the unhealthy foods you've been eating have been building up in your system for years.

My skin improved dramatically thanks to a modeling assignment I was on in Portugal with *Bride's* magazine when I was nineteen. The hotel we were staying in didn't have a single dessert on the menu that appealed to me (that's hard to imagine, since by now you know that all desserts appealed to me), and for three weeks I was forced to eat healthy: eggs, fish, vegetables —oh and just a *little* junk food so I wouldn't turn sullen. At the end of the trip, my skin was clearer than it had been since I was a babe. I was beginning to win the battle! Incidentally, on my travels I've noticed that the residents of underdeveloped countries, where refined sugar and flour are not an accepted part of the diet, aren't afflicted with acne; none of the East African tribes I visited had it.

VISIT A DERMATOLOGIST, PLEASE

Don't try to cure serious skin problems on your own. A change of diet alone won't do it, nor will over-the-counter medications and assorted home remedies. Certain types of skin scar more easily than others, and a serious infection can leave your complexion unevenly pigmented (to put it kindly). So why take the unnecessary risk? A clear skin enhances your appearance far more than an expensive new coat or dress is likely to. Too many people wait far too long before seeking medical help for a disfiguring skin ailment, and just keep hoping against hope that it will vanish all by itself. It won't.

MAKING DULL SKIN DISAPPEAR

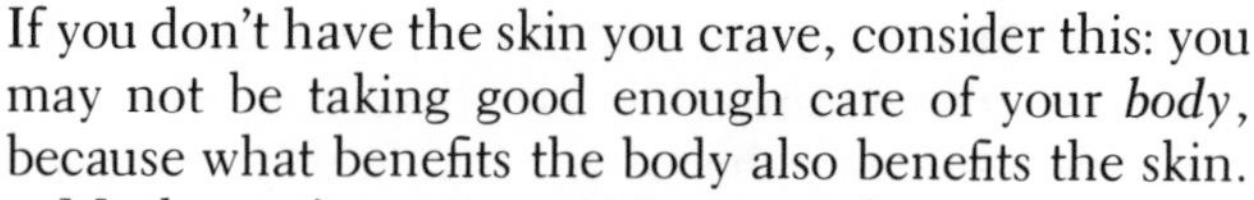

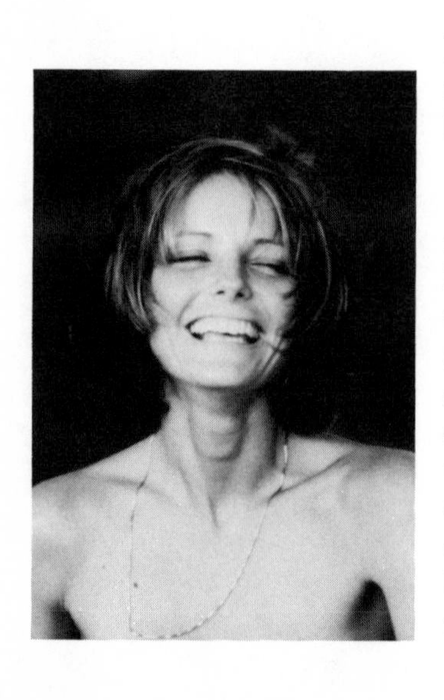

If you don't have the skin you crave, consider this: you may not be taking good enough care of your *body*, because what benefits the body also benefits the skin.

Maybe you're not exercising enough.

The growth of skin cells depends on oxygen and moisture received from the blood. When your circulation is sluggish, your skin receives less nourishment than it needs, and this in turn slows down cell growth and elimination of such waste products as carbon dioxide and fatty acids. So exercise those impurities out of your system; and feel and watch the color and texture of your skin improve along with your blood circulation. A ruddy complexion may be an indication of high blood pressure, and dull or sallow skin of low blood pressure. Exercise can help normalize such irregularities.

Maybe you're not getting enough sleep.

Lack of rest slows down blood circulation to the skin. When I'm tired and tense, my skin looks a sickly gray. Rest refreshes the skin every bit as much as it refreshes the body and mind.

Or maybe you really shouldn't be smoking.

When you smoke, you're doing almost as much harm to your skin as to your lungs—by cutting off the source of oxygen. The nicotine in tobacco causes the small blood vessels in your skin to shrink and thus cuts off circulation. If you continue to smoke, your skin will get duller and coarser as you age. Many experts have hazarded the guess that smoking is partly responsible for crow's-feet around the eyes. That's a heavy trip to lay on smoking, but there you are. Whatever the truth about this calumny proves to be, smoking *can't* be very good for you.

THE BEST DO-IT-YOURSELF DEEP-CLEANSING FACIAL IN THE WORLD

Aida Thibiant is the most celebrated and sought-after skin-care specialist in all Hollywood. Many a California beauty owes a real debt of thanks to Aida's European techniques and "secret" formulas. I love going to her salon for a deep-cleansing and moisturizing facial. I lie back in a reclining chair, close my eyes (blast and damn the *real* world!), and just totally relax as Aida works on my skin with her practiced hands and sweet-smelling lotions, creams, masques, steam treatments, and unique massages. This is the life they used to lead in palaces—no wonder I feel like a princess. And the results last for weeks.

Ideally, I would like to have a facial by Aida once a month, but I'm usually traveling. I pleaded with her for years to give me her recipe for a special deep cleansing facial that anyone can do for herself, and the other day she divulged it. So here it is, and it's *guaranteed* to give your skin and your psyche a tremendous lift.

Do it before going to bed at night, so your just-cleaned skin can have eight hours to relax, breathe, and otherwise respond to all the good things you've done for it. A do-it-yourself facial takes about an hour, so you'll probably find the time to do it only once a week or so. But that's okay.

There are six basic steps—one or two of them may

turn out to be especially effective, but try to practice them *all* as often as you can.

1. The Gommage

Gommage is a French word meaning "the erasing of dead cells on the surface of the skin." For this you'll need a cleansing cream that contains lysin, a plant extract that helps melt the dead skin cells, making them easy to remove. Most salon lines of cosmetics carry a cream of this type. Apply it to the skin and wipe it off with cotton balls. If for some unaccountable reason you can't find a gommage cream, begin your facial with step 2.

2. Scrubbing and Steaming

Fill a pot with water and add a tablespoon each of the following ingredients: Rosemary (it has great toning properties); camomile (it's relaxing); fennel (it's a decongestant); dried rose buds (they're soothing and sweet-smelling); and camphor (it's both a decongestant and an antibacterial agent). Herbal treatments such as this one are an important part of the European tradition of skin care. Now cover the pot, bring it to a rollicking boil for several minutes, then remove the cover, bend over the pot, and let the sweet-smelling vapor penetrate your pores. Don't cover your head and the pot with a towel—it will only make the concentration of steam too hot, and it *may* irritate your skin and break delicate capillaries. While the steam is cleaning out your pores, massage a honey-almond scrub into your face with gentle, circular movements of your fingertips. (You can make your own scrub by grinding four ounces of blanched almonds in your blender and mixing the powdery meal with four ounces of honey.) Don't pull your skin up and down, and don't massage so roughly that before you know it you've scratched your face. This pure, organic mixture softens up the skin better than any soap I know. And if you haven't eaten in a while, it also *tastes* delicious. Steam and scrub for five minutes, then wipe off the scrub with a washcloth soaked in warm water.

3. Toning

Apply a skin freshener to your face with a cotton ball. Aida believes that not even oily-skinned people should use an alcohol-based astringent. "Too harsh for the skin!" is the clarion note of warning she sounds.

4. Nourishing

Apply a light-textured cream to your skin with your fingertips. The right cream should not be oily or form a film on top of the skin.

5. Pincement Jaquet

This is another French term, meaning "pinching the skin lightly between thumbs and middle fingers." So now, pinch your entire face to step up blood circulation and help the nourishing cream penetrate the skin. Then tap your chin and jaw area with the back of your hand.

6. Using a Masque

This is the final step in any facial. Masques shrink your pores, stimulate and nourish your skin, improve your blood circulation, and "trap" the skin's moisture so it can't evaporate. The result is a plumped-up, shining, soft skin that looks young and well rested. The benefits last for several hours after you remove the masque.

Quick Money-Saving Masques

1. Beat an egg white with a few drops of lemon juice to tighten your skin.
2. Liquefy a cucumber in the blender with a few drops of lemon juice, which will also help clear your skin.
3. Mix a tablespoon of brewer's yeast with a teaspoon of vegetable oil or water till it's the consistency of a thin gruel (very good for oily skin, but watch out that it doesn't cause dryness and irritation).
4. Soak a couple of cotton pads with the juice of a fresh orange and apply to your skin.

Masques for Dry, Delicate Skin

1. Apply plain yogurt to your face.
2. Liquefy an avocado, which is rich in natural oils, in the blender and mix with a few drops of lemon juice.
3. Cooked, cooled oatmeal, which may also be used as a scrub.
4. Liquefy the pulp of a peach in the blender and mix with a few drops of avocado oil or a liquefied mixture of avocado and peach.

Put your masque on, lie back, close your eyes, and enjoy. After fifteen minutes, remove the masque with warm water and a washcloth. Then tone your skin once again with a freshening lotion. Apply a moisturizer or a night cream (and to all a good-night cream!).

CARING FOR BODY SKIN

The skin on your body, which has far fewer oil glands than the skin on your face, needs special care to stay soft and smooth.

I don't want to cause any anxiety to American mothers, but—here goes: bathing is not always as cleanly and godly as it's been made out to be. In fact, very dry skin improves with less bathing—and in direct proportion to how little you bathe (Pew!).

When I bathe, I try to make the bath a really relaxing experience: I want my nerves calmed as well as my muscles eased and my skin smoothed.

C.T.'s RECIPE FOR A SENSUOUS BATH

Don't make the water too hot unless your muscles are feeling all achy after an exercise session. Take the phone off the hook, so you won't be tempted to leap out of the tub to answer it. Lower the lights, put on your favorite record, and sip some topsy-turvy champagne.

When I'm in the tub I like to breathe in sweet smells, so I take some of the herbs I used to steam my face, wrap them in a porous cloth bag (a pocket from an old dress or skirt, tied at the top, will do just fine), and float them in the bath. Then I add my favorite fragrant bath oil. It's easy and inexpensive to make your own bath oil—just add a few drops of perfume or oil extract (musk or patchouli oil) to a bottle of unscented coconut or almond oil. This, by the way, was one of Cleopatra's favorite recipes and, as we know, "age cannot wither nor custom stale *her* infinite variety." Stay away from bubble baths that contain drying detergents. Some women like to stir a package of instant powdered milk into the water. To each her own.

Now: Lather your body with a mild soap. The rough surface of a loofa sponge, an aloe fiber bath mit, or a bath brush will slough those dead cells right off your arms and legs.

Wring out a washcloth in the warm water and lay it over your face, gently steaming it. This opens and cleanses the pores, and moisturizes the surface cells as well.

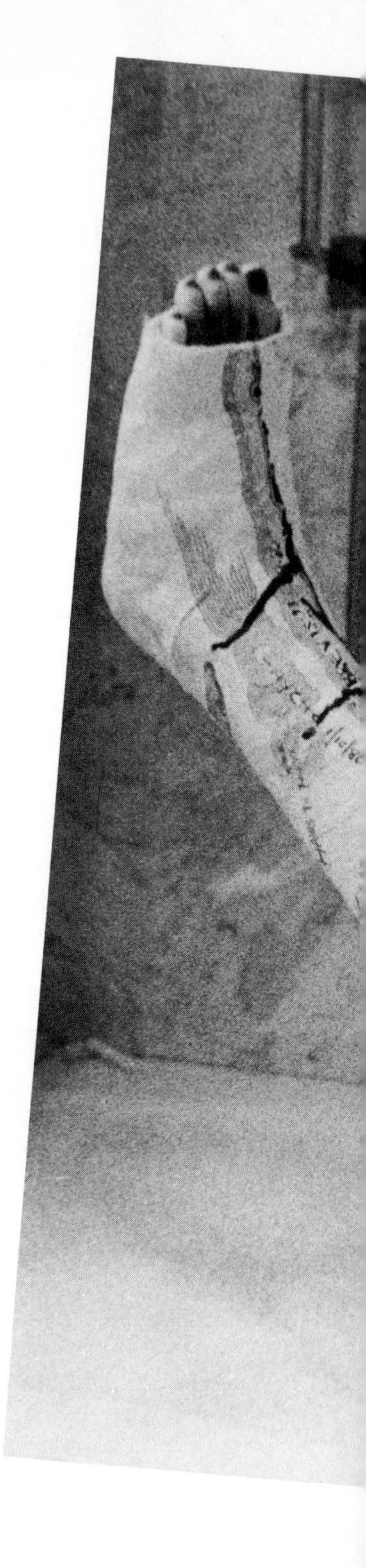

— to a cast of characters

If your legs feel achy, move both hands over the muscles in long, gliding strokes.

But, as one of my favorite Robert Lowell poems puts it: "Dearest, I cannot loiter here in lather like a polar bear." So:

I step out of the tub and immediately I smooth on a generous amount of moisturizer while I'm still damp. The water on my skin helps the moisturizer slide on, especially in the first five minutes after I'm out of the water. Take the extra time to make your bath a real luxury, the snug and watery cradle wherein you gather your thoughts, read a book, write a poem, or hum a favorite tune.

SKIN TREATMENT PRODUCTS

Because there are rows and rows of skin treatment products on the market, each one of which promises to work miracles, it's awfully hard to distinguish fiction from fact. How, you wonder, will I ever find the one that will work for me? It must exist somewhere, in the heart of that heartless shelf, because you know that others before you have found it.

What I advise is buying a cleanser, toner, and moisturizer all with the same brand name. The cosmetics industry is extremely sophisticated today, and basic products in a single line have been designed by technicians to work together for the good of your skin.

And give the products you select a chance. Unless you're allergic to a lotion or moisturizer, or find it has an instant bad effect on your skin, use it for a month or so before discarding it in favor of another.

Some skin products contain costly ingredients such as fruit extracts, turtle oil, and even mink oil, and there are experts who swear that these additives have no more effect on the skin than do ordinary, down-to-earth cosmetic ingredients such as lanolin and mineral oil. Other experts claim that special oils and extracts can greatly improve your skin. I use a night cream containing an esoteric little substance called collagen, which is a liquid protein that is supposed to firm the skin. There's no denying that expensive products have a scent and texture that are far more enticing than their cheaper counterparts. I mean, who wants to use Crisco on her face?

The most important thing to realize is that no cream yet invented, no matter how expensive it is, can replace a wrinkle with unlined skin. When and how much and how badly you wrinkle is determined largely by hereditary factors and by the amount of time you've spent suicidally overexposing yourself to the sun. Creams soften skin, yes, but they don't perform miracles.

Today, most products are required by law to list on their labels every single ingredient they contain. But unless you happen to know for a fact that you're allergic to some specific substance, the information on the label will be of little use to you because the ingredients usually have indecipherable chemical names—there's no way you're going to know what most of them are or actually do. One thing you can do is avoid alcohol-based products; another is to keep your eye peeled for ingredients like mink that you just know have got to raise the price of the product, or look for those ingredients that you know from past experience will improve your skin.

HYPOALLERGENIC COSMETICS

A hypoallergenic label doesn't guarantee that the allergy-prone will be immune to every ingredient in the formula. The main difference between hypoallergenic and other products is that the hypos are unscented and packaged under sterile conditions. Many people are allergic to some of the ingredients in perfumes, so using a milder scent will reduce the likelihood of reactions. Here's a Catch-22 for you: you may turn out to be just as allergic to an ingredient in a hypoallergenic product as you are to one in a regular product.

MAKING YOUR OWN COSMETICS

This is not the greatest idea you never had. It can be very expensive to make your own cosmetics. Besides, homemade products might not work as well, and certainly they won't smell and feel as nice as those you can buy. Given the time it's going to take you to go out and buy the many ingredients necessary for making your own astringent, you'd be better off buying one formulated by professional chemists to last a month or more. But if you're hell-bent on beating the system, then by all means go right ahead and give it a try. But remember, "cosmetics making," like baking and fancy cooking, takes time and energy and doesn't always turn out right.

C.T.'s MINUTE-TO-MINUTE TIPS FOR BEAUTIFUL SKIN

Humidify Your House

A humidifier is one of the best investments you can make if you live in either a very dry climate or a steam-heated house. Hot air absorbs all the moisture it can find, including the moisture in your skin, and can dry out the membrances of your nose and throat. Pans of water near the heating ducts or on the radiators can serve as homemade humidifiers (you can dress them up a bit with rocks or flowers). Or try lowering the thermostat in the winter. And don't forget your plants—they need a squirt of water from time to time, too.

The Airplane Facial

I am more dependent than most on airplanes, and I'm the first to admit that they have their place in the sun, in the scheme of things, but they certainly were not designed with "saving the skin" in mind. The atmosphere on planes is exceptionally cool and dry, and may dehydrate the skin, mouth, and throat. My little remedy is to drink club soda with lime throughout the trip; and of course I also carry some moisturizer in my purse. I dab a little extra on, even when I'm wearing makeup, so my skin doesn't completely dry out.

The Breakfast Masque or Guess Who's Coming to Breakfast

If you're alone one morning and want to begin the day with a smooth, glowing skin, then apply a masque at breakfast. There are quick-acting masques on the market which can revitalize your skin in a matter of minutes. Just be sure to wash it off with warm water, and then tone your skin and moisturize.

Misting Your Face

Living in a humid or foggy climate is great for your complexion (but hell on your clothes and spirit). However, you can create your own moist climate by filling a small spray bottle with mineral water. Or if you're lazy, there are fine mists sold in aerosol cans. Misting will set your makeup and keep your face soft and moist. And also refresh your thoughts, cool you out.

C.T.'s Telephone Hand Treatment

As the skin on your hands is especially thin and prone to dryness and chapping, you should apply hand lotion throughout the day. The way I remember to do this is by keeping a small bottle by the telephone. Every time I see that little bottle staring at me, reproaching me for my dereliction, I rub some lotion in.

C.T.'s Luscious Lips Insurance Policy

Don't let sleeping lips lie—they're sensitive, and they need your protection in order to stay soft and moist. I use a lip protection stick all year 'round under lipstick or gloss. Another way to moisturize lips is to wet them with a damp washcloth and then apply a gloss. Lips burn in the sun, so if you spend a lot of time out-of-doors, use a lip protector or look for a lipstick that contains a sun block.

The Water Cure

My skin tends to dry out when I'm tense and reeling from the pace of life in New York ("There's a neurosis in the air that the inhabitants mistake for energy," is how Evelyn Waugh described New York's vibes in his novel *Brideshead Revisited*), or when I've spent too much time in wildly overheated rooms. What I do then is go to the water faucet every chance I get, and drink down as much water as I can. After just a few days of this internal moisturizing treatment, my skin is smooth again.

MISTAKES PEOPLE MAKE

Sun Baking

These days, there is nothing more OUT than a dark, leathery tan. Baking your body in the sun without using a sun-blocking lotion is the best recipe for both wrinkling your skin and contracting skin cancer. The consensus among dermatologists is that the *only* effective method for keeping skin smooth and young is to protect it from the sun as much as humanly possible. I'm an active person with a genuine love of the out-of-doors and I refuse point blank to swathe myself in scarves and hats. But I wouldn't dream of not applying a good sunscreen with PABA to the exposed parts of my body, along with nosecoat, before facing the sun. The sun-block deflects the sun's damaging rays and at the same time allows me to get a light tan that actually protects my skin. If you do get sunburned, here's what to do: draw a tepid bath, and add two cups of oatmeal

"Extase du Perrier"

to the water—and, as they say in the comic strips, *no soap*. Afterwards, apply a heavy cream to your wet skin, followed by a masque consisting of one ounce yogurt and one ounce buttermilk. It's as soothing as it sounds.

Sun Protection

Baby oil does a good job pampering and lubricating your skin but when it comes to protecting you from the sun, forget it. Ditto for mineral oil, and even for some of the highly touted suntanning oils on the market. To guard against sun damage, you'll have to buy a sun block containing PABA. The only natural oil capable of adequately protecting your skin from the sun is sesame oil.

Too Much of a Good Thing

Women who apply countless creams and medications to their skin—who steam it, masque it, and buff it as if it were a pair of penny loafers—run the risk of ending up with drier, duller, or oilier skins than women who practice the little praised art of sensible moderation. Too much steaming and hot-water cleansing can stimulate your oil glands to overproduce, which in turn can aggravate an acne condition; too much buffing can remove the cells that serve to protect the skin; and too much moisturizing can clog your pores and give your skin an altogether dull finish. Yes of course, work for a beautiful skin, just so long as you don't make the common mistake of thinking that more means better.

Overfocusing on a Blemish

When I was having problems with, ahem, "grog-blossoms," I used to think about them all the time, and even a single "blossom" could make me feel terribly self-conscious; my whole world was circumscribed by that "flaw." Now, when the inevitable happens from time to time, I try to remember that it's my entire face that people will see, not just the "spot." So if your skin breaks out, remember this: others will be focusing on your eyes or your smile or your facial expressions and probably won't even notice the "trouble."

When to Have a Professional Facial

A facial does not always improve your skin right away; sometimes, when the treatment of blemishes is involved, the skin becomes temporarily redder and more inflamed. So schedule your facial for at least a day or two before a special occasion.

Using Tissues on Your Face

Don't ever use tissues to apply creams, lotions, or toners; they contain tiny woody fibers that will scratch your skin. Use cotton balls or pads.

The Danger of Believing Everything You Read

There is enough propaganda about skin products and skin care around today to overwhelm, if not actually bury, you. It seems as if every dermatologist and cosmetician in the world is flogging a different system of skin care— each of them completely foolproof. It's no wonder that so many people are confused. All you have to remember is that the best judge of what's good for your skin is, first and finally, you.

So: experiment (within limits), and *observe* how your skin is responding. Before long, you too will be comfortable and safe in your own saved skin.

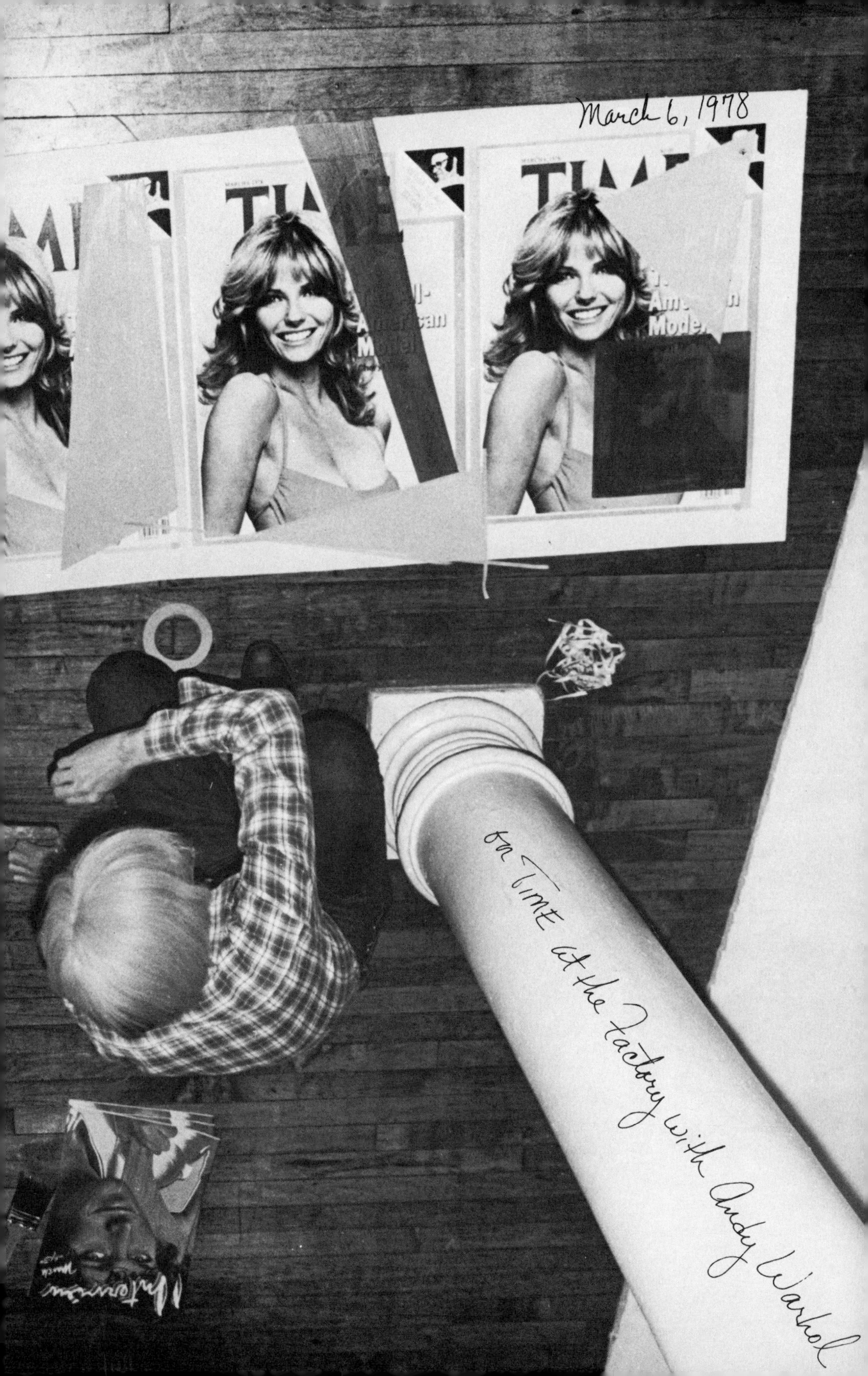

March 6, 1978

On TIME at the Factory with Andy Warhol

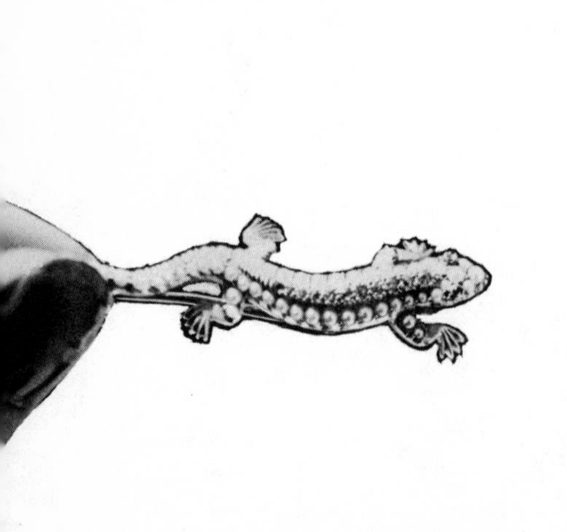

8

Life Is a Dressy Occasion: How to Get It Right

Sugar

e all know women who go to great expense and trouble to dress very badly and, what's more, "derive a kind of puzzling authority from it." The woman who knows her stuff takes care to choose clothes that communicate her unique self to the people she encounters; she knows that, as Virginia Tiger has written, "clothes may make the man but woman *is* the world she wears." She uses her clothes to enhance her best features and draw attention away from, if not artfully conceal, her second-best. She realizes that fashion is not only a mysterious but a very revealing form of human expression. If she *really* wants to dress to kill she'll wear clothes that run toward greater and greater simplicity so that people notice *her* rather than *them*.

Most women have a closetful of clothes, and yet they're never satisfied with what they have; they spend a lot of unnecessary time and money shopping for the latest styles—often not even bothering to insure that the clothes go well together. Others summarily (and boldly, given that life itself is a dressy occasion) dismiss fashion altogether, in favor of comfortable old standbys—till the day when a job interview or something equally momentous pounces and they panic because they have—and how many times have you heard or said these words yourself?—"nothing to wear." (And, if she's the world she wears, just what does *that* make her? No, fashion is not at all as frivolous as it looks.)

■ *Do you find yourself buying new clothes and then almost never wearing them?*

■ *Do you buy new clothes only to discover that you have nothing in your wardrobe to complement them?*

■ *Do you shop only before special occasions—and then frantically, like one possessed?*

■ *Do you feel your clothes are out of style, uninteresting, or inappropriate?*

■ *Do you shop only in the budget departments of local stores because you've convinced yourself that you can't afford designer clothes?*

1964

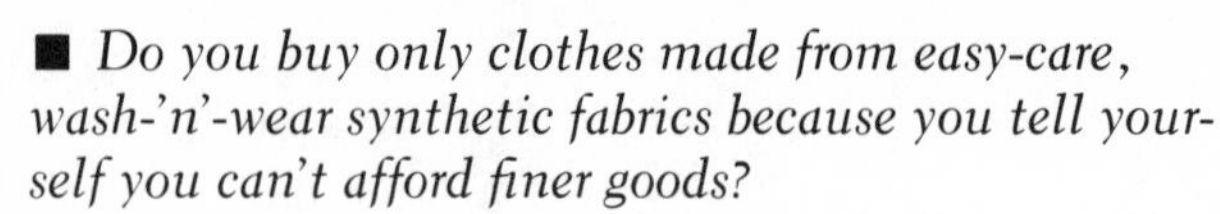
■ *Do you buy only clothes made from easy-care, wash-'n'-wear synthetic fabrics because you tell yourself you can't afford finer goods?*

If you've answered yes to any of the above questions, it will pay you many times over to read the rest of this chapter.

First of all, I've always felt that so-called good taste is something that anyone with a head on her shoulders can learn. Subscribing to a fashion magazine is one way to begin—notice I said "begin," because you don't want to let the fashion magazines have complete dominion over what you wear. I look to them for guidance and new ideas.

One of the biggest discoveries I made was that updating a wardrobe is not as expensive or time-consuming as is commonly thought. Even if you really can't afford designer dresses, you should try them on anyway, if only to see firsthand what a beautiful cut and a tasteful fabric can do for you. It's not a wasted day when you discover, as I did quite late in the game, that clothes made from beautiful fabrics are not as far out of your price range as you imagined and that they're just as economical to care for as those grungy synthetic wash-'n'-wear materials.

1965

In fashion, it's the overall effect that counts. The truly well-dressed woman will look just as smart in casual wear as she will in formal evening clothes. She has learned, probably by trial and error (few of us have unerring instincts), which color combinations, textures, and fabrics are the most flattering to her skin and hair and personality.

THE WAY I DRESSED BACK THEN

1965

Every time someone compliments me on my "fashion sense," I have to stop and sort of pinch myself, because until very recently it never even occurred to me that I had any. I went through most of my life not knowing what to wear, or even what I really wanted to wear. As far as clothes went, I more or less ran with the pack. A few years ago, however, I began to wake up to the fact that fashion sense is not a special talent some women are born with and others are not, but rather—like most other things—a matter of effort, self-education, and—again, trial and error.

All through my teens I stuck to the most conservative styles and rarely strayed from the color blue (actually, truth to tell, it's still my favorite color). When I began to model and came into contact with the fashion world, I developed enough self-assurance to experiment a little with clothes. I said a faint good-bye to the safe approach—a little too quickly, as it turned out, because—I can tell you—I had my fair share of disasters. I'll never forget the time I went out and spent a fortune on a pair of special plastic see-through, high-heeled shoes. Oh they were the last word—or the next-to-last, anyway—and I felt proud of being brave enough to sport a pair. I put them right on and went to a fraternity party. After I was on my dancing, sweating tootsies for only about an hour, those chic plastic attention-getters steamed up and clouded over so you couldn't tell my toes from twigs. My ungracious chums slapped their knees over the hilarity of it all—making me even more self-conscious (if that were possible). One of them even had the nerve to ask me if the shoes had come complete with windshield wipers! I *almost* managed to be formidable in my distress.

Another time, I really branched out and got a wonderful pink mini-dress, which I wore with white knee socks, flat shoes, and a little pink purse. All dolled up (literally!), I was sure I looked more "in style" than anyone on campus. As I strolled along to English class, my cute little purse got caught in my cute white knee socks and it took me half an hour to disentangle the various parts of my oh-so-fashionable outfit—much to the amusement of passing students.

When I began to model for *Glamour*, I found my mentor in fashion editor Julie Britt. She had a great flair for clothes, and soon I was slavishly copying everything she wore. If Julie came to a shooting in a beautifully fitted A-line dress and Gucci shoes, I'd rush out and buy an A-line dress and buckled shoes that looked as much like Gucci as I could afford. I wouldn't buy anything without first asking myself "Would Julie buy this?" or "Would Julie ever wear that?" There's no question I learned a lot from Julie, but copying is never as edifying as developing a sense of style of your own.

For years I would wear anything I could see was in fashion regardless of how it looked on *me*. I kept telling myself: "I must above all things be snazzy." So I wore the hip-hugger pants and the skintight tops that were so popular in the sixties (despite the fact that I was then pretty heavy, and long-waisted to boot). I also followed the crowd and wore the most extreme versions of the mini-skirt, although at the time my legs were far too thick to be out there where everyone could see them.

As a model I was constantly being exposed to the most beautiful clothes created by the top designers. It was like pressing your nose up against the window of your very favorite pastry shop—temptation incarnate. When I was a very naïve twenty-one, I bought an incredibly snazzy, very expensive, vampy black dress—slit all the way up. In the designer's showroom the dress had made me look like the glamorous, soignée woman I thought I wanted to be. I coveted it, so I bought it. But when I got it home and tried it on in front of my tell-me-no-lies mirror, I saw that it made me look like a little girl wearing a costume. It was a gorgeous, languorous dress, but better leave it alone, Cheryl, I said to myself, it isn't for you. I had a hard enough time getting up the nerve to take it back.

THE WAY I DRESS NOW

Now that at least to a certain extent I've developed a fashion sense of my own, I realize that I feel most comfortable in classic and simple clothes for daytime wear. Who wants to get all dressed up in the morning, anyway?

I prefer to put on one outfit that I know will get me through the whole day. Well-cut jeans in different fabrics, one-of-a-kind silk shirts, T-shirts, classically tailored skirts and blazers, vests and sweaters in subtle colors—these are my favorites for daytime. I'm a strong believer in wearing parts of the same outfit several days running (but not, however, if you've been running for several days!)—a common practice in Europe, by the way—but with different accessories; that way, I don't have to make a decision about what goes with what *every* morning. I prefer the milder styles to offbeat, zany outfits, because coming up with a really successful offbeat look takes a lot of time, thought, "creativity," and also, unless you get it exactly right, it usually comes out exactly wrong. Whatever fashion imagination I do have blossoms at night (in this sense, I'm quite the opposite of a morning glory), when I can spare the time to put some real effort and ingenuity into the way I dress. I love the fantasy aura of evening clothes—shiny fabrics, satins, velvets, rhinestone belts, and high, strappy, sexy sandals. One of my favorite outfits for a champagne evening (which you can have either with or without the champagne) is a pair of tight turquoise velvet jeans that I wear with my shameless purple fox fur. There's also a shimmery sequined traffic-stopping silk shirt that I love—it's a hot

C.T. with friend
c 1979

Cheryl
in
St Martin

shade of rose and I wear it with white satin pants and gold sandals: ooh-la-la.

Because I'm sometimes in the eye of the public, I *have* to own more clothes than the average person; but I still don't believe in overdoing it, and my wardrobe happens to be smaller than that of most of my friends. I have a great weakness for anything from that classic American designer Calvin Klein, and from St. Laurent, whose imaginative designs have refurbished the fantasy lives of so many women the world over ("grasshopper notes of genius!"). I adore Ann Klein's colors and fabrics and Oscar de la Renta's fabulous evening silks, and Giorgio Armani's elegant *and* practical clothes. Another of my big fashion heroes is the inimitable Halston. These designers are all friends of mine and they have all helped teach me to select and appreciate what looks good on me.

Here are some suggestions for how to develop *a new approach to what you wear* (kind of a long-winded way of saying "fashion sense").

FIND A MENTOR

As I've said, my fashion mentor was Julie Britt, and you should be so lucky. If you know a beautifully dressed woman, someone whose fashion sense you admire, watch what she wears, notice how she combines colors and fabrics, how she puts her clothes together, and how she uses jewelry, belts, and scarves. Observe how she chooses clothing to display her figure and coloring to their best advantage. Don't only ask her advice, try to get her to come along with you on your next shopping trip. I bet she developed her fashion sense through careful thought and study, and not through any accident. Even now, I "study" the women I consider exceptionally well-dressed. I no longer feel the need to copy what they're wearing but I'm still very much open to ideas and inspiration; I may go out and buy a particular dress I've seen them wear—but only if I think it will look right on me, and then what I'll do is wear it with completely different accessories and in a different way from them, because no two women wear a dress the same way. Your goal, then, should be not to copy but to discover what exactly it is that governs how well-dressed women dress.

SUBSCRIBE TO FASHION MAGAZINES

As I travel throughout the country, I'm surprised to see how few women are aware of what the current style is. And there's really no excuse for this; the many excellent fashion magazines published here and abroad can keep every woman up to date. Their function is to educate you to absorb from them and to help you catalyze (not cauterize) your own ideas.

I used to get awfully discouraged leafing through the fashion magazines, looking at models like Verushka in her height and glory. I would think, "Are you kidding? I could never look like that in a million years." Now, of course, I realize that I'm not supposed to look like the layout in a fashion magazine (unless of course it's me, Cheryl Tiegs, who's in it). Don't attempt to reproduce the outfits you see, don't strive and toil to look like the model on the page. Believe me, she's *too* put together for everyday life, she's a living doll, just perfect—for a dollhouse! Fashion layouts are designed to provide a fantasy-inducing ambience, and the *last* thing they should be taken for is a prescription for reality. So use them wisely. Let them suggest new lines and styles to you—broader shoulders, narrower pants, an authentic peasant image, or the sleek, glamorous look, whatever. They're meant to give you ideas that you then modify to suit yourself. Let's say the look for spring is the va-va-voom "gypsy look" complete with shawls, petticoats, turbans, full skirts, ruffles, and bangles. This may give you the license you need to bring a shawl with you in the evening, or get your old full skirt out of the back closet. Pay attention to the silhouettes, fabrics, and colors the magazines are promoting, then decide which of the current trends are right for *your* figure and *your* personality. It's a mistake to totally ignore current trends; being rabidly anti-fashion may be chic—for about ten minutes!

SHOP WITHOUT BUYING

If you're dissatisfied with your wardrobe, yet can't imagine an alternative, experiment in your local department store and boutiques. Try on styles and fabrics you've never worn before. Put together unusual combinations. Try on designer clothes you know you could never afford, and evening clothes you think you'd never wear. Have a ball. Indulge yourself. Be bold—but not too bold: leave your checkbook and credit cards at home or in your back pocket. Your mission this trip is not mission impossible, because you're there not to buy but to discover. Keep your eyes on the mirror, that's you in there—look at yourself realistically. Your goal is to see what *different* clothes can do for you, so don't stick obstinately to old favorites, don't be a donkey—new vistas are opening up before you. By examining what is available, without feeling the psychological pressure to buy, you'll form a new impression of yourself in relation to fashion with a capital "F." Later, think over the different yous that you saw in the mirror and ask yourself how you felt about each of them. Then—and only then—return to the shop and make your selections.

WHICH COMPLIMENTS TO TAKE AT FACE VALUE

When you have something new on, listen carefully—and discriminatingly—to what others have to say about it. Don't fish for compliments—the heartfelt ones will come of their own accord and you'll know them when you hear them. Sometimes the admiring (or envious) expression in a friend's eyes will tell you more than an over-enthusiastic exclamation.

ANALYZING YOUR CLOTHES

Make it a point to analyze the clothes you have before going out and buying new ones. Many people fail to make good enough use of the clothes they already own. These are the same people who make the same mistakes every time they shop.

List Your All-Time Favorites

Everybody has her favorite outfit that she wears and wears and wears because she knows she always looks good in it. One of my favorites was a black silk St. Laurent shirt, which I'd purchased in the men's shop. I wore it till the cuffs were practically in shreds and the collar was completely, triumphantly frayed. Think about clothes you've owned that you loved and wore into extinction. Which clothes in your closet right this minute get the most wear? Why? You'll probably find that your favorites all have a similar mood, style, or fabric. Ask yourself why you love these particular clothes, and how you felt about them when you bought them. Sometimes it's the dress you were ambivalent about in the store that spends the least time in your closet. It may be that the clothes you love are connected to happy moments.

One FiFteen

in Lake Powell for Cover Girl

LIST YOUR MISTAKES (ONE TO TEN THOUSAND)

Go ahead, don't hang back—make a list of the clothes you bought that wound up hanging unworn in the back of your closet. Take the extravagant white Austrian peasant dress with the lace-up bodice that I bought five or six years ago. It looked wonderful, positively irresistible, in the designer's showroom. I wore it once and felt like a misplaced milkmaid. When you're in a store, surrounded on all sides by exciting fashions, your fancies and fantasies can often get the better of you and you may buy something that really has no place in your life (as you discover sooner rather than later). Or your mistakes may take the form of choosing colors that once they are on you, you find too flamboyant for comfort, or very tailored clothes that seemed perfect for the job but make you feel unfeminine after working hours. And clothes whose textures irritate your skin, or those that don't fit well, no matter how beautiful they are, are always a mistake. Analyzing the kind of mistake you're likely to make will make you less prone to making those mistakes again.

Giving Away the Clothes You Never Wear

A lot of women keep their closets full to bursting with clothes they would never in this life be caught dead in. The mistakes hanging there may be expensive ones, but give them away. Be generous. It may help to remember that clothes that have gone out of style seldom come back in; if you're sick of something, don't keep it in the bound-to-be-blasted hope that you'll see it resurrected five years hence in the pages of *Bazaar*.

BUYING NEW CLOTHES

Shopping is a bore—and can be a trauma—for many women; for others it's an obsession, a compulsion second to none, an actual demon. Some women buy clothes they can't really wear because they have a warped self-image—they see themselves as younger, older, fatter, thinner, or more or less sophisticated than they really are. Some get high on the atmosphere in the store and buy clothes that will never fit properly. Millions and millions of dollars—*your* dollars—go down the drain every year, courtesy of all the clothes you soon decide you don't want, need, or enjoy.

Department stores have always kind of overwhelmed me. I feel the same way when I'm in a fancy restaurant and a waiter hands me a menu so big it blocks out the whole world. Working for ABC, I couldn't afford to remain oblivious to fashion—I mean, it's part of my job to be in style—so every year, in the spring and in the fall, I update my limited wardrobe. In Los Angeles I gravitate to two boutiques, Maxfield Blue and Charles Galley, where I know the sales personnel and they know me, which I like. I will occasionally go out of my way to shop for an evening dress, something with a melting effect. Over the years I've picked up or invented some shopping tricks and techniques that may be of some help to you as you go about the potentially killing business of building a wardrobe within your price range.

UPDATING YOUR WARDROBE

It is definitely not necessary—or "NN," as a good friend of mine always says—to buy a whole new wardrobe every year in order to stay in the so-called swim. You should be able to successfully combine a few new things with the clothes you already own. But before shopping, go through your closet and single out the outfits you're really going to wear that year. Make a list of styles, colors, and accessories that would go well with the clothes you have. When you hit your favorite boutique or department store, look for the type of clothes in the colors and fabrics you've determined you need. And whatever you do, don't buy something just because it's marked down.

When I buy clothes, I always lay them out on the counter and mentally combine them with the clothes I have at home, before I even take them into the fitting room.

FABRICS

Fabrics should never be underestimated. Everybody loves the feel of soft clothes and few can stand fabrics that are rough or itchy to the touch. A beautiful fabric makes the person who's wearing it feel sensuous, and has even been known to make other people want to reach out and touch it. I go so far as to automatically write off clothes that even *look* as if they might be irritating; a scratchy-looking unlined jacket or a coarse sweater communicates a downright uncomfortable feeling—anyway, that's the message *I* get. Another plus for soft, flowing fabrics is that they reveal the lines of your body as you move in a way that's—frankly—sexy. Whenever I buy a dress or skirt, I choose a fabric that subtly reveals the shape of my legs.

How to Judge

You have to educate your fingertips to tell the difference between a fine fabric and an inferior one. A good material should feel soft, cool, luxurious. The better it feels, the better it most probably is. Cottons, silks, wools, linens, and synthetics are all made in different weaves and grades. Silk is a strong, long-lasting fiber, whatever grade it is, but the finest weaves will feel as soft as butter. A good wool garment will also feel good enough to eat, and it has the added advantage of not wrinkling easily. Anything made of fine wool will hang in a neat line and fold smoothly. Material that's 100 percent cotton is finer in texture and wears better than a combination of cotton and synthetic blends. I prefer natural fabrics, but there are some modern synthetic materials that are very fine and resemble silks or elegant cottons. Rayons, for example, are made from tree fibers and are nice and soft, and rayon and acetate blends combine into a beautiful fabric that also feels good. Some polyesters, a material often used by designers, feel and look exactly like silk, satin, or polished cotton. Here again, use C.T.'s twenty-second touch test to identify a fine synthetic; the best of them will feel luxurious and slither between your fingertips, while a poor-quality one will be practically untouchable.

Good fabrics, needless to say, are more expensive and require a bit more care than poor-quality ones—as they should. In my opinion, this country places far too much emphasis on practicality—with the result that both men and women in droves buy polyester drip-dry-type synthetics that feel and look cheap and stiff. I strongly encourage you to purchase the best fabric, even if it means you have to settle for fewer things. You will look sexier and more elegant in beautiful fabrics, and they'll certainly last longer.

"What about my dry-cleaning bills?" you're probably

getting ready to ask. Contrary to popular belief, good fabrics don't really have to be dry-cleaned, even when they're labeled "Dry clean only." Silks and fine fabrics were invented eons before the dry-cleaning industry was even a gleam in somebody's avaricious eye, and they can perfectly well be washed by hand. Most silk blouses, fine synthetics, linens, rayons, wool sweaters, and even cashmeres can be laundered in *cold* water and Woolite. And there's a good all-fabric bleach for hard-to-remove stains. Washing, in fact, gets fabrics cleaner than dry-cleaning, which in the long run can be destructive to fine silks.

HOW CLOTHES ARE CUT

A good garment is both well-cut and well-made. Here are a few techniques of workmanship to be on the lookout for.

A *properly set zipper* should lie flat and even. If the zipper is puckered or curling, chances are the entire garment has been sloppily put together and won't ever hang right.

A *well-sewn seam* sometimes has two lines of stitching. If the item you're planning to buy is torn along the seam, turn your back on it, even if it looks like it can be easily mended—it has either not been well made or not been inspected.

Hems of a skirt or dress should hang evenly (many don't), and the stitching should be secure.

Consider the fit. Too many women buy clothes for style or color without bothering to take into consideration the way they're cut or how they fit. Unless something fits, and fits well, it won't do much for you no matter which fashion luminary designed it or how much it cost. If you would like to be a smaller size, *diet*; then buy clothes that fit you. Don't, as some diet experts recommend, buy a smaller size dress than you take—as an "inspiration" or incentive—it may never quite fit your reduced contours and you'll have thrown your money away.

Pants. Let's face it—I have—most of us have trouble finding pants that fit. Fortunately, pants can usually be altered by the tailor at your local dry cleaner's for a reasonable fee. Make sure they fit properly in the hips and crotch; bend and sit in them to see if they're comfortable. If the hips fit, but the waist or crotch is too loose, a tailor can easily take the pants in along the back seam and in the legs. Never buy pants (or any

松下電器
仲見世

Shopping in Tokyo – 1979

garment, for that matter) that are too tight, planning to "let them out." Clothes are not as amply made today as they used to be, and it is all but impossible to make them larger. As for length, pants just have to be the right length or forget it. When you shop for them, wear the type of heel you want to wear with them. Shoes with different heels can't as a rule be worn with the same pants. This is a small point, I grant you, but oh what a difference it can make.

Shirts, Jackets, and Sweaters. I like the look of a blouse, sweater, or jacket that's reasonably tight under the arm—it gives a neater, rangier, girl-of-the-limberlost look, with the seam of the shoulder falling on top of the shoulder line. When you're buying a jacket, make sure the hem falls beneath the buttocks, because if it's any shorter, it will tend to look too small. The cuffs of a jacket should be short enough for the blouse underneath to show. As James Cagney once said, "I like to show a lot of linen." (This was maybe after he shoved that grapefruit in Mae Clark's face.) If you have on a short-sleeved blouse, just push the jacket sleeves up above the elbows.

The Cut of the Garment on the Figure You Cut or Cut Up in. A well-designed, well-cut dress—and the two are for all practical purposes synonymous—should be able to be worn in a certain size by many differently shaped bodies. As I've said before—and brace yourself, I'm going to say it again, the only way to learn what well-cut clothes can do for you is to try them on; from time to time, it will pay off to pay more and go for quality instead of quantity.

What I admired most about Julie Britt's wardrobe was its dramatic simplicity. I made a point of learning how she achieved the effect she did. One time, during a *Glamour* trip to Paris, she took me shopping and taught me, as only she could, to appreciate the difference between a Sonia Rykiel sweater and an ordinary one. And, let's not kid ourselves, there *is* a difference. Designer names and prices may not be in our league but that's no reason to automatically reach for the copies. This is going to sound as old as the rushes of the Nile: *use your own creativity* (ten to one you've got some if you only knew it) and be your *own* original.

YOUR, AHEM, BUDGET

Judiciousness—that's the key requirement here. You don't have to be rich to be well-dressed—remember what I said before about women who go to great expense and trouble and come out dressed "importantly" but very badly. Not that good clothing is cheap—those who want a beautiful wardrobe have to be prepared to invest their fashion dollar carefully. My best cut and most expensive clothes are the ones I can wear year in and year out without wearing *them* out because they're so well made. I advise buying fewer garments but ones of good design instead of accumulating a large trendy wardrobe that is doomed to eventual, if not instant, obsolescence. Some traditional clothes, like your good old Chanel, stay in fashion forever, for what is a tradition, anyway, but a fashion that has lasted? On the other hand, the silhouette of skirts, dresses, and pants may change in the course of a single season. Obviously it is more practical to spend money on garments that will stay in style at least long enough to stabilize your wardrobe (these shaky days a wardrobe is one of the few things you *can* stabilize—barring earthquakes, tidal waves, and other natural phenomena).

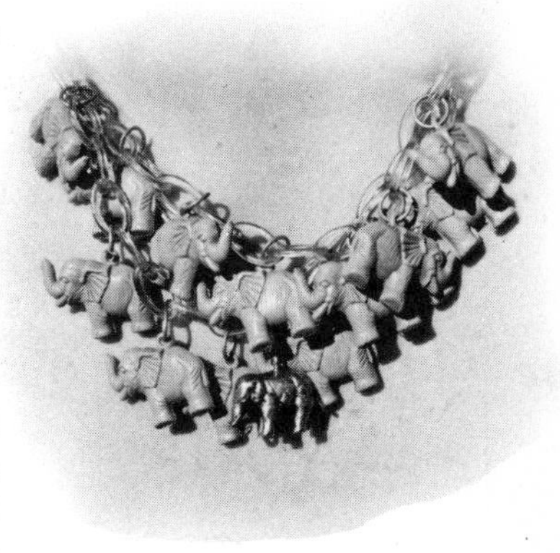

HOW TO KNOW WHAT TO BUY

Me, I always know when I want to buy something. I remember reading in high school that the critic and anthologist William Rose Benét knew when a poem was good when the hairs on the back of his neck began bristling. And it's something like that with me and clothes. By now I have sort of a bristle-sense for the kinds of clothes that suit me best. If you have to keep asking yourself, "Do I need it? Do I even really want it? Does it *really* look good on me?" you probably shouldn't get it. It helps to get to know salespeople in the stores you frequent. The people who work in the shops I go to the most often know my tastes at least as well as I do. I've gotten to the point where I can rely on them and just disappear into a dressing room and wait for them to present me with the latest goodies, and they have yet to disappoint or betray me. If you're trying to change your "fashion image" and can't decide whether or not something looks good on you, take along a friend whose taste you trust. Apart from whatever advice she gives you, she'll make the whole business more like a junket.

HOW TO CREATE AN "ORIGINAL" OUTFIT

Even if you do have a closetful of pretty clothes, maybe you don't have the know-how to put them together in terrific combinations. Here are some suggestions that might just work.

Select the Silhouettes That Flatter Your Proportions

Since few people's figures are ideally proportioned, to look good in clothes they are going to have to wear styles and combinations that emphasize the best parts of their figures and give the desired illusion—whether of thinness, fullness, or longer lines. Here's a rough guide to putting together outfits geared to your particular figure.

Heavy: If you're heavy or big-boned, avoid both skintight clothes and voluminous, tent-like garments because neither is going to make you look smaller. Fairly loose clothes, with tops that fall from the shoulder, will give the illusion of softness and length. And so will V-necks. Lines should be relaxed and flowing, fabrics should be fluid. For the full figure, well-tailored clothes are a must. Pants should have a smooth front and a natural waistline. Don't make the mistake I did of buying pleated pants—they only added fullness at a time when my old thin self was in exile. Avoid pants with a high waistband, baggy pants, and again and above all, tight pants. And, if you don't like the size of your backside, don't buy pants with large back pockets.

Thin: The Duchess of Windsor is reputed to have said, "You can never be too rich or too thin." Well, she was wrong—about the thin part. You *can* be too thin, at least for some styles of clothes. If certain parts of your body—chest, collarbones, legs—are spare and bony, what are you waiting for? For Heaven's sake, cover them up! And stay away from halters, low necks, bare midriffs, and short shorts. Go for full-cut clothing in textured fabrics to fill out the curves of your body. If you're partial to straight skirts or skintight jeans, then wear a top with soft, full lines. You should be able to wear pants that are exaggeratedly full at the waistline. Almost all clothes look better when draped on a thin figure.

Short: If you're small, short jackets, narrow skirts, and pants with straight-cut legs and high waistbands are a safe bet to make your legs look longer. Also wear your skirts a few inches below the knee if you want to make your legs look longer. Such accessories as heavy jewelry, big purses, broad-brimmed hats, and bulky mufflers will bury you. Also avoid T-strap, thick ankle strap, or chunky-heeled shoes, because they'll give

golden Cobras with turquoise eyes

Tiffany teardrops

antique frog

Masai bracelet

waterproof

"Willy"

your legs the appearance of being shorter than they are. Stick with high heels in simple styles.

Tall: (C.T. answers to this one). Just relax and make the most of it, don't hide your height by slouching or wearing flat heels. I trafficked in my tallness even as a teenager; I wore high heels, I was proud to be tall. Tall women can get away with wearing almost anything, especially if they're on the thin side. I say "almost anything," because you'll surely want to stay away from long straight dresses in one color. Color contrasts in "separates," and vests, belts, and textured stockings will break up the long lines of your body.

Short-waisted: Avoid separates, and high-waisted pants, skirts, and dresses (they'll emphasize your waist). Tunics, vests, the blouson look, and loose-fitted clothes will all suit you, as well as dresses and skirts with a dropped or gathered waistline. A thin belt worn slightly below the waistband of a skirt or pants will give the illusion of a longer waist. And go for pants or skirts with a thin waistband.

Long-waisted: That's C.T., too, and I find it much more of an asset than a liability. You can easily wear skirts or pants with high waistbands. I confess that I don't even mind a dress with a waistband that rides up an inch or so more than normal.

USE ACCESSORIES TO THE HILT

Anyone who's become skilled at taking outfits and creating a "look" knows how accessories can add that inspired personal touch without which you might as well have been dressed by a computer or a chart. Here are some tips on how to wear accessories.

Jewelry

Days, I usually wear a snake ring with turquoise eyes, a green art-nouveau frog ring with ruby eyes, a gold elephant on a chain around my neck, an African bracelet, given to me by a Masai who in affection bent it so compellingly around my wrist I've never been able to get it off (not that I'd want to), a Rolex watch that I can get wet and bang around all I want without fear of breaking, and small diamond teardrop earrings. Occasionally I do take all these baubles and bangles off (except for the untakeable-off African bracelet) and put on a single large, heavy ivory bracelet. All my jewelry, as you can see, is highly personal—and also mythic, since it's connected in one way or another to

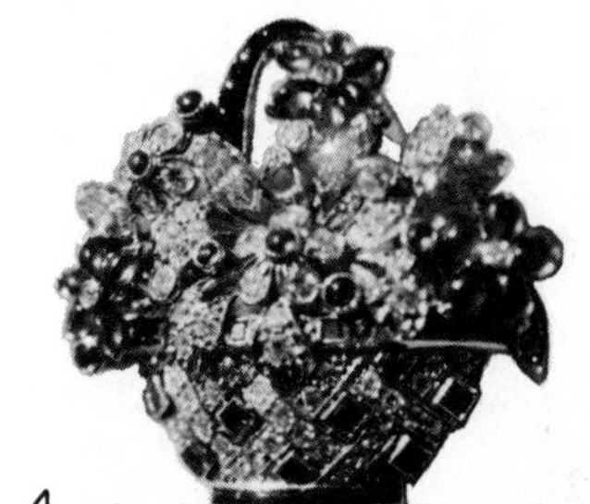

Cartier flower basket Circa 1890

various people's pasts, and gives me a special feeling that goes way beyond the delimiting universe of fashionable appearance. For evenings, I have some wonderful antique watches and bracelets, some of which were given to me on nights when the wind kind of spreads your sails. Many people just pile on jewelry that has no real meaning for them except for what it all too obviously cost. I think your jewelry should represent some event or person in your life. I often remember a woman by the jewelry she wears; it tells me a lot more about her than how much money she has to spend on herself. Try using one or two pieces of jewelry to make a simple statement about yourself, or else wear one kind of jewelry, such as bracelets, earrings, rings, or special chains as your trademark. And then you'll wear the taste your trademark confers on you, not like a uniform, but like a badge.

Belts

I must have the world's largest collection of belts. I'm convinced that a belt can do more than just about any other accessory to change the mood of an outfit. A rhinestone belt, worn with a pair of velvet jeans and a silk blouse, for example, can give a simple daytime outfit a glittering nighttime excitement. Double-wrap belts, rope belts, ties and cords can, one and all, change the line and look of whatever you have on. Use your imagination to create unusual and striking belts; try winding scarves or pieces of suede or cord from the yardage store around your waist. One of my most eccentric belt purchases never fails to make a hit. In St. Paul de Vence, over in the South of France, at a simple little leather goods store, I bought a belt whose buckle was made of the parts of a 1930s radio, so tune in to what I'm saying, okay?—and don't stick with the matching belt that comes with the outfit.

Scarves and Hats

I seldom wear any of the many scarves I own. The best accessory is one you can put on and forget all about, and a scarf always seems to need redoing—at least mine does, I'm always having to put it back in place. If, however, you're stuck on scarves, practice wrapping and tieing them. But promise me you won't wear a scarf with a designer name on it—talk about insecurity. As the clever ad says, "When your own initials are enough."

There's one type of scarf I can't live without, though —the huge, oversized ones that come in soft cotton or silk. I travel with them and wear them as cover-ups on beaches or as robes in the blank, anonymous hotel rooms I sometimes have to stay in.

As for hats, I feel comfortable in them only if they're serving some purpose—otherwise I feel like I'm trying too hard. They can be fun, and even terribly flattering, but make sure you get the size right. If you have small features, go for the smaller brims—only people with large features can afford to wear wide or big-brimmed hats.

COLOR AND TEXTURE

The color of the clothes a woman wears doesn't just bring out the tones of her skin and hair, it tells a lot about how she's feeling, what she's thinking, how friendly a face she presents to the world. Many women are timid when it comes to color; they buy clothes in the same shades over and over again, or else they wear colors in grimly limited combinations only. The foundation of a really great outfit is often an unexpected and surprising use of color, enhanced by the texture of the fabrics. Every color reflects differently on every face and, as you know, there are innumerable shades of the same basic color. You may discover that an off-shade of a color you always thought you hated looks fantastic on you and provides the perfect accent for some of your other garments as well. I've never liked the color yellow—it's always reminded me of kitchens and canaries (though don't get me wrong, I've got nothing against dishes and birds), but once I bought a mustard-colored blouse which turned out to go with everything I owned. I wore that blouse to death. So if you can't wear red, how about maroon; if you're wary of wearing purple, give mauve the old college try.

Don't play it safe by deciding that two colors are an automatic clash. How do you know till you've tried them together? When you buy a dress, hold it up to other dresses in the store. You may just spot that interesting color combination you've never before worn. Do the same with the clothes back in your closet.

As a general rule, bright colors work best as accents in blouses, sweaters, and scarves. One thing I always avoid is big bold prints too overpowering and, in the end, just plain boring. If muted colors appeal to you, select them in fabrics that have something a little out of the ordinary in the texture or weave. The pants and blouse of one of my most prized evening outfits come

SO
SONY
Enjoy
Coca
5:05

in lustrous beige satin—I call *that* a little out of the ordinary. The shininess of the satin takes the dull beige and makes it interesting. Sometimes I wear separates all in one color—like a dove-gray sweater with a dove-gray skirt, which I think of as an interesting non-combination.

FEET, DO YOUR WORK!

When you're out shopping for shoes, it's sometimes hard to envision what kind will go best with the clothes you have. Moreover, when you get them home you often find they're a lot less comfortable than you imagined they'd be. I can't overemphasize the importance of wearing comfortable shoes, because when your feet hurt, they hurt and the whole evening is sacrificed.

I love high glittery sandals for evening. During the day I can't wear high heels because I do such a lot of walking. As one of my good friends said as she was about to run out to the store for groceries, "Feet, do your work!" and it wasn't high heels she had on. Did you know that if you wear high heels too often, you can throw your whole back out of alignment, and even distort the shape of your foot? When you buy high heels, make sure they're balanced correctly and can offer your foot the support it needs—otherwise you'll teeter-totter in them, a walking (sic) advertisement for the Old Comedy of Faults.

CARE FOR YOUR CLOTHES AND SHOES

When a button pops or a zipper goes, repair the damage before you toss the garment in your closet or drawer. Or else what will happen is you'll forget all about it till you pull it out to wear, and then you'll be mighty disappointed. There's nothing that detracts from a well-groomed look more than unshined, run-down-at-the-heels shoes and boots. Keeping your shoes shined and in good repair also gives them a new lease on life—and a longer run for *your* money.

MATERIALS FOR ALL SEASONS

Heavy cottons, rayons, ultra-suedes, velours, fine silks, corduroys, and many synthetics are comfortable in almost all seasons. Stretch your fashion budget and concentrate on long-lasting clothes that can be worn more than a couple of months a year. For warmth, simply add layers.

CHOOSE YOUR OUTFITS IN ADVANCE

Don't wait till you're about to rush out the door to find the perfect outfit in your crowded closet. The afternoon or night before, try on your clothes in varying colors and textures. How does that silk skirt look with your favorite sweater? How well do your well-cut jeans go with that silk shirt? Consider wearing one silk shirt over another as kind of a jacket. Use your imagination. Ransack your drawers for accessories you haven't worn very much and put them together with your new clothes. When you've concocted a few exciting outfits, you won't have to ask before every big appointment or glamorous date, "What should I wear?" Oh me oh my!

YOUR NOT-SO-CASUAL CASUAL LOOK

Audrey Hepburn knocked me out in *Two for the Road* wearing simply a pair of jeans, tennis shoes, and a T-shirt. I've always worn jeans and casual clothes—who hasn't?—but I discovered that there's a chasm deep and wide between a casual elegant look and a sloppy, thrown-together outfit that does nothing for me and less for the people who have to look at me. Never was this brought home to me more annihilatingly than the day I ran into my old friend Ali MacGraw outside Aida Thibiant's oasis of a salon in Beverly Hills. I had on tennis shoes, jeans, and a sweatshirt—an outfit I felt completely comfortable in and with—and one I always assumed I looked perfectly presentable in. Ali was wearing a cotton top, cotton pants, and sandals in magical shades of mauve and rose. The simplicity and clean lines of her outfit, combined with its sheer *practicality*, made me feel messy, which is about the last thing I like to feel. I kept my eyes glued to my dirty sneakers hoping she wouldn't notice what I was wearing (Fat chance!). That encounter led me to reconsider my casual look; by observing Ali, I learned that it was just as easy to put on an attractive casual outfit as it was to put on my sloppy clothes and dust-furred sneakers.

There's nothing cleaner, fresher than jeans and a cotton shirt, so long as the jeans fit and the shirt is pressed and well-tailored. This is another place where a single piece of jewelry can turn a neutral uniform into something stylish, another of the little creative "pushes" you can give to your look.

I've worked out some methods for dressing well and spending less time and money at it. They said it couldn't be done?

DAY INTO NIGHT

Most of us are at work all day and don't have time to zip home and change before a cocktail party, dinner, or theater engagement. One good idea is to wear a simple skirt and a silk blouse to work and under the blouse a lacy camisole. Now unbutton the first two buttons of the blouse just as the evening begins. You might also keep a gold or rhinestone belt in your desk, and a small evening purse that's a snazzy nighttime alternative to your daytime pocketbook. Be sure to wear high-heeled sandals to work that day (or, once again, keep a pair in your desk). A velvet blazer can also turn a practical daytime look to one of instant evening elegance—garnished, perhaps, with a piece of your favorite jewelry. Well-tailored velvet jeans are always equally at home in the office and in a nightclub or discothèque.

STOP 'N' SHOP IN YOUR FRIENDS' CLOSETS

Extend your wardrobe by trading and borrowing clothes. You may love a friend's fuscia blouse that it turns out *she hates*—and vice versa. I'm always borrowing and lending clothes. I had to go to Chicago on the spur of the moment a couple of years ago for a very important meeting, and found I had nothing really suitable in my overnight case. Instead of taking to the streets the first thing the next morning and shopping in a panic for something new, I borrowed a full, flattering pink dress from a friend. And I got the job!

TRY A DO-IT-YOURSELF KIKOY

When I was in Kenya filming my ABC-TV special, I "discovered" a fantastic thing called a "kikoy," which is a brightly colored piece of cotton fabric about 5′ x 4′. I wrap it around my waist and tuck it in, and it makes a wonderful casual skirt, or I use it as a lounging outfit or a beach shawl. I often tuck it around my bikini bottom if I'm going straight from the beach to lunch. You can make your own kikoy by taking any scarf or large piece of fabric and simply wrapping it around your waist.

A Kikoy that was worn as a beach robe in Jamaica
can also be worn as a skirt in the middle of winter.
— yes, your legs do get cold...

PACKING IT IN

Because I travel so much, I've had to work out a real system for packing. I *always* pack three pairs of pants, one pair of jeans, two skirts, three sweaters, six blouses, and a couple of evening things. I make sure that most of the separates can be worn together. If I'm going to a cold place, I bring shirts, vests, and sweaters that can all be worn in layers for extra warmth. I always check out the climate before I go-go-go!

MISTAKES PEOPLE MAKE

Overdoing It

I've seen many well-known women, women with every possible advantage in life, pile on so much clothing and jewelry that all they succeed in doing is hiding the beauty or chic they would otherwise have in spades. This is just as bad as piling on too much makeup. The best-dressed woman knows that the most dramatic personal statement she can make is through simplicity. If you want to wear the latest hat, fine—just don't also wear the latest vest, the latest pants, the latest shoes, the latest stockings, the latest man's tie, and the latest stickpin. "Don't let your clothes walk in front of you," the saying goes.

Shopping Madly Before a Special Occasion

I've made *this* mistake a lot myself. I was once invited to a fancy dress ball and told, "We're flying people in from Europe in private jets and everyone's going to be wearing one-of-a-kind designer dresses." I spent the entire day madly rushing around from shop to shop in a quest for the one dress that would take everyone's breath away. I couldn't find it. On an impulse I turned up wearing a very simple black evening dress—and you know what, I looked as good and chic as any of them. So don't knock yourself out shopping before a special occasion. You may find something spectacular all right—that will sit in your closet all the other 364 days of the year. Far better to wear an old favorite you feel completely at home in, completely yourself in (no, don't go in a "kikoy").

Buying a Coat First

First of all, don't buy a coat before assembling your wardrobe. And when you do buy, buy one that fits over your jackets and sweaters and is slightly longer than your skirts and dresses. Choose a model that has good lines and a great fabric, but don't go overboard and buy a purple coat with tangerine flowers—pick a shade that has staying power.

Looking Inappropriate

No matter how beautiful your outfit is, you'll feel pretty silly in it if it's not appropriate to the occasion. A few months ago I appeared at a party in a soft wool skirt, cotton blouse, high heels, and bow tie. Everyone else there was dressed to kill—it was a big bow-wow party—in silk and satin evening clothes. I knew I looked good but I felt almost criminally out of place, so naturally I didn't enjoy the evening—for one thing, I couldn't quite bring myself to hit the dance floor out there among all the sleek silhouettes under the twinkling lights and toy balloons. Take the trouble to phone your hostess and find out beforehand what kind of dress to wear.

Buying Pre-Selected Outfits

Don't blindly buy a skirt or pants with a top or vest manufactured to go with it. These "perfectly matching" outfits can be altogether perfectly depressing and unimaginative and show that you *prefer* running in a pack. There may be safety in numbers, but there isn't much style. Trust yourself a little and choose an outfit that reflects *your* taste. Mixin' and minglin' is always more fun than blindly matchin'.

Fretting Over Minuscule Wrinkles and Spots

We Americans are much too involved with ironing and Clorox. Many women reject beautiful fabrics out of the misplaced fear that they won't have time to keep them perfectly pressed. They worry too much about wrinkles and spots too tiny for a naked eye to see. Of course, keep your clothes clean, but don't relinquish quality for drip-dry, non-wrinkle polyester.

Underestimating the Importance of Your Clothes

Whether you like it or not, you are going to be judged partly by how you dress. Psychologists say that people who pay absolutely no attention to their wardrobes may be suffering from a poor self-image, and that the reason they wear sloppy or anonymous clothes is that they subconsciously long to advertise the negative way they feel about themselves; some go so far as to wear clothes *calculated* to diminish their sex appeal and keep them secure in the background—they're that afraid to project themselves. If you're totally indifferent to clothes and all your life have been claiming you just couldn't care less, there are more important things to worry about, maybe you should ask yourself a very uncomfortable question—"Why?"

Mind you, I'm not saying that I think clothes are the be-all and end-all or even the most all-all-all of them all. Everything in its place. Shopping can be frustrating, vexing, maddening. But the result is often worth the trouble. It was no less august a figure than Emerson who wrote: "the lady declared that the sense of being perfectly well-dressed gives a feeling of inner tranquility which religion is powerless to bestow."

9

Odds & Ends: You're Only as Good as the Finishing Touches

he quality called attractiveness is a function of the whole person; you can't be, like the curate's egg, only "good in places." You must be aware of all parts of your body: how your shoulders sit, your smile, fidgeting hands and feet, your fragrance, and—the sum and extension of all these parts—your attitude, which is, after all, the image of your image. Neglect the "invisible" basics of grooming and health care and they won't stay invisible for long; they will emerge with a force all the greater for their suppression and ultimately sabotage whatever efforts you've made with your wardrobe, makeup, and hair.

Here are the things I've learned to watch out for when it comes time to polish up my appearance.

THE IMPORTANCE OF STANDING STRAIGHT

All through junior high I hated dancing class because I was so much taller than all the boys. Back then, those extra inches felt like miles. Fortunately I had a mother who encouraged me to take pride in the fact that I was a tall girl, and thanks to her, I learned to stand straight, and bypassed the tall girl's slump: the rounded shoulders and curved back that many short girls also manage to saddle themselves with. Today it feels even better than it did then to be tall, and when I really want to get way up there I put on my high-heeled gold sandals and tower over everyone, "taller than the tallest building!"

Good posture has certainly been a big plus in all my modeling jobs. (Bad posture can disqualify an aspiring model on the spot.) Many girls seem to have completely forgotten how to walk normally. And that's a great shame, for aside from doing a lot for any outfit, good bearing makes *you* look better—slimmer and more assuming, someone with real "presence." If you're apt to become nervous when you enter a room, straighten those shoulders, hold your head up, and move on in, as if the room belongs to you. Good posture can give the lie to whatever self-doubts might be consuming you in your personal life and holding you back in your career.

Too many people these days don't have the slightest awareness of the way they sit and stand. After you've

answered the following questions, you should have a pretty good idea as to just how good your posture is.

■ *Are your shoulders sometimes tense and all hunched forward?*

■ *Does your chin jut out? Or is it tucked down and pushed back? Or does it tilt up?*

■ *Is the part of your back just below your neck straight or slightly curved?*

■ *Is there an S-shaped curve in the small of your back?*

■ *Do you always have a pot belly, no matter how thin you are?*

If you answered yes to any one of these questions, the chances are you did to all of them—because poor posture has a chain-link effect on how your body looks. Tense, hunched shoulders make your neck tense, which in turn gives your head a slightly lopsided look. And, if your shoulders and head aren't held in a straight line, your back won't be straight, either. And a curve in the small of the back almost always means there's going to be a pot belly out there somewhere. Or, as the poet might have put it, if a pot belly is here, can a curve in the small of the back be far behind? Seriously, you run a big risk of having every part of your body become slightly deformed, and these deformities can become permanent with time: the old lady's hump is the fearful legacy of her lifelong habit of slumping. And did you know that really bad posture can cause back pain and headaches as well as cramp the style of the lungs (and the style of the lungs, in case you didn't know, is a little function called breathing!). You owe it to yourself to stand up straight—that is, unless you want to look like a hovel and feel like one. Don't let bad posture become a metaphor for your whole life.

HOW TO DEVELOP GOOD POSTURE

Exercise

It shouldn't come as any great revelation that women who've been doing ballet for years have better posture than other women. Not every woman can (do ballet), but there are many other kinds of exercise that not only make you conscious of the way you stand, but develop the muscles that hold your body up: swimming, yoga, calisthenics, and *any* kind of dance training will all strengthen your supporting muscles as well as make you fully aware of how they work.

Vigilance

Even though I have fairly good posture, I make a point of checking it out in the mirror: Are my shoulders back and down? Am I holding my stomach up and in? Are my head and neck poised directly on top of the spine? If you make a posture check at specific times every day, you'll begin to see your bad habits standing out in bold relief. And knowledge of them is the first step toward correcting them. Check your posture when you're sitting down, too. If you have a desk-oriented job, try keeping your feet on the ground, your chin in, and your back straight. By sitting straight when you're at your desk, you'll feel less tired when your workday is over.

Posture Exercises

Close your eyes and imagine that someone is pulling you up by a string attached to your head. Unless you're John the Baptist, you should be able to feel your whole body lengthen and straighten.

Now lie on the floor on your back and bend your knees. Press your whole back, and also the back of your neck, right into the floor. Now slowly, slowly straighten your legs, continuing to press your back into the floor.

Ahhh . . . !

FLASH THE WHITE TEETH OF THE HAPPY GIRL

I was shocked when I read recently that roughly one half of all Americans don't bother to visit a dentist even once a year. God! I always have my teeth checked and cleaned at least twice a year.

Many people lose their teeth and, worse, become the victims of gum disease: the guaranteed result of improper brushing and flossing. Achieving and maintaining good dental hygiene require almost as much in the way of time and attention as your makeup application does. But it's worth it, since there is nothing more costly, inconvenient, frightening, and painful than the elaborate procedures necessary to restore your teeth and gums. It's not called tooth "decay" for nothing: they go downhill fast, once they begin to go, and down you go along with them, down into "the country of the general lost freshness." So practice these four cardinal rules and save your teeth—and your beautiful smile.

1. Sugar

Like the rest of your body, your teeth and gums need a varied, nutritious diet. It's the same foods that make you fat that destroy your teeth. And the main enemy, an unnatural enemy if there ever was one, is *sugar*. It joins with the bacteria in your mouth to form acids and plaque that eat your teeth and gums away. If you just can't help yourself and you do eat sugar, then get it out of your mouth as fast as you can. And eat a lot of crunchy, fibrous raw fruits and vegetables, which help clean your teeth.

2. Brushing

Make sure you get the brush as close to the gumline as possible, and brush *all* the surfaces of your teeth. Use a fluoride toothpaste, but stay away from special teeth whiteners, which are said to be too harsh on the enamel. For a special whitening treatment, brush once a week with baking soda, which makes for a good old-fashioned, slightly abrasive toothpaste, in addition to your regular brushing. Brush twice a day—and always before bedtime, because bacteria remains longest in the mouth—doing its nasty work—while you're fast asleep.

3. Flossing

Brushing is not enough! To prevent the dreaded plaque from building up on your teeth, you must use dental floss. Your toothbrush alone cannot possibly remove food particles from between the teeth and close to the gums. Flossing is no joke: it prevents gum disease more effectively than any other form of home dental care.

4. See Your Dentist

Don't see your dentist only when you have a toothache, because by then you're already in trouble. Most tooth decay and gum erosion begin with no betrayal of discomfort. A good and easy way to practice preventive dental care is simply to have minor work done on a regular basis. If your home dental care habits are not what they should be, then by all means have your

teeth professionally cleaned at least a couple of times a year.

FINGERNAIL POWER

A model's hands are one of the most pliant, expressive, and revealing parts of her body. I'm often surprised how my hands stand out in photographs, and how the gestures I make with them add or detract from the general picture. It goes without saying that there is no way your hands can be appealing if your fingernails are not well-groomed. A lot of women seem to be under the unfortunate impression that "well-groomed" means long, red nails (the better to maul you with, my dear?). I was once the victim of this misconception myself. When I stopped working and didn't have all that much to do with myself, I became a slave to nail polish. It sounds like a joke, but believe me, it wasn't. Every week I had a manicure, and if one of my holier-than-thou nails so much as chipped or cracked or—heaven forbid—actually broke, I dashed back to the body shop for repairs. My nails finally got so long I couldn't zip my zippers or button my buttons by myself—I mean, I might just as well have been on a life-support system. As soon as I got out of the house and went back to work, I dispensed with the nail routine.

There's no question that perfectly manicured, painted nails are fun for all the world to see. Beyond that, though, they raise some troubling questions, since they obviously mean you're not doing anything very strenuous or life-enhancing, like gardening or sailing. I think a good solution is a short, well-groomed nail, clean and glossy, coated with a clear polish, which can be every bit as beautiful as a long, red talon and which has the added advantage of making your hands look *capable* and *natural*.

The Ten-Minute All-Natural Mini-Manicure!

Flash! Here's a five-step manicure that takes only minutes.

1. Remove your old polish.
2. Gently push your cuticles back with an orangewood stick, covered with cotton.
3. File with a nail file or emery board in one direction only. Round the corners, but don't file the sides (this will make your nails weak). Try not to cut your nails with scissors (this will make them brittle) or to

file after a nail has been immersed in water and is soft and fragile.

4. Buff your nails with a natural hide buffer to give them a natural shine. Buffing also improves the circulation of the nail. (For a maxi-mini-manicure, stop here! Do not proceed to 5.)

5. Apply a clear polish. If you like a bright polish, apply a base coat of clear polish first. Different polishes wear off at different rates. You'll just have to experiment till you find one that stays on.

MISTAKES PEOPLE MAKE

Using a Cuticle Clipper

Cutting your cuticle will only make it big and tough, which is probably not what you had in mind. So always push your cuticle back, then just leave it alone. Treat any ragged cuticles with a cuticle cream. To soften your cuticles and prevent rough, red hands, rub Vaseline into your entire hand; if you want to go to extremes, wear white gloves to bed.

Removing Polish Too Often

When a nail chips, instead of removing all your nail polish (this will dry the nail), just add a touch-up coat.

The Gelatin-Cocktail-Hour Syndrome

You can drink a thousand and one unflavored gelatin cocktails and still they will not make your nails grow longer. Polish actually does more to harden and protect your nails than anything you could ever eat. (A protein-rich diet, however, is important for both hair and nails, which are composed of a protein substance.) If you want long nails and, no matter how hard you try, you just can't seem to grow them, ask your manicurist to wrap them in a paper shield to protect the growing nail.

Be Kind to Your Fingers

If you pull at hangnails, bite your fingernails, or jam your fingers into a jammed-up handbag, you have some bad habits to overcome. Remember, "Don't make frazzled nails the mirror of frazzled nerves."

FEET, BEAUTIFUL FEET

One's feet are usually visible only at intimate moments (many men by the way, find a beautiful foot a real turn-on) or at the beach. Unlike your hands, your feet have limited powers of expression (this side of kicking!), and to look good, they must be pampered. I rub the rough, dry areas of my feet with a pumice stone and try not to overlook my feet when I'm applying lotion to my body. A painted, well-groomed toenail is a must in an open-toed sandal. Clip your toenails to a smooth oval, then smooth the rough edges with a file, and separate your toes with cotton pads before you apply the enamel so it won't smudge.

Don't sacrifice your feet to good-looking, but constricting—even killing—shoes. They'll just give you corns, bunions, and other unsightly ailments. If you've already gone and bought a pair of fabulously expensive and unbelievably uncomfortable high heels, I guess you're going to feel you have to wear them just to get your money's worth—but wear them for a couple of hours at a time only! The agonies of having aching feet, along with the tiresome grumbling you're bound to do, will eventually show up graven on your face. Try soaking your feet in very hot water and then plunging them into a cold bath. In summer, when they're apt to get overheated, spray your feet with a light cologne; the alcohol will cool them off.

THE SWEET SMELL OF . . . YOU!

The perfume you wear creates an aura, like a sub-light; lingers in the air, and in the memories of those you come into contact with. I always wear perfume. My favorites are Oscar de la Renta, Madame de Balmain, and Chanel #5. I usually finish a bottle of one of these before I switch my allegiance to another, because it's nice to identify with a single perfume for a while, let it mark a time in your life, the time of your time which if you're lucky may even be the time *of* your life.

Back in my salad days, I once took the advice of a fashion magazine and set my hair with perfume before a party. When the curlers came out the scent hung over me like a cloud, like a reproach that reeked. Too much perfume is much worse than none. Any insistent odor can ruin an appetite, yours and others'. A touch of scent behind the ears, a dab on the neck or along the torso, is far more provocative than an envel-

oping fog of the stuff. For a very light scent, spray your favorite perfume into the air and walk through the shower of tiny droplets.

Selecting a Scent

Don't choose perfumes just because they're new or "different," or have seductive names, or smell good on your friends. Body chemistry very subtly changes the fragrance of perfume; also, the longer you keep it on, the more it changes. The seasons also have an effect on scent, so when it's hot, you should use a light fragrance in preference to a heavy, exotic one. By the same token, it's a good idea not to wear perfume in the sun—some of the ingredients can spot your skin when exposed to ultraviolet rays.

Instead of Perfume, What?

Use a few drops of good bath oil, that's what. Bath oil scents are often quite heady and, used as a substitute for perfume, make your bath all the sweeter.

A great-smelling soap is an inexpensive way to smell fresh. And use a bar of it, left in its wrapper, to scent your lingerie drawer. For a really spicy fragrance—if you want him to feel that old, warm, spicy breeze blowing—switch to a man's cologne.

SLEEP, BEAUTIFUL SLEEP

"Blonde Waiting"
Roy Lichtenstein—1964

Lack of sleep not only makes you look a bit out of it, whatever "it" is, but also fosters a sort of worm's-eye view of the world that doesn't exactly help either the world or you. Irritation, lethargy, and lassitude are some of the more attractive results of insomnia. Each of us requires a different number of hours of sleep, "sleep that knits up the ravelled sleeve of care," and our requirements change as we get older. Most of us, for example, need more sleep during periods of stress, and less when we're doing something we enjoy.

Stress keeps us from falling asleep easily. When I'm on the road and working hard, or socially overindulging myself, or not getting enough exercise, it's sometimes a real struggle for me to get the sleep my body needs. I've had to work up a few tricks and routines to get by on.

C.T.'s Never-Say-Die Cures for Insomnia

Every night before I lay me down to sleep, I wash my face, straighten my apartment up, and close all the doors, even the closets. (Everybody has some little neurosis about the sleeping ritual and mine is closing all the doors. Indulge yourself!) The point I want to make is that if you follow some regular bedtime pattern, your psyche will come to associate it with deep slumber.

And how about a glass of milk before bedtime? It contains a sleep-inducing amino acid called "tryptophan," that's especially helpful if you suffer from acid indigestion. If you don't like your milk cold, heat it with a quarter teaspoon of vanilla and add a teaspoon of honey—it's yummy. Calcium tablets also are a great natural sleeping pill. Even a little old aspirin can relax your muscles and help you fall asleep. Avoid barbiturates at any and all costs: they can be addictive and, gobbled in large doses, can actually *prevent* you from getting to sleep (and if and when you do, you may have the foulest nightmares). On the very few occasions when I've resorted to sleeping pills, I've paid the high price of being too groggy the next morning to function effectively, to perform at the top of the tent, so to speak (so *not* to speak?).

Just before turning in, I organize the following day in my mind, and then write down all my appointments. I think through the problems that are preying on me so that half-baked plans and nagging worries can't keep me awake and fretful. If I find my mind getting stuck on all my problems while I'm trying to find sleep, I concentrate on one thing at a time, instead of letting everything gang up on me.

I imagine—or, depending on the weather outside my windowpane, fantasize—that I'm lying on a beach in the unwavering heat of noon, so that my body is infused with that peaceful, somnolent feeling born of sun and sea and good clean air. Sometimes I imagine —or, again, fantasize—that someone is rocking me slowly in a hammock. Another trick I have for defeating, or at least subduing, tension: I relax one part of my body at a time—toes, feet, ankles, calves—right on up to my head, which is often in the clouds because my castle's in the sky. It works! And why shouldn't it? Because what is sleep if not a question of mind over matter? If my plane lands in New York from Los Angeles at night, I adjust to East Coast time simply by telling myself, "It's midnight and time for bed!" instead of panicking, "How will I ever get to sleep?" Thinking makes it so!

I keep a "dream pad" beside my bed, and every morning I write down whatever I can remember from the night before. God, the things you can learn about yourself! Looking forward to dreaming can be an incentive to get to sleep.

If you really, really can't sleep, don't surrender to the misery of tossing and turning. Don't just lie there, *do* something! Get up, for a start. How about a few stretching exercises? There's always the TV, or a good book. Try to relax. You have a lot at stake: your peace of mind.

Exercise: Again and Then Again!

At the risk of becoming the nag of all time: now *is* the time and this *is* the place to reiterate that few people who exercise regularly suffer from insomnia. Exercise rids your muscles of the tension that keeps you awake.

Create a Room That's Good to Sleep in

A cold room begets a cold, shivering sleep. I painted mine a warm, relaxing color and I sleep well, with all my plants and books and thoughts and things around. A humidifier helps keep the lining of my nose and throat from drying out, and the hum, surprisingly, is soothing. Make sure your mattress is firm and that the bed board under the mattress is three-quarters of an inch thick. This also makes for both a comfortable night and a strong back. Despite the dozens of decorative pillows you see piled up in magazine layouts of bedrooms, don't ever sleep on more than one, because if your neck gets over-elevated, it may be stiff in the morning—and for several days running. And a stiff neck is not the finishing touch you want. You want to wake up sweetened by your good night's sleep—and holding in your hand the key to all life's secret little graces.

But alas, the knowledge of how to make yourself attractive doesn't arrive in a dream, at least not in any dream I know of.

> *To be born woman is to know—*
> *Although they do not talk of it at school—*
> *That we must labour to be beautiful.*
> —*W. B. Yeats, "Adam's Curse"*

Oh, it may be a struggle, it may even be a fight, but to quote Colette again, "It is the fight itself that keeps you young."

Photographs are reproduced by the kind permission of the following:

Tommy Mitchell: 17, 32 bottom. *Secrets*, Macfadden Women's Group: 20. Sante Forlano/*Glamour:* 24, 26, 28 bottom, 30, 46, 62 bottom, 146, 147 top and center, 149 top row/third from left, 152, 153, 158, 166 bottom. Sante Forlano/Bonne Bell: 200. Bill Connors/*Glamour:* 33, 48, 141, 142, 145, 147 bottom, 151 bottom, 157, 172–173. Bill Connors/*Good Housekeeping:* 47. Hanna-Barbera's Marineland, Los Angeles: 27. Cole of California: 28, 274. Pendleton Woolen Mills: 29. Eastman Kodak Company: 29. *Seventeen* Magazine: 32 top. Steve Horn: 34 and lower two, 35. Menken/Seltzer Studio: 35 top. Philip Morris Incorporated—All photographs and registered trademark "You've come a long way, baby" used by permission: 34–35. Barry McKinley/*Vogue Australia:* 36–37, upper left and lower right. Helmut Newton/*Vogue:* 37 lower left, 38 (1972). Kourken Pakchanian/*Vogue:* 37 upper right, 160 bottom, 167 bottom. Walter Iooss, Jr./Time Inc.: 40 top. Jay Maisel/Time Inc.: 40 bottom. Jay Maisel/*Sports Illustrated:* 188–189. Jerome Ducrot: 41 top. Bill King/*Harper's Bazaar:* 41 bottom, 109, 115, 116–117 all photos except extreme upper right, 190, 223, 277. Bill King/Time Inc.: 225. Bill King: 179 left, 236. Roxanne Swim Suits: 63. The Mike Douglas Show, Group W Productions Inc./Westinghouse Broadcasting Company, Inc.: 79 left. American Broadcasting Companies, Inc.: 83 top, 85 bottom, 111 bottom, 242. Bob Landry, *Life* Magazine, copyright © 1941, Time Inc.: 84. Arthur Elgort/*Vogue:* 86. Alan Lewis Kleinberg: 93–99. ABC Sports: 108. Tony Costa: 112, 113. Philip A. Pessoni: 117 extreme upper right, 139, 143, 151 top, 175, 182, 183. Art Kane/*Sports Illustrated:* 133. John Zimmerman/*Sports Illustrated:* 144. Jim Houghton/*Ladies' Home Journal:* 148–149 bottom row, center. Peter Beard/Warner Bros. Records: 150 bottom. Roger Prigent/*McCall's* (October 1975), The McCall Publishing Company: 155. David Woo: 162. David Bailey/*Glamour:* 165. Bourdin/*Elle-Scoop:* 166 top. 3M: 167 top. Barry Lategan/British *Vogue:* 170. Hiro: 179, 209, 255. John Ford/*Eye* Magazine: 192–193.

Collage on page 64–65 by Peter Beard. Painting on page 282 by Roy Lichtenstein.

All other photographs are by Peter Beard or from the private collection of Cheryl Tiegs.

Photographs on the endpapers are reproduced by the kind permission of the following.

FRONT ENDSHEET: *Top row, left to right:* © *Woman's Own;* Jim Houghton/*Fair Lady Magazine;* Time Inc.; British *Vogue*, Time Inc.; *'Teen Magazine* (June 1966); *Bride's;* Tori Lenze/*Elle-Scoop. Second row, left to right:* Rico Puhlman/*Harper's Bazaar; Glamour;* Bill King/*Harper's Bazaar;* Time Inc.; Time Inc.; Tony Costa/*Us* Magazine; *'Teen Magazine* (Sept. 1966), *Redbook* Magazine. *Third row, left to right: Glamour;* Carrara/*Elle-Scoop;* Hispard/*Elle-Scoop;* Marco Glaviano/*Harper's Bazaar; Brigette* Magazine; Jim Houghton/*Ladies' Home Journal; Glamour;* Rico Puhlman/*Harper's Bazaar. Bottom row, left to right: Secrets*/Macfadden Women's Group; Phillip Dixon/*SportAmerica* (Denver, Colorado); *Bride's; Glamour; Secrets*/Macfadden Women's Group; *Glamour;* Bill Connors/*Harper's Bazaar;* © *Woman's Own*.

BACK ENDSHEET: *Top row, left to right:* Rico Puhlman/*Harper's Bazaar;* Barry Lategan/British *Vogue;* Bill King/*Harper's Bazaar;* Carmine Schiavone/*Seventeen®* Magazine (copyright © 1967 by Triangle Communications Inc. All rights reserved); Time Inc.; Douglas Kirkland/Burda Publications; Rico Puhlman/*Harper's Bazaar;* Bill Connors/*Elle-Scoop*. *Second row, left to right:* © *Woman's Own; Bride's;* Tori Lenze/*Elle-Scoop;* Bob Stone/*Harper's Bazaar;* Jaeckin/*Elle-Scoop;* Rico Puhlman/*Harper's Bazaar*. *Third row, left to right:* Sears, Roebuck and Co.; *Weight Watchers Magazine; Hairdo & Beauty* (Dec. 1968)/Dell Publishing Co., Inc.; Carmine Schiavone/*Good Housekeeping; Glamour;* Peter Beard/*Look* Magazine (copyright March 1979); *Modern Bride*/Ziff-Davis Publishing Company (copyright © 1968); *Glamour. Bottom row, left to right: Glamour; Family Circle* Magazine/Family Circle, Inc. (copyright © 1979); Rico Puhlman/*Harper's Bazaar; Glamour;* Bill King/*Harper's Bazaar;* © *Woman's Own;* Carmine Schiavone/*Seventeen®* Magazine (copyright © 1967 by Triangle Communications, Inc. All rights reserved); Bill King/*Harper's Bazaar*.

VOGUE
APR 1
40p
the prettiest time of your life
silks chiffons and April flowers
40 best looks in fashion and beauty now
BAZAAR
AUG $1.50
YOU & YOUR JOB
LOOK GREAT, MAKE BIG MONEY & ENJOY SUCCESS
THE NEW YORK HOSPITAL'S ANTI-ACNE GUIDE
Plus the Good-Skin Diet
CHERYL TIEGS
MODELING, MONEY & MEN
CLOTHES THAT WORK BEST
RONA JAFFE
THE SEVEN-SISTERS SCHOOLS:
FALL COLLECTIONS
THE NEW YORK LOOK!
FASHION TURNS ON THE PRETTY POWER
THE RETURN OF THE RINGLET
CONVERSATIONS TEENS NEVER HEAR
BEST NEW
ERICA UNDER $25
BARGAIN DIET:
N COST, HIGH IN HEALTH
P YOUR HAIR
FALLING OUT
ORCE IN SUBURBI
SUMMER NEWS
ON LINGERIE SANDWICHES SUNGLASSES
How Important is VIRGINITY?
BRIDE'S
$1 AUGUST
40 DREAMY NEW BRIDAL FASHIONS
HOW TO LOOK BEAUTIFUL ON YOUR WEDDING NIGHT
PERFUMES, LINGERIE THAT TURN HIM ON
WHY THINGS GO WRONG IN MARRIAGE
BY DR. LAURENCE PETER
WORKING WIVES
HOW TO MAKE THE BEST OF BOTH WORLDS
THE KITCHEN SCENE
WE ANSWER THE 25 MOST ASKED QUESTIONS ABOUT COOKING
UNE VRAIE GARDE-ROBE VACANCES EN 15 BONS MAGIQUES ET 13 COULEURS
DÉCORATION : L'ART DE VIVRE A L'ITALIENNE
AMERICA'S
YOUNG CAREER GIRL
TO THE TOP
FOOLPROOF GUIDE:
LOOK GREAT & LIVE WELL ON $150 A WEEK
TOP DESIGNER CLOTHES YOU CAN AFFORD
NOBODY'S PERFECT
WHAT TO WEAR IF YOU ARE TOO TALL, SHORT, THIN, HEAVY
BAZAAR'S
SPAGHETTI DIET:
LOSE 5 POUNDS ITALIAN STYLE
HOW TO BE
SEXY, FEMININE & ASSERTIVE ON THE
Sears
Weight Watch
Cheryl Tiegs
America's Top Cover Girl:
'I Was Too Fat To Model'
50 Fabulous Burgers
Land A Glamor Job!
Advice From 9 Experts
Compulsive?
How To Put Your Energies To Work
We Tested The Old Saying:
'The Way To A Man's Heart...'
HairDo
December · 50c
GREAT LOOKS THAT TURN MEN ON
What Men Really Hate about Make-up & Hair
Newest Fad: THE BROW-BAND HAIRDO
WHAT MAKES A GREAT HAIRCUT-WHAT MAKES A DISASTER
&Beaut
JOYCE BROTHERS:
FIGHTING THE FEARS THAT RIOTS BREED
18 PAGES–
GREAT INFORMAL OUTDOOR DINNERS
BOB HOPE, JOHN LINDSAY, HUGH DOWNS AND OTHERS DESCRIBE "THE DAY I WAS PROUDEST OF MY WIFE"
HUMPHREY & McCARTHY:
CAMPAIGN ORDEALS FACED BY THEIR FAMILIES
APRIL 50¢
SPOT-REDUCING WITH CLOTHES
HOW TO KNOW IF YOU NEED A PSYCHIATRIST
STAY THIN FOREVER!
Family Circle
How to get it wholesale
Mouthwatering cookies, candy, snacks—without sugar
50 big & little home-improvement projects
The 30 best plants for hanging!
Beauty cures from Mother Nature
Princess Grace's technique for pressed flowers
20 proven ways to save money
Bonus: The card that could save your child's life
Magic with muslin
NATURAL
GREAT LOOKING INEXPENSIVE CLOTHES AND HOW TO WEAR THEM
TOP BEAUTY EXPERTS SHOW
HOW TO CUT YOUR HAIR, MAKE OVER YOUR LOOKS
NOV 50¢
YOUR PARTY LIFE
SKI-MANSHIP